THE BADLANDS SERIES

NATALIE BENNETT

D1526046

Edited & formatted by
PINPOINT EDITING

To the badass tribe that always supports me.
#TPR

Savages

Playlist

1. Let You Down—NF
2. Whore—In This Moment
3. Sick Like Me—In This Moment
4. The Beautiful & The Damned—G Eazy
5. What's Wrong—Pvris
6. Imperfection—Evanescence
7. Madness—Ruelle
8. The Devil In I—Slipknot
9. Homemade Dynamite—Lorde
10. Gangsta—Kehlani
11. Take Me to Church-Hozier
12. Bad at Love—Halsey
13. Heaven in Hiding—Halsey
14. Him & I—Halsey
15. What Sober Couldn't Say—Halestorm
16. Praying—Ke$ha
17. Cut the Cord—Shinedown
18. Wrong Side of Heaven—5FDP

19. Cradle to the Grave—5FDP
20. Pray—Sam Smith

Servatis a periculum, servatis a maleficum

Prologue

There are no heroes to be found here, only monsters.

I am not an exception.

I am the devil's confidante.

I am guilty of unimaginable sins.

I was better off without him, and he was better off alone, but the red string of fate tied us together. No matter how much it tangled or stretched, it would never break.

In him, I found my absolution.

He saved me from the light by showing me the beautiful depravity that could be found in the dark.

My beloved devil made every withering parcel of my being bloom and thrive by nurturing it with his sinister mind. He tattooed himself across my heart and took up permanent residence inside my head.

Ours is not a story full of sickly sweet nothings, nor is it a fairytale built on illusions. The world we lived in had long ago turned cold, and our hearts turned with it. Love was a four-letter word neither of us had ever learned, and trust was a foreign concept we didn't know the meaning of. The odds were stacked against us on all sides of the spectrum.

Our dark paradise could only be reached by paving the way with blood and corpses.

Some might find it hard to understand how mere human beings could do all that we did: kill without mercy. Lie through our teeth. Take what we wanted just because we could.

It came to down to nothing other than DNA, the genes that made us who we were. The blood pumping through our veins carried a beautiful madness only we understood.

He was born sick.

I was fucked in the head.

Together, we were Savages.

Part One

Chapter One

Calista

He set her on fire, but it was me he watched burn.

Within seconds, her body was drowning in an inferno. The blaze glowed red, bathing the night sky in blood. A sheet of flames danced across her naked skin, shrinking and splitting open flesh, leaving body fluid to expel. They reached for her dark strands of hair and singed them to the scalp.

Her mouth had been sewn shut after she was forced to repent for her sins, silencing her shrills of agony and fear. The familiar aroma of charred flesh permeated the air, filling my aching lungs with every ragged breath I took.

The Order stood by, watching with bored expressions on their faces as the faux nuns held hands and whispered their synthetic prayers.

I wished it were a dream, but I was wide awake. I wished

nothing more than to take her place. I wished someone would have saved us from the hate, but not one person stepped forward.

I had tried so hard to warn her away. I'd begged her not to come back for me. Why didn't she listen?

My body shook with silent sobs, constricting my heart in my chest. I couldn't move. It hurt to breathe. I felt like I were burning with her.

I was forced to watch on as the life vacated her body, leaving her limbs dangling limply above the flames. The bones that had been exposed were slick with the greasy residue of melted flesh.

As two men moved forward to begin extinguishing the fire, still no one said a word.

I tried not to picture what would happen to what remained of her blackened body, knowing she was to be discarded for crows and wild animals to feast on.

"It's unfortunate it had to come to this," my father sighed, removing his heavy foot from my spine. "You let me down, Calista."

He stepped over my body and knelt down, lifting my battered face from the dirt. His skewed logic made him believe that if my pain wasn't visible, I wasn't hurting—yet he was the one who'd taught me to handle abuse.

I looked into his cold, grey eyes and hoped he saw the hatred I no longer bothered to mask. If I had the strength, I would have torn out his jugular with my teeth.

I had done everything he'd asked of me, even when I didn't want to, when the aftermath always killed me a little more each time.

I suppressed parts of me to appease him, but no matter how hard I tried, it was never good enough.

Once upon a time, all I wanted was for him to remember I

was his baby girl. Now, I wanted him dead. I wanted to feel his blood between my fingers and keep his head as a trophy.

"Feel better…now?" I wheezed out, choking on phlegm.

"You've learned nothing from any of this; you are truly hopeless." He squeezed my cheeks and then shoved my face back in the dirt, a look of disgust twisting his features. "Your sins will eat you alive." With one last shake of his head, he chuckled and regarded me with unfeeling eyes before standing up and strolling away.

"Take her past the border and leave her," he demanded over his shoulder to my brothers, who had been standing by, watching the events unfold.

"If you don't kill me…I *will* kill you," I called out to him.

He continued walking away, not bothering to give me so much as a backward glance.

My hope that he would turn around and end it all was gone just as quickly as it had arrived.

My brothers rushed to obey his command. They each grabbed an upper arm and began dragging me face-down across the ground. I gritted my teeth as my hands were secured behind my back with strips of twine.

"Let's get this over with; I haven't eaten supper yet," my eldest brother grumbled, lifting me up and tossing me in the bed of his truck with an irritated sigh. I let out a soft grunt as my side impacted with the plastic floor.

A second later, the engine revved, and I was flying forward as the truck sped off into the night.

Much quicker than I expected, signs warning that we were about to leave a safe zone began to appear on the trees.

I remained on my stomach, trying to come up with a quick plan of action.

I knew once we reached our destination that the inevitable would be moments away from happening.

And I was right.

Seconds after the truck came to a full stop, one of my brothers dropped the tailgate and grabbed hold of my habit to pull me out.

"We could fuck her now," my younger brother, Noah, whispered, pressing his elbow into my back to keep me pinned down.

"No, Judy is enough for me. Besides, look at her, she's filthy."

At their words, my stomach twisted into a knot, acidic bile rising in my throat. Judy was our thirteen-year-old cousin.

How did I not know this was going on? When did my brothers start feeding on the bullshit our father spewed like every other brainwashed acolyte? This shouldn't have surprised me as much as it did.

The entire Order was made up of one giant, incestuous family exchanging bodily fluids.

"Suit yourself; I don't care what she looks like. I only want what's between her legs," Noah laughed. He gripped the dark fabric around my waist and started sliding it up.

"Make it quick; I'll wait in the truck."

The sound of retreating footsteps had one of my worst fears quickly becoming a reality. I was really being left alone to be violated, which was normal under usual circumstances, but never by my brothers.

"Don't," I choked out, struggling to move away.

"Shhh," he blew in my ear, pressing the side of my face into the bed of the truck.

Grabbing my cloth underwear with one hand, he easily tore it away. His heavy cross amulet pressed into my back as he crushed me with his weight.

I heard the telltale sound of his belt being undone, and my stomach turned to stone.

"Stop," I pleaded a little louder, my voice chock-full of emotion.

He cleared his throat and spat into the palm of his hand, rubbing the DNA we shared between my ass cheeks. I swallowed repeatedly to hold down vomit, but when his disgusting, hard cock pressed against my sensitive hole, it erupted from my mouth and dribbled down my chin, leaving an acidic taste on my tongue.

I thrashed from side to side, trying my damnedest to dislodge him, failing miserably. My haggard body protested at the movement, radiating with pain.

Louis Armstrong began to croon out the words to 'What a Wonderful World' from the truck's cassette player, overshadowing my pleas and sobs.

"Hold still," Noah growled, flipping me over so I was on my back, forcing my head to lie in my own vomit.

My shoulders screamed in their sockets, and the twine cut into my wrists.

"Please don't do this," I begged as he settled between my legs.

He covered my mouth with his hand and managed to shove half his length inside me.

Vigorously shaking my head back and forth, I freed my mouth and sucked in a breath, releasing it on a broken scream as he pulled out and pushed back in. Friction coupled with dryness tore the delicate tissue, making me bleed. My mind blanked, unable to believe that this was happening, that my sweet little brother was moving inside me, moaning his pleasure in my ear.

Nausea tossed my stomach. I couldn't get out from

beneath him, and I was wasting all my energy trying, but I had to do something. No one was going to save me.

Adrenaline had my pulse racing at a hazardous speed. I could hear my heartbeat thundering in my ears. With a single-minded focus, I lurched up and brought us nearly mouth to mouth, catching him by surprise.

I snagged his lower lip between my teeth and bit down as hard as I could.

"Ah, fuck!" he garbled, immediately pulling out of me.

His fist and pain simultaneously hit the right side of my face. The impact forced me to let go, but not without tearing a soft piece of flesh from the inside of his mouth. I spat it out, along with the blood I tasted on my tongue.

He jumped up and swiped his face with the back of his arm. With nothing to balance me, I fell off the gate of the truck. Before I could get my bearings, his boot kicked me square in the stomach.

Gasping, I managed to roll onto my side, receiving another kick to my back. I bent my spine, pulled my shoulders in, and tucked my chin to my chest to form a protective ball.

"Fucking bitch. You're not even worth it." A glob of spit landed on my cheek, and his hand came down and attempted to tear the necklace from around my neck.

When he failed to remove it, he kicked me one last time in the back of my head. Pain exploded in my skull, and I saw stars.

A door slammed, and then they were gone. As the tail-lights faded, darkness eagerly swallowed me up.

Chapter Two

Calista

When the sun rose, the heat rose with it.

Sawdust and little bits of grass clung to my sweaty, swollen face. I was still on the side of the road, battling with myself not to give up.

My father would never expect me to survive, and that had me realizing for the first time in nineteen years that I was free. This was not where my story would end—not when it hadn't even begun yet.

I was so goddamn tired, though. The thought of moving almost gave me anxiety, but I couldn't continue to idle on the side of the road. If someone out here found me in such a pathetic condition, I stood no chance against them.

I tugged at the twine around my wrists for the hundredth time to no avail. Gritting my teeth against an onslaught of pain radiating from my ass, I used my core muscles and legs to push off the ground, hissing as my ribs protested.

Once on my feet, I swayed and fought to stay upright. Glancing around through one good eye, I took in the scenery surrounding me.

I'd never been to the Badlands before. I'd never been allowed to venture away from The Order. I had no idea where to go. Left and right were both long stretches of road surrounded by fields of…nothing.

Taking a gamble, I chose right. I avoided the smoking blacktop by walking along the edge of the street. I didn't know what the hell I was going to do, but at least I was moving—albeit slowly. I walked and walked and walked.

My chest heaved with every strangled breath I took as I attempted to get some saliva in my mouth. Sweat rolled from my brow to my cracked lips.

How long would it take for my heart to give out? Every pump of blood it pushed through my veins was like a solid rasp on a bass drum reverberating in my brain. All the aches and pains from the day before were now stiff and sore. My left eye had swollen to the size of a golf ball, limiting visibility. My habit only added to my struggles, the heavy black garment weighing me down and serving as a beacon for the sun.

Eventually, I stopped to rest against a tree that offered some semblance of shade, telling myself it was just for a few seconds. My vision was fuzzy and my legs could barely hold me up. The view looked the same as when I started, making me feel like I hadn't really gone anywhere.

I knew I could survive this. I just needed to keep walking for as long as I could without falling down.

I willed myself to believe that everything would be all

right; no negative thinking, no analyzing or processing anything that had happened.

When I began to doze in and out of consciousness, my inner voice failed to get me moving again. It wasn't until a cool rag was placed over my face that I woke enough to realize I was in a moving vehicle and my hands were free.

"Is that her?" a man whispered. I think my head was on his lap.

"I'm not sure. Is she doing anything yet?" another man answered, sounding a little farther away.

"Well, she's breathin, isn't she?"

"Smartass," the distant voice grumbled.

"Why do they make them dress like nuns? This holy shit fries my brain."

"You know they're a bunch of freaks, bro. I just hope they don't have Tilly."

Tilly! He knew Tilly?

She's dead! I tried to tell him, but my mouth wouldn't work.

Hearing her name broke open the floodgates I was trying to keep closed. The memory of her body burning to a crisp was all too fresh. It was an ugly, festering wound I didn't know how to begin fixing.

I wanted to scream. I wanted to give myself a minute to fall apart and mourn the first person I had found friendship with, but I was too mentally and physically exhausted.

As I began to slip away again, I felt grubby fingers back on my skin, finding their way to the cross around my neck. I must have made some sort of sound because the gentle touch disappeared when my head lolled.

"Can you hear me? Can you tell me who you are?"

I *could* hear him, but I couldn't tell him who I was because I didn't know. I could tell him what I was supposed to be and what I was made to do; that ever since I was a little girl, my daddy had used me as a pawn to further his agenda, passing me around to men three times my age since I was a ripe eleven to perform sexual favors. I was a living, breathing sex doll for a colony of men and women. I was condemned and convicted for being different and misunderstood.

If I could have spoken, I would have told him the only thing that mattered anymore.

I am the monster they created. I'm the whore they're ashamed of.

They took my heaven away.

Now, I would bring them hell.

Chapter Three

Calista

It was another sleepless night beneath burning sheets. The large electrical fan rotating back and forth wasn't doing shit to cool down the room. I restlessly toyed with the inverted cross I wore around my neck before finally giving up with a frustrated huff. Insomnia was such a clingy little cunt. While normal people slept soundly, my demons decided to strike up a conversation.

Kicking the sheet from my legs, I glanced over at Jinx, making sure I didn't wake her. When she didn't move or speak, I slowly slipped out of bed.

Spotting my clothes bundled up on the floor, I scooped them up and tiptoed into the small bathroom.

After I had my shorts and tank back on, I went over to the basin attached to the wall and drank some cold water from the faucet, sighing as the cool liquid alleviated my throat's dryness.

Twisting my lips around, I cocked my head and stared at my ghostly, pale reflection in the shattered mirror. Dull blue eyes surrounded by smudged black makeup stared back at me. White-blonde locks framed my face. I looked alive, my body breathed, and my heart still beat—but inside, I was dead. Most days it felt like I barely existed.

Placing my fingers on the glass, I began tracing over the lines. No matter which way I went, I always wound up right back where I had begun. My life was nothing but a hamster wheel spinning in place, making no progress, going nowhere.

I pressed my index finger down on a protruding shard, smiling when blood began to spill from the tip.

I watched it try to retrace my path in the twisted cracks, just for it to simply break free and make a crimson trail of its own.

Was it really so easy? I couldn't seem to find my way out. No matter how hard I tried to break away and venture out on my own, I always ended up right back in a twisted maze, trapped.

I wanted to know where I went wrong. There was a black hole growing in my mind. I hated what I'd become, this empty shell of a girl who had spent so much time hiding who she was that she now had no idea who the fuck she was supposed to be.

I had no issue remembering the things I wanted to forget. The mental prison I was stuck in kept all the memories from my past trapped with me in a cold and lonely cell.

I fucking hated it.

No, that was an understatement.

I was sick of being sick of it.

Sucking my bloody finger into my mouth, I turned away from the mirror and walked out of the bathroom.

Tiptoeing back through the room, I slipped out into the dimly lit hall and pulled the door shut behind me.

Expecting everyone else in the compound to be asleep at such a late hour, I immediately headed in the direction of whispering voices. The closer I got, the clearer they became. Rounding a corner, I came to a stop in the doorway of the living room.

Tito and Grady stood over a table with their heads bowed together. I watched them for a few minutes, wondering if they would notice me standing there, waiting to be acknowledged. There was a mass of papers between them that I couldn't see clearly from my vantage point. It was glaringly obvious they were up to something, just like they had been every other night for the past few months.

Their stealth level was shit.

"We have to do this on the low. No one else can know," Tito whispered.

"No one else can know what?" I asked, strolling into the room.

They jumped apart, both spinning around to face me. Tito's brown eyes met mine, and as always, I was reminded of Tilly, his twin. They had the same Polynesian features: shoulder-length curls and flawless brown skin. The only difference between them was that one was alive and the other was dead.

"How long have you been standing there?" Grady asked.

"Long enough." Forcing myself to look away from Tito, I focused on the table they seemed a little too determined to block from me.

"What the hell are you two doing in here?"

They stood rigid and silent, prompting me to walk around

them to see whatever they were trying to hide for myself. "What is this?"

"Research," Tito answered, turning back around to watch me.

"Research, huh?" I looked down at the tabletop that was littered with notes, article clippings, and polaroid pictures. "You're full of shit, and you're lying to my face. Why would you be researching them?"

I snatched up one of the many sheets of paper that had 'Savages' scrawled across it.

"I told you we shouldn't have done this here," Grady spat at Tito before turning his attention to me. "Cali, this isn't what it looks like."

"So I'm just dreaming that you two assholes are meeting in secret to plan something that involves them?" I grabbed another sheet of paper, letting it flutter to the floor when I couldn't decipher the sloppy handwriting scribbled all over it.

One picture in particular caught my attention. It wasn't like any of my others.

I reached for it at the same time as Tito, slapping his hand away before he could pick it up. He wasn't in color, the man in the photo. Whoever took the shot had snapped it without his knowledge.

There was a scowl on his face as he looked at something not visible to the lens. Tattoos covered every visible inch of skin. 'Savages' was inked over his right temple, and directly beneath the corner of his eye was a tiny but noticeable inverted cross. I absentmindedly stroked my necklace, unable to look away from him.

"He might know where David is," Tito eventually said.

"Might?" Suddenly, he had my full attention.

He sighed. "They've been abnormally quiet for the last

few weeks. They could be working together. I *think* they might be about to do something big.

"My paranoia needs to know what the fuck is going on so I can be prepared if a shit storm is coming, and we won't get caught in the middle.

"I need someone on the inside. It was either Simon or Grady, so I'm sending him." He hitched a thumb in Grady's direction.

"I get why you would keep this from everyone else, but why me? Why would you hide this from *me*?"

I was pissed, and he knew it. I had been searching for David—my sperm donor—for years. It was damn near impossible to find him, because he never stayed in one spot for longer than a few months. I'd heard through the grapevine that The Order was growing and his mindless followers seemed to be increasing with it.

"The fewer people who knew, the better. This isn't a personal conspiracy against you."

"This could all be a bunch of bullshit; like he said, it's just paranoia," Grady added, backing him up.

"I don't care if it's paranoia. If you so much as thought there was a miniscule chance of finding him, why wouldn't you tell me?"

"Maybe because you aren't the only one in this room who lost someone because of that piece of shit," Tito snapped.

"Lost *someone?* I lost everything, but that's beside the point. It's not a competition. Why would you send Grady in, of all people? And why was Simon ever an option? He wouldn't be able to find his dick if it wasn't attached to him."

"Well, I can't trust many people with this. I don't want anyone getting killed or falling into that lifestyle. Whom do you suggest I send? You?"

I shrugged. That's exactly what I was suggesting. He

started to laugh, stopping short when he saw how serious I was.

"Absolutely fuckin not. No. Are you out of your goddamn mind?" He picked up a recent article clipping and held it up for me to see. "Do you see what they do to women? Look at this!"

Huffing out a breath, I carefully studied the news photo. The breasts were the only thing left to confirm the person's gender. Everything else was mutilated or gone.

A large inverted cross had been carved right down the center of her naked torso. He clearly didn't see what I did.

I saw someone trying to make a statement.

They were sending a personal message.

Whoever had taken the shot did so long after post-mortem. The body had begun to decay, but pointing out that anything or anyone could have taken her apart was a moot point with him.

I wasn't sure how he expected me to react, but this didn't deter me.

My mind was already made up. I had nothing to lose and nothing to fear, which made me the best candidate.

I looked up from the picture with another shrug. "This doesn't change anything. I'm not this woman."

"This doesn't bother you at all?"

He looked at me in disbelief, glancing at Grady as if he needed confirmation from another person that I didn't care.

"What's going on with you?"

I didn't bother voicing a response; he wouldn't like my answer. At one point in time, the horrific image would have had some effect on me. Maybe the kick to the back of my head had knocked something loose. I couldn't pinpoint when I'd changed, or really describe how I knew I wasn't the same.

Something had just shifted, and I had made zero effort to shift it back.

They had no idea who they let live under their roof.

There was a secret side of me I never let them see, keeping her hidden under lock and key. The strange creature that lurked just beneath my skin was caged and waiting to be let out.

I usually took better care hiding my harsher nature, but as of late, I was struggling with being good. My angels and my demons kept crossing signals.

"Actually, Cali is perfect for this," Grady hesitantly said.

"What the fuck?" Tito voiced my exact sentiments, whipping his head around so fast his neck cracked.

"Hear me out on this," Grady continued, holding up a hand to silence any protest. "She may be a smartass, but she *is* smart. And stubborn. And she doesn't trust anyone. Oh, and she's a she, which works about a thousand times more in our favor—you know, cause the whole 'helpless woman' thing." He ticked off each point on his fingers.

When neither of us immediately spoke, his hazel eyes bounced between us, a smug grin spreading across his cherub face. I had half-expected him to repeat what everyone else in the compound whispered about me when I walked by. I should have known better than that, though.

Ever since the day he and Tito had found me, they'd done their best to look out for my wellbeing. They were the only people aside from Jinx who never spoke ill of me. They had never judged me for my obscurity or religiously told me I didn't belong with them because of my ties to David.

Everyone else needed somewhere to direct their hatred and misery, and I happened to be the perfect target. I was a villain they could blame; they were afraid of me. Sometimes,

I didn't blame them. I knew there was a flaw in my code. The simple truth was that I didn't give a fuck.

"Those sound like reasons not to send her," Tito finally said.

"No, those are the reasons you *do* send her. Plus, she doesn't like dick," Grady slipped in. They stared at one another, some silent battle of wills taking place between them.

I felt like I was missing something, but with these two that wasn't unusual. I didn't bother adding my two cents, mostly because what Grady said was true—except for me not liking dick. I didn't particularly care for anything anymore. I had slept with too many men in an effort to prove to myself that I wasn't broken. It never worked.

I got nothing from the experiences but a free three minutes and twenty seconds of wasted time. I was left feeling empty and used, just as I had years ago, and it wasn't worth it anymore; not when I knew what I really needed.

Jinx was strictly a friend—the only real friend I'd ever had.

She was a gorgeous, but despite what Grady refused to believe, I harbored no secret desire for her.

I stood, watching them discuss my pros and cons as if I weren't in the room, shutting them both down when I couldn't take it anymore.

"It doesn't matter what either of you thinks *she* should or shouldn't do, because *she* is going to do whatever the fuck *she* wants."

They stopped going back and forth and stared at me with slightly open mouths.

"The Savages aren't a gang of gentlemen trying to do the world a favor. They live by their own code. This isn't the goddamn Boy Scouts we're talking about!" Tito preached, throwing his hands up in frustration. "They're outcasts. They're undesirables. They're sick in the fucking head."

He wasn't saying anything I'd never heard before. Quite honestly, it sounded like he was describing *me*.

"No one wants to do this world favors, T, and I don't blame them. It's a real fucked-up place to live."

He opened his mouth to respond, promptly snapping it shut, unable to refute what I had just said. We lived in a world where the human race had no humanity, were merely animals who hadn't been taught how to behave.

There was a place referred to as The Kingdom. Supposedly, the grass was a vibrant green, it was always sunny, and love conquered all—a real fucking utopia that had no use for bad batches like us.

Outside those towering walls was the Badlands, and in the Badlands, the weak struggled against the strong.

Anarchy reigned.

The world had been like this long before I was born. If The Order and the Savages really did have some diabolical plan for the rest of us, there wasn't shit me or Tito could do to stop it.

"You're not going to let this go, are you?" he asked me outright.

"Highly unlikely."

"You should probably grab a seat, then. We have a lot of shit to talk about."

He turned around and shut the door, letting out a deep breath before facing me again.

"Let's start with his name."

Chapter Four

Calista

His name was Romero.

That was the first time I had ever heard someone say it. People were too superstitious to speak it, as if he were some demonic entity that would appear and slit their tender throats before dragging their fragile souls straight to hell.

We'd spent hours discussing risks and potential outcomes. With time being sensitive, we had to do the best we could, converting their months' worth of information into a last-minute plan.

Sighing, I looked out the Touareg's window and watched all the empty fields, vast open wasteland passing us by.

We were getting farther and farther away from anything remotely civilized.

Into the wild. That's how I thought of it—away from petty moral barriers and society's fragile sensitivities.

"This could all be nothing," Tito told me for what had to be the tenth time in less than two hours.

"Or it could be everything." I pursed my lips and narrowed my eyes. I wished we could play the quiet game until I was no longer stuck in a car with him. Our eyes stayed locked in the rearview mirror until he was forced to look away or risk veering off the road.

"I just don't want you to end up like his last girl."

His last girl? That instantly piqued my interest and further irritated me. I didn't know about any girl.

"Why? What happened to her?"

"That isn't relevant to your situation. He's just trying to change your mind," Grady interjected.

"Trying to chit-chat me out of this is a waste of your precious breath. This is the best lead I've had in four years."

The only response he gave to that was a shake of his head. I knew the only reason he caved on this was because he knew I'd just take their information and do it anyway. I didn't particularly like being told I couldn't do something because my balls were on my chest and not between my legs.

For the first hour of our drive, he had told me every horror story about Romero that he could think of, not realizing what he was doing. The brutality didn't scare me; it intrigued me. Truthfully, I wanted to see who these people were and the way they lived. Every scrap of information, no matter how disturbing, only made me want to meet him more.

I needed to get away, needed something to pull me out of the murky cesspool of the thing I called life.

Every day I felt like I lost another part of the woman I shunned in order to assimilate. I *needed* to do this. It was everything I'd been waiting for.

I couldn't tell them any of that, though. They would never understand the parts of me I hid. Jinx was the only person who had ever tried, and I'd just had to leave without telling her goodbye. I sincerely hoped she would understand why.

"This is it." Grady pointed in the direction of a tree line looming in the near distance.

Squinting, I peered through the front windshield, trying to spot what he was referring to. Tito drove a half mile farther before pulling over. We sat in silence for a few moments. I couldn't say for sure what they were thinking, but it was more than likely about how crazy this whole thing was.

I was going to solicit the lions that ruled over a land of sheep. They would either sink their teeth into me or let me into their pride.

When Tito's brown eyes met mine again, I knew on some level that he did understand, and I knew he wanted to find David just as badly as I did.

"All right, let's do this," he said, climbing out of the SUV.

I put one hand on the door to follow him. Before I could even push it open, Grady reached back and snagged my wrist.

"If things start to go south, you get away, Cali. Run like hell, and I promise I'll find you."

I could only nod my head. Vocalizing emotions had always been one of my weak points. He nodded back before letting me go and turning around, allowing me to get out. Shielding my eyes from the sun, I walked to where Tito stood.

"You'd better not get yourself killed," he teased, attempting to break the tension between us. He rolled his shoulders and looked upwards at the clear sky. "Sometimes I forget how sheltered you've been. I'm going to give you one last bit of advice."

I readied myself for another rant and received something much simpler—also, a tad confusing.

"They don't do anything for free. They don't give without receiving. The worst thing you could do is make a deal with one of them that you can't retract."

What? "You've been telling me for the past however many hours that I should move as quickly as possible to figure out what's going on. Wouldn't making a deal be doing just that?"

I rolled my eyes when he pinched the bridge of his nose dramatically before answering the question.

"Romero isn't called the devil for shits and giggles. He'll eat your soul and then shit it out."

Frowning, I studied his body language and for the first time noticed how distressed he was.

"Why are you so afraid of him?"

"I know *you're* not afraid of anything, Cali, but in this case, I really wish you were." He paused for a few seconds before continuing. "I'll find a way to contact you after a week or two. If I can't, I'll assume you're dead. If shit goes bad, try to get back to the compound. Never let your guard down, and don't let them get in your head."

"And if I can't find them?"

"That's not probable. You just go straight. You see that?"

I turned ever so slightly in the direction he was pointing, never seeing his other arm move.

It happened so fast all I felt was the blade piercing my skin and an odd tingling sensation, followed by an intense, searing heat.

"Why did you do that?" I instinctively wrapped my arms around my middle and backed away, glaring up at him.

"I'm sorry; it had to be done. You're the perfect picture of health. They'd never believe you were out here on your own.

I have to get back, and you need to go. We don't know who could be out here." He rushed past me, getting back in the car with the bloody knife in his hand and peeling off before I could fully process what had just happened.

"Shit," I muttered, pressing a hand to my side. Blood seeped through the small hole in my shirt, running down my stomach and staining my fingers crimson.

Knowing my only option at this point was to get out of the open, I looked at the tree line and began to move towards it.

Five minutes into my foray, I deeply regretted wearing jeans. It was so damn hot my thighs began to sweat.

I made it to a small creek and rested my sticky hand on the nearest tree, pausing to catch my breath and evaluate my situation.

Tito didn't even tell me exactly where to go. How the fuck was I supposed to walk straight when there wasn't a straight path? "Damn," I hissed, pulling up my shirt so I could get a better look at the stab wound that was starting to hurt real fucking bad.

I pressed around the tender area, trying to determine just how deep it was. If he'd hit something vital, I would have already bled out.

I had no damn clue if that were true or not, but I was going with it.

There was too much blood for me to see anything. Wading into the shallow water, I slowly crouched down and scooped some into my hand. I did my best to clean the area off.

So focused on myself and how unsanitary the water was, I ignored nature's blaring warning that something was wrong.

There was no sound. No birds, no bugs, and no tiny creatures scurrying through the undergrowth. Not even the wind carried. It was utterly silent.

I was still examining myself when I heard the rapid sound of footsteps, as if someone were running. Not a millisecond later, a solid body was barreling into me from behind. The abrupt impact gave me no time to brace myself and sent us both to the ground.

"Fuck!" I screamed, getting a mouthful of murky water. I ignored the pain shooting through my side and focused on the man damn near straddling my back.

"I been watchin ya fer a good minute now," he confessed with a thick accent.

When his weight lifted away, I attempted to move, but he quickly grabbed hold of my ankles and flipped me onto my back with a little splash. Swallowing a yelp, I blinked up at a bear of a man with a head of unruly brown hair.

"What do you want?"

"Got what I want." He flashed me a smile of stained black and yellow teeth before turning around. He started walking in a different direction than I had been going, dragging me along behind him.

"Let me go!" I yelled at his back, twisting and turning in every direction, clawing at the ground in an effort to break free.

"Calm down, darlin. We'll be home soon," he laughed.

Home? Where the fuck was home?

Chapter Five

Romero

Most people had a morning routine.

The fortunate ones got to sit down and read the paper in a comfy, cozy house, and enjoy a cup of espresso. They sat in some plush ass chair in the fleece robe or plaid pajamas they had slept in. Maybe they propped their slipper-clad feet up in the process.

Thank fuck that wasn't me. Espresso tasted like pig shit, and I slept naked.

The unfortunate ones had to figure out if they were going to be able to drink a glass of water or eat that day. Then they had to double check that the boogeyman hadn't snatched up a family member in the middle of the night.

They couldn't even piss in safety.

Gotta say I'm real fucking glad not to be one of them, either. Having to worry about my life while my dick was in my hand would really fuck up my day.

Then, there was me.

Every morning, I looked out at a world that had rotted and gone cold. A world responsible for taking away the parts of me that ever dared to care. I had nothing left but a cyclone of endless rage constantly churning thorns and venom through my veins.

I didn't give a shit if someone's family member went missing in the middle of the night. I had my own people to take care of.

If I wasn't so deranged, I might have pretended I wanted to change. I was better off like this, and I refused to hide from what was inside me. In my anarchy, only the strong survived. I had the scars beneath my ink to prove it. The bodies buried all around my domain only solidified it.

The weeping that burst through my monitor and had me turning away from the window, putting an end to my daily morning reflections, sealed the deal.

Without bothering to look, I bypassed the screen and left the room. The warehouse was silent now that I was away from the monitors; not even the woman's cries could be heard.

I made my way down to the lower level of the building, reminding myself I still needed to get rid of the dead redhead on my bedroom floor.

Beyond a metal door that sat alone at the end of a short hall was my unhappy new friend. The door groaned and squeaked when I pushed against it, slamming shut with a loud bang after I stepped through.

I glanced around the barren room, noting that the pliers had been moved from their resting place on the wall. That meant Cobra had come in after I left the night before.

Looking towards the woman restrained in the center of the room, I began to approach her with slow, measured steps.

Her husband's naked body was directly across from her. His arms were still tied to the poles that had pulled them from their sockets, his tibia stuck clean through his right leg, and dried blood coated the backs of his thighs and ass. He'd bled out sometime the previous day after he was fucked for a solid hour and then had his wrists cut open.

The woman stopped wailing and started trying to swing her suspended body in my direction. I had purposely secured the ropes around her so there was no give in them, making sure she couldn't find a way to ease her discomfort or look away from her husband's brutalized asshole.

A fresh line of drool hung from the side of her busted lip. On the floor beneath her head lay Cobra's handiwork—a small pile of bloody, broken teeth.

She looked up at me with swollen green eyes I wanted to carve out of their sockets. The blind would see a helpless woman made to dress like an old-style nun, hanging from the ceiling. I saw a lamb waiting to be slaughtered.

"Do you remember where David is now?" I interrogated.

"I'll never tell you." She tried to sound strong, but with spittle flying from her mouth and her voice almost gone, I was severely unimpressed.

"That's funny. I swear a few hours ago you said you couldn't remember."

I grabbed her cheeks and squeezed, applying pressure on her tender gums. Her pained bleat was a fucking delightful sound. I knew she would never tell me where her precious prophet was. None of them ever did. I'd lost count of how many people I had killed trying to get a solid answer. The motherfucker had his followers brainwashed.

These people's weak, corruptible minds believed his interests and theirs were the same. The Order wasn't a religious group; it was a widespread cult with a made up doctrine that revered David like a god. They had their own convenient definitions of sin that matched their bullshit religion, which made the fact that David used a fucking cross of all things as his insignia comical.

I used the symbol in a much more appropriate way. It was my endearing way of saying fuck him. I could never embrace that shit. The only gods I believed in were myself and death, and she had always been on my side.

As I watched, blood began to pool between the woman's lips. I wondered how many children she had helped steal. How many men and women were killed in front of her. It wasn't that I cared—I was just curious.

I was still squeezing when Cobra and Grimm walked in, carrying sandwiches.

"Get rid of her. We have a problem," Cobra announced around a mouthful of food.

"Lena still hasn't come back," Grimm clarified.

"Well, that doesn't fucking surprise me." I let go of the woman's face to retrieve the Browning knife I kept in my back pocket. With one fluid motion, I flipped it open and inserted the seven-inch blade into the side of her neck, then just as smoothly pulled it out.

She gurgled, choking on own her blood. Her body swayed, twitching involuntarily as it died. I placed the palm of my hand over her heart and shut my eyes. It was beating to an erratic tempo, fighting so desperately to cling to a life that was already lost.

I expelled a quiet breath and opened my eyes to watch the

blood run down her face, turning her honey brown hair a vivid maroon before dripping in a steady pattern onto the concrete floor.

Death was such a beautiful thing. She could take everything in the blink of an eye, or draw the suffering out for as long as she desired.

I wiped my knife clean on the woman's habit and then turned to face my brothers. "I guess we need to go find Lena, then. I'll get her down later."

"I'll drive, you eat," Grimm replied, tossing me a sandwich on our way out of the room.

We searched the only place someone could get lost: the woods that sat twelve miles down the road. The longer we were out playing *find the needle*, the more our irritation grew.

I could admit that for the most part, society had kept its shit together. We weren't considered part of that society, though. We didn't live in the fancy fucking houses that had twenty-four seven patrols and a fence to keep people like us out. You know the ones who tie up Daddy, terrorize the kiddos, and then fuck Mommy to ramp up the despair? We are those people.

It was dumb to go anywhere alone if you weren't

someone people knew not to fuck with. I wanted to believe Lena didn't come across someone that fucking stupid, but the evidence was not in her favor.

"I don't think she's out here," Grimm said, breaking our companionable silence.

"Do you think that's human?" Cobra pointed to a flattened plant with a small amount of fresh blood on its leaves. Looking beyond the plant, it was obvious someone or something was recently dragged through the dirt.

Guess we were about to find out which one it was.

Chapter Six

Calista

He secured a chain around my neck and knocked me on my ass before walking away.

I immediately wrapped my hands around the thick metal and pulled to no avail, agitating the raw skin on my palms.

"This can't be happening to me." I gritted my teeth and tried again, yanking with all the strength I had.

"It's not going to give. Trust me, I've tried."

I stopped and looked across the barn in the direction the voice had come from.

A girl who looked to be a few years younger than me was chained to the adjacent wall. The sun filtering in from outside bounced off long, chocolate brown hair and illuminated a pair of cognac colored eyes.

Various flower and henna tattoos were inked on her bronze skin.

"How long have you been here?" I asked, taking a good look around.

"Two days, maybe three. She was here before me." She gestured to a dead girl strapped down on an old table near the back of the barn.

The rancid smell emanating from a quad of rusted oil drums lining the front wall was self-explanatory, as was the rotting torso lying in front of them. Only the head was left; the rest of whomever it had once been was either in one of the barrels or someone's stomach.

"He's coming back," she warned quietly.

I pressed my back against the wall to give myself a full view of what was going on, wincing from the sharp pain in my side. The lumberjack entered the barn with a hacksaw in one hand and a little boy's in the other.

We watched in silence as they walked right by us to the table in the back.

"Grab the buckets, Dex."

The little boy did as he was told, taking off and returning with two round, bloodstained pails. He sat them down by the edge of the table before climbing up on a stool so he could watch the man I assumed was his dad work.

"Remember to keep your hands off," the man warned the kid as he began sawing into the dead woman's arm.

You could hear the blade sliding back and forth, cutting through bone and muscle.

"I saw that man stab you," he said after a minute. "Shame. If I weren't a married man, I might keep yer for myself."

What a goddamn nightmare that would be.

"I acquired Arlen over there when her uncle was kind enough to stop and offer me a ride. That's him."

He gestured towards the decapitated torso lying by the oil drums. I glanced at Arlen; she was now staring down at the ground.

Generally, I didn't feel bad for people, but I hoped for her sanity's sake she didn't have to watch that happen.

The man resumed his sawing, occasionally saying something to the kid as he stripped the body down and tossed random bits into the buckets.

"Now, yer never wanna eat the brain. It ain't good fer nothing but C-J-D. That's Creutzfeldt-Jakob disease," he explained, loud enough for us all to hear. "Ribs? Well, who doesn't like a good barbeque?" he joked.

"The forearms are tough meat. My wife likes to use those chunks for soup. The shoulders need some work to make tender, but once yer do then yer get a nice blade steak. Oh, and anything on the back is gonna give yer some good choice cuts. Now, can either of yer pretty ladies guess what my favorite part is?"

He glanced between me and Arlen with a disgusting toothy smile as he flipped the body onto its stomach.

The arm he'd been working on dangled by a small band of tendons that slowly pulled apart.

"It's the buttocks!" He laughed and slapped the dead girl's ass. "Put it in a slow cooker for a few hours, and it reminds me of my momma's Sunday roast."

Neither of us said a word. I had no idea why he felt the need to share all of this, but it was information I never needed nor cared to know.

I'd heard all about cannibals before. They refused to be simple outliers, and no one else would accept them. The

Savages didn't exactly have an open door policy, and there was no way in hell they could live in Centriole—the megalopolis.

Like everyone else though, they usually cliqued up in groups; safety in numbers and all that jazz.

They were unable to get food through connections or other means, so animals and people were their only options.

Nevertheless, hearing about something and seeing it were two entirely different things.

I listened to his heavy breaths as he grew tired and began to sweat. I turned away when he started to strip down individual bone, using the claw of a hammer to pull and pry.

After another stretch of silence, he began to whistle as he worked. Tuning out the noise around me, I leaned my head back and stared up at the ceiling.

A giant cockroach darting down my arm woke me up.

I smacked it off and watched it skid across the dirt floor. The chain around my neck clinked at the sudden movement, instantly reminding me of where I was.

Looking out the open barn door, I saw it had begun to drizzle. The hazy blue-gray sky signaled it was early dawn.

I'd lost a full day thanks to a cannibal.

I took my first real breath and had never been more grateful for having a strong stomach. The smell of decaying flesh was so potent it burned my nose hairs.

Just for the hell of it, I tugged on the chain again, knowing it wasn't going to magically unlock itself or come off the wall.

"He keeps the keys on a belt loop," Arlen flatly commented.

She seemed resigned to the fact that we would be sautéed like fillets and then eaten with a side of flesh rolls. I was determined that wasn't going to happen. This was just a minor setback I should have foreseen.

Every time I thought I was finally getting somewhere, this bitch called life decided she would try to break me down again.

I thought she would have fucked off by now and realized it would never happen.

I had already been to hell and back, and now it was a part of me. There wasn't much she could throw my way that I wouldn't overcome. I think she forgot all the cards I'd already been dealt.

"Okay, Cali, you got this." Looking around, I studied what was left of the woman on the table. Damn near all the flesh had been stripped from her bones, except for her face, which was untouched.

Not only did this make a plan begin to form in my head, but it made the inverted cross tattooed beneath her eye stand out like a beacon in the night. If she were part of Romero's group, that meant they had to be around this area, just as Tito had said.

"You look like you might have a plan," Arlen said, suddenly sounding much more alert.

I looked back at her and smiled.

I didn't know shit about this girl, but I wasn't going to leave her here to become someone's midnight snack.

Glancing out the door to make sure Lumberjack wasn't coming, I began to explain.

Chapter Seven

Calista

I bit down on my lip and pushed two dirt-clad fingers into my stab wound.

"Fuck, this hurts." Breathing through my mouth, I blinked to clear away gathering tears.

Arlen made a sound in her throat, watching me with a frown. Blood quickly seeped through my already stained shirt. I pulled my fingers out and pushed down on the inflamed skin, leaning over so blood would drip down on the ground, stopping when my head grew fuzzy and it felt like I would throw up.

I'm not sure how long we sat before Lumberjack showed up, reacting just like I thought he would.

"Oh, no, yer don't!" He rushed towards me, grabbing for his key. "If yer dying I gotta skin yer now or the meat will go bad."

I didn't move from where I'd purposely slouched on the ground. I let him unlock the padlock, remove the chain, and drag me towards his table.

As I played half-dead, I couldn't help but wonder how many people had been alive and fully aware of what was going on as they were dismembered limb by limb. Not that I cared; I was just curious.

His mistake was underestimating my will to survive. He lifted me up and dropped me down right on top of the bare torso. Bones shifted and collapsed beneath my weight, pressing into my back. I swallowed repeatedly in an effort not to throw up from the smell.

As soon as he turned to grab one of his buckets, I reached for the hacksaw he'd left near the edge of the table.

There were still pieces of tissue and flesh embedded between the ribbed blades.

I gripped the blood-crusted handle and swung without hesitation.

He screamed and bowed forward as the blade made contact with the back of his upper thigh. Before he could get up, I swung again, sucking in a breath as pain shot up the entire left side of my body.

This time, the blade hit the back part of his neck. Instead of pulling it out, I pushed in, making a seesaw motion to wedge it in place.

"You cannibalistic fucker!" Arlen yelled triumphantly.

I swung down off the table and pushed him over. He reached for his neck and I went for the key, ripping it right through his worn belt-loop.

Key in hand, I ran to Arlen, letting out a quick breath of relief when it easily fit into the padlock holding her chain on.

"Bill?" someone called from outside the barn just as her chain hit the floor.

We froze and looked at one another. The person called out again, sounding a little closer. Bill stood up and stumbled forward, making an attempt to yell for help.

With the saw no longer wedged in his neck, blood flowed freely, spurting around meaty fingers.

"We need to go," Arlen rushed out.

She grabbed my hand and pulled us closer to the wall, using shadows to cover us.

"Bill!" a woman screamed from just outside the barn's doorway.

She barreled right past us and we wasted no time slipping out. I still heard her screaming as we took off through a field to the right of the depleted building. A screen door slammed shut shortly after.

"They went that way," were the only clear words I understood over the loud commotion.

"Shit! How many of them are there?" I asked as we zigzagged our way through the tall grass.

"Five…four…" Arlen responded, before gasping out, "Woods!"

We made a break for it, hearing multiple male voices calling out behind us. My heart felt as if it were going to beat out of my damn chest. Adrenaline had my brain so focused on getting away I almost forgot about the bloody hole leaking down my side.

The drizzle had turned into a light rain and the ground was wet. I saw the steep embankment but Arlen didn't. I managed to slide into a stop; she fell forward and grabbed for me, taking us down together.

A list of expletives flew from my mouth as my body

rolled over hers and we tumbled like logs. Leaves and mud clung to me like Velcro. The pain in my side suddenly hit me like a hammer to a nail, slightly blurring my vision.

"Come on girl, we gotta move." Arlen recovered first and grabbed my upper arm, practically dragging me until I was running beside her again—barely.

She was in pretty good shape for having not eaten the past two or three days. The ground was uneven and neither of us seemed to have a clue where we were—not that it mattered, because we sure as shit didn't make it very far.

They had to have seen us long before we saw them. This time, there was no stopping. I slammed right into him, and it was as if he'd been waiting for me to do just that. His hands gripped my forearms to steady me, not push me away.

From my peripheral, I saw Arlen apprehended by a redhead and another dark-haired man with a beard. I attempted to turn my head to make sure she was okay, but I was stuck. I had never stepped in quicksand before, but I imagined the sensation was similar to this.

He had the darkest eyes I'd ever seen. I blinked, thinking the pain was affecting how I saw what was right in front of me.

Nope, I was still staring into two black holes with endless depth. I saw sorrow, pain, and so much anger sunken within them that it was almost like looking in a mirror—a shattered mirror with jagged edges.

I smiled. I was a bloody, muddy mess, but I smiled, and he smiled back. That alone would have knocked me right back on my ass if he wasn't holding me up. It was like déjà vu; he felt so familiar to me.

Before I could open my mouth to speak, he had a hand tightly wrapped around my throat. He spun me around and pressed his brick chest against my back. I reached up to remove his damn hand when two men came sliding down the embankment much more gracefully than we just had.

"Those lags belong to us," one of the men said as they approached, unmistakably kin to cannibal Bill.

"Do they?" Romero challenged lazily.

The deep timbre of his voice sent a chill straight down my spine.

"If she belongs to you, why is my hand wrapped around her throat?"

The other man opened his mouth to respond but was swiftly cut off.

"We don't belong to no bottom feeders!" Arlen yelled, struggling to break away from the dark-haired man who was now holding her in a chokehold.

"We don't want any trouble, Romero. We just want the girls," the more intelligible one conceded. There was a nervous hitch in his voice that reminded me of how well known the Savages were, and how people purposely avoided them at all costs.

"There was a girl with y'all's tattoo. They ate her. They ate your friend," Arlen rushed out.

None of the men reacted. Her confession was met with resounding silence from both sides.

"So she's yours?" Romero asked again, cupping a tattooed hand over my mouth when I tried to speak.

"They both are."

"All right then, take her." He pushed me forward and stepped back. "And her." He nodded to Arlen.

She barely righted herself from being shoved forward when the man's companion grabbed her by the hair and started dragging her along as if she were a ragdoll.

"No, wait!" I shouted as I was partially lifted over the man's shoulder. I hit the back of his head with a closed fist and he let me go. I stumbled backwards, tripping over myself as I tried to get away, landing right at Romero's feet. The air whooshed out of my lungs and I reflexively grabbed for my side.

With an angry growl he reached for me again, this time going for my ankles. The situation flipped in a matter of seconds.

I stared in confusion as he jerked away and blood began to spill down the front of him. Romero stepped around me and I watched as he pulled a knife out of the man's chest, shoving him to the ground in the process.

"Go get the other one," he said to his friends, placing his black boot on the man's stomach to prevent him from getting up.

Without a word, his comrades walked off after Arlen. Romero looked at the cannibal and began pressing down. The man's pained scream echoed across the treetops as Romero dug his steel toe into the chest wound. I watched him suffer with a deep feeling of self-satisfaction. The fucker deserved it.

"Stop, ple—"

Romero lunged down and drove the silver blade straight through the center of the man's forehead, cutting his plea short. His muscles flexed beneath his shirt from the force it took to penetrate the man's skull.

My lips parted as I stared at them both in fascinated awe. A silent crimson river made its way to the forest ground. The knife made a faint squelching sound and then a 'pop' as he removed it.

With a flick of his wrist, something chunky and pinkish-red flew off the blade and landed on a nearby plant. He looked at me then, his onyx hues drilling into mine—dark meeting light—and gave me a beautifully devious smile.

"I changed my mind." He shrugged. "Finders keepers."

His words had the breath evaporating from my chest. As I stared into his eyes, I saw myself falling right into the void.

I was so fucked.

An angry scream in the near distance broke me from my tunnel vision. I blinked and looked away, glancing around in hope I would catch a glimpse of Arlen. Remembering my objective, Tito's voice resounded as a warning bell inside my head.

"They can't know you found them willingly. They'll know something's up and won't hesitate to kill you."

Well, fuck. Realizing I'd almost completely screwed everything up, I began to half scoot/half crab-walk backward.

Our eyes locked once more and he grinned, flashing a set of perfect white teeth. Somehow, this smile was darker than the last one, because now he seemed to be amused.

"Where are you going?" His tone was mocking—child-like. He tilted his head to the side, making no effort to come after me. He simply tracked my every move with his coal-black eyes.

My back hit a tree and I used it as leverage to pull myself up, keeping one hand over my injury. We were only a few feet apart. My ragged breathing filled the silence between us.

Arlen's yells grew louder.

Male laughter signified his friends had caught her and were bringing her back against her will.

I tried to spot what direction they were coming from but I still couldn't see anyone.

Is he getting closer?

I glanced back at Romero and swore he'd moved from where he'd just been standing. His face gave nothing away.

"Why are you still here?"

"Why am I still here?" he repeated.

"That's what I said, isn't it? I don't know what you want. I have nothing to give. So why are you still standing there?"

"The odds must be in your favor then, babe, cause I don't want anything from you yet. You don't even have to thank me for saving your pixie ass, *but* you're coming with me."

His friends came up behind him, and the redhead smiled at me. The one with darker hair carried an unconscious Arlen in his arms.

"What did you do to her?"

'I shut her up," he replied, a little too happily.

Fucker.

I fixed my face with a glare and looked back at Romero.

"I'm not going anywhere with you, and neither is she, so you can just put her down and be on your merry way."

He flashed me another dark smile before sharing a look with his friends.

"Not only is she a fucking idiot, but she's mouthy, too? Huh. Guess I shouldn't be surprised, though. I mean, look at her." He turned away from his friends, letting his eyes slowly travel up and down my body, landing back on my face. "All beauty and no brain," he sneered.

Did this shithead just call me an idiot? I was filthy, hurt, and aggravated, and a million different variations of the word asshole were flying around in my head. He had just insulted me multiple times in the span of five minutes.

"Hypothetically speaking, say I leave you out here with your little friend. What's your next move? You're hurt. She's unconscious, and you're in the middle of the woods. Where are you going to go?" His tone was way too smug.

I mentally attempted to count to ten, only making it to three. Tito and Grady had laid out a plan and a strict set of rules, making me swear I'd follow both before agreeing to send me out here. I was supposed to pretend I was scared and helpless. In other words, *do not poke the beast*. They should have known that wasn't going to last long.

Screw the plan and screw the rules. I had never been any good at abiding by them anyway. I was going to do this my way. Besides, their plan should have gone right down the drain the second Tito stabbed me. Somehow, he had left that important detail out of our discussion.

"Look, asshole, I'm not some poor damsel in distress. Thanks for your help; greatly appreciate it, but I don't need you—"

I suddenly found myself pressed into the tree with his hand back around my throat.

"You don't need me? Prove it. Break free," he taunted, starting to squeeze.

I covered his clean hand with my filthy one but didn't try to pull it away. Maybe it was from my lack of oxygen and the warm feeling spreading through my brain, but I swear something happened between the two of us.

Something shifted, something clicked. It wasn't love. No, it was the same familiarity I'd felt just moments ago, like I was reuniting with an old friend. Our eyes met and there was an inexplicable understanding between us. One dark, damaged soul fully recognized another, reaching out and beckoning to play with the other.

His mouth moved and I counted four words but didn't hear what was said. Spots began to dance before my eyes.

He let me go and stepped back. I spluttered and braced myself as I plunged forward.

The ground rushed towards me but I never made impact. He caught me before I completely fell and supported my weight with ease.

"You're coming with me," he repeated, taking hold of my left wrist and guiding me towards his friends.

One day, I would look back on this memory from some far away vantage point and realize how significant it was. I would recall that this precise moment was when it really all began. My story did not start until I met him.

Chapter Eight

Calista

I was exactly where I intended to be, albeit utterly exhausted and craving something to take the edge off my pain.

I couldn't say the same for Arlen, who had woken up mad as hell. She stayed close to me, not looking any direction but straight.

We were surrounded. The redhead was to our left, and Romero was on my right. The third man walked close behind us. I indiscreetly studied them whenever I got the chance.

They looked like they were around the same age, all covered in various ink with the same inverted cross tattooed below one of their eyes.

They were all dressed in black: black shirts, dark jeans, and black boots—like a small army of shadows.

For the most part, we walked in silence; I put all my focus

on placing one foot in front of the other. My brain was churning at a mile a minute, but I couldn't analyze anything yet.

By the time we cleared the woods, I was even more of a mess. My shirt was clinging to certain areas near my open wound, the mud coating my skin had dried and was starting to itch, and I was about to perspire into a puddle.

We emerged from the trees and approached a matte black Jeep that looked like it had been customized to drive through anything.

"Wait." Romero held an arm up, stopping us in our tracks just outside of it. "Sack em."

"What does—? What are you doing?" I yelled as something black was placed over my eyes.

"Safety first," the redhead joked, making sure I couldn't take the damn thing off.

"This is bullshit; just let us go!" Arlen snapped, blindly bumping into me.

We were both ignored and roughly placed inside the Jeep. Neither of us knew where they were taking us or what they planned to do when they got us there.

It didn't take long to get to wherever they went. We were removed from the vehicle after approximately twenty minutes. A door—a large one, from the loud groan it made—opened and then slammed shut behind me. I breathed through my mouth, trying to listen for any kind of sound, but there was none aside from our footsteps. Another door opened and I was hit with a cool draft, led a few steps forward, and then stopped.

"Down you go," the redhead said, pushing on my shoulders.

I blindly felt out around me, encountering something smooth and metal.

Before I could guess what it was, someone shoved me all the way down to my back.

"What are you doing?" I asked in alarm, choking as something was pushed beneath the sack and shoved in my mouth. "No," I protested, realizing it was some type of pill.

"Swallow it," Romero demanded, covering my mouth with one hand and rubbing my throat with his other. "Cobra, grab me some liquor."

With no other choice, I swallowed the round, dry pill and his hand disappeared. I began turning my head from side to side to try and get the cover off it. When I attempted to sit up, I was instantly shoved back down.

"You do that again, I'll tie you up," Romero warned.

"Here," the redhead—Cobra—said from above me a moment later.

What the fuck are they doing?

"Stop it!" I shoved someone's hands off just to have mine stretched and pinned above my head.

"Ugh," I growled, finally managing to get the stupid cover off my head.

The first thing I noticed was the metal beams running across the high ceiling, and Cobra being the one holding me down. Then, I turned my head and saw two bodies.

I recognized the habit immediately as one given by The Order, but I didn't know the woman wearing it. Someone had slit her throat open in a ridiculously tidy fashion and done some damage to her mouth. She hung upside down from thick pieces of rope wrapped around her arms and legs. The dead man across from her looked like he'd received the worse end of the bargain.

Finally looking towards the end of the table, I was greeted with the sight of Romero holding the knife he had just stabbed through a man's skull in one hand and a bottle of liquor in the other.

"Shit," I gasped when his soulless eyes met mine and he began approaching me with purposely slow, even steps.

I had pictured my death in a million different scenarios. Being gutted or cut up had never crossed my mind. I hoped this wasn't karma catching up to me.

"Easy," Cobra warned as I wriggled around, tightening his grip so I couldn't go anywhere.

Without a word, Romero grabbed the hem of my ruined shirt and sliced it right up the middle, easily pulling it off. I was left in nothing but a dirty bra. I hissed when he tore the leftover pieces of fabric off me, detaching them from my skin.

Shit. Following his stare, now aimed at my stomach, I saw the puncture wound was surrounded by inflamed purple skin and slowly leaking pus.

"This is gonna hurt," he warned, flashing his eyes to mine.

"What's going to hurt? What the hell do you think you're—"

He didn't let me finish before he leaned down and dumped liquor right onto the wound, using it as irrigation.

It. Was. Excruciating. Firewater was raining down on my flesh.

"Sonofabitch!" I sucked in a breath and swallowed a scream, unknowingly squeezing the circulation out of Cobra's forearms.

I could hear the area sizzle and managed to catch a glimpse of blood, pus, and clear liquid running together. When he did it again, I planned his death in my head. The smell was horrible. I couldn't tell if it was coming from me or the dead nun across the room.

"Take a sip," he demanded, a little more gently, pressing the bottle to my lips.

I didn't have to be told twice. I eagerly welcomed the burning sensation in my throat over the one on my torso.

He wordlessly pulled the bottle away after a few seconds and disappeared from view.

Leaning my head back, I swallowed, staring straight into Cobra's smoky-grey eyes.

"I think he likes you." He smirked down at me.

I attempted to furrow my brows to say, *"Are you shitting me?"*, but whatever I had just been made to swallow was starting to kick in.

Unfortunately for me, it wasn't fast enough. When I looked down again, Romero was heating what looked like a large fishing hook with a lighter.

"Don't even—" I began to protest, just as Cobra covered my mouth with the palm of his hand and dropped his elbows on my shoulders, essentially blocking my view with his upper body.

I felt Romero's fingers near the wound a second before the pressure began. He pushed until the end of the hook popped through my skin, tugging something on the end of it and then pushing it through the other side.

I don't know if it was from the pain of having a hook shoved through my flesh over and over again, the pills, or both. Either way, I closed my eyes to hide my tears and didn't open them again.

Chapter Nine

Romero

Where the fuck did she come from?

Her screams were on a repeating soundtrack inside my head. I still had her blood on my hands. *And when was the last time my dick was this hard?*

I took another swig from the bottle and then passed it to Grimm. It was almost dawn, and none of us had slept. I couldn't sleep because, well, I rarely slept, and because I couldn't stop thinking about the potential problem I had placed in my bed.

It was a problem that had long blonde hair, skin as white as snow, and a cesspool of rage and pain that mirrored my own behind a pair of cornflower blue eyes.

She reminded me of an angel that had been stripped of its wings. It was a fitting description when I thought about the circumstances surrounding her, and I'd been doing that a fuck of a lot.

"You were right about her," Grimm acknowledged. His neck was bent forward, and he was staring at the liquor bottle as if it held all the answers to his questions. A strand of his dark hair hung partially over his forehead.

"Where did she come from?" He looked at me for an answer he knew I would eventually have. I suspected this would be the most emotion he showed on the topic until he was ready to talk about it, which could be never, and that was more than fine by me.

The first time we saw Cali, we were ten, and she was five. She had been wearing a pink nightgown, and her hair was in two long pigtails. The kid was so fucking pale she looked like a ghost.

I didn't know where she'd been for the past few years, but it made a lot of shit make sense now.

"So, are we keeping both of them?" Cobra asked, as if we were talking about a pair of puppies.

"Do we really want the loud one?" Grimm asked, referring to the brunette currently sleeping in the dog pen.

"She might be leverage."

He grunted in response.

I already knew what I was going to do, but I never wanted them to feel like their opinions didn't mean shit to me, so I always heard them out and then laid it all out for em. Rarely did they disagree.

"I think it could be good for a while. We could use a woman's presence around here now Lena's gone," Cobra added.

Ah, Lena. The stupid bitch more than likely ran off having a temper tantrum and got herself killed.

We had yet to discuss what we were going to do about her death, but we would be doing something in due time.

Leaning forward, I rested my elbows on my knees and made sure I had their attention. "Until I know the who, what, when, and why, I'm keeping Cali close to me."

Grimm shot me a skeptical look while Cobra's expression turned smug. They knew what happened the last time I kept a woman close to me, and it didn't end well between us. They each played a role in her eventual downfall. That was years ago though, and I got what I wanted out of that situation. This was different.

I had selfish ulterior motives. I hadn't been this intrigued in a very long fucking time—not by a woman who was supposed to be dead.

We had come across bitches before who would beg to be let in without actually knowing what it was they were asking for, swearing they were like us at heart, but it was all bullshit. After they were used a few times, they eventually buckled and had to be killed. It was pure entertainment, watching them all try to be something they weren't.

I never made it easy for anyone to get in; I never accepted anyone at face value. I had too much shit at stake to ever be stupid and careless. Too many people relied on me.

This girl, though? She was different, so fucking different to what I had imagined. When she looked up at me and smiled, I saw insanity dancing behind hypnotic blue irises. It was the kind that made people scared shitless. I saw her look the devil in the eyes and accept what everyone else feared.

The immediate pull between us almost felt magnetic. It sure as shit wasn't love, but definitely lust, and maybe something else. I couldn't fully wrap my head around it and I honestly wasn't sure I wanted to.

. . .

"Cali lived with The Order for nineteen years. She knows something that can help us." Cobra spoke up first, handing the bottle back to me.

"Yeah...well, The Order also said she was dead. We don't know what happened in the last however many years. They could have sent her themselves," Grimm pointed out. Bitterness we were all familiar with laced his tone.

The fucking Order was a major pain in my ass. I had so much shit that needed to be handled and David was fifty percent of it. We all had our reasons for wanting to find the motherfucker, and we were close, *so* damn close.

"We can use this to our advantage. Just let me think for a minute." Because all I had was a minute. We were running out of time, the clock was ticking faster each day, and this was something I hadn't prepared to handle.

I meticulously planned my shit. I knew exactly when every bump, twist, and turn was coming my way, but I never saw this one.

I didn't know a dove was going to land amongst the crows, and while her white feathers represented purity, her jet black heart gave life to a beautifully insidious soul.

Calista

He was the first thing I saw when I opened my eyes. For a few seconds, I thought I was having one of my rare good dreams again. He was facing away from me, getting a shirt from a dresser. His body was...*incredible*.

The patterned ink and his well-defined physique made him look like a living, breathing piece of art.

His hair was perfectly styled, undercut and combed back on the top with tattoos running around the trim line. I was still appraising him when he turned around, giving me a quick view of his solid abs that were also covered with tattoos, one being of a nearly obscured Sabbatic goat head, accompanied by a quote that read *Flesh of Blood of Bone*.

His fitted black T fell into place and slowly brought things back into perspective. I tried to swallow and nearly choked on dry air. My mouth felt like it had been stuffed with a handful of cotton-balls. In the midst of my coughing episode, my bladder made sure to let me know it was seconds away from busting wide open.

"Bathroom?" he asked, plucking the thought right from my head.

I looked at him and nodded.

"It's through there. Do your thing and clean yourself up. There's shit in the box."

He pointed to a semi-open door to my left before heading out of the room, barely paying me any attention. I heard the telling sound of a lock clicking into place and then his boots carrying him away.

Shoving the comforter away with my legs, I slowly sat up and looked down to see I was wearing an oversized black t-shirt, much like the one Romero had just put on. My bra was still on—not that I would have cared if it wasn't; Daddy dearest made sure I was comfortable being naked around strangers. I just wondered who'd taken the liberty of starting to scrub the dirt from my body.

Scurrying off the (surprisingly comfortable) bed as quick as I could, I tested the waters with how I felt pain-wise, relieved that though I was sore, it wasn't nearly as bad as it had been.

I still took my time walking to the bathroom, glancing around the room as I went.

There was no real character to it. The gray walls were bare and the bed linens were all black, as were the few pieces of furniture. The bathroom was just as dull with the same cold, sterile feel to it. Nothing about either room gave away anything about the man they belonged to, except the smell.

It was *his* smell. I'd inhaled it the second he stopped me from falling on my face—twice. It wasn't synthetic, but all natural. It was exotic, a little indulgent, and, after sleeping in his bed, intoxicating.

My bare feet carried me across a cool slate floor. I plopped down on a steel seat and shut my eyes. Warm sunlight filtered down on my face from an oval window above the toilet.

"Shit, I got in." My eyes popped open as if I were just now coming awake. I did my business and then rushed over to the sink. The flare-up in my side barely registered.

I was too focused on the fact that I had gotten inside whatever the hell this place was.

My excitement slightly waned as I reminded myself that getting inside was supposed to be the easy part. Nothing about what I just went through was a cakewalk. The hidden obstacles before me were slowly but surely making themselves visible.

I studied my reflection in the mirror above the sink, frowning at the woman staring back at me. My blonde locks were a tangled, bed-headed mess, and I had a few colorful bruises from my recent escapade that harshly stood out against my skin. I didn't like this mirror very much. There weren't any cracks in it.

Skimming my fingers along the hem of the t-shirt, I lifted it up and examined my puncture wound. Romero had done a surprisingly good job of stitching me up. Bits of crusted blood and scab still clung to me, but that was to be expected. The area was still tender to the touch, on top of being an ugly reddish color.

Letting the t-shirt fall back into place just above my knees, I turned the faucet on and finally peered inside the cardboard box on the counter. It contained various sizes of men and women's clothes, and a few pairs of shoes. Unless Romero and his buddies were gathering clothing up for a rainy day, I could only assume it all belonged to some poor, dead, unfortunate souls.

I pulled out a long-sleeved plaid shirt that was about two sizes too big and set it to the side. After a few more seconds of digging, I had a pair of black boots and someone's lacy bralette. I held the peach number up and shrugged. It would be a little snug on the girls but it looked clean and it wasn't like the original owner could object.

After pulling Romero's shirt off, I quickly washed my face the best I could with the corner of a balled-up bandana, sparing a few seconds to drink from the tap.

The end result was far from perfect, but I wasn't trying to win any beauty competitions.

Tiptoeing toward the door, I tried to see if I could hear anything. Only the silence remained. With every second counting and a clock ticking, I tried to get my thoughts back in order.

David would not be in the same spot for long. If Romero knew where he was, he would have to make some kind of move soon. That is, if they weren't working together. This had the potential to get all kinds of messy. I took a good look around and asked myself the game changing question: *What the fuck now?*

Heading back towards the toilet, I shut the lid and used it as a stepping-stone to the upper tank. Gripping the barely-existent window rim, I stood on my tiptoes and stretched up as far as my side allowed me, squinting from the sunlight. "What the hell?"

Narrowing my eyes, stretching a tad bit more, I tried to pinpoint where I was, but all I could see was wasteland.

Looking as far left as I could, slightly leaning in the process, I saw little black specs floating in the air above a circular pit full of visible corpses.

To the right was nothing but a view of the building I was in: some kind of refurbished warehouse. Old boxcars were stacked on top of one another and served as a fence that connected to a large pair of chain-link gates. They were secured together by what I was guessing was a manual lock. Clearly, they had two objectives: keep people out, and keep people in.

So much for running if things went south.

Dammit.

"Tryna find an escape route?"

Yes. "No, I'm trying to figure out where the hell I am." Not letting on to the fact that he had just caught me completely off guard and that my side now hurt like a sonofabitch, I slowly lowered my booted heels and climbed off the toilet.

I turned around and crossed my arms, openly perusing him from head to toe. He was enigmatic and sinewy, leaning against the door jamb with an unreadable expression on his pretty face.

The skull ring on his index finger looked familiar, but I couldn't place it. When my eyes drifted back up to his face, there was a cocky little smirk waiting for me.

"I've found many women outside those gates before, and none of them have been anything like you."

"You didn't find me, I found you, and I'd appreciate it if you let me leave now." I tossed out a partial lie, readying my arsenal of false pretenses.

"Leave? Why would you want to leave when you just got here?" He pushed away from the door and took two steps towards me. "Do you think I saved you out of the kindness of my heart?" His voice turned serious. If possible, his eyes got a little darker.

It didn't take me long to conclude that it was best to tread carefully with this man, but where was the fun in that?

It also didn't take me long to conclude that I'd made the right decision earlier. Tito and Grady's plan was shit. I could not pretend to be weak or helpless in front of these people; they would eat me alive. Yet being too headstrong, being myself, could get me killed. It was a crossroad I really didn't want to be at, so I chose the most logical path to take.

"Didn't we already go over this? I never needed your help. You didn't have to *save* me." Boldly mimicking his actions, I took two steps forward.

"See, that thing you just did has me wondering if you were really lost in the first place." His eyes traveled up and down me in a way that had goose flesh spreading across my skin.

"You think I purposely went off into the woods so I could meet a cannibal?"

"I'm not sure. Maybe. Why don't we find out?"

He stepped forward, bringing us chest to chest, forcing me to tilt my head back so I could look up at him. In one swift motion, he had his thumb over my trachea, gently applying pressure.

"What were you doing in the woods?"

"You saw what I was doing."

"Come on now, Cali, I know you're smarter than this." He shook his head and tsked at me.

Once again, I had to keep my face impassive. *How did he know my name?* He leaned in so close I could smell traces of menthol on his breath. His proximity had my discomfort levels off the charts for reasons I wasn't accustomed to.

I wrapped a hand around his wrist and placed the other against his firm chest, keeping my eyes locked with his, letting him know I wasn't intimidated.

"Is this making you feel better about yourself? Interrogating a helpless woman?"

"Now, we both know you're far from helpless. But yes, it is kind of making my dick hard."

I coughed to cover the laugh that almost slipped out. His raised brows told me he heard it anyway. Thankfully, he didn't comment on it.

"I'm still waiting on an answer, Cali." He said my name like it was something decadent.

He began to run his thumb up and down my throat. His skin against mine gave me a feeling I couldn't describe. His touch didn't make my heart race with anxiety, my limbs didn't shake from nervous energy, and my knees didn't grow so weak that I fell at his feet. His touch made me feel unexplainably calm and warm at the same time, like at any second my skin would burst into flame, but it was okay as long as his hand stayed wrapped around my throat.

"Such a fragile thing, you," he murmured. When he leaned in again, I thought he was going to try to put his mouth on mine. I was well prepared to high-knee his balls into his stomach for calling me fragile.

Instead, he spoke directly in my ear. "What were you doing in *my* woods?" His warm breath trickled across my skin, his voice low and menacing. He pulled back but kept his thumb in place, studying my face. His dark stare penetrated right through me, daring my lips to spill the lie that sat on the tip of my tongue. For a second, I forgot how to breathe.

"I got lost. I…"

With the slightest tilt of his head, I knew he didn't believe me.

"I was with a guy. He dumped me off on the side of the road after doing this." I pointed to my stab wound. "All I was trying to do was get away from the main road."

He looked at me a few seconds before saying, "Okay."

"Okay?"

"Yeah, now let's try this again, and this time don't fucking lie, or I'll snap your pretty little neck."

Chapter Ten

Romero

I used my body to back her against the bathroom wall, pinning her wrists down on either side of her.

"You have a super original method of handling women," she quipped.

I couldn't stop myself from laughing in her face. What the fuck was wrong with this girl? Either the people we killed were Academy Award winning actors who willingly pissed their pants in fear, or she was a little more off than I thought. No one had the balls to be this brazen.

Maybe she was psychotic. I *liked* that.

Her throat bobbed as she swallowed.

The tip of her tongue darted out and she licked her lips. I tracked the movement like a goddamn wolf stalking a deer.

Using my knee, I nudged her legs apart and moved her

wrists upward, forcing her to make a T, inadvertently lifting the shirt she chose to wear. A dead man's shirt—she turned a dead man's shirt into a dress.

I had to look down to see it because of how much smaller than me she was. Everything about her was tiny, exactly like a fucking pixie. And she wasn't wearing any fuckin underwear.

Her bare pussy was right on top of my denim clad knee. As if realizing the same thing, the faintest little gasp slipped through her lips and sent blood rushing to the tip of my cock. I studied her pinched features and grinned.

"You like that, don't you? Cause if you like that, you're going to love the way I fuck."

"You know, men who lack balls and need to compensate for their tiny dicks always have the biggest egos."

"Is that a challenge? Do you want to find out what I can do to you? Because I'm happy to oblige but I promise, baby, you'll never be the same after I'm done." I gave her a devilish grin and made sure she felt my dick against her lower stomach.

"I'll fuck you hard enough to rip you apart, and I'll keep fucking you until the base of my dick is covered in your blood."

Her pretty pink lips parted and she tried to twist away. I pressed into her a little more.

"I'll fuck you so hard Jesus Christ will make his second coming before I make my first."

She immediately responded to my words. Her knees fell farther apart and she licked her bitable lips again, making a sexy growling sound in her throat as I brought my mouth just close enough to skim over hers.

She nipped at my bottom lip, making me chuckle.

Switching her wrists to one hand, I brought the other up

and roughly cupped her jaw, forcing her mouth open and slipping my tongue inside. Our eyes remained wide open and locked together.

She gave me a stormy, heated glare that went straight to my dick and began to kiss me back, shocking the shit out of me. Smiling against her mouth, I recovered and amped up the intensity, watching her work to match it as if she'd never done this before.

The sensual groan that spilled from her mouth had common sense trying to evade me. This crazy fucking bitch had a taste that overwhelmed me. She tasted like every immoral thought I'd ever had.

When I felt her tense up against me, I had to force myself to let go and step back. Her chest rose and fell but she kept her breathing quiet, rolling her lips together.

For a second, she looked up at me with confusion before her expression changed to one that was equally terrified and aroused.

I knew that if I placed my hand between her legs, I would find her pussy wet. Being a gentleman wasn't my forte. Part of me wanted to wrap her legs around my waist and force my dick inside her just to feel her tremble in fear from the inside out, to hear her beg, to scream at me to stop.

As I looked at her face, I knew. I knew someone had done something to her, just as I knew she would be mine. The beast inside me reared his fucking head and set a claim on her without my permission.

I wanted to know the name and location of every motherfucker who had hurt her so I could take him or her apart piece by slow, agonizing piece.

I only kept my composure because this wasn't the time to

fuck her against the wall and make her tell me everything I wanted to know.

Turns out that wasn't mutual.

The little minx launched herself at me. One second she was staring at me with hatred, and the next, her hands were on my face and her mouth was back on mine.

I had my tongue shoved down her throat before I knew what the fuck was happening. She was stretching up to reach me and I knew it had to hurt. Grabbing two handfuls of ass, I wrapped her legs around my waist and she clung to my neck like it was a lifeline.

She pulled away and looked me dead in the eye and said the two words I knew all too well. "Fuck me."

Maybe I should have warned her about what she was asking for. It would have been kinder to mention what my true intentions were, but that would have been the right thing to do, and I wasn't a do-the-right thing kind of person.

Chapter Eleven

Calista

He didn't hesitate to oblige.

He said he'd tear me apart and make me bleed. I'd heard those words in my head so many times it was like a trigger being pulled, a switch being flipped as a curtain was yanked open.

He made my body come alive with a plethora of foreign feelings I didn't think were possible anymore. I'd be damned if I let that slip away from me.

He carried me back into his room and dropped me onto the bed.

"Don't fucking talk. Just strip." His voice was iron, his eyes cold.

I bit my lip to stifle a giggle and did as I was told. I knew he'd be like this; just this once, I didn't mind.

I never willingly gave up control, but this was different. I wanted him to dominate me and take everything I didn't willingly give, just like I imagined in my head. I wanted his shameful hands around my throat and his dick buried inside me.

His eyes traveled over every inch of my skin. When the word *beautiful* fell from his mouth, I looked down, trying to see what he did.

I would have thought my pale, bruised skin, thin body, and overall disheveled look would have had the opposite effect. I was almost at my ugliest point and he called me beautiful. By the look on his face, it wasn't a word he used often. I shifted uncomfortably, unsure how to feel about it.

He didn't look away once as he peeled off his shirt and dropped down his pants and drawers, not completely removing them.

Mmm, this man was *gorgeous*. I scanned over his perfectly muscled arms, down his stomach, and stopped at his cock. I bit my bottom lip, seeing how thick and long it was. The metal bar going through the head had me fixated.

Something dipped in my lower stomach; the ache he elicited between my thighs had my arousal at an unbearable high.

He made a sound in his chest and grabbed my ankles, pulling me to the edge of the bed. My legs were hooked over his forearms and his dick was pushing into me by the time I'd exhaled a single breath.

A quiet grunt left my mouth at the stretch and slow burn of his intrusion. I reached down and used two fingers to spread myself further.

He pushed all the way in and the air dispersed from my lungs on a scream.

There was a temporary disconnect between my mind and

body, coming back with an overwhelming hysteria of emotions.

I hadn't done this in so long, and I'd never been with a man like him before. My body worked to accommodate his size, stretching around him. That didn't stop him from setting a grueling pace. He cursed beneath his breath and dug his fingers into my flesh.

I shut my eyes and struggled to hold back the moans building on top of one another in my chest. It wasn't until I truly focused on his face that a wisp of clarity trickled through my lusty haze. His midnight hues were zeroed in on my face. He was moving inside me, but it barely looked like he was breathing.

With each passing second of his eyes boring down at me, a heady feeling had my gut telling me to stop this, even if I didn't want to. The way he was looking at me made it seem as if he could see everything inside me, like he was analyzing me for something.

"Stop," I breathed, trying to push myself up with my elbows.

"There we go. I was waiting on that." His face split into a sinister smile. "Why would we stop? We haven't even started."

I swallowed, sucking in a breath as he pulled me further down the mattress until my ass was left hanging between him and the air.

His words were loaded with a double meaning, I was smart enough to know that, but he didn't give me time to think about what it was. He placed my legs on his shoulders and bent my knees towards my chest, folding me in half. A soft whimper left my mouth as my side protested.

"Stop."

"Shut the fuck up." He shoved my upper half down and

pinned me by the neck. "Stop sounds a lot like no. I don't know the meaning of that word and now, neither do you." He thrust his hips, planting himself so deep his balls rested against the groove of my ass.

"I can't," I half moaned, half pleaded.

I arched my back in an attempt to lessen the intense pressure and fullness of him inside me, making it worse and adding more strain on my side.

"You wanted to be fucked, remember?"

He cruelly laughed at me.

The man who starred in all my dirty, degrading nightmarish fantasies finally made his appearance.

He drilled into me. The louder I moaned, the harder he fucked me. The mattress creaked beneath me, skin smacked against skin, and his grip grew tighter around my neck. It felt like I was being ripped apart, straight down the middle, from the inside out.

Something pulled and snapped. I cried out in pain, feeling something wet run down my stomach. I couldn't do anything but lie still and let him have his way with me.

I'd been here before but never like this. My body burned with pain and pleasure.

I clenched the sheets between my fists like they were a lifeline as he made good on his promise of fucking me hard enough to tear me apart. The metal bar began stroking something inside me I didn't even know was there.

My pussy flooded with arousal, growing wetter than it already was. I felt his muscles tense and knew he was holding back for my benefit.

"Come for me, Cali," he ordered in a low voice, tightening his grip even more, restricting my airflow. I grabbed for his hand, unable to pull it away. My chest heaved with strangled breaths and choked moans. I tried to do what he said, but I didn't know how. I'd never gotten off with a cock inside me.

"Fucking come and I'll let you breathe again," he snapped, cutting off my air supply completely.

He shifted his hips and dropped one of my legs, angling himself as deep as he could.

Something rapidly built in my core, pervading through me like liquid lightning as he hit that sweet spot with brutal thrusts over and over again.

Oh my god.

He let my throat go and leaned down to catch my barrage of moans in his mouth as I came apart around him. I couldn't see. A black curtain drew across my vision. I stopped breathing completely. I never knew I could feel pleasure in every part of my body strong enough to leave me shuddering and pulling him into me to go deeper, clawing at his back.

Fuzzy specs of white danced before my eyes as he continued to fuck me into the mattress. When his dick swelled, he immediately pulled out with a low groan, spurting warm come all over my breasts. With a swirl of his fingers, he massaged it into my skin.

"Fuck," he softly cursed.

Still trying to breathe again, I lifted my head and looked between us, seeing his come mixed with the blood between my thighs and trickling from my wound.

Chapter Twelve

Calista

He pushed my hands away so he could examine where his handiwork had come undone.

"I've got a first aid kit—"

"You don't need one, it's not that bad," I lied.

His hands landed on my shoulders to prevent me from hopping off the sink where he had sat me. "I'm gonna ignore the fact that you just spoke over me. You're gonna sit your ass on this counter until I get back with the kit." He stepped away, giving me a warning glare before exiting the bathroom.

As soon as I heard his bedroom door shut, I stood up, steadying myself on trembling legs.

Holding my head in my hands, I tried to make myself regret what had transpired between us but the feeling wouldn't come. So many men had used me and none of them had ever made me feel like he just did.

I should have seen this coming. The powerful frequency between us had our souls fucking before we ever touched. No, I could never regret the painfully sweet ache he created between my thighs.

Ever since I'd discovered who he was two years ago, he'd done the impossible. He intrigued me like no man had ever done before. He was beautiful and sick, like me—the star of all my obscene fantasies.

The throbbing in my side steadily reminded me he was real. He was more than pictures and the erotic nightmares I craved late at night.

This lust though, my secret obsession, was dangerous. I had yet to see just what he was capable of, but I knew he was merciless, ruthless. He had an aura around him that was so dark it could blot out the sun. It seeped into everything around him. I knew I wouldn't be the exception but that didn't bother me; I harbored my own demons inside me.

Through the white noise inside my head, I distinctly remembered Tito warning me, *"You don't want to end up like his last girl."*

Now that I thought about some of the things he'd said, it was alarmingly obvious Tito had known more than he'd let on. Some of the things he'd told me could never be learned from a sheet of paper or in-depth research. They were too personal. The Savages were notorious, but they were also highly secure and private.

Of all the things I'd found out about him, no woman had ever come up. So how did Tito know there ever was one? I mean, she clearly wasn't around anymore. That's if she ever existed in the first place. He could have easily made it up in his failed attempt to ward me off.

I was inclined to believe she was either no longer breathing, or their relationship had ended on an unpleasant note.

A chain of truth tried to form in my mind, but there were too many goddamn links missing. I couldn't ask, either, not without giving up information on the other and risking being lied to. Right then, I barely even trusted myself.

"Didn't I tell you not to move?"

"I didn't like the way you asked." Lifting my head, I clenched the shirt covering my waist a little tighter and took a quick inventory of the things in Romero's hands as he re-entered the room.

"I didn't fucking *ask* you anything. You know what? We need to get a few things clear." He brushed past me and sat everything in the sink. Then, he scooped me up as if I were a ragdoll and deposited me right back on the counter, parking his muscular body between my legs.

"You gorgeous girl," he murmured, brushing strands of hair out of my face. "I don't want to hurt you...wait. That's not how I want to start." He gave me a skewed grin and shook his head. "I *do* want to hurt you. There are so many... things I want to do to you. And I will. You'll love every torturous second of it...eventually." He smoothed the pad of his thumb across my bottom lip. "I don't want to hurt you for pissing me off, Cali. Not this early in our relationship."

Early in our...

"We don't have a relationship," I objected.

"We have whatever I want us to have."

"You can't do that. You can't just make decisions for me."

"I can do whatever the fuck I want. It's *you* who no longer has choices."

My eyes floated to the slate floor and then back up to his. Not yet up for a battle of words, I asked him the question that was still swimming around in my head.

"How do you know my name?"

Should I have asked how he knew my name before demanding he fuck me like a needy whore? Probably.

He smirked. "I was wondering how you knew *my* name, seeing as you just repeated it like a well-versed prayer."

Shit, did I really do that? I pressed my lips into a straight line and looked up at him, refusing to give myself up. "You need to work on your art of seduction."

He reached out and pinched my chin. "Do you want me to seduce you, Cali?"

I choked on a swallow and knocked his hand away. Since he was still shirtless, I chose to intently focus on his Sabbatic goat head.

Yes, yes, yes! I excitedly repeated in my head. He could be mine and I could be his. I couldn't give up the plot so fast, though. I may not be able to follow Tito's plan, but I could never be disloyal to him.

Okay, deep breaths. Fake it till you make it, Cali. I hated rejecting him, but I couldn't so freely give in. Letting out a little sigh, I smiled and placed a hand on his broad shoulder.

"I want you to stop doing…whatever it is you're doing. I don't know you well enough for you to be my…boyfriend. I've never even had a boyfriend. What makes you special enough to be my first?"

He threw his head back and laughed. "You knew me well enough to let me inside your tight little pussy and come all over my cock. You'd be amazed what you can learn about a woman when you're balls deep inside her.

"And where in there did you hear I wanted to be your *boyfriend*? That's fucking juvenile. Boyfriends are temporary; I'm not."

Keep going, I thought, secretly thrilled by his words. The hairs lifted on the back of my neck. I brought my free hand up to his other shoulder and slightly leaned back. "I don't understand what you're trying to say."

"You let the devil inside you, baby. And he isn't leaving anytime soon."

I blinked up at him, hearing his words but not fully processing them. It couldn't be this easy-peasy. Romero Deville was not rumored to be a nice man. Like Tito said, the Savages didn't give without receiving, so what was it he wanted from me, and why wasn't he saying something?

Taking my silence as his cue to continue, he gripped the back of my neck, ensuring he had my full attention.

"I don't know what the fuck this connection is, but I'm not letting it die before we give it a chance to live. Don't focus on me being your first when I'm going to be your last. I have your whole life to tear you apart and then put you back together again."

Well, the first part sounded a bit romantic, but the ending could use a tad more work. I needed a minute to reflect, needed to retreat somewhere quiet so I could think.

There were a few parts of his proclamation that stood out, but what did it even matter when we both seemed to be on a similar track?

"You have no intention of letting me leave here, do you?"

He looked to the ceiling with a sigh. When his eyes met mine again, I saw the answer before he repeated the two simple words that had damned me from the beginning.

"Finders keepers."

Chapter Thirteen

Calista

Something was about to happen; I could feel it. My mind kept going to worst-case scenarios.

Romero cleaned my wound and covered it with gauze before leading me from the room. We walked down to the lower level in silence.

I immediately spotted Arlen sitting at a long farmhouse table. She was still filthy, and it looked like she had yet to fall asleep. A teeny trickle of guilt ciphered into my psyche. How had I forgotten her so fast?

Grimm and Cobra calmly stood on either side of her, as if they'd been instructed to do so.

I licked my lips and shot a quick glance at Romero. Something just wasn't right—not that it ever was.

Grimm slowly approached us, holding something in his

hand. He passed it to Romero and then whispered something I couldn't hear in his ear. Whatever he said had Romero's gaze turning stony and his jaw clenching.

"What's going on?"

"I think we need to discuss a few more things in detail." His voice housed no emotion, giving away nothing. He'd had a swift change in demeanor in the span of ten seconds.

As he walked me towards the table, we bypassed a large circular sectional. Painted on the floor directly in front of it was an inverted pentacle. The five-pointed star had a single downward spoke, turning something once righteous wicked.

Before I could question what the deal was, I spotted the large skull of a ram with the same pentagram painted on its forehead in red, serving as a centerpiece.

Were they Satanists?

"Have a seat." Romero pulled out a chair for me at the end of the table and I cautiously sat. Arlen was at the opposite end, staring at me with a warning in her cognac eyes and maybe...fear.

"You've been a busy girl, Calista."

He stood behind my chair and laid my necklace on the table in front of me. I hadn't even realized it was missing.

The black inverted cross starkly contrasted with the brown tabletop. I heard him move away, but I didn't turn to see what he was doing.

"You haven't told me what you were doing in my woods yet, but we can get to that later. What I really want to know is how long you've been a fan."

I stared down at each picture he slowly placed in front of me.

Four detailed pictures of four mutilated bodies with a cross carved straight through their centers.

"Was that question too hard? Do you need a few minutes to come up with a reasonable explanation?"

"You have an excellent photographer."

He knotted a hand in my hair and pulled my head back, forcing me to look up at him.

"Do not fuck with me, Cali. I am exactly the kind of person you don't fuck with. You wanted my attention, and now you've got it. Why. Are. You. Here?" He pulled my hair a little more with each word, making pain ripple down my scalp. My eyes burned with unshed tears from how far he had the skin around them stretched back.

"How did you know I liked my hair pulled?"

There was laughter from the opposite end of the table. He didn't find it nearly as amusing.

He kicked the chair out from underneath me, lifted me by the head, and slammed me down onto the table.

Strands of hair tore in his hold. When my jaw hit the wooden surface, I bit my tongue so hard I tasted blood. His body covered mine, making sure I couldn't go anywhere.

"Girls like you don't wander around in the woods, and you sure as fuck don't get dumped off. I'm going to ask you one last time. Why are you here? I know you didn't do all this just to get a sample fuck, though you wouldn't be the first—definitely the craziest."

What a cocky fuckin asshole.

I tried to knee him in the balls but I couldn't lift my leg high enough. "You haven't ever met a girl like me, cause if you had you wouldn't have just made that dumbass statement. I only wanted your help!"

"That is definitely a new answer," Cobra commented from the other end of the table.

"It's an honest answer," I growled.

"You did all that in hopes that I'd help you because I'm a good guy?" Romero sneered.

"No. I thought you'd help me because it's fucking David and you're the only one with balls big enough to go after him."

He stared down at me with an unreadable expression.

"I'm telling you the truth," I snapped.

And I was. I had snuck out at night for months to kill those women in hope I would come across one of the Savages, always sticking to the same area. I always chose women who were followers of David.

It took me hours to take them apart and make sure they were in places journalists would find. Having to sneak in and out of the compound, ditch my bloody clothes, and hide a murder weapon got old—fast.

Tito and Grady were my lucky break. I had stumbled upon their secret meetings entirely by accident.

I'd been trying to make it back to my room before Jinx woke up and saw the bloodstains on my hands.

Romero looked at his friends and did some sort of silent communication bullshit before taking a step back, letting me go. I sat up, just to be pulled off the table and spun around. My palms hit the wooden surface as he gripped me from behind.

The scene at the other end of the table had me clenching my jaw and balling up my fists.

Grimm had a machete resting on top of Arlen's head. She had her eyes trained on me, looking rightfully terrified.

"What do you have to offer that would benefit me in any way?" Romero asked.

"I know where my uncle meets with his delegates."

At my words, a pregnant silence ensued.

"Okay, now we're getting somewhere. I'm going to make

you a deal, Pixie. Listen to me very closely. You're going to take me to this supposed meeting place." He pressed himself into me and slightly lifted me up by the throat. "And you're going to give me something I want…"

When he didn't immediately finish his sentence, my thoughts ran wild. If he asked for where I'd been or where I came from, I couldn't tell him—I wouldn't.

Outside of that, I had no idea what he was playing at. I didn't have anything. I had no home, no money, and no resources. Come to think of it, I was a bit pathetic. I truly had *nothing* and I felt the need to apologize for it.

"I'm sorry, but—"

"I want you."

My brain froze, hitting an embankment of confusion. I was quickly becoming irritated with his blunt responses. The manhandling didn't bother me much. I actually kinda liked it, though I preferred it to be under different circumstances.

"You already—what do you mean, you want me? We just did that whole thing…upstairs."

"*I* did that whole thing upstairs. You just sat there. Why wait to make it official? We even have three attentive witnesses."

"Witnesses…you want me to marry you?"

"This goes deeper than marriage."

His tone was so serious I fell off my train of thought. No one laughed or commented at his statement.

What could be deeper than marriage?

If vowing to honor, forsake, and cherish till death wasn't enough for this man, then he was a little too high maintenance.

I was so damn confused, and it was hard to think clearly when his hard dick was pressing into me through his jeans and Arlen's life was a blink away from ending. I tried to articulate my uncertainty in a way that wouldn't offend him and get me potentially killed, along with her.

"You want all my knowledge *and* you want me in a way you're being purposely vague about? That doesn't seem like a very fair deal to me."

"I'm not a fair person."

"Oh, you don't say? I hadn't noticed."

"Cali, let me tell you what's about to happen if you don't agree."

He forced me to arch my back, making me feel every bit how hard he was.

"I'm going to make you watch my brothers destroy every hole on your friend's body before they take off her head while I fuck your sweet little ass.

"And after all that, I'm still going to get what I want. I'd just treat you like all the other bitches that come here and beg to be a part of my world, a world they wouldn't last sixty seconds in. Do you know what we do to them, pretty girl?

"We use them. We break them down until they have nothing left to offer. We take what was once whole and break it into a million unfixable pieces. Half the time, our dicks are still inside them when we snap their fucking necks."

Holy shit. By the time he was done, his words had me soaked, damn near ready to ask him to fuck me again.

I didn't want to be broken. The thought of breaking someone else with him, though…that sounded like my kind of party. But if I went down that road, I knew how it would end, which was precisely why I could never let him know just what it was he did to me, the way he made me feel.

Not to mention Arlen's life was in my hands. If I thought for one second he was bluffing, I would call him out on it, but I knew he would act on his threat in a heartbeat. I could only hope she was strong enough to survive the ride of insanity we were about to climb on. After all, I would be fucking the conductor to ensure we survived.

I knew a deal was the equivalent of handing over my soul, but I didn't have any soul to give anyway.

"I'll do it."

"Cali, it's not worth it. Don't you dare take that deal!"

I took it—and everyone in the room seemed to know something I didn't.

Part Two

Chapter Fourteen

Calista

He let me up but didn't let me go.

I was still between him and the table when he told his friends to take Arlen to get cleaned up after assuring me she might be hurt, but not killed, which wasn't really that reassuring at all.

"There's something I need you to do before we discuss a course of action, but first, turn around."

I turned to face him, rubbing my jaw, wondering what he was going to do next. Peering up at him, I was once more in awe of him.

His beauty was the best illusion I had ever seen. Whoever taught him how to mask his true nature had done a phenomenal job.

He was flawlessly gorgeous on the outside, vile and revolting on the inside.

He was perfection.

I didn't need anybody to tell me he was a bad idea that would more than likely end with me being killed. I knew that —it was part of the allure. I knew he would hurt me, but that's what I wanted. It would make up for all the other men who did it without my permission.

I was willing to give myself to a merciless killer, knowing full well what the ramifications could be. I was a grown woman making her own decisions, and no one could take that right from me ever again.

I'd followed the rules long enough. I just wanted to find myself. This was too new to know if it would last forever, and it would never be considered normal, but it was my present and I wanted to indulge in it.

He was a hazardous risk and a mystery; I'd never been more certain about anything in my life. Whatever this connection was between us, I fucking needed it.

He stepped forward and raised my chin with his knuckle, gently brushing his lips down either side of my face before hovering them over mine. "Sit on the table and spread your legs."

Keeping my eyes on him, I backed up until the rim of the wooden table was at my ass and hopped up. Still watching him, I parted my legs. With no underwear on, my arousal was put on display.

"Cali," he tsked at me, gnawing his bottom lip and closing the small distance between us. "Which part made your pussy this wet?"

He braced his hands on my bruised knees and skimmed his lips down my neck. I sucked in a shaky breath, curling my fingers into my palms, fighting the urge to touch him.

"Was it the visual of me fucking you in the ass, watching my friends fuck yours, or the idea of me tearing another woman apart?"

"All of it," I breathed, turning my head to catch his mouth. I ran my tongue over his lips, seeking entrance, intertwining it with his when he granted it. His large hands gripped either side of my face and he slightly pulled away. "I'm going to push you straight into madness," he whispered in my ear before dropping to his knees.

"This is mine," he growled, burying his face between my thighs. He took his time sliding his tongue up and down my slit. "I love the way you taste," he soughed against me.

I jerked at the feel of him pushing two of his digits inside me and then slowly pulling back out, still freshly sore from the way he'd taken me less than an hour ago.

He latched onto my clit and held it between his teeth, massaging it with the tip of his tongue.

I bit down on my lip to stifle my moans, starting to move my hips against his mouth in rhythm with his languid strokes.

The sound of him feasting on my wet pussy and my untamable whimpers reverberated in the air.

His tongue was just as magical as his dick, making me see colors I didn't even know existed. I panted as I felt a familiar heat coiling inside me, spreading up my spine.

"Rome," I groaned and grabbed the back of his neck, grinding myself against his face. He responded by pulling his fingers out and burying his tongue so deep inside me I felt myself clench around it. He looked up at me with the same intense expression he had when he fucked me on the edge of his bed, and bit down on my clit.

"Oh, Rome," I repeated on a low moan, falling back to my elbows as the second strongest orgasm of my life washed over me.

He continued, lapping up my come as I writhed against him.

He used his thumb to toy with my swollen nub, pushing me into another orbit of pleasure.

When he stood up and wiped my juices from his face, I was still trembling. He gave me a skewed smirk as I pushed myself into a sitting position and unhurriedly squeezed my legs back together.

His gaze floated to the floor where my necklace had fallen. He scooped it up and secured it back around my neck. I sat still, closing my eyes as he moved my hair and buckled the clasp, smelling myself on his breath.

I opened my eyes when he stepped away and instantly missed the warmth of his body. "What about you?" I gestured to the visible bulge in his jeans. I admittedly wasn't a fan of blowjobs, but I wanted him to feel good, too.

He smirked and held out a hand. "You'll make it up to me later. Come with me."

I grinned at the obvious double entendre.

After helping me down, he led me back through the refurbished warehouse towards a short hall with a large metal door at the end of it.

I could still feel him between my thighs as I walked, making me want him even more. This mercurial man had the sole ability to turn me into a crazed nymphomaniac.

He'd taken a sex drive that needed a hard kick to sputter at best and smashed it straight to full-throttle. Glancing at him from the corner of my eye, I felt a bit foolish for where my thoughts were drifting. I'd just met him, felt like I'd known him forever, and was already craving more than the lust and attraction.

"Where are you taking me?"

I already had a pretty good idea but I needed something

else to focus on besides the way he made me feel, the deal I'd just made, and how totally fucked everything was.

He waited until we reached the end of the hall to answer me.

"I want to show you where I play." He flashed me a devilish smile and pushed open the door.

Chapter Fifteen

Calista

Expelling a steady breath, I shoved all my bullshit into a corner of my mind until I had time to sort through my confusing, chaotic feelings.

The door slammed behind us, shutting me in the same room he had stitched me up in. The draft from the air conditioner was stronger in this part of the building. It made the tiny hairs on my arms rise. An ambient glow illuminated the large space.

Both the dead bodies had been removed, replaced by a man who was tied to a steel chair in the center of the room.

He had a familiar black sack over his head and was dressed in the white robes of David's followers.

Seeing him was like being doused with a bucket of cold water.

It affirmed one of the answers I was sent here to find and replaced it with another. The Savages would not be kidnapping and killing off The Order members *and* working with them.

"Why are you killing them off?"

"Same reason you were. Figured I could get answers and get David's attention. Two birds, one stone."

I nodded and took a good look around the room. One wall held an array of tools. All the others, with the exception of one, were plain. On the back wall directly ahead of us was a Leviathan cross smeared with bold red paint inside another inverted pentacle. There was an eye drawn above the infinity symbol and bottom bar of the cross.

This room had a sole purpose. People were brought in here to suffer and die before a symbol that destroyed the pipedream of heaven.

"Is there a reason you have the official symbol of Satan all over your house…and your body?"

He was quiet for so long I almost thought he was ignoring me.

"I thought you knew," he eventually answered, turning his entire body towards me and giving me a look I couldn't decipher.

His stare was so intense I took a step away from him. On a scale of small to big, it was minuscule, but he saw it. When it came to me, the man saw everything. The smile that graced his face was so sinister I had to stop myself from flinching. My breath caught, and I felt the prickling of my skin.

"You have no idea what you're in for."

I hadn't the faintest idea what he meant, and he didn't seem inclined to offer me an explanation.

I knew the inverted cross was the Savages' symbol, but

I'd always thought of it as more of a logo. I mean, I wore the same cross around my neck.

I knew Romero was referred to as the devil, but I thought that was because he was a cruel and heartless asshole.

He couldn't be the actual entity—this was fucking reality. So what was I missing? What did it have to do with the markings?

"Oh, you're a Satanic." I snapped my fingers and pointed at him.

Without a word, he sniggered and walked past me towards the man in the center of the room.

"Are you going to explain?" I called to his back.

He spun around and started walking backward.

"If I told you how to pass all the trials and tribulations and gave you all the answers, I'd ruin half the fun. Just stay curious and keep a smile on that pretty face."

I crossed my arms and huffed out a breath. "So you're spinning riddles, now? Seriously?"

He winked and turned back around.

"Come here, baby, we need to properly send off our friend."

Hiding how much I loved hearing him call me that—how much it warmed me—I rolled my eyes to the ceiling and made my way over to the chair.

Romero pulled the sack off the man's head and tapped his cheeks a few times to wake him up. He jolted awake, turning his head every which way. The moment he saw my face, his eyes almost popped out of their sockets.

"Calista! What have they done to you?" he gasped.

Even tied to a chair, the guy had the nerve to sound appalled when he was just as bruised as me, if not worse. I tried to find a hint of recognition somewhere in my memory, but I simply had no idea who this man was. However, he certainly knew me, which further screwed with my mentals because I had been out of The Order for years.

I looked at Romero and saw him watching me in all his intensity again. Was this one of those trials or tribulations he'd just mentioned? Finding out if I was secretly working with David?

My eyes fell to the shiny black amulet around the man's neck.

I snorted at the sight of it. "I see David's still preaching his made-up gospel."

Just like that, he shut down, and a tic appeared in his jaw. A tiny click brought my attention back to the gorgeous man beside me. In his hand was a smaller version of the knife he'd used the day before, outstretched in my direction.

"Take this and slit his throat."

"Um, okay." That was easy enough. Shrugging, I took the knife from him and slashed at the bishop's neck. He closed his eyes and braced himself but was spared at the last second.

Confused, I looked down to where Romero gripped my wrist. "That's not what you wanted?"

"You're moving too fast."

He let me go and circled behind me, gently resting his hands on my shoulders.

"I have a gun, but I rarely use it. It hinders the creativity I would normally have with my knife. I like to kill slowly. Draw it out and watch them break, look them in the eyes as they suffer and their lives fade away."

Using one hand, he gripped my waist. The other moved my hair to one side so he could speak into my ear, using his breath to caress my skin.

"I want you to relax. Lean into me and look at him. Look at him real fucking good and then tell me what you feel." His voice was soft and soothing, and he nipped at my lower lobe.

Letting out a shaky breath, I stared down at the man in front of me. A bead of sweat rolled from his graying temple to his chin. He did his best to keep a blank face, but the look in his brown eyes conveyed the panic he was trying to hide.

It took me a minute to block out everything but the safe embrace of the man behind me and solely focus on the one in front of me.

As I looked at him—*really* looked at him—my cold prison cell of memories began to bustle with activity. His robes, his transparent loyalty, and the way my stomach began to turn with every passing second of him being in my sight brought everything back to the forefront of my mind.

I never intentionally faced my past. I'd always looked to the future for the day I could make them suffer like I did. This, though, made me realize how unprepared I was. This was the closest to it I'd ever been.

When I snuck into the church where my uncle preached his bullshit to his delegates, he was always in the front. I hid as far away from him as I possibly could, waiting for the perfect opportunity to drag one of his mindless bitches off to dismember. His voice alone was enough to make my skin break out in a cold sweat.

I started to see them all again—smell them and taste them, their voices in my ear, their breath on my neck, the way they took turns fucking me in both holes until I bled.

Shaking my head back and forth, I clutched at the arm wrapped around my waist, suddenly feeling as if my chest was going to cave in.

"Uhn-uh, no." My voice quaked, and I loathed myself for showing a sign of weakness.

Ignoring the way I was clawing at his arm, Romero brought a hand up and gently clasped it around my throat. He kissed my temple and started speaking softly in my ear. "Easy breaths. I got you, babe. I'm right here. He can't fucking touch you."

He gripped my waist tighter, purposely squeezing my wound. Whimpering, I pushed back against him, taking comfort in his security and drawing it from my pain.

"Look at him, Pixie. How do you feel?"

Focusing back on the bishop, I leveled him with a fevered stare. With a heaving chest, I could only muster up one emotion to feel.

Hatred.

I hated him.

I didn't know him from a hole in the wall, but I truly fucking hated him. I hated what he represented, I hated the way he made my blood freeze over, and I hated what they did, hated that they'd siphoned every bit of my innocence with their pedophile cocks.

I hated him for everything they took away from me and the irreversible damage they caused. I wasn't sure how he got caught, and I didn't care—he was a parasite that needed to be terminated.

"I…I *hate* him," I spat in a scathing tone.

"Good girl." Romero breathed his praise in my ear. "Hold onto that hatred, baby. Make him bleed."

It was like being put in a trance.

Stepping forward, I zeroed in on the bishop in the chair and turned the knife's handle in my hands, tightening my grip.

I reached down and roughly grabbed him by the hair, making sure he couldn't turn his head as I plunged the thin silver knife into his left ear.

He started to scream, but it wasn't loud enough. I ground my teeth together and continued to push in, passing the pinna, twisting through the canal, and rupturing his eardrum.

The knife was like a bottle opener. The instant I pulled it out, blood spurted as if a cork had been popped off, hitting my shirt, running down his earlobe, and landing on his white garment. His skin turned a dark cherry red as he began to weep. He was in obvious pain, but he wasn't close to dying...*yet*.

I ran my bloody fingertips down his face and used his tears to clean them off.

He choked and gagged from the intensity of his sobs, rocking so hard the chair almost tipped over.

I loved seeing this man helpless, bawling his eyes out as blood dripped freely. The only thing that could make this moment more perfect would be him begging for forgiveness at my feet.

With the palm of my hand, I pushed his head back until he was staring up at the ceiling. "You're looking mighty pathetic, Mr. Bishop." Straddling his lap, I glanced back at Romero and gave him a shy smile. "Will you hold him still for me, please?"

Without a sound of protest, he circled back around the chair and took a firm hold of the bishop by his graying hair.

I placed the tip of the knife at the base of his throat and slowly twisted it in. The bishop let out a low wail between his sobs.

"Aw, does it hurt really bad?" I cooed, poking out my lower lip.

With a forceful shove, I broke through the skin, inserting the blade directly where his trachea was.

His brown eyes widened as he was forced to gargle his own blood. Removing the knife, I squeezed the slippery handle and began blindly driving it home anywhere I could penetrate, finally getting a reaction that was worthwhile.

His dying, garbled screams echoed inside the room and

urged me on. The serrated blade sliced into his flesh with minimal ease. I didn't stop until my chest was heaving and his neck looked like a crimson dipped honeycomb.

I felt his blood on my face, in my hair, and saw it all over my hands up to my elbows. There wasn't a mirror in the room so I could only imagine what I looked like. The bishop's hair was no longer gray, and his head hung at an odd angle. Licking my lips, my tongue swiped up the sweet metallic taste of a sufferer's blood.

I blinked and looked away from him, realizing Romero was no longer behind the chair. He had taken a few steps back to watch me.

That seemed to be a habit of his—watching everything I did like he was analyzing me for something.

Peering up at him through lowered lashes, I offered him another shy smile, feeling a bit self-conscious.

"Whoops, sorry. I got a little carried away."

"Come here." There was no change in his vocal inflection; I couldn't read his mood. Wiping my bloody palms on my ruined shirt, I went to him without hesitation.

The second I was within reaching distance, he had a hand knotted in my hair, slightly tilting my head back so that I was looking up at him.

"Tell me how you feel."

"I feel…better."

"Beautiful." He gave me the smile I was quickly coming to adore and dropped his mouth to mine, slipping his hand from my hair to the back of my neck.

He kissed me hard and deep, speaking to me without saying a word. I felt like I'd known him for a thousand lifetimes.

Walking us backward, we got all the way to the other side of the room without detaching from one another. Without warning, he spun me around and I found myself bent over the metal table he'd stitched me up on.

His leg came between mine and spread them apart. The unmistakable sound of his zipper going down had my body elated with anticipation. I hummed my approval when he slid the smooth head of his cock up and down my lips, gathering my arousal.

"You're a dirty little bitch. Fuck, Cali, your pussy is drooling all over my dick."

"I'm only dirty for you, Rome," I moaned and pushed myself at him, trying to slide him inside me on my own.

It was apparently the right thing to say. With a growl, he grabbed a handful of my hair and drove his dick into me.

My pussy gripped his thick length like a vise. I spread my legs a little further and gripped the edge of the table to keep me grounded as he hammered into me.

"Your pussy feels so fucking good," he ground out. "Put your hands between your legs, baby. Touch yourself."

I eagerly responded to his command. Snaking one hand between my thighs, I fondled my already sensitive clit, no longer recognizing myself. Dirty talk had never made me wet before; killing someone had never given me such a lust-filled rush. As the blood sprayed, my arousal spiked. I needed to be fucked—hard—and Romero gave me exactly what I wanted.

He fisted my hair with one hand and brought the other one to my waist, pushing down on my wound. My legs almost buckled from underneath me.

"You like that?"

"Yes! Don't stop!" I pleaded, bucking against him.

"Tell me what you need." His demand was rhetorical. This man knew what I needed before I did, but I was so delirious I would have recited the alphabet if he asked me to.

"I need you, Rome. Fuck me—hurt me."

With another growl that sounded much more beast than man, he gave me exactly what I asked for.

He wrenched my head back to the point I could barely swallow, pressed his palm down, and bit my shoulder just hard enough for my endorphins to go crazy from the pain. The table tilted and fell from the force of our bodies repeatedly thrusting against it, hitting the floor with a loud bang.

"Rome!" His name spilled from my lungs and echoed around the room. I came on a soundless scream, clenching around him as my eyes rolled to the back of my head.

He cursed and pulled out before I could fully come down.

"Knees," he rasped, spinning me around by the hair. Immediately dropping down, I let out a soft hiss as my knees hit the concrete.

"Mouth."

As soon as my lips parted, his slippery dick was hitting the back of my throat. Gagging, I gripped his thighs and let him fuck my mouth, taking him as deep as I could, sucking my juices and come off him.

His cock jerked twice. He let out an almost inaudible groan as I hungrily swallowed every drop of come that shot into my mouth, swirling my tongue around the tip to make sure I got all the salty fluid off.

When he pulled away, I rolled my lips together.

Clasping my hands together in my lap, I gazed up at him as he tucked himself away, all the while looking down at me. Both of us fought to keep our chests of heaving breaths quiet.

Holding my hands out in front of me, I stared at the blood coating them and thought how terribly wrong Tito was when he said I wasn't afraid of anything. I remembered my father saying I would be eaten alive by my sins.

I hated that one was wrong and one was right.

This—whatever this feeling was between us—was terrifying. It was growing at a disturbingly rapid rate. Was it possible to fall this fast? Could I stop it? Did I even want to?

It felt instinctive, like breathing. It was completely unexpected and unexplainable. He made me feel so much inside my chest, feel things that were indefinable.

I was hurtling head over heels—obsessively, addictively, stupidly, over-emotionally hurtling.

This would be about the time it was smart to run away from him as fast as I could, but like a suicidal moth to an eternal flame, I moved closer.

His clean hands covered my filthy ones and he helped me up. When he touched his forehead to mine, I knew I was doomed.

Romero was an inferno of tantalizing sin, and I wanted him branded on every inch of my skin.

Chapter Sixteen

Romero

It took a lot to impress me, but Cali had been doing just that from the moment we met.

She reminded me of a lioness, stunning and fierce as fuck. Now I understood why her skin was white as snow: it was a canvas meant to be covered in red. She looked like a goddess covered in blood, a homicidal angel with devil horns.

She'd surpassed my expectations and passed her first test. I had to be sure she wasn't with The Order, and now I knew. Her hatred was a beautiful tool. Her pain was power.

There was no way to fake her kind of madness. I could see it boiling beneath her surface, eager to emanate. I didn't need to push her into it; it already swam in her veins.

"So the madness got her, too," Grimm mused, staring across the room to where Arlen was sleeping on the sofa.

"If she wasn't with The Order, she was with another group," Cobra theorized, blowing out a ring of smoke. "A group that either isn't up to par on this century or they were keeping shit from her—specifically, shit about us. We all know she didn't end up in those woods by accident."

I crossed my arms and nodded. I wanted to know who kept her so sheltered that she didn't know the one thing about me the entire world seemed to know. Unless she was as skilled in the department of duplicity as I was, then she truly was clueless. It was both a blessing and a curse for her to be so naïve. The blessing was, of course, in my favor. I was going to take everything she had to offer until I possessed her mind, body, and soul.

The feeling she invoked in me was primal.

If I was a shark, she was the blood in the water. I was the wolf and she was the rabbit. I wanted her so immersed in me that when she was faced with truth of my world, she would be immobilized.

"She's…" Cobra trailed off, stubbing out his joint.

"Childishly maniacal," I finished for him, opening a cabinet.

"Yeah, that."

Handing him a bowl, I rolled my shoulders. "I don't think that's intentional." I leveled him with a look that warned him to choose his next words carefully.

"I'm not judging; I was just pointing out your girl might be crazier than you."

"David had her cut out of her mother's stomach and raised her on his own. Who the fuck knows what went on during that time?

She wasn't fucked up when we saw her; maybe it's her head's safe place," Grimm said. "Are we sure we want to deal with this?"

"Damn, Grimm, I feel your emotions so strongly," Cobra joked.

I knew why he was really asking us that question and didn't bother answering it. Cali was not Tiffany. I didn't need to use her to that extreme, and I sure as fuck would never share her. The thought of another motherfucker touching her was enough to make me see red.

A soft ping had us all looking towards the stairs, watching Cali make her way down them. She was freshly showered and dressed in an over-sized white tank and black lacy knee highs she tied together with a fitted leather jacket and the same pair of black boots from earlier.

She definitely had a certain way she liked to dress; pulling it off with a box of dead people's clothing was impressive, but I'd rather she have whatever she wanted at easy disposal.

With a smile and wave, she made her way into the kitchenette where the three of us were, giving Arlen a quick once over.

She impaled me with her blue gems and smiled a little bigger. I felt that shit in my gut.

I did a lot of sick shit. I killed without remorse and ruthlessly took whatever I wanted. I didn't believe in any of that love at first sight bullshit—I didn't even know what the fuck love was—but I was fucking positive Cali was my soul mate.

"Hey y'all." She greeted all of us but came straight to me.

If any other chick tried this with me, she would have been drop kicked to the other side of the room. I didn't do clingy, emotional, or needy. I did do Cali.

Pushing a few stray strands of blonde hair out of her face, I gripped the back of her neck and pulled her into me, sealing my mouth over hers.

She placed her dainty hands on my chest and sighed, parting her soft lips and twining her tongue around mine.

I loved the way she smelled because she smelled like me —like she was mine.

I felt like a goddamn Neanderthal as much as I kept repeating that word in my head.

My dick was constantly engorged since I'd met her. Fucking had never been a must on my to-do list, and now it was at the top of it. Cali was a pain slut, and I was more than happy to give her what she needed. Everything about this woman made me feel more insane than I already was.

"When you two finish mouth fucking, the chili is done," Cobra drawled.

"I'll wake the brat up," Grimm volunteered, giving Cali an appraising look as he turned away.

"You need to eat." Breaking away from her, I took the bowl from Cobra's hands and nudged her towards the table.

She eyed the ram-head centerpiece but didn't comment on it.

"You could have done that a lot gentler, you shithead," Arlen snapped as she took a seat beside Cali and glared at Grimm, who was holding her shoulder.

He gave her a rare smile and placed another bowl in front of her.

"This is really, really good," Cali enthused, licking her spoon and giving me all kinds of visuals.

"Compliments to the chef, who also happens to be a pretty badass redheaded dude." Cobra grinned and Cali beamed back at him.

I reached into my back pocket and pulled out a weathered picture that was creased and wrinkled from how many times I had folded and unfolded it.

While it would be ideal to stay buried in Cali's pussy all

day and eat chili all night, that wasn't realistic. I still had shit to do and the clock hadn't stopped ticking.

As soon as she took her last bite, I placed the picture in front of her. "How many of these people do you remember?"

Her reaction was instant. An onslaught of emotions flashed across her face and I knew every one of them intimately, starting with anger, shame, and disgust, before the pain was masked with indifference.

"All of them," she answered in a flat tone.

"Which one hurt you?" Grimm interjected, asking the question I had never planned to ask but was going to.

Her blue hues darted around the room. Before she could have another episode like she did in my playroom, I brought her focus solely to me.

I gripped her jaw and turned her face towards me, blocking everyone else from view.

"Who was it?"

"All of them," she whispered.

Calista

I refused to make eye contact with him after I answered. Grimm making a sound in his throat gave me the perfect excuse to look away.

No wonder he knew my name; he had to know I was David's daughter, too.

The last thing I expected him to do was pull out a photo of David and his most trusted followers—me being amongst them.

I'm sure we looked every bit like a happy father and daughter from an outside perspective with the smile he had painted on his face and arm wrapped around my waist. No one but him and a few of his friends knew he was forced to hold me up so the picture could be taken because I had been ass-fucked the entire night before.

"Even the women?" Cobra asked. "Never mind; don't answer that," he backpedaled when Romero and Grimm both glared at him.

"It's…okay." I shrugged, trying not to think about it as I answered him. "The woman who raised me taught me how to give blow jobs and eat pussy."

"All those fuckers deserve death," Arlen spat. Her angry response was the only sound in the room for a good five minutes.

My face flushed and I looked down, using my hair as a curtain.

"She's right." Romero stroked the top of my head and expelled a deep breath. "How did you watch your uncle's meets without getting caught?" he asked, steering the conversation in a better direction.

"They keep extra habits in one of the old confessional booths. I just wore one of those and hid inside it until he was done, and waited for one of the sisters to walk past alone."

"That was really fucking stupid of you. If he'd known you were right under his nose, what do you think he would've done?"

"Stop calling me stupid!"

"Then don't do stupid shit. What time does he do his meets, and how far is it from here?"

"He meets every night at eleven, and I don't know how far the church is from here because I don't know where I am."

"He meets in a church?" Grimm laughed darkly. "Does it have a lake behind it?"

I furrowed my brows, eyeing him suspiciously. "Yeah… how did you—"

"We can make it there if we head out now. There are robes and habits in the storage room."

I let out an annoyed breath. They kept cutting me off. "All right, so we're going to church. Let's hope it doesn't burst into flames the second we all walk through the door."

"Do I have to go?" Arlen piped up, drawing everyone's attention to her.

"Fuck yes, you have to go. You're not Cali; you don't get a deal. You need to ask yourself, do you really want to be in? Because this is how you start earning that right.

"And be careful how you answer, cause if you say no, then we have a problem we need to immediately rectify," Cobra stated.

"I'm not leaving Cali, and you sure as hell ain't killin me, so yes, I want to be in," she snapped back at him. "And before we go runnin off to some church, where is everyone else?"

"We are everyone," Romero swiftly responded, pulling out my chair.

"There's only…three of you?" she asked, her voice full of skepticism.

"Strength is in unity, brat, not numbers," Grimm answered.

"Only five people live in this house," Romero cut in with a hard tone, ending the discussion.

Arlen and I glanced at each other with the same knowing expression—he had just majorly deflected the question.

He was hiding something.

Chapter Seventeen

Romero

The ride was uneventful.

Arlen and Cali sat in the back on either side of Grimm, and I drove with Cobra riding shotgun. Every time I looked in the rearview mirror, Cali's eyes met mine.

She had on a habit and hood with her cross necklace tucked in. She looked pure as ever, tempting the strongest man to wanna sin.

I parked the Jeep hillside, partially obscured and still able to see the lone church that sat center field.

"You got this?" I asked Cali and Arlen at ten till eleven.

"I can do this," Cali answered with heady determination.

"That's my fuckin girl."

She beamed at me and climbed out of the car, blowing a kiss before shutting the door.

"What about you?"

"I got her back," Arlen retorted, climbing out and circling around to walk in step with Cali. We watched them fall in line with the rest of the nuns rushing towards the church in the mirrors. The bright light made them all look like scurrying black dots.

"Did you bring it?"

"It's right here," Cobra said, pulling a utility bag from beneath his seat with an excited grin.

"You're such a child, Bow-bow," Grimm taunted from the backseat, using the nickname we'd given him when we were kids.

Cobra gasped dramatically and turned in his seat. "Is that a compliment from the reaper? Thanks, man. I got love for you too."

Ignoring their banter, I kept my eyes trained on the rearview mirror.

Patience was never my strongest virtue to begin with, but where Cali was concerned, the shit didn't exist at all. I knew she could do this—she'd done it multiple times before I entered the picture—but that didn't make me feel any better about her safety.

Exactly on time, a figure dressed in all black appeared at the back of the church. I was more relieved than I was willing to admit.

"Let's go."

I was out the car before the last word finished coming out of my mouth, jogging towards the door. Cobra and Grimm fell in step beside me.

As people began filing out the front of the church, thanks to Arlen we were able to slip in the back. She held a finger to her lips to silence us and took the lead back the way she came.

The building went peacefully silent after the large doors slammed shut.

The moon shone through the stained glass windows and served as the only light in the hall.

"You look cute, brat, like a school girl." She glanced over her shoulder and shook her head, flipping Grimm the bird as she walked.

At the end of the hall, she paused and put an arm out to stop us, pointing around a corner.

Peering around her, I searched the pews for Cali, spotting her kneeling in front of the altar. Father Azel—her uncle—was making his way towards her.

We filed into the room just as he reached her and touched the back of her head. Like a jack-in-the-box, she sprang up and turned around with a shit-eating grin on her face.

"Hello, Father. Did you miss me?"

Her sweet voice echoed across the room. Azel faltered, visibly surprised. Cali stepped forward and shoved him so hard he fell back and tripped, landing on a pew.

"Lock the doors," I directed Arlen as we moved past her.

Hearing my voice, Azel whipped his head around. His wide eyes took us all in and he blanched, hopping up and attempting to run.

"Hey!" Cali yelled, sticking a foot out to trip him. He fell into the aisle, landing at Grimm's feet.

"You're aging like shit," Grimm told him, bending down and lifting him up by the head with one hand covering his mouth.

Cobra bypassed all of us, giving Cali a high-five. He went to the altar and began unloading his utility bag.

"Come here, baby." I held my hand out. She took it and linked our fingers together as I draped my arm over her shoulder.

"Doors are locked; coast is clear," Arlen announced, pulling her hood off.

"Where do you want him?"

"You're letting me choose?"

"This is your show. We're just the muscle." Her eyes lit up like saucers and she did an excited shimmy.

Slipping out from beneath my arm, she spun around like a ringmaster and pointed to a large silver cross leaning against the wall.

"Can you use that to *cross* him up?" She looked at me and laughed at her own joke. "With that," she clarified, pointing to the long metal chain Cobra had placed on the altar.

"We can make that work." Grimm answered before I could, dragging a struggling Azel towards the altar.

I went and retrieved the cross. I carried it to the altar and propped it up.

"Lift, strip, tie." I pointed to each of us and grabbed the chain. Cobra cut Azel's robes off and partially assisted Grimm holding him up as I secured his left and then his right arm on the bars of the cross.

"God, we're all going straight to hell," Arlen groaned.

Cobra paused and looked at her with a mischievous grin.

"Take a good look around you, sweetheart, cause you're already there. This world is hell and that psychopathic asshole is the devil." He pointed to me with the tip of his knife.

"So what does that make the rest of us?" she scoffed.

"Well, I'm clearly his most trusted, loyal, advisor," he hyped, tearing the last piece of robe from the now constrained Azel. "Grimm is self-explanatory. He kills shit without discrimination, takes no bribes, and never fails to get the job done."

"That's actually pretty accurate," Grimm approved, pulling Azel's drawers down to his ankles.

"Cali is his beautifully insane, dark, maleficent queen." He sighed dramatically and looked to the ceiling. "Even the devil needs love."

I shook my head and looked at Cali. She stared back at me with an unreadable expression on her angelic face.

His spot-on definition did crazy shit to my head.

She just didn't know how serious he was.

"That's sickeningly sweet, but y'all aren't that bad."

"Of course you would say that, Arlen, because you don't know us...yet. But you're more than likely dead anyway, so tough shit for you."

"Y'all don't know us—"

"I know Cali." I cut her off and put an end to the discussion. No one said anything; Grimm and Cobra didn't even attempt to act surprised by my words.

Did I know what her favorite color or her favorite food was? Fuck no. Did I know every sordid detail of her past? Also fuck no. Did I give a shit about any of that? Again: fuck no.

I knew she was so broken she didn't even realize it. I knew what she saw when she looked in the mirror was nothing but confusion.

I knew she was drowning inside herself and struggling to figure out who she was while the demons screamed at her to let them out.

I knew all of that because once upon a very shitty, unfortunate time, that was me.

I was her.

I knew her.

We reflected off one another.

She was *my* beautifully dark motherfucking queen.

She was *mine*. I wasn't letting her go even when it was all said and done and she hated my fucking guts—because she would. That was inevitable. I destroyed everything good that I touched. She'd just have to hate me with her pussy sitting on my face.

"Why...did you tie him that way?" she asked, breaking the silence and staring at Azel's shabby, pale ass.

"We're going to make him suffer until we get some answers."

She nodded and approached me, holding on to Arlen's arm to move forward.

"Calista, sweet girl—"

I was behind him, slamming his face into the cross before he could finish. "You don't get to address her! The only time you get to open your mouth is to answer questions or fucking scream."

"He's pissin on himself." Cobra pointed to the stream of urine running down Azel's pale leg.

"Typical." I stepped away from him with a look of disgust. "Pick a tool, Pixie."

Without a word, she studied the altar and hummed beneath her breath, selecting the yellow drill. She clicked the button and smiled at me when it whirred.

A shocked cry had all of us turning our heads to see a nun had come around the corner. She screamed and took off for the door.

"Fuck, I got it," Grimm grumbled.

He hopped down the small step and took off after her.

Just before she reached the door, he lifted her up by the waist and flung her through the air. She bounced off a pew with a resounding boom and cried out when her body smacked the marble floor.

Grimm being Grimm, he wasted no time picking her up by

the neck and squeezing the life from her body. She wildly swung her arms at him, gasping and kicking her legs. It took thirteen seconds for her to pass out and another two to kill her. She died so fast, if it wasn't for him carelessly tossing her body over the back of a pew, it would be easy to believe it never happened.

"You have three strikes to tell me where David is, starting now." My impatience was starting to kick in, and I was tired of being inside the church.

"I don't know—"

"Strike one—just because I know you're about to bullshit me."

Cali stepped up beside me with the drill in her hand and looked to me for instruction.

"Make it hurt."

"Make it hurt," she repeated. Her eyes travelled over every inch of him, landing on his hands. She stepped closer and raised the drill to the back of his left one and held the button down.

The drill bit spun around, only twisting his skin at first, gradually drilling into his flesh.

"Stop! Please just stop!" he screamed in agony.

I gently pulled Cali's hand away, revealing the tiny hole she had started to make on the back of his hand.

"Stop crying and pull your shit together. We haven't even hurt you yet." I sighed and patted the top of his head. "What kind of man pisses himself and cries because of a little good old-fashioned torture?

"Same question, Azel—where is David?"

"I haven't seen him in months," he whined.

"But you've talked to him. You always talk to each other on the phone. You know where he is; I know you do!" Cali interjected, yelling in his face.

"I'm telling you truth. Why would I lie?"

"Because you're a sorry sack of shit."

"Because you're at strike two," I added behind her.

She sighed and raised the drill again, pulling back with a shake of her head.

"Why are we even wasting our time on this sicko when he keeps a ledger of addresses in his office? He's not gonna talk. They never talk. We might as well just make him scream, make him bleed, and then kill as many of them as possible. David will show himself if you start killing off his most important members. With the ledger, we'll know exactly where to find them."

"She has an excellent point," Cobra agreed, smacking a hand over Azel's mouth to muffle his screams.

"What do you think?" I asked Grimm.

"I think it's rhetorical. And why did it take her so long to get lost in the woods?"

"Do your thing." I gave her the green light, curiously watching for what she would do now.

I fucking loved seeing the way her mind worked, figuring out exactly how badly she wanted to make a motherfucker scream. That pretty little head of hers was full of a festering sickness. When she finally broke free of her chrysalis, she would be fucking incredible.

She smiled at me and grabbed for Azel's flaccid cock. The tip was still wet from his piss.

With no forewarning, she jammed the drill bit into his urethra. He was screaming before she even held the button down. My own cock couldn't decide if it wanted to shrivel itself inside out in fear or stay rock solid while Cali drilled a hole into another man's dick.

Cobra looked at me and I nodded.

Within a second, he had his own cock out and was spreading Azel's ass cheeks apart, lining himself up.

"Let's see how you like being on the receiving end for once." He shoved himself in dry—just like they used to.

Cali immediately stopped and dropped his bloody member, peering around with large eyes as Cobra pounded into Azel's ass.

"Holy shit," Arlen sputtered.

"Don't think his shit is gonna be too holy anymore," Grimm joked.

Azel twisted in his restraints, crying out for mercy and not receiving any. Cobra's dick became tinged with blood as he drove in and out of his ass.

Cali's mouth opened and shut. She licked her lips and stepped back. Feeling my stare, she wiped her bloody hand on her habit and set the drill down.

"I'm going to get the ledger." She excused herself and took off quicker than a mouse.

I watched Cobra for a few minutes but quickly grew bored. Azel had turned into a whimpering broken record. "Let's wrap this up."

"Thank fuck, finally. My dick was getting chafed." Cobra pulled out and jumped back as Azel defecated all over the floor.

"God, that is disgusting," Arlen shrilled, darting towards the back hall, shielding her eyes.

I yanked the cross amulet from around his neck and stood in front of him. Grimm placed one hand on the top and the other on the bottom, pulling his mouth wide open, breaking his jaw apart.

I shoved the amulet in Azel's mouth and Grimm slammed it back together, pushing the cross straight through the roof of his gums. Blood dripped down onto the silver pendant and leaked over his lips.

Glancing down, I laughed at the sight of his bloody dick. We'd done this same routine so many times it was nice to have it shaken up a little bit.

"Bleed him out and then find Arlen."

I left them to it and walked off in the direction Cali had gone.

Chapter Eighteen

Calista

If I was his, did that mean he was mine?

Why was I even asking myself that when I couldn't get a firm grasp on my emotions?

I'd just brutalized someone's genitals and all I could think about was sex. Something was wrong with me—outside of me already knowing I was a tad fucked up.

My sigh skirted over the church's vaulted ceiling. Clutching the black ledger in my hands, I bypassed the wooden confessional booths, noting that Azel wasn't crying so loudly anymore. Maybe Cobra was done—and good for him.

I could see myself befriending him, and maybe even Grimm one day, if it weren't for the fact that Tito was still out and about somewhere and I just couldn't bring myself to snub him.

"What the hell am I even doing this for?" I mumbled to myself, turning the corner and running right into Romero.

"What are you doing what for?" He grabbed my upper arm and turned me around, all but dragging me into one of the dark, dusty confessional booths.

"What are you doing?" I whispered.

"Is that the book?"

He reached for it and I twisted away. "Why do you want David so badly?"

"Cali, if I don't tell you something, it's because I don't think you should know."

What could I say to that?

I couldn't demand he give me one hundred percent transparency when I wouldn't do the same, and if we couldn't trust one another, then where did that leave us?

He reached for the book again, this time snatching it out of my hands.

"Was that your pathetic attempt at blackmailing information out of me?"

"I'm smarter than that."

"Are you?"

"You're such an asshole," I breathed, squeezing past him to push the thin wooden door open.

"Uhn-uh." He pulled me away from the door and caged me between him and the wooden bench.

"What do you want?" I growled. The box was stuffy and I could barely see his eyes from the lack of light.

"What if I told you to confess your deepest, darkest sin?"

"*You* are my deepest darkest sin."

"Maybe I should fuck you in here, then. I've never been given the honor of defiling a nun."

"I'm not a real nun."

"Don't ruin the fantasy, baby. Just spread your legs for me."

He knelt to set the ledger down on the floor, lifting my habit when he stood back up.

Gliding his fingers along the skin of my left thigh, he gripped it tightly and hitched it over his hip.

I wound one arm around his neck and dropped the other to the zipper on his jeans, working it down until I could reach in enough to free his cock. He abruptly spun us so he was sitting down on the bench and I was straddling his lap.

"Put my dick inside you and ride it. Hard."

"I don't—"

"Do it."

I hovered above him, my heart beating at an uneven tempo. Exhaling a shaky breath, I curled my fingers in the confessional's divider and slowly sank down, easing him into me.

"Like this." He gripped my hips and thrust up, burying himself to the hilt, filling me with him entirely.

I choked on a scream that quickly morphed into a moan as he controlled me below, setting a rapid pace for me to keep up with. "Goddamn, Cali, your pussy's so fucking wet; so fucking tight. So fucking *mine*." He slid his hands to my ass, grabbing a globe in each hand, and began drilling into me from underneath.

When he urged me to take over, it took me a minute to find a rhythm. I kept my grip on the divider and rolled my hips, bouncing up and down on his cock. My uninhibited moans echoed inside the church and filled the small confessional booth.

My leg muscles began to burn. Sweat beaded between my heaving breasts. My breaths started coming loud and ragged, intermingling with my pleasure-filled gasps.

"I can't do—'

"Don't tell me you can't. Just fuck me," he growled.

Dropping my hands to his shoulders, I adjusted my position and began rocking into him, taking him deeper, harder.

"Rome," I whimpered, dropping my forehead to his.

"That's it, baby. Use me, make yourself come." He pressed the pad of his thumb down on my clit and slowly massaged it in a circular motion.

My lower stomach began to tighten and warmth rifled up my spine. He leaned in and swiped his tongue up the side of my neck and bit me. He pushed up into me with one solid thrust. I came so hard I forgot to breathe.

"Fuck!" I could no longer move. My muscles tensed and I shut my eyes, reveling in the sensation only he could draw out of me. He pulled out a few pumps later, staining the center part of my habit with his come.

"Now seems like a good time to discuss contraception," I stated, smearing his semen into the black fabric.

"You just fucked me raw inside a confessional. That's what makes you think of birth control?"

"Rome," I stressed.

"Why are you worrying about this when all our kids have either gone down your throat or landed somewhere on you? When I want to get you pregnant, I will."

"Ugh, you're so poetic," I deadpanned. I tried to stand up and his hands clamped down on my hips to hold me in place. The wooden bench creaked beneath our shifting weight.

"I don't need to see you clearly to know you're pissed off. I can sense it. Don't be a girl, Cali. Tell me what the problem is."

"How many girls have you said that to? Are you even—"

"Clean?" he interjected. "If this is you being jealous, you can shut that shit down now. I don't just stick my dick in anything with a hole. I'm actually pretty picky. And I don't make a habit of going in raw.

"You're mine. I want nothing between us. I'd never let any dirty shit touch you. And there is only you, Cali."

His words were the balm to my irritation. I swallowed and nodded. "Okay," I whispered in case he couldn't see my head moving.

He gripped the sides of my face and placed his forehead against mine. "The shit you do to me makes no fucking sense."

The strain in his voice wasn't surprising enough to catch me off guard. I felt the same way. Maybe that was the way relationships were meant to be, indefinable with unbreakable bonds. No words were needed to convey what our warped hearts already knew.

I was his, and he was mine.

I was curled up in a corner of the sectional when he handed me the mason jar.

"What exactly are we celebrating?"

"The ledger you gave us, and Romero not being such a dickhead," Cobra said.

I laughed and brought the jar to my mouth, regretting the

decision to partake in this activity as soon as the moonshine hit my tongue.

"This is disgusting," I sputtered, pushing the jar at Romero. "It burns." I wiggled my tongue around, tasting nothing but rubbing alcohol.

"You can do better than that," Romero challenged, nudging the jar back in my direction.

"Hold it for three seconds," Grimm looked up from the ledger and advised.

"Ugh, fine." I took the glass jar back and held my breath as I tilted it back and counted to three. "Ah, how do you drink this?" I coughed, shaking my head and squeezing my eyes shut.

"You get used to it," Romero said, taking the jar from me and passing it to Arlen.

"You didn't drink any."

"I don't drink."

"Then why did you tell me to?" I glared, wiping my mouth with the back of my arm.

"Maybe I want to see what drunken truths you'll tell."

Arlen snorted. "Not everyone has something to hide."

"Everyone in this room does," Grimm countered.

That was a sad goddamn truth, and nothing good would come of it. Everyone knew that lies hurt, but secrets killed.

Sighing, I snuggled deeper into the leather couch cushion. Romero shifted beside me and lifted me onto his lap, placing my head on his shoulder.

"I can't believe y'all left that man strung up," Arlen mused from the opposite end of the couch, knocking her sip back like a seasoned pro. "What?" She shrugged when she realized everyone was staring at her.

"What else can you do?" Cobra inquired, leaning towards her.

"I'll share mine if you share yours," she teased.

"I'm almost positive you're not old enough to drink," Grimm scolded.

"I'm old enough to watch y'all turn the holy house into a snuff film but not take a drink of alcohol?

"And what happens after y'all take out David, anyway? Is this a revolution or somethin?"

"Don't you have to give a shit about the people to start a revolution?" Cobra retaliated, stretching himself out and placing his sock-clad feet on her lap, taking the moonshine back.

"It's the beginning of paradise." Romero responded in his usual way of deflecting a question with an answer that wasn't really an answer.

I frowned and stared down at the pentacle on the floor, asking myself once more what I was doing this for. I wanted Romero. I wanted to know him, but he didn't seem inclined to let me in, and, if Tito ever popped up on his radar, I was certain he would kill him.

Everything was such a jumbled mess inside my head. When I got the jar back, I didn't hesitate to drink that time. It tasted horrible, but misery loved drunken company.

Chapter Nineteen

Romero

I carried her upstairs and laid her on the bed.

I thought she was asleep until she reached for my hand.

"I was trying to get away." The fuck?

"In the woods, I was trying to get away," she whispered.

"Away from what?" When she didn't say anything or open her eyes, I realized how fucking dumb it was to converse with a woman drunk off her ass.

"The man who looks like her, my past, myself."

"Go to bed." I walked to the door and got as far as one step into the hallway.

"Don't leave me in here alone."

The needy tone in her voice had me glancing over my shoulder. Her blue eyes were wide open, staring at my back.

"It's lonely in here. Stay with me."

I was almost one hundred percent fucking positive this was her crazy ass mind talking for her, but she patted the empty bed beside her and that was that.

I kicked the door back shut with my boot, pulled my shirt off, and stretched out beside her. She immediately rolled over and threw her leg over mine.

I waited until I was certain she was asleep before climbing back off the bed, pausing at the door to double check. I scanned over her tiny body and was struck with how surreal it was that she was materialized in the flesh—the ghost I'd thought about off and on over the years.

Slipping out of the room, I made my way downstairs and found Cobra and Grimm at the table.

"She's down for the count." Grimm answered my silent question about Arlen, who was no longer sleeping on the couch.

"So, are we on for tomorrow night?" Cobra asked me.

Thinking it over, I nodded my head. "Yeah, that gives us an extra day to set up for everything else."

"Okay, now that all that's out the way, does anyone wanna discuss the elephant in the room?" He looked between us and waited, but neither of us spoke.

"You haven't seen your sister since you two were kids, and you don't have anything to say?" Cobra questioned him.

"My *sister*," Grimm repeated, adding extra enunciation. "You two are more my family than she is. I don't know her and she doesn't even know I exist. She has zero recollection of me, and I don't feel the need to let her know because *I* don't know if I can trust her."

He gave him a flat look, which was him saying he no longer wanted to discuss it.

"And what about you?" he asked me next.

"I agree with him. I don't know if I can trust her, but she's mine regardless."

"Yeah, I know what that means. Means you two fuck-sticks have your heads up your asses," he grumbled.

"Maybe you should go take a shower." I was more telling than suggesting. He was half drunk, so I was going to give him a small pass instead of wiping the floor with his ass.

"Don't fuck shit up." He stood up and fixed us with a pubescent glare before stumbling off.

"That shit is exactly why we don't let him drink," Grimm said as he stood up. "I'm going to shower and pretend to sleep." He clasped my shoulder on his way past.

I knew he was irritated because Grimm was like me, whereas Cobra still had a bit of good left in him.

If someone were on fire, he'd be more inclined to put it out, while we would use their burning body to light up a smoke.

This was the unplanned part of bullshit I didn't have the patience to deal with. I didn't need the two of them at odds over something we had no control over.

Cali was the last thing I needed to deal with right now. She was an unstable hurricane threatening to destroy everything in her path. Any sane man would have run for cover, but I had never fucking been sane and I'd always had a thing for storms.

I sat at the table half-assed, reading the ledger, thinking about how many things had changed so drastically and how fast they were going to continue changing in the extremely near future.

Shit was about to hit the fan.

Chapter Twenty

Calista

I woke up with a raging headache and Romero in my face.

"Do you always fucking sleep this heavy? I was about to drown your ass in the shower."

"Stop yelling at me. Jesus." I threw an arm over my eyes in hope he'd go away.

"Babe, I don't think Jesus would appreciate being confused with me. I dragged his sister with my Jeep for about ten miles last summer."

I peered at him through one eye from beneath my arm. "You have severe psychological issues."

"I also have an extremely hard dick, so unless you want a headache and a sore pussy, I suggest you get the fuck up."

I definitely wasn't up for getting destroyed. With a groan, I rolled across the mattress and reluctantly got up. When I couldn't sleep, I was stuck awake; when I could sleep, I was stuck awake. A girl just couldn't win.

Smothering a yawn, I began combing my fingers through my hair. "How late is it?"

"Super late. It's almost six."

I gave him a dirty look. Six in the morning was not my definition of late. "Is there a particular reason you're waking me?"

"There is. You're gonna help me with the body pit, and like I said, my dick's hard and there was this sexy fucking blonde lying in my bed, begging to be violated."

I just couldn't even deal with him. Shaking my head, and then regretting it, I pulled my boots on and headed for the door.

The sooner I helped him, the sooner I could go back to sleep. "Next time, use your hand, Romero."

"Next time, I'll just stick it in between your lips. I get off and you stop snoring. Two birds, one stone."

I paused on the staircase and glared back at him. "I don't snore."

"Yeah you do." He grabbed my hand and took the lead, walking us towards the front of the warehouse. As we passed through the door, he snagged a metal slugger leaning against the wall.

The humidity wasn't so bad yet due to it being so early, which I guess made it make sense why he was waking me then. Heat or no heat, the smell was horrible.

I peered down into the hole without really needing to and got a nice whiff of death. Pulling my shirt over my nose, I backed up and tried not to gag, swallowing hard. "It smells like swamp ass!"

"Interesting description." He twirled the end of the bat a few times and then used it to start smashing corpses down like one would a composite pile. Things mashed I didn't know could mash, and the smell of fly larvae overwhelmed me.

"What did you need my help with?"

"Nothing, this job is filthy and you're not to get filthy doing something I'm fully capable of. I just wanted you with me."

Then why did…ugh. Could I even be mad at the guy for that? He woke me up to spend time with me. It's not his fault I sipped on moonshine.

"Wow, that's actually really sweet."

"All we do is fuck or fight. I figured I could take a day off. So after dinner, that sweet pussy of yours is mine."

Rolling my eyes to the sky, I moved a breathable distance back and watched him work.

"So who's the guy who broke your heart?"

I gave him a blank look. "Guy?"

"Last night you said some things," he clarified.

"Have no idea what you're talking about because it wasn't a guy—it was a girl."

He froze and gave me his full attention. "You like women?"

His tone didn't convey whether this bothered him or not —not that I would give a shit either way, but I didn't want to start a 101 about my sexuality either.

"The only thing I like is you."

My answer seemed to placate him for the time being because he went back to smashing bodies. It didn't dawn on me that there were at least twelve people in the large ditch and the majority weren't from The Order until a redhead's body shifted into corpse oblivion.

"Who are these people?"

"Not sure, to be honest. Some are from The Order, obviously; some are from our beds."

He didn't look at me once when he answered.

"So you mess with a woman and then put her in your pit of bodies after you're done with her?"

"You mean when I actually touch a woman, yes, but that isn't always the case. The redhead all the way to the right tried to climb in my bed after leaving Grimm's. I snapped her neck."

"Okay, that's understandable, but what about the others? Why wouldn't you just let them go?"

"Once someone has been touched by me and gotten to experience the tumultuous life-altering experience that is my dick, there is no letting them go."

"Did you really just call your cock life-changing?"

"I called it life-altering. You know it's true because I can see you changing too, and you've only had the sample edition."

The intensity of his gaze had me looking back down at the body pit and rubbing the back of my neck.

Was I changing? I didn't feel any different, but maybe he could see things I couldn't. He did call me beautiful when I didn't even consider myself pretty.

Aware he was watching me in the annoying testy way he always did, I crossed my arms to keep them from making any nervous movements. Meeting his eye, I swallowed and adjusted my stance.

"Are you going to kill me?"

"Didn't you hear what I just said? For that to happen, I'd have to let you go. So no, baby, I'm not going to kill you. I'm just going to make you wish I had. I'm going to hurt you real fucking bad."

He didn't say another word to me. He poured a canister of gasoline on the bodies and we watched them burn.

I didn't have artillery strong enough to win a fight against a man who was severely unhinged.

His vast mood swings made me feel as insane as he was.

I decided to give everyone around me a large berth so I could reflect and think for once. I needed to reestablish order in my madhouse of thoughts. My chosen method of self-therapy was taking a hot shower and letting my mind wander.

I'd gone from a life of dull repetition to one of resonant uncertainty in the blink of an eye. Looking forward, I saw nothing, had no idea where my life was going. Looking backward, I saw routine, knowing exactly what to expect every day I woke up.

I had to remind myself why I was here. I had come here for answers and I had them. I had come here because I was struggling to find myself, and, in the midst of my struggles, I found Romero.

I started adding *what if* questions to certain scenarios. Cool air rushed into the cubicle, replaced by the heat of

Romero's naked body as he stepped inside behind me. Surprising myself, I calmly turned around to face him.

His perfectly styled hair came undone and curled up at the ends. He palmed it back and looked over every inch of my body. "You're fucking exquisite."

"Is it dinner time already?"

"It's noon—close enough."

Placing the palms of my hands on his slick chest, I peered up at him through wet lashes. "What are we doing?"

He looked at me for a few silent beats as if he needed to carefully pick and choose his words. "You have this truly shitty inability to just let things be. I can see the thoughts churning inside that pretty little head of yours. You're a victim of your own mind. Stop over-thinking, stop over analyzing; just let shit be. Live in our present before you fuck it up worrying about the future."

"I have to overthink when it comes to you, Rome—I have to avoid certain situations if I want to live at all."

A dark smile slowly spread across his face.

"Situations? You gave yourself to me. You're already in a situation that's permanent. You're going to live for me. As far as you're concerned, you don't even get to breathe without my permission."

"Why are you being a bigger asshole than usual?"

He answered me by dropping his mouth down to mine, biting my bottom lip hard enough to draw blood when I didn't let him in.

Pushing against his face, I pulled away and soothed the pain with my tongue, glaring up at him with mounting frustration. "What if I don't want to belong to anyone else?"

"Too fucking bad, cause your ass is mine and I'm not going to pretend I care how you feel about it. I know you're going to hate me, baby, but I guarantee you'll love me more and fuck me harder."

He gripped my jaw so hard something popped. When he brought his mouth within the proximity of mine a second time, I grabbed a handful of his hair and bit him back. He laughed and wrapped a hand around my throat, slamming my head into the slate wall.

I swallowed a hiss of pain, expelling it on a scream when he lifted one leg over his forearm and buried himself inside my pussy. He didn't give me any time to adjust, driving into me over and over again, fucking me into the wall.

I grabbed at his hand, unable to pull it away. My chest began to burn as my lungs were deprived of the air they desperately needed. He watched me choke and fight to breathe with a serene expression on his face.

"You know what you have to do."

He sounded far away. I couldn't respond. I swore there was no way in hell I was coming, not when my brain started to go fuzzy. I thought he was going to kill me, but, at the last second, he forced what he wanted out of me.

His hand fell away at the exact same time my body went numb. I sucked in air as pressure burst in my core. I had no recourse, forced to let the orgasm sweep over me as his cock bottomed out. Without a sound, he buried himself to the hilt and froze. I felt him jerk twice, releasing his come as far inside me as he could.

He stepped back, slowly easing out his flaccid dick. I looked down and rubbed at my neck. My mouth went dry as I watched excess semen drip down my thigh. He couldn't have changed his mind so quickly from our discussion in the confessional.

"Why would you do that?"

"Why would I not do that?"

He reached out and swirled his fingers in the seedy liquid and then brought them up to my mouth. I mechanically sucked off every drop the shower didn't wash away, barely tasting it. His soulless eyes tracked every flick of my tongue.

"We have somewhere to be." Without another word, he reached for his body wash and began lathering it on my skin.

Chapter Twenty-One

Calista

At some point, I must have dozed off because when I opened my eyes again we were no longer moving, and it took me a few seconds to remember where I was.

"There's my girl." Romero's voice broke through my disoriented haze. I turned my head and was greeted by his perfect smile. I reached up and touched the side of his face, as if I needed reassurance he was real.

Was he going to pretend the last few hours never happened? Apparently so. He kissed my open palm before pulling my hand away from his cheek, waking me all the way up.

Unsticking my cheek from the leather seat, I peered through the windshield.

Once my eyes adjusted to the darkness around us, I saw a single light on up ahead and instantly knew where we were.

"What are we doing here?" I asked as soon as I was out on solid ground.

He looked down at me with a sinister smile and wrapped an arm around my shoulders, turning me in the direction of the old farmhouse. "They took one of mine, so I'm going to take all of theirs."

"Let's get this done," Cobra hype-manned, coming around the back of the Jeep with the bloody pillowcase he had stashed in the hatch before we left. He turned it upside down and a severed goat head hit the ground with a soft thud.

I wrinkled my nose and frowned. "That is fucking sick."

"Sick like rad? Or sick like ew?" he asked, picking it up by its tiny horns.

"Definitely the latter. Where did you even get that? And where is the rest of it?" Arlen asked, curling her lip up.

"I don't remember." He shrugged.

"Come on." Romero dropped his arm from my shoulders and grabbed my hand, setting off at a rapid pace.

As we neared the wraparound porch, the only sound that could be heard was faint sobs coming from inside the barn.

"Are you going to break in?"

Grimm walked up the stairs and turned the door knob. He strolled into the house like he lived there and spun around to face us. "We don't need to break in; they never lock their door." He smirked and disappeared out of sight.

If life were a movie, this was the part that would be paused as a wise narrator explained just how fucked I was about to find myself. This was the part where they would say I should have turned and ran as if hellhounds were on my heels.

It was the part where I would understand why they called my lover the devil. It was his kind way of giving me the pamphlet version of an introduction to the world he talked about that normal people couldn't survive in.

Going into this house was the beginning of my end, the catalyst for everything that was yet to come.

Romero kept his hand clasped around mine as we walked forward with Arlen and Cobra. The tip of my boot was barely over the threshold when a woman screamed and a man landed at an awkward angle on the hardwood floor a few feet ahead of us.

"That's one!" Grimm called down from the upper level.

Blood began to pool around the man's head. He wasn't wearing anything but a pair of drawers. His lifeless, wide-eyed stare was locked on us.

Cobra walked around him, goat head in hand, and entered the kitchen.

Doors slammed from upstairs and footsteps thundered across the floor, making the ceiling fixtures rattle.

Romero looked towards the staircase and let me go, giving me a little nudge forward. "You two, go set the table."

"What the hell do we need to do that for?" Arlen asked from beside me when we could no longer see him.

"Romero's methods only make sense to himself."

"And him." She gestured to the kitchen where Cobra was dumping cooking oil into a saucepan.

I walked forward, chalking my jitteriness up to bad nerves and Romero's precarious mood. The kitchen and dining room were side by side. Spotting a china cabinet in the back corner, I steered Arlen with my shoulder and made a beeline for it.

"This place is filthy."

"That's an understatement," Arlen muttered.

Clutter and dirty laundry were everywhere. There was a thick residual stench of cooked flesh in the air.

Searching the dining room for a light switch, I swept my gaze past the kitchen and saw it was even worse.

Dishes were piled a mile high in the sink, chunks of black grime were smeared on faded yellow tile, and a plastic pitcher with questionable content was tipped over on the counter.

Finding a light switch, I flicked it up with the tip of my finger, having zero desire to touch anything around me.

"Table's already set," Arlen pointed out.

"Good, we can get started then," Romero responded, walking into the room half-dragging a woman by the back of the neck. I instantly recognized her from the day we escaped.

"It was Bill. You know I know the rules! I would never be so stupid, Romero." She clutched at his arm but he simply shook her off.

"Martha, we had a deal and you violated our terms. You had no business being in my woods in the first place. Did I not provide your family with enough to eat?"

I crossed my arms, watching their interaction with furrowed brows.

These people were cannibals. The only way he was giving them food was by giving them other people. Why the fuck would he do that?

He sat her down in a chair and reached in his back pocket, retrieving the Browning knife he always carried. "Place your hands on the table, Martha."

She looked up at him with tears rolling down her face and shook her head. Chewing my bottom lip, I glanced back into the kitchen to check on Cobra.

He was rifling through the drawers, placing things I assumed he intended on taking with him in a pile.

"I need your help, Cali."

Bringing my focus back to Romero, I uncrossed my arms and made my way around the table, stopping beside the woman.

"Place her left hand on the table."

Wondering where he was going with this, I pried the woman's stiff hand away from where she clutched it to her chest and held it down as he instructed.

"I'm going to count to three."

At his words, the woman began to struggle and push at me with her other arm. Arlen grabbed it and held it identically to the way I was.

"Three," Romero said calmly, driving his knife through the side of her left hand, removing it and plunging it straight through the back of her right. I winced and turned my head away as she screeched in my ear.

Her blood quickly made its way across the table, some making it onto my skin.

"Pin em down," Romero instructed in the same level tone.

Searching for something that could do what he wanted, I swiped up the steak knife from the now bloody table setting beside me and pushed it through the hole he had just made, sticking it into the wooden table with a twist.

Arlen didn't hesitate to do the same.

The woman dropped her chin to her chest and moaned, more than likely slipping into shock. I wiped my bloody hand on the back of her shirt and stepped back.

"Look what I got." Grimm came from the opposite direction with an unconscious man in a choke-hold and the little boy from the barn like he was a sack of potatoes.

"Give me the kid." Romero held out his arms, taking the crying little boy from Grimm.

As Grimm situated the man across from the woman who had yet to stop groaning, I gave Romero a questioning look.

"What are you doing?" I asked with a calmness I didn't feel.

"What do you think I'm doing?" He shifted the kid around so that his back was pressed into his chest and his feet dangled off the floor.

"Grease is ready!" Cobra called out over the sound of the oven door slamming.

"Let him go." I kept my eyes locked with his, my voice low but demanding.

"Why would I let him go?"

"He's just a kid, you fucker!" Arlen lunged forward in a stance meant to snatch the kid away, but Grimm moved quicker. He let the man fall out of his chair and snaked an arm around Arlen's waist, hauling her backward.

Not so much as batting an eyelid, Romero lifted the boy higher and gave a sharp twist to his neck, strong enough to sever the connection between brain and nervous system, before dragging his knife across the boy's throat. He dropped the body right beside his mother's chair, and then proceeded to torture her further by removing two of her fingers.

I was cemented to the floor, watching everything happen as if through a periscope. Arlen's screams were muffled as Grimm smothered her mouth with his hand.

Cobra walked in, carrying the saucepan of oil, and placed it down on the center of the table. Romero dropped the severed fingers in and they immediately began to pop and sizzle.

I watched the man on the floor wake slowly at first, startling awake when the scene before him fully settled into his brain. Grimm swapped Arlen for him, letting her break away from him.

She wasted no time taking off out of the room. I heard her footsteps hit the porch and knew she was making a run for it.

I looked at Romero and he already had a knowing smile on his face, two steps ahead of my thought process. With a slight, almost unnoticeable nod of his head, he dared me to run.

Chapter Twenty-Two

Calista

I spun in a circle, thin branches grabbing at my skin as I pushed through them, trying to find my way in the dark.

The screaming from the farmhouse stopped and then started again, making me believe I had more time to get wherever it was I was going, but I heard someone moving in close proximity.

"Arlen?" I whispered, peering around trees and foliage.

"Cali, it's me."

I paused and searched for the voice's owner, jumping back when he emerged on my right.

"What the fuck are you doing here, Simon?" I hissed, listening for any other sound.

"Tito sent me to watch out for you. I set up camp in the

woods by the warehouse trying to see you, but I never did until now. I overheard where you were going."

He answered all the questions I hadn't asked, but it was ridiculously foolish to send him so close, which was probably why Tito sent a guy he didn't care for. If he died, no biggie. Tito was a pain in my ass. He meant well, but his ideas were never foolproof.

"He wants you to come back."

"I can't do that...yet," I tacked on for good measure, noting that the screaming had stopped.

"What? Why would you...holy shit, you crazy cunt, you switched sides? You've no idea what that prick has planned, do ya? Ask him about—"

Too much chit-chat.

He ended his sentence on a scream as I jumped on him, wrapped my legs around his waist, and bit down as hard as I could.

He pulled at my hair and swung his fists into my side, trying to get me off. It fucking hurt, but I persisted nonetheless. There was no chance in hell he was making it out of the woods without being caught, and he would sing like a bird with the blues from the slightest bit of torture.

I didn't need to see Romero to know he was in the woods somewhere; I could sense him, and I would never be able to explain why a stranger was talking to me in the middle of the woods.

Biting through someone's neck looked much easier in movies. The skin was rough and firm; I couldn't bite it open like a vampire.

He started spinning in circles, slamming me into a tree and dislodging me. I hit the solid ground with an "Oomph."

Rolling away, I barely missed his shoe connecting with

my face. I scrambled to my feet and he landed in the exact spot I had just been.

"No, no, no!" His scream cut through the air as bone made a loud pop and Romero broke the leg he'd just kicked at me. His fist connected with his face, breaking his bottle cap glasses and knocking him out.

"You don't touch her." The calmness in which he delivered the words was completely contradictory to the way his muscles were bunched in anger.

Grimm came trampling through the trees a minute later and quickly surveyed the scene. His gaze paused on me and he shook his head.

"Take him to the Jeep," Romero bit out.

"You and that lil brat are a real fuckin handful," Grimm muttered, grabbing Simon by the shirt. He turned back the way he came and dragged him off.

Shit! If they took him back to the warehouse, Tito would be a lot more screwed than I was.

"Did he hurt you?"

"No…" I brought my hands together in front me and stared at his back.

"Are you going to tell me why?"

I knew what he was asking me and I had an answer…sort of. I wasn't ready to explain it to him, though.

It didn't matter how far I ran or if I ran using every last ounce of my energy. I could run from my past. I could run from the things I had done and had yet to do. I could run from the illusion of the woman I'd tried to portray to everyone. I could not run from him or the sick bitch inside me I was finally getting acquainted with.

One went harmoniously with the other.

I didn't voice any of that, though.

I allowed him to believe whatever conclusion he wanted,

let him think I ran because I was unable to handle this side of him.

He made a humming sound in his throat and walked off without looking at me once. "Bring your ass on."

Scrubbing a hand over my face, I stared up at the starless sky and expelled a deep breath before following him.

When I caught up to him again he had the passenger side door open and helped me climb into the Jeep, still not looking at me.

Arlen gave me a weak smile from the back seat. My eyes floated over her shoulder to where a blonde sat with her head on her knees. I didn't bother asking what they were doing with her; I didn't care.

"Your friend's riding in the back," Romero said once he was back in the driver's seat.

"That girl is not my friend."

He started the Jeep and pulled off, driving around a stick in the middle of the lane that had the goat head staked on top of it.

It wasn't until I heard the screams five minutes in that I understood what he meant. Simon was riding in the back. Romero was dragging him behind the Jeep.

Chapter Twenty-Three

Calista

He pushed the speedometer to seventy and kept his dark gaze trained straight ahead.

I could partially see Simon in the rearview mirror trying to keep his head up, being brutalized by the asphalt.

"Who is he?" he asked me, speaking just loud enough I could hear him over Simon's screams.

"I don't know, but you're going to make a mess," I replied flippantly, twirling a strand of hair around my finger.

"You fuck him?"

"What?" I started to laugh. "Are you for real?"

"You think this is funny?"

"You're jealous because I may or may not have fucked that guy, but I've fucked lots of guys. I've fucked my dad, my uncles, and I was kinda-sorta fucked by my baby brother. I'm a real bona fide whore."

"Cali," Arlen choked from behind me.

"Don't feel pity for me. I've had as many cocks between my legs as I've had in my mouth. Oh, and a few women got the VIP treatment too, so no one was left out." I forced another laugh and looked down at my lap, clasping my hands together.

Romero swerved sharply after a minute, sending Simon's body to the far right. The chain around his ankles snagged as his head hit a culvert and detached from his body.

Quietness settled over the Jeep.

I had no desire to see what was left of Simon's body. As soon as we were back at the warehouse, I was out of the Jeep and darting inside.

"Don't ever fuckin call yourself a whore again."

I paused on my way to the kitchenette.

"And here I was, thinking I was your special whore now." With a sigh, I resumed walking, adding a little skip.

He came up behind me and spun me around. "What the fuck did I just say?"

"I think I forgot already. Will you repeat it?"

Slipping out from between him and the counter, I put space between us by circling to the opposite end of the table.

He looked at me for a minute before scrubbing a hand over his face.

"I'm waiting." He crossed his arms and gave me a leveled stare.

"Why did you kill that little boy? He was just a kid, Rome."

"So she does have some morality left in there," he sneered at me. "That wasn't a kid; that was an animal. He would've eaten your fuckin face off in your sleep. I've seen dozens of kids just like em."

"You're an animal, too! You're a…"

"Savage. I know. I make no excuses, and I have no regrets. This is who I choose to be and I don't care if you don't like it. You're either with me or against me."

"And what if I'm against?" I asked quietly.

I wasn't, of course. I was with him through and through, but I could already picture Tito in my rearview mirror.

If I knew with complete certainty that there would be no issue between them, I would put it all out in the open. My gut told me that wasn't the case, though.

"If you're not with me, then I guess you *would* be a whore." He spat the word at me like it tasted vile in his mouth. "Get your ass upstairs, the fuck out of my sight." He walked away, back towards the front of the warehouse.

"Shit," Cobra muttered, taking off after him, leaving the clueless blonde beside Arlen.

Sucking in a breath, I stared after him, looking down when I felt a tug on my wrist. "Come on," Grimm coaxed.

I let him lead me up the stairs, surprised when he followed me into Romero's room.

"I'm not looking for a pity fuck," I clarified right off the bat.

"I don't want to…I would never." He looked mortified at the very idea of it, the most emotion I'd ever seen from him written all over his face. He shook his head, stroking his beard.

"I would never fuck you because you belong to my best friend, and he would do things to me not even I could imagine—and I'm real imaginative, just for some clarification. I would never fuck you because nothing you said in that car was true.

"You're not a whore, Cali. You were just a little girl and no one was there to protect you. I promise you there are a lot of people in this world who regret that."

The sincerity laced in his words knocked against my stone exterior. Dropping my gaze to the floor, I sat on the edge of the bed and let out a dry laugh.

"That's real sweet of you, Grimmy, but no one in this world has ever apologized for what happened to me, and I no longer expect them to. I just want to find a place where I fit in."

"You already did. I don't have any issues with you staying, as long as you're in it for the long haul. We haven't got to the good parts yet."

Toying with my hair, I gave him a small smile. "Thank you."

His regular inexpressive face was back but I could swear the man almost smiled. He nodded and headed for the door, pausing after he pulled it open.

"You're crazy and a pain in the ass. He's insane and always fuckin moody, but the connection is undeniable. Everyone sees it. You fit—you're a fucked-up pair of star-crossed lovers."

With that, he walked out of the room and shut the door, leaving me to wallow in my thoughts.

Falling back onto the bed, I looked up at the ceiling, blowing out my cheeks.

Me and Rome.

Rome and I.

We were unhealthy, dysfunctional, toxic.

I could flip through both an encyclopedia and a dictionary and still wouldn't find words to describe us.

Beyond the excitement, beyond the lust, he gave my aching heart a place of comfort that I'd never known. This thing between us was certain death, all smoke and darkened skies with no sign of a sunrise, but I wanted what I wanted, and that was him.

Romero

Her moans grew louder and louder, and the headboard hit the wall in a steady rhythm, echoing down the darkened hall.

I glanced over at Arlen and snickered.

"It ain't funny."

"Either the sound of fucking makes you irritated, or who's doing the fucking has you irritated. I'll take a wild guess and say it's the latter."

"I don't need you to play couch therapist, and Cobra fucked her too, so that trumps your theory."

She tossed the blanket off and sat up, crossing her inked arms over her chest.

"What's your story?" I already knew it. I just wanted to hear her answer.

"Don't got one. I was tryna find my sister and got taken by them cannibals."

Huh, that was almost true.

"Shouldn't you be kissin ass right now?"

"I could be bending you over—"

"You got bout three seconds to fix that sentence. Don't give me any reasons to take Cali your balls in the form of a necklace."

I laughed for what felt like the first time all day.

"I was fucking with you, baby girl. I don't juggle women."

I was actually making sure her loyalty was in the right place. If it wasn't, I was going to kill her quick and tell Cali she ran off.

Fucking Cali.

I needed a drink, and I didn't drink.

This was the part about giving shit that bit me in the ass. I had a track replaying in my goddamn head of every person she named, and I was gunning for their asses.

My beautiful girl thought she was a whore. Those mother-fuckers created thorns on a flower that never had any.

I could see the real her, feel her trapped inside a dark fucking sinkhole that they shoved her in.

Cali knew exactly who she was. She was ashamed of it. She lashed out the only way she knew how because of it. Her head was irreparable because of it. Why had no one told her she was fucking perfect?

I'd never seen damaged look so good. Never seen bruised knees look so pretty. She was so perfect I didn't deserve her. A better man would've let her go, but that wasn't me.

Arlen's drowsy voice pulled me out of my head.

"Can I ask you something?"

"You just did."

She gave me a flat look.

"Shoot your shot."

She got so damn quiet I thought she'd fallen back asleep. Her back was to me and the blanket was almost over her head. Her question almost threw me off guard—almost.

I wondered if she asked because she wanted to know or asked because she wanted a man nicknamed after the personification of death.

"What kind of evil are you?"

"The kind no one can save you from. If there's a god, not even he could help you."

"Okay, you can go fix your screw up now." She adjusted her head on the arm of the couch and sighed. "You two, you're like fire and gasoline. You're perfect for one another so quit being a dumbass and go strike the match."

I smirked at her back. If my sister were still alive, I could see her being a lot like Arlen. Standing up, I gave her the only advice I could offer.

"If you're going to run, run now, because after tomorrow, everything's going to change."

Chapter Twenty-Four

Calista

He had deep scars beneath his tattoos. I'd never seen anything sadder than that. I'd never been so upset since watching Tilly burn.

If I had a heart left to break, it would have broken right then. Who hurt this man and where could I find them?

"Don't fucking look at me like that." He rolled from his stomach to his back, giving me something much better to stare at.

"You know, I could never sleep until I came here. It could be your bed, but I think it's you."

"I'm going to assume you're talking to me, even though you just said that to my dick."

Flashing my eyes to his, I offered him a timid smile.

"I failed your second test. I'm sorry, and I'm sorry for being a mess…I'm not sorry about the kid, though."

"Is that why you stopped running?"

Chewing my lip, I began tracing imaginary patterns into the blanket. "I was never running from you, Rome. I was running from…myself."

When he didn't say anything, I quietly continued. "Before I ever met you, I had a box of pictures and articles—all of you—and I…used you."

"You used me."

"You're my muse. I have dirty…sick fantasies, and they all feature you."

"Keep going," he encouraged, wrapping a hand around the base of his hardening cock.

"I like hearing them scream, making them bleed, and watching the life leave their bodies…torture though, even psychological, it makes me *so* wet. And you're always beside me, touching me, fucking me in the bloody mess we made."

The bed creaked as he fisted himself, keeping his eyes locked on me. I reached out and cupped his balls, gently rolling them in the palm of my hand.

"My daddy always told me I was sick and full of sin. The last day I saw him, he said those same sins would eat me alive. I never got the chance to tell him I'm a natural born sinner and the devil lives inside me."

I shifted onto my knees and stopped his hand. Before I could start, he grabbed me by the leg and pulled my lower half towards him.

He sat my pussy on his face and I sucked his cock into my mouth.

We face fucked one another. His cock hit the back of my throat, bringing tears to my eyes as I struggled taking all of him. His tongue explored me everywhere, delving in and out and toying with my clit.

Leaning lower, I used my hand to stroke him hard and fast and my tongue to toy with his balls, lifting them individually and gently suckling them into my mouth.

When I felt pre-come run onto my hand, I sat up straight and licked it off. He flipped me over onto my back, locked me down with a hand across my waist and buried his face between my thighs.

He plunged two fingers inside me to work alongside his mouth. It took me a good few minutes to realize he was apologizing. He wrote he was sorry on my clit with the tip of his tongue.

He kept repeating the motion and then backing off just before I came. Clenching his sheets, I lifted off the bed as far as I could and pushed against his mouth.

"I forgive you," I moaned. He bit down as soon as those words left my mouth and I repeated them like a chant, coming all over his tongue.

I was still shaking when he rose above me and pushed his dick in. I clenched around it, immediately coming again.

He grabbed me by the top of the hair and clenched his teeth.

"Fuuck, Cali," he growled in my ear.

Wrapping my legs around his waist, I dug my fingers into his shoulders and licked my juices off his face as he rocked into me, taking me to a place only he could.

I finally wandered out of the room an hour after he left.

He wouldn't tell me where he was going, only that he would be back soon. Grimm left with him and Cobra was playing mechanic.

The blonde had not so mysteriously vanished. My guess would be straight into the body pit. That left me and Arlen to our own devices, which was admittedly not much despite how large the warehouse was.

"Let's go this way." With her arm linked through mine, we went down the only hall we hadn't ventured yet, passing a bathroom and an open broom closet full of cleaning supplies.

At the end of the hall was a large shutter that was lifted up, revealing a chain link gate. On the other side of the gate was a room full of neatly organized crap. To the far left was a wall and tables lined with boxes like the one I had gotten my first shirt from, and straight ahead were shelves of canned goods, boxed foods, and condiments.

Two deep freezers were running in the back, and to our right was another gate that led to what appeared to be a garage.

"Where did they get all this from?" Arlen asked in awe.

The feeling was mutual. I hadn't seen anything like this... ever, not even when I lived with The Order. Romero had a connection, a good one from the looks of it. Tito had a connection too, but the most overstocked item we had was tampons; everything else was the bare minimum basics needed to live semi comfortably.

"Well, we were clearly meant to find this room so we could go through em," Arlen commented, nudging me in the direction of the boxes. She took one side and I took another.

"I never got a chance to thank you for taking up for me." I spoke softly in an effort to keep or conversation as quiet as possible.

"Are you serious? You saved my ass when someone else would have only worried about themselves."

She had a point there. I could have made a run for it as soon as cannibal Bill hit the ground. Finding a pair of denim shorts that would fit me, I kicked my boots off and pulled them on beneath my long shirt.

"I was looking for my sister," she added after a beat, turning around and beginning to dig in the boxes behind her.

Slipping back into my shoes, I rose and continued searching through another box. I started to respond but glanced around, and for the first time, I noticed the suitcases piled beneath the table and some of the more expensive clothing in certain boxes.

Finding a wallet in a pair of jeans, I flipped it open and stared at the identification card still inside. *James Wallace*. He was an official from Centriole.

"That's not good," Arlen whispered.

"Understatement of the year."

There was only one possible explanation I could come up with. Romero was not finding random people to torture; he was making people disappear—many people, by the looks of it. Whole families, if the few diaper bags meant anything.

The wallet had to have been left by mistake. None of the

other boxes contained belongings that were indicative of where they came from or whom they belonged to.

I was struck with the cold reality that though we were connected on a level only we understood, that connection didn't give me the magical ability to read his mind and know all his secrets.

What the hell was this man up to?

"So you never told me…is he good in bed?" she suddenly asked me, a wide grin on her face.

I was about to respond but saw the warning in her eyes and dropped the wallet. She quickly kicked it beneath the table.

"She never told me either," Romero said from behind me, sliding his arms around my waist.

Locking the newfound information in my head, I spun around and wrapped my arms around his neck, accepting his hungry kiss. His skin was warm; wherever he'd gone, it was outside.

"Are you ready?" he asked, pulling away.

"Am I ready for what?"

"We're going to play."

This was insane. Period.

I looked at the large church and shook my head for the hundredth time.

"So, do we have a plan?"

"Yeah, kill everyone, make sure they're dead, and go home," Grimm tossed out.

"Gabe isn't a loner like Azel; there's going to be lots of other people in there."

"I called in some friends," Romero finally said.

I looked at him for an explanation, but he didn't give one.

"Do your friends wear creepy hooded robes and walk like cult members?" Arlen asked in a dry tone. "Cause they're here."

Turning in my seat, my jaw slackened as a surge of people in black robes washed through the parking lot and headed straight for Gabe's abode.

"Let's go."

With no other choice, I climbed out and barely missed getting plowed over by a group of four…people.

"So creepy," Arlen mumbled, coming to stand beside me.

It was majorly creepy. Everyone in a black robe had a white mask on and a large Leviathan cross hanging around their neck. The inverted cross tattooed beneath Romero and his friends' eyes was painted in the corners on either side of the odd masks.

My mind was screaming something at me but I couldn't hear it or I didn't understand. Where had all these people come from?

"Come on," Cobra said, jogging ahead of us.

We were almost at the doors when a group of people in the black robes rushed through them, and they all began stampeding in. Glass shattered from others breaking in through the windows. A symphony of screams filled the air soon after.

By time I was able to walk in, complete pandemonium

had erupted. Bodies lay on the floor, in the aisles, and over the backs of pews. The cross that hung on the back wall had been knocked down, tearing a chunk of drywall down with it.

Spotting Father Gabe in the back of the church trying to sneak away, I zeroed in on him and took off after him. I hopped over a woman who had had her neck gouged open, and a man whose nose was half gone. Blood coated the marble floor, making me slip more than a few times.

I was a little surprised to find Gabe in his office alone, pacing back and forth. It wasn't until I slipped in and shut the door that I saw he had a silver gun in his hand. Shock, recognition and anger played out on his features as he immediately recognized who I was.

"You've got to be shitting me. Calista." He gave me the same smile he used to give right before sticking his dick in me.

I stepped forward and he raised the gun. I stepped forward again, and he narrowed his eyes. "So, this is what you've been doing?" He laughed a brittle laugh and shook his head.

"Where are your friends, Father? I was hoping we could all play." I used the same line David had taught me, and the same innocent voice; he slightly wavered.

Smiling, I persisted.

"Would you like me on my knees, Father, or do you want me bent over the desk?"

"I know what you're doing, Calista. I wasn't born yesterday. Don't take another step unless you want a bullet in your skull."

"I promise I'm harmless." I held my hands up in a defensive gesture, slowly turning in a complete circle, facing him again with a smile. "See, I'm still your sweet candy girl."

His beady eyes roamed up and down my body. I could

guarantee if he touched his dick it would be hard—but then, he'd have to find it first.

"Where the fuck have you been?" He slackened his grip on the gun, quickly tightening it again when I moved forward.

"I'm just gonna have a seat, okay? My legs are sore. I've started this really intense exercise regimen. It involves my legs being around someone's neck while they shove their cock inside me so far and so hard I can barely breathe."

I hopped up on the desk and crossed a leg, propping my chin in my hand. "Sounds fun, right? You should try it sometime. It almost sounds as good as all your delegates being brutally slaughtered right now."

He snarled at me and flew across the office. Grabbing a fistful of hair, he pointed the gun right at my temple. "You always were a homicidal slut."

"Aw, thank you."

I winced as he shook me a few times back and forth, hitting me in the side of the head with his gun.

"Ouch. That really hurt." I scowled at him, blinking away tears of pain, feeling a trickle of blood rolling down the side of my face.

"If this church is going down, so are you and I. Open your legs." He glanced at the door, keeping the gun trained on me.

I stiffly spread my legs apart, reminding myself of what I was doing there.

"Do you wanna hear a secret?"

He moved forward until he was in between my legs. "Tell me your secret, Cali."

Eager to oblige, I wrapped one arm around his neck and leaned towards him.

"I found a lover, Father. I found a lover in the devil and

any second now he's going to come through that door and fucking tear you apart."

He immediately stepped back. I grinned up at him. On perfect cue, his office door flew open with such force it left a hole in the drywall.

I watched his facial expression and stature go from smug and confident to shocked and terrified. His fear was tangible. Using his distraction against him, I kicked him in the balls and snatched the gun from his hand.

"I guess I'm right on time." Romero stepped into the room and shut the door with his foot. He had bloodstains on his face and his clothes.

Gabe breathed something under his breath that I couldn't make out clearly. He was looking at Romero as if the reckoning had arrived and this was his Judgment Day. Well, I suppose it kinda was.

Romero's eyes dropped between my legs, bouncing back up to study my face. I offered him a smile and the gun.

"Get in the corner," he directed Gabe, who scrambled to comply.

He came to stand in front of me and gently skimmed his knuckles near the area I'd been hit with the gun, taking it from my hand.

Beyond the office, I could hear the remaining windows shattering, the echoing boom of pews being overturned, and the occasional scream of someone new being discovered by the robed figures.

I reached up and touched the side of Romero's face, feeling his rage building in his veins.

"There's two left in the chamber."

"You hear that, Gabriel? I'm gonna give you that many more chances to live." He brought the barrel of the gun to my mouth. I closed my lips around it and ran my tongue up and down the cool metal. Pulling it out, he mimicked my action before lowering it between my open thighs. He grinned at me when he saw I had no underwear on.

I placed my hands behind me and gripped the edge of the desk as the hard metal was eased inside me. Gabriel's breath audibly hitched when I groaned.

"You're beautiful," Romero mused, pulling the gun out and pushing it back in. My inner muscles stretched and clamped around it, a little gush of arousal lubing the barrel.

"Rome," I sighed, bringing one hand to my clit as he slowly fucked me with the pistol.

The first empty click seemed louder than the carnage outside the door. My breath stitched, my arousal heightened.

"That's one," Romero counted. He twisted the solid metal inside me, going a little deeper. I increased the speed of my fingers, rolling my hard nub faster. The second click sounded. I whimpered and propped myself up on my elbows.

"Two," he counted again, his voice a little deeper.

"You're both fucking insane…mad in the blood," Gabriel spat from his corner, not daring to move.

"We know," Romero said just before the third click.

I felt a tightening in my lower stomach but fought the feeling. There was hard metal inside me when I wanted him.

"Kill him and fuck me, please," I begged. The gun immediately disappeared, covered in my juices.

I reached for his pants and fought to free his erection.

"Please, Deville, we can—" The gun went off twice, sending his blood and brain matter spraying up the wall. Romero tossed it to the side and entered me with one solid thrust before the priest's body hit the floor.

"Fucking beautiful," he murmured, kissing on my neck before wrapping a hand around it. I gripped his perfect toned ass and pulled him deeper, wrapping my legs around his waist. His cock filled me up, creating a deep suctioning sound every time he moved in and out.

"Harder," I demanded, and immediately received.

I stared at the fresh blood running down the gray wall and felt the same tightening in my lower belly.

"I need you to come, baby." He lifted me by the neck, bringing me to the edge of the desk so he could go deeper. His mouth hit mine hard, and animal instinct took over.

We bit and sucked at one another, having the same carnal need to devour one another. I rolled my hips, meeting him thrust for thrust.

Things poured from my mouth I thought I would never say. The smells, sighs and moans suffocated us until the pressure inside me unexpectedly burst, sending electric shocks up and down my spine, and my come soaked his dick, running down the crevice of my ass.

He followed after, coming with me when his cock jerked and triggered another rush of pleasure.

We stayed pressed together; body to body, soul to soul, breathing each other in.

He pulled back and gripped both sides of my face, planting one last lingering kiss on my lips.

"We're gonna be legends."

I pecked his cheek, feeling warmth in my chest from his words. He helped me off the desk, steadying me on my trembling legs. We walked back through what remained of the church, passing hooded figures that stopped what they were doing when they saw us.

I was blissfully unaware of what was really happening.

When the church went up in flames, we stood and watched, and I loved the way the fire warmed my face.

Chapter Twenty-Five

Calista

I think I was starting to befriend the strange girl who dwelled within one part of me.

The devil on my shoulder reached out a hand to my fallen angel and they formed a truce.

Over the next two weeks, things were relatively peaceful. Every day, I fell a little more for my beloved monster. Our demons played at our feet while we got lost in one another over and over again.

I chose to live in my bubble of bliss for just a while longer before summoning the courage to bring up Tito. I hadn't heard from him, but I figured if Tito knew anything about Simon's death, his common sense had kicked in and he was playing it safe.

It wasn't until the third week that things got strange.

I was woken up by the noise.

It sounded like the biggest block party of the century was taking place inside the warehouse. Swinging my feet out of bed, I walked across the floor, feeling the bass vibrate through my soles.

Flipping on the bathroom light, I frowned at Arlen's cosmetology job in the mirror, lifting my temporarily dyed strands of hair. She'd been struck with the idea after hearing Romero tell me I brought color to his world. His exact words: *"It's always so fucking dark in my head. You make me see color again, vivid colors: pink and blue, green and purple."*

He said this while we were in bed so I wasn't sure if I'd fucked him so hard he saw a rainbow when he came or he was just being sweet.

I splashed some water on my face, swirled some mouth-wash, pulled my shoes on, and left the room.

People were everywhere.

Some wore the hooded robes from the night we burned down the church; others barely wore anything. They all had the inverted cross tattooed beneath their eye, or somewhere else visible on their bodies.

Five Finger Death Punch's 'Cradle to the Grave' blasted through the air at a deafening decibel.

I shoved my way through dancing, writhing bodies, from people openly fucking and rude assholes who wouldn't move when I said excuse me.

Glancing over the banister, I saw Arlen's usual resting spot on the couch occupied by Cobra and a busty brunette. Hanging down from the ceiling was a large flag with the official symbol of Satan printed on it.

By the time I made it to the lower level and headed towards the back of the warehouse where the doors were wide open, 'Cut the Cord' had begun to play and I'd tripped over two dead bodies—both nuns.

I reached the doors and took a minute to gather my composure, not wanting to believe what was obviously right in front of me.

There was a large crowd gathered around the man sitting like a king on a throne in the middle of a clearing. Someone had painted a pentacle in the dirt. There were four wooden stakes hammered into the ground at different points of the star.

"Here's the woman of the night," a soft voice said, almost right in my ear.

I sidestepped and did a quick once over of the redhead who had come up behind me, noting her tattoo was located on her neck.

"Oh, he got you good," she laughed, staring at Romero a little too intently for my liking.

"Can you speak like a regular human?" I cut off her view and leveled her with an unimpressed stare.

"Calm down and look around you. Everyone looks at him the way I do. That's what happens when you start sleeping with a man with power."

I blinked at her, not saying a word.

"You had to know you were consorting with the devil," she scoffed.

"I…" I let the sentence die, looking back out at Romero. She was completely serious. I'd already established that the Savages were a fucking gang of cult worshippers of all things —worshippers of Romero to be more exact.

Having knowledge of something and physically seeing it, though, were two entirely different things. The man I adored was revered as the actual devil. It wasn't just a nickname. I felt like I'd taken acid and was still on a trip.

"He has you now, sweetheart. I can already see the web he's woven around your poor little soul. One minute he adores you, the next you're scared shitless he's going to kill you for blinking wrong." She tossed her cigarette down and snuffed it with the heel of her shoe. "Whose fucking idea was it to give him something so pure? Your corruption was unquestionably going to happen."

"I was never pure."

"You have a heart, darling. That's good enough." She brushed past me and walked into the crowd.

"Goddamn it." I dropped my head and closed my eyes, pressing my hands to my temples. I didn't yet fully understand what any of this meant.

Lifting my head, I locked eyes with his, and, like a tethered ball and chain, he pulled me to him. People openly stared at me as I walked by, eyeing me with curiosity.

"What the hell is this?" I wasted no time asking as he turned me around and sat me on his lap, pressing my back to his chest.

"It's a celebration."

"Of yourself? When did you have time to do all this?"

"I told you, I have connections. This celebration is for you...us."

"Why would we celebrate with your cult? What are we even celebrating?"

I tried to stand up but he locked his arms around my waist.

"I thought you'd be happy about this. I'm letting you in."

"I am...I think. I need a minute." I kissed his cheek as a reassurance that I wasn't all the way freaked out—yet. I went to stand again and this time he let me, only to motion two robed men over to take hold of me.

My heart lurched into my throat as I found myself on the

ground, my arms and legs each secured to a wooden stake in the pentacle.

"What are you doing?" I tugged at the rope around my wrists but couldn't break free of it. "Rome?"

I wriggled around in the dirt as hooded figures surrounded me, all wearing the silver Leviathan cross around their necks.

I looked all around me but could no longer see him. A man stepped forward, holding a wriggling baby ram in his hands.

He held it above me so another man could slit its throat.

"No!" I protested, turning my head as blood rained down on me from above, coating my chest and neck, some inevitably landing on my face.

The circle parted the smallest bit, and I lifted my head up to see a shirtless Romero back in front of me, wearing a mask a little different from everyone else's.

"What are you doing to me?" I screamed at him, furiously tugging at my restraints. He covered my body with his, pressing me into the dirt. I felt a sharp pinch, then a sting, followed by something wet running down my legs.

I sucked in a sharp breath when the same thing was done on the other side, and then repeated twice more.

Dropping my head back, I closed my eyes and focused only on breathing, trying to ignore the way my body was reacting and the endorphins swimming through my brain.

I still had my eyes closed when he shoved my underwear to the side and pushed into me. I was so wet he slid in with ease. I had no choice but to take every inch of him as blood ran down my legs.

The men around us begin to quietly chant *ave satanas* as he fucked me harder, making me break my silent pact not to make a sound.

Romero

The music pouring from her mouth emanated pleasure and pain, her muscles flexing every time I touched her with the tip of the knife.

I loved seeing her like this, coming apart; it was beautiful. Ever since we'd met, she'd fed the beast in me, teased him and damn near begged him to come out.

I wondered what she would think of all this when she woke up, when she wasn't so high off pain and my dick making her come that she could think straight.

What we did was animalistic. It was dirty. It had to be done; I had to shove her headfirst over the edge and straight into my world. They needed to know she would be by my side—forever. This was deeper than marriage. It never ended until we were both buried twelve feet under.

This thing between was still begging to be explored. She had no idea what the near future had in store for her. She wasn't done being molded just yet.

All that aside, she was it for me.

She wasn't classically gorgeous, wasn't what anyone would think of when they thought of centerfolds.

She was a sick bitch.

Maniac.

Homicidal harlot.

And that's what made her so fucking beautiful—a motherfucking queen. Her devious, filthy fucking soul stole the air from my lungs.

I wanted her forever under my compulsion.

Chapter Twenty-Six

Calista

Maybe it was all a dream.

And then I sat up and realized how badly I wished it was.

My legs were on fire. My labia were so swollen I wasn't sure my clit was even attached to my body. There was an inverted cross tattooed on my inner thigh.

The entire night before was a blur in the background of a raging headache. I wanted to lie back down but knew I needed to get up.

Stumbling out of the bed I didn't remember being put in, I made it to Romero's dresser and tugged open the upper drawer.

Propping my head up with one hand, I lazily dug through, looking for a shirt that would cover all my bruised assets.

My fingers slid over something metal and broken.

Shoving clothes out of the way, I picked up the frame and flipped it around to see what was inside. Popping the back off, I removed the photo and studied it.

There was a tightening in my chest, and my throat constricted when I tried to swallow. Suddenly, the clarity of where I'd seen the skeleton ring before came rushing back to me.

Tilly had it on when this picture was taken, and she'd had it on when I first met her through the border fence. All of them were pictured together: Cobra, Grimm, Romero, Tilly, and a brunette.

"What are you doing?"

I turned, still holding the picture in my hand. I opened my mouth to say something, unable to find words.

His dead eyes looked at the picture, then back at my face with an understanding so clear I almost believed he was a mind reader, forgetting that fast how well he knew me.

"That's the girl."

"Tilly. She has—had—a name," I bit out.

His brows raised and he laughed. "Her name sure as fuck wasn't Tilly. Her name was Tiffany, and she was one of the most fucked-up bitches I've ever met."

Tiffany?

"She wasn't, she was good," I refuted.

"No, she was an unstable and untrustworthy narcissist who happened to be obsessed with me. The problem was her thinking she was better at mind games than I was. She ended up being the perfect puppet. She was *not* anything remotely good."

I knew in my gut he wasn't lying, which meant she had, like everyone always did. I let the picture flutter down and tried to move past him.

"Shit, Cali. I didn't know, baby." He wrapped his arms around me and smothered me into his chest.

I didn't want to find comfort in his embrace, not when there was an ocean between us and so much that hadn't been said. I shoved away, almost falling on my ass.

"What the hell is this? Last night, us, and now this? Who the fuck are you?"

My brain felt like it was going to split in two. I never wanted to unravel, never wanted him to see I was weak, never wanted any of the bad shit that happened to me. I wanted to live. I wanted the yesterdays full of happiness back.

I angrily swiped at my face, feeling the first tears spill over.

"Who are you?"

"Yours."

That made it worse.

"Tito wanted me to find you," I blurted out. "Is this why? Because you fucked his sister? What did you do to her?"

"Everyone fucked her, Cali. If you want to know what a real whore was, it was Tiffany. I didn't do anything but give her enough rope to hang herself, and she did." He paused and looked me over with an inexpressive look on his face. "This isn't the time to tell you about this. I promise I didn't know, Cali. It wasn't a fucking secret; I just didn't think it was relevant for you to know about."

"Tito is the one who sent me into the woods." I said it in a way meant to lash out. My gut instinct about bad blood between them had been right and was the only thing I had to throw back at him. I regretted it the second I said it, because I knew Rome wasn't trying to hurt me.

When his facial expression didn't change, I repeated myself, fully accepting that he might hate me and think I was using him.

"Did you hear me?"

He looked at me another minute and then finally came forward. He scooped me up like I was a doll and carried me into the bathroom.

"I'm going to take care of you now." He kissed my fore-head and turned the water on.

I didn't bother trying to stop his hands from cleaning and massaging every inch of my skin.

I didn't bother pointing out that with every touch, he made me more his than I wanted to be. I was too busy going around and around with the madness in my head.

When he was done, he took me back to his bed and sat with me in silence, staring at one another, neither of us bringing up anything that needed to be discussed. I was okay with that right then; talking would make it all worse before it got better.

The longer we stared, the harder my heartbeat started kicking. I reached for him at the same time he reached for me.

It was the right thing to do at the wrong time. I indulged in the taste of him. His hands were everywhere, gently teasing my skin, leaving me no choice but to focus on him and nothing else.

When he finally brought our bodies together, he made it hurt in a different way.

It wasn't brutal or cold. He fucked me lovingly, and the pain went deeper than anything I'd ever felt before. It was beautiful agony. He was tearing me open and digging out the soul I didn't know I had, taking it for himself, permanently tying us together.

Chapter Twenty-Seven

Calista

He was gone when I woke up again.

I dressed, trying to stuff my thoughts in a cell of their own and keep a positive outlook.

Shit would be okay; I always found a way to make things okay—that's what I did, fixed my shit with duct-tape and super glue. It was never perfect or pretty, but it was together.

Leaving the room, I listened for sound, hearing nothing. The building was eerily silent.

Halfway down the metal grated stairs, Arlen and Cobra came around a corner.

"Sleeping Beauty lives!" Cobra exclaimed.

"Are you okay?"

I ignored him and focused on Arlen, who had a bruise that looked like it went down the whole right side of her body.

"I should be askin you that, but we should go."

"Grimm and Romero already went ahead so we don't lose em, but turns out David isn't happy about his buddy Gabe and all his delegates kicking the bucket. He's trying to move again; we're playing interception," Cobra explained.

I sucked in everything he said with rapid thought process.

"Why didn't he wake me up?" I asked, already walking towards the door before either of them could answer.

"You look like you need as much sleep as you can get."

"Shut up, idiot," Arlen snapped at him.

"It's fine. When do we leave?"

"Are you sure you feel up to this after the—"

"I wanna go," I cut him off.

"Okay, you're the boss."

When derelict buildings began to appear, I had a good idea where we were heading.

"Is this really a good place to meet?" I glanced in the rearview mirror at the trail of cars Cobra had met up with a few miles back.

Narcoosee Bridge only had two different directions you could go, and stone barriers on either side to prevent someone from driving into the water.

I leaned forward when I spotted black Jeeps up ahead, and a few pickups on the other side of the low stone divider.

Cobra stopped his Pontiac behind a few other cars and cut the engine.

"Where are they?" I asked, searching for him.

"He's right there." Cobra pointed and I followed.

"Why…what is he doing?"

I stared across the bridge to where Romero and Grimm stood with three robed figures behind them, and a brunette between them.

Wasn't she in that picture?

"That's my fuckin sister," Arlen choked out from the backseat.

My brain was screaming at me to get out, that something wasn't right. David appeared from behind a pickup with Noah and a man I'd never seen before, slowly walking towards Romero.

I watched the scene play out in slow motion, wanting to scream but unable to open my mouth.

When they were finally right in front of each other, they embraced, hugging like the best of friends.

"What the fuck is goin on?" Arlen yelled, opening the back door of the car.

I twisted to tell her to get down, but I wasn't fast enough to beat the gunfire that erupted up and down both ends of the bridge, both sides shooting at their own people. I glimpsed David and Romero calmly walking away as if none of it was happening.

"Ah, fuck!" I dropped down to the floor as bullets peppered the windows, covering my ears with my hands.

When I got back up, blood was smeared on the seat where Cobra had just been sitting, and he was gone. Taking a deep breath, I climbed across the front seat and through the open driver side door.

Who the fuck was the enemy of whom?

People with the cross tattoos were shooting at both each other and David's followers, and vice versa.

As I crawled on my hands and knees, using cars as shields, I couldn't spot Arlen anywhere.

My stomach turned to stone as I heard the arrival of more vehicles and round two transpired.

Bodies were dropping left and right; glass and blood were everywhere. Deciding to take my chances, I rushed to the barrier and pulled myself up, barely missing a stray bullet.

Looking down at the navy-blue water, my stomach fluttered, and I started counting to three. I made it to two before someone shoved me from behind and came over with me.

Deviants

Playlist

1. Breaking Benjamin—Angels Fall
2. Breaking Benjamin—Feed the Wolf
3. Bring Me The Horizon—Empire
4. Adele—Love in the Dark
5. Trivium—The Sin and the Sentence
6. Bastille—World Gone Mad
7. Five Finger Death Punch—M.I.N.E
8. Five Finger Death Punch—The Bleeding
9. NF ft. Ruelle—10 Feet Down
10. NF—Remember This
11. Yelawolf—Till it's Gone
12. Banks—Judas
13. Halsey—Him & I
14. In This Moment—Scarlett
15. In This Moment—No Me Importa
16. Ruelle—Monsters
17. Halsey—Gasoline
18. Natalia Kills—Devils don't Fly
19. Disturbed—Stricken

20. Creed—Overcome
21. Kendrick Lamar—Pray for Me
22. Eminem ft. Ed Sheeran—River
23. Skylar Grey—Tragic Endings
24. Fall Out Boy—Bishops Knife Trick
25. Gin Wigamore—Willing to Die
26. Avenged Sevenfold—Hail to the King

The devil asked me how I knew my way around the halls of hell.
I told him I did not need a map for the darkness I know so well.
-T.M.T

Prologue

When derelict buildings began to appear, I had a good idea where we were heading.

"Is this really a good place to meet?" I glanced in the rearview mirror at the trail of cars Cobra had met up with a few miles back.

Narcoosee Bridge only had two different directions you could go, and stone barriers on either side to prevent someone from driving into the water.

I leaned forward when I spotted a few black jeeps up ahead, and a few pickups on the other side of the low stone divider.

Cobra stopped his Pontiac behind a few other cars and cut the engine.

"Where are they?" I asked, searching for him.

"He's right there." Cobra pointed and I followed.

"Why…what is he doing?"

I stared across the bride to where Romero and Grimm stood with three robed figures behind them and a brunette between them.

Wasn't she in that picture?

"That's my fuckin sister," Arlen choked out from the backseat.

My brain was screaming at me to get out, that something wasn't right. David appeared from behind a pickup with Noah and a man I'd never seen before, slowly walking towards Romero.

I watched the scene play out in slow motion, wanting to scream but unable to open my mouth.

When they were finally right in front of each other, they embraced, hugging like the best of friends.

"What the fuck is goin on?" Arlen yelled, opening the back door of the car.

I twisted to tell her get down but I wasn't fast enough to beat the gunfire that erupted up and down both ends of the bridge, both sides shooting at their own people. I glimpsed David and Romero calmly walking away as if none of it was happening.

"Ah, fuck!" I dropped down to the floor as bullets peppered the windows, covering my ears with my hands.

When I got back up, blood was smeared on the seat where Cobra had just been sitting, and he was gone. Taking a deep breath, I climbed across the front seat and through the open driver side door.

Who the fuck was the enemy of whom?

People with the cross tattoos were shooting at both each other and David's followers, and vice versa.

As I crawled on my hands and knees using cars as shields, I couldn't spot Arlen anywhere.

My stomach turned to stone as I heard the arrival of more vehicles, and round two transpired.

People were dying; glass and blood were everywhere.

Deciding to take my chances, I rushed to the barrier and pulled myself up, barely missing a stray bullet.

Looking down at the navy blue water, my stomach fluttered and I started counting to three. I made it to two before someone shoved me from behind and came over with me.

Part One

Chapter One

Calista

I made a deal with the devil and let him subjugate me in his hell.

It turns out that was *exactly* what I needed.

The numbness he left me with gave me a blissful moment of serenity, and with it came the rage that broke the lock on the prison cell housing my insanity.

There was a pitch-black hole in place of what should have been my heavy, dirty soul. I felt the darkness seeping down to my very core.

I held up my end of the bargain, but he didn't do the same with his. He walked away and took part of me with him. I was gradually coming undone, falling into a tediously slow tailspin down the rabbit hole.

I had these murderous cravings and an undeniable need to sate them. It had been over one week since I'd spilled blood, and I was jonesing for a kill.

If I were to look at my reflection in my mirror of broken glass, I would see that the animal inside of me was closer than ever to being free.

On the outside, I looked the same—I was alive, my body breathed, and my heart still beat—but inside my head, demons sang softy, telling me it was time to face who I really was.

Oh, there were still times I doubted myself and struggled to reason with all the voices of logic telling me not to give in to the debased maniac that had woken from a long twenty-three-year slumber.

Suffice it to say, I wasn't quite so lost these days. I was more like a rabid caterpillar fighting like hell to break free of my suffocating cocoon.

At this point, it was too late for remedies. There was no going back to the girl I used to be.

There wasn't a special cure for what ailed me; I wasn't broken, so there was nothing to fix, and I didn't want anyone preaching to me about redemption. Atonement wasn't an option when all I wanted to do was dive into a river of sin.

I was addicted to bloodlust, violence, and depraved, immoral fucking. I had an obsession with a man revered as the devil—an obsession that was growing like a malignant tumor. I blamed him for how detrimental it had gotten. He single-handedly cultivated my sick infatuation into something virulent.

He'd pulled my ashen heart and pumped it full of his narcotic poison so he could be the one to incinerate it.

For two whole days, I told myself he would never forsake

me, he would never leave me for dead, but there was no denying the scene that had played out before my very eyes.

I watched him walk away with the same man who'd turned his back on me years ago. I had to admit he was a brilliant, deceitful asshole. He was the most lethal man I knew. He was beautiful and so undeniably sick, like me—the star of every debauched fantasy I had.

And I refused to him go.

I couldn't allow him to slip through my fingers. Not when I'd spent so much time and effort trying to find him. Maybe I was heading for a mental breakdown. Maybe I'd already had one. I couldn't really tell. Did crazy people know they were crazy?

It was fucked up, but he was what I needed, even if what he did still hurt like a sonofabitch.

I shed a few tears before telling myself to get my shit together and persevere, doing whatever I had to do to keep myself alive.

I knew I'd eventually figure it all out, because I *always* figured it out, regardless of how much of a fucking mess my head was.

Speaking of deceitful.

"Cali, you have to talk to me sooner or later. This is childish," Tito grumbled.

"Oh, I didn't realize being used by everyone you know was child's play."

"I just saved your life," he scoffed.

Pausing midstride, I squeezed my eyes shut, pulling in a deep breath and slowly letting it back out through my mouth. I whirled around to face off with him, and he wisely took a step back.

"You *stabbed* me. I could have been eaten by a fucking cannibal because of you!

"You sent Simon after me, the same guy who wouldn't be able to find his dick if it wasn't attached to him.

"He's dead now, by the way. I'm positive he felt every piece of his skin tearing from his body as he was dragged behind a car before his head disconnected from the rest of him. If he'd been made to talk, that could have easily gotten me killed on the spot.

"You shoved me off a goddamn bridge. And before you say anything, no, I was not going to jump. My brain kicked in and reminded me that I don't know how to fucking swim."

He didn't say anything to defend his actions, which only irritated me further.

I let out a humorless laugh. "Doesn't it almost seem like you've been trying to kill me far more than you've been trying to help me?" With a shake of my head, I turned away and continued walking.

Did the guy want a trophy for preventing me from drowning? I could still feel the harsh impact of my body breaking through the chilled water before I got a mouthful of it in my lungs.

If I had died from his pathetic attempt at playing superhero, I would've risen from the dead and came back to devour his shitty soul.

I pushed through the thick overgrowth, blocking out the asshole behind me, doing my best not to focus on the hunger pains cramping my stomach so badly I was damn near light headed, and ignoring how filthy I was.

There wasn't an inch of my ghostly pale skin not covered in sweat or grime. The blood from the man I'd gutted with a broken beer bottle stained my clothes and caked beneath my nails with a layer of dirt. I'd completely given up on the rat's nest sitting on the side of my head in a frizzy braid.

I longed for a shower, a bed, and warm food. Physically, I knew I could push myself beyond the fumes I was utilizing to stay mobile for just a little while longer. Mentally, I didn't know where to begin.

Feelings were severely overrated.

If someone offered to cut my withering heart out from my chest, I'd happily draw the dotted line for the incision. The stupid thing had only ever caused me problems and I couldn't deal with any *woe-is-me* bullshit at the moment.

"Cali, look mamas, we have to figure out what we're going to do."

Did he just say *we*?

I faced him again with a glare, breathing heavily from exertion.

"There is no *we*, Tito. How can you stand there and pretend everything is fine between us? I told you to stop following me days ago."

"Look, I know things look bad, but they could be worse."

"*Things* look bad? Everything is fucked! We've been living like wild animals for the past two weeks.

If you've already forgotten, let me remind you that I killed a man with a beer bottle and you nearly pissed yourself."

"He was just trying to survive. Like we were–*are*. And I did *not* almost piss myself."

"He was trying to *rob* us, you dumbass, and you just stood there shaking like a goddamn leaf; pissing wouldn't be far behind that. His gun wasn't even loaded." I smirked. "It's okay T, we both know my balls have always been bigger than yours."

We were surviving off a depleting supply of MRE's from the backpack he'd managed to keep attached to him when we free-fell from the bridge. Splitting one pack between us wasn't exactly adding to my nutritional needs. We slept in shitty abandoned buildings or the woods, and slunk around like stray dogs with our tales between our legs to avoid being spotted by anyone from The Order.

He clenched his jaw and took a step forward.

"You know what? This entire situation was avoidable. I told you not to go! I *knew* this would happen.

"If I was scared, it was of you. You were *smiling* while he was dying! You're different now, and it's the Savages' fault. The devil himself got inside your head. What happened to you being able to handle it?

"Things wouldn't have snowballed like this if you didn't fuck him. You should have left him. Can you really not see what he's turned you into?"

Judgmental asshole. I wanted to tear his throat out, so much so that I started visualizing it in my head. He was talking out of his ass about a situation he had no real knowledge of.

Romero would never have let me leave him, which added even more confusion to the fact that he'd turned around and left me. Still, though, I couldn't allow him to be incriminated for my irreparable moral compass.

"First of all, I can fuck whoever I want, however want, whenever I want. You don't get to dictate who I spread my legs for.

"Second of all, don't blame him for the way I am. I've been this way from the beginning—you've just never seen it. You have *never* known me, Tito.

"You believed the façade just like everyone else did. Just like I believed you would tell me the truth about your sister and not use me for your own benefit."

"Jinx knew," he immediately deflected, choosing a topic that would sway the conversation away from what he'd done.

Guilty sonofabitch.

I was hoping he'd trip up and spill what actually went down with that whole situation, because I had yet to get all the details.

He wasn't the least bit shocked or surprised about Tilly-slash-Tiffany's involvement in all of this.

That had me wondering just how much he was keeping from me.

"Jinx showed me the pictures and articles you hoarded when she found out who had you. She's the one who knew you were, uh, different. I chose not to listen."

I rolled my eyes at his nice way of saying Jinx knew I was fucked in the head. Showing Tito my memorabilia of Romero sounded exactly like something she would do, hoping he'd come get me. As if I'd needed rescuing. I had never been more content in my life. I'd been happy.I had just started to feel like I finally belonged somewhere with a man no one sane would dare climb into bed with.

Fucking Romero and his soulless eyes. I felt him every-where, and he was nowhere to be seen. His smell, his touch, and the way he tasted in my mouth—how he watched me with his predatory eyes when he was buried between my thighs. The vivid memories were a battering ram to my once stone-walled mentals.

Nothing that happened on Narcoose Bridge made sense, because I *knew* him just as eerily well as he knew me.

I knew he would never work with David without having a damn good motive. And then there was the issue of delegates turning on delegates while others still went after Romero's people and vice versa. Toss in that there were outliers on the bridge too, and it left a major question unanswered. Who was the enemy of whom?

Thinking of it all over again brought something Tito had just said to the forefront of my mind. "Where are Jinx and Grady? Were they on that bridge?" I asked suddenly, staring Tito down.

"Where are they?" I repeated when he didn't respond.

"I'm not sure what happened to Grady. We were never together. Jinx...was taken," he answered slowly, palming strands of dark curls off his sweaty face.

I narrowed my eyes. "What do you mean, she was *taken?*"

"The redhead Romero runs with took her."

"Cobra? He's alive?!" I couldn't keep the elation out of my voice.

That meant Arlen could be alive, too.

"I don't know if he is now...when Jinx and I were running towards you, he was running away. They collided. By the time I turned back to help her, they were gone. He'd been shot at least once or twice."

"Damn," I muttered, scrubbing a hand over my face. My head felt like it was going to implode. Thoughts began whipping back and forth like a game of jungle pong.

Arlen could be anywhere, but I refused to believe her heart wasn't still beating. She was resilient. As for Jinx, I had not the slightest idea why they would take her, and even less faith that she was alive.

This was such a damn clusterfuck.

Looking up at the hazy-orange sky, I stared for a moment before squinting, making sure my eyes weren't deceiving me —that I really saw what looked like smoke.

There wasn't any real civilization left near Narcoose Bridge, which meant it had to be from people. The Badlands had no good souls left. It was yet to be determined how dark these ones were.

A snap of my fingers was my only warning to Tito that he needed to move his feet or be left behind. I figured I might as well keep him around. He'd be perfect as a scapegoat.

Chapter Two

Romero

Her sobs and screams were damn near inaudible now.

She writhed in pain, unable to clamp her legs closed due to the way I'd tied them open using the bedpost. I thrust inside her one last time, lifting my hand from where I'd knotted it in her hair so I could wrap it around her throat.

She feebly clawed at me and the bed sheets, croaking like a frog as she fought for air I refused to give. Her fear was tangible, drenching all my senses. It was the best kind of aphrodisiac. But this wasn't about pleasure—not this time.

I continued pumping in and out of her until my muscles were sore and she stopped breathing, the life slowly fading from her brown eyes.

I pulled my knife from between her creamy thighs and cleaned the bloody blade with her habit. I couldn't help but laugh at the irony of David sending me a virgin of all things, a stiff whiny bitch that could have never handled my idea of fucking.

I'm not sure what century he was living in, but those weren't magical beings. Not that it mattered; I never had any intention of sticking my dick in her. She wasn't privileged enough to know what I'd feel like buried inside her.

It took a particular pixie-sized, crazy ass blonde to do it for me anymore, one who knew how to fuck like she killed —mercilessly.

Reaching for the glass of water on the nightstand, I poured it over my hands and wiped them off as best I could with a different part of the black fabric.

Just as I tucked my knife away, the door swung open and David himself strolled inside. His face blanched at the scene. I smirked.

The nun he'd sent for Grimm was down on her hands and knees in a puddle of her own piss–being used as his personal footrest. Cobra was smoking a joint and finalizing tonight's move on the other side of the room. His wounded left arm sat comfortably in a sling.

David swiftly regained his composure and gave me a flat look. "How many of them are you going to kill?"

"As many as you send."

Swiping my shirt off the floor, I pulled it over my head and walked towards him. He gave me a level stare that was meant to show he wasn't afraid of me. I knew better. He was seconds away from shitting down the back of his fraudulent holy robes.

I smiled, showing teeth this time just to make him a little more uncomfortable.

He cleared his throat and slightly shifted from left to right.

Fear was a drug I administered effortlessly. I didn't even have to try; it always happened naturally. I wondered if he knew how little time he had left alive before I cut him into individual pieces and gave his head to Cali in a box.

"I'm not going to keep sending you girls if you don't know how to take care of them," he stated.

"We've only killed four, but who's counting? None of us give a shit about the bitches you send in here. I have too much to do if we want this all to go smoothly. You said have fun with them…" I paused and stepped to the side so he could get a clear view of the mutilated pussy I'd left on display just for him. "That's my definition of fun."

He bought every word I said, sighing and nodding in agreement, refusing to stare at my craftsmanship.

"You're right. I should have considered that and…your specific taste," he added dryly, diverting his grey eyes to the floor.

I knew what he was doing. He thought he was testing me, and in his eyes, I was passing with flying colors. He wasn't intelligent enough to outsmart me. I was twelve steps ahead of him. I'd planned this entire charade out meticulously; there was only one variable unaccounted for.

Cali. She was my unpredictable wild card.

Once she was back by my side, I couldn't care less if he knew just how mine she was. That was inevitable; the world would know. The few acolytes I could depend on knew already from witnessing her initiation.

But as things stood right then, I didn't give a shit about her, and had him believing she was the one who had orchestrated the killing off of his delegates by manipulating some of my people.

Of course, he bought it. He was the one who taught her how to use herself to take advantage of men and women.

With her sinful blue eyes, white-blonde hair, and snow-white skin, she looked like a sweet, innocent porcelain doll. No one who saw her would ever suspect that she was a crazy fucking bitch who loved the feel of blood on her hands.

"What do you want?" I stopped a few feet away from him, not so subtly watching the way his Adam's apple bobbed. It was times like these I wondered how David had risen to the top of The Order. I knew it was passed down to him from his father but the man was a gaping pussy. Giving him the metaphorical keys to the castle was a dumb as shit move.

"I just wanted to ensure everything was coming along for this weekend."

"I've been working at this for day and night. You don't think I'd be well and fucking prepared?"

He sighed again, nervously smoothing his palms down his robe. I was going to burn him in the motherfucker.

"Was that all?"

"I guess so. I'll see you in the morning." He turned and did one last slow sweep of the room, freezing when his gaze landed on Cobra.

"Tell me again why he's still alive?" he hissed back at me.

Knowing David was talking about him had Cobra looking up with a giant grin on his face, purposely antagonizing the situation.

"You had one simple task, and that was bringing Calista back to me. Please share what you find so amusing about your screw up," David snapped at him.

I forced my jaw to remain slack when I felt it beginning to clench. I had a primal urge to constantly claim Cali like the Savage I was, and this stupid motherfucker actually believed I was going to hand her over to him.

I couldn't do shit about it though, not yet. In due time, he would get what was coming to him. I was going to bestow upon him my own version of karma.

Cobra cleared his throat and let out a loose chuckle. "Dave. Can I call you Dave? I think we got off on the wrong foot. I'll say sorry for fucking up the delivery of your daughter if you tell me why you want her back after she's been gone so long."

David looked at the three of us and scoffed. "Why wouldn't I want her back? I was devastated when she went missing."

His head snapped to Grimm, who laughed loudly and didn't bother covering it up.

"We both know that's not true, David." He removed his boots from the nun's back and roughly kicked her away from him. She whimpered and crawled to a run, taking off out of the room with the smell of urine chasing after her.

David had a deep hatred for Grimm.

I didn't bother trying to understand it because any reasoning behind it would be bullshit. David's beef was with our father, over a woman of all fucking things.

His hatred didn't extend to me, though; it never had. Fucking ironic, considering my people killed his for sport.

He and Grimm eyed one another, years of barely restrained hostility thickening the tension that hung in the air.

Cobra cleared his throat to break up their silent duel. "She's like one of those vintage editions of a Mattel Barbie: perfect and priceless when you're looking in from the outside of the box, but then you naively open it up and out comes this psychotic blonde in high heels equipped with a meat-cleaver."

I laughed quietly under my breath. He was definitely high, fucking idiot.

"Did you sleep with her?" David asked. A vein throbbed

in his forehead, giving away how pissed he was in spite of how calm he sounded.

Cobra turned his entire body in his chair so he was facing me with an ornery grin.

"Nah, I wanted to. Who wouldn't? I bet she's wild in bed. Romero said she wasn't allowed to be touched."

David looked directly at me for elaboration, but I refused to give him any.

"I'll deal with him on my own terms. Now if you don't need anything…" I left the sentence hanging.

He gave a slight nod of his head and left the room without another word.

"Send someone to collect this body," I called after him, kicking the door shut with my boot.

"Dude is determined to ride your dick," Cobra spat, his smile instantly morphing into a scowl. "You think he knows the truth?" He asked before I could say anything about him implying he wanted to fuck Cali.

"No. If he did, we wouldn't be at this *humble* abode." I waved my hand around the room we'd been placed in.

It was nicer than some people's houses, equipped with a living area, kitchenette, and a bed. We'd been there for two fucking weeks, playing the good alliance to buy some time.

Unbeknownst to David, we would no longer be staying there after that evening. I'd had a few spotters pinpoint Cali's whereabouts, and I had a plan already set in motion to trap her.

Had things been different, I'd just have her snatched up and brought to my rendezvous point, but I couldn't risk her doing something stupid in the state she was in, and I couldn't fucking make a scene to get her myself.

I wasn't sure who the fuck was playing on both teams,

relaying information that was meant to be private, but I would find out.

I had the few people I knew I could rely on working at it without taking so much as a piss break.

It was this person's fault Cali wasn't safely by my side.

Instead, she was who the fuck knows where in the world she'd been way too sheltered from. If this person were smart, they'd take themselves out before I discovered their identity.

"Rome," Grimm repeated my name, pulling me back to the situation at hand.

"Yeah, I got it." I don't know what I supposedly had, because my head wasn't where it needed to be, and they both knew it.

The thing about having a mass amount of people counting on you and putting you on a pedestal was the responsibility that came with it.

But I had those same people's respect and devout loyalty —why would I give that up?

I'd worked my ass off and done shit that would make the strongest man's stomach turn itself inside out to get where I was.

Nothing was handed to me.

I was constantly planning, manipulating, and killing to get what I wanted. This was the beginning of the end, and I was going to make sure it turned out exactly as it needed to.

My life wasn't a movie or piece of fiction. I was and always would be worse than any made up villain. Love wasn't going to make me turn into fucking Saint Nick. I didn't want to save this world. It was exactly how it should be. I damn sure didn't want to start a revolution, I wasn't a teenage girl, and I couldn't give two fucks what happened to strangers.

I wasn't seeking a way to the light, only peaceful eternal

darkness. If I somehow didn't make it out of this alive, I would be happy knowing that whatever was left of me would forever burn in the hell I had created.

"Are we ready for tonight?" I asked them, getting my head back in the game.

"More than ready. This sets everything in motion. It's been a long time coming; we deserve this. You deserve this. My sister deserves this," Grimm answered, openly accepting Cali as his blood for the first time.

I looked at the two men who had grown up with me, who had backed every decision I ever made, and who were just as fucked up as I was. We were a family, and Grimm was right.

We fucking deserved this.

Chapter Three

Calista

The smoke was coming from a fire right in the middle of an abandoned intersection.

From our vantage point, we could see everything without completely exposing ourselves. Tito grabbed my hand to prevent me from going any closer. I was so transfixed on the scene in front of us, I didn't pay him any mind.

"What the fuck?" he whispered, summing up my exact sentiments in three words. We stared at the gathering of men —and, I assumed, some women.

They wore black robes and white masks marked with inverted crosses on either side, so I couldn't tell who was male or female.

Every pair of eyes was trained on Romero—including

mine. My legs burned to run to him, but I wanted to watch this play out.

Standing directly to his left were a man and woman with thick pieces of rope around their necks. Another man knelt at his feet.

It wasn't until I followed the burly ropes up and over the metal base of decrepit traffic lights and back down again to where Grimm and Cobra each held an end with gloved hands that I saw Jinx.

I couldn't say I was relieved to see she was alive because I had no idea what the hell was going on. She was staring at the ground, and her dark hair was curtaining her face.

Romero was speaking, but I wasn't close enough to hear him. I shifted slightly and strained my ears.

He lifted his right arm, and the setting sun glinted off a metal blade.

I caught the words *"punishable"* and *"death"* right before he reached down and grabbed the man in front of him by the hair, pulling his head back before lowering his knife to the man's forehead.

The crowd seemed to ripple the second he began screaming. You could feel their antsy excitement in the air. Their murmuring grew loud enough for me to hear, but I couldn't make out the phrase they kept repeating.

"Cali," Tito whispered, nervously taking a step back, tightening his hold on my hand.

I ignored him and kept my eyes on Romero, watching him work. He was dressed just as he usually was: dark jeans, black boots, dark shirt. He looked just as gorgeous, too; better, actually. My stomach twisted into a gnarled knot.

His inked hand moved left and right, up and down, carving something into the man's flesh.

His unfortunate canvas could do nothing to stop it; his

hands were bound behind his back, and even if he tried to stand up and fight, he knew his death was inevitable.

Blood rolled down his forehead, dripping onto the white robe I belatedly realized he was wearing. He was one of David's. The other man was Romero's, and the woman looked like a run of the mill outlier.

I tried to piece together what the fuck he could be doing, but I couldn't determine what his end goal was. It was becoming increasingly obvious Romero had never truly let me in.

Because he doesn't trust you, an inner voice chided. I couldn't even be pissed about it because I didn't exactly trust him, either.

Breaking my hand free of Tito's, I cautiously moved down the embankment so I could get a little closer.

"Cali," he hissed in warning, following me anyway.

Romero stepped fully behind the man and gestured down to the bleeding leviathan cross he had just carved. From the infinity symbol that made up the bottom of the uneven bars that sat above it, he'd engraved the design perfectly.

I stopped walking, shooting Tito an annoyed glare when he grabbed my hand again.

As people began to cheer, I looked back to see the man and woman with the ropes around their necks being stripped of their clothing by a few robed volunteers.

As soon as they were fully nude, Cobra and Grimm, both began lifting them into the air. Romero forced the man in front of him to look down, and started speaking again.

"Disloyalty will not be tolerated." He placed the edge of his blade on the back of the man's neck, and then looked up when the bodies now fully lifted, beginning to sway.

The pair struggled for air as the nooses compressed around their tracheas, squeezing their carotid arteries and blocking the oxygen from their brains. They fought hard, writhing and kicking out against the weight of their own bodies being entirely supported by the neck and jaw.

Two robed men stepped forward on either side to help Grimm and Cobra keep them suspended; everyone else continued to chant.

Romero watched with an inexpressive look on his face, keeping one hand on the back of the man's neck still kneeling at his feet. I knew he was impressed by the hangings because I was impressed my damn self.

Their deaths were anything but quick. They both suffered through a painfully slow process of strangulation.

The pressure from the blocked oxygen continuously mounting with nowhere to go caused both of their capillaries to burst, making them break out with red and purple splotches as the skin bled from underneath.

It took approximately ten minutes for their hearts, brains, or lungs to decide enough was enough and give up. They became nothing but limp scarecrows with fixed, bulging eyes.

Romero's voice ensnared my attention again, and this time I heard him crystal clear.

"You're either with me, or against me." He shoved his knife clean through the back of the man's neck with one fluid motion, severing his spine. His coal black eyes flashed to mine, and I swore he knew I'd been watching all along, making me wonder if his last words were solely meant for my ears because he'd said them to me before.

His followers began to chant their earlier words louder now, *Ava Satanas*, over and over again, growing higher in volume with each repetitive cycle until it seemed to echo through the ruined city.

Tito was seconds away from having a meltdown, and I was frozen in place.

The power Romero had over me with just a single gaze was daunting. I felt like I couldn't breathe, and everything around him faded away.

It was an overwhelming déjà vu to get lost in him like this again, a stark reminder of the magnetic, indefinable bond that was between us, like a flicker of a flame in the dark, one that had been lit so I could find my way back home—because home had become wherever he was.

I knew it wasn't one-sided. The asshole looked like he was smirking at me. I wanted to go to him; I *would* have gone to him, but he turned away again and the ashen little pieces of my brain-dead heart followed right behind him.

He turned his back on me so he could talk to the brunette Arlen claimed was her sister.

When she laid her hand on his shoulder, I promised then and there I would remove every single one of her fucking fingers.

The atmosphere shifted after Grimm and Cobra let both bodies carelessly drop to the ground. As soon as they cracked against the asphalt, a large flag unraveled from the old stop-light and I found myself staring at a Sigil of Baphomet, the official symbol of Satan. The Hebrew characters running counterclockwise around the ring framing the goat head had been made to spell out Romero's name.

If I hadn't already known the man I was enamored with was the king of the Savages—a satanic cult masquerading as a gang—I sure as fuck would have just been made aware.

One prominent question still took precedence over all the others. What the hell was he planning? So lost was I in my tumultuous thoughts that I missed the two people in masks who had broken from the crowd and were charging right for us. Tito didn't.

"We need to go!" He jerked me backward so hard my arm almost popped out of its socket.

"That hurt, you dick!" I stumbled, catching myself whilst trying to pull away from him.

Seemingly not satisfied with my reaction, he picked me up despite all my protests, no doubt garnering the full attention of the crowd, and booked it back into the woods.

Chapter Four

Romero

I wasn't a huge fan of guns. They curdled creativity and ended people too quick. I liked taking my time when I killed, savoring the affliction of pain, but I wasn't in the mood to play right then, so I pressed the barrel to her palm and pulled the trigger, burning a perfect hole right through it.

Cobra's good arm slightly jerked from the kick-back. She screamed, and I sincerely hoped it was loud enough for Cali to hear.

She'd been right in front of me and I turned away.

I never did dumbass shit but I suppose there was a first time for everything—and a last.

I knelt down and pressed the warm, now crimson barrel right to Beth's trembling mouth, telling her to shut the fuck up without needing to say a word.

She had this idea in her head that she would be the next Tiffany, and it was about time she realized it was never going to happen.

"That looks like it hurts." I nodded to her bloody palm. She made a low keening noise and continued to sob. "The next time you touch me, I'll take off the whole fucking hand. You should thank me for being in a semi-good mood today and not killing you here and now."

I stood up and tucked the gun away. No one stopped to stare at what I was doing. Everybody continued milling around, getting ready for what came next and keeping watch over me like junkyard guard dogs high on meth.

"I can cauterize this. Go handle shit," Cobra said, already pulling Beth towards the fire where two of the corpses were burning.

I wasn't going to object. I needed some peace but that wasn't likely to happen. The rage I constantly felt simmering beneath my surface was close to erupting.

All because of one damn girl.

"We'll find her again," Grimm said, falling into step beside me.

I had no doubt she would be found. The issue was her being out in the woods with Tito of all fucking people. He was no better than his sister. It didn't help that he knew I was the one who had indirectly killed her. How it eluded me that he was the one who could have sent Cali was another major fuck up on my end.

The past was the past, though, and shit could be done to change it. Focusing on my present would secure my future. I needed to get everything back on track—and fast.

That included getting my girl back before Tito opened his mouth and spilled his guts.

Cali only knew partial truths of sordid secrets about everything and everyone.

I'd weaved my wicked web so thoroughly for a reason. I could only imagine the thoughts already spinning around her psychotic little head.

"I know," I finally responded to Grimm, pausing to look down at the naked woman still lying on the ground. Her clit was engorged and discharge was pooling between her legs.

I didn't feel an ounce of remorse. I didn't believe in mercy so no one would be given if they fucked with me. It was the way I'd always done things.

Now I was no longer making my moves behind a curtain of obscurity, word could spread as a reminder that the Badlands was *my* domain. The time had come to restore some order and get rid of all the motherfuckers who mistakenly thought I liked to share.

"Toss her in the flames, too," I commanded the man closest to me before walking off again.

Grimm remained diligently beside me, keeping silent. He knew my mind had wandered straight back to Cali.

Time apart hadn't lessened whatever the fuck was between us. It made it stronger. That was a good thing; it solidified that it was real and not fleeting.

Something was different about her. She was so close to breaking free of her chrysalis. I felt it. I saw it in her eyes, and it was about fucking time. There was a demonic beast that lived inside every single one of us. It lurked in the darkest parts of the human mind, locked away in fear of judgment or ostracization.

I had only ever known how to let that motherfucker rein free. Cali's was dormant, slowly coming alive, clawing and tearing away at the part of her mind trying to restrain it to a dark iron cell.

When it fully emerged, my beautiful girl would desire only chaos and anarchy.

I ignored Beth's screams as Cobra held her hand in the fire, and I didn't look back to see my acolytes loyally trailing after me.

I had to get Cali's ass back where she belonged.

A king wasn't shit without his queen.

Chapter Five

Calista

He grabbed my ass without permission, so I bit him.

That got him to let me go and remove his straying hands —two birds, one stone. I closed my mouth around his shoulder and clamped down on the flesh, throwing in a growl for added effect.

I was airborne the second he managed to dislodge me. I hit the ground with an *"oomph,"* losing the air in my lungs just as a scream echoed through the trees, sending a wave of black crows with it.

"What is wrong with you?!" Tito yelled at me, covering the spot where my teeth marks glistened.

"You should be asking yourself that question," I retorted, pushing myself up off the ground. "I told you to put me down, not throw me."

"I'm not just talking about this, Cali. I'm talking about back there." He jerked his head in the general direction we'd just come from, huffing and puffing, still trying to catch his breath. "You were turned on. I saw the way you looked at him. Your hand started to sweat, and your cheeks flushed."

With a heavy sigh, I brushed the dirt and sticky leaves from my shorts–forcing the naseau I kept getting at the most impromptu times away. "What would you like me to say to that?" I waited for a snarky response and only got stared down.

"What did he do to you?" He slowly shook his head with a look of disappointment.

He knocked down my barricaded walls and made me his in every sense of the word. It wasn't like I hadn't practically dared him to. After all, I'd demanded he fuck me the second he put his perfect body against mine. I definitely wouldn't be joining any women's equality movements in the future.

"What *didn't* he do to me?" I snickered. "Don't you think we should be worrying about what just happened back there?" I pointed over his shoulder.

"They were hailing Satan as your *lover* had three people killed, all while you were sending out huge fuck me signals," he gritted out through his teeth.

"Oh, okay. Thanks for clarifying." I turned away and his jaw unhinged.

Staring through the breaks in the treetops, I looked up at the rapidly darkening sky as if it could solve all my problems. Of course, that would never happen, because life was too busy trying to power-bomb me in the ass.

What was Romero up to?

The Hail Satan and flag with his name on it were self-explanatory. It was him hanging people from different factions that I didn't understand.

If I didn't know any better, I'd say he was preparing for a hostile takeover or something equally as deadly—or this was a normal occurrence, and I was just too damn sheltered to know that.

Whatever it was, I needed to hit a pause button on my brain until after I slept. Exhausted, I dropped my butt to the ground and my head to my hands. With my back cushioned against a tree and Tito finally shutting the hell up, I had a minute of blissful silence.

It was the quickest minute in history.

"You can't stop now. We have to get going; those people are still in these woods trying to find us," Tito rushed out. "You can't go back to him, Cali. I know you're aware of who he is. I refuse to believe you're as fucked up as him."

The only words that rang with clarity through my foggy brain were *you can't*. He didn't ask me; he was telling me.

Everyone was always telling me what I was going to do, never asking what I *wanted* to do. I lifted my head and tilted it to the side, studying the man who was now talking down to me and trying to make me feel ashamed for being the way I was.

I never thought he'd judge me like this—screwing his enemy aside. It helped bring a few things into perspective. In the early beginning, I said I would do whatever the fuck I wanted to do, but that wasn't true, was it?

I chose to keep Tito's best interests in mind, and Romero's, too. I struggled to find a balance between fully giving in to a man who made me relish in sin without damning the other.

I could be a truly fucked up person. Okay, I'll own it, I *was* a fucked up person, but I never wanted my loyalty questioned.

Look where that had gotten me. Look where the hell I

was. I think it was time for me to be selfish and take control of my life.

I was well acquainted with the demon that lived inside my head, and if I stopped waging war against her, that sick bitch would ensure I got everything I wanted, and everything I deserved.

Tito stopped pacing when he finally realized I wasn't paying attention to a word he was saying.

"You're not even listening."

I stood from the ground so fast he was still looking at the spot my ass had been when I stepped up to him and placed two fingers on his lips.

"What—"

"Shhh," I hushed him. "You're done talking. It's my turn now." Keeping my digits pressed to his mouth, I continued. "I don't think you understand just how unlike you I am.

I want you to forget that girl you thought you knew. She doesn't exist. She never did. I'm not a good person. I'm as unholy as they come, and your opinion of me is not going to make me change who I am." Dropping my hand, I took a step back, holding his gaze.

He stared back at me, and I could see the silent questions burning in his eyes. When did I get so cold? What happened to my soul? That was proof enough for me that he had no idea who he'd let live under the same roof as him.

The gullible fool tried to use me as the key player in a game he never had a chance of winning. Unfortunately for him, I was done being anyone's pawn the day he found me. I refused to be a goddamn stepping stone.

After giving him one last unimpressed look, I turned around and walked away. His hoarse voice called after me; I ignored it. I was *so* over judgmental, hypocritical assholes.

Our world had gone mad long ago.

We lived in a perpetual hell that was only going to get worse as time went on. Survival meant you were a hunter, or you were prey.

There was no reason for me to keep playing a role anymore. Fuck my morality, and fuck what anyone thought about me.

I would find a way to get to David, and when I did, I would rip his heart out of his goddamn chest so I could feel its final beat in my hands.

I would lay his faux holy delegates out in shallow graves after I cut their throats and watched them choke on their own blood.

I would bring the devil to his knees and put that silver tongue of his to work between my thighs. If I was meant to be a queen, then it was time to wear the fucking crown.

Chapter Six

Calista

My first course of action was to find somewhere to sleep and something edible to fill my neglected stomach.

I'd originally tried finding my way back to where Romero had been, but thanks to Tito's zigzag pattern, I wasn't sure which way that was exactly. The smoke was no longer visible in the sky, so I just walked and hoped for the best.

As the sun got lower and darkness took over, the woodland creatures began to shift about and the temperature dropped.

I got lucky after I made my way up a small embankment, using the moon as my nightlight.

I paused, taking in the square structure in front of me. It was such a random place to build a house, but despite the fact it was smack dab in the middle of a small clearing of trees, the old home had managed to withstand the elements.

There was a light on inside, the grass around the house was low, and the windows weren't boarded up like the majority of the homes near Narcoose Bridge. It obviously wasn't abandoned, but there weren't any cars, and there was no sound or movement.

I took a few steps forward and abruptly stopped. "I know you've been following me, so you can come out now."

At my words, Tito pushed his way through a leafy shrub and stared at me with his big brown eyes, looking like a wounded puppy.

"You've always been shitty at being stealthy," I pointed out, cutting off whatever he had opened his mouth to say.

My calf muscles protested with every step I took up the porch stairs. The front door was wide open, so I took that as invitation enough. I strolled right in like I lived there.

"Anybody home?" A heavy silence answered.

The place wasn't overly large. The word cozy came to mind. Aside from the kitchen also serving as a dining room with atrocious striped wallpaper, the rest of the house had mahogany wood paneled walls and dull hardwood flooring.

I could sense that something was off here. Doing a slow sweep through both rooms, I approached the table and took in four place settings. There were half-eaten sandwiches that still looked relatively fresh, an empty glass on its side, and a dead fly floating in a pink kitten cup full of water.

The million dollar question was what happened to the people?

"Shut the front door and lock it," I called to Tito just as he stepped inside. He did what I asked for once without any rebuttal.

I walked into the main part of the kitchen and searched the drawers, finding a large cutting knife.

"Coming?" I asked him, making my way back to the foyer and slowly starting up the staircase, taking in the golden framed pictures of a family that lined the walls. The steps creaked behind me from the pressure of Tito's weight.

At the top landing, I took a moment to survey the hallway. There were two doors on one side and two on the other. All four were closed.

"I don't think we should be up here. We have no idea what or who could be in one of those rooms," Tito whispered.

"Then go back downstairs."

This man needed a testosterone shot in his balls. His fear was driving me bat-shit.

I had no idea he was this emasculating.

Moving forward, I opened the first door on my left, finding an empty room that clearly belonged to a little girl. There were unicorn stickers all over one purple wall.

Seeing nothing out of the ordinary, I moved on. The next room was plain with no real character to it. There was an old basketball in the middle of the floor and a weathered desk beside a window. The first door across the hall revealed a small bathroom. The final room was where the bodies were.

A man, a woman, and an adolescent boy lay on the floor. All three had bullet holes in the center of their foreheads.

The little girl from the pictures was missing. I knew she wasn't inside the house, which meant she was more than likely taken or dead somewhere in the woods.

"Who do you think did this?" Tito asked from behind me.

Crouching down, I reached my hand out and swirled two dirt clad fingers in the blood to get an idea of the texture, ignoring the sound Tito made in his throat. Next, I stroked the man's face. His skin was taut but rigor mortis hadn't fully set in yet, and the room was lacking the smell that came with decaying bodies.

"It wasn't Romero or his people, if that's what you're thinking, and they haven't been dead for very long," I responded, standing up.

"How do you know any of that?"

"Because I'm an expert when it comes to death, and no one was tortured. There's also no inverted cross or sigil anywhere, and you know the Savages always leave behind a charming token of their presence."

Stepping back, I turned around and walked out of the room to head back downstairs.

"And the little girl?" Tito asked, following me.

"She's obviously not here."

"Okay, so what do we do about that?"

"*You* can do whatever you want. I'm going to raid the cabinets for food and sleep in one of those beds."

Turning the kitchen sink on, I grabbed some soap and began washing my hands, scrubbing beneath my nails.

"Are you serious?"

"What do you suppose I do? Go hunt down whoever took her so I can be the next to get a piece of metal in my brain?"

He didn't respond, so I dried my hands on a cloth towel and then busied myself finding something to eat. I ended up with two pathetic pieces of wheat bread, a dish of strawberries from the fridge, and water from the tap.

"Look, I'm hungry, I'm tired, and so are you. There's food, and there's a place to sleep here. Sounds like two plus two to me."

"Yeah, and the people who lived here are all upstairs."

"Well, until they ask us to leave, I'm sure they won't mind," I quipped over my shoulder, heading back to the upper level.

The heavy contempt in his voice every time he spoke to me grounded what was left of my nerves down to my brittle bones, and I had no energy left for a battle of words.

I made my way into the room with the desk and sat the pitiful lackluster meal on the bed. It took me fewer than five minutes to consume my food and chug the water.

I could hear Tito grumbling to himself when I got back up to shut the door. I'd left him some bread and strawberries so he'd have something to eat; he should be grateful and kissing my ass for not gutting him with the kitchen knives.

Grabbing the desk chair, I positioned it beneath the bedroom doorknob when I saw there wasn't a lock.

Plopping down on the bed with a heavy sigh, I shut my eyes to revel in the feel of a mattress beneath my back instead of dirt or concrete.

The shower across the hall beckoned and my feet screamed to be free of my worn down boots, but with the bodies across the hall, I felt better being completely clothed. Letting my guard down wouldn't be the wisest thing to do. If shit were to hit the fan, being ass naked or barefoot wouldn't do me any favors.

I stared up at the white textured ceiling, my muddled mind sloshing in every direction. Even beyond the brink of exhaustion, sleep still chose to evade me and insomnia taunted. I didn't have this issue when I slept with Romero.

Frustrated, I threw an arm over my face and tried to force myself to a dreamland.

I could still feel Tito's disappointed eyes on me. He assumed I was a heartless bitch for not showing anguish over the missing girl.

It wasn't that I didn't care; on the contrary, the situation had memories trying to resurface from when I was younger that I was doing my best to suppress.

The girl could be no older than ten at most. I hated all the possibilities of what could be happening to her. It killed something inside of me even thinking about it, because I knew there was nothing I could do.

I couldn't help anyone else without helping myself first. I had to ensure the potential life growing inside me would never have to go through what I did.

Chapter Seven

Calista

I was going to ignore him, but the urgent tone beneath his whispered words had me rolling out of bed.

Pulling the chair away from the door, I cracked it open and felt my glare morph into a frown, seeing Tito as distraught as he was.

"Come with me," was all he said before spinning around and zooming back down the stairs.

Grumbling in the back of my throat, feeling far less than energized, I followed.

"What is it?" I asked, stepping off the last stair.

He wordlessly waved me forward without turning away from whatever he was looking at. I crept up beside him and used my hip to bump him out of the way so I could peer out the storm door.

I was immediately taken back to an old movie called *Children of the Corn* when I saw the little girl from the pictures on the wall staring back at me. I felt the hairs rise on the back of my neck.

"How did you know she was out there?" I asked him, never taking my eyes off her.

"She knocked and then ran back down the stairs."

I hummed in response. She didn't look to be under duress. Her clothes were clean, and her dark hair was neatly parted down the middle. Everything about this was off to me.

It was the middle of the night, her family was behind me with bullet holes in their foreheads, and she was wandering around the woods playing ding-dong-ditch?

Not fucking likely.

"We can't leave her out there," Tito said before he bumped me back out of the way and tried to open the door. I threw my weight on the wooden surface, slamming it shut with a loud bang.

I turned my head and glared at him. "That's exactly what we need to do."

My warning either went right over his head or his flawed compassion meter was at maximum capacity. With a look of abhorrence aimed at me like a weapon, I was shoved sideways, almost falling on my ass. Tito threw open the door, charging out before I could stop him.

The gunshot sounded like it came from the right, but I knew it was the left. Tito's leg buckled just as he hit the first step, his bellow echoing louder than the gunfire as he fell in an awkward heap on the walkway.

Arterial spray peppered the gray paint on the stairs and the cracked concrete.

The little girl looked at him and smiled as four people stepped from the surrounding darkness.

A man stroked her head and told her, *"Good job"* before settling his gaze on me. I quickly assessed the scene. Tito held his hand over a leg that was gushing like a geyser, doing his best not to show he was in pain.

There were three men and a chick with dirty blonde hair standing around him in a semi-circle, all looking up at me, and all carrying long black guns hooked over their heads.

This obviously wasn't good.

Taking a silent breath, I stared into the cerulean blue eyes of the man straight ahead. I locked down my poker face, forcing myself not to look at Tito.

It was always friends and family that wound up used as leverage against you in dire situations—precisely why it was best not to have any.

"Why don't you come on out." Blue Eyes spoke, breaking the tense silence. It wasn't a question as much as it was a politely spoken demand.

Damn Tito and his stupidity! How did he miss the fact that the little girl was bait? Her demented ass was *still* smiling down at him. He walked himself into this. I didn't feel an ounce of sorrow for his suffering, because now I was in shit with him.

"What if I don't want to?" I asked innocently.

Blue Eyes barked out a laugh, flashing his teeth. Surprisingly, they weren't the color of urine. His clothes were clean and he was unmistakably healthy, letting me know these weren't your average band of outliers.

"I could come in and get you," he said calmly.

Yeah, no, that wasn't happening.

Knowing I couldn't run without likely being shot in the back had me begrudgingly stepping out onto the porch.

None of the others with him spoke, so I assumed he called the shots.

I moved down the stairs, keeping my hands by my side, flicking a careless glance at Tito. He had torn a piece of fabric off his shirt and was securing it around his wound. "Skinners," he groaned through his teeth, not bothering to look up.

I briefly wondered if the pain was making him delusional, but I didn't have time to discern that. Ignoring the other three people with him, I kept my eyes locked with the man in front of me, slightly tilting my chin up to accommodate our height difference.

He looked pretty damn good if I was honest, with his odd blue eyes and dark curly hair.

He didn't hold a flame to Romero because, also being honest, he was the perfect specimen.

On the bright side, if Blue Eyes decided to use his gun and paint the house behind me red with my blood, I'd get to look at something pretty as I died.

"Get down on your knees," he commanded in the same tone, snapping me out of my intrusive stare down.

"Wow, straight to foreplay?" I replied, not making any effort to do what he said. If he wanted me on my knees, he would damn well have to put me there. Call it stupidity on my end, but I wasn't going to bow to any man.

He smiled as if reading my mind and gave the slightest lift of his chin. It was almost unnoticeable, but I caught it. Not a second later, the butt of a gun was slamming into my jaw and I was on the ground just like he wanted.

Pain exploded up the right side of my face; a metallic tang flooded my mouth.

Holy fuck, it hurt. I swallowed a mouthful of air to drown out my whimper and blinked three times to clear the tears away.

I glanced up at the blonde who was now smirking down at

me. Keeping my head was an incredible test of my willpower. I tampered down the urge to lunge up and wring the bitch's neck. Attacking her would only cause me more harm.

"Now, that wasn't very nice." I gave her a big smile, feeling blood dribble down my chin. I spit the back tooth she knocked out, right onto her black boots.

I heard a laugh, and then someone told her *"no,"* not a fraction of a second before her gun came down again on the back of my head.

Chapter Eight

Calista

The heat was unbearable.

Perspiration gathered on my brow and slowly rolled down and pooled between my breasts. It was only a matter of time before I'd be sitting in a deep puddle of my sweat.

I could feel a solid lump on the back of my head, and the side of my face was painfully swollen. There was a throbbing ache every time I swallowed or moved my tongue.

A man had been screaming and begging for his life for what seemed like hours on end, abruptly cutting off just minutes ago.

Now I could hear someone pitifully sobbing.

A solid brick building was at my back offering no shade, and I had loose rusted chains around each of my wrists, but I wasn't going to complain about that. Not when the two women beside me were completely nude and hanging upside down from some manmade contraption.

They weren't moving, and both of their eyes were shut. I stared at their naked bodies until I saw the slight rise and fall of their chests. Their skin was covered in raised heat blisters and had an ugly red tint. They were slow roasting in the sun.

I shifted on the concrete when my ass started to fall asleep. If the abundance of old bloodstains splattered across it was anything to deduce, this wasn't going to go well for me.

"Hellooo?" I called out for the hundredth time. My voice sounded like two pieces of sandpaper being rubbed together. Unsurprisingly, no one answered me.

Pulling my legs up to my chest, I rested my cheek on my knees and tried not to breathe too deeply.

The smell of body odor and death was potent, and I only cared for one of them.

I had no idea where Tito was. The man screaming had too deep a voice to have been him. I couldn't see anything but a manicured grassy field and a house in the far distance.

Studying the two women beside me again, I noted how drastically different they looked. The one on the very end had purple hair and was heavyset. The one next to me had brown hair and was almost as thin as I normally was, aside from the protrusion in her midsection.

I wondered how long it would take me to look like they did, and why I hadn't been hung the same way.

My throat was parched, my body ached, and my stomach churned with another bout of sickening nausea, but I held it together.

I was so damn tired of ending up in situations I had no control over.

Lifting the rusted-orange chains up so I could examine them, I couldn't see a way to get them off. I was stuck.

Fighting was always my number one option, but I had no idea what I'd be up against—or who—and I wasn't exactly in the best physical condition.

I knew I had to consider a few added limitations. I wasn't an idiot. But the position I'd found myself in didn't make me a delicate wallflower, either. I wasn't the first woman in the Badlands to end up this way. Hell, some women popped kids out like they were pinball machines. I couldn't even be that far yet.

Regardless, if it really was set in motion and meant to be, I could handle it.

What I couldn't do was magically escape a set of chains. There was only one person I could think of who could get me out of this, and he was nowhere near the facility.

Groaning, I leaned my head back and shut my eyes. I just needed him to save me one last time.

I was almost entirely out of it when I felt the rim of a plastic water bottle at my lips. Slowly peeling my eyes open, I saw a woman in front of me, encouraging me to drink.

"Come on," she whispered encouragingly when I coughed the first bit of water right back out. Her next attempt paid off. I guzzled down the soothing liquid like a newborn calf whose life depended on it.

All too soon, she was pulling away with whispered words that sounded an awful lot like *"He's coming for you,"* Then, she was gone, disappearing around the corner so fast I wasn't able to get a clear look at her face.

If it wasn't for the slight relief, I felt I would have chalked it up to me hallucinating.

Elation was the first emotion that rushed through my veins when her words repeated in my head. I naively thought she meant Romero.

That idea was wiped out when a guy came strolling

around the corner of the building with a thick garden hose clenched in one of his hands, and pushing a bright red wheelbarrow.

Suddenly alert, I scanned the contents of it and a small trickle of worry ciphered into my conscious—not for me, but for the woman right beside me.

Shifting slightly, I found my eyes traveling up the body of a man who was the same size as me, all the way up to his mohawk and then back down to his honey brown eyes.

"Sorry blondie, I'm not allowed to play with you. Boss' orders." He winked, completely misinterpreting why I was looking him over. The little smile accompanying his statement had a brittle laugh slipping out of my mouth.

"You should probably move as far right as you can." He flashed another smile, gently setting the wheelbarrow down.

"What are you doing?"

"I'm prepping them.". He turned the hose nozzle and then proceeded to spray down the two women. Neither of them reacted beyond quiet whimpers.

They must have really been out of it because the water was scalding, hot enough that steam visibly lifted from their flesh and burst some of their heat blisters, leaving milky pus to run free.

I scooted as far away as I could, just like he'd advised, sucking in a sharp breath when a few drops of water landed on my knee.

I wasn't expecting what came next but I wasn't all that surprised, either. It made Tito's grumbled phrase make a helluva lot more sense. The stick figure of a man put earphones in, pulled a pair of leather gloves on, grabbed a thin knife, and walked towards us.

He continued to pay me no mind, getting straight to work.

He started with the woman farthest away, the one with purple hair.

With an incredibly steady hand, he began carefully cutting and peeling the skin away on her face, starting at the center of her chin.

His blade cut clean through, as if it were garnering softened butter. I watched him, torn between feeling sickening awe and repulsion.

With the bloody knife handle clenched between his teeth, he used two hands to lift off almost the entire surface of the woman's face.

It was gently tossed it into the plastic covered wheelbarrow where it landed with a wet splat. His facial expression was set in a glare of concentration, the woman's blood not bothering him at all. There was so much. It hung from her barren face like thin strings of long ribbon.

He continued. Every cut he made was specific and calculated. From what I could see, they weren't incredibly deep, but they were enough to separate the skin from muscle.

He sliced into the woman's arms, wrists, feet, and chest. I quickly realized the goal was to remove the skin in as few pieces as possible.

Crimson rained down to the ground like a steady waterfall. The sound of dripping blood coupled with him slowly peeling flesh reminded me of snapping Velcro and rain boots jumping in mud puddles.

The visual oddly reminded me of someone having their clothes taken off. My stomach churned, and my throat painfully tightened, but I couldn't look away.

If the purple haired woman weren't already damn near dead, she would be completely gone in a few minutes. Perhaps that was a good thing. A lethal infection or exsanguination would kill her far quicker than hanging upside down would have.

When he was done with her, he moved on to the brunette.

The leather gloves he'd pulled on were a dark shade of maroon, and so slippery they squelched every time his fingers flexed.

Maybe I should have tried to thwart his attention so he'd focus on me. Maybe that would have miraculously spared his next target.

I didn't.

I was never the hero. I was always the villain. I was selfish and unashamedly stingy when it came to self-preservation.

The knowledge that I could potentially have my own bump soon meant a fuck load more to me than either of these unfortunate strangers being flayed alive.

I wasn't afraid of death but I wasn't quite ready to accept her loving embrace. I wanted to live. I'd never gotten the chance to do that yet. With that in mind, I knew I was going to get out of this. I didn't know how, but I would. I had to.

The man continued with his work, humming to the beat of a heavy metal song blasting through his ear-buds loud enough for me to hear. Black Sabbath? *Seriously*? It was almost comical.

I watched him skillfully maneuver around the chains and wondered how many times he'd done this. He didn't so much as bat an eyelid when he had to lift the section of skin that covered the bump.

"Jesus Christ." I shut my eyes and looked away, unable to watch, wishing I had something to block out the sound.

"Ugh, fuck." My eyes flew open when something wet touched my legs. Her blood seemed to gravitate towards right where I was sitting. I hurriedly crab walked further, not stopping until the chains around my wrists reached their limit.

I hoped that she couldn't feel any of this, that her nervous system was screaming for help and misfiring so many different warnings that her body was shutting down.

I wisely kept my smart ass mouth shut for once, not wanting to draw any more attention to me than necessary. If I were a normal woman, I would have been a hysterical mess and projectile vomiting all over myself.

I wasn't, though, and I was really happy about that right then. Falling apart was the last thing I needed to do.

Fortunately, he sped through the rest of the process and walked off with his wheelbarrow full of bloody flesh, only acknowledging me with a slight nod.

His process had been so different from the cannibals. Why did he only take the skin? Were there people who only ate human flesh? I found that more disturbing than broiling someone's arm.

When empty silence descended, I found myself studying the carcasses beside me, doing my best to avoid the brunette's torso for obvious reasons.

It was morbidly educational to see tendons and muscle mass exposed. They looked like large slabs of raw meat left out to dry. The smell was an entirely different story. It was like cheap perfume had been dabbed on a rotten piece of beef.

The steady blood flow eventually turned into a light trickle, and then a drip.

I eventually had no choice but to shimmy my pants down to urinate on the ground or risk pissing myself. There was nothing I could do about my growling stomach.

No one else came by.

Day turned to night, and I was left alone.

Chapter Nine

Calista

Every time I shut my eyes and managed to sleep, he was there waiting for me. This time was no different, even when my dozing off wasn't intentional.

He knelt right in front of me, his onyx eyes boring straight into mine, searing right into the tar black soul that exclusively belonged to him.

His infuriating as hell signature smirk was in place, and made my heart beat off kilter. One look in his jaded eyes made me want to forgive everything.

I was so lost to this man, trapped under his wicked spell. He would forever be my beloved devil.

When he finally spoke, the familiar deep timbre of his voice sent delicious chills down my spine.

"You look like complete shit, but you're still the most

beautiful thing I've ever seen." He clicked his tongue and reached out, gently trailing his knuckles down the swollen side of my face.

It wasn't until a door slammed in the distance and I became extremely aware of how real his touch felt that clarity came rushing back to my mind and I knew this wasn't a dream.

The natural exotic smell of him and the heady scent of blood and old piss filled my lungs as I sucked in a harsh breath. I wanted to wrap my arms around him and kick his ass at the same time.

I wasn't ready for, or expecting, the wave of emotion that came crashing down on me now that we were right in front of each other.

I felt like we'd just ended the most fucked up game of hide-and-go-seek in history.

All I had to do was lift my hand and I'd be able to touch him. My brain started churning at a mile a minute. I suddenly felt ultra-awake. Adrenaline flowed like lava through my veins.

There were so many things I wanted to say; I'd planned this out in my head a thousand times, but I could never bring myself to tell him how I felt, and that didn't miraculously change in the short span of two weeks.

I buried it and did my best to act indifferent. That could all wait. All I needed to focus on right then was getting far the fuck away from wherever I was.

Glancing to the left, I was glad to see that someone had at least had the decency to take the bodies away.

I leaned forward to stretch and every muscle in my body screamed in protest; I was so sore, it even hurt to flex my toes.

I was okay, though. I'd been in worse pain when he found

me the first time and saved me from becoming someone's dinner.

Romero shifted and rose back up to his full height. I stared at his shiny black boots, taking my time to appreciate what I'd been missing as my eyes drifted up his body. He had on dark jeans that hugged his amazing ass, and a dark shirt covering all his beautiful tattoos.

When I got to his face, I was greeted with a smug as fuck grin. "That's just a preview. If you're an extra good girl, I'll let you have a private showing."

I scoffed to hide a smile as if I didn't know every inch of him by heart.

"Are you going to get these off me?" I lifted my wrists up, shaking the chains.

His hand reached down and took hold of the rusted links on the left. He gave a gentle tug but made no effort to remove them.

"You're good for my ego. This whole damsel in distress thing you have going on almost makes me feel like a hero."

So, we were jumping right back into it were we? I huffed out an annoyed breath and told myself to count to ten.

I couldn't make it past zero.

"I'm not a fucking damsel, asshole! I wouldn't even be in this situation if it wasn't for you, so just take the goddamn chains off and I can go."

He immediately dropped the links and stepped back, crossing his arms. Ugh. It should have been a sin to be so damn gorgeous. "You shouldn't talk like that, babe. It's unbecoming of a lady. And don't you mean so *we* can go?"

I ground my teeth and glared up at him.

Goddamn it.

"What do you want from me now?"

"Not much." He smirked, and I knew whatever came out

of his mouth next was going to piss me off more than he just had.

"You don't have to do anything drastic, like thank me for saving your ungrateful ass *again*. Just admit that you need me, and this can all go away."

I did need him. I needed him to feed the addict in me. I needed him to fill the bottomless void inside me so I could feel whole again. We were tied together from the second we met.

He was already aware of all this. The fucker just wanted to hear me admit it aloud. Was I going to? Hell no. I was stubborn, and didn't appreciate ultimatums.

"Go fuck yourself."

The grin he gave me was full of devilry. He laughed and took hold of my chin, forcing me to maintain eye contact. "Not only is she a fucking idiot, but she's mouthy, too? Huh.

Guess I shouldn't be surprised, though. All that beauty and no brains," he sighed with forced exasperation.

It was almost verbatim of what he'd said when we first met.

He moved his hand, rubbing the pad of his thumb across my bottom lip. If my mouth didn't hurt, I would have bitten him.

"Since you don't need me, you shouldn't have any problems breaking free," he taunted. "I have to go handle something. You wait here." He winked at me before walking off.

I was tied up. Where the hell was I going to go?

"Fucking asshole!" I called after him, getting a laugh in response.

Chapter Ten

Romero

I banged on the steel door twice and waited.

I listened to the running water, the scraping of graters, and the hum of an old ventilation system. Bugs repeatedly flew into the bulb of the floodlight hanging above me.

Not a full minute later, the heavy door was slid open just enough for the noxious fumes inside to escape and for me to see inside.

Piles of human skin sat ready to be processed and either discarded in the old dumpster I knew was out back, or unhaired, degreased, desalted, and then soaked in water.

Luther stepped out and quickly closed the large room off again, still wearing his plastic overalls and face mask.

"Didn't I tell you it would work?" He pulled his mask down to reveal a wide ass grin.

"You should probably commit this moment in history to memory, considering it's the first time you've been right about anything in sixteen fucking years."

He threw his head back and laughed.

"Actually, *My Liege*, if the blonde chained up outside my stable is the infamous Calista, I've been right about two things. If I remember correctly, I was adamant you'd find her eventually."

"You're right. I'll add a golden star to your special chart."

"I've sincerely missed you and all your royal asshole remarks." He laughed again, holding a gloved hand over his heart.

"Yeah, now we've caught up, go take those fucking chains off my girl."

"Come on, Dhal has the key." He grinned and set off towards his house. "You sure you don't wanna leave Tito behind?"

There was no love lost between the two of them. Tito just wasn't a well-liked individual these days. I smirked in amusement at his anger on my behalf.

"Nah, his ass is mine to handle. I'll send Grimm to collect him. And I want whoever it was that knocked Cali's tooth out. You can have Janice for the kid. It'll save you a body."

He stroked his chin and nodded. "Yeah, that works for me." I knew he would accept the offer. He'd been teaching his niece how to flay on cadavers and could always use another one.

We walked in silence. I laughed to myself. Cali would be mad as fuck. Knowing she was safe and would soon be back by my side where she belonged calmed the beast inside me.

I swear I could breathe easier, knowing my beautiful girl was coming home.

I should have come to see Luther first, but my feet had

carried me to her. The pull was magnetic. It was only after I checked her over that I realized I needed a key to get her chains off. If I didn't already know Luther had only done what was necessary, I would have crushed his fucking spine for tying her up.

"I like her."

"Uh huh, so do I," I replied, feeling the need to state what was plain as fucking day.

"She's tiny a little thing—"

"If you're trying to make a point, make it," I warned.

"Hey, chill, man. I value my life." He held his hands up in surrender and took a small step away. "I was going to say she has spunk. If she's anything like what I've heard, you two are gonna be fuckin great together. This is what we needed."

I didn't have anything to add to that. Shit was weird and way too far out of my comfort zone.

Cali represented a lot of things I'd never had before. I was not accustomed to discussing her. She wasn't some random fuck. I had balls big enough to admit she mattered to me.

Luther knew she would play a pivotal role in my life, but this felt way too much like an opening for a heart to heart, and I didn't do that bullshit.

We walked in silence for a few minutes. Away from the spotlight, the rest of property was blanketed in darkness, but from what I could see, Luther was still doing a bang-up job of maintaining it.

"You have a good system." It was the closest thing to a thank you he was going to get. He'd had his trap-house set up for almost nine years now. The place was wired to alert him when anyone entered.

Usually, he had scouts nearby to go in and wrangle the people up but, Cali wasn't just people, she was mine.

He staged it to look ransacked or abandoned, swapping

out the pictures on the wall to finish off the whole thing. It was morbid and fucking brilliant.

"I learned all I know from the master of debauchery. I'd be ass up without you, man." He rubbed the inverted cross tattooed on the back of his neck.

I shrugged it off. I'd known Luther since I was twelve, a year less than I'd known Cobra. Grimm, I'd known my whole fucking life. The four of us, along with Dahlia, the only bitch we let in our inner circle, grew up together. We were as close as four fucked up degenerates who hated emotional attachments could be.

I was the one who turned his odd hobby into a tool for profit. Money would always be a powerhouse in its own right.

I forged the connection between him and a buyer, and next thing next, business was booming. The house was just a way to lure stock. It had yet to fail.

When I suggested he initiate his niece into the family business, the motherfucker almost pissed his pants in joy. That was all the motivation he needed to off his sister and her sack of shit boyfriend the next day. It all worked out in end. Annie was eight now, and had been happily acing her role for four years. The kid was a chip off the old block.

"We sure as hell have come a long way. We're the best damn sinners and thieves in the Badlands now," he reminisced aloud with a huge ass smile on his face. He was right, and we'd continue to be so for years to come.

That was the thing about sick fucks like us—our repertoires were endless. We took pride in all we did and we had our own ideologies about how the world should be.

It was that belief and with their backing that paved the way for my future. I took over a motherfucking cult at the ripe age of sixteen. We didn't let where we were from or how we were raised cripple us. We were the rejected rebels who lived by our own set of rules.

The Badlands was considered hell on earth, and I had used it to build up an empire. Now it was time to ensure the motherfucker never crumbled.

Chapter Eleven

Calista

I'm not sure how long I petulantly sat with my back against the wall. With nothing to do but stew, I absentmindedly stroked the inverted cross I wore around my neck.

That fucking dickhead really left me chained up.

I couldn't confidently say I was safe considering Romero was my rescuer—*again*, as he so eloquently reminded me—but it was a fuck of a lot better than having my skin removed for who knows what reasons.

I didn't trust him as far as I could throw him, but I wanted to.

I wanted to be able to confide in him and know without a doubt that he would never betray me. At first, I had just wanted to be understood. I'd been lost when I met him, having no idea who I was. I'd spent so much time hiding her from everyone that even I started to forget.

Things were different now. The twisted maze I always ended up lost in had finally presented a new twist for me to travel. It was a twist that led me straight into the arms of the devil, entrapping me in a devious dance that never ended.

I was no longer a prisoner of my mind. I was now a prisoner of my addictions and obsessions. It was his entire fucking fault. He changed me. He gave me something I couldn't live without.

So much was up in the air between us but one thing would remain forever set in stone.

In the end it would always be him and I.

I jerked out of my dark thoughts when the heavy silence dilapidated into a barrage of sounds rolling in from different directions. Looking towards the house, I saw the robed followers of Romero. I had to have been pretty damn distracted to have missed their arrival.

As if conjuring him up, I spotted Romero walking towards me with the man who'd brought me here. The sky had a purplish-blue tint to it, signifying dawn. Where the hell had he been this whole time?

"Oh, look. She's still here," Romero jeered when they were just a few feet away.

I glowered at him, cursing him a thousand times over in my head.

The instant they reached me, Blue Eyes came to me with a bright grin on his face and quickly undid the chains around my wrists. "Sorry about your tooth, sweetheart," he said softly.

I heard the sincerity behind his words but I didn't understand why he was apologizing to me. He could have saved himself the breath.

I smiled back as sweetly as I could manage. "You can shove your apology up your ass."

His dark brows rose to his hairline and he chuckled.

"Well, I'm Luther, and it's nice to officially meet you too." He grinned and then moved out of the way so Romero could take his place.

I rubbed at my wrists where the shackles had been to get feeling back in my skin. Romero offered me his familiar inked hand, keeping his eyes on my face. It would have been stupid and petty to prolong the inevitable, I knew just as well as he did I was leaving with him, if I wanted to or not.

I placed my palm in his, and it was like linking two puzzle pieces back together.

"Can you walk?"

"Well, you sure as hell aren't carrying me," I snapped.

He smirked and pulled me up with a firm yet gentle tug, making sure I was steady on my feet before tucking me into his side. I didn't bother trying to be discreet as I breathed him in.

"Come on." His mouth tilted slightly up and he turned me in the direction of the house.

We walked in silence. Luther was on one side of me and Romero was on another.

I solely focused on placing one foot in front of the other. He was so clean and put together, while I was filthy. This seemed to be a common theme.

As we walked up a pathway passing the house, I looked to the driveway where four vehicles were parked. Three were large SUV's with a texture that reminded me of a chalkboard.

His followers stood outside them. I couldn't see their facial expressions due to the masks but I knew they were all looking at him.

Leaning against the rear passenger side door of Romero's

heavy duty jeep was a dark haired girl. I was positive she was the one who'd given me water.

When she saw us, she pushed off the jeep and lifted a hand to tuck a strand of her silky, coal black hair behind her ear. The bangle on her wrist shifted and revealed an inverted cross tattoo I was very familiar with. My mind buzzed with implications.

As we got closer, I saw one of her eyes was toffee brown and the other was pine green. Her hips had a bit of a curve to them and her tits were large and perky. She was pretty—more than pretty. I wouldn't touch her, but by the way she smiled at the man beside me, I knew he had.

"You sure about this, Dhal?" he asked when we reached her.

"What's she supposed to be sure about?" I dove right in the conversation, knowingly going into territorial bitch mode.

"She's coming with us," Romero answered.

"Why?"

She blinked at me, looking a little taken aback by my forwardness. From that alone and her shifty disposition, I knew she was the type who thought bad things about you but wouldn't dare say them aloud. What a perfectly clichéd match they would have been: the good girl and the bad boy.

"Change of scenery," she offered up with a small shrug, looking between me and Romero, who had yet to say anything.

"Right," I quipped. "Can we go?" I asked Romero, already heading for the passenger side of his vehicle. I wasn't up for being hospitable.

Pulling the door open, I glanced over my shoulder and saw Luther smiling so hard I was surprised his face didn't break.

Romero was watching me with an inexpressive look on

his face. He said something I couldn't hear and then made his way to the driver side.

I climbed in and shut the door. It felt so good to have something soft against my back after spending all night outside on the ground.

Dhal waved to Luther and then got in behind me as Romero took over the driver's seat.

"Tito was there somewhere," I said a few minutes after we'd been on the road.

"I got him out."

"K," I hummed, not really caring either way. After thinking it over, it didn't matter to me what happened to him. Sure, he'd saved my life once, but it wasn't because he was a stand-up guy; he'd had an agenda of his own.

I was over worrying about him. He was a grown ass man who could fend for himself.

.

I kept my mouth shut the rest of the ride, even though I had a million questions and certain things needed to be said. I wasn't going to open another can of worms when my mind was already crawling with parasites.

I needed a minute to think. I needed a minute to breathe. I hunkered down and shut my eyes. When Romero put his hand on my dirty knee, I felt a calm wash over me.

I was alive, free, and had a man who redefined what it meant to sin by my side. I was not going to waste time dwelling on what happened. My experience wasn't even that traumatic. I'd been through so much worse.

If I wanted answers, I had to make him inclined to give them to me. With that, my eyes popped open and I took his hand in mine, forcing our fingers to intertwine.

"I was going to wallow in self pity," I began. "But fuck

that. I have a list of demands, and don't interrupt me until I'm done, because I'm not allowed to interrupt you."

"I won't interrupt you. I'm not even going to let you start. You seem to have forgotten how our relationship works. I know what you want, and I know what you need.

"We're going to talk about what happened on the bridge and all the other fun shit that correlates with it. But first, you're going to get cleaned up. You're going to eat, and I'm going to give you something to relieve some stress—and I'm not talking about my dick. I know how much you love him, but don't worry, baby, you'll have a reunion soon.

"It's been two weeks and my balls are bluer than your eyes. I need to remind you what it feels like to be buried inside you. I'm going to fuck you so hard your tight little pussy will be left with a permanent imprint of me inside it. And then, you're going to have to ride my face so my tongue doesn't feel left out.

"Did I miss anything?"

I stared at him a full two minutes, the wetness between my thighs overriding all my other senses.

Dhal shifting in the backseat snapped me back to attention. He'd made me forget all about her while nailing every bullet on my list.

"Cocky fucking asshole," I muttered, clenching my legs tighter and glaring at him.

Chapter Twelve

Calista

The sun was high in the sky by the time we finally arrived at our destination.

I peered through the windshield as Romero and Dhal got out. The building in front of us had once been a hotel—a nice one, if the architectural details were anything to go off.

People were lingering in the courtyard, some lining the walkway, guarding it. I spotted a few more up on the roof. If anything, Romero was always secure.

What I found a little surprising was that not all of them were donning their masks. Quite a few had their whole face exposed.

My door popped open and Romero reached in to help me down.

He took my hand and started leading me towards the

entrance of what was once *La Monte Suites*, according to the weathered sign I could now see.

I faltered when I realized how easily I was going along with him into a strange place. I froze, leaving him with the option to either drag me or stop walking, too. "Is he in there?" I asked in reference to David, trying to pull my hand out of his.

He shared a look over my head with Dhal, some unspoken message passing between them. Before I had a chance to ask what the hell it was, he seized my upper forearm and swept my feet out from underneath me.

"What the fuck are you doing?" My sudden outburst snagged the attention of the few people nearby.

A fraction of a second before I hit the ground, he caught me. I was so close that if I puckered my lips I could kiss the ugly orange concrete.

He pulled me up to my feet, roughly, and forced me to continue forward. "Let me go," I snarled at him, trying to twist away. The effort was wasted. There was zero strength left in my reservoir. I was like a kitten trying to take on a Doberman.

I had no idea what he was doing, intended to do, or why he felt the need to suddenly drag me. I attempted to spin around mid-step and wound up being jerked so hard I bit my tongue, pissing me off even more.

"Don't fight me, Cali, you won't win," he warned, turning me so I could see his face. There was an edge to his voice but his dark eyes were telling me something different.

My brows furrowed as I looked at him. What the hell was he was up to now? Knowing he wouldn't—or couldn't—outright tell me, I had no choice but to play along.

"Okay," I harshly breathed out, before repeating myself a

little quieter. "Okay, please don't drag me anymore. I'll be... good." I almost gagged on the word.

"See, I knew you weren't as stupid as you looked," he whispered softly before glancing away, urging me forward albeit gently this time. It truly was déjà vu; the cocky fucker had said just as much the day he saved me from being a cannibal's meatloaf.

Dhal opened one of the glass doors ahead of us without being asked. As we passed, her gaze clashed with Romero's. I wanted to take her to the ground and crack her skull open. She hadn't really done anything, which meant she'd done enough to make me want her heart to cease beating.

I didn't bother trying to play therapist with myself and rationalize my crazy. I was out of my fucking head and perfectly fine with it.

The lobby of the hotel was open and airy. Bright light flooded in from the glass dome roof, and activity bustled all around.

Some people curiously stared. Most continued on with their business. They all wore the black robes I associated with the Savages.

"I'll catch up with you in a few," Romero directed to Dhal, steering me towards the elevators. She finger waved at him and walked off, giving me a small smile. It was not returned. Why the hell was she even here?

I stood beside him, not saying a word, not knowing where to start, and still playing my role until he told me otherwise. Even when we stepped inside the four walled box, I said nothing, and neither did he.

My ignoring him didn't stop him from staring at me, breathing down my neck, and twisting my insides up even more.

Was it wrong that I wanted him to slam my face into the wall and fuck me from behind?

I wanted him whether I was dirty, clean, pissed off, or happy. In sickness and in health, I always wanted him. I should have hated him—but even then, I would want him. I wondered how good a hate-fuck would feel.

When the old metal doors loudly squeaked open, I stepped out into a long, empty hallway and felt like I could breathe again. That was the longest elevator ride of my life. Romero exited behind me. "Come on."

I walked with him to one of the rooms. He opened the door without a key-card and moved aside so I could go in first. The room was bigger than I expected, with one magnificent single king sized bed, a sofa area, and a bathroom.

I moved farther in when I heard the door shut and a lock click. Taking a small breath, I turned around to face him, making sure there was space between us.

"What the hell was that?" I snapped, referring to the little incident in the lobby.

He laughed softly and closed the gap I'd made.

I frowned when my pulse quickened and crossed my arms. "You think this is funny?" I angled my body away from his, flattening my lips.

All traces of amusement fled his face as he tracked the subtle movement. "I just bought us a little more time."

"Time for what? And what happened on that bridge?"

"I left you on the bridge so I could have a steak dinner with David and Arlen's sister."

I felt my muscles quiver, but I wasn't aware I'd lunged at him until I was spun around and pushed against the wall.

He didn't let me utter a single syllable, smothering his hand firmly over my mouth.

"We're not doing this right now. You've had a whole two weeks to let everything build into irrational anger.

"You need to chill the fuck out and get yourself cleaned up before you go on a tirade." His voice was pure ice.

I hated him right then for knowing me so well.

I shoved his hand away from my mouth and stared back at him with flinty eyes. "*We* don't have to do anything. *You're* the one with a fuck ton of explaining to do."

"I don't have to explain a motherfucking thing. Answers are a privilege, not a right. I just told you I knew what you needed. Now trust me to give it to you."

"You can't expect me to trust you after you left me behind." There wasn't any spite in my voice, just a dull resignation. He gave me a look I couldn't decipher.

"I'd never leave you behind. Not when you have this."

He moved in closer until our noses were practically touching, and placed his hand on my thigh, tracing over the inverted cross he'd branded on me without my consent.

"We made a deal. You belong to me until you take your last breath, even if it's me who steals it from you."

He ignited my blood with that one soft caress. My body was a traitorous bitch when it came to him.

"Stop it," I hissed, knocking his hand away.

"Long two weeks?" he taunted, reaching out to finger a tangled strand of my hair. "Deal or no deal, you and I will never be through. You can't walk away from me any more than I can walk away from you."

"Funny, I recall you doing just that."

He regarded me closely with an inexpressive look on his face.

. . .

"You know you're important to me. And you know what happened on that bridge isn't anything like what it looked like. Appearances can be deceiving."

Of course, he was right about everything. I hated that I was lashing out at him when I rationally knew all that.

He stepped back and ran a hand over his mouth. "All the shit you need is in the bathroom."

I didn't bother objecting again. I desperately wanted to be clean; I could smell myself and it was a miracle he was able to breathe properly with the stench wafting between us. Besides, I still had an inkling of common sense and knew when to pick my battles.

I moved into the bathroom, closing the door and doing a quick sweep of the spacey area. It was just as nice as the room. There was a glass shower and a cast iron tub against the far wall.

On the vanity, I spotted a travel sized toothbrush and toothpaste of the same variety. I attacked it like a madwoman, physically cringing at my reflection.

I really did look like complete shit. Road-kill could have given me a run for my money. I was a few pounds away from being classed as emaciated. Dark circles formed half-moons beneath my eyes, and my hair was a knotted mess. I was grateful that the swelling in my face had gone down considerably.

I looked like something that lived in the bottom of a swamp. Brushing my teeth made me feel a little more human and effectively slayed my dragon breath.

I scooped up a washcloth and all the mini toiletries, carrying them to the shower. Once I had the water heated to near scalding, I stripped down, stepped in, and shut the door. I went to war straight away with my mess of locks, ripping long strands out in the process of untangling them.

The water washed away weeks of sweat, dirt, and all the hair I shaved off my body. I watched it all go down the drain in a chaotic swirl, taking a heavy weight off my shoulders with it.

This was exactly what I needed.

I was studying my flat stomach, thinking about how that conversation was going to go, when the shower door opened.

When he stepped inside in all his naked glory, I studied him like it was the first time I'd ever seen him naked. He was the most beautiful man I'd ever laid eyes on. The sinister dark aura that emanated from him only added to the allure.

He was so goddamn perfect it hurt. My resolve was crumbling to pieces and he hadn't had to do a thing but stand in front of me.

I pressed my palm against him just so I could feel his heartbeat. He lightly gripped my hand and slid it down his slickened chest, making me feel every hidden scar and solid ab. My eyes followed the path he made, faltering at the sight of his thick dick.

I swallowed and bit down on my lower lip, unable to look away and pretend it wasn't taking up a space between us.

His barbell had a compulsion of its own. I wanted to feel it on my tongue. I think my mouth watered.

Romero's smug voice was what finally broke me out of my trance. "It's a masterpiece, I know."

I looked up at him and felt my face flame as I realized I'd just been ogling his dick like it was the Holy Grail.

"You're so fucking arrogant."

"Not arrogant, just confident enough to know that every time I fuck you, I turn your world upside down." Shifting his grip to my wrist, he pushed me backward and used his knee to spread my legs apart, pinning my arms on either side of my head.

The hood of his piercing rubbed against my clit and a tiny gasp slipped through my lips.

I knew we needed to talk. He didn't deserve to be inside me but that's where I wanted him.

As if reading my mind, he let me go and gripped my jaw, dropping his lips to mine. I eagerly let his tongue through, sighing contentedly at the familiarity of it.

I wound my arms around the back of his neck. His hands grabbed my ass. He stole every breath I took as he devoured my mouth, nipping my lower lip and roughly kneading my globes. His hard cock pressed into my lower stomach, hotter than the water coming down on us. An over-whelming ache only he could elicit burned between my thighs.

"Fuck me," I breathed. "Hard."

He didn't have to be told twice. He lifted me up locked my legs around his waist,

"Goddamn, Cali. My dick isn't supposed to be anywhere near your pussy right now.

The shit you do to me," he growled, pushing into me without a second's hesitation.

I sucked in a sharp breath and held onto his shoulders. His rough intrusion stung, and I could feel the metal barbell against my walls as they stretched to accommodate his size. He didn't wait for me to fully adjust.

He cursed beneath his breath and dug his fingers into my flesh, setting a brutal pace as he fucked me against the tiled wall. Wet skin met wet skin, mixing with the sound of running water and my unrestrained moans.

My hands went everywhere, feeling the muscles in his arms, firm and solid as he effortlessly held me up, thrusting with no mercy. I let my fingertips travel over every inch of his beautifully inked skin that I could reach before threading my fingers through his dark hair, making him more than just a memory.

"Harder," I moaned, trying to bring him closer.

He pulled out but didn't let me go. I groaned at the loss of him.

Without turning off the water, he stepped out of the shower and carried me dripping wet to the bed, dropping me right in the middle.

He positioned himself between my legs and stared down at me. His dark, unreadable gaze made my breath hitch in my chest.

I focused on a bead of water running down his chest. I didn't know if I'd ever be able to handle him looking right through me. He could see beyond my veil to the woman I'd just started to accept. He'd known who I was long before I did.

"Look at me." His voice compelled me to obey. In the time it took my eyes to find his, he had my legs hooked over his forearms, slamming back into me with no warning.

Air dispersed from my lungs on a scream, my hands immediately going to his shoulders where my nails burrowed into skin.

He snatched them off, pinning them down on either side of my head as he pounded into me.

"Let me go!" I meant for it to sound assertive and strong but it came out as a breathy moan.

"No." He flashed me a wicked grin. I opened my mouth to respond and he lurched down, shoving his tongue inside to intertwine with mine, grinding against me.

I curled my fingers into fists, the nails digging in so deep they started piercing the skin. When he moved his mouth to my neck and bit, my pussy clenched around his dick.

Oh my god. I lifted my hips to take him deeper and

wrapped my legs around his ass. He didn't let me go, not once, and every time I shut my eyes or attempted to look away, he thrust hard enough to make me bleed and his grip on my wrists got a little tighter.

His expression stayed the same.

His breathing slightly changing was the only thing that confirmed he was affected by what we were doing. I felt exposed, like every part of me was on display.

He knew exactly what he was doing. He knew where to bite, where to bruise, and the perfect spot to hit inside me so I would come apart around him. He continually brought me right to the edge and then eased off, letting the feeling slip away.

He used our bodies as a gateway to re-establish our physical connection. I felt pleasurable pressure mounting inside me, starting right at my core.

"Rome." I moaned his name for the hundredth time.

"Beg," he bit out, drilling into me and hitting my G-spot.

"Please," I whimpered as my legs numbly slipped from around him and fell limply to the side.

"That's not good enough. Beg me to let you come, Cali. Tell me how badly you want to nut all over my dick."

Triggering a mental response, desperate words poured from my mouth.

"I want it so fucking badly, please let me come, I'm begging you...Rome."

He grinned down at me deviously, snaked a hand between us, and began rolling my clit, picking up his pace, fucking me so hard I thought the bed would break.

"Come for me, baby," he demanded in a low voice. The sentence hadn't even fully fallen from his lips before my body was arching into his and I came screaming his name, heat searing through my limbs. He continued rocking inside me, finding his own release as I trembled beneath him.

My shallow breaths and running water were the only sounds in the room. My heartbeat echoed in my ears.

He pulled out and rolled onto his back, taking me with him. With my head on his damp chest his arms caged me in an almost suffocating embrace. He didn't have to say a word.

I knew some part of him needed this just as much as I did. He placed a kiss to the top of my wet head.

"What did you mean when you said you bought us more time?" I found myself asking after an elongated silence persisted.

His fingers ran up down my arm, leaving goose-bumps in their wake.

"Someone told David I had you. He thought I was going to hand you over. I had to make him believe it was true. And in the lobby, I needed to make it look like I was bringing you in against your will. If someone runs to tell him I've got you back, it helps me narrow down my rat. I know the names of every acolyte here. After tomorrow though, it won't matter. He'll know you're mine."

"What happens tomorrow?" I smothered a yawn and curled further into his warmth.

"Everything changes," he answered quietly.

Chapter Thirteen

Calista

He was gone when I woke up.

I lay there for a minute, letting the events of the past two weeks and everything leading up to them flicker through my mind.

Beneath me, the comforter was still damp, and the setting sun cast a warm, hazy glow inside the suite.

I felt more rested than I had since everything went to shit, apart from the lingering soreness between my legs and the bruises on my wrists.

I still had that sick feeling in the pit of my stomach, the one that made me long to hurt someone.

Across the room, a table lamp was on. Beside it was a small pile of clothes that hadn't been there before. Not knowing where Romero was or when he was coming back, I left the comfort of the bed behind for another shower.

I combed out my hair and lathered on an entire little bottle of peppermint lotion before getting dressed.

The pants looked like a black pair of skinny jeans but were really some type of stretchy material. They were a perfect fit. Of course, Romero didn't bring me any goddamn underwear or a bra, so fortunately, the tank top was the same material and snuggly hugged the girls.

After pulling on a pair of socks, I wandered into the room with a much clearer mind to find I'd been locked in.

It wasn't until I looked down that I saw why Romero didn't use a keycard to get in. The lock had been flipped around.

"Asshole." I smacked the door and walked to the window.

I stood there for a good ten minutes trying to decide what to do next, thinking over what Romero had told me. Who the hell would tell David he had me, and why? And why would he want me back?

I was cast out and left to die. It had been four years ago, but it all felt fresh. I remembered the stolen innocence and the things they did to me, all for the benefit of getting their dicks wet or pussies eaten. I would never forget that it was my father who made me drop to my knees or spread my legs on command, always taking his turn last.

I wondered what little girl had replaced me and how many of the others were impregnated by an uncle, cousin, or sibling.

The Order needed to be annihilated.

I couldn't change my past, but their blood staining my hands would still make me feel better. I wanted to do it nice and slow, draw it out and prolong their suffering as they did to me. I wanted them on their knees, begging for mercy as death lingered in the shadows ready to drag them purgatory.

Hell was too much of a paradise for these kinds of people.

We'd already taken out two of the Bishops, so that left six —David included—and when they fell, their delegates would follow.

"Pixie."

At the sound of his voice, I spun around. He stepped in, holding a pair of boots and a metal thermos, shutting the door with his shoulder.

His hair was back in its perfect combed-back style. He was wearing a navy T-shirt that hugged him in the best way possible, and dark jeans.

He perused me from head to toe. "You look good."

I scoffed in the back of my throat. "Flattery will get you nowhere with me."

"Cali, I just had my dick buried in you for over an hour. I don't need flattery to get anything from you."

I scrubbed a hand over my face and a heavy sigh released from my lungs. "Is that all you want from me? Because we did make a deal, and you have yet to hold up your side of it."

He sat the boots and thermos down on a chair and came to stand in front of me. His palm cupped the back of my head, and he brought his mouth to mine.

The kiss was rough and possessive, telling me I belonged to him regardless of whether I consented or not.

He pulled away but kept his hand on the back of my head. "I could give you words of bullshit reassurance, but words fade away and are often empty. You're just going have to sit down and enjoy the ride. Eventually, you'll see what I want you to.

"And I always uphold my end of a deal. David will be handled. How many times do I have to tell you that?"

"You'll have to explain how exactly, because did you or did you not leave me behind on a bridge to potentially die? And isn't David still alive after you were right in front of him?" I braced my palms on his chest and glared up at him.

"If I fucking wanted you dead, I wouldn't set up a big elaborate show for it, I wouldn't be doing everything I can to make sure your future is secure, and I damn sure wouldn't be standing here right now."

His words were coated in truth. I believed him when he said he didn't want me dead.

"But you hugged him. I saw you. You walked away without looking back once…For steak dinner—your words, not mine."

"That was fucking sarcasm. Yes, I left you. I fucking walked away from you, but I would go to the ends of this earth to ensure you stayed by my side. You're not asking the right questions. I don't do shit on a whim, and I don't do shit for no reason." He grabbed my hands and pulled me closer, letting go to link his arms above my ass. "I'm the only motherfucker on this planet that would never abandon you."

Something twisted inside me. I softly swallowed and looked up at him, unable to decipher what he was feeling. I heard his words, but I didn't trust them.

In the end, he did find me, and he did take me with him, but the damage had already been done.

His onyx hues roamed over my face, and then he stepped away, walking over to the chair. "We're on a timetable and I need you to be relaxed for the conversation we need to have. So shut the fuck up, stop thinking, and put these on."

He thrust the boots at me.

"Has anyone ever told you you're an asshole?" I snapped, taking the shoes and walking to the bed to put them on.

"It's known to be one of my finer qualities."

"And cocky."

"I have a big dick, I look good, and I have power. I'm not cocky, baby. I'm the devil, and you love it."

I tried to suppress the laughter in my chest, failing miserably. "I can't deal with you. You're fucking impossible."

As soon as I had both knee-length boots on, the thermos was practically shoved in my face.

"Drink this. It will fill you up for a minute, and it has protein and shit in it."

I took it without question, biting down on my inner cheek to hold back a smile.

His mouth had no filter.

Chapter Fourteen

Romero

All I felt like doing was burying myself between her thighs. I wanted her to scream my name until she lost her voice and could no longer feel her legs.

But I had the rest of her life for that. Right now, just being beside her was enough for me. It was soothing, almost.

"What are you thinking?" I asked without looking over.

She didn't bother to, either, lost in the world inside her head, a world I loved to manipulate.

"That I really have no fucking clue about your past, and you know all about mine," she responded somberly after taking a drink. I bit back a laugh.

"That's not exactly true." I didn't elaborate on my answer; didn't need to. She knew more about me than almost any woman ever had. I only knew her better than she knew herself because she was so lost when I first found her. She wasn't now, though.

My beautiful girl no longer wanted to fight her demons, she wanted to embrace them. Tito had all but told me that, but I didn't believe him.

She'd struggled with it before, warring with herself about who she was. I knew there would still be ups and downs to come.

Cali was, if nothing else, vexing and an unstable pain in the ass, but I was prepared to deal with it.

I bypassed the elevators and led her down the stairs. She didn't question why, she just accepted it. On some subconscious level, I knew I had her trust. I also knew she wouldn't outright admit it, not when she herself wasn't aware.

Sometimes I wanted to warn her away, tell her to run as far from me as she could. A good man would have. Lucky for me, I wasn't classified as one of those and had no fucking desire to be.

It was too late now anyway. Inside these walls we were in a fragile bubble; outside, anarchy was already reigning in the streets. We'd be in the fray soon enough. We were already half-way through the day and I had so much fucking shit left to do, too many moves left to make.

I had to give her some of my time, though. I'd just gotten her back, and in her condition the last thing I needed was her questioning my loyalty to her.

Had she been any other woman, I'd have snapped her neck or slit her throat to spare myself this emotional ping-pong bullshit.

"How did you know that guy?" Her soft voice pulled me back to the present.

I instantly knew who the 'guy' was she was asking me about. "I grew up with him. He was brought to my camp when I was twelve. He's a skinner. Skin-farming is his livelihood. He make goods from human flesh; leather exclusives… belts, wallets."

"Did you just say it's his livelihood?"

"His and a good amount of others. The mayor makes it worthwhile." From the corner of my eye, I saw her brows furrow.

"The mayor of The Kingdom—Centriole—*pays* people in the Badlands for human skin?"

"Not people. Luther. And he isn't as powerful as he makes himself out to be." I knew my answer only added to her never-ending list of questions.

She was struggling to rein everything in, trying to process it all. I could've helped her, but damn if I didn't love watching the gears turn in her pretty little head. Cali did stupid shit but she was truly fucking brilliant.

It was only a matter of time before all the things she'd been naively ignoring gave her some answers to what she wanted to know. Only some, though. It was the unanswered questions that were better for her to wonder about and draw her own conclusions.

She finally glanced at me and took her time, openly staring at me and using the metal hand rail to guide her along. I would never get tired of that. She looked at me and saw the beast beneath the surface, and she'd never run.

If she did, I'd chase her. It wouldn't matter how fast she ran, I was faster.

Men like me didn't get women like her, the kind of women who embraced our every flaw, let us freely sin, and never tried to change us.

The last time I was given anything that held significant value was on my tenth birthday. My mother gave me the tactical knife I always carried with me. Exactly a week later, I used that very knife to sever her lifeline.

I believed this was a twist of fate. The God of Death herself made sure I would have a queen to my king. An angel that was exiled and stripped of her wings before she ever got the chance to fly. That had to be why I just so happened to be in the woods the day Cali dramatically rolled down that fucking hill. She never did anything half-assed.

All the men in her life had failed to protect her. They never realized they had something as rare as gold in the palms of their hands. Instead, they shoved her in a bottomless sink-hole to wither away. Now, I got to watch her rise from the ashes like a goddamn phoenix.

She was a dark rose finally learning how to wield the wicked thorns she'd been forced to grow.

She was everything, and she was fucking mine. I didn't need a deal to do what was right for once. I was going to tear apart every motherfucker that hurt her.

Her shameful truths became my vengeance. Destroying The Order would never be her burden to carry alone.

I wouldn't lose sleep over the things I planned to do. I knew the truth about myself. I chose to be who I was without any regrets. I was worse than fabled demons, the sickest kind of monster. I wasn't ashamed to admit it. Soon enough, she'd learn that I was more fucked up than even *she* could imagine.

And she was perfect for me in every sense of the word. Her dark soul was always meant to be mine. It was something to possess and to cherish. A newfound madness.

Chapter Fifteen

Calista

He held a solid steel door open for me, and I stepped through.

I wanted to go back into the room and just sit down so I could think for a minute. Every time I thought my head was clear, Romero muddled it up again. Sometimes, I thought he did it on purpose. One second, I felt like I knew him just as well as he knew me. The next I realized how much I still didn't know at all.

"Where are we going?" I finally asked, needing to break the silence that had settled between us and focus on something other than the chaos growing louder in my head.

"Right here." He gestured to a door on our immediate right.

We were on the first floor of the hotel, in a long empty hall. I gave him a wary look. "What's in there?"

He took the thermos from me and sat it on the floor. "You can go in and find out," he taunted.

Rolling my eyes, I pushed past him and walked through the swinging door, right into a large laundry room.

My gaze immediately went to the bitch responsible for knocking my tooth out. She was in perfect health, aside from her arms being secured around a thick pipe running from the floor to the ceiling. There was a metal lip refractor wedged in her mouth.

A jolt of excitement ran down my spine.

"Aw, Rome." I looked over my shoulder and gave him a genuine soft smile. The smirk I adored appeared in response.

"I figured this would help you relax."

I didn't need a lengthy explanation. I knew why she was here.

He would have asked who'd hurt me, and sometime between me being unchained at the skin-farm and brought inside the hotel, she was delivered.

"Come on, pretty girl." He snagged my hand and walked me towards the blonde, who, to her credit, tried not to show she was afraid. Tried and failed. Her fear hung in the air.

He positioned me in front of him just a few feet away. Using one hand, he gripped my waist and pulled me backward to mold against him. The other moved my hair to one side so he could rest his chin on my shoulder.

"I wanted you to relax, relieve some stress." He placed a soft kiss on my neck. I angled my head to give him better access that he didn't hesitate to take.

"Ah," I hissed when he bit down, slightly jerking from the sting. He soothed it with his tongue, lightly swirling it over the bite mark.

His solid body was a pillar of strength behind me. I could feel his hard dick pressing into my ass. "I know it's been a while, so I just wanted to remind you, we kill slowly. We draw their pain out and watch them break. I want you to look her in the eyes as she suffers."

I audibly swallowed, pulling in a lungful of air and then quietly releasing it. In other words, don't bash her head in using the pole.

"I got it," I confirmed, turning my head to kiss his cheek.

"Make her bleed, baby."

My grin was unrestrained as I stepped forward. I could feel his eyes watching my every move. The blonde's throat bobbed and her eyes slightly widened. Funny, she didn't look so entitled anymore.

I knelt down and traced my fingers around the dental tool forcing her mouth to stay open. "You're always so prepared. Where did you get this?" I asked, looking over my shoulder.

"I usually always have one with my tools; I've used it for other purposes." He proudly grinned, making me laugh.

"Is that how you know Dhal?" I didn't intend to ask him about her that way, but what was done was done. It slipped out. We'd never had that talk. Obviously, he had a past, and I wasn't bothered by that at all.

I honestly wanted to line some of the girls up and high five them for giving my man experience, but from what I did know, the majority of them were dead, so that wasn't going to happen. I was curious about her, though, and I wanted to kill her, but that wasn't important.

"Ah, no," he chuckled. "Dhal didn't like things that rough."

I stared back at the retractor. He always did that, worded things a certain way. It wasn't by accident that he just confessed to fucking her. Rome was smarter than that.

"You've been holding out on me? You don't play with me like that," I fake pouted.

where a thin strip of fleshy gum came away with it. Romero held her head through the whole ordeal.

Her voice had turned hoarse, and her sobs were dry, all the tears spilled from their ducts. After pulling out another two teeth at random, my wrist was way beyond the point of starting to ache. Furthermore, snot was running from her nose; there was saliva and blood all down the front of her and on my hands. It was disgusting.

With a sigh, I tossed the pliers down and stood up. "I'm getting bored and my wrist hurts," I sighed, looking for something to wipe my hands off on.

Romero let the blonde's head go and whipped a dark green cloth out of his front pocket, pressing it into my hands.

He then wordlessly turned around and pulled a familiar knife from his back pocket.

"I'll finish it," he said, taking up my prior position. Without preamble, the tip of the blade met her gums and began to dig in. Suddenly finding her voice, she squealed like a pig being slaughtered. Romero held a handful of her hair to keep her head still.

Neither of us was affected by her sobs.

The sounds she made while choking on blood were an indication that Romero was doing something right. He cut his way into the whole top portion of her mouth, mutilating the gums in a way that the pliers never could.

I watched without commentary. This woman skinned people alive. In my opinion, what we were doing was child's play, mercy she didn't deserve. I even felt a little vigilante.

Rome stopped after he finished the bottom, accepting his cloth back to wipe off his own hands and the knife.

Her mouth looked like it had been put through a paper shredder.

She'd passed out from the pain when he started on the right portion of her gums.

Romero dropped his cloth to the floor and then nodded his head toward the door.

"Why are you leaving her alive?" I asked, walking towards the exit.

"I'm letting her suffer for a little bit. I'll off her in the morning."

I nodded and entered back into the hall, heading straight for the dark stairwell. I felt better, more clear-headed. The violence gave me peace.

Romero grabbed my hand and linked our fingers together. I was half-way up the first set of stairs, walking slightly ahead of him when I abruptly stopped and turned around. I smiled happily at him.

"Thank you for that."

He let go of my hand and cupped my chin, His soulless eyes held mine, drowning me in their endless depths.

"Don't ever thank me for shit like that.

I told you, you're mine, and that makes me yours. It's my job to handle anyone who hurts or disrespects you."

I rolled my lips together and placed my hand over his. Rising on my tiptoes, I brought our mouths together, and he instantly responded, letting my tongue through to explore.

Cupping the back of his neck, I nipped at his lower lip, letting out a small gasp when without warning he forced me to sit down on the stairs. I giggled like a fucking girl when he roughly started tugging my pants down.

"Ugh, what are you doing to me?" I groaned.

"I haven't done anything yet." He reared back and flashed me a devious smile. "I'm going to make you come in my mouth, and then I'm going to fuck you in this stairwell."

"Can you let me pretend to be mad at you for five minutes?"

"No." He removed everything in his way before placing his hands on my knees, spreading my legs so far apart it burned.

His eyes met mine, and then he was burying his face between my thighs. He dragged his tongue from back to front, circling it around my clit. I lost count of how many times he did that before plunging it inside me.

"Your pussy is a fucking narcotic," he growled, hooking my legs over his shoulders, holding them in place with his hands clamped around my thighs.

"Fuck, Rome," I moaned and grabbed the back of his neck, bucking my hips uncontrollably against his face while trying to push his tongue deeper.

He slightly lifted away with a soft chuckle, his warm breath fanning over my sensitive nub a second before his mouth closed around it and two fingers slipped inside me. His teeth gently bit down. I cursed and let his hair go to grab his shoulders as an orgasm came rushing in out of nowhere.

He continued to pump his digits in and out of my pussy, massaging my clit with his mouth as I writhed against him.

I was still trying to come down when he rose up, sucked his fingers into his mouth, and then partially slid down his jeans.

Grasping his dick with one hand, he slid it up and down my slit, coating the head in my arousal before driving into me.

"God," I half moaned, half whimpered.

"Romero," he arrogantly corrected, pulling all the way out and pushing back in, burying himself to the hilt. He angled me so that half my ass was hanging off the step.

Bending my knees towards my chest, in true Romero fashion, he fucked me ruthlessly.

The marble stairs painfully dug into my back. He was so deep it felt like he was trying to fuse us together. It hurt in the best way possible.

"Watch us, baby. Watch how my dick slides in and out of your pussy."

I managed to glance down, watching his slick cock slip in and out of me. The sound of skin slapping skin and my screams of pleasure echoed up the empty stairwell. His barbell repeatedly met my G-spot.

Through my euphoric, lusty haze, I felt him watching my every reaction in his intense analyzing way. I fisted his shirt and pulled him closer, bringing his lips to mine.

He greedily swallowed my obnoxious sounds. I could taste myself on his tongue, turning me on more than I already was.

In the recess of my mind, I knew I was entirely too hooked on him.

It wasn't healthy but I didn't give a fuck. Nothing else mattered to me when we were killing or fucking, and with us, they always went hand and hand. A psychologist would have had a field day.

I yelped when he dropped my right leg to wrap his hand around my throat, and the back of my head hit the step, forcing my body into an awkward arch.

My mouth opened but only a cough came out as he pressed down on my windpipe.

"Tell me you're mine," he demanded in a level tone, pressing down a little harder, continuing to drill into me.

My stomach dipped. Had I ever admitted that aloud before? I couldn't remember. I wasn't ready to vocalize that or tell him he was everything to me, that he was everything I ever wanted. He was the oxygen in my blood, a dangerous toxin I would willingly inhale over and over again so I could feel alive.

Some would claim this made me weak, but what the fuck did I care what people thought of me? I didn't. I never would again. I had tunnel vision and Romero was my glitter in the dark.

He watched me struggling for air and fighting to deny him. I wanted to glare, but my eyes started to water. I could feel my heart beating against my ribcage. Blood roared in my ears.

"I...I'm yours," I croaked, just barely.

"Good girl," he soughed, leaning down to bite my lip so hard he drew blood.

"Now you're either going to come, or you're going to pass out. I'm not letting you breathe until your pussy is clenching around my dick."

I may have whimpered, earning another devious grin from him. I focused on the feeling of him moving inside me, lifting my hips as best I could.

The pressure built at a dizzying speed as black dots danced across my line of vision.

My fucking chest burned with every attempt I made to drag air in, a throbbing started in the back of my head.

He lurched down and licked the tears that had broken free from my cheeks, kissing along my jaw-line. "Beautiful," he breathed in my ear as he bottomed out. Heat spread up my spine, pervading through my core.

Just when I thought he was truly going to choke me out he let go I came apart around him with a soundless scream, my mind going blank and my vision turning a fuzzy black as I dragged air into my desperate lungs.

Chapter Sixteen

Calista

I could feel the soft mattress beneath me, and my pants had been replaced with what felt like boxers.

My head hurt, my throat ached, and my body felt like it had been hit by a car.

"Fuck," I groaned, rolling to my belly.

"Uh, I think you've done enough fuckin," a familiar voice drawled.

Arlen?

I momentarily forgot all about my pain and whipped my head around. My blue eyes met with a pair of cognac ones at the foot of the bed.

I immediately sensed something was different about her, knowing the bruises spread across her once flawless bronze skin came with a story.

Biting back my questions, I chose to concentrate on the fact that she was right in front of me. I hadn't realized how much I'd missed her presence or had even liked her until that exact moment. I felt a little more weight lift off my shoulders knowing she was alive.

"I was so worried about you," she exhaled, rushing forward and engulfing me in her arms.

I fought the urge to shove her away. I didn't do touchy-feely unless it was Romero, but I awkwardly patted her back so I didn't come off as a total bitch. She smelled freshly showered. Her chocolate hair was piled on her head in a messy bun.

"How long have you been here?" I asked, gently pushing her backward.

"Grimm brought me a few hours ago. I can't go anywhere without that damn man followin me. He stood outside the bathroom the entire time I showered and then locked me in the room," she growled.

So they were locking her away too? Huh.

I studied her various tattoos, unsure what to say next. We hadn't known each other long, but she was one of the only women I'd allowed myself to get close to. I guess I considered her a friend.

"You look thoroughly fucked. Y'all certainly didn't waste time goin back to your kinky ways." She made a hand motion around her throat.

"I think I need to see what you do." Pushing the comforter away from my legs, I slowly stood and walked into the bathroom.

"Holy shit," I muttered when I saw my reflection.

My bottom lip was slightly swollen, my hair a mess, and there was an obvious hand shaped bruise on my neck that matched the ones on my wrists.

Lifting my tank top, I saw there was another from the stairs digging into my back. I was in fact wearing a pair of plaid boxer shorts rolled up at the top. Seeing as Romero was usually commando, I sincerely hoped these were his retro just-in-case drawers and not some random man's dick huggers.

I picked up the comb I used earlier and smiled at myself, combing out my blonde locks.

"Where is Romero?" I called out and asked.

"Not sure, he said he'd be back and not to upset you." She snorted as if the possibility of that happening was absurd.

I had just sat the comb down when I heard another familiar voice.

"Room service!" Cobra yelled enthusiastically.

I practically levitated out of the bathroom, taking note of his blue sling and his freshly trimmed carrot head.

I beamed at him and gave a little wave.

"Girl, the fuck was that? Get over here and hug me," he demanded good-naturedly.

I slipped past the food cart he'd wheeled in and reluctantly let him give me a one-armed hug.

"Thank fuck you jumped off that bridge. If anything happened to you, I'd be dead," he admonished.

I didn't think Romero would take out a man he considered his brother because of me, and I hadn't actually jumped, but I wasn't going to point that out.

"Cali." A timid voice spoke from the open doorway. I looked past Cobra to see Jinx standing with her hands nervously clasped at her waist.

Clearly, this was a night of reunions. Yay me.

"Go head and do the girly thing. We'll catch up later, but make sure you eat every bite. You got this waif thing going on right now. You're already too skinny and your ass is shrinking. I gotta go talk to Rome." The smile he gave me reached his silver eyes and I couldn't help but return it. I had no anger for him; I was glad he was alive.

He gave Jinx as wide a berth as he could, pulling the door shut behind him.

"Babe," she breathed, rushing at me.

Great, another one, I thought as she flung her arms around my entire upper body, almost knocking me down.

I allowed it for a total of three seconds before stepping away. She looked as healthy as could be. Her jade eyes were bright and there wasn't a mark on her dark skin. A heavy frown settled on her face as she looked me over. "Calista," she murmured. "What the hell has he done to you?"

Arlen made a sound in her throat that sounded suspiciously like a laugh turned into a cough. I refrained from rolling my eyes.

Two people had obviously seen them and hadn't responded by looking at me like they just found out that I killed puppies for fun.

I followed Arlen's lead and cleared my throat.

"He fucked me really hard, Jinx." I said slowly.

"And...you let him do this to you? You *like* this?" Her tone was incredulous. I saw the heavy judgment in her eyes and I didn't appreciate it. She'd likely faint if I told her murder and torture made me wet.

I wasn't sure how to answer her questions. It wasn't like I could stop him, and as for liking it, hell yes. I wanted more. I was a greedy pain slut when it came to him. My body felt like it had gone through the wringer and I was still craving more.

"I love it," I shrugged, wheeling the food cart over to the bed so I could sit down.

I didn't care if she liked it or not, I was done hiding who I was to spare someone's sensitivities.

"You said you were her friend," Arlen cut in when Jinx continued staring at me with a frown.

"I *am* her friend, which is exactly why I can pass judgment," Jinx snapped.

"Well, I'm her friend now, too, and you don't see me being a judgmental cunt. Let her get off however she sees fit," Arlen retorted. "As long as she's okay with it, you should be too. We both know Romero wouldn't legit fuck her to death. Not literally," she added as an afterthought.

I bit my cheek to stop from laughing as they eyed one another with open disdain.

"Girls, no catfights," I interjected, lifting the silver lid off my platter.

I was so hungry I didn't even care what kind of meat was in the soup in front of me.

I dug in with vigor. It tasted amazing and it was warm. Arlen took a seat on the window ledge and Jinx sat in the chair.

"So what's it like out there?" I waved my hand, indicating outside.

"It's full of your boyfriend's cult members. And Tito's here, if you were wondering," Jinx answered, disapproval heavy in her tone. From the corner of my eye, I saw Arlen shoot daggers at her.

"I wasn't wondering, actually. Whatever he got himself into with the Savages started far before I came along." I dropped my spoon and reached for my bottle of water, feeling the sudden need to clarify something she'd just said. "Romero is more than my boyfriend. He's my soul."

"You mean soul-mate?"

"No, he's my soul."

Jinx eyed me like I'd officially lost the plot.

Arlen grinned at me, understanding my sentiment perfectly, maybe because she was there the day I made my deal with him. More than likely, it was because Arlen fit right in without trying.

"Right," Jinx drew out. "So what's the plan? We have to get away, you know that, right? We can't be sitting ducks while we wait for Romero and his band of merry men or army of misfits to decide what they're going to do with us. And the sooner we go, the better. It's getting crazy out there."

"Misfits? Is that what they're calling them these days?" I took another bite of soup and met her gaze head on. Hers was frustrated, mine was glacial. I couldn't pinpoint why I suddenly felt so defensive over Romero's followers, but hearing her so openly judge them pissed me off. They were part of Rome's life and that made them a part of mine. Not to mention, she might as well have been talking about me.

"Cali isn't going to leave Romero. She's fuckin in love with him," Arlen scoffed.

What? "Um, no I'm not."

Jinx didn't hear me. She was on her feet raving.

Me and Arlen shared a look.

We both knew there was no getting out of here, not without heavy planning. And where the hell would we even go? Three women out on their own in the Badlands with no goods to sell except their bodies and zero funds, it was pitifully comical.

I'd just survived two weeks and that was begrudgingly with Tito's help. I didn't want to struggle for survival day in and day out. And then there was the whole pregnancy detail I hadn't breathed a word about. I'd be far safer in the lion's den.

"We have to leave," Jinx finished with a huff. I wondered if she knew she'd just said that fifteen times in ten minutes.

"Leavin here would be a fuckin suicide mission," Arlen retorted. "I saw the shit just about to hit the fan as Grimm was bringin me here. It's safer for us under the Savages' protection. And you know she can't go for obvious reasons, so I don't really understand you suggestin she do."

I agreed, but I wasn't going to try and reason with her; that would be pointless, so I kept it simple. "I can't. Even more so, I don't want to."

"Callista. Yes, you can." She ignored the last part of my sentence completely.

"She isn't going anywhere."

Shit.

"Shit," Arlen echoed my thought aloud.

Romero strolled into the room followed by Grimm, Cobra, and a guy I'd never seen before.

He was a little shorter than Rome, well built, had a head full of brown hair and the brightest pair of green eyes I'd ever seen.

Grimm's dark orbs fixed on my face and his mouth tilted up on one side, offering me the closest thing to a smile I'd get. I quickly returned it just as Jinx did the stupidest thing she could've done.

She whirled around, glaring at Romero, and stepped over the line I considered personal space. "You can't keep her here like some hostage. What do you even want her for? Who do you think—"

The rest of her sentence was cut off with a loud and painful yelp. Romero lifted her up by the throat and slammed her back into the wall.

"I don't know who the fuck you think I am, but if you

ever talk to me like that again, it'll be the last thing you do. Consider this your only warning, courtesy of Cali."

Jinx made a keening sound and scratched at his hands. I slowly rose from the bed, earning a slight headshake from Grimm, warning me not to intervene.

"Cali's a queen. You're nothing but a hole for Tito to dump his come in. Judgmental bitches like you don't deserve to breathe the same air as her. Just know from this point on that she'll always be well fed, she'll always be safe, and she'll always be thoroughly well fucked for the rest of her life." He tossed her across the room like she weighed nothing; she nearly landed in the hall with a small sob.

"Lock her up," he ordered.

"I got it," the brown haired man volunteered, striding right back out of the room.

"Brat," Grimm called to Arlen.

She went to him without rebuttal, squeezing my hand on her way past.

As soon as they were gone and the door shut with Cobra following behind them, Romero turned to me. "You don't love me?" His voice was as tense as his muscles. The question sounded like a threat, and I wasn't expecting him to ask it.

It was the first time I could say I'd ever been tongue tied. I wish I could rewind time and take it back.

I couldn't just split open my chest and spill my guts. Not when it came to discussing that. Nothing had ever scared me more than what I felt for him. I wanted to give him everything but I knew if he abused it or didn't feel the same, it wouldn't just crush me; it would severe my lifeline.

But, I wasn't going to avoid the herd of elephants in the room any longer. I once wished I could be with him without having to pretend otherwise, and now I could. It was freeing, liberating, to think of myself and what I wanted without worrying about betraying someone.

"You don't trust me. I don't trust you, not fully. I know you'll keep me safe, fed, and *thoroughly* well fucked," I teased to lighten the mood, "But I don't know if you have some hidden agenda to screw me over."

He studied me like the idea of what I was saying was preposterous.

"You left me to 'die' on a bridge and walked off with David without looking back."

"Cali, I'm not good at heart to hearts and we really need to get past this little hang-up so we can focus on what we're going to do next. I need you to use your fucking head and put two and two together.

"Why would I leave you and my brother together if I wanted you dead? He was in that car with you. He was shot. None of that was supposed to happen. That situation could have gone so much fucking worse. I could have lost both of you. And I know I hurt you, but there wasn't anything else I could do.

"I tried to protect you and fucking failed. I was trying to stop David from getting you back." He shifted and then straightened to his full height, staring down at me with cold eyes.

"I fucking hate that I had to walk away. I apologize for not telling you what was going on. I don't apologize for a single thing I've done."

Swallowing, I tipped my head back and let out a breath I hadn't realized I was holding. Romero Deville just apologized—sort of. Where was the confetti? I looked back at him and met his penetrating gaze head on.

"You didn't fail because he doesn't have me, and now I'm even more…" I trailed off. How did you tell someone you no longer gave a shit about right and wrong? I wondered if he knew about the chaos festering inside me or the venom running through my veins that ached to be released.

Turns out, I didn't have to question any of it. I should have known better. This was Romero I was dealing with. He was the reason I was strong as I was. When I'd been down, he forced me to get up.

I learned to face my past the day he locked me in a room with a bishop and handed me a knife.

He'd pushed me towards the darkness from the very beginning, patiently waiting in the shadows so I wouldn't be alone.

"Like me," he filled in after an elapsed silence stretched between us. "You're even more like me."

I nodded, tracing invisible patterns into the comforter. "It doesn't ever end, does it?" I knew he'd pick up on what I was really asking. Would I always be stuck on this fucked up linear timeline of grief? I'd gone straight from acceptance to anger and depression.

He shook his head and released a deep sigh. "Nothing ever numbs the pain. No matter how deep you bury it, it always fights its way back to the surface, so you learn to live with it."

I looked up at him in surprise, almost falling off the bed. I'd expected him to be a lot more vague.

He didn't discuss feelings—at least, not his.

The Badlands grapevine would attest that he had none. All anyone seemed to focus on was the reputation that'd made him so notorious for all these years. He was an outcast, an undesirable, and sick in the fucking head. He had his own law and his own rules, taking what he wanted and never apologizing for it.

None of that was untrue.

He was supposed to be this unstoppable force that never showed emotion and didn't feel anything. But at the end of the day, he wasn't made of stone. The devil felt pain just like the rest of us. He turned it into power.

At my prolonged silence, he continued.

"We did make a deal, you and I, but all fourof the other bishops are in hiding. There's been no sign of them, and David went back underground as soon as he found out that I have no intention of ever giving you up."

Well, fuck. I should have known that would happen. David was like a phantom when he wanted to be.

That was one of the reasons I'd needed the Savages' help in the first place. Where the fuck did the man go when he was off the grid?

"How did you lure him out this time?" I asked.

"Me and David had been in contact for months when you came along. He has a pattern. Every six months, he moves to a new location. I fucked up the first time. He reached out to me again when he found out I had you. Knowing all he does now, don't count on that happening again."

Great. We were on a strict timetable and hunting a ghost. Four ghosts.

Wait…"Four *other* bishops? We already got rid of two. Shouldn't there only be four total?"

"No, his son is a higher up now. I think his name's Noah."

"Noah?" My stomach rolled and my heartbeat turned sluggish at mention of him. He was a fucking bishop at twenty-one?

The last time I saw my baby brother, he was forcing his dick in my ass and then kicking the shit out of me. I tried to school my features but must have failed because Romero paused mid-sentence.

"What did he do to you?"

The hair on the back of my neck rose at his tone. I sent a thank you up that it wasn't personally being directed at me.

"He was my brother, but that didn't miraculously make him any different from the rest. He's the one who left me on the side of the road." I shrugged, glancing away. I'd never hidden what was done to me but it was still hard to talk about.

I had to tell the man I belonged with that half my colony had had a turn between my legs. There was no way to dress up the truth and make it sound pretty. It was what it was.

"So we need a plan, then. Do you know why David wants me back?" I smoothly redirected the conversation.

I could tell he wanted to push me on what I'd just confessed, but fortunately, he dropped it.

"David's been looking for you for a long time, Pixie. You've just been left in the dark for way too fucking long."

"Why has he been looking for me?" I asked incredulously. I didn't expect him to know the answer, but I should have.

"You're the spitting image of your mother, and he's still hung up on her."

I opened my mouth to respond, and then closed it, running a hand over my face. What the hell? "How do you know...you knew my mom?"

I didn't know how that was possible. Maybe he was aware of who she was; I mean there, were only five years between us. He couldn't have known her too well.

From what I'd been told, I was removed from my mother's stomach without her having a choice in the matter.

The second I was cut out of her womb, she was left for dead on someone's dining room table. It wasn't a huge secret in The Order; it was a tale I'd heard numerous times. I was a black sheep born to be a whore. That's what I was taught, and I was treated as such.

"Tell me how you two know each other. You and David." I said after a beat when he didn't answer me.

He cocked his head and tsked. "I thought you would have figured that out by now. Where do you think I came from, Cali?"

Chapter Seventeen

Calista

I blanched and my stomach dropped. "What? No. No fucking way." I vigorously shook my head back and forth, looking him over from head to toe.

He was covered in tattoos and built like a Greek god. He was the leader of the Savages, king of a cult. Men in The Order didn't look like him and they sure as hell didn't get to branch off like he did.

"You never wondered how Grimm knew exactly where the church by the lake was? The one where Azel held his meets?"

I stared at him long and hard and suddenly felt like I should have figured this out long ago.

It semi-explained the inverted cross tattooed under his eye

that served as the official symbol for the Savages, why he had his own vendetta against David, and how they knew one another.

But even as the pieces clicked together, I couldn't wrap my head around it.

"H How did you get out? How did three of you get out at once? The Order never lets anyone go. Those who don't follow David's bullshit doctrine are immediately executed."

"My father was told to get out, and he took me and Grimm with him. Cobra wasn't part of it. That's not where we met."

His. Father.

I pulled in a quiet breath and softly let it out. I knew he wasn't lying because that wasn't his style. He just liked to spew facts in a not easily decipherable way.

There was a sleuth of missing details in what he was telling me, like how the hell they got to leave alive and why they were told to go in the first place.

I wasn't going to push him about it, not when he didn't push me about the Noah thing. Eventually though, he would be telling me all about it. He never spoke about his past or his parents, but he logically had to have come from somewhere. I knew he had a closet full of bones.

And now, with answers came so many more questions. And fucking shame.

I knew his reaction when I told him things was genuine, but knowing he was part of that world meant he was a little more keyed in to the inner workings than I thought.

I guess because I was David's flesh and blood, outsiders thought I'd be spared, when that only made it worse.

My past was a heavy book I never wanted anyone to open up.

The pages were full of ugly stains and smudged finger-prints. There was still so much I hadn't told him about.

What would he think if he knew they used to make me come? That when they realized I'd never get off with their dicks inside me they'd switch to using their mouth or hands. Sometimes, they used a sister so they could watch. Rarely was I with just one person a day. Whether I was sick, sore, or bruised to the point I couldn't move, they used me.

It didn't matter how many days passed or how many showers I took; I would always be that unclean, filthy little girl.

He shoved off the wall and took my face in his hands, forcing me to look up at him. "I don't give a shit about the things in your past. That would be pretty fucking hypocritical on my end. All I care about is the gorgeous, dope ass queen in front of me right now."

"How can you say that? Do you know how many people have seen me naked?"

"They saw you naked. They never saw *you*. I do. Grimm does. Shit, even Luther and Bryce do. Cobra and Arlen do, too. We fucking see you, baby."

"Get out." I pulled his hands off my face and looked away. "You're going to make me cry, you poetic asshole."

He laughed deep in his chest and sat down beside me. "Tomorrow, we're going to leave here and find these mother-fuckers one by one. I vow to you that I won't stop until they're all twelve feet under and David's head is a decoration on our mantle."

Hearing the sincerity in his words, I leaned my head on his shoulder. He lifted me up and sat me on his lap, just holding me.

We spent the night like that, talking about mundane

things, simple things, things that didn't weigh so heavy. It was uncharted territory for both of us, but it felt…nice.

He was a living nightmare feared by everyone, and I'd never felt safer than I did wrapped in his arms.

Chapter Eighteen

Romero

It was the first day of our forever.

I stared down at the toothless blonde and she stared back. Her mouth looked like a hotdog that had been cooked in the microwave for too long, swollen and split in different directions.

Tiny pieces of mutilated gum and teeth littered the floor around her. My fingers danced around the handle of my knife. She screamed as I wrenched her head back as far it would go.

With time not on my side, I flipped my tactical blade out and lodged it straight through the bottom of her jaw, forcing it through the floor of her flayed mouth to the roof.

I managed to get her flailing tongue in the process, making her screams garbled.

I bent at the knees and placed my hand over her heart,

letting out a contented breath. It was beating in the erratic tempo I knew all too well, fighting desperately to cling to a life that was already lost.

Beautiful crimson leaked around my blade, spilling from her mouth in a steady, rapid downpour. It pooled onto my hand and dripped onto the old linoleum floor. With her throat tilted back, blood flowed straight down, making her choke and gag.

After twisting the handle in a full circle to widen the hole, the blade slipped right out. I let her head loll and bounce off the pole.

I was still looking down at her when Janice walked into the room with Grimm on her heels. She didn't bat an eyelid at the dead body, keeping her attention solely on my face.

"You wanted me?"

Grimm snorted in amusement at her eager tone.

"I just wanted to say you did good yesterday."

"Oh." Her face fell but she quickly forced a smile for my benefit.

If I hadn't wanted to kill her before, I would have now for the simple fact that she was supposed to be Cali's friend and she kept hoping I would fuck her. I'd sooner stick my dick down a garbage disposal.

"Thank you. I thought it may have been a tad bit overkill."

I grinned and reached my bloody hand out. She took it and allowed me to bring her closer. What a fatal error on her end, especially when she knew better.

I was never one to be a wolf in sheep's clothing. I always had my fangs proudly on display. It never stopped foolish little lambs from coming closer. They seemed to like it when I made them bleed.

"No, it was good. So good that I knew it wasn't all an act.

If Calista really wanted to leave me, you'd help her. Wouldn't you, *Jinx*?"

I felt her pulse jump beneath her skin. She looked at me in equal parts fear and surprise. "No, I would never do that."

"Just like you swore you were reporting back everything that happened at Tito's?"

She shook her head back and forth, denying the obvious right to my face. I turned her around, bringing her back flush with my chest, and settled my hands on her shoulders.

"Let me guess, you were so busy protecting her, you forgot to tell me that the woman I'd been searching for shared a room with you. Am I correct?"

"I didn't—"

"You did know." I cut her off, and took hold of her head.

"Romero," she started to plead, but I didn't need to hear anything she had to say.

I snapped her fucking neck before she could lie to me again. I wanted to tear her apart and remove her vocal cords, but I didn't have time—Cali would be up soon.

"Well, thank fuck that's done," Grimm commented, stroking his beard.

"I should have killed her ass long ago."

I'd sent her into a large group of outliers under an alias, and she'd intentionally failed. Now, she was just another body in my cleaning house regimen.

I could have men do my dirty work for me, but half the respect I got was for doing shit myself. I *needed* to kill. I needed to hear the screams and hopeless pleas when I tortured.

I needed to see the blood and feel the hearts struggle to continue beating as I took a life away. Looking into someone's eyes as they died was like drinking a warm glass of milk before bed, or a good fuck.

"What do we do with the bodies?" Grimm asked.

"That one can go in a dumpster." I pointed to the toothless blonde. "I told Luther he could have Janice for Annie. I'll stuff her ass in one of the double-loaders for now."

"Look at you, being creative."

"Shut the fuck up."

He laughed as I grabbed Janice by her hair and dragged her towards the washing machines. It only took a few minutes to get the traitorous bitch inside, though she had to be bent into an unnatural shape to fit. Her elbow had popped all the way through her skin by time I finished, clacking against the glass door when I slammed it shut.

I left Grimm with instructions to get Arlen ready, and slipped back into the room. She lay in bed, naked, completely defenseless, trusting that the devil she allowed to ease his demons between her legs wouldn't kill her while she slept.

She was even more gorgeous like this. I could slit her throat and her pretty blue eyes would fly open in confusion as the blood streamed down onto the sheets. I could tie her up and take my time removing every one of her soft limbs piece by piece.

I was going to punish David by taking the life away from his one and only sick, twisted vice. But I couldn't. I wouldn't. I could never hurt her or take her life without taking my own. Cali was my perfect disease–I craved the sickness in her like I needed air to breathe.

I never intended to keep her.

Then, she looked at me and changed everything.

She tilted my entire world on its axis. Now, it was time to rule that world together.

I was king of an empire for the damned and Cali was going to stand by my side like the motherfucking queen she was.

We were going to be legends, a tale of two gods who let their demons reign free. Chaos, anarchy, bloodshed…it would all be right in our backyard.

I could never give her heaven, so it was a damn good thing she coveted hell.

Chapter Nineteen

Calista

When I woke up, Romero wasn't beside me.

I took a much needed walk down memory lane, smiling to myself when the night before flashed back to me.

From the moment we met, our relationship had been go, go, go. We fought hard. We fucked harder. We killed without remorse. Being separated didn't change what was between us. If anything it felt more solid than before. The devil on my shoulder was my sole voice of reason on the matter, and the angel wholly agreed with what she wanted.

I rolled onto my stomach with a groan, my sub-conscious reminding me of what was growing in my womb. Another conversation that needed to be had, and the only one I wasn't ready for. I didn't regret it for one single second but the timing was *all* wrong.

Life just kept slinging curveballs at me and being a moody bitch, but whatever, I was a bigger one. Closing my eyes, I let out a breath and tried to get my thoughts in order.

I didn't hear Romero enter the room but I knew he was there. The hairs on the back of my neck rose and I felt his eyes on me. He did that a lot, watched and studied me while I slept. I always wondered what he was thinking but never asked.

"I know you're up, Pixie." I heard the humor in his voice. His fingertips were on my bare skin a second later. I shivered from his touch, his soft laugh letting me know he saw it.

Rolling over, I opened my eyes and sat up excitedly, taking the sheet with me. "It's tomorrow."

"Good morning to you too," he sarcastically quipped.

"We've never said good morning to each other; we're not that domestic. *Please* don't try and be domesticated."

"You're right, my day always starts off better after my face has been between your legs and your come is on my taste buds."

"There ya go, honey." I grinned up at him.

"I love seeing that smile." He looked at me for a brief minute and his eyes darkened. I had barely blinked and he was ripping the sheet away, pushing me down onto the bed.

"What are you doing?" I laughed.

"Figure it out," he responded, shoving my legs and apart and covering my tender pussy with his magical mouth. He pressed his forearm down across my navel, forcing me to stay how I was.

His tongue swiped up from my ass to my clit in carnal, frenzied strokes.

"Rome," I breathed, trying to wriggle away.

He lifted his hand and began massaging my clit with the pad of his thumb in a steady circular motion at the same time he started easing the tip of his tongue in and out of my pussy, humming in the back of his throat.

"Your pussy tastes so sweet, Cali," he soughed.

I threaded my fingers in his silky hair, struggling to swallow the moans building in my chest. I lost the battle the longer he licked and sucked, fucking me with his tongue and teasing me with his fingers.

"I want you inside me."

"You can't feel my tongue?" he teased.

I would have glared but it was hard to be mad at a guy when his face was between your legs.

"That's not what I meant," I growled in frustration, sucking in a quiet breath when he obliged me and placed a gentle kiss on my swollen nub, moving slowly up my stomach until he was settled over me and his erection was pressing against my apex.

He placed the pad of his thumb on my lips. I nipped it, smiling up at him and breathing in my scent. I was putty in his hands, a marionette that moved in perfect sync with her marionettes.

My hands flew to his zipper; he kicked off his boots and helped me work him out of his jeans, pulling off his shirt last. He was commando underneath. His metal piercing proudly protruded through the head of his stiff cock.

"Let me ride you," I nearly whispered.

He apparently liked that idea, because I was on top of him before I could take my next breath. I laughed, which he didn't appreciate.

"Don't play with me, put my dick inside you and fuck it."

"Oh, you're so romantic."

"Stop talking and start fucking," he growled, smacking my ass.

I had to bite my lip to hold back another laugh. I adored

his crude mouth. Spinning around so he only had view of my back, I lined myself up with him and sunk down before he could change his mind.

"You feel amazing," I moaned softly, feeling myself stretch around his cock.

He gripped my hips tightly, urging me to move. It took me a second to find a rhythm but when I did I rode him hard, gripping his toned thighs for support.

I could hear the suctioning sound my pussy made every time I slid down. I cupped his balls, gently rolling them in my hand as I rocked on top of him.

"I need to do this," he abruptly said, easily forcing me forward.

He kept himself inside me as he took over, switching us into a new position. He fisted my hair and roughly pulled my head back until I was arched how he wanted me.

"You're so fucking tight," he groaned directly in my ear before biting down on my shoulder hard enough to break the skin.

"Rome!" I cried out, feeling my pussy clench around him from the pain.

Shifting his hips, he began fucking me like he had a point to prove. The position let him go as deep as he wanted, his balls smacked against me, mixing with the sound of my heady moans.

Without letting go of my hair he paused momentarily and reached for something, forcing my face into the mattress so I couldn't see what it was. I tried to lift my head but his grip was too tight

I yelped when I felt a sharp sting, a trickle of wetness followed and my heightened arousal drenched his dick.

"Did you just fucking—" He did it again, this time a little harder. As if having a mind of their own. my hips pushed back, urging him to move. He did it a third and fourth time, slowly dragging his serrated blade across my upper back.

He tossed the knife away; I heard it hit the wall, hissing when he reached down and smeared the blood into my stinging flesh.

"You bleed so pretty," he said quietly, all the while holding me in place, still buried inside me. "Please just fuck me," I pleaded, desperate to come.

He used my hair to drive my body back into his, fucking me with zero restraint. My scalp prickled and burned. It hurt in the best kind of way. This kind of pain was beautiful. He could've done anything he wanted to me.

I couldn't think straight with him pounding me into the mattress. I could barely breathe. I could feel my blood dripping down onto the white sheets.

I slightly tensed when he pushed two fingers into my ass. He moved them in and out at a slower rhythm than he was thrusting, ignoring my protest.

He added a third finger, stretching the muscle as he continuously pumped in and out of both holes. I whimpered and moaned uncontrollably, fisting bloody fabric.

I wasn't going to be able to walk at this rate. My body trembled, every nerve ending on fire, the heat going to my very core and the ecstasy overwhelming me.

When he finally finished, I felt boneless, little tremors continuing to course through my limbs. He kissed down my spine, removing his fingers, and slowly, without a word, pulled his flaccid dick out.

I collapsed the second he stopped supporting me. I didn't know how he was so quiet when he did all the work. At the sound of his clothing rustling, I forced myself to move.

Looking down, the bed looked like someone had covered themselves in red paint and then rolled all over it.

I stood up, feeling a tad unsteady; he wrapped an arm around my waist to ground me, bringing me flush with his firm chest.

"Let go of me," I calmly demanded. "Please," I added when he didn't budge.

"Only because you said please." He kissed my temple and dropped his arm.

"What the hell was that?" I asked, now nearly bouncing on the balls of my feet from the elation I felt.

I hid a wince as I twisted my torso, trying to see my back. Between my thighs felt raw and exposed. If I looked down, I could easily see how swollen I was.

"You liked that, huh?" he smirked.

"Yes! You've never done that before," I shot back, pointing to the ruined sheets.

"I needed to compromise."

"Compromise for what?"

His eyes traveled up and down my body as he finished pulling his jeans on. "You're sexy like this. The roughly fucked look really works for you." He grinned and then, like a switch flipping, his usual mask of indifference slid back into place. "I don't fuck women and keep them. I fuck women and then kill them after I come."

His words had goose pimples erupting across my flesh, my elation deflated like a popped balloon. "You want to kill me?"

"That's not what I meant. I'd never take your life now... definitely not while I'm fucking you. I thought you wanted to play?"

Instead of gaping at him, I quickly pulled on my poker face and simply blinked.

"Don't look at me like that. I took it easy for your first

time." He laced his boots back up. "Wait until I'm fucking you with the blade against your throat."

I ignored the tiny spark of excitement that sprang up in my gut.

We were definitely a match of epic fucked up proportions. Even our pillow talk was screwed up.

I stood naked with blood running down my back and asked a question I wasn't sure I wanted an answer to. "So you *did* want to kill me? What changed?"

"No, not exactly. It's a long story. You weren't supposed to mean anything to me." Pausing, I could tell he was hesitant to say his next words. "I remember the tears in your eyes the night I left. You never saw me, but I saw you.

"I look at you now and no longer see that broken little girl. I see a beautifully fucked up woman who's finally growing into her skin. You're just like me. You're everything this world loves to hate. You're everything I want and I'm everything you need."

Letting out a long exhale, I gave a curt nod and fought to withhold my emotions.

He was right; I needed him. He'd once told me that I let the devil inside me and he wasn't leaving anytime soon.

I think he took up permanent residence when he evicted my soul. He'd been right all along. It would take an exorcism to take back what I willingly gave away.

"Why were you supposed hate me?"

"That's a conversation we don't have time for. Like I said, it's a long story. Just know I don't and I never actually did. But you do an excellent fucking job at pissing me off badly enough to make me feel like I do."

"How were you going to do it?" I persisted with genuine curiosity even as his confession warmed my chest.

He studied me, his eyes lingering on my stomach before meeting my stare again.

"You're not ever going to try and leave me so it isn't important anymore.

If you ever do, I'll find you, and the things I'd do to you would make your worst nightmare seem like a daydream."

"You're a goddamn psychopath."

"And now you're being a hypocritical bitch." He began moving towards the door. "You have fifteen minutes to get yourself together before I fuck you again and use your body to act out all my psychopathic fantasies."

I wasn't going to give him time to change his mind about that. I walked into the bathroom, pettily slamming the door behind me just to look in the mirror and see the red R he'd carved between my shoulder blades and throw it back open.

He was already gone.

Chapter Twenty

Calista

I bit into the apple he'd had Arlen bring for me while I was in the shower, along with a bowl of oatmeal.

She leaned against the dresser, looking much better than she had the night prior; I sat across from her Indian style at the edge of the bed, dressed in an outfit almost identical to the one I'd worn the day before.

"Where's Jinx?" I asked after I swallowed my bite.

"No idea. I haven't seen her since we left this room."

I nodded, wondering if she was going to avoid me because of what happened, shrugging it off. I'd talk to her eventually. What I wanted to discuss was better off not heard by her ears, anyway.

"Tell me how you are."

She laughed and huffed out a breath. "I should be askin

you that. Grimm found me three days after that little bridge incident and kept me at some damn shack. I'm only here because you are. When I heard you'd been found, I raised hell until he brought me to this shithole."

I scanned over her fading bruises.

"He didn't do this." She gestured up and down her body but didn't elaborate on what *did* hurt her. "Do you think his balls would still be attached if he put his hands on me?" She quirked a perfect brow, making me laugh.

"I'm glad you're here," I admitted.

"I already told you; I go where you go. Now, tell me what the hell happened to you."

Taking a small breath, I told her everything from the time I went over the bridge up until the present, excluding the R on my back, and it felt good. I'd never had another woman I could talk to like this. I wasn't this open with anyone, not even Jinx. She didn't say much until I was finished, only adding a curse word here and there.

"My sister is here and I'd love to know why they won't let us near one another. That bitch acted like she didn't know who I was. Ya know me and my uncle left to find her and she never needed our fuckin help? He died for nothin," she fumed.

I watched as she paced back and forth, understanding her anger completely. Her uncle was shredded apart right in front of her and then consumed as someone's breakfast, lunch, and dinner. She had every right to be enraged.

"Cali, I don't know how the fuck you're still sane."

"I'm far from sane." I laughed but I was being serious. Nothing about me was remotely stable. I was a high functioning psycho on my good days. On my bad days, no one was safe.

"That's not all," I sobered, keeping my voice low. With a soft exhale I let the cat out of the bag. "I'm pregnant."

"Huh?" She whirled around so fast she almost spun into the wall.

"Shhh," I hushed her, nodding my head in the direction of the door.

"Are you for real? I mean, you're sure? You don't look any different." She zeroed in on my stomach as if she had x-ray vision.

I was ninety percent sure. I didn't have nausea and I wasn't any bigger than I had been, but I highly doubted Mother Nature decided to be kind and take my period away just for the fuck of it. They'd always been regular and Romero wasn't exactly wrapping his dick. I told her as much, leaving out the fact I'd been through this before.

"I figured he'd be comin on you, not in you. He doesn't look like the bareback type," she mused. "Holy shit, you're gonna be a mom. Does he know?"

I scoffed once my brain caught up and defined her terminology. Twisting my lips, I thought back to how his gaze lingered on my stomach and a few oddities in his behavior. "I think he does, but he hasn't said anything. I have an idea on how to fix that."

"He's crazy possessive over you. Lord knows what he'll do if this comes full circle."

Nodding in agreement, I went to speak when the door flew open with such force that it hit the wall.

"Get out," Romero ordered her without looking at me.

Sensing his dark mood, Arlen glared at him, not moving an inch. "Are you calm enough to be left alone with her?"

"Get the fuck out."

His expression didn't change but she must have seen something in his eyes because she held her hands up in surrender and edged past him, shooting me a look that said, *"See what I mean?"*

I let out a breath I didn't realize I was holding once she made it into the hall unscathed. He shut the door and walked to the window.

I knew this wasn't the time to bring up the R now scabbing over on my back. One: I liked it. Two: Romero gave zero fucks and did what he wanted. The argument would end with his dick inside me again and my body couldn't handle that.

A stifling silence filled the room and I internally groaned. At least our relationship was never dull.

"Romero, you can't go around terrifying all my friends. That's not right," I explained in a voice that didn't sound like my own.

"We both know you don't give a shit about—"

"Well, maybe now I do."

"Don't interrupt me again."

"Don't talk to me like that, asshole," I snapped.

He turned away from the window and the look in his eyes almost made me flinch. I was smarter than that, though. You never showed a monster your fear; they fed off it. I was recklessly unafraid of him because, if nothing else, he was *my* monster.

I never claimed to be smart when it came to dealing with him. Even as my heart thudded in my chest like a thoroughbred in its final stretch and my mouth dried, I didn't run. I let him approach me and wrap his hand tightly around my throat.

"For someone who doesn't trust me, you're real fucking comfy. I could snap your neck and be done with you right now.

I could slit your wrists and fuck your dying body until

your heart stopped and you bled out." His voice was normal but the threat was loud and clear.

I stared up at him and my breath caught. His eyes were like windows to the darkest pits of hell. That alone should have terrified me, but I happily breathed him in and accepted every part of himself he laid bare.

"You could, and you already told me you want to, but you're not going to," I said confidently. "Because you wouldn't hurt the baby."

He studied my face for beat and chuckled softly. "Cali, you're fucking crazy." His lips met my forehead and his hand fell away.

"I told you, I trust you not to hurt me like that. Just because your demented ass has fantasies about killing me, it isn't going to change my mind."

"And what made this come about?" he asked, cupping the back of my neck.

"I'm the queen to your king. If I go down, you're going down with me." I grinned and placed a soft kiss on his lips. "You're a Savage psycho, and I fucking love that about you." I stepped back. "Now, tell me how long you've known about baby S."

"I don't know if I want to fuck you or kill you right now." He grabbed hold of my ass and pulled me into him. "I've known for a while, Cali. How could I notice everything about you and miss something that fucking important? I told you pregnancy was nothing to worry about when all our kids were either going down your throat or landing somewhere on your body. I've been coming inside you for a while now. How did you know I knew?"

"Um, the nasty protein drink you keep giving me, you keeping me locked in here when I've always been by your side, and the way you stared at me earlier. You're okay with this? I mean, you do know what a baby is, right?"

"Cali, shut the fuck up," he sighed. "I'm okay with it. I wanted this. The timing might not be ideal but my fucking kid is inside you so I don't give shit."

Oh my god.

I felt tears welling up in my eyes and scowled at his chest. "Goddamn it, Rome, look what you did." I swiped at them, glaring when he laughed.

"Everything will be okay, baby. We're going to take care of all this Order shit way before you're so big I have no choice but to fuck you from the back."

Ignoring the fucking part completely, I honed in on the finer details of that proclamation. "You're going to let me in still?" I looked at him in surprise. I thought for sure I'd have to fight for that right.

"I'm not doing it without you. You're not fucking handicapped or suddenly made of glass. And as shitty as this is to rush, we need to go."

"Where are we going?" I asked as he guided me towards the room door.

"I'm going to take you to see someone before we head out, and on the way, I'm going to give you the Cliff Notes version of events."

Chapter Twenty-One

Romero

A sweet metallic pungency assaulted my nose the minute we stepped into the room.

The smell of blood…it never got old.

Cali wrinkled her nose in disgust and eyed the man partially suspended from the ceiling. When the door clicked shut, he opened his good eye and attempted to lift his head.

He was ass naked, the heavy odor of must, piss, and shit mixed with the other aromas in the square room.

"Tito, how are you my friend?"

"Fuck…you," he rasped out through cracked, peeling lips.

"Hey, don't say that. I might get jealous." Cobra feigned hurt as he entered the room with Grimm and Bryce, shooting Cali a bright smile.

His red hair was still dripping wet. He never dried off

when he got out the shower, one of his many quirks. Just like his preference for breaking men.

I didn't judge him; none of us ever would. I'd had my fair share of experimentation in that department. Cobra could be an eccentric motherfucker but at the end of the day, you wanted him on your side.

"Fuck, he stinks," Bryce coughed, pulling his black robe up over his nose.

"Ah, come on now, Bryce, man up," Grimm scolded him sarcastically, laughing when he gagged and back-pedaled into the door.

"No, he's right. It smells like swine ass in here," Cali coughed.

I chuckled under my breath, letting her hand go so I could tighten the pulley holding Tito's arms above his head.

His muscles strained and he groaned in pain, a fresh line of sweat breaking out on his brow. I was waiting for his shoulders to dislocate. If he hung here long enough, it would happen on its own, but then I wouldn't be around to see, and that diminished the entertainment significantly.

"Grab me a rag, Grimm," I called to him, looking down at Tito's bullet hole. The area was swollen, surrounded by dried old drainage and seeping with new.

"I know this seems like the shit end of the stick, but Luther wanted to keep you for himself, and between you and me, being skinned alive would hurt a fuck of a lot more than this. So, you're welcome."

"What are you doing with it?" Grimm asked, walking over to where I stood.

"I'm going to shove it in the bullet hole, unless you want to do the honors?" I looked at my gorgeous girl.

"If Grimm wants to do it, I'm happy to watch." She gave her brother a soft smile.

He nodded and balled the end of the dirty white cloth up so it was easier to push in.

"Cali…please," Tito gasped, no doubt sensing how much worse things were about to get for him.

"Tito, he told me all I needed to know about you, your sister, and Jinx. You're a grown man and you got yourself into this bullshit way before I came along. You're on your own."

"Cal—" His strained sentence cut off in a high-pitched scream.

When Grimm knelt down and started pushing the rag into the gaping wound, the smell of dead skin, puss, and blood wafted from it.

"No, no, no," Tito thrashed, trying to kick his leg away.

Grimm easily subdued him, holding it in place with one hand and twisting the rag in the other. "Why?" He hung his head and groaned, his body shaking with a silent sob.

"Are you fucking serious right now?" Cobra laughed, swaggering up to us with a bottle of bourbon in his hand. "Get the fuck over here, Bryce."

"No, I'm good," he called out, standing securely in a corner.

I laughed and shook my head. The man would crush throats with his bare hands but couldn't stomach torture.

"Because you're no good to me now. Because you and your sister have been nothing but pains in my ass." I responded to Tito.

I held my hand out for the bottle in Cobra's hand. He handed it over without comment, pulling a gold lighter out of his back jean pocket.

"The real issue is that he didn't want to give Calista up." Grimm picked up where I left off, rising to his full height.

"Good help is so hard to find." I untwisted the lid of the

bourbon. "You're easily dispensable. How many times have I told you that? There are a hundred fucking men vying to do what you did for me. I've already replaced you."

With that, I began to pour the liquor over his wound, drenching the rag hanging out of it. I made sure I coated some of his skin for added benefit.

Some men would have felt an ounce of remorse for discarding someone who had worked for them for so long. He was my eyes and ears of the outliers, feeding me information and keeping me updated.

It was his idea to use his sister to further my agenda.

When I made sure the stupid bitch got burned at the stake, he suddenly wanted to feel regretful. He didn't care when she was fucking me, my brothers, and anyone else that gave her an illusion of power, never defended her when I made her ass bleed and then locked her in a dog cage because she pissed me off.

I fucked her mind to the point of insanity and then fed her to the wolves. When he discovered Cali, it was because of me. I gave him the fucking order to drive down the road she was dumped on when I found out what David had done.

"You made me think she was dead." I took the lighter from Cobra and looked at the sack of shit dangling in front of me. He told me he'd found the body; he'd lied to my face.

"Listen," he began to plea, grunting when Grimm's fist met his mouth, jerking his head to the side.

"Shut the fuck up. There's nothing left for you to say," Grimm leveled in an even tone.

Tito's head lolled back down and he whispered an apology that wasn't good enough to wipe my ass with. I never trusted him but I relied on him for information.

It was only when word reached me that David had started searching for Cali that I knew Tito had lied. Sending Janice in had proved to be a waste of time. For four fucking years, they kept the wool over my eyes and fucked one another.

Never again would I be so comfortable in my position. I needed to stay hands on and ride all these motherfuckers so hard that they had heart palpitations if they even thought of going behind my back.

I flipped the lid of the lighter back and lit up the rag. Flames consumed the cloth within seconds, reaching into his bullet hole and burning the surrounding flesh.

"Damn," Cobra laughed, jumping back as Tito wailed.

Cali watched on in silent fascination.

His agonized screams filled the room. He looked like a worm on a hook, twisting around uncontrollably.

An audible pop was heard as his shoulders dislocated. With his contorted body hanging in the pulley and flames eating his flesh, his screams cut off and he passed out.

"It was just getting good," Grimm mused, walking to the sink in the back of the room, his heavy boots thudding across the concrete floor.

I breathed in all the different smells, feeling a sense of comfort from being in my element.

"You good back there, Bryce?" I couldn't keep the humor out of my voice.

"Never better," he deadpanned.

"You sure about what we're going to do?" Cobra asked quietly, watching Grimm as he lazily doused the fire close to consuming Tito's balls.

"You know our plan is solid. We'll all be right there," Grimm reassured me.

He was right. We'd gone over a million possible outcomes and tweaked the plan so we could control how it all went down.

"We need to get going," I turned and made my way towards the door, taking Cali with me.

I wanted to chain her up in a fucking cellar until her dying day but the need to have her beside me was too damn compelling. I despised that she made me care so fucking much. Hatred was so much easier to cope with than whatever the fuck it was I felt for her.

One woman was wreaking havoc on my iron-willed control, but she was carrying my child and accepting it without argument. That only solidified the fact that I'd made the right choice in keeping her.

Now it was time to end this shit once and for all so we could move forward with our lives. It was time to rack up our body counts and stain our hands red.

Chapter Twenty-Two

Calista

Everything was about to change.

We were actually going after The Order, I was going to be a fucking mother, and most of the people from my past were dead.

All in all, life wasn't too bad.

I was damn near frothing at the mouth knowing I'd get to spill blood. We came back to the room to do one last sweep and Romero felt the need to give me an unnecessary number of safety rules and tips.

I'd never jeopardize Baby S, but like he said, I wasn't handicapped.

I could cut someone's throat open and drink a protein smoothie at the same time.

"You ready?" he asked, hooking a duffel bag over his shoulder.

"Can you put that down a sec?"

He gave me an imploring look, slowly lowering the bag back down to the floor.

I took his hands in mine, tilting my head back and never breaking eye contact. My skin suddenly felt sensitive and there was a flutter in my stomach.

"You've made me such a girl," I grumbled.

"You're welcome," he smirked.

I think we were having a moment. That thought had me ready to run to the other side of the room. I didn't. I gathered my lady balls and gave him the truth, hoping like hell I wasn't fucking myself.

"You asked me if I loved you the other day and I wanted you to know, I don't know what love is. No one's ever loved me. I'm not even sure if I believe in it. But if there was anyone that could make me, it would be you. I love chocolate. I love dick. And whatever I feel for you trumps both without any question." It wasn't some deep proclamation. I couldn't force myself to vomit flowery words out of my mouth, but it *was* something.

Whatever I felt for him was overwhelming. It consumed me. He was all I could think about no matter what I was doing. I wanted to say it was love, because what else would it be?

What I felt for Tilly, who was really a lying bitch named Tiffany, wasn't even on the stratosphere of what I felt for him.

He didn't say anything for what felt like hours, staring like I hadn't just made myself vulnerable. My brain told me to backtrack. This was Romero, the man that took pride in turning the Badlands into his own personal hell. Did I really just confess to wanting to love him when I didn't know the real definition of the word?

I wished I'd had a mother around to teach me how these things worked.

It was bad enough realizing how damn sheltered I'd always been from the real world.

It was hard going about life when I'd been left to figure it all out on my own.

"I don't know how to do this. I've never...I'm sorry."

"Don't fucking apologize. You haven't done anything wrong." He pulled his hands free and his arms wrapped around my waist.

"I don't believe in any of that love at first sight bullshit—I don't know what the fuck love is, either—but ever since you looked at me with those big blue eyes, I've been fucking positive you're my soul mate.

"You're mine, I'm yours. It's that fucking simple, baby. We can figure everything else out together."

"Together." I confirmed, trying to contain the ridiculous grin ready to explode across my face.

"Ugh, this is over the top cheesy. I feel like you should call me a slut, bend me over the desk and then fuck me so we're normal again."

He let out one of his rare laughs and it warmed my entire being. I could sit and stare at him for hours on end but when he laughed or truly smiled, I was completely captivated.

"You and I will never be normal, but if you want to be a slut, get down on your knees and wrap your lips around my dick."

I smirked and did just that, sinking down to the carpet.

It took me a full minute to free him from his jeans with no assistance. I gripped his dick in my hand and stroked with my thumb. It was soft and smooth, encased in a patch of dark hair.

With the tip of my finger, I traced a circle around his barbell and then down a vein. He twitched against my palm.

"Cali, stop teasing me and suck my dick before I choke you with it."

Biting my cheek so I didn't laugh, I looked up at him and without further preamble, I swirled my tongue around his tip before swallowing him whole.

He made a sound in his throat and tangled a hand in my hair. I wrapped both my hands around his base and worked them up and down in succession with my mouth, toying with his piercing every time I glided up.

"Just like that. You look beautiful with my dick in your mouth." I felt the muscles in his thighs tense. His grip on my locks grew tighter the faster I worked and harder I sucked.

He started fucking my mouth, forcing me to repeatedly deep throat, holding my head in place. I let go of his dick and gripped his thighs to keep myself up.

Doing my best not to gag and choke on the saliva rapidly building up and running down my chin, I slurped what I could, occasionally coughing around him, feeling the rest coat his balls. My eyes watered and spilled over. I sucked harder as he thrust down my throat.

He didn't warn me before he came. The only sign I had was the hair along my scalp feeling like it was about to rip out and his dick jerking a second before his semen coated my taste buds.

I caught and swallowed every last creamy drop, flicking my tongue out just to be sure I'd milked him bone dry. His dick left my mouth with a wet pop.

I rolled my lips together, watching him tuck it back in his pants, and wiped my saliva drenched hands on my jeggings.

In the blink of an eye, he had me on my feet and his mouth on mine, no doubt tasting himself. Not seeming to care, he cupped my ass and pulled me into him, nipping my lower lip.

When he finally pulled away, his forehead rested against mine and he held my face in his hands.

I dared imagine a future with him, something I'd never had the guts to do because happily ever after wasn't meant for girls like me.

Regardless, whatever happened, I knew walking away from him wasn't an option.

I wasn't ever letting him go, even when keeping him meant I'd soon be standing beside him in a war where I would be forced to partake in a bloodbath, fully embracing the dirty twisted bitch he always saw me as.

Part Two

So if the devil ever asks you to dance,
You better say never,
because a dance with the devil may last you forever.
-IMMORTAL TECHNIQUE-

Chapter Twenty-Three

Romero

I'd done and would continue to do a lot of wrong fucked up shit in my life. Cali was one thing I did right.

I looked over at her every so often, watching the rise and fall of her chest as she slept and clutched a pack of peanuts in her hand. The girl was so unmistakably human and in a way it rubbed off on me. Not a lot, but nonetheless it did.

I saw her as I had in the beginning but with a little more flare.

She reminded me of a lioness, stunning and fierce as fuck, now leader of the pride. She looked like a goddess, but she was a maleficent queen. And she was the mother of my child.

There were lots of nice words I could dress up for her but I knew from experience that words were often empty. I planned to show her all the shit I couldn't say as soon as this was over.

She told me she wouldn't do anything purposely reckless that could hurt our baby before reminding me that being pregnant didn't mean she couldn't kill anyone who fucked with her. Her bloodlust made my dick hard, and I fell for her a little fucking more.

I turned onto the temporary last leg of our trip and prepared myself to see a face I had left behind years ago to build up the Savages.

The truck ahead of me pulled to the side of the road when I turned off again, moving to an area that would cover my jeep.

My front end dipped down and came right back up, moving smoothly out of a ditch, forcing thick leaves to part as I drove into a small clearing.

Cobra followed right behind me, stopping when we were fender to bumper. I slid out, making sure I didn't wake Cali. Grimm shifted in the backseat, careful not to wake Arlen, whose legs were stretched across his lap.

"Didn't think we'd ever come back here." He waved his hands to the woods we'd be walking through once we formed a mini huddle.

"You two assholes remember to keep your mouths shut," Cobra directed at Bryce and Dhal.

"You have nothing to worry about on my end. I'm here to keep her safe if things go haywire, not give a history lesson," Bryce replied indignantly.

I wasn't real worried about him.

He'd been closer to us than anyone else had for the past two years. It was Dhal I expected to fuck up and tell Cali things I didn't want her to know.

I had enough to bullshit to deal with. I'd never handled

her with kid gloves, never needed to. That didn't mean I wouldn't shield her from shit sure enough to fuck up her already fucked up head.

Hearing car doors slam on the other side of the clearing was my queue to get shit moving.

"Let's get them up."

It was time to take a step back into my sordid past.

Chapter Twenty-Four

Calista

If there was anything I'd learned in life, it was that traipsing through the woods usually led me right into a shitty situation.

At least those times had been partially my fault. Since Romero was the one leading us like a good little duck and ignoring me when I asked where we were going, if anything went wrong, I was blaming him.

"You get used to it," Cobra snickered when he caught me side-eyeing one of the acolytes walking on my left.

"Right," I said slowly. Being followed by someone in a long black robe and satanic mask wasn't really something I saw myself adjusting to, but I was sucking it up.

Arlen walked on our right with Grimm. A triangular formation of acolytes was behind us and there one on each outer ring of our little group.

"Hey, I need you to know that I wasn't trying to leave you behind on the bridge. I thought I could divert the attention off the car."

"No hard feelings C, you'd know if there were." I smiled at him, watching as once again, his eyes flickered to Bryce.

I couldn't blame him for that. Bryce wasn't overly tall and he had only a few tattoos, the inverted cross being one of them. But he was well built, his face could make a few panties drop, and he seemed the most normal out of all of us —aside from Dhal, who was so sweet I legit couldn't stand it.

"I like puss—"

"You don't have to explain it to me. Ever. Don't forget that I'm in the same boat." I swiftly cut him off. I didn't want him justifying his sexuality to me of all people. I didn't care if he wanted to suck off Adam on Thursday and ride Eve on Friday. That was his prerogative.

He nodded, letting my words sink in. "You're a pretty cool chick, sis."

"I know, right?"

We walked a little further, following a well worn path through the woods. Soon enough, the sound of voices met my ears as the trees began to flare out in a circle and a clearing came into view.

"We're going to a trailer park?" Arlen asked incredulously.

"We're going back to where we grew up." Grimm answered.

Grew up? The closer we got, the more I wondered how that was remotely possible.

If they left The Order and ended up here, did that mean Rome's dad was around?

"I didn't know meeting O.G Grimm was on today's task

list," Arlen muttered, wiping chocolate tendrils off her sweaty forehead.

Romero abruptly stopped walking, making me run into his back. Without turning around, he slipped an arm around my waist and pulled me into his side. His mouth was on mine before I could ask what he wanted.

Like a puppet with its string being pulled, I responded without a second thought. I wrapped my arms around his neck, happily accepting his hungry kiss. Suddenly desperate to feel his body, I molded against him. He shamelessly grabbed my ass, pressing his hard dick into my lower stomach. Neither of us gave a shit about having an audience. This man turned me into a nymphomaniac.

"Well, damn," Arlen sighed wistfully.

Someone laughed. It sounded like Grimm.

Romero pulled away just as Cobra told everyone we would catch up. I grinned up at him, keeping my arms around his neck.

"What was that about?" I asked, clearing my throat when I heard how breathless I sounded.

"I haven't been inside you in hours. What if I told you I wanted to bend you over and fuck you right here with everyone we consider a friend just a few feet away?"

"Well, I would tell you that since we're in the middle of the woods, you'd better make it dirty and fuck me hard enough that they hear me screaming your name."

His midnight hues almost seemed to darken. He put his hands on my hips and forcefully walked me backward, already pushing down my jeggings.

Without warning, he spun me around and pushed my cheek against a tree. My pants were pulled down to just above the knee, and my feet were nudged apart.

At the unmistakable sound of his zipper going down my body elated with anticipated pleasure.

I whimpered and gripped the tree-trunk when he slid the smooth head of his cock up and down my lips, teasing me with his barbell.

"Fuck, Cali, your pussy is already soaking my dick." He gathered a handful of my hair into a tight ponytail and drove into me, forcing me up onto my tiptoes.

The height difference made him feel incredibly deep. My legs attempted to spread further apart on their own, getting trapped by the fabric of my pants.

I curled my fingers into the rigid bark, feeling every thick inch of him sliding in and out of me, hitting the cushion at the end of my pussy.

"Jesus, Rome." I tightened my grip just as he tightened his. The muscles in my legs burned fiercely and my cheek was starting to sting.

"You like it?"

"Yes!" I cried out, struggling to breathe around the moans building in my chest.

He leaned in, burying himself deeper with a grunt. His mouth found my shoulder and bit down. Not a second later, he pulled me away from the tree without a word and shoved me down to the dirt on all fours.

He bore down on me, easily sliding right back in, fingers digging into my hip so hard I knew I'd have a new bruise but I didn't care. Sweat rolled off him and dripped onto me. My own perspiration had the dust settling on my skin.

Arousal slid down my inner thighs and formed a vacuum around his dick. I clawed at the dirt and tried to shift off the twig digging into my knee.

"Come for me, baby," he cooed, letting go of my hip to assault my clit. His name spilled from my lungs and echoed across the treetops. I felt my pussy lock down on him like a vise, squeezing his come out as he came with me.

"I could overdose on you." He nipped my ear and slowly pulled out.

When he stood, he took me with him. I leaned my head back on his chest as he righted his jeans and then mine. "Your cheek's bleeding," he said softly, stroking it with his thumb.

"Good." I turned my head and kissed his palm.

"Come on." He took my hand and led me forward. A few steps later, we were in the clearing, where a small crowd was waiting.

Chapter Twenty-Five

Calista

Everyone at the camp would have heard me being fucked like a bitch in heat, and that had been his intention from the start.

Romero was a territorial beast.

I loved it.

Being told to sit on a wooden log serving as a bench by a fire pit while he went to talk with someone, however, I didn't. Bryce stood a little ways back, keeping watch with two acolytes.

"Girl, that was hot as fuck," Arlen whispered, glaring at a woman who kept doing double takes at us.

"It felt even better," I sighed, still feeling my just fucked high.

"You know people are staring at us?"

"Kind of hard not to see them. It's even harder to pretend I care."

The looks on these people's faces when they saw my boys (yes, *my* boys) again ranged from shocked to elated, and some even shed tears. Now that all three had slunk off together, me and Arlen were open season.

I ignored it and focused on our surroundings. There were trailers haphazardly placed everywhere. Some looked like they should have been junked decades ago. Others looked in their prime and had small flower beds in front of them.

In a section all its own, a group of kids played on a manmade jungle gym.

There was an awning across the property with two raggedy washing machines beneath it, but no dryer. The people clearly lived in poverty, but just a look at their faces showed they didn't care.

Everyone who wasn't gawking like they had no common sense was wearing a smile. I spotted a few that could use a good lesson in hygiene, and a couple of the women were wearing tops that exposed their tits completely, but all in all, everyone looked clean and well fed for the most part.

After studying them for a good ten minutes, something wiggled at the back of my mind. There was a scent in the air that smelled so familiar, but I couldn't pinpoint what it was.

"You smell that?" Arlen asked, as if she'd heard the thought inside my head.

"Yeah, it kinda smells like…bacon?" No, these people could never afford such a commodity. That much was obvious. Maybe they had their own pigs somewhere.

We were still trying to figure it out when there was a soft thud behind us.

"Afternoon ladies, nice to have you here," a tall man greeted, stepping past our log and dragging the body he'd just dropped by the ankle. There was a large knife with a curved, jagged blade strapped to his thigh.

Looking to the square-shaped pit and four posts evenly spaced around it, my brain quickly supplied why this whole scene had a similar feel to the one in the cannibal's barn.

Arlen tensed beside me, going ramrod straight.

"Hey, now, you're safe here. I wouldn't touch Brock's family." He held his calloused hands up in an I-mean-you-no-harm sort of way.

Who the fuck was Brock? Shit. Romero grew up here. Was Brock his dad? Oh, hell no.

Don't judge, Cali. I chastised myself just as Arlen hissed, "Not only are they psychopaths, they're cannibals too."

It was then the man on the ground's head lolled and he looked up at me with hazy, unfocused eyes. He'd been drugged, and whatever he was given was some strong shit because he couldn't lift any of his limbs.

The tall man went about his business, not looking the slightest bit offended at Arlen's response. I hid my reaction, trying to process the fact Romero possibly ate human. Well, that possibly was a definitely if this was where he grew up. I could kill him for bringing us here and not giving a heads up about what this place was—a trailer park for cannibals.

The man prodded the coals and lit a fire before coming back to the grab what I assumed was his dinner. He stripped the man of his mud covered clothing and then stretched his arms out in a T.

"Might wanna take a step back," he warned, pulling the knife out of its sheath.

I darted to the side, taking Arlen with me.

He cut the man straight from his neck to his ribcage, splitting him apart before making another slit a little lower from the navel to the man's balls, digging deep and grunting loudly from the force it took to break the man's pelvis.

Blood went everywhere, spreading over the dirt and spurting like a fountain. The man never had a chance in hell of fighting for himself. He didn't even get to scream.

"Okay, let's go." I grabbed Arlen's elbow and began leading her away just as the man started cracking apart the ribs.

Bryce trailed after me with the two acolytes that could have been mimes, and even he looked sickened by what he'd just seen.

Arlen clung to me like Velcro, unusually quiet. "Are you okay?" I asked once the fire pit was no longer in sight.

She opened her mouth to answer, snapping it shut when we turned a random corner.

What the hell?

There was a chain link fence in front of us, caging a small area in like an animal pen. Inside with chains around their necks were seven people.

None of them reacted to our sudden presence. They all continued staring aimlessly with gaunt expressions on their faces. I didn't blame them. They had to be well aware of what was going to happen to them.

These were outliers. This is what they had to fear most: being snatched up and never seen again. Their families and friends wouldn't bother looking for them after a day or so. Everyone knew the ways of the Badlands.

There were animals, too. A few goats and a few chickens were inside the pen with them.

"I don't understand why people do this…it's sick. Everyone struggles; we don't all start eating human beings because of it. I…I need a sec."

She bolted, disappearing around the side of a trailer. The acolytes followed after her, leaving me with Bryce.

"Well, what am I supposed to do about that?" Placing my hands on my hips, I debated for a minute or so and then went after her.

"Her reaction isn't completely unfounded," Bryce offered up quietly.

"I know that, but I don't deal with things like this," I huffed. She wouldn't like my response if she asked for it. The cannibals were just another way of having a safety net for some people. They resorted to human meat because it was either that or starvation. Or, they were born into it.

I didn't condone it. It was a rock bottom place to be, but I couldn't stand and point a finger when I wanted to kill people for fun and they killed them for nourishment. Yes, it was fucked up, but this was the Badlands, the wonderland of hell.

I couldn't find her, but I did find the missing links of our fucked up entourage.

I heard their low voices and found them behind a green trailer. Their conversation ceased when they all saw me.

Cobra was leaning against a picnic table, Grimm stood beside a man I barely looked at, and Dhal was standing way too close to Romero. If she got any closer, her tits would be smashing into his arms.

"What the fuck are you doing?" I went right up to him, shoving her away from his side. Unprepared for my assault, she stumbled backward, landing on her ass.

Romero instantly wrapped an arm around me and pulled me flush with his chest. "Cali, I don't have time for your jealous shit. We were having a private conversation."

"Wow, things men shouldn't say for dummies," Arlen quipped with heavy sarcasm, walking around the corner like she hadn't just stormed off.

"Grimm get her the fuck away from me," Romero bit out.

With no objections, Grimm made a sound in his throat and moved towards her.

"Don't fuckin touch me," she growled at him.

"Move your ass." He ignored her demand, roughly grabbing her arm and forcing her to walk away.

Dhal gracefully stood up and gave me a pitiful look, dusting her jeans off. "Look, Calista, you have nothing to be jealous of or worry—"

"He's full of shit. I'm not jealous of you," I scoffed. She fucking wished she could have that delightful honor. "And I'm not worried, either. It's a matter of respect. You should get some before you become a casualty. You're here because he thinks you can play midwife. You need to get your head out of your ass and stop pining for a man you can't have."

She swallowed but wisely kept her mouth shut. Pregnancy wouldn't stop me from choking the shit out of her. I didn't say the last part to be catty; she looked at my man like he hung the stars and moon. Sadly for her, I was the stars and moon, so she was shit out of luck.

Cobra made a cat fight sound, laughing when I flipped him off. "Come on, Dhal, let's leave them to 'talk'." He winked at me on the last word.

By now, everyone knew how Romero and I handled our issues.

We argued, he sometimes degraded me, I called him a few derogatory names, and then we fucked like rabid rabbits and got on with our lives. Our love story was one of dysfunctional perfection.

I was stronger than all the men I knew, except for him. His cold, jaded eyes and Judas touch were my kryptonite, but that didn't exclude him from pissing me the hell off.

"A *private* fucking conversation? Why are you still leaving me out of things? Goddamnit, you get on my nerves!"

"Who the fuck are you talking to?" He jerked me around and grabbed my jaw.

"Clearly you, asshole!" I pried his hand away, preparing to high-knee his balls into his stomach.

"Calista." A deep voice spoke my name.

I whipped my head around and saw the man I'd barely glanced at. I had to blink twice.

He was Grimm's double, minus the tattoos. Mirth danced in his brown eyes.

"I thought he was your father?"

"He is my father. And he just gave me our first solid lead. One of the bishops is staying at an Order owned cabin with his family. It's secluded but easy to get to."

I didn't want to skip over the fact that this man was who got Romero and Grimm away from The Order, and it was obvious he wasn't Romero's real dad.

He and Grimm weren't blood related, and there was no way this man hadn't played a huge role in Grimm's creation.

He said he had a lead though, and I was wired. I was ready to shed blood.

"Nice to meet you," I lied. "So we're leaving?" I asked Romero.

"Cali, chill out. You need food and sleep. Once we get on the road, there will be no stopping. We'll leave before dawn so we can get to the cabin while the sun's still up."

He spoke with a finality that had my hackles rising. I wanted to go right then, but I knew arguing with him wouldn't make that happen.

"Whatever, you have it all planned out, I'm sure." I tried to pull away from him but he wouldn't let go. Why did he feel the need to keep a lead from me? I didn't understand; we were supposed to be working together.

"You don't storm off because of your feelings. Don't be a little fucking girl. Tell me what the issue is."

"Rome, if you like your ability to piss standing up, you'll let me go."

"Goddamn, Cali. I can't handle your emotional bullshit all the time. Go, run off. Get the fuck away from me. I need to talk to Brock."

Cock sucking asshole.

He pointed like I was child and I proved his point by storming away.

I'd almost forgotten Bryce was playing body guard until he stepped out of a hiding spot and trailed after me with an amused smile on his face.

Grimm's double let out a boisterous laugh and I heard him say, "Ah, son, you're going to have your hands full with her."

"I already fucking do," Romero snapped, and it sounded like he punched the trailer.

I smiled to myself, losing it the second I thought about what he considered food.

If we were going to eat anything here, his ass better have some more peanuts.

Hell would freeze over before I added cannibal to my list of attributes.

Chapter Twenty-Six

Romero

She glowered at me from the other side of the fire. Her hypnotic blue eyes were lit up like the moon.

I knew I'd fucked up the second I called her jealous. If looks could kill, my dick would've been twelve feet in the air and incinerated. And she thought I was keeping a lead from her, of all things. Brock did in fact give me one, but what we were discussing wasn't remotely related to that.

What came after being out of your mind? That's what she made me.

She was under my skin like a parasitic poison. I fucking hated her. I was addicted to her. I fucking loved her. I think.

She was the one thing I couldn't control, and it only made me want to control her more.

Her hand held one of the cans of tomato soup Brock had

given to her and Arlen, who was right back by her side, blatantly avoiding Grimm.

If she wasn't so loyal, I'd gut her and immensely enjoy it, but Cali needed at least one female friend that wouldn't fuck her over.

It sure as shit wouldn't be Dhal. She hadn't said two words to me since getting knocked on her ass. I'd already told her we would never be a thing, not to mention that thing we were was years ago. I didn't stick my dick in every hole available. I had too much respect for myself to do that. And Cali, she was everything to me. I would never give a bitch something to hold over her head.

But, how I felt on the subject was irrelevant. She still wanted to kill Dhal.

Most men worried about their woman killing an old flame in a metaphorical way. I actually had to make sure Cali's crazy ass didn't knife mine in the middle of the night.

Keeping my gaze locked with hers, I tore a piece of barbequed flesh from the finger bone I was holding and slowly sucked it into my mouth.

I couldn't hold back my grin when her lips parted in shock. Human didn't taste bad. It tasted strongly like pork, actually. The taste was sometimes so similar one could swap the two and someone who didn't eat people wouldn't know the difference.

It wasn't something I'd go out and eat on my own, but I wasn't not going to consume it because of a prejudice.

I was raised eating this shit.

Grimm, Cobra, and Dhal were all doing the same, used to the acquired taste.

Cali was so focused on watching me eat that she was oblivious to Brock staring at her.

Couldn't say I blamed the man. He hadn't seen his

daughter in over ten years. The last time he had, she was crying because he was leaving, taking Grimm and I but not her.

She had no recollection of any of us. We never forgot her, the sad little girl in a pink nightgown who was so pale she looked like a ghost.

I'd tell her one day, maybe, but not that day. It would fuck with her head and lead to places I didn't want to go just yet.

Brock agreed that it was for the best, even more convinced when she said something about Dhal being a midwife and he easily put two and two together.

I stood up and rubbed my hands on my jeans, ready to get the fuck away from this whole scene. I'd left it all behind for a reason. Brock wanted that whole deep father-son thing, and I gave him crumbs.

I couldn't do any more than that. None of us ever had.

"We leave at three; that's seven hours away. Arlen, Grimm will show you where you're sleeping," I announced and turned back to Cali, crooking a finger. She said goodnight to Arlen and came straight to me.

Even pissed and more than likely disgusted, she looked at me like I was the only man in the fucking universe. No matter how twisted or deranged I got, she was always right there, accepting every dark, vile part of who I was.

She let me take her small hand and lead her to the trailer we'd be staying in.

"Ladies first," I gallantly gestured after unlocking the door.

"I don't see any ladies around here, good sir," she responded in a shitty English accent, taking the two steps inside.

"Wow," she breathed, taking it in.

Not that there was much to see.

There was one old ass plaid couch that pulled out into a single bed, a bathroom with a single shower, and a mini fridge with a microwave balanced on top of it. The only light that worked was the dull yellow one currently shining from above the toilet.

"It still smells like you."

"What the fuck? Is that good or bad?" I flipped the flimsy lock on the door and pulled the two couch cushions off, tossing them aside.

"Good. You smell exotic; it's hot."

"That's weird, babe. Anyway, there's a shower you can wash up in. The water's only setting is lukewarm."

Her sudden laugh caught my full attention.

"How old are these?" She held up a box of rubbers that had been sitting on the night stand. "There's only two left. Rome, I know you didn't bring me to the trailer you and Dhal used to have basic ass sex in."

"How do you know it was Dhal?"

"That weir...your father said something about seeing her again after some crazy number of years. Once he took a break from staring at me." She twisted her lips, looking deep in thought, then shook whatever it was away. "And I was just joking, I'm not that petty. I mean, I am, but I just want to cuddle up with you before we get all bloody."

I cocked my head and studied her impassively. She sounded sincere enough but this wasn't her go to MO.

"No demands that I tell you everything you want to know and all about my past? I at least expected you to say something about me having an acquired taste for human meat."

She sighed and planted her hands on her hips. "I want to know everything there is to know about you, Rome. I want to know how you got those scars under your ink, and how you ended up here of all places with that man. I don't give a shit about your acquired taste. This is how you were raised.

"As long as there are no human buffets, I'm good, even if it's gross. Like, really vomit inducing gross. " She wrinkled her nose. "I want to know how you became the head of the Savages. And why you keep things from me as simple as cellular phones, and how you feel about the baby we seem to only talk in circles about.

"I want to know so many things, and if you don't want to talk about your past, then at least let me know what's going on in the present.

"I never got to have a life; you know all there is to know about me. I was treated like a show animal. I was told when to perform and how. When I wasn't, I was locked in a room with shelves full of porcelain dolls. I fucking hated those dolls. You're my do over. I get to have a life with you."

Fuck. I felt like an asshole for once in my life because I didn't have the words to reply to any of the shit that just came out of her mouth. And for Cali, that was some next level maturity speech she'd just given.

She'd gone right into the kind of logical, emotional rant I avoided like the black fucking plauge. Half-assed honesty was the best policy, right?

"I don't know how to respond to half the shit you said. There are just some things I'll never tell you. Not anytime soon." *Or fucking ever,* I added silently.

I stood from my position over the pullout bed and went to her. Cali was strong, I would never deny that, but she was fragile too. I'd known it from the first day she woke up in my bed.

If it were some regular bitch that was the catalyst for all this, I wouldn't have spared her, but this was my queen. I couldn't tell Cali the deal with her mom because it tied too heavily into my past. I'd reluctantly told her about the deal with Janice.

I didn't tell her the real truth about Tiffany, or as she knew her, Tilly. I'd added bits and pieces of half a puzzle so she wouldn't try and save Tito. She took it all in with almost no reaction, simply because they'd all used her.

Tiffany never gave a shit about her. She used her to get close to David based off my order before I knew Cali still existed.

I told him who she was when I could no longer predict her next move. I sent her that night, knowing he would burn her alive.

David had been fucking her for months, thinking she was an outlier slut craving a man with power. Cali never knew about their relationship, and for whatever reason, David didn't tell her.

He didn't tell her a lot of things.

How did I fix that? Simple, I wouldn't. There was so much she didn't know about it. I constantly pushed her in the direction *I* wanted her to go in. I was a selfish manipulative motherfucker who had no shame.

I was doing her a favor in the big picture. Cali was out of her head. There was no question about it. She was child-ishly maniacal and didn't even realize it. Sometimes, I felt like I was like walking a tightrope of dos and don'ts with this girl.

Fortunately, I knew how to handle her. She was a shat-tered reflection of myself. She just never knew what to do with the broken pieces. *I* did that for her.

Making sure the void inside her stayed dark and dirty was for her own good. Depravity soothed her mind better than any medicine ever could.

In the beginning, it may have been easier to kill her and

put her out of her misery, but it was too late now. I couldn't let go.

Her beautifully twisted soul was mine and I was never giving it back. She made a deal with the devil without knowing the stipulations. I never told her it would be fair, only that it was never-ending.

Our baby was an entire different story. I'd wanted this for a very long time with a woman just like her.

I put my hands on her hips and gave a light squeeze. "I'll start with the most important thing you said. Don't ever think I don't want our baby. I don't jump for joy and shit when I'm happy, Pixie, you know that. But he is *more* than wanted. I knew what I was doing when I put him inside you."

She smiled up at me and I kissed the tip of her nose. What I didn't tell her was that I had a pretty good idea of how she knew she was pregnant in the first place. It made me want to kill those motherfuckers ten times more than I already did. I knew what they'd done as soon as it came to light. I had to let her know he would be fine.

"Don't worry about him. Once we're back home, I'll have the best doctor I can find on standby." Dropping a kiss to her forehead, I went back to preparing the bed.

"And for the record, I was only fifteen when me and Dhal happened. The last time, I was twenty-two. It was years ago and…" Why the fuck was I explaining this to her? "You're all I see, I don't want anyone else. "You're a crazy bitch, but you're perfect for me."

"Ah, Rome. That was the sweetest thing you've ever said to me. I heart you."

The room grew quiet as we both paused and eyed one another. That was the closest she'd gotten to telling me the three words I already knew she felt.

"And your dick was not this big at fifteen; nice try. How

many times did you have to wrap these around?" She laughed, and just like that, we were out of an awkward as fuck situation.

I grinned and cupped myself. "Baby, you know my dick's always been legendary."

"You did not just say that." She laughed louder and launched the box at me. "I'm going to wash up now."

She came out ten minutes later stark naked. From the long blonde hair that covered her tits that fit perfectly in my hand to her perky round ass, she was ethereal. My dick immediately jumped to attention.

She hadn't gained all her weight back yet, but she looked better, and the bruises I'd left on her were still visible—that was a plus. The scar from where I'd sewn her up had healed nicely.

This wasn't about me right then, though; it was about her and her up and down emotions.

It could have been my inexperience dealing with a woman for this long without killing her, but I knew it had more to do with the need to spill blood.

You could only hold off the darkness for so long before your demons took over and destroyed everything in their path.

She was ready to let loose, a ticking time bomb that would detonate as soon as I hit the right button.

In the morning, her chains would come off and the hellish beast lurking beneath the surface would be set free and never locked away again. I wanted every corner of her sinful mind engaged and ready to play.

For now, I'd settle with making her feel good. I wordlessly took hold of her hips and walked backward until I was sitting on the pullout bed.

"What are you doing?" She giggled when I laid back and

took her with me, pulling her tiny body up the length of my torso.

"I want your pussy on my face."

"Oh." Her whole demeanor changed. I could damn near smell how aroused she just got.

Grabbing hold of her frozen frame, I spread her thighs, gripped her ass, and positioned her over my mouth. "Spread yourself open for me, Pixie."

Instantly complying, she placed one hand on the back of the couch and used the other to pull her lips apart.

Holding her globes tight, I slowly dragged my tongue from her clit to her ass and then back up again, flicking at the little nub. Her breathing was already changing, growing choppy, and I knew it wouldn't take her long to get off.

"Ride my face, baby. Feel my tongue inside your tight pussy and fuck it."

My words set her off, arousal coating my taste buds. She had a tangy taste. I worked my tongue in and out of her, roughly kneading her ass.

"Rome," she half gasped-half whimpered, rocking on my face so hard, every time I breathed her scent went right into my nose, and my chin was drenched in her juices. She reached down and grabbed hold of my hair.

She fucked my mouth like her life depended on it, moaning so loud I wouldn't be surprised if the entire camp heard us again.

"Right there," she cried out, grinding her hips down on my tongue as I moved it around inside her hole, pushing in as deep as I could. The second I put pressure on her clit, she came, her legs locked on either side of my face, her tiny frame quivering above me.

I kept my tongue moving inside her, lapping up every drop, savoring the way she tasted in my mouth. When she finished shaking enough to move and catch her breath, her body slid down mine like a snake and she licked her arousal off my face.

"Rome…" she trailed off, straddling me right above my painfully hard dick.

"It's—"

"Don't you dare say it's okay. You took care of me. Now, let me take care of you."

She gave me a saucy smile, turning around so I had full view of her creamy ass and wet thighs.

My dick was out and in her mouth in less than a minute flat, and that's where it stayed until my come was hitting the back of her throat.

Chapter Twenty-Seven

Calista

Sure enough, Romero had me up and out of the trailer before dawn.

Arlen walked beside me like a member of the living dead, not at all a morning person.

I felt fine—lighter, in a way. I'd slept like a rock and woke up with Rome's words fresh in my mind.

"Where are your people?" I asked, belatedly realizing the acolytes were missing.

"You mean *our* people. I sent them ahead. I need to tell Brock goodbye."

I nodded, trudging along. There was a chill in the air and the faint scent of impeding rain.

As if conjuring him up, Brock stood by the entrance of the trailer park with his hands in his pockets.

"Heading back out, huh?" He stepped forward, offering Romero his hand.

"I'll keep in touch. If you need anything, you know how to get hold of me." They shook hands like they were business partners instead of father and son. He turned his gaze on me and almost looked like he was going to hug me. My body instinctively stepped into Romero's.

Brock nodded as if I'd just confirmed something. "She'll be okay with you, kid."

What the hell? Was I not standing right in front of him? It wasn't until we were back in the woods, heading up the trail, that I realized he could very well have remembered a semblance of me if he was in The Order like Romero had said.

I almost regretted not saying more than ten words to the guy, but he'd rubbed me the wrong way. The three of them may have been brought up by him, but they were nothing like him. I wanted to question it but that would be asking about his past again, and I needed to stop pushing if he was going to ever say anything.

Our group reached the jeeps in breakneck speed, only the sound of our footfalls interrupting the peaceful silence.

Arlen dozed back off as soon as we were on the road, leaving me, Grimm, and Romero wide awake.

"We know for certain that someone is at the cabin," Romero explained.

"Okay," I processed. "Do you know who?"

"Bishop Marco. You remember anything about him?"

"Well…." I'm guessing he didn't mean remember, as in, Marco couldn't fuck his way out of a paper bag.

"Marco has a wife, Veronica. She used to visit me with him. I don't know much outside of that." I fidgeted for a second, feeling a fresh wave of excitement. "So what's the plan?"

"There is no plan, aside from killing all these motherfuckers so we can go home."

We huddled at the edge of the property like soldiers about to go on a raid. The only person missing was Dhal, who didn't partake in such acts of brutality. Those were her exact words. I had no idea why she even came. It's not like she was needed to perform a medical exam or anything. I felt great, health wise.

"Just to clarify, we don't have a plan?"

We'd spotted two delegates standing guard outside the cabin's front and rear entrance, so walking right in wasn't an option.

"I got this, sis," Cobra said, speaking for the first time since we'd arrived.

He gave us all a cheeky wink and then darted off.

"What's he gonna do?" Arlen asked before I could.

"He's going to kill them before they have any idea he's there. It's how he got his nickname. He's fast and venomous."

Sure enough, he took out the delegate out back first. I didn't see it because I was too busy watching the one out front. When I looked to the back again, I saw the man on the ground in a puddle of blood.

"You ready to do this?" Romero asked me with a knowing smirk already on his face.

"Do you really need to ask?"

I felt like a predator getting ready to fuck up some prey.

My demons danced beneath my skin eager to play with his.

"Let's go, then." Rome gently took hold of my elbow and urged me forward, keeping me between him and Bryce.

"Some things never change," Grimm laughed as screams filtered out of the cabin.

We went right through the front door Cobra had left open, shutting it behind us.

"Look, they're here," Cobra announced, swinging a blonde around by her hair so that she was facing us. He no longer had his sling on and was using his hurt arm to hold her in place. I'm positive a doctor would frown upon that.

Grimm headed straight for the stairs, confidently striding up them.

"Hi, Vicky." I finger waved with a smile. "Where's Marco?"

A door slammed from upstairs, something fell, and a millisecond later, a body was rolling down the steps.

"Shouldn't people know by now that hiding under the bed is the dumbest thing you can do?"

Grimm sighed, his heavy boots resounded off the wooden stairs as he rejoined us.

He stepped right over Marco, who looked around in what appeared to be shock.

"You left your wife to hide under the bed? For real?" Arlen snorted and sat down on the leather couch.

"What do you want?" Marco asked.

"What the fuck do you think we want?" Romero asked in a bored tone.

"Pixie, why don't you explain to this beautiful couple what's going to happen?"

"Oh, okay, sure." I cleared my throat and opened my mouth, shutting it when Marco attempted to run.

"You can't be that dumb." Grimm grabbed him by the back of the neck and bounced him off the wall like a yo-yo.

He hit the floor again with a loud thud and pained groan, blood running from his nose. "Go ahead," Grimm encouraged, placing his shoe on Marco's chest to keep him down.

"Oh, you're going to die." I looked down at Marco and shrugged. Vicky choked on a sob, whatever she yelled muffled by Cobra's hand.

"Don't be so dramatic, Vicky. You are, too."

"It's your show, baby. Tell us how you want this handled." Romero put his arm around me, waiting for me to speak up. All of them stared expectantly, even Arlen.

"Look," Romero turned our bodies inwards, placing us chest to chest, "there's no wrong way to kill someone. Relax and let that crazy fucking head of yours do all the work."

"You're right, of course." Nodding, I inhaled, and then exhaled on a light bulb moment.

"How often does David check in with them?"

"Once at noon the other delegates arrive at four to do a shift change." Cobra answered, tugging on Veronica's hair.

"Okay, well, we should probably try and get one of them to talk. And, um, I need a needle and thread, please."

None of them so much as asked what the hell I was planning to do. With the exception of Romero, they all took off in different directions.

"How do you want to make them talk?"

"I thought one of you would work one while I worked the other."

"See, just let your mind do the work for you. You're a natural." He kissed my temple and stood protectively by my side. I looked around the open cabin as Veronica and Marco were gagged and bound in the center of the room, facing one another in large distressed dining chairs.

It was simple and quaint, nothing real special about it. Everything was rustic.

"Got the bags," Bryce announced, walking back inside with the two large duffels.

"Got your needle and thread," Arlen called from the bathroom in a back corner, lifting a sewing kit in the air when she walked out.

"Thank you." I took it from her and moved to where Veronica sat. Romero moved with me like a silent shadow.

Grimm and Bryce moved to separate windows to keep watch.

"Okay, I'll bite. What are you doing?" Cobra asked, leaning down with his hands on his knees.

"I figured I could start with this. The message that was left in Woeford gave me an idea." I flipped open the sewing kit and looked at my color choices. Veronica was a blonde with brown eyes. I held a spool of dark pink up next to her face. "Mm-uh." I shook my head and grabbed purple next, swiping one of her tears away with it.

"What do you guys think?" I asked the room, but looked to Romero.

"If you like it, I like it." He ran a hand through my hair and gave me a little more space.

"Well?" I glimpsed around at the others.

"I think we're gonna go with what Romero said," Bryce finally answered.

"Y'all are so typically male," Arlen huffed. "It looks good, Cali."

Giving her a thankful smile, I got busy threading my needle, carefully selecting which one I wanted to use.

"What's *typically* male?" Grimm asked her.

"That's like her asking Romero how she looks in a dress and he gives that answer; typically male. Never wanting to be offensive," she sighed.

It was dead silent for all of two seconds before they all laughed.

"Are you fucking serious? We're probably the most offensive men you'll ever meet."

"If Cali ever asked me how she looked in a dress, I'd tell her it didn't matter because it would be around her waist soon enough."

"Rome!" I feigned indignation, feeling my face warm.

"You know I think you look beautiful in anything."

I nodded, not giving a shit that there was a room full of people witnessing a disgustingly tender moment between us.

"Great. Now, if Cali could give my bro his balls back and move along," Cobra drawled.

"Shut up, that was definitely getting laid worthy," Arlen retorted.

"Is that all it takes?" Grimm asked her with zero amusement.

She glared and flipped him off.

"I got it!" I jumped up excitedly from where I'd been kneeling on the floor. I glanced back at Romero. "Can we play now?"

"I thought you'd never ask."

Chapter Twenty-Eight

Romero

She wasn't half-way done and Veronica was already screaming loud enough to break the windows.

"My goodness, shut the fuck up," Cali mumbled, pushing the needle through her upper eyelid and looping it through the lower, pulling the thread taut before starting another.

Marco writhed in his chair across from us, yelling around his gag until he was red in the face. Cali worked at a quick speed, weaving the thread in and out. Her fingers were coated with blood, along with the needle.

"All one of you has to do is tell us where to find the other bishops, and this can all be a thing of the past." She forced the gag back in Veronica's mouth and stood up, leaving the spool of thread attached to her eyelid to dangle. "I have to use the restroom. Cobra, maybe you should try."

He dropped the hunting magazine he'd been engrossed in and hopped up. "I'd love to."

I laughed at his enthusiasm. Cali vanished into the bathroom and shut the door. A second later, the sink turned on.

"So, how do you want to do this, my *liege*?" he asked me.

"Do your thing." I crossed my arms and stood calmly behind Marco's chair.

"Okay, then." He took hold of the dangling spool and jerked it so hard the needle tore straight through Vicky's eyelid.

I watched her and Marco both yell behind their gags, but I knew he wasn't ready to talk just yet, and Vicky was following his lead.

I gnawed my bottom lip and we shared a look, paying no attention the piece of eyelid now on the floor. We shared a look and I shrugged. "You up for it?"

"I'm always up for it." Cobra grinned.

"Brat, come take my spot."

She looked up from the table where she'd been going through all the paperwork they'd brought to the cabin.

Once she was at the window and Grimm was in position, we made our move. Even with one eye full of blood and missing a chunk of her eyelid, Vicky quickly figured out what was going on. Marco didn't get it until it was too late.

"Calm down, sweetheart, he might enjoy it." I patted the top of her head and smirked.

Cobra had just dropped his pants when Cali stepped back out of the bathroom. She made her way to me, taking in the new scene with curiosity.

Marco was bent over the chair, his ankles were tied to together, and his wrists were bound. Grimm kept him pinned with his strength to make everything a little easier.

Cobra lined his dick up, spreading the man's ass wide

open and plowing in dry. Marco screeched and tears spilled down his cheeks. He tried to move his upper body to fight off the assault, but Grimm's grip was ironclad.

"You ready to talk yet?" Cali asked Vicky, running her hand down the woman's tearstained face.

"I think he's done this before," Cobra laughed, lazily moving his hips.

With the exception of Arlen and Cali, we'd all seen Cobra do this so many times we couldn't pretend to be surprised.

I pulled the gag from Vicky's mouth and the first word she said gave us our second lead.

"Jericho? I thought that got torn down."

Cali looked from me to Grimm, the only two people in the room who would know what Jericho was.

"If it didn't, it's old as shit and…" I let them fill in the blanks.

"The perfect hideaway," she and Grimm said at the same time, sharing a rare smile with one another—rare for Grimm, that is. The motherfucker grinned less than I did.

"J-J-Jonah," Vicky stuttered, beginning to shake. Marco slouched completely, crying louder than any bitch I'd ever tortured. His wife had just signed and delivered their asses.

Cobra patted his back and slowly pulled out. His dick was still hard and tinged red.

"Alright." I nodded. "What now?" I looked at Cali, giving her the go head to let loose.

She gave me a slow smile. I could see the gears already turning her head. "It's only nine-thirty. We have over two hours."

Calista

He stood back and watched me work.

Letting my mind lead me, I straddled Vicky's lap, placed my hands on either side of her face, and stared into her eyes. Her breath smelled sweet, like toffee. She whimpered when I ran the tip of a finger over her ravaged eyelid.

We kill them slowly.

"It's okay." I gently ran my thumbs up and down her cheeks in a soothing motion, luring her into a false sense of safety.

Taking a small breath, I placed my lips on hers in a slow, sensual kiss.

Vicky sobbed but reciprocated pretty damn fast. I could feel everyone's eyes on me, each wondering what the hell I was doing. When her tongue hesitantly touched mine, I bit down on it as hard as I could.

Prolong their suffering.

The first thing she tried to do was turn her head. I dug my

fingers in until I could feel skin beneath my nails, and held her in place. I ignored her ear rupturing scream, jumping up when I tasted blood. Immediately, I spit it right into her bad eye.

I dropped down to my knees in front of the black duffel bags. Looking up, I measured the distance from the square banister overlooking the lower level to the floor.

Make them bleed.

It would suffice.

Romero crouched down beside me as I dug, lost in my own little world.

"What are you looking for?" He reached out and tucked my hair behind my ear.

"String or rope and a blindfold."

He unzipped the bag I hadn't gotten to yet and took out a roll of twine and the same type of black cloth he'd placed over my head the day we met.

"I want his socks off." I pointed to Marco. "And then you'll need your knife." His dark eyes studied me for a beat and then he moved towards Marco's chair.

"Is there a shovel somewhere, to dig a hole?" I asked the room, unrolling the twine.

"I can do that," Bryce volunteered. "How big does it need to be?"

"Big enough to hold a body."

"It'll be faster with two people," Grimm said, following Bryce out of the cabin.

I looked at the clock and took note of the time, scooting towards Marco with the blindfold in my hand.

"What are we doing, sis?" Cobra asked. He stood with Arlen, both watching me with open curiosity.

Instead of answering him, I looked up at Romero. "I want you to cut both of his Achilles tendons."

He didn't so much as bat an eyelid at my request. I watched him remove his knife from its hiding spot and crouch down.

Marco yelled something unintelligible through his gag.

Romero was fast. He lined his blade up and cut into the spot at the back of Marco's ankle, right above his heel. He sliced right through the springy band of tissue and then did the second foot just as fast.

Blood went everywhere. The back of his feet now resembled gaping, toothless mouths as the tendons separated and tore.

Marco and Vicky's cries mingled together, filling the room and making my heart do a little jig.

Devoting my full attention to my next task, I held the blindfold into Marco's right wound and harshly pressed down.

When it was drenched in his blood, I bounced up and slipped it right over his wife's head, pulling it taut, making extra sure it added pressure over her hurt eye.

Next came the twine.

Romero watched me closely as I snatched it up and quickly wound it around Vicky's neck twice, making sure a decent length was left for me to work with.

I waved Romero over to me and whispered in his ear, keeping an air of suspense for the benefit of our two new friends.

"Damn, Pixie, that's brilliant." He gave me a rare smile.

"We wanna know, too," Cobra whined.

"Let it be a surprise," Romero answered for me, already untying Marco's ankles.

He could no longer stand and had remained pitifully slouched over the chair while I tended to his wife.

His pants were still down, making the next part of my

plan easy. Romero held him up and I knelt in front of him. Lifting his flaccid cock, I wrapped the slack end of twine around it as many times as could before cinching the end.

I beamed up at him. His face was paper white and his jaw was clenched, his entire body trembling uncontrollably.

"Oh, damn, that makes my dick hurt," Cobra mused, laughing and covering his crotch.

"Arlen, untie her legs." Romero gestured to Vicky. "Cobra, go up top."

"Oookay," he drawled out, heading for the stairs.

"I can't believe I'm part of this," Arlen mumbled under her breath. "Let's go, lady." She pulled Vicky to her feet and looked to us expectantly.

"Ready?" Romero asked, already hoisting Marco over his shoulder, unperturbed that his cock was touching him.

Still blindfolded, gagged, and unknowingly tied together with her husband, Vicky stumbled forward when the twine reached its limit, digging into her neck and, simultaneously, Marco's flabby dick.

The three of us went to the upper level where Cobra waited, bouncing on the balls of his feet.

"Stand her here," I pointed to a spot on the floor right in front of the banister.

Arlen led Vicky to it and stepped back. Romero kept Marco as far back as the twine would allow. "Free ride's over, motherfucker," he announced, unceremoniously dropping Marco on the floor.

He was covered in sweat by this point, his chest heaving as if it pained him to breathe.

"I think I know where this is going," Cobra crooned.

Laughing, I stepped back. Romero wrapped his arm around my shoulder and tucked me into his side.

"Do the honors." He waved to Vicky, giving Cobra the green light.

Having the foresight to know what was about to happen, Marco writhed on the floor like a wounded animal.

Cobra lifted Vicky over the banister like she weighed nothing and sent her airborne. The fact that she never saw it coming made it ten times more enjoyable.

The real entertainment and payoff was watching Marco's dick go from an ugly pink to a dark purple as the twine angrily dug into it, cutting off all the blood flow and circulation.

He couldn't walk and was in so much pain he just lay there and screamed in agony, being dragged across the hardwood floor. Just as he reached the banister that would have stopped him from following his wife to the lower level, the twine broke apart.

I stepped right over him and peered down to see Vicky lying motionless at an odd angle. Her neck was bleeding and her right leg was clearly broken. The bone had shifted to an obtuse angle, almost pushing clean through her flesh.

"Well, alrighty then." Cobra nodded.

"That was like, cathartic, in a really weird fucked up way," Arlen agreed.

"What do we do with him?" Romero asked, resting his boot on Marco's side.

I looked down at the man and studied him, committing this moment to memory. I imagined it wasn't quite so fun with the tables turned.

When you went from being the strong to the weak, helpless, and completely at someone else's mercy, and you could do nothing to make the pain and degradation stop, death would be a welcome relief.

He and his wife had made me feel like that many times.

This—what I was doing to him—was an act of kindness compared to what I had planned out in my head. But my options were limited in this cabin so I had to do the best with what I had.

Did it change my past and erase years of being an abused fuck toy? No. Did it make me feel better and thirst to hurt someone more, do something crueler? Hell yes.

I hated these assholes.

I wanted them dead.

"Let's go check on your hole" Romero's voice filtered into my head, bringing me back to the moment. Our bloodied fingers intertwined and we walked away together.

Cobra and Arlen followed, dragging Marco behind them.

Chapter Twenty-Nine

Calista

The grave was shallow perfection.

Cobra dumped Marco right into it and managed to squeeze Vicky in slightly on top of him.

Being buried alive with your dead wife had to be a nightmare. Fortunately, I was the dream-maker and not the victim.

"How did you do this so fast?" I asked Bryce, toeing the soft dirt.

"It was already started. We haven't found whatever it was they wanted buried."

I hummed and stared down into the hole. It was caddy-cornered from the cabin with a clear view of the upper master-bedroom.

I wondered if that was planned.

"He looks damn pitiful," Arlen sighed.

She was right, he did. He was naked from the waist down, his dick was engorged, he had crusted blood on his nose, and the gaping wounds on the back of his feet rested squarely in the dirt.

"Let's bury him and get our asses to church," Grimm said.

As he and Bryce got busy filling the grave with dirt, Cobra went to drag the delegates to where we were.

"You need to relax. You know, the more you panic, the quicker you'll use up all your air," Romero explained as if he were speaking to a child. He tossed a cellular I hadn't seen before down on Marco's chest and grinned. "Tell David I said hello."

I shook my head and smiled. He knew full well that call was going to go unanswered. Marco still had a gag in his mouth and his arms were left bound. He turned his head left and right, yelling up at us, trying to shift from beneath his Vicky's body.

"You know how paranoid he's going to get?" I laughed just thinking about the look on David's face when he couldn't get hold of Marco.

"I know." Romero smirked, crouching down so he could look Marco in the eyes. "In just a few minutes, all your open orifices are going to be filled with dirt. It's going to crush your chest and your ribs. You won't be able to see, and you won't be able to breathe. You won't even be able to move. You're going to suffocate." He titled his head and grinned. "Slowly."

I rested my cheek on his shoulder and watched each mound of dirt bury Marco a little more. It was a small victory.

Whatever was lurking beneath my surface was far from satisfied. She didn't want slow, methodical torture. She hungered for fast, spur of the moment brutality. And I was going to find a way to give it to her.

"How the hell are we going to get in there?" I studied Jericho, popping another tortilla chip in my mouth from the bag I'd taken from Marco's.

"I can't believe this place still exists," Grimm commented, rubbing his beard.

Jericho was supposed to have been torn down before I'd ever been born. The church was more like a fortress. It looked ancient.

There were heavy padlocked chains in the shape of an X across the large double doors, and the windows were barred.

"I think they learned their lesson about windows," I mused, thinking back on how easy the acolytes had broken out the windows from the last church we showed up at.

Speaking of acolytes, I could see a few of the ones Romero had called on the other side of the property, which meant somewhere behind us were more.

"Where do they go when they're not with you?" Arlen asked him.

"I have the entire Badlands to keep track of. Who do you think helps shit stay in running order? Contrary to what you believe, I usually don't run around after fucking bishops or spend my every waking moment thinking of David. I do have an actual life. All three of us do."

"Not to mention this small thing called war that's going on. Who do you think's been dropping delegates and outliers left and right as we speak?" Cobra added when no one said anything.

"So they're like your employees."

"Close, but no," Grimm cut in, stealing a handful of chips from my bag.

Cobra sighed and waved his hand at Romero. "The devil is king here. The Badlands is his kingdom. The crazy as fuck blonde beside him is his queen, and all the insane fuckers wearing masks? They're hell's army."

"Yeah, yeah, I get it. And you're the greatest, his best friend, and simply just fuckin amazing, while Grimm's the dark and broody as hell Reaper, collector of souls," she deadpanned.

"I don't fucking brood," Grimm scoffed at the same time Cobra said, "You think I'm amazing?"

He grinned, placing a hand over his heart. I half-listened to their conversation, eyeing Jericho for another entrance.

"The back of the church has a crawlspace that leads to the wine cellar right by the rear doors," Bryce said out of the blue.

I'd almost forgotten he was with us. The man didn't go out of his way to say anything to anyone.

"He's right, there is," Romero confirmed, running a hand over his chin. He didn't question how Bryce could possibly know that, so I assumed there was another untold story there.

"And if this door is chained up, the rear isn't," I concluded, staring in that direction with a frown. This place was old as dirt; I could only begin to imagine what underneath it looked like. Dhal chose that moment to open her fucking mouth. I hadn't forgotten she was standing there but I was petty enough not to acknowledge her.

"If this crawlspace is limited on size, we should probably send the smallest person here in there." She made it sound as if that idea wasn't appealing to her.

"You could have just said send Cali in. None of you are smaller than me." *Bitch.* I added in my head. Romero glanced at me and smirked like I'd said it aloud.

"You know she's right, baby."

I pouted for a full ten seconds. On one hand, I was over-joyed he wasn't trying to wrap me in bubble wrap and treat me like glass because I was pregnant. On the other, I would have liked a little more resistance on his end about me crawling around under a church. The damn thing would prob-ably crush me just for being on holy ground.

"Let's just figure out how we need to do this," I sighed.

Chapter Thirty

Calista

This was the epitome of bullshit.

Cobra had snuck up first, finding the crawlspace and removing the grate. He'd returned and the first words out of his mouth were, *"It's dark as shit under there."*

That wasn't an issue. I liked the dark; it had always made me feel safer than the light.

I was given a mini flashlight, a knife, and a swat on the ass as my send off. "No bullshitting," Romero had warned.

There was an acolyte named Jeremy coming me with me. We were the same damn size, so him fitting wasn't an issue ,either.

We'd made it to the crawl space without being spotted, and were now crawling in what I hoped was the right direction.

The bullshit was the smell, the spider-webs, and the moldy dirt underneath me. I held the flashlight in my mouth and moved at a steady pace.

There were some fallen beams and spiders the size of my hand watching me from them. Their beady eyes seemed to say, "*You aren't supposed to be here.*"

Going out on a limb and adding mice or rats as another species that lived under here wouldn't be a far stretch.

"You good back there?" I whispered to Jeremy. I didn't want to turn and blind the kid with my flashlight.

"Yes, my liege," he answered respectfully.

I rolled my eyes and huffed.

Little pebbles pressed into my palms. I shuffled forward, dragging my jegging-clad legs.

The crawlspace opened up after another few minutes into a circular area. Aiming the light, I spotted the old door in the ceiling that led into the church.

To get to it, all I had to do was crawl over a small grave-yard of bones. My flashlight beam bounced off three skulls, one much smaller than the others. The rest of the bones I couldn't offhandedly identify. None of them were together anymore, and the skulls all sat in different places, coated in dirt and cobwebs.

"I would like to go first, my liege," Jeremy said softly.

"Its Cali," I reiterated for the fourth time since we'd been down there, moving out of his way.

He crawled past me towards the door. I kept the flashlight aimed up so he was able to see better.

I had no idea how he was moving so gracefully and not passing out from heat stroke, wearing his black robe.

The door lifted right up, which I found anticlimactic as fuck. Jeremy slowly eased himself up and out of the crawlspace.

I listened for a few minutes and waited. There was a soft thud right above me but no voices. Just when I began to think he'd been caught, his head popped back down and he gestured me onward.

Moving to him, I did my best not to crush any of the remains. I wasn't that disrespectful as to screw with someone's resting place. Even if this more than likely wasn't their number one pick in terms of burial sites.

Jeremy lifted me out of the crawlspace with ease, gently shutting the hatch behind me. "The back end of Jericho seems to be empty as of now, but there are voices coming from the front. I believe it's some sort of meeting," he quickly explained, opening the door of the small wine room we were in.

I shut off the flashlight, no longer needing it, and followed him out into an open foyer. "You get the back door open and let the others in. I'm going to eavesdrop." I took one step towards one of the halls that split off the foyer before he blocked me.

"I was told to stay with you. I—"

"Well, I'm telling you to go open that door. They could say something useful, and every second you stand here trying to stop me is another second wasted."

He stared at me without saying a word—or I imagined he was. I couldn't see his eyes beneath the mask. "Don't worry about me, I've done this before," I reassured him, and didn't wait to see if he responded or not. I darted down the hall.

I set my pace at a quick jog, trying to keep my steps quiet on the old wooden floor. Jericho's age showed everywhere I looked. Old woodwork and arches portrayed a design from a different era.

It was beautiful in its own special way. Too bad, really, because I wanted it burned down.

The place was just as large on the inside as it looked on the out.

I slowed when I got as close to the front room as I dared, hearing voices just like Jeremy said. Peeking around the corner, I saw the room was set up to my advantage. The pews all sat horizontally in the opposite direction.

I'd just spotted Bishop Jonah at the front of a group of delegates when the room exploded into a flurry of activity. Acolytes rushed in from the opposite hall.

Jonah didn't waste one second, taking off at a run for a stairwell in the back of the room. I debated what to do for only a split second. Pews were shoved backward, screeching across the floor and slamming into the ones behind them with loud, echoing booms.

It had gone from a meeting to a bloodbath in a matter of seconds, and the Savages had nothing to worry about.

The acolytes were ruthless. They were an impenetrable shadow that moved as one.

Anyone in their way was heinously cut down. This wasn't even a fraction of them; I couldn't picture dealing with the entire army.

I took one last look at the scene before me and then made a mad dash for the stairs.

Chapter Thirty-One

Calista

He'd beat me upstairs by taking another staircase.

The fucker was always ten steps ahead of me.

I crept down the hall towards their voices, snagging a heavy bronze chalice off a decorative podium.

"You were always my favorite, Romeo."

What the fuck? I froze just a few doors away from where they were.

"Look at you," Jonah wheezed. "Your father is so proud of you, my boy."

Confusion clouded my brain but I didn't get much time to dwell on his words. The telltale click of a gun had my legs moving on their own accord.

I peeked through a slit in the door and saw Jonah aiming a tiny black gun at Romero. My heart stumbled and sped up.

This fraudulent fuck had the balls to point a gun at *my* beloved devil.

Before I even realized what I was doing, I had the door flying the rest of the way open. Jonah's head whipped around and he gaped in what looked like confusion. It gave Romero the small distraction I knew he needed.

He grabbed hold of Jonah's arm and wrenched in a full circle, bringing the man to his knees. There was a loud crunch, followed by a gunshot.

I moved up behind Jonah and swung the chalice like it was a bat, crashing it into the side of his head. An audible gong sounded from the heavy cup and he fell to the side.

Romero looked at me for a split second before taking over. He flipped an unconscious Jonah onto his stomach and jumped up.

He seemed to be searching the room for something, seeing as it was a study of some sort; I was lost as to what.

His eyes were impossibly dark. I could feel the anger rolling off him in suffocating waves. It didn't take a rocket scientist to figure out the first part of Jonah's words. There was only one reason why a man like him would have called a younger Romero his favorite.

Sick fucking asshole.

I didn't say anything. I moved to the corner where a desk was and lowered myself onto it. There were no words I could say to make this okay for him.

"I'm sorry they hurt you too," just seemed so meaning-less, and an apology would never fix us. Whoever said violence isn't the answer was full of shit.

Violence soothed our demons and gave them a semblance of peace. I sat and watched the man I loved unleash his. There was no doubting that anymore. I didn't need to know the definition of a word to feel its meaning.

I think I loved him before we met. We'd been together only a moment, but it felt like a thousand lifetimes. Even then, as my brain slid pieces of a puzzle together that made my chest hurt, I still loved him.

Romero was irrefutably deranged and diabolically astute. He was a lethal fucking cocktail that came with a hazardous warning label, and I would die being blissfully inebriated by him.

I watched him strip Jonah of his robes and throw them in the fireplace. He grabbed a lit candle from the candelabra sitting on the mantle and shoved it straight up Jonah's ass, flame side up.

The act had Jonah screaming himself awake. He never got the chance to move. Romero's steel toed boot met his side, and something else cracked. Giving the man no time to reciprocate, he grabbed hold of his hair to lift him up. He dragged his heavy body like it weighed nothing to the other side of the room where he grabbed a cross off the wall.

Grimm flew into the room, quickly assessing the scene, falling right into a role he must have played a hundred times. He approached Romero cautiously, like one would a raging bull, taking hold of Jonah by the back of the neck.

Romero relinquished his grip as they shared a look. In one second flat, Jonah was on his back, the movement wedging the candle deeper, tearing the sensitive tissue in his rectum. A trickle of blood ran from between his legs.

Grimm grabbed hold of his upper and lower jaw in a familiar move. His muscles flexed and he pulled as hard as he could.

He kept hold of it as Romero slammed his boot down on Jonah's chest and the metal cross he'd snatched off the wall in his mouth, forcing it to fit.

They proceeded to tag team him. Jonah's wide hazel eyes met mine only once.

"You don't get to look at her, you piece of shit," Romero growled, sounding like a possessed beast. I thought he'd forgotten I was even in the room.

By the time they were finished, he was no longer recognizable as a human being. He was missing chunks of blonde hair. His skin was black, blue, and bloody. His body looked unnatural and clearly broken. They'd finished him off by carving a large leviathan cross down his stomach.

Both men were breathing heavily, covered in blood and sweat. Unsure what to do, I slowly stood up with the intention to give them a minute alone. They'd clearly needed this one kill much more than I did.

Romero's eyes flashed to mine and cemented me to the floor.

"Get the torques ready. We need a minute." He spoke to Grimm but continued to stare at me. Looking between us, Grimm nodded, grabbed Jonah's large, broken body, and left the room.

"You were going to come in here alone with him."

Okay. That wasn't the first thing I'd expected him to say, but I understood why he'd be pissed. I had never seen Romero lose control of himself, but there was a first time for everything.

He wasn't a get-angry-in-your-face kind of psycho. He was a silent killer. He raged inside and only showed it through his actions. He'd just brutalized a man and barely spoken a word the entire time. His eyes told a different story.

"What the fuck were you thinking?"

"I wasn't," I admitted. The steel in his voice had part of me ready to hide under the desk, but I refused to cower, and I honestly hadn't been thinking. All I knew was that he couldn't get away. Now that it came back to me, I saw how reckless it was.

"I shouldn't have done that. I won't do it again."

"I know you won't, because I'm taking you home," he replied, cool as ice.

"You're going to keep me at your warehouse while you—"

"That's not our home." He cut me off. "This isn't a debatable topic. I don't give a shit what you do once you're there, but it's the best place for you. There's a fucking tiny army of Savages that will die for you there. There's a doc on standby. I need you to do this without fighting me. It makes me fucking crazier than I already am every time you go off on your own.

"I'd tear this whole motherfucking world apart if something happened to either one of you. I can't lose you."

I swallowed, opened my mouth and then shut it again. He hadn't said a damn thing wrong. He'd said everything right. The rawness in his voice tore at my heartstrings.

"I will bring David to you alive. We can still end this together," he added in a quieter voice.

"Okay. I'll go."

"Okay?" he asked in disbelief.

"Yeah, okay. It's the best thing for Baby S, and you just said you'd bring David to me. You took all my ammunition away before I could even load it."

I wouldn't play at his emotional state. This was rare form for him, and that would be wrong on so many levels, so I eased back into his comfort zone with wit. I was becoming quite good at that.

"Cali." He gave me a whole different kind of look and I knew exactly what it meant.

"Rome," I retorted, pretending to be oblivious and failing.

He was covered in blood and had just destroyed a man in front of me; he'd never looked fucking better. I don't think I'd ever wanted him more.

"Get up and turn around. I want you bent over that fucking desk."

Chapter Thirty-Two

Calista

It was painfully intense.

I was completely naked.

He was behind me on his knees with his tongue inside my pussy and the handle of his knife easing in and out of my ass.

I'd already come once. He pulled away and sunk his teeth into my right cheek. I bit my lip to stifle a moan. The knife disappeared and something wet replaced it.

I glanced over my shoulder to see him holding his freshly cut fist over my ass, letting blood drip down the crevice. I could have come again from that visual alone.

"Rome, hurry up." I pushed back at him, arousal making my pussy clench when his onyx hues looked into mine. "Can you take your shirt off?"

His pristine grin was full of devilry, disappearing as he

pulled his bloody T-shirt off and let it drop to the floor. I drank in his wildly inked body, wishing I was facing the other way so I could stroke the wicked looking skull.

He eased behind me, smearing his bloody fist up and down his dick before spreading my ass cheeks apart and shoving inside with no warning. The immediate pressure was overwhelming. I was so full of him, I thought I was going to rip in half.

I choked on a scream, grabbing the desk to brace myself. He grabbed hold of my throat to keep me upright; his other hand lifted my leg and hooked it over his arm, leaving me to balance on one.

He pummeled me. His dick drove into my ass like it had committed a crime against him and this was punishment. The blood quickly lost its slickness and all I felt was every solid inch of him thrusting in and out. It hurt in a beautiful agonizing way, a way only he had ever made me feel.

"Fuck, Rome!" I gripped his wrists so hard my nails dug in.

"Say it again," he breathed in my ear, kissing down my neck.

"Romero," I moaned, as he picked up his pace, leaving me a quivering, screaming mess.

"Play with my pussy, baby. Touch what belongs to me."

My hand immediately flew between my spread legs. It was a miracle I could concentrate. I fucked myself with my fingers while he dominated my ass.

"You feel so fucking good. This will always be mine," he growled, biting down on my shoulder and bottoming out.

"Yours, all yours," I agreed, feeling heat gathering in my core.

His grip on my throat tightened, and he dug his fingers into my thigh. I felt his solid abs against my back. I moved my fingers to my clit, rolling it in a circular motion. "Holy shit, Romero! I'm—"

I grabbed hold of his wrists with my hands, unintelligible words poured from my mouth, mixed in with a barrage of unrestrained moans.

I saw colors I didn't even know existed.

It felt so good, I started crying while I was coming.

"Cali." I heard him laugh and opened my eyes.

I was leaning my head back against his chest, missing the part where he came and it was now running down my ass crack. He stood me up and kept his arms around my waist.

Slowly turning in his arms, I laid my cheek on his damp chest and shut my eyes. When I finally looked up at him, I placed a soft kiss on his lips.

Being in his arms brought back the things in my head I'd temporarily pushed aside. I needed to process all it meant and ask a question I already knew the answer to, because it made too much sense. First thing first, though; I needed to get out of damn Jericho.

"You ready to burn a church down?"

His soft laugh was the only response I needed.

We watched the church burn together. Jonah and the delegates burned with it.

His broken body was secured by the padlocks on the front door. The roof groaned and shifted as parts of the old building caved in. Flames reached into the darkened sky as our sign of victory. We had no lead on the other bishop or David, but this was still a pretty big deal.

"Romero, who is your real father?"

I kept my eyes trained straight ahead. I didn't think he was going to answer me.

"David made me, but that pathetic piece of shit will never be my father. Or yours."

From the corner of my eye, I saw Grimm shift beside him, uncomfortably.

That had me turning my head to meet his stare. "Brock is."

What?

"Brock is what?"

"Your father," he said calmly.

"The cannibal? Grimm's—that would make—"

"I'm your half-brother," Grimm cut in.

What the entire fuck?

This wasn't what I was expecting. I was expecting Romero to admit David was his father; the evidence of that was astounding. David hugged him, and David had only ever hugged his sons. He didn't let any man that close to him without making a power play. That's why the hug had always bothered me so much.

He came from The Order. He and Grimm weren't blood brothers, and Brock clearly was Grimm's father, making the signs point back to David.

One of the most obvious red flags was the fact that he was able to leave the Order at all, and only David would have allowed that. If it were anyone else ,they'd be dead, but Romero was his son, and David's sons were like gold to him.

He and Brock weren't close. Jonah told him his father was proud of him—referring to David—and that's what really honed it in for me.

Romero owned the Badlands. He was strong and lethal. He was everything David would be pissing himself in joy over, because he was *his* son.

My brain was ready to implode. Romero did a lot of morally questionable things, but I knew he'd never touch me if I was his sister. I didn't ever consider the possibility of my real father being a goddamn cannibal. Or that the man I thought was my father might have no relation to me at all, depending on who my mother was.

"This is…this is…"

"It's a lot to take in, I know. Why don't you and Arlen ride with Grimm? We need to go, and I know you want space."

Glancing up at him, I wasn't sure what to say.

We all began branching off, leaving the burning church behind us.

Romero remained silent as he walked me to the passenger seat of the second jeep.

"I love you. Just thought you should know," I said softly. I didn't need a special moment or shining stars, and I was likely to kick his ass if he tried to give me a candlelit dinner, so what better time than the here and now?

What better time than when I needed him to know I was still all in? It would always be him in the end, even if the foundation beneath our feet caved in and the walls came tumbling down around us.

"I know you do, baby." He wrapped his arms around me and pressed his lips to my forehead. "This shit won't always be easy. Love…is just a word to me, but you taught me how to define the feeling. It's how I feel inside, and how fucking insane you make me. I want to kill you half the mother-fucking time, but the need to keep you is overwhelming.

"You're the queen to my king. I'll worship the ground you walk on as long as you always walk beside me."

"I'll always be beside you. I don't need perfection, Rome. I just need you and all your insanity."

He cupped my face in my hands, kissing me hard before stepping back again to open my door. I climbed inside and watched him walk away.

Chapter Thirty-Three

Calista

We drove for hours.

The first two, it was awkward as hell.

Three was unbearable, and I had to say something.

"I don't want to talk about it," I tossed out honestly.

That apparently was the right thing to say; Grimm seemed to relax visibly. I studied him from my peripheral. We looked nothing alike. His skin was tan and covered in tattoos. His hair was dark brown with naturally lighter strands on top.

He kept it brushed back or trimmed short. Same with his beard; it was either full or freshly shaven. His eyes were dark, too.

Everything about Grimm had an edge of darkness about it, just like the man himself. He was quiet and hard to read. I could easily see how he and Romero had ended up so close.

He let out a sigh and glanced at me a brief second before giving the road his attention. "I meant it when I said someone should have been there for you. I'm not sure how this all works, but I'm here now. Always."

I nodded, finding it hard to voice a worthy response. The feelings talk had drained me enough already, and this was something I needed to process in my own time.

Silence reigned again, but it was different. Companionable.

By the time we reached where we were going, my head was still all over the place, and my ass was numb from sitting for so long.

It all momentarily faded away as Grimm approached a twelve-foot barbed-wire fence. All I saw was an expansive desert-like field.

There was a guard shack on either side of the lone gate. Three acolytes manned each one. They had guns similar to those the skinners had carried.

Two held what looked like thin tow chains turned into leashes for the beasts at the end of them. They were funny shaped and had spots.

"Are those fuckin hyenas?" Arlen asked incredulously.

"Max and Toby," Grimm answered, almost affectionately.

"They're kinda cute," I mused.

A buzzer went off, and the gate slid open with a clicking sound. Our small fleet of vehicles pulled through and continued down a long road.

"Where exactly are we goin?" Arlen asked after a minute rolled by.

"Home. The house is just up ahead."

"You sure it's not a prison?" I mumbled.

He laughed aloud and shook his head.

"Holy shit." I stared up at the monstrous house rising in the distance.

"Your man's been holdin out," Arlen breathed.

The place was gorgeous, but I wouldn't call it a house.

I heard a whirring noise and turned my head to see a golf cart heading off across the field.

"There are acolytes at the gate and four sets of two that constantly circle the fence," Grimm explained.

"His following is crazy," I said, more to myself than them.

"He's loyal to those loyal to him," Bryce stated. "They have homes on the rear of this property and everything they could need: food, water, clothes, and electricity."

"So he has a compound full of devil worshipping psychos?" Arlen sarcastically drawled.

I smiled and shook my head.

"Romero is the devil, so I guess he has an army of worshipping psychos."

Before she could say anything else, we were pulling around a circular drive and stopping.

Romero was at my door the second my seatbelt was off. He pulled me out and looked me over from head to toe.

"What do you think?" he asked once he was satisfied I hadn't harmed myself on our journey.

"I think you need to explain why she's here." I not so discreetly pointed at Dhal. I had full confidence he wanted nothing to do with her in that way' she still wasn't living us under one roof.

"I wasn't making a pit-stop to drop her ass off. She's not staying, so don't start your girly shit," he smirked and took my hand, leading me towards the front door.

We were the last to enter the house. Cobra was already leading Arlen up the stairs, boasting about her being his new housemate. The second the conditioned air hit my skin I noticed a few key elements.

1: The house wasn't actually that much larger than his warehouse and had the same setup—almost.

2: Romero had a lucarative lifestyle because of his position; he had nice, luxurious things.

3: The whole satanic theme was ten times worse here than at his old place.

The main ceiling fixture was a black ram head in the center of an inverted pentacle that held four light fixtures.

The large flag was on his open dining room hall, but black and white and instead of red and white. And the wall fixtures were deep golden ram heads that served as placeholders for candelabras in the shape of inverted crosses.

Everything else was normal, if not a little too masculine—all dark brown hardwood and charcoal coloring.

Romero didn't bother giving me a tour or explaining his décor; he led me straight up the stairs and through a set of black double doors at the end of the hallway. He had me shoved against the wall with his mouth devouring mine without giving me a chance to look around. I kissed him back, greedily.

He let me go and stepped away, running a hand over his lips. I inhaled the smell of him and looked around the room. The bed was black, large, and wrought iron. There were matching dressers and leather loveseat. A flat TV hung on one of the charcoal-colored walls.

"It's very you," I said, taking note of the Sigil of Baphomet on the ceiling above his bed.

"You don't find it creepy to have the symbol of Satan staring at you while you sleep?"

"That symbol represents my life."

Right, he had a point.

"We need to talk." He peeled me off the door and led me to the sofa, sinking down with me on his lap.

"I have the doc arriving tomorrow to check you over. I'll be here until I get a lead, but I've got a lot of shit to catch up on. You're free to do whatever you want here."

I nodded. I wanted him superglued to my side, but that really wouldn't be the best idea for us considering how up and down we could get.

Plus, someone had to make sure the Badlands stayed in order—that someone being him. There had to be something left to keep.

"I get it." I trailed a finger across his jawline.

"And there's a gathering tonight. I wanted to give you a heads-up."

"A gathering? Oh, fuck that!" I jumped off his lap and glared down at him. "You're not doing that freaky goat shit with someone else. You can just cut off your dick right now if you expect me to be okay with that."

His mouth twitched, giving away the fact that he was trying to hold back a smile.

"I would never let anyone touch my dick but you, Cali. That was an initiation; I won't be claiming any other woman like that in this lifetime. This is just a gathering because I've been gone so long. I need to update them on what's happening and let them see your face."

"Oh." What else could I say? I was beginning to see this whole devil/king thing wasn't a role or him playing a character; it was real life, our reality. I could accept it—no, I *did* accept it. I would proudly stand by his side like the queen I was.

"How are you handling everything?" he asked.

"Honestly, I don't know." I shrugged.

I hadn't given myself a chance to analyze what anything

he'd said earlier meant. "I don't consider either of those men my father. One used me, and the other left me. I'm more concerned about what was done to you."

He looked up at the ceiling for a minute and then nodded to himself. "Sit down, Cali. I need to tell you something you should've known a long time ago."

Chapter Thirty-Four

Romero

There was a ton of shit I would never tell Cali.

But then there were things I figured I'd been wrong about her knowing that maybe she should.

I told her Brock was her dad because I didn't want her thinking she'd been getting fucked by her brother.

She looked at me, her blue eyes never shying from my onyx ones. There was a slight frown on her face, and I hadn't even started yet.

I hadn't the slightest fucking clue where her mind was.

Cali's brain operated on its own wavelength; sometimes, it was damn near impossible to know what shit her head had spinning around in it.

Cobra and I had gone over what I should and shouldn't tell her on the drive back from Jericho. That was the only reason I'd had her ride with Grimm. I wasn't a 'give space' type of person. She could be as mad as she fucking wanted right beside me.

Grimm knew his baby sister was a whole different kind of fucked up than he and I were, but just like our father, he trusted me to take care of her and tell her what I thought she could deal with.

It was Cobra who miraculously wound up being the voice of reason. He pointed out how open-minded she was, how she didn't judge anyone, how she could walk in a room with two people that destroyed her innocence and remain calm and outwardly collected.

She was so fucking strong.

I knew she could handle the parts of my past I was about to share with her. I walked to the window and rolled my neck.

"Time…it doesn't change shit. No matter how many years go by, I still remember it like it was yesterday. My mom was David's third wife. I was never close with him. He thought my mom had an affair because I didn't have his eyes.

"Things were shitty but about as bearable as they could be in The Order. Then, your mom came along, and David got fucking obsessed. He fucked her on the side. I was young, but I can remember my mom crying a lot. It wasn't until I got older that I pieced some of this together.

"Your mom got pregnant. David thought it was his. He found out it belonged to the man who was supposed to be his best friend—Brock. I think that's when he fucking snapped.

"He had you removed from your mother. That same night, he put me in the Shiloh. I was five. The scars are just remnants of my time spent there.

I was allowed out once a month. Other than that, I was fed there, slept there, and spent my time in solitude. Men came to see me—a few women, too."

I glanced over my shoulder and saw her hanging onto my every word.

"My mother gave me my tactical knife. I was ten by this time. A week later, in the middle of the night, I was taken from the Shiloh and brought into a room.

"Jonah was there, and David too, of course. And three others. They had a woman down on the floor with a veil around her head, taking turns raping her. Beating the shit out of her until her ribs cracked and her jaw broke. When they were done, they left me in there and told me to clean up their mess.

"I pulled the veil off the woman's head and was met with the face of my mother. I killed her, used the knife she'd given me to slit her throat. I couldn't fix her, and I couldn't leave her to die like a wounded animal.

"Fucked up thing is, by that point I felt nothing for her. I still can't bring myself to feel bad about it. I remember staring at the blood and placing my hand over her heart. I felt it beating hard at first, fighting to keep her alive. It slowly faded away.

"And you were right, David never told us to leave. Brock took me and Grimm in the middle of the night and got us out. He couldn't get to you. You've always been untouchable. He went back to try, but David had moved the colony by then. The rest is ancient history.

"I grew up a cannibal. Brock did what he could to make me human again. He became something like a father; Grimm *is* my brother. We found Cobra a year later. "

I sighed and turned to look at her, making my way back to the couch. I needed a fucking drink, and I didn't drink.

"Rome, I—"

I hushed her with a kiss. "I don't talk about this shit,

Pixie. I don't need to and I don't want to. This was just something I wanted you to know."

I expected her to push me. She didn't.

"Okay. I understand. I won't bring it up again, promise." she held up her little pinky.

Fuck, she was perfect for me.

Like a pussy, I looped my much larger pinky with hers. She smiled as if I'd just given her a pony. "But you can tell me about your cult, right?"

"My cult?" I raised my brows. I guess she would've caught on to the fact that the Savages weren't some street gang. I never told her much about it at all.

I'd just tossed her ass in my world without a lifejacket, and made her learn to swim in it. She hadn't drowned yet, so I'd like to say things were going good.

"Really?" She tried to mock my look and failed.

"I'll tell you about that another day. In the meantime, why don't you get cleaned up? You have clothes in the closet. Come down when you're ready." I kissed her cheek and reluctantly moved away.

I could sit and talk with her for hours. Right then, though, I just wanted to talk to my brother.

Chapter Thirty-Five

Calista

When his door clicked shut, I went to the closet and peeked inside. He'd had a whole section of grunge clothes and a few dresses brought in. He was always paying attention to the little things.

Smoothing my fingers over all the different fabrics, I thought over everything he'd just told me. The ache I felt for him was both physical and mental.

The Shiloh was a like a round metal water tower without the legs. There were three of them on the edge of The Order's property.

They had one small circular window in the ceiling, dirt floors, and no toilets. I have no idea what my state of mind would be like if I'd been locked away as he had. I knew things couldn't have been good for him, but he'd had it far worse than me. And now, David wanted to be his friend? Fuck that.

I wouldn't pretend I knew what any of that was like. His admittance to killing his own mother didn't even surprise me. Maybe that should've bothered me far more than it did, but I couldn't force myself to conjure up feelings that weren't there.

All I had was this bubbling fissure on my heart of pain, and heartache for the little boy he'd never got to be and what was done to him. I understood why he didn't talk about it.

There was nothing pleasant in reliving those memories, and I didn't need specific details to make the right assumptions.

I grabbed a simple black t-shirt dress, some knee-high boots, and finally some damn underwear from a drawer.

His bathroom was something from a dream. It was dark and warm, comforting and clean. I hadn't sat down in a bathtub in months, so I went straight for the big ass soak box in the middle of the room.

Kicking off my shoes and clothes, I padded across the cool slate floor to the vanity, where a basket of bubbles sat. I'd never had bubbles before. I looked in one of the double mirrors as I waited for the tub to fill, trying to compare what I'd been to what I'd become.

The thing about mirrors is that they only showed us reflections of how we saw ourselves. They didn't show what was inside us.

I used to want people to believe I had a light inside me, and in doing so, I made myself empty.

I knew the woman staring back at me was far from perfect, but at least I was no longer at odds with the stranger she'd been.

Maybe in a different world, I would have been fortunate

enough to have a life full of laughter and love from the beginning. My hands wouldn't have been permanently stained red.

But I didn't, and I was okay with that, because I would have never belonged in that world. It didn't matter who my mother was, because I never knew her, and nothing would change that.

I didn't care who my father was, because I'd never had one. I felt nothing, only relief that I wasn't an incestuous fuck toy, although that didn't make me feel better about what was done to me.

Submerging myself in warm water and a variety of bubbles, I leaned my head on the rim of the tub and shut my eyes.

It felt good being able to think clearly without going into a tailspin.

My mind wasn't so much of a chaotic war zone with the animal inside me wide awake and learning to thrive, no longer locked in a cage. I was exactly where I needed to be. It took a lot of dead bodies to get here, but I'd do it all over again if I had to.

I was born a freak, now turned into a deviant Savage.

I was the devil's queen.

The devil was my king.

I'd found my peace in his world of darkness.

I woke up beneath a warm comforter and a semi-dark room. I hadn't meant to fall asleep; I'd sat down for two minutes after getting out of the tub.

I could hear voices—lots of voices.

Hopping out of bed, I quickly dressed in the clothes still in the bathroom. My skin smelled like the variety of bubbles I'd dumped in my tub water. After a quick brush of my teeth and hair, I smoothed on black eyeshadow and left the room.

The second I shut the door, I spotted Romero. He was standing on the stairs addressing a house full of people. Some wore the masks and robes; some didn't.

I stood back and watched him work the crowd. It was obvious that these people adored him and everything he represented. When he talked, they listened as if they were entranced, and when he moved, they followed as if they were compelled. I leaned against the door, content to stay in my little bubble for a few minutes longer.

"Cali."

I blinked when he popped up in front of me.

"You zoned out on me, baby." He linked our hands together and led me towards the stairs. Music was playing from somewhere, and the smell of food made me weak in the knees.

"Did I miss something?"

"Only that everyone is losing their shit because you're home and having my kid."

"I missed *all* that?" I had to damn near yell to be heard.

"Cali, you should have your skinny ass in bed and be pigging out. You're exhausted. And don't try and fucking bullshit me, I can see it."

Fucker.

He led me to the sofas and sat me beside Arlen.

"Stay here; I'll be back." He disappeared into the masses without explanation.

A few minutes later, he was back with a plate of delicious goodness and a bottle of water. He dropped down on my other side and handed me the plate.

I bit into the juiciest burger in existence and almost moaned. I didn't even care there was an onion on it. The meat was thick and healthy looking, unlike the flat mystery burgers The Order used to consume.

I swallowed my mouthful and looked over at him. He and Grimm had their heads bent in conversation. As I turned my attention back to my plate, Dhal caught my eye.

This chick was weird—and that said a lot, coming from me. She pretended she hadn't just been staring at Arlen and me, making herself that much more obvious.

Finishing off my plate and water, I searched for a trash-can, only to have the plate lifted by an acolyte. He or she gave me a slight nod and simply walked away.

"Stop glaring." Romero nudged me with a soft laugh, instantly making me melt. He'd been doing that a lot lately—laughing, that is. I loved it.

"They like doing shit like that," he explained.

"Being garbage collectors?"

"I have to go to the pot," Arlen said. She'd been speaking specifically to me, but Grimm heard due to the volume.

"Let's go." He stood up and held his hand out like a well-refined escort.

"I'm not goin to argue with you about being my shadow, because I don't wanna piss my pants." She took his hand and huffed out an exasperated breath.

I stared after them with furrowed brows.

"That's going to happen," Romero stated with something akin to amusement. I'd like to have agreed with him but I didn't see it.

"Didn't you all have a thing with her sister?"

"You mean, didn't we all fuck her bitch of a sister at the same time?"

"Yeah, Rome, that's exactly what I meant." I rolled my eyes and shoved his shoulder. "What happened to her?"

"She'll be at the hotel until it's laundry day."

I wanted to know what he meant but that would have to wait. I followed his gaze across the room where Luther stood with Dhal, both staring back at him expectantly.

"I'll be back." He rose from the couch, dropping a chaste kiss on my lips before making his way through the masses. Unsurprisingly, people got the hell out of his way without him saying a word.

Unsure of what to really do with myself, I just sat there, receiving more than a few weird hand signals and genuine grins, one of them from a redhead I remembered being at my initiation.

"Wanna girl chat?" Arlen asked, bounding up to me and wiggling her brows.

I had no idea how to do that, but one could try.

"Sure." I grinned and let her pull me off the couch and

through the crowd. Surprisingly, people were quick to move the hell out of my way, too.

We passed a man that had a woman sitting on his lap, stroking her hair. She was naked, and her throat was split open. He smiled at me, so I assumed he was lucid.

She took me through the back door, out into the warmth of the night. We walked to a patio set and sat down.

Across the lawn, I saw teepees of flames with some of the Order delegates and sisters being burned alive within them thrashing around in pain. Their screams were full of agony.

I'd seen much of this from my initiation, so it was easier to take in stride this time around. It would take a minute for me to adjust to this fully, but it was easily doable.

"How are you doin with everything?" she asked, tearing her gaze away from the fires.

"Well, I know my father went from being the head of a bullshit religious cult to a cannibal, but…I don't really care. I've never had parents. This Brock guy doesn't change that."

"I totally get it. My sperm donor would rather run the Kingdom than be a dad," she shrugged.

"Run the Kingdom as in…?"

"He's the mayor," she answered slowly, as if this was common knowledge.

"Your dad is mayor of Centriole?" I confirmed.

"Shit, you didn't know?"

I shook my head. No wonder no one seemed surprised when she dropped Kingdom knowledge left and right.

I think people tended to forget my limited knowledge of the world. How would I have known who she was? I didn't watch the televised news segments, or have cellulars.

The only news I'd ever been interested in was about the Savages. I only discovered my music preferences and clothing style four years ago.

" It's not something I ever discuss freely, but it's not a secret. I thought you knew."

Her tone was apologetic, so I believed her. I just couldn't see it, and I didn't understand why she was still in the Badlands, along with her sister. After Romero's cryptic response about Beth, I was positive something was going on with that whole situation and they were both tight lipped about it.

I wasn't going to dive into her business—that included raging at Romero to tell me what the fuck it was, because I knew he knew. If she wanted to tell me, she would.

"You know what's crazy?" she asked.

"Hmm?" I responded absentmindedly.

"If people in The Order are turning on each other and either joining the Savages or branching off, and the same is happening with everyone else, where are these rouges aligning? No one wants to be alone in the Badlands. That's fuckin suicidal."

I replayed her words in my head twice.

She was right.

"You're right. There's someone else, a third player!" Goddamn, why hadn't I thought of that? It was the same question I'd asked myself long ago: who the fuck was the enemy of whom?

I sat up in my chair, already spinning through who it could be. I began speaking aloud. "Whoever is feeding people info is on the inside and close to this person. So close that they knew Romero had me the first time and exactly when he had me the second time. Now, who would run off and tell David Romero had found me?"

"That little bitch, Dahlia." Cobra's venomous voice cut through our conversation.

Chapter Thirty-Six

Calista

Everything that happened after Cobra eavesdropped on our conversation was a blur.

He was there one second and gone the next, no doubt going straight to Romero.

I waited around with Arlen, but nothing happened. She wanted to confront her; I knew it was best to give the bitch her illusion of safety and let her gut herself.

She was lingering and interacting with people when I went back to the room.

I ended up in bed without Rome, figuring he was out pillaging villages in a rage, or drowning puppies.

What sounded like a foghorn woke me at three in the morning.

Before I could make it down the hall to investigate,

Romero carried me—literally—back to our room and fucked me back to bed.

Fast forward a few hours later, a woman with silver hair and a pudgy face quickly lost her smile when neither of us seemed to have the reaction she was expecting.

"Heartbeat is one-fifty-four." She wiped her fetal Doppler off and then the goop on my stomach. "That's good," she added when I stared blankly.

Romero squeezed my hand, and I squeezed his back. We were happy, of course, but neither of us were sentimental people. I was so in love with him that I'd lie, steal, and kill without hesitation. Yet, I'd only said it once.

I just found out the asshole who spent my whole life playing god wasn't my real father, but that a man who literally ate prime rib was. I wasn't going to break down over a heartbeat.

I never thought there was anything wrong with Baby S to begin with. He was alive and healthy. Excellent.

I was barely over two months, according to some weird wheel thing the doctor spun around. She asked me a shit load of questions about being sick, tired, cravings.

Aside from sleeping more, I felt the same as I always had. Blood samples were taken, she gave me pills that looked way too big to swallow, and then we left her to set up whatever she'd need to stay around until D-day.

"Sucks about your, um, person," I said twenty minutes later as we entered the open living area.

Not responding right away, he walked to the fridge and retrieved two bottles of water, handing one over when he joined me on the couch.

"I'm not surprised she did it, but I wish I were."

Shit. This was not my department of expertise. I awkwardly reached out and patted his back.

"What the fuck are you doing?" He stopped staring at the Sigil on the wall and glanced at me.

"I was trying to be comforting, asshole." I snatched my hand away, placing it on my lap.

"You comfort me with your pussy or your mouth, occasionally your wisdom."

What a dick. I bit my cheek so I wouldn't smile.

"Arlen confronted Dhal last night, and now she's missing," he tossed out lazily, as if he were telling me the sky was blue.

"Missing as in, you need to find her within forty-eight hours, or missing as in, she got super pissed and left?"

"She couldn't leave if she wanted to; that's not how this works. Missing as in, we have no trace of her to begin a search. The alarm went off, and I knew it was triggered on purpose. Dhal used the distraction to get Arlen out with an acolyte. This wasn't random, Cali."

"So she was just waiting for Arlen to kick her ass?" I assumed that's what he meant.

"Dhal was set to leave tomorrow, and she knew beforehand about the gathering," he explained in a slow tone, like I should've known that already.

"Are you telling me this was going to happen regardless? Why would she take Arlen…oh." I trailed off. "Goddamn it. Why do you have to fuck with crazy bitches?" I stood up and started to pace.

"Don't blame this shit on me. I don't give a flying fuck about Arlen. She could be getting her ass and pussy wrecked right now, I still don't give a fuck."

"You're such a pigheaded dick. And if this was going to happen regardless, how do you know Cobra wasn't the one who confronted her?"

"Cobra's not that fucking stupid. Don't insult his or my

intelligence. I watched the cameras—I saw it happen. He came to me, and we were going to get all we could get out of her with a *plan*. We don't know who she's working with. Arlen should never have confronted her on her own."

Oh, this asshole. He was not blaming my friend for his ex's suicidal choices.

"Well, you always have everything figured out, so I'm sure you'll have no issue getting together a *plan* to get her back, you arrogant—"

"Cali." He lunged like a viper and grabbed the back of my neck.

"This isn't a game, Ro—"

I squeaked, finding my upper half bent over the couch.

"I wasn't aware I was joking." He reached beneath my shirt dress and roughly pulled my underwear left and right until they tore from the strain. "I'm burning every single pair of these motherfuckers."

"We can't do this—"

"Shut the fuck up." He kicked my legs apart and easily pushed two fingers into me. "Clearly, your pussy wants to do this. You're fucking soaked."

He made me delirious. I was always ready to go for him. The world could be ending and I'd still be ready.

I growled and pushed back, jumping forward with a little hiss when his hand came down on my ass. The sound of his zipper going down seemed to echo in the open room.

"You know what?" he asked, pushing inside me with one swift motion. "Why do you always have to open your smart ass mouth?" His grip tightened on the back of my neck as he flexed his hips, making sure every thrust was hard, smashing me into the leather couch. I tried to answer him but my brain seemed to have erased its knowledge of the English language and left me with nothing but the ability to moan.

"You like the way I fuck you, Cali?"

He slightly shifted, driving himself deeper, forcing me on to my tiptoes. I made a muffled sound in response, curling my fingers into the leather fabric.

"If you want to come, you'll beg for it. Make me think you deserve it."

"P-please," I managed to gasp out. It was the best I could do. I don't know how he expected me to beg when I couldn't even talk.

My body jarred against the sofa as he showed no mercy. His balls slapped painfully against the groove of my ass.

I felt a cooling sensation trickle down my spine. I came on a soundless scream, turning rigid in his hands. His cock jerked twice. He let out an almost inaudible groan and found his own release.

He rested his forehead on my shoulder, replacing it with a feather light kiss before he pulled away.

"I was trying to tell you I think I know where they might be."

I slouched onto the couch, trying to catch my breath. Why didn't he just lead with that?

Chapter Thirty-Seven

Romero

I'd been revisiting my past a fuck of a lot the last week, and can't say I enjoyed it.

I stared at the rundown house with the patched roof and recalled the cold nights when rain declared open season on all our shit, and days when I'd come back to find racoons with their faces in our bare supply of food.

"I can't believe we lived here," Grimm mused, stepping up beside me.

"Thank fuck we don't now," I agreed.

We'd been teens then.

It was a year before I killed the old leader and took his place as the head of what was now the Savages.

It was pitch black outside, but two of the lights and a television were on inside, showing me all I needed to see.

Dhal sat right at the fucking table, laughing with someone I couldn't see clearly; two more men were on the couch. In a back bedroom, a couple was fucking right in front of an open window.

None of them signified where they'd come from, but each single one of these dead fucks was in a building that belonged to me.

Tallying up how many motherfuckers I was about to kill, I walked back to the hatch of my jeep.

It was just a small group of us: Cobra, Grimm, me, and Luther. Like the good old days. I could have sent the army, but I was the motherfucking army.

I'd assumed Dhal had gotten over whatever weird bullshit dilemma she'd gotten herself into a few months back. Obviously, I'd assumed wrong.

Now here I was, playing the fucking rescue role again. I genuinely didn't give a shit about Arlen, but I did give a shit about my girl and Grimm, who had a soft spot for the loud mouthed fugitive.

And then there was the principle that the bitch had been taken right out from underneath me, which, in my eyes, was stealing. And in my world, when you stole from me, that was delivering your own death warrant.

For once, I didn't want to do this shit nice and slow. I wanted it hard and fast. My gorgeous girl was at home trying to bake cookies with Bryce on guard duty. She'd probably burn the fucking house down.

I handed Grimm a buckshot shotgun and took one for myself.

Shutting the hatch, I made my way back to Luther, who took the gun in with little surprise.

"It's showtime." I jerked my chin towards the back of the house where Cobra was slinking up.

He carried a freshly severed ram head in his hands. He crouched right under the open window of the couple still going at it and gave us all thumbs up.

"Fucking goof," Grimm chuckled, heading for the back door with Luther as I went for the front.

I made it to the house without any issues. Peering around the porch, I jerked my chin to give Cobra the okay.

The ram head sailed through the window, no doubt smacking right into the chick's chest or landing on the man she'd been riding.

Cobra was gone before she even started screaming, coming up on my ass as I kicked the front door open.

Luther and Grimm kicked open the back.

I side-stepped the naked bitch trying to run out the front. Cobra raised his leg and kicked her straight in the stomach, sending her careening backward.

He took hold of her hair and dragged her to the couch, tossing her naked ass right on the two men already sitting on it.

"Stay the fuck down." I aimed at Dhal and the man she was sitting with.

Grimm shoved the missing link to our couple forward by the hair. The man was stark naked, covering his dick with one hand, and trembling so hard you might think he was seizing.

"Where the fuck is she, Dhal?" I made my way towards her, wasting no time with casualties.

I wasn't in the mood for the rambling shit; I wanted answers. I circled around her buddy sitting beside her, held the base of my gun to his head, and pulled the trigger.

. . .

"I was only trying to help you, Rome. You wanted David gone for so long. I—" She screamed, cowering and getting hit with blood and chunks of brain matter.

He fell to the floor with a decent sized portion of his head missing. She'd crack before they were all dead. Dhal could never handle this shit.

The people on the couch huddled together, as if that would do anything to protect them.

"He's pissing." Grimm nodded, raising his gun and firing a round at the naked man who, sure enough, was pissing himself.

His face made a perfect O as he dropped in place, a red hole forming in his stomach.

The bitch on the couch flinched and covered herself but didn't seem all that upset, in my opinion.

"Romero p-p-please, let me exp—"

"Shut the fuck up."

I pressed the barrel of my gun into the side of Dhal's head. If she thought she still meant something to me, she had life all the way fucked up. I didn't let someone fuck me over and then sit back to see if they were dumb enough to do it again.

I sniffed the air and smelled something cooking. Glancing into the kitchen, I saw a large red pot on a burner.

"Grimm." I nodded towards the pan.

Cobra grabbed the naked girl off the couch and walked her over to the table to sit down.

"She's next," Cobra sang, cupping the woman's tits and squeezing until she whimpered. Luther approached and nudged her legs apart, placing the barrel of his own gun right against her pussy.

"Dinner!" Grimm walked in and sat the pan of boiling

eggs in the center of the table. Steam wafted off it and the water still bubbled.

"You're going to tell me where Arlen is and who the fuck you're helping."

"I just want—"

"You know, I don't like repeating myself. I asked you the same question twice now. I don't give a shit why you did it. You made a choice, and now you're going to pay the mother-fucking consequences."

I handed my gun off to Grimm.

"Are you hungry, Dhal? Is that it? It must be impairing your hearing." Lifting her up by the back of the head, I fisted her bloody hair and slammed her face first into the pot of egg water.

She screamed, flailing her arms and kicking out with her feet. Her face was tinged bright red when I finally pulled her up. She coughed and sputtered, grabbing at her cheeks.

"Do you need a little more?"

"No, no!" she cried.

"Good, we can move on then."

Only a soft sob came from her throat as Grimm made quick work of both men on the couch, swiftly coming up behind them and slitting their throats.

"He doesn't want the B-Badlands, he just wants it to be over. You were pitted against one another on purpose. I told him you had initiated Cali, and he said it was the perfect reason to start a war. He knew you'd win, Romero. You always win." She was crying so loud it was hard to under-stand what she was saying.

"He doesn't care about Arlen, he just needed her as a token of good faith that you wouldn't come after him. It was her or Cali. I left you Cali! He's terrified of you, Romero.

And the army. He just wants out to start over somewhere else."

We all shared a look. David wanted out?

"I don't fucking know what you're trying to say, and my patience is gone." I rolled my neck. "Get rid of that bitch, too."

Luther lazily lifted a shoulder. "I'm gonna keep this one. Her skin's perfect." He smoothed a hand down her stomach before standing up and wrapping it around her throat.

Cobra kept her hands at her side so she couldn't move. Her mouth opened and closed but no sound came out. "Just take a nap, doll," Luther soothed.

"Noo!" Dhal wailed and attempted to lunge at me.

I still had hold of her fucking hair so I wasn't sure what she thought she was doing. I slammed her face down onto the table. "The cellar!" she screamed out suddenly, "Check the cellar."

I wasn't sure how the fuck she'd got into it, considering it had been closed off for years.

"Go," I said to Grimm.

He and Luther quickly took off out the front door.

Cobra lifted the now unconscious blonde up and dropped her on the floor so he could have her seat.

"Don't kill me," Dhal pleaded.

"I'm not going to kill you, Dhal. Cali is."

Grimm appeared in the doorway with a look I couldn't read on his face. "You need to see what's down there."

"Let's go." I stood Dhal up and made her walk in front of me.

We went to the side of the house where the cellar doors were pulled open. A dank smell floated up from below.

Forcing Dhal down the old concrete stairs, I ducked my head and let my eyes adjust to the shitty lighting. The ceiling slightly lifted up ahead, but I didn't need to stand straight to see the bodies stacked and piled on top of one another.

"Shit," Cobra breathed from behind me.

I took in the outliers, acolytes, and delegates. Hanging on the wall and partially draping over the corpses was my flag, the Sigil of Baphomet.

"What the fuck is this?"

"I think the better question is what the fuck is he doing here?" Grimm pulled open a door I'd overlooked to reveal a man tied up, gagged, and passed out.

Fucking David.

"You said he wanted out. What the fuck is going on?" I spun Dhal around to face me, grabbing her up by the throat.

"Your brother wants out. Your brother did it," she wheezed.

My brother?

Fuck. "Noah?"

Chapter Thirty-Eight

Calista

This wasn't how I saw this going, but nothing in life was ever guaranteed.

He came back two nights ago and handed me a box. Inside was memorabilia that put mine to shame.

Noah was obsessed with his big brother. So obsessed, he rose his way up the ranks and helped disband The Order from the inside.

He planted his own seeds and then sowed them when he got what he wanted—a reaction from Romero.

He knew he could never take The Order out by himself, so what better way than to get the army and us to do it for him?

He was our third player.

David never would have suspected him. He was his golden child.

We never suspected him.

I couldn't even wrap my goddamn head around it.

"Are you ready?" Romero asked, slowly opening the door.

"As ready as I'll ever be."

He reached down and took my hand, leading me inside the devil's playground once again.

I'd pictured this moment countless times.

The anger I'd expected to feel was simmering on low. I hated him, I loathed him with my entire being, and there was no doubt in my mind he would suffer as he died.

He deserved that much.

No, he wasn't my real father, but that was the role he'd been meant to play, and he let me down every day in every way he could.

He hurt the man I loved, his own flesh and blood, because his pride had to come first.

In the end, he did this to himself.

He should have killed me when he had the chance. Instead, he let me go. I recovered and grew stronger. Now, he was fucked. I promised him this day would come.

I thought I'd do it brutal and fast, but like I said, nothing was set in stone. My demons wanted to revel in his sorrow.

Looking into his terrified grey eyes and seeing his tattered robe, I couldn't believe I'd ever been afraid of him.

"You ready?" Romero asked from across the room.

"Let's do it." I stood up and moved to the large Leviathan cross.

Cobra and Grimm helped Romero lift David up and carry him to the metal work table. Luther and Bryce entered the room, jogging over to help. His body was extended to fit the cross. Two people on each side held him in place as we got to work.

Romero placed the first steel stake mid-center of his wrists, right over the median nerve. "Make him bleed, baby." He gave a devilish smile to egg me on.

Tightening my grip on the metal mallet I'd picked up, I swung it down onto the stake. blood gushed all over the cross bar and onto the floor.

The bone crumbled with swing number two. David screamed until his voice gave out, and his face turned beet red.

"Let's hear him," Grimm said, plucking the gag from David's mouth so his screams filled the room.

We did his other wrists just the same, paralyzing both his hands.

Rome took over the ankles, holding the stake and swinging the mallet on his own, crushing the bone just the same as we did with his wrists. David passed out before the first foot was finished. He was drenched in sweat, breathing heavily.

Grimm, Luther, Cobra, and Bryce lifted the cross up. The thick wood groaned from the weight of David's body but held steady. Without any saying a word, they carried him away.

Epilogue One

Romero

She knew if she moved, the knife would slit her throat. Trickles of crimson were already running in rivulets down her porcelain skin.

Not that it mattered, because she was wearing it like warpaint on every other inch of her it could spray. This was our new routine.

We played, and then we fucked. I had to admit I'd never enjoyed bloodshed this much, even on my own. The kill was twice as fun when my queen stood beside me covered in blood.

I rode her harder and deeper, fucking her so good nothing coming out of her mouth made sense.

The bed sounded like it was going to go through the wall.

She had a death grip on our ruined sheets, a light sheen on

her body from struggling to stay in position so she didn't come and die at the same time.

I could have fucked her until my lungs gave out. No one compared to my beautiful girl. The way she made me feel couldn't be put into words, so I showed her through my actions as best I could.

When she finally came, her body fucking quaked around me. Her pussy locked down on my dick and didn't let go until I was coming balls deep inside her.

I slowly pulled my knife away from her throat, laughing under my breath when she collapsed and let out a loud, *"Holy shit."*

Removing my dick from his favorite place in the world, I pressed my lips to the O and M I'd added to her back.

When she pissed me off to the point I wanted to do things no man should imagine doing to the woman he loved, I wrecked her ass and added another letter.

Reaching under the bed, I carefully slid out the box I'd placed beneath it. I sat it right beside her before she could roll over.

She glanced at it, feeling the bed slightly dip from its weight, and then she fucking squealed like a girl.

When she bounced up on her knees, my eyes immediately dropped to the slight bump protruding from her stomach that I already had plans to make permanent.

She smashed her nose against the glass, meshing it down like a little kid.

"You like it?" I laughed again. I did that shit more times than I ever had in my life.

"Rome, I fucking love it! I love you!" She launched herself at me—something she'd been doing a lot more fucking lately—which as a man I could never complain about because it always ended with my dick down her throat or inside her. And sometimes, it just felt good to be loved by her.

"How long have you had this?" She lifted David's preserved head onto her lap.

It'd taken me for fucking ever to find someone to do it. He was already a nice charcoal color and deformed; I figured if he rotted, anyone at least I could say the motherfucker was once on my mantle.

Burning him alive was cathartic.

I would've given her Dhal, too, but she didn't make the ride home in the back of my jeep.

Reaching back under the bed, I pulled out the second box.

Without asking—because, like I'd already told her, what we had went deeper than marriage—I pulled her hand onto my lap and slid the square ruby on her finger.

She stared at it for what felt like hours when one tear finally slid down her cheek. I beat her to it, swiping it off with my thumb and then sucking on it.

"Fucking asshole, making me cry," she mumbled and wrapped her arms around me, burying her face in my neck.

"I love the fuck out of you, baby." I kissed her temple.

I meant that shit. This crazy fucking woman was everything to me.

She was hellfire and holly water.

The savage queen to my deviant king.

I would do anything to keep her by my side, even if meant always keeping her in the dark, because if she had any idea what I was really up to and all the things I'd twisted around or never told her, we'd go to motherfucking war.

And I would win, because I always fucking win.

Epilogue Two

Calista

I sat on the balcony with Bryce.

He was a constant companion of mine these days. The man didn't say much, but he was still somehow good company.

My ring glinted in the setting sun. I traced over it, still not believing he'd actually slipped it on. I never thought I'd have a black wedding.

Rubbing the back of my neck, my thoughts went from everything from Grimm leaving the next morning and finding the only thing I'd ever had close to a best friend, to whatever the hell Romero was up to these days.

I worried he was working with Noah because of some fucked up brotherly bond. Noah, who was still helping him grow stronger every day by wiping out straggling delegates or sending him leads on resources. Romero never responded, at least not that I knew of.

I still had so many questions. I still felt so much hate inside me and I couldn't find it inside myself to forgive those who had wronged us.

It was time to move forward. I would grow from this. I had to. There was someone else who would need me soon.

The sliding glass door opened and we stared at one another, his all knowing gaze locking with my passive one. In that moment, I thought how unfair it was for one man to be so damn gorgeous. The devil came disguised as everything I'd ever wanted, a beautiful mirage meant to lure the darkest sinner.

Romero was my plus one, my other half. He was my reflection in a mirror full of cracks and missing pieces.

His darkness was mortally terrifying to most, yes, but to me it was a hidden heaven. His actions were repugnant and unforgiveable.

He was kingpin to a society of savages that revered him as the devil, but I loved his psychotic ass with every part of my being.

We found our dark paradise

And this was the end of our story...for now.

Outcasts

GRIMM X ARLEN

Playlist

1. Gin Wigamore—Black Sheep
2. NF—10 Feet Down
3. NF—Mansion
4. BHM—Can You Feel My Heart?
5. Trevor Moran—Sinner
6. Coldplay—Fix You
7. Lacey Strum—Rot
8. The Neighborhood—Heaven
9. Disturbed—Down With The Sickness
10. 5FDP—The Devil's Own
11. The Fray—Never Say Never
12. Stone Sour—Song #3
13. Tove Lo—Moments
14. Halestorm—The Reckoning
15. Fall Out Boy—Bishops Knife Trick
16. Three Days Grace—The High Road
17. Three Days Grace—Painkiller
18. Three Days Grace—Animal I Have Become
19. Wasteland—10 Years

20. Evanescence—Imperfection
21. Shinedown—Cut the Cord
22. Sam Smith—Life Support
23. Niykee Heaton—Lullaby
24. Halsey—Gasoline
25. Halsey—Roman Holiday
26. PVRIS—Separate
27. PVRIS—Fire
28. The Weekend—Pray for Me
29. Breaking Benjamin—Red Cold River
30. Breaking Benjamin—Save Yourself
31. Breaking Benjamin—The Dark of You
32. In This Moment—Sick Like Me
33. In This Moment—Forever

Prelude

pulvis et umbra sumus.

There is no light to be found here, only darkness.

Our world is full of monsters that no longer bother wearing friendly faces.

The saints and the uncorrupted have either perished or hidden away. Sinners and the dearly depraved have gladly taken their place.

I am not an exception.

I am a lover of death.

It came to me in the form of a man revered as the Grim Reaper himself. They call him a demon, something straight out of nightmares; a loyal solider in the devil's army.

He was the reckoning I never saw coming.

I am the Persephone to his Hades.

He is the misery I crave.

He became my absolution by showing me that hell, too, had beauty.

I became his salvation by accepting him for who and what he was.

We are not soul-mates, but one eternal flame split in two.

We were going to set fire to anything and anyone that stood between us and the way back to our dark paradise.

Our story is passionate, sometimes painful, other times brutal.

I advise you leave your morals at the door.

You will find we outcasts have none.

Part One

Chapter One

PAST

Arlen

He told me to sit taller, look softer, keep my mouth shut, and smile.

Clearly, he forgot who his daughter was. I *never* shut the hell up. My mouth was a pistol, my tongue a silver bullet.

It wasn't the best trait to have, but it'd come in handy quite a few times.

I figured this'd be one of em.

"I'm not marryin this man." I cut right into the conversation, no holds barred.

The room grew so quiet you could hear the leaves swaying on our golden wattle tree in the front yard. My ma shot me a warning look, which I ignored.

"Arlen," Dad chastised.

"You told me she understood," Rodrick, the groom in question, sighed.

"I understand just fine, Dick. I'm not marryin you. How about findin a woman closer to your own age?"

See, I thought this was a great suggestion. Dick didn't. He scoffed, but couldn't open his mouth to dispute me. At thirty-nine, Rodrick (Dick) was a fairly attractive man, with swoopy blonde hair and money green eyes.

He was also two decades older than me, and the furthest thing from my type. I didn't really have a type, actually, but if I did, it wasn't a man in a suit who ate garlic bread with a fork.

That wasn't normal.

My ma rubbed her brow, diverting her gaze as if I'd just sat the weight of the whole damn world on her over-privileged shoulders.

"Why don't we move this discussion into the den?" Dad was already standing to do just that before Rodrick could agree or disagree, shooting me a scathing glare that spoke volumes.

Dad didn't hit; he used words. He told me I'd be no good to anyone bruised up and skittish, so he would break me in another way, like I was a damn colt or somethin. I could tell the last thing Dick wanted to do was go off and have a conversation with him, but he followed regardless.

They left behind their pipin hot lasagna. I wanted to yell after them that there were families who would (literally) strip the tanned flesh from their bodies for the same indulgence.

Hell, some families would eat it, too.

"Arlen, you cannot ruin this deal," Ma hissed the second she heard the door click shut. I whipped back around and shook my head at her.

I studied her from across the table and frowned. She was always so put together. I didn't understand how she could wear those long thin heels all hours of the day, every day.

And she never let her hair down. I wish she laughed like she used to. She'd changed so much over the years. Her main goal was being the best wife, the best cook, and the best hostess.

She forgot how to be my mother.

The opinions of strangers held too much weight in this household. I learned to quit caring long ago. I didn't give a rat's ass what anyone thought of me. Ma had been like that once, but now she was stuck.

I could grab her by the shoulders and preach about old times till I was blue in the face; I knew it wouldn't change a thing.

"You hear what you just said? A deal, Momma. You want my marriage to be a *deal*?"

"Sweetheart, she's gone now, and it's important to maintain a healthy working relationship between your father and Rodrick."

"You mean Be—"

"You know you're not to say that name," she interjected.

"Beth. Her *name* is Beth, and she's *your* daughter."

"*Was* my daughter, until she brought shame on this family by running off like some hoodlum in the middle of the night. It's only natural the responsibility move to you.

"Rodrick wants to ensure he has an in with the wealthiest family in Centriole before he agrees to your father's terms. You know how hard he works to hold his position."

I had to refrain from rollin my eyes. I'd heard the 'dad works hard speech' so many times I could recite it in my sleep.

What he did that was so strenuous was beyond my understanding.

Seemed to me he got dressed up every day just to sit on

his ass and make phone calls so everyone else had to work for a livin.

Attempting to tuck a strand of hair behind my ear, I grunted when I remembered it was already pinned back in some extra fancy hairdo Ma insisted on.

"Maybe you should tell me what this big deal is, if it's that important."

"You know I can't do that."

What was with all the secrecy?

"I'm not sure if this is the part where I say we're ahead of such times, or times are changin, since no one around here seems inclined to give me a history lesson."

She sighed—dramatically, I might add—but I still didn't get any real explanation. I never did.

"Dick's meant to be marryin my sister. That's probably why she left in the first place. It don't matter now though, does it? Ya'll won't give me the option of makin my own choices."

When she let out her signature musical laugh, I knew exactly where this conversation was goin.

"Your choices have resulted in all those tattoos covering your body in a poor attempt to rebel, screwing the pool boy, and failing every aspect of etiquette—your speech, especially."

There was no reasoning with this woman. I was tired of wastin my time trying to explain who I was to someone committed to misunderstanding me.

How many times did I have to tell her the ink on my body was art? That the pool boy had an actual name, and was my first of everything?

"You keep trying to change me into everything he hates."

Her swallow was audible, and suddenly she had a bit of invisible lint on her skirt.

The *he* in question was another subject I was not to discuss—a lesson drilled into my skull from the time I was nine years old.

"You could be happy," she solemnly deflected.

I huffed in defeat. We always ended up back at this, forever talking in circles.

"Where are you going?" she asked as I pushed away from the table and stood up.

"Goin to wash this gunk off my face, and then I'm goin to bed."

"Your father will want to speak with you."

She knew full well I wasn't going to wait around for *that* conversation.

I made my way to my room and, once inside, immediately headed for the bathroom.

I laughed at my reflection the second I saw it. I looked like a walking scuff mark.

Ma had wanted to hide some of my tattoos and lathered me in some sort of cover up. It was a hot mess, and extra pointless.

I'd been the subject of gossip and ridicule for years. Everyone in this judgmental city knew I was inked.

I removed the pins from my hair and ran my fingers through the long wavy strands to give it back some life. The few lighter highlights I'd been permitted to have boldly contrasted with the natural dark brown.

Letting the hideously dull teacup dress billow to the bathroom floor, I took a quick shower, and threw on my plaid pajama shorts and an old metal t-shirt, instantly feeling much more like myself.

After shutting the lights off, I turned the lever on the window to let some fresh air in, and settled beneath my abstract comforter. I rolled onto my side, and stared out at the pretty night sky, where the moon sat by her lonesome.

Our backyard seemed to stretch on forever, ending where a solid brick wall wrapped around Centriole as a whole began.

I felt trapped here in every way. I knew Ma loved me, and I liked to imagine Dad did too, but they would never accept me as I was.

It hurt that I couldn't be what they needed, and it hurt I couldn't be what I wanted. I was fed and watered daily, but something told me there was more to life than this. My cage may have had bars of gleaming gold, but it was still a cage.

Many referred to this place as The Kingdom, a utopia of sorts. I could understand why, but that's not how I saw it.

Our grass was lime green, the water was a shimmering blue, our stores were stocked with food, and people could safely go for walks in the middle of the night, knowing the wall was constantly being patrolled. You could even score some happy pills, if that was your thing.

On the other side of the wall was the affront to my morbid curiosity.

The Badlands: a prettied up hostile desert wasteland.

The pinkish plains were home to various gangs of undesirables and an enclave of cannibals.

I suppose that was the purpose of the wall in the first place: to keep 'them' out. The deviants and outliers: people deemed not good enough to live among us. Outcasts. Those rejected by society.

I couldn't help wonderin how vastly different their lives were from mine, reckoning I was the only person in the whole city who wanted to know what life would be like outside that eyesore of a damn wall. It wasn't like I'd never asked someone these questions neither. I had—many times.

No one ever gave me a real answer. Just like Ma wouldn't share any knowledge of history with me.

Thinkin of the loaded up duffel bag stowed beneath my bed, I knew I'd be leavin this place behind sooner than later, and Ma and Dad didn't have the slightest clue. Nobody did but the man who shared my secret with me.

My reputation had never preceded me.

To anyone outside looking in, I was Arlen Prosner— spoiled rich bitch that did everything her daddy told her.

None of that was remotely true.

That girl would have never considered her uncle's whispered offer to leave The Kingdom in two weeks time.

I knew once we left, we weren't goin to ever return. Coming back meant going through a lengthy process, and most were immediately shot or turned away. There were two ways in and out of the city, both heavily guarded. No one was forced to stay in, but once you got beyond a certain point… that was it.

There were even signs posted; I'd memorized them by heart.

Warning: Beyond this fence is no longer the territory of Centriole. Thereafter no person within the territory beyond this fence is a resident of our city or shall be acknowledged, recognized, or protected by the governing body therein.

You are now entering the Badlands.

Good luck.

It was debatable if the 'good luck' was genuine or not, but I had questions, a wayward sister, burnin curiosity, and an itch to break free.

Even knowing what was out there, how dangerous and foolish the choice would seem to anyone else, I was goin.

When I looked at the Badlands from the comfort of my

bedroom, I didn't see mutilated bodies or a war brewin between two powerful men.

What I saw was the lack of a wall, and freedom from a life of being a Stepford wife, popping out babies for a man twice my age.

I didn't see how damn naïve I was.

I didn't see myself befriending a tiny blonde who was a full blown psycho beneath her flawless exterior. I never foresaw the path my life would take from that day forward.

I made a life changin decision, and I didn't have the foresight to see how drastic it would be.

I could have never foreseen all the ways I was goin to suffer on a precipice of insanity, before death finally gave me peace.

Chapter Two

PRESENT

Arlen

Red wine scented breath was on my neck. There was pressure between my legs and a weight on my chest.

Lucidity washed over me and I knew I'd been drugged again. The stiff mattress beneath me barely creaked as he thrust in and out. Raw. He was always raw when he forced his cock inside me when I couldn't give consent. My fingers twitched as my body became as awake as my brain.

I did my best to ignore his groans of pleasure, feeling the acid bubblin in my stomach as I had no choice but to lie wide open. I felt like a starfish, sticky and stuck.

Willing all feeling to come back, I flexed both fists as a test, reacting before it had fully sunken in that I could move.

"Get the fuck off me, Noah!"

He was so caught up in releasing the pleasure in his tiny balls, he hadn't realized I was awake. His face was the perfect picture of surprise as he fell onto the floor, leaving behind a nausea-inducing wetness between my thighs.

"I was almost done," he sighed, as if I'd majorly inconvenienced him, already grabbing for the cattle prod I could never get to in time.

"You're a sick fuck!" I closed my legs and sat up, preparing to fight him off best I could if he tried comin at me again.

I wouldn't rush him. I'd learned my lesson the first and second time he'd shocked me with the damn stick in his hand —the one he'd acquired after he had to have me pulled off him. The first time we fought, we were like two men in a ring goin for a championship belt. His precious ego hadn't taken that loss too well.

That's when the prod came into the picture. He'd blindsided me with it, shocked the hell outta me and brought me clean to my knees. I never wanted to be on the business end of that thing again.

If I ever got hold of it, I was gonna jam it straight up his ass and fry his shitter from the inside out.

"Petals, I don't know why you deny what's between us."

"Ain't anything between us, you sick, shrivel dicked asshole." I glared at him. He shut his eyes and sighed, tightening his grip on the prod. You'd think I would've learned to shut the hell up, considerin my mouth was what got me in this situation.

"Petals." He sighed again.

I curled my lip at the stupid name. Why the hell did he choose it?

He muttered something unintelligible beneath his breath, and wordlessly readjusted the ridiculous white robe he always wore. His father's order had been disbanded, largely thanks to him, so I didn't see his point at first, but after being stuck with him for so long, I'd overheard quite a few things I shouldn't have.

"Denial can only hold out for so long. You know you're not leaving me, so you might as well make the best of our relationship."

He stared at me expectantly, and I stared back in pure disgust.

I *hated* him. Not just for what he did to me, but what he'd done to Cali, too, the sweet girl who was supposed to be his sister—turned out she wasn't, but that was still damn sickening.

I *hated* him touching me the way he did. I *hated* this feelin of helplessness.

"You're pathetic. Get out of my room."

Swiping a hand through his short, dark hair, he frowned and gave a shake of his head. He looked nothing like Romero, his brother. And they couldn't have been more different.

One was a rat placed in a maze and made to do another's bidding, while the other was the head of the Savages. Romero was a king, the very devil I'd heard so much about, and the Badlands was his personal hell.

After a brief hiatus, he was back, and making that known to everyone and anyone who tested him with my newfound best friend, Cali, at his side.

Noah desperately coveted the power Romero had. He wanted the adoration and loyalty his brother's acolytes willingly gave.

He would never have it. What was it with men in their need to have big ol dick measurin contests? Noah was strong, but debilitated next to Romero. He was occasionally smart; Romero was ten times smarter.

None of that had stopped his thirst for his brother's throne, and that in itself made him a damn fool.

Not to mention the army that stood between him and making that happen, and the other key players he'd have to go up against. Last time I pointed all that out, he'd almost punched my head off my shoulders. Lesson learned.

"I've been trying to make it work between us for the past three weeks. I don't know what else to do." He went to the door, keeping his front towards me so I couldn't jump him from behind, the prod out in front of him like a shield. "You'll change your mind by Thursday morning."

The door was open and shut with him on the other side before I could ask what he meant. I didn't even know what day it was.

One lock clicked, followed by the second, and then finally, the chain was slid into place.

As soon as his footsteps faded, I was off the bed like a fire had been lit beneath my ass, straight into the lemon scented bathroom.

It was tiny with dull yellow tiled flooring, and only contained a toilet and sink, but all I needed was running water and a bar of soap.

Turning the little silver knob with an H embellished on the top, I grabbed one of my wash rags from the wicker basket Noah had placed on the toilet's tank.

Steam rose from the stream of water. I drenched the rag, fighting the urge to pull my hand back even as it shook uncontrollably from nerves and turned a dark pink from the heat. My heart was beating so fast, I thought for sure it was going to come right through my chest.

"Ignore it all," I whispered to myself.

I rolled my lips together in a firm line to keep the hysteria ready to empty from my lungs quiet. I'd cried too many times already—ugly, terribly loud sobs.

I wouldn't give him any more of my tears. I couldn't, anyway; the pain was there, but the well had run empty.

I never let Noah see how severely his actions sabotaged my psyche.

It excited him and made things worse for me. I'd yet to decide if it was a small saving grace when he raped me and I awoke to feel nothing but the come and soreness he left behind, or a disadvantage not to feel everything from the beginning.

There were times I woke up. Others, I didn't. Often enough, he woke me up for the pure entertainment of fighting his way inside me. I'd been taken advantage of so many times at this point, I wasn't sure it mattered anymore. I just wanted it to stop.

I'd never felt more trapped than I did now, and sometimes I thought I deserved this.

I was the one who ran away from home, so desperate for a taste of freedom.

Watching my uncle cut open and dismembered for a family of cannibals' weekly supper wasn't penance enough.

I didn't miss the city, though—not even a little bit.

I suppose life was now punishing me for the company I chose to keep. She was a mean bitch like that.

Grabbing the soap and making good use of the rag, I began to vigorously scrub between my legs, ignoring how badly it burned. I had half a mind to shove the soap inside me to clean away where he'd been.

I was so damn grateful his intent wasn't to get me pregnant. He made me take a contraceptive with the only drink he allowed me to have—water.

It was always a gamble if he'd laced it or not, but it was either risk pregnancy by refusing the liquid, or drink it to receive the pill.

I was real familiar with the package it came in. My ma made me take the same ones.

As far as I knew, they were only available in Centriole. To get something like that in the Badlands, you would need a pretty penny or solid connection. The fact that Noah had some told me more than he might have thought.

That kind of thing is what made him so stupid. He had loose lips, and never seemed to realize I heard everything that went on when I wasn't drugged. Didn't he know I was foe, not friend?

I retained as much information as I could because I still had a small sliver of hope I'd be gettin out of this shithole. I knew if it were up to Cali, she'd have stormed the building with a take no prisoners approach already, but she wasn't in any position to do that. She was growing a baby.

She may not have been some mushy sentimental person, but I knew she wouldn't risk her child—nor would Romero ever allow it. Not for me. And I didn't want her to. She was Romero's queen—quite literally.

The man had a nasty attitude and seemed made of stone, but he adored her. I was envious of that. I didn't think epic love was in the cards for me, though.

The only person I'd ever felt drawn to like a magnet wasn't really a relationship kinda guy, and there was a whole unrequited mess between us.

Shutting the sink off, I wrung out my rag, avoiding my reflection. I didn't want to see the shame looking back at me. After re-positioning my slip—the only clothing Noah allowed—I went back into the bedroom.

The four wood paneled walls were different to the teal ones that had surrounded me a month ago.

According to what Noah had just said, we'd been here three weeks, which meant we'd be moving again soon. He never stayed in the same place for long. I had no real measurement of time in regards to how long he'd had me, but I estimated a solid sixty days, minimum.

Crawling onto the bed, I avoided the place my legs had just been sprawled apart. I drew my knees to my chest, and rested my cheek on them, staring at nothing.

The room was barren, aside from the bed and a small round coffee table.

The only window had a thick piece of plywood across it to prevent me from escaping or seeing out—probably both.

I sat there in that dimly lit cell with nothing to distract me. I sat there for minutes, hours, maybe even days, and with nothing to busy myself with, my mind ran wild. I never knew silence could be so loud.

I missed my friends.

And I missed *him*.

I missed my shadow, the reaper at my back who watched over me without wanting anything in return. I could make myself blissfully and deliriously numb to my surroundings if I filled my every thought with nothing but Grimm.

If I saw him in a dream, he was always torn away when I woke again, and I was never ready to say goodbye.

I'd honestly expected him to come for me out of everyone, but he hadn't shown up yet.

Noah's ominous taunt became the focal point of a slow growing paranoia. I had no idea what he had planned for me. I wasn't adept at dealing with things like this.

I told myself to think positive thoughts, but the hope I kept a firm grasp on was beginning to slip through my fingers.

Chapter Three

Arlen

Nothing tragic happened that morning.

I woke from the sound of the door clicking shut with heavy sleep in my eyes from fighting it off for so long. A silver tray with oatmeal and a fruit cup sat waiting for me on the coffee table—another regularity, and my only breakfast option.

Noon came around, bringing me closer to whatever it was Noah wanted. I was able to pretend all was fine for a few minutes as I brushed my teeth and hair.

My actions may have seemed pointless, but I knew I needed to eat for my own well-being, and keeping somewhat clean was my way of refusing to fall apart completely.

I guess you could say it was a façade.

As soon as I was done, I was left with the same problem I always had: nothing to do but sit on my ass and wonder what was gonna happen next. I leaned back on the bed, listening to the movement throughout the house we were holed up in.

I heard multiple voices, but that was nothing new. I theorized all the possible scenarios as to what Noah could be up to in the long run, but continued to pull a blank.

Keeping me was strange in itself. He knew who I was, and made no effort to contact my father for a ransom or power exchange. He'd once said I was his collateral, a reason for Romero not to hunt him down, but that didn't explain much, either.

We both knew if his brother wanted him dead, he'd be dead.

With no way of knowing what time it was, I tried to use basic math as a timetable for when the sun traded places with the moon. Still, nothing happened—not right away, anyway.

I was half-asleep when they showed up; four men I'd never seen strolled into the room with Noah right behind them.

My danger radar immediately went through the roof, as did the tempo of my pulse. I could nearly feel it in my throat. All of em had on the usual dark jeans and dark shirts men in the Badlands wore, but they were too rough around the edges to be anyone Noah regularly associated with.

"What is this?" I asked, sitting a little taller and pressing my back flat against the worn headboard.

"Petals, these are my new friends," Noah announced, making his way to the front of the little group, prod in his hand.

"We both know damn well you don't have any friends. Cut the shit and tell me what's really goin on."

Two of the men laughed at my accurate assumption, while the biggest one gave me a smile full of surprisingly white teeth. That's what I got for jumping to conclusions.

He looked rugged.

Looking at him a little closer, I took notice of the tattoo on his neck—a V with a black snake intertwined around it. I also realized he was much older than I was, but his overall hygiene didn't seem bad.

None of that explained why they were in the room with me. I looked at their faces, and suddenly had an inkling of where this was going.

Their aura was menacing.

The way they were lookin at me was as if they were starving and had just found a five-course meal.

"You definitely don't look like any Kingdom bitch we've ever seen," one of them commented, dropping his heated gaze to where my nipples were easily seen through the white fabric of my slip.

My stomach knotted in a million different directions, and a dull ache resonated through my entire body. I felt like one of the raccoons Dad used to catch in tiny metal traps. I had no way of escaping; I was stuck with danger staring me straight in the face.

"Why are they here?" I asked Noah directly, ignoring the quad.

He opened his mouth to answer but the man who smiled at me held up a hand, shutting him up.

"Arlen, my name's Vance. This is my brother Rex, and these are our boys, Hawke and Vitus."

He aimed a thumb at each of them without taking his eyes off me. Him knowing my name wasn't the least bit surprising.

Anyone who paid enough attention to any form of press knew I was the Regent—or, as he liked to call himself lately, *Mayor*—of Centriole's daughter.

"What do you want with me?"

"Well, I asked Noah here to show me he could make good on his word."

At my blank stare, he chuckled amusedly and partially turned to clamp the man he'd called Vitus on the shoulder and pull him forward.

"It's my boy's twenty-fifth birthday, and Noah promised some exclusive one-on-one time between you two during a round of cards the other night."

"I'm not his to promise." I glared at Vitus. If he was really twenty-five, that sat him only six years older than me, but I could tell just by looking at him that whatever happened in his daily life had matured and hardened him beyond his age.

He had dark curly hair and a solid build. He stared me down with odd bluish-green eyes, one side of his mouth lifting into a grin when I scowled.

"Alright, everybody get out." His gruff demand was met with laughs from everyone but Noah, who had the audacity to look slightly concerned.

Nonetheless, he wordlessly trailed after the others as they filed out of the room, leaving me alone to fend for myself.

"You know, you're a lot prettier in person," he said, inching closer to the bed.

I edged away, wanting him nowhere near me.

My voice may have remained steady, and I could bravely look these men in the eye without crumbling to pieces, but that was only because my mouth seemed to move without approval from my brain half the time.

That ridiculous thing called pride wouldn't allow me to beg for mercy.

In all actuality, I was absolutely terrified. Natural fight or flight instinct had my entire body tensing in apprehension of

NATALIE BENNETT

what was to come. "There are plenty of pretty girls you could go and play with. Why pick me?"

"None of those girls *are* you, Arlen."

I scrambled off the bed, keeping as much space between us as I could. Fightin him wasn't the brightest option. That would do nothing but wear me out or get me hurt.

Vitus shook his head and held both his hands up like he was surrendering. He was quick to hold a finger to his lips when I opened my gob to ask what the hell he was doing.

He continued moving towards me in the same pose, giving a slight shake of his head when I side eyed the bathroom, easily understanding my intent. I took two steps back but didn't have room to go further because of the wall.

"Listen, forcing women to spread their legs isn't my forte, and I don't want to today, but my pops won't be very happy if I walk outta here without getting what we came all this way for," he whispered lowly, stopping an arm's reach away from me.

"How's that my problem? That seems more like a personal issue."

"It's actually just an issue for you. I'm trying to do the right thing. They're outside that door, listening, so you can get on that bed and willingly lie on your back for me, or I can do things the hard way for both of us."

What type of compromise was that? He was getting what he wanted either way. My only options were to fight and ultimately lose.

Maybe I'd miraculously hand him his ass, but then still have to deal with his posse on the other side of the door—or, I could steel my spine and take it.

There was really only one logical route to go: throwing the battle but still holding out for winning the war.

478

With a sharp jerk of my chin, I stormed past him and went back to the bed.

I refused to look at him as I laid flat on my back and spread my legs, willing him to just get it over with.

Ma told me being with a man never lasted very long. She'd been trying to prep me for the marriage I didn't want. I'm sure she never imagined her advice would be used for something like this.

It didn't take Vitus long to make a move. The sound of his belt jingling had my hands balling into fists by my sides. I focused on the paint peeling off the ceiling, squeezing my eyes shut when the bed dipped.

Everything inside me resented this, made me hate myself a little more.

I flinched when he placed a hand on my knee.

"It's alright," he cooed, settling between my legs. "I don't need any more Vitus Jrs. running around.

Noah told me you're on the pill, though if I had you to breed, I can't say I'd complain. I'm clean, by the way." He laughed a little, and my stomach pitched.

This asshole just said 'breed'. I'd never heard any man say that before, and I could wager I knew some damn shitty men. The Savages didn't even do such a thing.

It was a knockout right to the face when I realized the devil and his unholy family had more morals than common men.

There was a brief moment when nothing happened, but then I felt the bareness of firm pectorals.

Something rattled in my chest as my brain screamed at me to do something and stop this from happening.

Smashing my lips into a firm line, I tried to swallow the sob rising up, leaving some garbled sound to slip out in its place.

"Shh, it's okay," he soothed, running a thumb over my hairline. I wanted him to stop sayin that. This was not okay. It would *never* be okay. *I* was never going to be okay.

A second later, he was pushing inside me, forcing his cock in past the dryness.

He continued to whisper his meaningless reassurances in my ear. I lay there, feeling his unwanted caress, wishing like hell I was back in that pretty cage with the golden bars.

I felt his length plunging in and out of me, hearing his every little groan. He told me I was beautiful, and suddenly, I had never felt uglier.

When the first tear slipped free, my soul cracked. When my body began reacting to what he was doing, it cracked a bit more.

Breathin became a struggle. I was giving another part of me away to someone who would never in a thousand different lifetimes deserve it.

When he touched his lips on mine, my eyes flew open.

"No," I choked out.

"Don't be like that." He tried again, and this time, I turned my face.

His responding laugh was like nails on a chalkboard assaulting my eardrums.

I thought what happened next would be as bad as it could get—when he slid his hand down between us and began touchin a part of me not even Noah bothered with.

"Stop," I demanded, shoving at his arm. He ignored me, pinning a forearm across my chest and picking up his pace.

"Feels good, don't it?" he taunted, thrusting harder.

I ignored that.

My body thought it did; my mind thought it was the worst form of torture I could go through. I focused on his right bicep, where the same V tattoo the other man had was inked.

I'd come many times from my own fingers to know what was happening inside me.

There was the familiar tightening in my lower stomach, the pressure slowly building.

I willed it away, thinking every demented thought I could. I dragged the memory of Cali drilling into a man's dick to the forefront of my mind.

I thought of the precise way the cannibals had used a crowbar to break my uncle's ribcage apart right in front of me.

The distraction worked. It didn't take Vitus long to finish; I held onto those minutes like a lifeline. When he finally buried himself one last time, coming with a vomit-inducing moan, I forced his cock out of me before it had stopped twitching.

He hopped up with a smile I wanted to punch off.

"Damn, look at this." He grabbed his softening dick and thumbed off some of my body's obvious betrayal. Without warning, he reached out and wiped it down the side of my face, laughing when I knocked his hand away.

I pulled my dirty slip back down and diverted my gaze to my toes as he tucked himself away.

"Well, I can't say you're the best I've ever had. I'm not really into corpses, but the others might be."

I jack-knifed into a standing position so fast, he took a cautionary step away from me. "What do you mean the others?"

As he pulled his shirt back over his head and let it fall into place, I already knew the answer. Why did I think it would end with him? I was an idiot.

Without giving any indication I was about to bolt, I darted towards the bathroom, paying no mind to the semen slowly sliding down my inner thigh.

There was a flimsy lock on the door. I knew in the recess of my mind that the move was illogical and did nothing but buy me maybe a few minutes. I went for it anyway.

He didn't try to stop me. I made it inside, slammed the door, and slid the deadbolt into place.

A creak sounded, followed by footsteps, and I knew his family had filed back into the room.

"Where the fuck she go?"

"She locked herself away. I didn't have to force her. She willingly let me between them legs. I told her one of you was next. I don't think she likes ya'll as much as she did me," Vitus joked.

He made me sound like a whore. I sort of felt like one too. In my head, I hadn't willingly given him a damn thing. But that wasn't true, was it?

"Get her outta there," the man named Vance ordered. I assumed that directive was given to Noah.

"Petals?" his soft voice called out to me not a minute later.

My heart crashed against its cavity. I'd been terrified plenty of times, but never like this. My eyes darted all around the room, stopping on the toilet.

The whole pre-conceived notion I'd had of throwing a battle to win the war seemed so naively childish then.

I didn't have a chance of winning anything, so why not go down swinging?

"Petals, open the door," Noah tried again.

"My name isn't fuckin Petals!" I lifted the top piece off the water tank and curled my fingers around the rim. Scampering backward, I made my way to the furthest corner and slid down the wall.

I brought my knees to my chest and watched the door. Adrenaline had my clenched hands shaking around the chunk of porcelain. Too many voices began murmuring at once for me to understand what it was they were saying.

They ceased abruptly. A millisecond later, the lock hit the dull tiled floor, and the weak wooden door blasted into the wall. I rose to my feet as Hawke barreled into the room.

He came straight for me, taking notice of the toilet lid a breath too late. I swung with everything I had, connecting with his dome.

"Sonofabitch!" He clutched the side of his head and stumbled sideways.

Vance was right behind him, and I wasn't lucky a second time. I swung at him with a heaving growl spilling from my lungs. He dodged it, grabbing hold of the lid and easily pulling it from my hands after a four-second struggle.

I wasn't expecting him to return the favor. When the lid hit the side of my forehead, pain had my mind going blank long enough for him to grab me by the legs and drag my shock-slackened body almost clear out of the bathroom the second I hit the floor.

Noah was yelling now, and someone else was yelling right back. Whatever they were saying was of no interest to me.

I somehow managed to grab hold of the door frame in a pathetic attempt to get away from Vance.

"Let go!" I struggled to break free by kicking him as best I could.

"You little bitch," a recovered Hawk spat down at me, slamming his booted heel right where four of my fingers were resting, making me let go of the doorframe.

Pain seemed to be radiating from everywhere. Something wet was running down the side of my face, and I could feel throbbing in my left hand. I felt like a rose being trampled on the ground. Vance carelessly dragged me the rest of the way into the bedroom.

I was lifted up by my middle and dropped face-first back onto the bed, kept there by Vance pressing my face into the mattress.

I tried my best, tried with my whole heart and every ounce of fight I had within me to stop them from destroying who I was.

In the end, that's exactly what they did. Each of them participated. Vance went first, forcing his cock inside me just like his son had less than twenty minutes ago.

He was much rougher. The grip he had on my hair seemed to tighten with his every thrust, setting my scalp aflame.

I wish I could say I made it hard for him to enjoy himself, but truthfully, I wasn't any kind of match for him—or his family.

I thought it couldn't get worse, but I was wrong. Vance lifted me by the throat like I was nothin but a dirty dishrag. He lined himself up with my virgin ass as Rex took the front. They entered me after some sick countdown, both brutally unforgiving. The skin around the rim of my ass shredded, and blood leaked between my cheeks.

I felt as if a pole of flaming iron was searing me in two. I screamed and begged for them to stop, suffocating on my sobs.

My body wanted to turn in on itself but, even there, it hurt too badly.

I couldn't tell how long they passed me around like a chip bowl at a party, each of them taking however much they wanted.

In the end, it was Noah who gave me the water that led me to pass out.

He probably thought he was giving me some form of peace, but his help came after a round too many.

Everything changed for me that night. The cracks in my soul became too wide.

There was nothing left to hold onto.

Chapter Four

Grimm

I tossed the last body into the pit, and signaled for it to be lit up.

One of the acolytes shuffled forward and dumped kerosene up and down the deep, lengthy ditch. Another followed, casually dropping matches, keeping his black hooded robe clear of the flames that instantly erupted.

The man I'd just tossed in blinked up at me, his eyes wide. He tried to lift his head off the broken legs he'd partially landed on, but didn't have the strength.

He couldn't do anything but let the fire slowly eat him alive, thanks to Cobra crushing his vocal cords.

Leaving the acolytes to it, I made my way back inside the house, stomping my boots on the welcome mat my sister had demanded be put down. The last thing I wanted to hear was Cali's mouth because I'd tracked dirt across her immaculate hardwood.

The open floor plan gave me a clear view of Romero standing in the kitchen. I glanced at the contents of the blender he was emptying into a glass as I made my way to the sink. "Milkshake?" I guessed, turning the faucet on with my elbow.

"Always fucking milkshakes. Oh, let me correct myself—always *vanilla* fucking milkshakes."

I smirked to myself in amusement. Ever since Bryson, Cali's personal guard, left to help guard Luca's skin farm, Romero was on full-time Cali duty.

"She's like a fucking bear. All she does is sleep, eat, and chafe my dick—in that order.

"And I'm not complaining about the first or last one, but she's been talking to me like she's lost her motherfucking mind."

I shook my head. "Could have gone my whole life without hearing that bit about your dick. It's just hormones."

"Well, fuck hormones," he retorted before wordlessly passing me the dirty blender on his way to the fridge.

I rinsed it out and loaded it into the dishwasher. When I was finished, I leaned against the granite countertop and continued watching him.

"And what is that supposed to be?"

He ignored me at first, like he always tended to do. When I continued to stare, he set down the foil packet with little chocolate chunks in it and stared back at me with eyes so fucking dark it almost looked like he didn't have any.

"This is a glass. Inside this glass is a vanilla goat milkshake.

"On top of *that* is puffy white shit, and on top of *that* is expensive ass chocolate. Any other questions, Grimm?"

"Nope," I grinned. Fucking with him was one of the many highlights of my day—second after killing a few motherfuckers. "Just wondering if my baby sister still had your balls in the palm of her hand."

"You know, now that you mention it, I'll be balls deep inside your baby sister's sweet, perfect fucking pussy here—as soon as she's done with this drink." He lifted the glass up and a smug ass grin took over his face, matching the one now wiped clean off mine.

"You leaving soon?" he asked, changing the subject as he went over to a cabinet.

"Uh huh."

"Come tell Cali bye, and I'll walk you out," he more demanded than told me, grabbing a straw before making his way out of the kitchen.

That was how it worked, and I had no issues with it. I willingly and loyally did the devil's bidding. I was one of his few confidants.

It was the devil I found a brother in, who gave me a purpose, a home, and a family.

I stood in the kitchen a few seconds longer, prepping to say goodbye to the sister I felt I'd just gotten back. I didn't do freely emotional, and she'd turned into a hormonal typhoon as of late. She'd always been a bit manically childish—not her fault—but shit was at a def-con level so getting outta here for a few days sounded like a mini vacation.

Even though we weren't that close in the beginning, I couldn't see life without her crazy ass. She fit right in with our eighty degrees of fucked upness. She made my closest friend slightly human again.

It was something I'd been wondering if I'd royally fucked up for myself, by failing the only woman who'd made a lasting impression on me in every way that mattered.

"Damn, Grimmy, you set yourself up for that one," Cobra laughed, interrupting my self-reflecting, waltzing around the corner with a little blonde who was damn near dragging her feet. By the fussed up strands of his red hair, it was obvious what they'd been doing.

"I take it from the lack of crocodile tears she isn't aware of what's coming next?"

"Oh, nah, I'm gonna her take to the play room. Thirsty." He shrugged and pulled out a water-bottle, shaking it at me to emphasize his point.

The blonde looked my direction for explanation, no doubt wondering what the play room was and why it would make her wish she'd never set foot in this house.

She wasn't going to get one—not from me. I didn't give a shit how badly he was going to torture her.

She'd put herself in this situation; they all did. It was all about being fucked by a Savage.

Now Romero was permanently out of the running, it left three potential candidates close enough to him to count as bragging rights for spreading their legs for someone at the top of our hierarchy.

They never took into account that they wouldn't live long enough to tell anyone. Shit had only gotten worse after it was known Cali had a ring on her finger.

Things were finally dying back down to normal now. Maybe they realized she was a little worse off in the head than we were. That took some fucking effort.

"Go get her settled. I'm heading out."

I left him with those parting words and made my way to the second level.

One of the large double doors leading into their bedroom was cracked. Knowing that was done for my benefit only, I walked in without knocking.

The shit I felt seeing my sister on Rome's lap as he cupped her round bump was foreign to me. Fuck, it was foreign for him.

I could admit I was happy—maybe even as far as excited —to have a niece or nephew sooner than later. Love and all the other bullshit didn't mean much to me, but I wasn't numb to everything.

Someone important was missing though, someone who should have been around for all this maternal motherly shit Cali was going through.

"It's D-day!" Her bold blue eyes met my brown ones and she beamed at me, sitting her half-empty glass on the night-stand, right by the plexiglass casing that held the head of Romero's piece of shit of a father, David. There was a giant book of baby names resting on top of it.

"I'm about to take off."

"Well, where are your bags? Do you have food? Are you sure you—"

"I know where I'm going, and the sooner I leave, the sooner she'll be back." I wasn't going to mention who the fuck knew what shape Arlen was in. I didn't even want to think about it myself.

It took me twice as long as it should have to track her ass down to an exact location. The last bit of information wasn't something I would be sharing with my sister, whose child-hood was full of the same type of bullshit. Me and Romero had agreed on that without argument.

I would let him know when I got to her, and he could handle the rest. I would be doing enough damage control when everything else we were keeping from her came to light.

She stood up and made her way towards me, looking as tiny as she always had, with the exception of the bulge slightly lifting her black dress. Looking at the two of us, no one would ever suspect we were related. With the same dad, different moms, we were night and day.

She was white as snow—damn near an albino, her hair only a few shades darker. My hair was dark and my tan skin was covered in various tattoos, whereas she only had the inverted cross that marked her as a Savage.

I knew she was as much of a hugger as I was, so what her intention was for getting so close to me, I didn't know.

"You better be back soon then, or I'm coming to get you, and I don't care what the asshole behind me has to say about it."

"We both know your ass isn't going anywhere unless I fucking say so. You keep trying me and I'll tie you to the bed again," Romero cut in, coming up behind her.

She rolled her eyes, ignoring him. Then, she surprised me by grabbing my arm like a kid would their favorite teddy bear and squeezing it. Being I was a good few inches taller than her, I wound up looking down at the top of her head.

"I'll be back long before baby S is here," I said, knowing that would bring a smile to her face.

Romero took hold of her wrist and gently pulled her away from me. I stepped back, giving them privacy as he whispered something I more than likely didn't want to hear in her ear.

He kissed her, placed a light parting touch on her stomach, and then motioned for me to walk out, silently falling in step beside me when we were back in the hallway.

"Will you two kids be able to play nice while I'm gone?" I asked as we made our way out the front door.

"They got me here," Cobra butted in, pushing off the wall where he'd been waiting for us.

"I don't need relationship help from either of you dickheads."

We approached where my Fat Bob was sitting with saddlebags already secured on the rear end.

They stood back as I wrapped a black bandana around my mouth and nose, slipped on a pair of shades, and pulled my hood up. Normally, I didn't go to such an extreme, but the heat was bearing down and this was the best way to protect myself against the elements on the ride I had ahead of me.

Once my fingerless gloves were on, I slipped an atomic slug bag over my shoulders, making sure the handle of my ReaperTac was sticking out.

"We sticking to the same plan?" Cobra asked.

"Yeah, give me four days after tonight. Come through the parking garage."

He nodded and stepped forward to dap me. "Be safe, bro. I'll be seeing you soon. I got a reason to break the charger out now." His face lit up like a little kid's, and I shook my head.

"What?" I asked Romero when he crossed his arms and just looked at me.

"You know what," he replied flatly. "And you know I'm right."

I did know what he was saying, but I didn't have a response.

"She might hate me," I admitted out loud for the first time.

"Yeah, fucking right, she has no reason to hate you," Cobra scoffed, easily picking up on our roundabout conversation. "You're her stars and moon," he fluttered his lashes and stared at the sun.

I gave him a flat look.

Romero slightly shifted, pulling my attention back to him, and I knew whatever he was about to say had him feeling uncomfortable, which rarely happened.

"You know the only thing I want from Cali is her to never

stop loving me? She's a psychotic bitch and pisses me off a good ten times a day, but she's everything to me.

"I don't think I'd be able to keep going if I lost her. Maybe I'm pussy for having that big a weakness, but I quickly learned not give a shit. I love that woman; she's my fucking queen. From the day she and that annoying as shit, loud mouth girl you got a soft spot for came rollin their asses down that hill and running through the woods, I knew she was it for me.

"You knew it too; I know you did. Don't deny yourself something like this. Trust me when I say she's the best thing that's ever happened to me, aside from that squishy alien in her stomach.

"You've always been a king in your own right; don't come back here without your queen. If you gag her ass in the process, you'd be doing me a favor."

I could count on one hand the number of times I'd been surprised. This took two fingers. Cobra had the same expression on his face as I did. That was the most emotional shit he'd said to either of us since we'd been kids.

Hugging him would probably get me dropped on my ass and be taking shit way too far, but I felt the love of a brother just as strong as I always had, if not stronger—for the blessing I didn't need but he gave me anyway, and the man he became for my sister.

"I agree with all the shit he just said," Cobra commented, grounding us back to our usual self-preserved demeanors as he usually did when shit got to an awkwardly silent level.

"Call me as soon as you settle with her," Romero said, back to normal programming.

He didn't like saying goodbyes because they were often final. We three lived up to every fucked up expectation people had of us, but what no one knew was that when we cared about someone, we cared with the all parts of us that could still give a shit.

I was loyal only to my family; it was because of that I vowed to track down someone that had been stolen from us. And I had. And Rome was right.

I climbed on my Fat Boy, gave a slight nod of my head, and turned the engine over.

Now, it was time to bring her home where she belonged.

Chapter Five

Arlen

I'd had enough.

I could no longer feel the steady rhythm of my heart. I felt cold and damned. There were these constant moments where I would disconnect. I was either numb or feeling everything at once.

I needed someone to shove me over the fuckin edge, or put me out of my misery. I was sinking; something murky was rising. My sky was falling, and the tides were turning.

I didn't know how much time had passed since Noah gave me to those men wrapped up in a pretty bow.

My body still hurt, but whether it was all in my head or physical, I couldn't process.

I think it was two or three days ago he'd come in and announced we would be moving again soon. His voice sparsely registered—I wish he'd shut up and save his breath, choke on his own words. I couldn't bring myself to pretend I cared about anything he had to say. He needed to find a hobby and spare me one single second more of his company.

I'd been having beautifully morbid daydreams lately. Every time I heard him speak, and every time I flashed back to the men who took what didn't fuckin belong to them, I drifted off into a catatonic place.

I envisioned their ligaments scattered in pieces, their entrails greedily devoured by the crows cawing outside my window as I sang the counting song.

One for sorrow, two for mirth…

Those black carrion birds had become a source of comfort.

I imagined them arriving just to keep me company, as if they knew in their majestic little heads that this kind of loneliness was new to me.

See, I'd always been kind of a loner, but never intentionally. I laughed a bit too loud, and my soul was a tad too wild for me to ever really blend in with normal folks.

This was different, though. This kind of lonely came from feeling like I no longer knew myself. I'd known exactly who I was before, but I didn't know who I was becoming now.

I'd had typical vengeful notions just weeks ago. These twisted thoughts were foreign to me. I swear I'd lost my mind; it felt like I was slowly going insane.

My life had been completely shaken up and rearranged. I knew I would always be partially to blame for that, and that there was nothin to be done about the events that led me here.

I wasn't going to deny those facts.

I'd fucked up, but I was sick of thinking about all that was. I was tired of feeling lost.

I stood in the dull bathroom under a lackluster light and boldly dared to look at my reflection. Someone who didn't know what I'd been through would look at me and not see anything wrong, or anyone other than the same old Arlen Prosner.

The bruises between my thighs and missing patches of skin I'd scrubbed at too hard were only evident to me and the men who left them there. I couldn't shake the feeling of their heavy breath on my neck, or the way they felt me up.

No matter how many times I washed myself, I felt like I was coated in layers of grime and filth. My body was a temple, and they'd tainted it. Invisible scars weighed me down heavily.

Like a moth to a flame, my wings had burned away. I dug down deep inside myself, searching for the part of me that cared, but whatever it was that shifted had me caring a little less lately.

I wasn't sure about this new me. I thought I'd picked up all the broken pieces, but the ones I had didn't align anymore. This Arlen was a stranger, and she offered no explanation.

I'd waited for my shadow, but he never came. Turns out this whole surviving thing was pretty goddamn hard. It was even harder when you had nothing left to lose and all you felt was a cruel, never-ending wanting.

At what point did I stop facing denial and ask myself what I was struggling to survive for?

Chapter Six

Grimm

I rode for a full day and night to get where I needed to be, stopping only to refuel, knowing exactly the range my Fat Boy could handle before it would start to sputter.

On my final stop, I stashed the bike in the exact spot I'd mapped out the week prior, pre-fueling with the gas can I'd stashed under a caved in portion of the abandoned garage.

All that was left to do was wait.

I munched on smoked jerky and sipped some hooch to pass a little more time, before taking a piss and then prepping to move into a proactive position.

I snagged my ReaperTac from my bag, now secured with the others, and then attached the suppressor to my Glock 17 after checking the magazine. The black gun was simple to use, durable, ubiquitous, and took the most easy to obtain ammunition there was: 9 mm Parabellum.

Cutting through a few weed-covered yards, I moved

closer to the house I knew Arlen was being held at. The heat was a sonofabitch, but the oncoming shadows helped to shade me from full on exposure.

I'd lived in this fucking place my entire life, spent half that time on the road, and still abhorred the sun. I couldn't stand its intensity or its light. I was a creature of the night.

The dark was easier on the eyes, and much better for killing, hunting, and getting pussy.

And that was why I'd planned to make my move when the sky was a deep purple and the Badlands' natural terrain was only lit up by a crescent moon.

The house had been easy to find; it was the only dingy blue one in the entire run-down neighborhood. There was a dark green pickup truck parked right on the front lawn, and I watched a laughing Noah climb into it with three other men.

I wasn't there for him. Not this time. His hourglass was near empty enough. I couldn't wait to shred him apart with my bare hands. My objective right then was to get to my girl.

Not knowing how long they would be gone, I tracked the movement inside the house, trying to get a feel of the precise layout.

I needed to get Arlen out ASAP, but I was never one for rushing into shit without taking in as much detail as I could. Acting brashly got people killed for being complete dumb-asses and not using their heads.

Me and my brothers learned that at fourteen when we sat back and watched a group of cannibals get slaughtered trying to steal a dairy cow, of all things.

The family had set traps around their property to prevent that very thing from happening. Lucky it was those fuckers and not us, because that's exactly what we'd been there to do.

We still ended up with the cow in the end; we just took

out the family later that same day as they cleaned the bodies up. But it was still a beneficial learning lesson.

Carrion birds perched on the house's depleted rafters, and the dying tree off to the side of it. They had a habit of showing up when shit was about to go down around me.

I hadn't figured out why, and I couldn't lie and say it wasn't creepy the first few times this happened.

But as with everything else that shaped who I was, I'd come to like them, and it heavily attributed to my alias.

Estimating there were four people inside and that my girl was naturally being kept in the room with the plywood over the window like a caged animal, I moved.

Sticking to the darkest part of the shadows wasn't something I did intentionally. The dark had a way of gravitating towards me. I used it to cover me as I made my way to the side door and found my initial assumption correct: the dumb fucks inside hadn't locked it.

Easing the poor excuse of a barrier open, I slipped inside and reclosed it. Laughter sounded from the right…the living room. A pipe groaned as someone shifted closer in a room to my immediate left—a bathroom, I guessed.

Straight ahead of me were half missing stairs that led down to what had to be the basement.

Ascending the short three stairs off to the side of me that led to a small landing, I pushed another door open when I knew it was clear.

I stepped into a small hall that expanded outward into a filthy kitchen. There was a laundry room with a rusted washer and dryer caddy in the corner from where I stood, and another door was wide open across from it.

By the low grunt and pair of jeans I could see around a set of hairy ankles, someone was taking a shit in a toilet that didn't work. There was a distinct stench emanating through the hall that could only have come from other people having done the same thing before him, and leaving all the feces to build up.

I readied my Glock and eased towards the bathroom. The suppressor wasn't going to completely silence the shot—this wasn't an action film—but it would reduce the muzzle flash and confuse the others in the house as to what they'd heard or where it had come from.

The man had his head buried in his hands when I pulled the trigger.

I'd just done him a favor. The kill was fast, instead of fatally wounding.

He didn't have time to react, and even if he did, it wouldn't have mattered much.

The bullet burned flesh as it formed a circular hole rimmed with abraded skin right in the top of his dome. It slid right through his hair and muscle, as if it were a silken caress. The casing made quick shrapnel of his calcium, phosphorus, sodium, and collagen case before splitting apart tissue and fibrous membranes.

All that gorgeous handiwork from a little bullet, and he was gone in a fraction of a second, without getting a moment to admire it or feel the inside of his head being ripped apart. The only thing he left behind was the smell of shit and a spray of blood, bone, and brains on the wall.

Hearing what sounded more like a loud door slamming than a gunshot, the other people in the house immediately began to investigate.

I slipped across the hall to the laundry room and waited, placing the Glock in my waist band in place of my ReaperTac.

There was a loud "What the hell?", before one of them opened the front door, another took the stairs to the second floor, and the third came in my direction, calling out the name of his dead friend.

Not getting a response, he peered into the bathroom, recoiling like a spring the second he saw the body slumped at an odd angle.

Before he could react, I moved from my position. He never saw me coming. I clamped a hand over his mouth and nose to shut him the fuck up and muffle the expulsion of air I knew would be coming.

Instead of slicing into his neck, I stabbed my curved stainless steel blade into the side, going through an artery, and gripped the handle a little tighter, dragging downward.

Most of his blood ran down his throat instead of spilling out all over the damn floor. His body lowered with silent spasms. He tried to speak, asphyxiating on his own ichor.

This was always messy, and I tried not to make it too gory.

The method of the kill wasn't what excited me. Neither did the begging or the torture—not that I didn't enjoy those aspects of my work. It was the final outcome, death, that made all this worth it.

The moment when someone realized their life was slipping away was my favorite part of the job. No matter what they did or how they lived, death would always show up in the end. I merely helped conduct their souls to the afterlife.

I liked my job. I was *good* at my job—so fucking good even the devil admired my craft. I had to live in hell, so why not enjoy myself and purge some motherfuckers from it?

I left the man behind and made my way through the rest of the house. Whoever had gone out the front door was nowhere to be seen. He could wait.

Darting towards the stairs, I swapped melees again and

popped the man who'd started coming back down as I was going up, sending a slug right between his eyes.

I sidestepped as his body took a tumble past me, landing at an obtuse angle below and leaking blood onto the floor.

At the top step, I saw there was only one closed door out of three. I didn't even bother trying to undo the excessive number of locks on the outside. I kicked the piece of shit right in.

And there she was.

She was sitting in a barely lit room on a full sized bed with rope wrapped around her wrists. There was an almost crushing feeling of relief that coursed through my chest merely from seeing her again. I felt like I'd just found something I didn't know I'd lost.

Her reaction was delayed. I knew then that she was different.

I wasn't surprised by that—nor did we have time to sing a sad song about it, but damn did it fuck with my chest a little bit.

She studied me as if she wasn't sure I was real. I did my damndest to make sure my eyes didn't stray from her face. Whatever the fuck she had on left little to the imagination.

I focused on her eyes that reminded me too much of sunlight and spoke a vocabulary that was all their own. I didn't dwell on the fact that I understood the language because it was mine. I didn't dwell on what the darkest part of my sub-conscious mind already knew. That whatever just fucking happened between us when I kicked in the door was the magnifying of a spark that would soon be an inferno.

Instead, I told her to get the fuck up and that we needed to go.

Chapter Seven

Arlen

I was leaving the bathroom as he was entering the bedroom.

He had what looked like twine partially bunched up in his hands, and one of his cronies standing in the hall behind him.

My face gave away exactly what I was thinkin: wrapping that damn rope around his neck and cutting off every ounce of oxygen flowing to his brain.

I could watch him gasp for air, and when he thought it was over, I'd give him breath just so I could swiftly take it away again.

I spotted the prod in this new man's hand. I was the first to speak, surprising both of us, "He supposed to be your protection?" My voice sounded so hollow I tried to pinpoint when the last time I'd used it was.

"After this morning's incident, I thought it would be best."

Course he did. It was all fun and games until I was

launching bowls of steaming oatmeal at his face. But I thought that had happened days ago.

"I need to leave, and timing is kind of urgent, so if you could just…" He twirled his finger in the air, signaling for me to turn around.

I wasn't willingly giving him my back. Crossing my arms tightly over my chest, I slightly widened my stance, as if I were a bull preparing to charge. "Why is it urgent?"

"I don't have time for this. Turn around, or I'll have him give you a zap."

He took a step closer, instantly retracing it when I did the same.

Why had I never realized he was afraid of me? Vitus had done the same thing. I was just a girl, after all. I wondered where he was goin that had a light sheen of perspiration on his sullen skin. How much had I missed happening around me?

I silently held my wrists out in front of me and gave him a blank stare. If I was gonna be tied up, I preferred my arms to be in front of me. With no further demands, he quickly secured the rope, pulling so tightly I let out a small grunt as the brittle rope dug into my skin.

"I'll unbind you when I return. This is just a precaution."

I could've pointed out that I was locked behind a door in a house full of men…there wasn't much to be cautious of on my end, but I had nothing to say to him.

He turned and wordlessly left me alone with what almost looked like concern on his face.

I took my usual position back up, studying the rope to see if I could possibly escape.

I was still doing that when the first pop spilled through the ventilation system. Unlike the last time, I knew it wasn't a rat. Voices from below and rapid footfalls made me think it was just men rough-housing.

Someone came up the stairs, but didn't come into the room, and then I heard it again. It was much closer this time around, and followed by something—some*one*—falling down the steps.

When the door flew open, I didn't even jump. Staring at the massive hooded figure, I thought I'd either officially lost my mind or that I wasn't awake. He shifted only slightly, making himself appear even taller, and looked me straight in the eye.

I knew those eyes. I saw the beard. Saw the inverted cross I'd always wanted to touch.

I even remembered the scent of citrus sweet and spicy wood that was naturally his. The hairs rose on the back of my neck as we simply stared at one another.

I couldn't tell ya what it was that happened right then, only that I suddenly felt more awake then I had in days. Yet I still wasn't fathoming what was going on. Leave it to Grimm to open his mouth and give me some swift clarification while skipping over all casualties.

"Get the fuck up; we need to go." He glided towards me like he was floating on air, and pulled what looked like a mini scythe from beneath his black ensemble. The blade on the damn thing had to be a good seven inches long. And was that blood?

I instinctively brought my arms up, but it was more in defense than for him to slice through the rope like he did. It fell away, landing on the floor as if it were a dead snake.

It didn't truly register that his hand was wrapped around mine and he was pulling me out into the hall until I realized my legs were moving. He didn't launch into detail about what would happen next, but he wasn't a real talkative man in the first place. That clearly hadn't changed.

The striped wallpaper in the hall hung in peeled sheets, revealing moldy grey walls underneath. It sounded like the warped wood flooring was going to cave in from the pressure of our weight, sending us straight to the basement I knew the rats dwelled in. I'd been able to hear them in the vents when the house was quiet.

We were halfway down the stairs when I saw the body at the bottom. I couldn't bring myself to feel sorry for him. I didn't even try.

With no shoes on my feet, I made sure to avoid the crimson puddle just like Grimm did.

At the sound of footsteps, Grimm brought me flush against his back and pulled out a shiny black gun.

I didn't see the initial impact the bullet made with the man's face, but his screech of pain was somethin similar to the sound a cat made if you stepped on its tail.

When we started moving again, I saw him holding a hand over the spot his right eye should have been, blood rushing through the gaps in his fingers in a waterfall effect. He fell backward into the wall, making that same high-pitched sound.

I didn't feel sorry for him either. He deserved this serving of vigilante justice.

My nerves felt like live-wires ready to short circuit, like at any moment I would wake up. This would have all just been a corporal daydream from me being stuck in my head again. I barely noticed how hard I was squeezing Grimm's hand, and when I did, I found myself squeezin it harder.

He couldn't let me go. He had to take me with him.

I didn't care what his rep was; he was a much better alternative than being left behind with any of these men.

The first floor of the house was in the same condition as the second, if not worse. I didn't understand why Noah was even staying someplace like this. He was used to more luxuries than I had been; a true spoiled pig.

We went through a kitchen and entered a hall with a strong noxious odor I couldn't place. Bypassing two doorways, I saw a dead man on a toilet, and another with his throat split open. I would be a liar if I said I wasn't impressed with how fast Grimm got this all done.

He took me down two stairs and right out a side door. Darkness was waiting for us, as were the few carrion birds I'd made friends with.

Grimm looked back at me and, without warning, turned and scooped me up as if I were a ragdoll before proceeding to take off.

"What are you doin?" I asked, holding onto him as he nearly ran with me in his arms.

"No shoes," he answered, seeming to know exactly where he was going.

It didn't take all that long for us to reach a garage, leaning on its last leg. He sat me down and immediately went inside, still givin me zero explanation as to what was goin on.

When he came back out, it was from around the corner of the structure, and he was wheeling a blacked out customized bike. I only knew it was a Harley because it said so right on a black front panel. The tires were thick, and the pipes gleamed; had this been a different situation, I might've drooled over the damn thing. It was so fitting for Grimm to have such a thing.

"Put this on," he gruffly demanded, thrusting the large black hoodie he'd had on just a second ago into my line of vision.

I took a quick glance at him and saw he was focusing real hard on everything that wasn't beneath my neckline.

That filthy feeling I always had intensified.

He was probably well aware of what had happened in that room. Did it make him think worse of me? Unable to look at him a second longer, I snatched the garment and pulled it over my head. It was long, covering everything, and almost to my knees. And it had his familiar smell. I left my hair tucked down inside it and pulled up the hood, knowing I was gonna have to get on his bike.

"Come on," he said, swinging a leg over the side. I moved so I was behind him and tried to copy his flawlessly executed move with no help, but wound up gripping his shoulder.

"Easy," he warned.

Trying again, I lifted up my slip and his hoodie and was able to take root behind him on my next attempt.

"Hold on tight," he said over his shoulder, turning the engine over. I did as I was told and wrapped my arms around his middle, smashin my breasts into his back and clinging to him as he hit the gas and propelled us into the road.

Two kids and what looked like their grandmother stood in their front yard three houses down.

A bug zapper was lit up and illuminated what they were doing. They stopped mid-dig of whomever the person was they were burying to watch us pass. A tiny wooden cross stuck lop-sided out of the ground with the word MOM written on it in tiny red letters.

As Grimm sharply turned the corner, the older child lifted her chubby hand and waved at me, smiling in spite of death being right in front of her.

At her age, seeing something like that in my neighborhood would have been hard for me to wrap my head around. It would have never happened in Centriole in the first place.

For this young girl, it was just another day in the Badlands. A child understood reality much better than I'd ever had the chance to at such a young age.

Like many of the other folk out here, she had a family, and she was educated. She had to wake up every day and go to sleep like everybody else did. Only, unlike the people livin nice and comfortably in The Kingdom, she wasn't guaranteed to survive and see another day.

She understood what this world was really like, and still found it in her heart to smile. In my mind, she was already stronger than I ever was. And as I was taken away from that old neighborhood, I came to realize somethin.

That wall didn't protect a damn thing. It just crippled everyone behind it.

Chapter Eight

Arlen

When we hit the open road, he gunned us forward, roaring full speed ahead.

I waited for Noah to come crashing into my whimsical bubble and drag me back to the real world where my wrists were bound and I was alone on that bed, waitin for him to have his way with me again, but he never came.

It was just me and Grimm. Of all the people I thought would come and get me, I always knew it'd be him. He had always been my shadow.

Just when I was ready to give it all up, he came kickin doors in and remindin me he'd never let that happen. I held onto his waist a little tighter, but felt no fear in this moment.

The starless sky was like a black swirling sea overhead. It was the first beautiful thing I'd seen in months. The vast wasteland looked picturesque like this. Wind whipped at my face and made my eyes burn, but I didn't care. It was fresh and clean, filtering in and out of my corrupted lungs—another sign that I'd really been freed from my four-walled prison.

The faster Grimm went, the more I felt the little tick in my chest that had been long gone trying to sputter again.

There was a chill in the air, but his hoodie gave me comfort, and his solid body was like a mini heater. He was the realest thing of all, the final bit of proof that this was reality. I could feel his firm abdominal muscles beneath my palms and smell him with every breath I took.

I'm not sure how long we rode, but when he finally began to slow, my arms ached and my thighs burned. There were structures rising in the near distance and I belatedly realized I was looking at a city.

He pulled off to the side of the road and cut the engine. "You need to piss?" he asked, easily swinging off the bike and turning to face me.

For real? His face was so serious I had the absurd urge to laugh—and that was really somethin I was certain I'd forgotten how to do. How long had I been with him? An hour? Three? I could almost imagine that awful shithole of a house was months behind me already.

But my barren feet had felt the wind just as clearly as my cheeks. The slip I had on was covered by nothing other than his hoodie, and I still felt filthy. It was impossible to look at him for longer than a few seconds, and I'd never had that problem before.

His gaze was penetratin. I forgot how easily he could see right through me.

Then there was the whole other issue that I couldn't even believe was happening at a time such as this. The way this man pulled me in over and over again, like gravity I couldn't overcome. I tried damn hard, too. I had been since the day we met. He would be a bad habit I'd never break free of.

I was in no kind of state to indulge in him. My mind was too unstable, brimming with an ugly cyclone of hatred, pain, and rage.

My soul had divided in two, and somethin wicked had taken residence in the middle. I didn't want him looking at this version of Arlen Prosner, but I wasn't much of a fan of the old one, either.

All of that sobered me right up and killed my momentary joy. I was like a mockingbird that could no longer carry a tune. And what was a mockingbird without its song, now that its whole purpose was gone?

The strange part of me I wasn't real acquainted with yet had an answer, but she still withheld it. Grimm stood before me, strong as ever, like he was the one who would explain everything, as if it was his responsibility to shoulder my burdens and make it better.

And wasn't that bullshit? Hadn't I handled everything up until this point? A harsh resounding *no* swiftly echoed inside my head. I didn't understand that either, so I wasn't goin to bother trying.

Clearing my throat, I shook my head, putting on the best poker face I could. Not a second later, his hand was cuppin my chin and reorienting my face with his line of vision.

"When I speak to you with words, you give me your eyes and speak back. That's how a conversation works."

"Plenty of people talk without payin attention to what the other's doin, Grimm."

I scowled and pushed his hand away; he easily let me go, but then snapped his fingers in my face to make me focus on him again.

"Last I checked, we're not plenty of people. I want your eyes on mine. You got that, brat?"

It sounded like he'd left somethin hangin off his sentence, but I knew Grimm well enough that if he didn't elaborate the first time, he wouldn't be goin back to amend his words.

Besides, he'd just called me brat. I didn't think I'd ever hear that nickname again. To be honest, I'd hated it, but ya know somethin? Brat sounded a helluva lot better than Arlen at the moment.

"I don't have to go number one or number two," I answered, holdin his gaze a full seven seconds—I counted.

"That's an improvement, but you could've just said you don't have to take a shit."

"I don't talk like you, Grimm."

"Clearly," he grunted, going to the saddlebag on the opposite side of his bike.

"You shouldn't have an issue looking people in the eye. Why would you want to hide that face of yours?"

I blinked. Was that sarcasm? If he'd just complimented me, I might still be daydreamin. When I just stared at him like an illiterate fool, he opened the bag and pulled out a pile of clothing.

He wordlessly held the bundle in his hands, waiting for me to get off his Harley and put it on right there on the side of the road. I climbed down, feeling like I'd just stepped in a bowl of Jell-O.

"Careful," he warned, shooting a hand out to steady me by grabbing my shoulder.

"I'm good," I said after a few seconds, taking the small pile from him. I sorted everything out, surprised to find a pair of underwear and a bra folded inside the dark green tank top.

Seeing as we were on the shoulder and out in the open, I dressed as quick as I could.

I slipped the black underwear on, then the fitted charcoal pants. Next were the brown leather combat boots. A pair of socks had been shoved down inside them. I reckoned Cali was to thank for all the extras—the girl had smarts.

Once the shoes were laced, I pulled Grimm's hoodie over my head and turned around, giving him my back as I took off the slip and clasped the matching bandeau bra.

Little bumps peppered my skin as it was exposed to the night air. Snagging the tank top, I hurriedly added that last, and tried to ignore the feel of Grimm's eyes on me the entire time.

"What now?" I asked, turning to face him the second I was decent.

"I have to go into the city—"

"You ain't leavin me," I butted in.

"Never planned on leaving you, brat, I just thought you'd like to be dressed before we went."

That was logical. "Oh, well, here."

"Keep it." He ignored his outstretched hoodie and climbed back on his bike.

Shruggin my shoulders, I pulled it back over my head, pushing the sleeves up as best I could, and then climbed back on behind him, trying not to pay much attention to how sore my ass had become.

This was nothin compared to what it'd felt like…whenever that incident was. He gunned his engine again and we were off, leaving my slip of ruined material behind us.

Chapter Nine

Grimm

She didn't need to hold me so tight, but I wasn't going to stop her.

This was the only time I'd had a woman sitting on the back of my bike instead of dragging them behind it. Being held like this was different, but not as intolerable as I'd imagined.

I tried not to think about it too much, how right it felt. I focused on wondering why I'd said what I had. I'd been trying to tell her she had too pretty a face to hide it away.

That was an understatement, anyway. Brat was a bombshell. It knocked me off kilter to even think that. I had almost eleven years on her, but my moral compass hadn't spontaneously decided to start working again because of that.

This thought process was more along the lines that I'd been with women all over the spectrum—beautifully dark to pale, freckled redheads, and none of them looked like her.

They weren't even a fraction as enticing; they'd still be alive if that were the case.

I could only imagine how much better she'd look at this age. I could see it clear enough that my dick hardened as we tore up the blacktop, and I was in no position to fix it.

That was a good enough reason to concentrate on other matters, like getting inside her head on our trip home.

Not sounding like a pubescent little boy was a good start. That bullshit that just came out of my mouth was cringe-worthy.

Not only was it a corny ass line, but it didn't exactly translate what I'd been thinking clearly. Speaking to women wasn't in my repertoire of skills. I was usually telling them to shut the fuck up for screaming in my ear. That was in both instances: fucking and killing.

Cobra was the best at things like that; even Romero was smoother than I was, and he wasn't Casanova by anyone's standards—not even my sister's.

I could tell by the look on Brat's face that she didn't know if I'd been bullshitting or serious. That blank mask she always tried to slip on might as well have been invisible. She had always been easy for me to read, like a picture book—I didn't need to an utter a word, and neither did she.

I just got her.

I don't think she was aware of that until now. She hadn't been aware of a lot of things.

That was the problem with people from The Kingdom: they didn't live in reality.

They lived in a fantastical dreamland, and when reality showed up, they were fucked.

I wasn't blaming Brat for her lack of life experience, because neither of us could help where we came from. And though I was no better than the fuckers that had just had her

—in fact, I knew I was worse in a few key categories—I refused to condone what I was fully aware had been done.

I wasn't going to coddle her, though, and I wasn't going to ask if she was okay. That was a dumbass rhetorical question. There were some things you just didn't need to confirm. Her eyes were open windows that gave it all away.

I understood the language they continued to speak, even if she didn't.

The fire that had once lit up her entire being like a beacon now burned within a darkness inside her that could rival my own.

She needed to be educated.

She needed to learn that there was nothing in the dark to be afraid of. I wasn't going to save her from it.

I wasn't a hero. I never would be—not for her.

We were all born to live in this hell. I would teach her how to transcend and thrive in it. I would drain her, break her down if I had to, just so I could be the one to make her whole again. In my mind, it *had* to be me.

I'd felt the need to shadow her from the beginning, and this situation only strengthened that resolve. I'd lost enough in this world. I wouldn't let it take her, too.

I would show her that hell could be beautiful. This is where she belonged—right beside me. Even knowing what my lifestyle meant for her…it was too late for that now.

Ask me where the fuck all this was coming from and I wouldn't have an exact answer.

I'd never had anything to be selfish about until her.

No one had ever looked at me like Brat did, seeing more than a man who harvested souls for a living…like I was something worth giving a fuck about.

Cali and my brothers tried to show me that very thing, but it wasn't the same. I knew Romero would know how to explain it better than I could. Logic, reason, rationality…none of it mattered. I just had this uncontrollable urge to protect her. I'd failed before—completely.

Had I been paying attention to her like I'd always done up until that night, she would have never made it out of the house. Had whatever this was between us been out in the open, no one would have dared remove her from that house. People were too afraid of me to ever fuck with someone who belonged to me.

I'd taken my eyes off her for what seemed like only a minute, and then she was gone.

That wouldn't happen again.

I would make her unequivocally mine. May some divine power have mercy on anyone who ever had the balls big enough to try and get between us again. I sure as fuck wouldn't.

Chapter Ten

Arlen

A faded green sign welcoming people to Rivermouth rose up on our right. It was marked with the Sigil of Baphomet, an inverted pentagram with the horned head of a goat. I knew the counterclockwise Hebrew characters spelled out Romero's name. He truly was the devil in the flesh. To think I'd once been terrified of meeting him or any of his satanic acolytes…They'd wound up being my closest friends, my extended family.

Life was most certainly a pretentious bitch, but she had her moments. I shifted on the seat so I could have a better view.

I'd heard every other city had been abandoned, which was hard for me to believe when I took into account that the population of Centriole didn't house *that* many damn people—not to mention the fact that I'd also heard that others were still managing to thrive. Not on a scale such as The Kingdom, but still: they were active.

Grimm didn't slow like I expected him to; if anything, he sped up the second he flicked his high beams off, whipping past moss covered buildings, a car left in the middle of the street, and avoiding a large pothole. How the hell could he see so well in the dark?

I squealed when he took a corner so fast I thought we were going to tip. I could've touched the asphalt if I'd wanted to—easily.

I felt him vibrate with laughter as I hid my face in his back, snuggling down in his long hoodie.

When I dared look back up, it was to see him coasting into the parking garage of a huge brick building with pointed arches.

He went up to deck C and swung the bike into a parking space in a darkened corner nearest a steel door.

Soon as the engine was cut, he was off the bike and gently lifting me down to the ground, supporting me until he was sure I was steady on my feet.

Moving with fluid vitality, he detached the largest bag from the back of his motorcycle and took my hand. I stuck close to him, looking all around the expansive space, expecting somethin to jump out at us at any second.

"Why are we here?" I asked in a low whisper.

"Didn't trust you to stay awake the full length of the ride, and I don't think you'd like falling off the back of the bike."

I wasn't tired.

When he pushed open the steel door, I was even more awake. Why did he pick this of all places to make a pit stop?

I wasn't sure if my curiosity was in full effect because I'd been stuck in the same environment day in and day out, or because I'd never seen anything like this.

The curved moon was the only thing trying to light our way, and there'd only been one window at the top of the stairwell.

Obviously the old elevator didn't work—not that I would trust it in the first place—so we walked. I held onto Grimm, hoping I didn't trip over somethin right in front of me, and because I wasn't touching the railing beside us.

He pushed open another door and we entered a super long hallway, lit only a little better.

That was when I realized we were in a gigantic hospital. It looked like somethin straight out of a horror film.

I was immediately more intrigued. The air was dusty, the paint on the walls so chipped they looked layered in mulch.

He continued down the hall with me in tow, maneuvering around an old wheelchair I would have run right into.

Our boots crunched over sheets of paper, grime, and some trash littering the floor. A few reinforced windows lined the wall on our left, but they were so dirty it was nearly impossible to see out of em.

I was going to ask why we were there again when he abruptly turned, just as we reached the end of the hall and entered a room. When he dropped my hand, I grabbed his shirt.

If he minded, he didn't voice it. He silently pushed the door shut and unzipped his bag.

A second later, a soft florescent glow lit up our surroundings. He'd pulled out what looked like a kiddy lantern.

"Have you been here already?" I asked, noticing how tidy the room was. I answered my own question when I saw the semi-clean patient bed with a fresh floral blanket on it.

"When I had a general idea of where you were, I began planning out a route there and back. This hospital was the best place. It's more than fifteen buildings, empty, as you can see, and ideal to hole up compared to the abandoned, roach-infested motel around the corner. I sent one of the acolytes out to make sure it was clear and set up a place you could sleep," he explained.

I think that was the most words he'd ever spoken to me in one go. His voice was deep, but also a little gravelly. I'd say very manly, but I hadn't ever been around any men of his caliber to make such a statement.

He turned to face me, and I was able to hold his gaze for a full four seconds before I pretended there was somethin else more intriguing to look at. Course there wasn't. He had always been the most interestin person in my life.

Well, aside from Cali, who was a whole other special story, and the reason I'd met him in the first place.

If that cannibal hadn't carried her crazy self into the barn that day, I wouldn't be alive. I was sure his rotting corpse was thinkin twice about that decision.

I wondered how she'd dealt with all that happened to her. She'd been used since she was just a little girl, and that made me sick to my stomach. Sure, she grew up to be a lil different, but she did grow—and change—and she was the strongest woman I knew. But she'd also fully embraced the crazy inside her. She wasn't as unsure of it as I was mine.

"Brat," Grimm said, suddenly in front of me and pullin me outta my head. I had to tilt my chin to look at him.

"Don't do that, either." He said it simply enough, but there was an edge to it.

"You can't tell me not to think."

"I didn't tell you not to think. I told you not to keep it in, and that you can talk to me."

I was gonna point out that he most certainly hadn't said any of that, but I wasn't going to get lengthy dialogue from Grimm. I'd never needed it before. I just got him. Without really trying, it was like some natural phenomenon between us, just as the sun knew when to trade places with the moon.

Still, what the heck happened during our separation? Why did he now want me to confide in him? He was back to staring me down at this point, and I was close to having an emotional outburst from it, so I did the next best thing and hugged him.

I knew he wasn't any kind of hugger, but I didn't care. I smashed my face against his firm chest, purposely breathed him in, and tightly embraced him. I waited for him to shove me away, but he just stood there for a full minute. Then, he hugged me back.

I probably could have died right then from the sheer impact that had on my chest. His arms around me was the first thing that had felt right in a very long time.

He made me feel somethin other than numb.

"Thank you," I said, reluctantly pulling away. I dropped my arms but he kept his firmly on my back.

"Why are you thanking me?"

"You came for me."

He made a sound in the back of his throat and stepped away, turning back to his bag. I got the feelin I'd said the wrong thing. I didn't care. My mouth had gotten me this far; what was a bit of truth gonna do now?

Plus, we could both use some dosage of feelings in our lives.

"I know I was too late, and you might be wondering why I'm not treating you like a piece of glass, but that's not me, and I'm not going to do that."

"It's also not like you to be this open," I couldn't help but point out.

"Not being open was a mistake we're going to rectify. You only talk to me," he was quick to clarify.

"That sounds rather possessive of you."

"Should I warn you that I'm going to be selfish and protective over the only thing that's ever been exclusively mine?"

Yeah, I was probably still dreamin. I opened my mouth, or it was already hangin open in what was either shock or a confused state of cautionary joy—I wasn't sure. "Did you just call me a thing?" was my brilliant reply to what were potentially the best words I'd ever heard in my meager life.

He reached out and gently took hold of my hand, leading me to the bed. Without a word, he directed me to sit. I sank down on what felt like a plush piece of Styrofoam beneath the floral blanket, and focused on his chin.

He was onto me, and used his finger to aim my head up so we had eye connection before he said anything else. "You're *my* thing—pain in the ass, bratty hellion. Call me a possessive dick if it makes you feel better. Still my thing."

He returned to his bag, giving me his back to scowl at. What was I supposed to say to any of that? Why the hell did he have to come out all noble now?

"First of all, Grimm, I'm a woman, not a thing. Second of all, if I'm anything of yours—"

"You're my woman, then. Is that better? And I'm your man. I had some advice given to me, and was reminded that this was inevitable. You and me both know it, so let's not do that bullshit.

"Label it however you need to. I'll leave the room if you want so you can do the girl thing and cry, maybe throw a tantrum and break whatever you can pick up, but it's not going to change anything."

I went back to scowling, but I wasn't upset with him. Granted, the man could have worded that much, much better. I wasn't expecting flowery poetry from him, though.

I wasn't expecting any of this. I knew in the back of my mind he was right about this being inevitable—in the fantasy land I lived in, where my feels weren't one-sided, that is.

I hadn't ever been certain he knew how I felt. It was never discussed. It was just a shared look here or there. He saw right down to the bare bones of my soul. I should've known better. Course he'd known.

"You hungry?" he asked, standing up again from his crouching position.

"So we're gonna just move right along then? That's it?"

"Are you hungry?"

"No, I'm not hungry, Grimm. Don't change the subject, either."

"Eat this." He threw something through the air.

As it came towards my face, I instinctively reached up and caught it. A damn red apple.

"I just said I wasn't hungry."

"You lied," he confidentially retorted, and at that very second my stomach snarled in agreement.

I bit into the apple so I didn't launch it at his smirking face. I wasn't goin to admit it was the juiciest apple I'd ever tasted. He came over with his own, and a plastic bottle, sitting down right beside me.

I didn't pay close attention to the way his tattoos I'd committed to memory looked in the light, or how perfectly sculpted his body was beneath his black shirt. I didn't even notice the little strand of hair that had fallen out of place and now sort of rested on his forehead.

We sat there munching in silence until he lifted the bottle up and took a swig. I watched his throat bob as he swallowed. He held it out to me when he was done, and I slowly took it, staring down at the clear liquid inside.

I knew this wouldn't be laced—Grimm wouldn't do that —but it was a sure reminder of all the times it had been.

It's just water, I told myself. Somethin I'd drank plenty of times before Noah came along. Damn. Noah. He was still out there.

"You don't want me like this." That was the simplest way I could say I was a mess without having to go into detail.

He looked at the ceiling for a few seconds. "I'm not good at this shit, brat," he sighed, rolling his shoulders. "I want you whatever way I can have you. Any version of you is better than none at all, and this one is perfect for me."

See, I knew he'd understand what I was sayin without me having to elaborate. He didn't disappoint.

"Who told you you're not good at this? Romeo?" I teased with a smile.

"Romero is better at this than I am."

I nearly choked on the water I'd just bravely sipped when I realized he was being serious. I was tempted to drop kick him off the bed for saying somethin that stupid.

"Sorry to be the one to tell ya you're delusional, Grimm. He could never make me feel like you do." I leaned over, intendin to plant a solid kiss on his cheek, aiming for right above his beard, but then he turned his head and suddenly his hand was gripping the back of my neck and he had his lips on mine.

I gasped, unsure what to do. I mean, I knew what to do, but this was Grimm. My reaper had his mouth on mine.

I reiterated the *my* part of that thought as he took complete control.

I willingly let him have somethin I never pictured me givin someone ever again.

But again…this was Grimm. The man who told me less than five minutes ago that he wanted me whatever way he could have me—which was majorly confused, undeniably fucked up, and forever being a smartass.

It was crazy to trust death with life, but I'd never trusted anyone more than I did him in that very moment. His skilled mouth coaxed mine to part, and then he had his silken tongue caressing mine.

I admit it took me longer than I'd have liked to reciprocate, because no woman wanted to miss a single second when it came to kissing this gorgeous man.

That tick in my chest turned into the rapid beating of a heart as I kissed him back. He tasted like the sweetest sugar, dissolving on my tongue like a drug.

We were in a run down hospital, but we could have just as easily been standing on top of a mountain with fireworks goin off somewhere.

His hands didn't stray, and he didn't push for more.

I leaned into him and cupped his face, stroking the inverted cross I'd been eyeing since we met. His skin was so much softer than I would've thought. His beard stubble was rough on my palm.

It was *me* wanting more. I wasn't sure where that sudden urge came from, but it was vicious in its hunger, and carnal in its need to be sated. Maybe it was because I actually wanted him, or maybe it was simply one of those things that was always going to happen between us.

He pulled back before I could think about it too much with a grin on his face, keeping us nose to nose.

"Don't ever say you're not good at this again, you liar." I dropped my apple core on his lap and leaned back.

"That good, huh?" He shot the apple across the room, making a perfect score into the rusted sink. "That was just a sample." He gave me a roguish smile it was impossible not to return.

I was well aware of that. Grimm just had a look about him. It was like a flashing red warning sign about that bad habit I'd mentioned earlier.

He was the kind of man who fucked you so good you thought of it every single day for weeks on end and replayed every second of it as you were foldin the laundry.

Maybe I was more screwed up than I thought. I didn't know if it was abnormal to feel such a way after what happened to me, but *this*—having him look at me the way he was—it felt powerful and destructive. And *that* was preferable to that sick, weak, pathetic feeling that seemed like a parasite trying to plant itself in my brain.

"Here," he finally said, manipulating my body as if I were a porcelain doll so I was on my back with my head in his lap.

I felt an obvious hardness beneath my skull that was apparently goin to be the starved elephant in the room.

"We won't be here long, so we can talk later. You need to sleep now."

I crossed my feet at the ankles and snuggled further into his hoodie.

I didn't feel tired, but I didn't feel like fallin off his bike because I got no sleep at all. I couldn't doze off like this, though.

"All I had was silence; I want to hear your voice." *It's my new favorite sound*, I silently added.

When the quiet stretched on, I didn't think he was inclined to indulge me. I might have been pushing, but I soon found myself with a small smile as he began tellin me about the hospital we were in.

With a gentle hand resting on my stomach, he spoke while looking down at me, and I looked right back at him with something lodged in my throat. Timing was said to be everything, and my reaper had come back into my life at just right the moment.

Face to face like this, everything became meaningless. I forgot where we were. Who I was no longer mattered when it felt like I was staring at myself, seeing something harsh and cold but full of blaze reflected back at me.

It's like time stopped and then reset with a countdown for somethin much larger than I could fathom just waitin to happen. His pretty, soulless hues were like a bottomless well, and he had no problem dragging me down, straight to the bottom where Tartarus waited.

When I finally started driftin off, it was with the thought that this was one bad habit I didn't want to ever be free of.

Chapter Eleven

Arlen

When I woke, I saw sunlight.

It streamed through the dirty window and only made the room seem muggier than it had naturally become.

Grimm's voice came from right outside the door, and I knew he was on a cell. I sat up and tossed my legs over the side of the bed, and then stood.

Stretchin some kinks out, I pulled the hood down and went to the window. Standing on my tip toes, I peered out.

This wing of the hospital faced an old grocery store. I spotted an older man pushing a rusted shopping cart full of crates, and another man beside him with a bat.

"I thought ya'll took this city?" I asked, sensing Grimm back in the room. "I saw the Sigil on the sign."

"We saved this city. It was abandoned a little after I turned sixteen. I guess it wasn't big enough to have been salvaged. It took too many resources that could be used elsewhere."

"If it's abandoned, what did ya'll save it from?"

He came up behind me and clamped his hands on either side of my waist, peering out the window. I tensed only a little, swallowing quietly. I wasn't expecting him to take his time with us, but this would still take getting used to.

"You see how old they are. All they're trying to do is live in comfort. They were being killed off, bodies left to rot in the open. Romero solved the problem."

I turned all the way around at that.

"The Savages care about the elderly?"

"The Savages want peace. Only, our version of it is more like anarchy. The elderly in Rivermouth don't give a shit. They just want to be left alone. Think of it as a retirement community. Those men are taking the crates of perishables and passing them out to others, courtesy of that man you know as the devil," he said with a smirk.

Now I was full on curious, but he had other ideas than me askin questions. He pulled my body into his, bringin us flush together and dropping his mouth to mine. This kiss was different to the first one. I could damn near taste his own desire on the tip of his tongue.

He slid his hands around to my ass and squeezed the cheeks. The second a groan left my mouth and I pressed further against him, he was pulling away.

"What was all that?" I breathlessly asked.

"I wanted to see something," he replied with a straight face.

Well, that was ominous. "What—"

A door slammed from somewhere, making my stomach jump.

Grimm's whole demeanor changed. One second he was

right in front of me, and the next he was pushing his gun into my hand and movin away. The gun I'd forgotten about and didn't know how to use.

"Stay here," he commanded.

"You can't...leave me," I wound up sayin to myself as he disappeared in the blink of an eye.

Like hell I was stayin behind in this rinky- dink room. I slipped out into the hall, the sun allowing me to see everything but Grimm, and I couldn't hear him, either.

Damn, he was fast.

Chargin ahead, I jogged down the hall through a pair of double doors barely hanging on their hinges.

I popped out an arched bridge, overlooking the floor below on either side. Straight ahead was another set of doors leading to another wing.

Voices below weren't what had drawn my full attention. The fact I was seeing Grimm in front of two men with that unmistakable V and snake tattoo was.

I saw only the men from that room, and I saw Grimm. They didn't know I was there, but I reckoned Grimm did.

One of the men moved too fast for my liking, and I didn't even think about what I was doing—I aimed the gun and pulled the trigger.

The pop was louder than I'd expected, and I missed. Both looked up like idiots. I'd barely blinked, and Grimm had one of their throats slit.

Blood went everywhere. I watched the man clutch at his neck, as if that could make it better. An odd sound came flying from his mouth.

A light thump from the opposite end of the hall had me looking away. Another man had just pulled open the doors, pausing when he saw me. He had hair as long as mine and had clearly ran to get this to point, as he was out of breath.

I wasn't a hundred percent certain he was with the men below, but he damn well wasn't with me, so I shot at him too. I felt the bullet leave the chamber this time and was prepared, expected the sound it made.

"For real?" I asked aloud when red spread across his chest, staining clean through his brown jacket. I'd been aimin for his head.

"Little bitch," I heard him gasp, crystal clear. When he ducked back through the door, I caught a glimpse of the V on his neck.

It all happened rather quickly—I'm talking in a span of three minutes or less. So where the fuck had Grimm vanished? There was no sign of him below, and there was only one body.

The man whose throat he'd slit was lying on the floor twitching. I wanted to yell out his name but had no idea how many of these men were in the building. I was too shit of a shot to take on multiple people, and I didn't know how many bullets I had left to try. If one of them had a gun of their own, I was screwed.

Oddly, I didn't feel afraid. I was pissed. Me and Grimm weren't supposed to be separated. With what he'd just told me about this town, I had a good feeling these fuckers had come here specifically for me.

Rushing across the bridge, I pushed through the rusted door the man I'd shot had just gone through. He was using the wall as support, trying to get away. I could've gone about my business and let him eventually fall to his knees, sufferin, but fuck that. I wanted him to meet death then and there.

"Let's see if I can get you dead this time," I muttered, following after him.

He looked over his shoulder at me and shook his head. "You don't have to do this, little miss. I'm only doing as I was told." He coughed, leaving a small dribble of blood on his cracked lower lip.

Little miss? I'm positive the word he used a minute ago was bitch. I glanced at his tattoo and couldn't help but sneer. He was as pathetic as the others had been.

He stopped hobbling and leaned against the wall, huffin and puffin. I stepped right in his face, getting the eye contact I suddenly craved.

"Well, your shitty boss didn't have to stick his dirty dick in me, but he must not have been thinkin with the right head." I pressed the extended end of the gun to his temple and pulled the trigger. I saw the life leave his widened eyes as they looked straight back into mine.

I watched the blood and bone splatter on that filthy peelin wall, and the rush that gave me could only be described as euphoric.

I'd seen lives snatched away many times, but I had never been the one to send someone to the afterlife. If this was how Grimm felt, I could understand exactly why he liked his job so much.

That single thought of him had me hurrying away from my first fatality, runnin down the hall. At the far opposite end, something groaned. It sounded like rusted metal, and at least two voices followed right after.

Making a split decision, I veered toward a door that was half bent at the bottom, preventing it from opening any more than it was. I could see a semi-dark stairwell beyond and squeezed through it, knowing Grimm had been on the floor below this one.

I exited right out the door that led to the next floor, bouncing off an old wheelchair.

"Shit," I hissed, recovering as quickly as I could. "They're comin."

I hauled my ass to my feet and took off, away from the dead body Grimm had left behind.

The room I'd found myself in was circular and massive. I had no idea where to go. Grimm told me this place had everything from a chapel to a theater; I didn't know where he was, or if he was okay.

"Hey!" a voice called from behind me, carrying through the empty building. I heard the sound of footfalls, and poured on speed, dodging old medical equipment.

I swear I felt breath on my neck. Our footsteps sounded like a barrage of thunder coming from every direction at once.

To hell with this.

I darted through the next door on my right and stopped a few feet inside, whirling around just in time to get smacked into by the guy who'd been behind me.

I wasn't braced enough to take the hit, and he was too close to shoot. We went over the edge of the old in-ground pool I'd barely caught myself from falling into just a second ago.

Who the fuck designed this layout?

Naturally, the pool wasn't full, but there was enough murky rainwater that had come through the roof to coat the bottom so that whatever equipment had been tossed in was submerged. A drop was a drop, though, and this wasn't a kiddie's pool.

It hurt bad enough to knock the wind from my lungs. It smelled terribly, like rotten egg salad. I tried not to think about all the contamination and bacteria I'd just landed in.

I hit the grizzly bear of a man who'd tackled me in the head with the end of my gun as soon as I could steady myself enough to do so, albeit it wasn't a strong one, due to our new situation.

He cried out and lunged at me, grabbing hold of my wrists, sending me careening into a filing cabinet as we struggled. I internally cursed as my knee resonated with pain.

His intent was clearly to make me drop the gun. Mine was to shoot the fucker and not myself in the process. One shot rang out, hitting a decaying trolley. Another hit where bright blue graffiti was spray painted on the other end of the pool.

The tainted water was a hindrance to both of us. It soaked through my clothes; I tried my best to keep my mouth shut, not wanting to swallow a drop of it, when my feet were swept out from under me.

"You fucker!" I cried out, dropping the gun as my arm bent back at an unnatural angle.

It hit the black water with a depressing plop, sinking to a place I wouldn't be going to get it.

"Carter?"

"In here!" the man advancing towards me responded.

"I'm co—" Whatever his friend was gonna say ended abruptly, and a familiar voice let out a loud whoop immediately after.

There was another splash, and then Carter was gone. It took me a split second to realize the man with blood smeared on his face and down his arms was Grimm, currently gutting the man who'd tackled me.

I say gutting, because there was really no other way to describe what looked like a mini scythe slicing right up the middle of the man's stomach. The skin made a crinkly sound as it was spread apart. The muscles in Grimm's back and arms flexed from the strain of him dragging his curved blade upward, cutting through abdominal muscle and tissue.

Immediately, a smell much stronger than the stagnant water reached my nose, almost like a burning chemical.

Blood and somethin akin to grease ran down the man's front as intestines became exposed.

With a small grunt, Grimm all but kicked the man back off his blade. He went down but he wasn't dead yet. His body violently convulsed, making mini bubbles in the water.

"Ugh, that smell is—"

"Like roses!" a voice exclaimed from above.

I looked up and immediately found a pair of silver eyes.

"Cobra?"

"The magnificent," he beamed, holding a hand out to me.

I smiled back at him, glancing at Grimm, who was sloshing his way towards me.

He was covered in blood, corpse juice, and tainted water from head to steel toed boot, yet he looked damned good, in my opinion.

"Here," he said when he reached my side, hoisting me towards Cobra, who easily lifted me the rest of the way out of the pool.

Bless him for not mentioning the way I knew I smelled.

I was sat gently to the side so he could grab Grimm and one handedly help pull him out next. He wasn't breathin hard or nothin. I sat there feelin like a deflated balloon.

He looked down at me with a storm in his eyes. "Didn't I tell you to stay put?" he asked, pulling me off the dirty floor.

"I'm gonna go try and get a signal." Cobra was quick to interject, winking at me before making a hasty retreat. I only then noticed he had blood on his hands too, no doubt the result of that whoop I'd heard.

I stared at Grimm, doing another sweep to make sure he was really okay before shoving him in the shoulder. I put effort into it but he was like an immovable stone.

"You're a real dickhead, you know that? You can't hand

someone a gun who doesn't know how to use it, and then poof into thin air."

"I didn't think you'd be that shitty of a shooter. You aim and pull the trigger, brat, preferably not to shoot me next time."

I swiped strands of filthy wet hair off my face and glared at him. "Well, I sure as hell can shoot at close range, and this shitty shooter was the distraction that saved your ungrateful self. Why would you leave me in the first place!? You can't do that. You're not allowed to leave me behind, Grimm!" I reckon from the sound of my voice, I was close to hysteria at this point.

I really didn't like this. Being such a hormonal mess was embarrassin enough, but doing it in front of him was a million times worse.

When it registered that he'd said somethin about me shootin him, my eyes went right to his arm that had the most blood on it.

I didn't see a bullet hole, but neither of the men he'd shot back at that shithole of a house had gaping holes from where'd he'd shot them.

"I-I shot you?" I rushed forward, feeling all over him, not thinkin this through at all, like I could find the wound and magically heal it with my hands alone.

He had too much blood and was too wet for me to tell what was what. When his body shook underneath me, I stopped and looked at his face to see if he was about to collapse.

"Cobra!" I yelled, a split second before I saw Grimm was laughin.

"Brat, you only grazed me," he explained when he got ahold of himself with the audacity to keep givin me that gorgeous smile of his that showed all his perfect teeth.

"What happened?" Cobra yelled, bustin through the door like a man on a mission.

"Your friend is a goddamn asshole," I answered, shoving past Grimm.

"Your gun's somewhere in that shitty water. Have fun fishin it out," I called back over my shoulder.

Chapter Twelve

Arlen

I didn't get to make a dramatic descent back to the room we'd been in and perform a miracle on my filthy clothes.

"Brat," Grimm called. He caught up to me, taking my hand firmly in his. "We need to have a private discussion." He was pullin me away without givin me much choice in the matter, much to Cobra's amusement.

"Talk later," he mouthed at me just before I disappeared back into the stairwell I'd come out of.

"You're leaving Cobra alone with those men lurkin around?" I hissed, trying to pull away. I was well prepared to go back and kick ass if need be. My muscles protested at that idea, but Cobra was the brother everyone wished they had—unless he was tryna get in your pants; then, he was somethin else entirely.

"You're doing that pain in the ass thing," Grimm said. He let my hand go and proceeded to scoop me up at the knees.

"He can take care of himself, and actually hit his fucking target." He slung me over his shoulder.

"What the hell are you doin? Put me down!" My voice echoed in the stairwell.

He ignored my protests and carried me back to the room we'd been in the night before. When he sat me down, he pushed the door shut and caged me between it and his body.

"I'm going to ask you a question, and I want you to answer me with the first thing that comes to mind. Can you do that, Brat?"

Nervous about where this was goin, I wanted to drop kick him in the balls. Trustin him nonetheless, I slowly nodded.

"What is it I want you to do?" he asked again.

"You want me to answer a question with the first thing I feel and nothin else," I repeated, and he nodded.

"The man you shot in the head, the one whose blood you haven't realized is on your face. How did it make you feel when pieces of his brain came out of his skull?"

"Good. Powerful. Alive," I tossed out all three.

"And how does that make you feel?"

"Scared, like I don't know myself anymore. That you won't like me this way."

He nodded again like he already knew this, and cupped my face.

I turned my cheek into his dirty, bloody palm, not caring it was adding to my filthy face.

"Your imperfections make you perfect, brat. You're the most beautiful fucking thing I've ever seen. That darkness you've come to know…it has you feeling overwhelmed, but I promise you're not alone. I won't ever let you go."

Hadn't he told me he wasn't good at talkin? Every time he opened his mouth and said somethin meaningful, I fell for him a little more.

"Grimm. You are…"

"I'm basically a king, so by default, you're a queen."

"I was gonna say you're a goddamn idiot for not makin a move sooner than this. You've always been my dark, regal reaper," I teased, pulling his mouth down to mine.

He eagerly obliged, and I selfishly demanded more, attacking his mouth with mine, but he pulled away once again, leavin me keyed up with no relief—not to mention pissed off.

"I know you ain't celibate. I've heard you plenty. I can feel your dick is hard, so I know it's not me in general. So why can't you touch me?"

He gave me an inexpressive look and then turned away. "I want you to be sure," was his answer. I was seconds away from imploding.

"The men with the snake tattoos. How many?"

Now I was glad he couldn't see my facial expression when he asked that.

This was the question I was waitin on, the one I knew he'd eventually figure out. I reckoned that was where'd he'd gone off to.

He went to a bright orange duffel bag that must've recently been placed on the foamy bed, and unzipped it.

I could have pretended I didn't hear the question, or played stupid, but by the anger suddenly rollin off him in waves, he already knew, and just wanted me to verify it.

"He told me before I dropped him down an elevator shaft," he explained, responding to my silent thought.

I wanted him to know solely because I knew how this was goin to go. So I told the truth—the whole truth, and nothin but the truth, because that's what my Grimm wanted, and I needed to tell someone.

"It started with Vitus, but he didn't force me. I know that

makes me sound like a cheap whore, but I thought it'd be over with if I just gave him what he wanted. Then his dad came in. His…uncle went next. The cousin."

I swallowed and looked down at the faded tile, feeling my stomach roll as I recounted it all inside my head. I took in a lungful of air and rushed through the next part.

"They took turns fuckin me in the ass while another one had his way with me in the front.

"I was held up between them, or on my side on that damn bed. I begged them to stop, and Arlen never begs. Arlen was strong and they took her away from me for no fuckin reason!

"They didn't care about the blood, or how bad it hurt, and Noah just stood there watchin so he could make good on his word, of all things.

"Why did they have to do that to me? Why am I the one who feels ashamed and dirty for what those sick assholes did?" I was sobbin into his chest by time I was done. He had his bloody arms around me and stood there like an immovable force, letting me get it all out of my system.

"Sorry I'm such a mess." I gave him a sheepish smile when I dared look back at him again.

"Don't ever apologize for this, brat. If you can't cry on my bloody shoulder, what am I good for?" he joked.

I wondered if he knew he was the sole reason I was hangin on. He was supposed to be dead inside, yet here he was, making me feel alive.

He used his tongue and swiped a loose tear right off my face, and then stuck it in my mouth. I tasted my own filth and couldn't find a damn thing wrong with it. He bit down on the tip, not lettin up until I whimpered.

"What do you need from me, Brat?"

"I'm tired of seein their faces. I just want you to erase it. Make me feel better."

Taking my left leg, he hooked it over his hip and pressed his hard cock into my apex.

"This?"

"Yes," I groaned on a loose breath, grabbing his hips. I didn't give a damn where we were, that we had both just killed less than an hour ago, or that we were coated in blood. Who was goin to judge us that mattered? If someone felt any type of way, that was their own damn problem.

My moral compass had begun to glitch. I couldn't find it in myself to give a damn about that, either. And was that really a bad thing?

Grimm tore away from me and lifted his shirt over his head, droppin it to the floor. My heart did some weird twist in my chest, and heat flared in my lower stomach as it erupted with flutterin.

His tattooed body was flawless. Every bump and ridge interconnected like a secret pathway. I took a step towards him, doing the same thing he'd done with my tank top, standing in front of him in nothing but my black bra and pants.

He undid the top button of his jeans, still moving away. As if there were an invisible choker wrapped around my neck, he became the master of my body, pulling me towards him with silent command.

"You're not ready for my kind of fucking, so you're going to have to sit your pretty ass on my lap and fuck me."

Oh, lawd. Between my legs clenched. I felt myself grow wet from his words full of dark promise of what would come later. I hadn't been with anyone aside from the pool boy and the men who'd used me.

I shook my head as if to free them from it. They wouldn't steal this from me; this choice was all my own. I wanted to give myself to this wicked man and let him do whatever he wanted to me.

He was more than likely right, though. I'd never been with a man like him. I responded to his promise by placing my hands on his solid chest and pushing him down on the bed. The duffel bag fell to the floor.

The devilish smile he graced me with made me want to repeat the move ten times more.

I worked my pants down that had become like a second skin since being wet, taking my underwear with them.

His eyes tracked over the fairy tattoo that spread down to where dark curls had begun to grow back due to me not havin a razor.

"I'm killing whoever did that," he said with no hint of humor. "You're beautiful, brat." He reached for me, running his hands down my sides, around to the back of my thighs, cautious of the healin skin. "And that is the prettiest pussy I've ever seen."

He let me go, only to lower his jeans, revealing a pair of black briefs. The outline of his cock was painfully obvious, and without a hint of shame, he pulled it out.

He was rock solid, tan just like rest of him, and more than a lil impressive. I peered up at him through half-mast lids.

I knew this was it, sealing the deal between us for good, and so did he. This wouldn't be a quick 'out of our system' spin cycle fuck.

His eyes were dark, like raven wings.

They were the type of darkness that wasn't dark. They were my rapture. There was no promise of dawn, only an endless midnight sky.

The danger held within them only allured me all the more, fanning a slow-burning desire and turning that spark between us into raging hellfire. I wanted him to burn me from the inside out and spread his ashes on my skin.

Straddling his lap, I gripped one shoulder with one hand and his smooth cock with the other, circling the head with my thumb.

"I got you." He gripped my hips, ensuring I wouldn't fall when I let his shoulder go.

"Grimm," I barely whispered, hovering over his tip. My hands gripped him harder than necessary as I fought against my paranoia. This was my reaper. He wouldn't use me like those men had. Grimm was my safety net. I had to get them out of my fuckin system.

"You don't have to do—goddamnn, brat," he amended in a growly voice.

I took him inside me to the hilt, desperate to feel anything other than *them*.

I moaned loudly without embarrassment. He felt perfect; this burn was welcome. The pleasure and the pain had me clenching around him involuntarily.

He filled me entirely, stretching me as his cock slowly became embraced by my walls. I knew this wasn't his M.O. Grimm wanted control. I imagined he needed it to deal with the things that went on inside his own head. But he willingly sat there and gave it to me—somethin I didn't need.

I rolled my hips, tryna get a feel for this, and he flexed his hands. I did it again, watchin his face this time, and he glared slightly. His body was all tensed up, like iron.

"I'm not the kinda man you want to tease with your pussy. Fuck me hard, or I'll fuck you harder, and by time I'm done, you won't be able to walk in a straight line. Every crevice of your sexy ass body will be dripping with sweat, and you won't be able to remember your name because you were too busy screaming mine."

He gripped the back of my neck, slamming his mouth over mine, and lifted his hips, thrusting into me.

He bit down on my lower lip so hard he broke the skin. I cried out, and he slipped his tongue in.

His other hand was now firmly graspin my ass, guiding me up and down on his dick. He helped me find a rhythm, easing all the way up when I took over.

He caressed my back, ran his hands over my sides, and roughly took hold of my breasts—all as I rode him. The sounds comin from my mouth were unrecognizable.

"Harder," he demanded, with no change in his vocal inflection. With him soundin as normal as he always did, aside from his harsh grip, I thought I may have been goin about this the wrong way.

I straddled him a little more, taking him to the hilt every time I slid up then back down on his slick cock. It felt too good. He felt so good it hurt.

He suddenly leaned back so he could watch me, loosely resting his palms back on my hips.

His eyes were saturated with raw desire, and it was all for me. I worked him faster, my breath coming in short puffs. The shitty bed was swayin in place, solely supported by the wall where paint-chips were steadily fallin away.

"That's it," he praised, his tone a lil more gravelly. "Fuck me, brat. Use me. Take what you need."

As if those were the words I'd needed to hear, that's exactly what I did. Wrappin my arms around his neck, I rode him—hard.

Every moan, gasped breath, and whisper of his name from my mouth, and every occasional groan from him were like a balm. The way he was lookin at me, though, that was the salve—the numbing serum on scars invisible to the naked eye.

I felt whole, connected to him entirely—far beyond the physical.

Cupping his jaw, I traced the inverted cross beneath his eye. I wanted to commit everything about this moment, about him, to memory. His silky soft hair wasn't perfectly brushed back; he had growth to his beard, making him look more intense and rugged.

He smelled as good as he always did—he smelled of death. I felt the dried blood on his hands, saw the crimson stains on his face. I could still see his scythe ruthlessly slicing up the center of that man's stomach, smooth as butter, in my mind's clear lil eye.

Grimm was filthy, wicked down to his core, but he was the kind of filthy you wanted coating every fiber of your being, straight down to your bare bones. He used his bloody hands to keep me together when I wanted to break. He let me use his body to purge my heavy soul.

I wanted—needed—him to come inside me, needed him to replace everything those men took from me.

"Grimm," I moaned in his ear, trailing kisses down his neck. "Can you hurt me?"

"Give me your eyes." He tangled a hand in my hair and pulled so I was looking at him fully. "Now tell me what you want."

He made it impossible to glance away. I forced my lungs to constrict and retract. "I want you to hurt me." My voice was so clear, so steady in comparison to how I felt right then, like a tickin bomb that wouldn't be diffused unless it detonated. And only he could disarm me.

"I can make it hurt very, *very* fucking good, brat." He pulled out and flipped us around, not so gently easin me down so the foamy mattress cushioned my back. Being on top of him was great, but him standing above me between my parted legs made me feel twice as powerful.

It was all in his eyes. If I told this man to get down and eat me, I knew he'd have every inch of his silken tongue inside my pussy.

"You sure you want this?" He asked the question as a means to give me a warning.

"I need it."

"I'll go easy this time."

I wanted to tell him I didn't want easy, but when my mouth opened, a gasp spilled out. He slammed inside me, purposely placin his hands on the raw, tender flesh of my thighs.

There were no pretenses after that. He squeezed, adding pressure, makin the sore skin feel like it was on fire. I whimpered, liftin my hips to take him deeper. His cock hit somethin inside me I wasn't aware existed.

"More," I demanded.

He watched me closely and dug the pads of his fingers into the same spot, beginning to knead the flesh. It did hurt, in the best fuckin way possible. I bit the corner of my lower lip, and my pussy clenched around his cock.

"Too fucking tight," I heard him say beneath his breath, picking up his pace.

The bed sounded like it was going to give out at any second. I felt a familiar pressure rapidly building, and reached for him. He instantly lurched down, giving me his tongue.

Meeting his solid thrusts took stamina I didn't have, so I attempted to take him deeper inside me, clawing his back and pulling him forward. I wanted him to tear me open and make me bleed.

I never got to ask that of him. He knew what was about to

occur before I did. I'm certain it was him who made it happen.

"Damn, brat, you're gonna come," his gravelly voice nearly groaned. He moved to my neck, suckling on the juncture above my shoulder, and then he bit down. I think he broke through skin, but I couldn't focus.

Endorphins mixed with pain and I didn't know which one felt better.

Grimm's name hung in the air, spillin from my lungs like a chanted prayer. He was right.

I never knew it just how good it could hurt, not until him. My pussy clamped down on his cock as heat shot through my veins, makin me damn near convulse.

He kept goin. When he was right on the brink of his own release, he attempted to pull out. I locked my legs around him a lil tighter, digging my nails into his back so hard I felt his skin beneath them.

"Brat—"

"No," I breathed, refusing to let go.

"Fuck," he cursed, tensing in my arms. I pressed down, making sure I felt every twitch of his dick and as much of his come spurting inside me as I could. I held him close, never wanting to let go.

Chapter Thirteen

Arlen

I wasn't sorry about what I'd done, but I didn't expect Grimm to feel the same way.

I admit I was confused when I dared look him in the eye again and saw his signature dark stare—the one that gave nothin away.

I'd been expecting to see anger, at the very least. I mean, I'd just trapped his swimmers inside me, and he didn't know I was on a contraceptive.

Feelin something wet under my fingertips, I drew my hands around, letting out a soft gasp when I saw blood.

"I'm sorry, Grimm, I wasn't tryna hurt you."

"Hurt me? Brat, if that's your definition of hurting me, by all means, fuck me up," he laughed softly.

"That might scar," I pointed out with more than a hint of concern, tryna turn him around so I could see the damage.

Grabbing my hand, he captured my bloody fingertips on

his soft lips. Keeping eye contact, he sucked them into his mouth, right down to the knuckle, cleaning them with his tongue.

"You're so dirty," I laughed.

"Babygirl, this is me being clean." He gave me a lil smirk and stepped back, taking his semi-hard cock with him.

"I want you to scar me, make me bleed. Use me anytime you want. I'll be doing the same to you soon enough."

I wanted him to do that right that second, even as I sat there with burnin skin, an achin, swollen pussy, and his come drippin between my wide open legs.

But I knew there was too much we hadn't discussed. Actually, we hadn't spoken about a damn thing aside from cementin the fact that I was his and he was mine. Not that it was much of a discussion, considerin I'd been his from the very day he put me in a chokehold upon our first meeting.

"We should probably...discuss all the stuff that needs discussing," I said. "Like me bein on birth control, not that you seem too concerned. Should I be worried about that? Is this a typical thing you do? Cause you sure won't be anymore, so if there's some pretty lil thing waitin for you at home with her heart on her sleeve, let me know. I'll make sure she and I have a clear understandin of who the hell you belong to."

Not givin me an immediate response, Grimm grabbed the duffel bag we'd knocked on the floor and sat it on the bed.

"You've been my main priority since you went missing. If you want me to say that I didn't shove my dick down some-one's throat, I'd be lying to you. But none of those bitches are around anymore, and you know what happened to them."

He went back to being quiet after that, but I could tell he had more to say. I let him work it out in his head, not pushin. He'd been so open with me, I couldn't be upset. Grimm wasn't a talkative man. I would accept this for the simple fact that there wasn't a single thing about him I wanted to change.

I took the small bundle of fresh clothes Cobra had had the foresight to bring, and watched him tear open a packet of wet wipes.

He shook one out and stepped between my legs, gently wiping my face clean.

The thin piece of cotton was cool and smelled like lavender. I shut my eyes, letting him work, keeping them closed when he began to speak.

"You make me feel shit I've never felt before, want things I didn't think I'd want. I fucking hated that when I first met you.

"Why do you think I tossed your ass right back to the cannibal who was chasing you?" He began rubbing down my arms next.

"You were right. Maybe you ain't so good at this," I quipped, opening my eyes. "You also helped hold a damn machete on top of my head, but we can just sweep that under the rug."

"I was ready to kill you to prevent this. Look at us now, though, destined to be epically fucked up," he joked, laughing beneath his breath.

"I'm gonna have to shut you down, because I'm one hundred percent sound of mind," I deadpanned.

He tossed another wipe down and gave me a serious look.

"I'm not a poet, brat. I can't give you long, drawn out exclamations drenched in honey. Words always fade away, and eventually mean nothing. I let my actions speak for me."

Cue a mental eye-roll. "I know all this, Grimm. I get you."

"You get me, huh?" he asked, wiping his dick off and then removing his old pants completely to pull on a fresh pair with clean briefs. "Then you wouldn't have tried to skin me alive, you little hellion." He knelt, swapping socks and then relacing his boots. "I wasn't going to pull out; I was trying to switch positions. I know he was giving you a pill. Now, get dressed, because I do need to have a conversation with you about a few things, Noah included."

"Then what?" I asked, pulling the fresh black tank top over my head.

"I think you know what," he answered.

And I did, which is why when he asked me earlier, I'd told him everything, why I made sure I had the guts big enough to end someone's life. I wanted every single one of those men dead, especially Noah. I wanted him down on his knees, weeping for mercy.

He'd survived far too long.

But was I savage enough to do somethin like that over and over again? Realizing I'd gone off on a mini mental tangent and Grimm was now sliding my new shorts up my legs himself, I began tryna explain.

"I've never felt like this before. I'm not real sure how to deal with it…hate, anger, the pain. It's never-ending. I feel stuck in reverse, but I swear I'm trying to keep movin forward. You're the only thing groundin me right now. I'm not ashamed to admit that." I pulled my stretchy shorts the rest of the way up and did the top button.

Grimm began tying my left boot as soon as I had it on, clearly in a hurry to get on with this whole shebang.

"I won't tell you to get the fuck over it, but I am going to get you through it. I'm yours, brat. You don't need to worry. You don't have to hide. Trust me to take care of you. I'll be whatever you need, as long you don't let those fuckers be the reason you lose your soul."

He stood and took hold of my face, his gaze searching for

somethin he must've found, cause he smiled so beautifully I think my heart stopped all over again. "You and I are going to have so much fun together." He pressed a possessive kiss on my slightly parted lips, resting his forehead on mine. "Hold onto your hatred, onto the pain and the rage. I'm going to show you how fucking beautiful it all is."

I didn't have any idea how to take that promise. Cause that's what it was—a dark promise, maybe even a sworn oath.

But I was more than ready to find out.

Part Two

She who walks the floors of hell finds the key to the gates of her own Heaven buried there like a seed.
–SEGOVIA AMIL–

Chapter Fourteen

Grimm

I shone the light down on his broken body.

His upper half was bent back so far the exposed portion of his skull nearly touched his ass.

Cobra's impressed whistle echoed down the old shaft. He knew I'd rather go right in for a kill than drag anything out. The man lying scalped and broken on the top of the old elevator said otherwise.

"Damn, Grimmy. What the fuck did he say? This isn't yo style."

"You have a style?" Brat asked, still curiously peering over the ledge.

"Beth told him my name," I said.

"My sister?" Brat whirled around, glancing between us.

Having a third sense that her clumsy ass would misstep right down the shaft, I pulled her away from it.

Cobra stepped back as well, crossing his arms with

559

furrowed brows. "Arlen's sister," he pointed at Brat, "told one of Vance's men your name? Why? How the fuck is she still running those loose pussy lips of hers?" He glanced at Brat again. "I do mean that offensively, by the way. Your sister is a—"

"Cum-hoarder, I know. But what are ya'll talkin about? How would she know these snake dudes, much less talk to em? Romero had her locked away."

I stepped back and leaned against the wall, pulling her into my side.

"In light of recent events, I have a pretty good hunch Beth hasn't been locked up for some time. The acolyte watching over her is the only one allowed in and out of the freezer where she's supposed to be being kept.

"Look what just happened a few months ago—our own fucking informants were turning from the inside. Ask yourself why, and then take into account Beth just happened to come around when that crazy bitch Tiffany did. She spontaneously ran away, making it out of The Kingdom, and Noah's working with Romero out of the kindness of his heart?

"No one with even a quarter of a brain would fuck with the Savages. Yet, now these Venom fucks are involved. Noah isn't controlling them, so that tells us someone they feel is just as big as Romero is. And they have to be selling a pretty convincing dream."

I waited for them to catch on; it only took Cobra a minute.

"Well, fuck. Do you think Rome knows?"

"Knows that he could never trust Noah? Yes, no one is fucking trusting Noah. Does Rome know Venom is involved? No, me and you didn't even know that, which means it's on the DL."

Cobra ran his hands through his hair, letting out a deep breath. "So the coach is throwing a tantrum because he just lost his QB?" He spoke in code, shooting a subtle glance at Brat, saying all I needed to know without saying a word.

"Hold up a sec. Why would my father do any sort of business with Noah or the…snake dudes? What they could possibly offer him?" Brat asked.

She'd caught onto a good gist of what I was saying, but not the most important parts.

"It's a long story. I'll tell you on the road."

"I'll go find a signal to call Rome. You two get your shit," Cobra said, already zipping down the hall. "Meet me in the old chapel!"

Brat stared up at me with an expectant look on her face. She wanted answers to all the questions I knew she had, and I didn't want her to know about any of this. Now, I understood why Rome had kept so much from my sister. The truths, the lies, and the secrets all had the ability to destroy in the right hands.

I wasn't him, though. And Brat wasn't Cali. We were our own people. This relationship was just me and her. She hadn't held anything back from me, and I was going to give her the same benefit. Ignoring our reality wouldn't bury or erase it.

I reminded myself she'd blown someone's brains out, watched me gut someone, and made me come like a little fucking boy all within the past few hours. Without giving her a warning, I reached out and grabbed her by the throat.

Her small gasp of surprise was the only emotion she showed.

Forcing her to walk backward, I made her stand right on the edge of the old elevator shaft. If I dropped her, she would die, or break the majority of the bones in her supple little body.

Keeping my grip as it was, I waited for her to yell, delving straight down the front of her shorts with my other hand, sliding her back a little more. Now, the back half of her boot was over the ledge.

I pushed two fingers inside her tight cunt, and she moaned. I began to pump them in and out, ignoring how hard my dick was, how fucking beautiful she was, and I waited.

I waited for her to demand I let her go, tell me I was a sick psycho, scream, cry—show any sign that this was all some mental fluke.

I'd want her all the same, but maybe it wouldn't be to this extent. Every time I fucking looked at her, I was ready to get down on my knees and worship at her altar.

She made me feel, made me care, laugh, joke.

I made promises to keep her safe and make her strong, show her how beautiful hell was. She said I kept her grounded. Even if this were inevitable, it was happening faster than I thought it would.

She humanized me, and to some people that was no big deal, but when you spent damn near nineteen years dehumanized, killing every woman you fucked or didn't fuck for sport, it was unnerving.

It was having all my don't give a fucks come back at once in the form of a woman.

Whose bright idea was it to give death the seed of life? Didn't they know what I'd do to her? Make her a sinner. Be like my brother and think of myself as a king. Crown her my queen of everything dark and dead.

The intense fucking sunlight in her eyes was a siren's song that would tempt the strongest man.

I wanted to fuck her again and again until a red river was flowing from between her juicy thighs.

"Grimm." She swallowed audibly, flooding my fingers with her pussy's arousal, as if she'd heard my last thought aloud, getting more turned on the harsher my grip got.

I could end this all right now and let her go, try and go back to how my life was before. I couldn't, though. Swinging her away from the ledge, I pressed her into the wall, shoving her shorts down far enough that I could get my dick inside her.

She fumbled with the top button on my jeans, gripping my cast-iron dick and damn near forcing it inside all on her own. I knew she was sore from just twenty minutes ago, and how rough this would be with a wall of peeling paint and half spread legs to accommodate my size. I slammed in to the hilt.

My balls were already lifting to spill. I'd found heaven, and it was inside her pussy.

She clenched around me, grabbed my hair, and pulled.

I fought the urge to come like a little bitch and fucked her like she was a whore.

She began moaning so loud she could've woken the man with the missing scalp lying on top of the elevator just a few feet away from us.

I belatedly realized she was saying my name. I usually hated that shit, but Brat could do no wrong. It was a quick, thrusting in and out, pounding my balls into her cunt hard and fast type of fuck. She came when I bit down on the side of her neck and slammed her into the wall, like the good little pain-slut she was becoming.

I came with a low grunt, pumping every drop of my come into her. She shuddered against me, breathing heavily.

"Damn, we should have been doin this a long time ago."

She smiled up at me, and my chest constricted so goddamn hard it almost hurt.

The advice I'd been given echoed in my head—when you know, you know.

"I like that you're filthy. I like that you're mine." She smiled again, planting a kiss right at the corner of my mouth.

Maybe I should have done this shit a long time ago, but then we wouldn't be who we were right this second. My fucking emotions didn't know whether to be up or down. I stared at her with my usual mask in place. Maybe I'd gone crazy, maybe I was fucking weak, but I could never set her free.

I think she got it wrong, because I felt like she'd just grounded me—like an anchor wrapped around my balls. Looking at her like this, I found what I'd been searching for but saw it from a different angle. It wasn't sunlight I was seeing at all.

Fuck Romero for always being right.

Her halo was broken, but there was brimstone burning in her eyes. Her hatred was beautiful.

I'd give her a crown forged of blood and bone from every motherfucker who'd laid a hand on what was mine.

I hoped she was ready to paint some shit red. We weren't going home until their bodies were at our feet.

Chapter Fifteen

Arlen

Assume the worst. Expect it to be even worse than that.

That's how I was going to think of all the things Dad could've done. Grimm said he'd tell me on the road, and I was patient enough to wait. Besides, I wasn't really excited to know how much shit Dad had started. Cobra's ridiculous code talk hadn't gone over my head. I knew full well what a coach and quarterback was.

I wasn't surprised he'd had help from over the wall, either —just who it was helping him. Why Noah? What role did Romero have in it?

They were questions I didn't even know if I wanted the answers to, but couldn't afford to be naïve about.

I followed behind Grimm with a bottle of water, munching on a pack of old saltine crackers he'd procured for me out the duffel after a pee break. I had his atomic bag on my back, the straps tightened so it wasn't slouchy. I was

565

assuming we were about to head out; course, Grimm was being mysterious and didn't explain it, but he'd gathered up our minimal supplies, shoving them in the bag I now carried, so that was my guess.

The sun was starting to set, giving the old hospital a creepy aesthetic. We found the chapel easily enough.

Cobra hopped up from an overturned rotten pew the moment he saw us.

"They're here. Talk fast before I lose my signal again," he said into a cellphone that looked more like a giant walkie-talkie with a long antenna. I hadn't seen one of those in ages, but I'd heard they got reception best in situations like these.

"I'm sending some acolytes to Plymouth. Go to Lucy's and she'll have a lead waiting along with them." Romero's voice crackled over the line, and it didn't take a magician to figure out he was pissed.

"From there, you do what you have to do, but I want Noah alive. I'm gonna piss on him as he bleeds out like a fucking pig over a fire."

"I can feel the brotherly love from here," Cobra joked.

"Are you sure about this?" Grimm asked.

"Don't ask me stupidass questions, and Arlen, don't fucking die."

"Wasn't plannin to, fucker," I muttered.

"Smartass—" His voice cut off. I thought the line had gone dead, some secret blessin, but there were muffles in the background.

"Have fun, Arlen! I'll be here, round, depressed, and cheering you on." Cali's voice boomed through the speaker loud and clear, making me smile.

"Call me when you get to Plymouth," Romero snapped. The phone made an elongated beep and then cut off.

"Let's go," Grimm said, taking me by the hand.

"Where exactly are we goin, and why will there be acolytes?"

"You know where we're going. We're going to kill shit, girl. And wherever that is, Rome is sending us some manpower," Cobra answered.

The surrealism of the situation was quick to sink into my mind. We were really doin this. I had wished it, I had told Grimm, and now it was happenin.

"Who has a pre-game conversation before they go to kill people?" I asked, tryna distract myself from my inner thoughts as we made our way back towards the parking deck.

"People getting ready for a game, and you're on the winning team now, sis," Cobra grinned.

"Sis?" I asked. "So I'm no longer the random chick who was probably going to die?"

I was joking; we'd long surpassed that, but he'd said somethin along the lines of that to me upon the first kill I'd seen them do inside an old church. Such good times.

I could see he was legit excited about doin this, to the point the man was nearly bouncing on his toes.

"How does Romero know we'll need acolytes for...whatever you just said?"

"Romero is always twelve steps ahead, and never shows his full hand. He more than likely knows exactly what's going on by now, has a bloodbath pile accumulating, and is waiting on us to make our move," Grimm said.

"Sounds much too stressful. Speakin of, how's the baby?"

"Baby S is fine," Grimm answered.

Lawd, I didn't think the whole baby S, a.k.a., baby Savage would stick. That kid was going to be a ruthless little fucker.

A loud bang echoed from somewhere in the building. We stopped and looked at one another, none of us saying a word.

Then, at the same damn time, Cobra and Grimm each pointed in the direction behind us. Clearly, they'd heard somethin extra that I couldn't.

"They probably had a look out, and seeing as how not a single one of them exited this hospital, he went for help," Cobra said quietly.

"Venom," Grimm explained at my look of confusion. "The name of the gang with snake tattoos."

"For real? That's what they came up with? Venom is a really stupid fuckin name," I quipped.

"Yeah," Grimm laughed. "It is."

"You ready?" Cobra asked me suddenly.

"For what?" I asked at the same time Grimm said, "Take this," and passed me a pearl white switch blade he'd just removed from one of his back pockets.

"We're gonna take this staircase on the next left, go down the stairs, exit on the next level, go down the hall, circle back up, and haul ass to the parking garage," Cobra explained.

I had to walk myself through what he was saying twice in my head before I had it down pat. How the hell did they all think on their feet so fast?

"Why the hell would we run? I thought the Savages didn't get scared?"

"Excuse the fuck out of me, but it was to keep *you* safe, princess," Cobra drawled.

We entered the staircase and I wound up sandwiched between them, clearly on purpose.

"Why does Noah want me so badly?" I asked as we exited onto the next floor.

"Because he has a god complex," Cobra snorted, stepping through the open doorway that led to the next level.

"The same reason he was giving you those pills," Grimm answered.

I didn't know what he meant by that, and didn't get a chance to ask.

A woman's short scream blasted through the air. It was so unexpected, I almost fell over my own two feet. If we'd gone left, it came from the right. It was followed by a door slamming.

"Keep moving." Grimm nudged my lower back. "They might not be here for you after all."

What the hell? "So those fuckers are gonna hurt some other woman, and we're gonna keep going about our business?" I protested and tried to stop walkin, but Grimm was right at my back preventin me from doing so.

"There aren't any heroes here, sis. Don't go trying to change that," Cobra said, siding with Grimm, of course.

I didn't want to be a goddamn hero; I wanted to slit their fuckin throats open. I wanted to see how they liked havin the tides turned on them. I condemned every single one of those bastards by association.

They made me suffer, and laid me to ruin. They took pride in my pain, and took what didn't belong to them. It was because of them that I felt dead inside.

I never fuckin wanted this. I didn't ask to be forsaken and left to crash in the dark. But that's where I was now. Grimm wanted me to embrace my hatred, pain, and rage. Well, this was me doin just that. I could feel it pumpin through my veins like a bittersweet madness.

I stood and planted myself between my boys.

"They made a mess of me. They need to pay for their sins and atone with flesh and bone."

It was silent for all of five seconds.

"Well then, I can't argue with that excellent point," Cobra humphed, his demeanor swiftly changin. "She wants to play, Grimmy."

Grimm ignored him entirely, focusing solely on me, seeing everything I wasn't saying aloud. "I'm not going to try and stop you. If this is what you want, let the red crusade begin." He stepped back and opened the door we'd just come through.

"You won't see me, but I'll always be right behind you." He nodded down the stairwell. "Go, you're running out of time."

Knowing his words were full of promise, I darted through the doorway, planting a quick kiss on his cheek on my way past.

I stood on the landing for a few seconds, tryna get my bearings. When I glanced back, Grimm and Cobra were nowhere to be seen.

They would know just where to go. Unlike me, those two were well seasoned hunters.

Knowledgeable of how large this damn hospital was thanks to Grimm, they could've been anywhere. But as if I had some internal compass, I knew exactly which way to head.

I began making my way down the stairs, oddly thinking of Ma as I did. What would she say if she knew I was seconds away from making peace with the demon crawling up my spine like a black widow eager to spread its venom through my veins?

What would she think of me now that I'd kissed death and liked it?

She'd probably preach to me and tell me to get down and pray, not understandin it was too late. There was no redemption for the wicked.

I had nothin to repent for.

I wouldn't have any regrets.

I'm sorry Father, for I no longer give a shit.

Chapter Sixteen

Arlen

It didn't take me long to find her.

It would seem lady luck was on my side for once, because I saw them before they saw me.

The girl, who actually looked older than me, had just rounded the corner.

I stepped back into a doorway, trying to ignore the damn awful smell emanating from behind me. Whatever was inside the room had been rotting for a while now.

This situation was nothin like mine, seein as I'd been chained up in an old barn, but I still couldn't help but think of myself as I watched the dark haired girl make her way in my direction. The man behind her was large, but my height, and his hair looked white, but he wasn't old.

While I didn't want to go swoopin in like a white knight, I wouldn't forget it was Cali who saved me when she could so easily have left me behind. I was never supposed to have made it this far.

Engagin the switchblade Grimm had given me, I saw the white handle had an intricate floral design, and briefly smiled. He'd brought it for me. The blade looked like one sharp point, bout ten centimeters long, making the whole thing around twenty one centimeters.

The girl zipped on right past me, and I readied myself. I wasn't sure if she saw me standin there. I didn't have a plan, aside from making sure he stopped breathin.

Before he could pass, too, I kicked the old wheelchair I'd been eyeing right at him. It worked; he nearly tripped.

In the end, looking down was what cost him. By the time he looked up again, I was in his face and the blade was finding a home right in his left eye.

I couldn't even be surprised at myself for moving in so swiftly with no hesitation. It felt too natural. I made sure my thrust was strong. I needed to penetrate his cranial cavity so the blade could efficiently reach the brain. That was basic science.

What I wasn't expectin was the eye to be so weak. There was a lil wet popping sound as the blade went right into the center, as if I were slicing a piece of smooth, red velvet, the kind with that sweet tangy icing on top.

Blood didn't go in any particular direction; it just seemed to spray out, like a hydrant. The round orb squished, and I damn near gagged.

His scream was so loud, my eardrum suffered, ringing in response.

The girl, who I thought had kept runnin, was suddenly beside me, kickin the man square in the stomach. He couldn't find his balance, resulting in him falling backward, his eye socket sliding off my knife.

The eye was gone, shoved backward somewhere in his skull. A pit had taken its place, blood flowing down the man's face in streaks of diluted burgundy.

Unfortunately, the fucker didn't drop dead like he would've if this were a slasher film.

The girl charged and jumped on him like a damn banshee. He went down, tripping over the wheel of the decaying wheelchair, landing flat on his back, still screaming about his eye.

In nothing but a sky blue skirt, she sat right on his head, using all her strength to keep him pinned on the dirty hospital floor.

"Kill him!" she yelled over her shoulder at me.

Not havin to be told twice, I took her initiative and straddled his beer belly, plantin my knees on either side of his waist.

Adjusting my grip on the slippery handle, I did what I'd said I was goin to, driving it through the center of his throat, pulling it back out and slicing to the left, then the right, making sure I got the jugular and all the extra sensitive parts, ensuring death was his end result.

There was a loud whoosh of air and a red blob spilled from his mouth. His body twitched like I'd electrocuted him. Blood was goin everywhere, completely ruinin the girl's bright blue skater skirt. Why the hell she was wearing that in the first place was beyond my understandin.

Her whole outfit was. Looking cute while traveling through the Badlands didn't seem all that important to me. Her top was tight, black and floral, a halter like bodysuit.

She had shiny plum polish on her fingers, a few tattoos on her arms, and a Cruella Deville type thing going on with her long hair.

"Well, what do we have here? Room for one more?"

Cobra asked, stepping through the door I'd come through with Grimm and two others right behind him.

"What the fuck are you doing?" Grimm wrapped an arm around my middle, lifting me off the man's belly. For real? He was jealous of a dead guy?

"Me? What happened to you two being *right* behind me?"

"They happened," he answered, jerking his head in the direction of the two people behind them.

"They used our skill-set as their cover against the other two snake head fuckers," Cobra added, staring at the brunette's bloody legs longer than was acceptable. "Damn, sis. You did that?" He gave me a bright smile, gesturing to the man's face.

"That's nothin." I shrugged, trying to stay modest.

"You didn't have to filet his neck, Brat." Grimm said. His expression was blank, but there was a prideful look in his eyes that made me smile. "Come on, we can clean you up when we stop again."

"Is there blood on my face?" I lifted my hands up to check.

"No, but if you touch it with those, there will be," he said, grabbing my left wrist and starting forward.

"I'm Katya, but go by Kat," the dark haired girl said, steppin right into our path. She had a non-English lisp, and a small gap between her two front teeth.

"That's Blue and Parker." She gestured to her companions. The woman, Blue, actually had bold blue hair and could've been a pin-up girl in another life, and Parker had blonde dreadlocks with huge black gauges in his ears.

It was such an odd combination of people.

"We don't have time for this." Grimm kept walking, forcing Katya to step aside.

"Never say the Savages haven't done the world an act of

kindness," Cobra said, giving a two finger salute and falling in step beside me.

We went right past the room with the horrible smell coming from beneath the door. I knew whatever or whoever was inside was dead, and had no desire to find out how much worse that smell was with no barrier between us.

The only people I gave a damn about were either right beside me, or hours away in a compound somewhere—so sucks for whoever the hell that person was who had to die in an abandoned shithole.

The group followed, not making a sound. Cobra and Grimm must not have thought them a threat, or they'd all be dead, and there was no way in hell they'd let them walk behind us.

"So what's the deal with you guys? I mean, what are ya'll doin in here?" I asked after a minute or two.

I'd just killed a man with Katya; it seemed kind of wrong not to say anything at all.

"Those freaks with the snake tattoos are all over the city," Blue said.

"We were just making our way through, paying them no attention. They cornered our group off—we got away and they found us again. There used to be seven of us," Katya added.

She didn't seem torn up about the people lost, which reverted back to the old adage: safety in numbers. The Venom took out four of them, just because. That seemed to be a thing in the Badlands. It was survival of the worst. A human eat human world. There was no place for morals here. There was no law. The only rule out here if you wanted to live was simple: don't have any rules.

The silence had awkwardness settling between our two trios as we headed in the same direction.

I wanted to keep them with us simply for the fact that they didn't seem outwardly evil. They were just strangers who wanted to survive. Didn't we all? My judgment of character hadn't let me down thus far.

I waited for Grimm to tell them they needed to go a separate direction—he didn't.

He and Cobra shared a look, doing the brotherly bond thing they always seemed to do.

The sun was nearly gone, leaving only faint light to pave our path to the parking deck.

We passed a body slumped against the wall with a long metal pole—I assumed a piece of an old hospital bed—jammed through the bottom of his jaw. His fixed eyes watched us pass him by.

On a staircase was another body with no visible marks; his head was facing an unnatural direction. I knew Grimm was responsible for that one.

He truly lived up to his personification. Death could be swift, fast, and something you never saw coming. That was Grimm.

His gaze was focused on the path ahead of us, no doubt in his own head, being his usual quiet self as he planned the journey of mass destruction we were about to embark on. I studied his side profile, feelin familiar warmth in my chest that came from looking at his handsome self.

I know he was supposed to be this unfeeling, cold, cruel man, but there was a heart in there somewhere. He showed me that time and time again. It was dark and diabolic, just like the man who carried it, but it was still a heart. I had every intention of owning it fully and completely. I knew it would take work. It could be said we were just two strangers with the same hunger: to feel loved, to feel a lil less lonely, to feel anything at all other than numb.

Hell, I didn't even know this man's real name, but the way I felt about him, I couldn't care less.

And that was really what it came down to, because I felt as if I'd known Grimm for a thousand lifetimes and was just now findin him again—like my twin flame. He was mine, I was his, and this hell was ours.

"What?" Grimm asked, glancing at me from the corner of his eye.

"Just thinkin." I laid my head on his shoulder and hid another smile.

Cobra, clearly feeling left out, hooked his arm through mine on the other side as we went down the last hall to the parking deck staircase.

Who'd have thought lil ol me would be in the shittiest of situations, again, but able to smile and laugh as dead bodies piled up by the hour? I'd killed two men, and had never felt stronger. I had my reaper to thank for that.

I had a man I considered a brother back.

I felt adrenalized. This new me wasn't so bad after all; seemed she got shit done.

Chapter Seventeen

Arlen

I was a bit surprised Grimm's Harley was fine, as was the 4x4 muscle car sitting beside it with a giant metal bar across its grill.

They sat in the back corner of parking deck C in perfect condition.

"The engines are going to draw them to us like flies on shit," Cobra pointed out, leaning on the hood of his car.

"How big is this group? Are they like the Savages?" I asked.

"No one can top what Romero built, but even ten people is ten bodies that need dealing with. I'm going to go out on a limb here and say there's at least that many, since little Blue," he stopped and pointed at the trio standing a lil ways away from us lookin completely at odds, "already told us they're all over the city. They're so desperate to get their hands on you that they invaded one of our territories. I don't think we're going to amicably talk our way out of this," Cobra said.

"Negotiating is for pussies." Grimm finally spoke up, placing a now empty gas can into Cobra's trunk. "I don't negotiate, I send people to an early grave." He walked behind me and slid the bag off my back, casually tossing it in Cobra's backseat in exchange for another he secured on the back of his Harley.

"Well, we need to get to Plymouth. So let's head out and take different routes. That'll make them go two separate directions. They won't bother us once we leave this city."

"The Venom is nothing but a group of boys trying to play in a league of men. This is a safety zone for them. Romero won't bring a bloodbath here, not with all the old crabs that could get caught in the crossfire. We both know there are acolytes lurking beyond Rivermouth, waiting to take them out," Cobra explained.

"So you go left and I go right, and then we meet in the middle? That's all you had to say," Grimm replied.

Cobra sighed, shaking his head. "You three! Get in the damn car," he called to Katya and her friends.

"You're going to take us with you?" Blue asked, sounding as surprised as I felt.

"Thank your friend with the bloody thighs and perfect ass. She sat on a man's face so sis could dig a knife in his throat. That bought your ride out the city."

There was so much wrong with his sentence I didn't know where to begin.

"Is it any safer to go with someone like him? He's a Savage," Parker whispered, not as quietly as he should have.

He had a good point, considerin. But I still didn't appreciate his prejudice.

"He offered ya'll a ride. Haven't you ever heard the

saying don't look a gift horse in the mouth or somethin? Don't be a prejudiced dick. You don't know him, so get in the car, or get the hell out of the way."

Cobra thanked me with a bright smile, climbing into his driver's seat.

"Or something?" Grimm laughed, guiding me to his bike. He climbed on and waited for me to do the same.

"My hands are dirty."

"Your hands are bloody, and I think that's sexy. If we didn't have somewhere to be, I'd sit you on my bike and spend the next few hours doing the same to your pussy."

"Da-yum," Cobra laughed, cause, of course, he heard every word of that.

Grimm needed to dirty talk twenty-four seven, I'd realized. The thought of fuckin this magnificent man in front of an audience was more than a little temptin, but I'd rather do it somewhere we might not die as we were coming.

I grabbed his shoulder and climbed behind him, wrapping my arms tightly around his middle, breathin in his spicy smell.

The trio approached Cobra's black muscle car and got in without another word of protest. We were pullin out the deck in a matter of what felt like seconds.

"Race you out the city!" Cobra yelled through his passenger window.

"The fuck? Nooooo!" I yelled at Grimm, drawn out as he hit the throttle and we shot off down the street.

I was terrified for a good two minutes until I slightly relaxed my lethal grip and let myself be in the moment.

The city was so quiet, Cobra had been right. You could hear the engine of the motorcycle and the muscle car crystal clear.

All was well until he began steering with one damn hand and whipped out his scythe like blade with the other.

"What are you doing!?" I yelled over the wind and engine.

"Up on the right," he replied, speaking louder than I'd ever heard him.

I looked over his shoulder, and sure enough, there were two of the men Blue had been talking about, darting towards a rusted out bucket they'd probably stolen from someone else.

Knowing Grimm's intention, I held on a little tighter and braced for impact. He zipped around a huge pothole, right onto the sidewalk.

I was positive he ran over the bones of someone, hearing the loud crunch as they crumbled.

With one hand out, he rode right past the man closest to us, maneuvered around the front of the car, and never slowed down.

I didn't think anything had happened at first, until I felt the fresh blood that had blown back onto my face. Quickly glancing over my shoulder, I saw the man on the ground and his comrade standing over him.

I rubbed my face clean on Grimm's shirt, feeling him laugh.

Aside from that, we almost made it out scot-free. Grimm was moving too fast for the Venom to do much but stare stupidly after us every time he abruptly went down an alley, or evaded them by taking a narrow route they couldn't. A few old people sat on the porches of their houses, enjoyin the show. I reckoned this was the most excitement they'd seen in years around here.

There was only one incident more, and it was quickly handled by Cobra.

A man came spinning out of an alley on his own bike, much too close for comfort. So close that if he wanted to reach out and grab me, he'd probably succeed.

I thought that was his intention, but at the last second, Grimm banked left and Cobra's car came from the right, smashing into the man. He and his bike went in two separate directions.

The red motorcycle screeched and sparked as it spun into an old stoplight on its side. The man might have lived if Cobra hadn't driven right over him as if he were a mere speed bump.

We left Rivermouth behind, and the sun had long set. We were a lil bit closer to being able to end all this and get back home—if it were every truly over.

Chapter Eighteen

Arlen

It wasn't possible to make it in a day.

We rode for what felt like ever, and then stopped, finding a semi clearing in the woods to rest in.

Katya and her friends were still with us. I had no idea what would be done with them come the end, but they were good company.

Cobra had started a fire, tossed down a bag with food in it, and then went off to speak with Grimm, standing where I could see them and they me.

I leaned against a tree, using Grimm's atomic bag as a cushion, munching on hard tacks dipped in peanut butter to add flavor to the bland crackers. I had Grimm's hoodie on so I wasn't cold.

I'd never been campin before, but I reckoned it was similar to this. Blue and Parker were fast asleep on the other side of the fire, using one another as pillows.

"So what's the deal with you and them?" Katya asked from beside me, nodding her head in Grimm's general direction. She had on a jacket I was certain belonged to Cobra, and was still wearin her bloody blue skirt.

I should've warned her she might not want to go that route, but they were both older than me. Who was I to tell either of them what to do?

Her question had a barrage of answers I could have given; I chose to keep it simple, with a Cliff Notes version.

"Grimm is mine, Cobra is my brother, and the woman who started this all isn't with them. She's at home about to have the devil's spawn."

"You mean Calista, right?" she asked, helpin herself to my peanut butter.

I grinned, because that was such a me move.

"I forget how widely known she is. To me, she's just Cali." I sat the peanut butter between us so she could stop stretching over my lap to get it.

My line of vision was cut off by Grimm's return. He wordlessly sat down, and nearly dragged me onto his lap.

"What's the deal with you and them?" I asked her, shiftin to get comfy.

"We kind of just banded together. Blue and I know each other from being in the same city. Parker was a tag-along. We didn't have a destination until now."

"They're coming with us to get Noah." Cobra joined us, answering my silent question.

"Why would you do that?" I asked Katya directly.

"An initiation." She shrugged. "We have nowhere to go, no real protection. Why not join the cult no one wants to mess with?"

"Understandable," I said slowly. I'd understood long ago.

What else was there for people to do when being a loner often equaled death? Safety in numbers seemed a logical solution, in my humble opinion. Wasn't that why people had banded together inside Centriole?

And who better to join than the gang that dominated the Badlands, just like Katya said? But... "What initiation?"

"Do you remember when you wanted in? We made you come with us to the church and the cannibal farm. They'll be coming with us to wherever we get sent," Cobra answered.

"Oh." I didn't know what else to say. He didn't seem to care if they made it in or not; neither did Grimm.

"Blue and I spontaneously left the city because it sounded better than the norm. We had families and friends try and talk us out of it, but we just wanted to see what was in the great beyond. You see how well that's worked out for us?"

She was making light of their situation, but I obviously knew what it was like to be smacked with reality.

"What city are ya'll from?"

"Prescott, you know, the one with the blue trees?"

I blinked like an idiot, course I didn't know, because Dad said there was no other city aside from The Kingdom.

"If you had all that, why come here?"

"We have rape, murder, thieves, and corruption. The slick streets just pretty it all up."

"This may be hell, but it gives you more freedom than what many consider heaven."

I didn't have a response to that, but I heard the sadness in her voice. I had the distinct feelin she'd killed long before the hospital hallway.

We each had our own story to tell.

We all had our own demons, and the option of making peace with em or vanquishing em in our own way. At the end of the day, it didn't matter, because we all had to go to sleep and wake up again until we died.

Hopefully, they'd survive long enough to figure it out. Katya and Blue seemed like the type of women you'd want around.

"Come with me, Brat," Grimm suddenly said, lifting me off him.

He took my hand and led me a little way from our group. Leaning himself against a tree, he pulled me to stand in front of him.

"Just spill it, Grimm," I huffed when it became clear he was hesitatin.

He rolled his shoulders, tightenin his grip on my hand as if he were worried I would bolt.

"Do you remember at the old compound? There was a room full of belongings: clothes, identification cards—"

"A wallet belonging to James Wallace? The missing Centriole Inspector?"

"Exactly like that. I know you're aware of the men being sent outside of the wall," he said.

I nodded slowly, already formin a hunch.

Armed men were often sent out when a power grid needed servicing, or a waterline needed a weld. Very rarely did that whole batch of workers return. How absurd was the notion that the council men would risk their own lives to ensure they had electricity and runnin water? Those glutto-nous fuckers didn't even pick their own strawberries.

Honestly, I'd never thought of the two in any relation but now that Grimm brought that specific room up, it was damn impossible not to put the pieces together.

"Keep goin," I said, feelin a small bubble of apprehension as I waited for him to confirm my theory.

"Your father added in people who he felt opposed something he was doing, or disagreed with him on whatever he wanted to bitch about for the day, ensuring they wouldn't be going back home."

"And that's where Romero comes in," I finished, answering one of my earlier questions. "But what does he get out of it?"

"What he got was a shitload of food, clothes, fucking bubble bath….the buyer for Luca's skin farm."

I took a step back to process what he was sayin. That my dad had been sendin entire families to their deaths…all to hold a fuckin position? I knew he was a power hungry hypocrite, but he was a murderer, too?

I *knew* the answer, had seen the facts, and it sickened me.

James Wallace had a place on the city council, he disappeared, and one of Dad's idiot friends took his place.

James also had a six month old baby, twins, and a wife— who all mysteriously disappeared. And he wasn't the only one.

When one family left, another took its place. But they weren't leavin on their own free will.

"Grimm, that's…. like fuckin genocide. No wonder the goddamn population never changed." I pulled my hand free and began to pace, wishin that sonofabitch was in front of me right that very moment.

Pausing, I turned back towards Grimm. "What happened to those lil babies? Did you…?" I couldn't even finish that sentence. "I know you've done a lot of sick shit, like the cannibal farm, and I've accepted that, but if you've been—"

His mask slipped for a brief second and he looked a combination of pissed and disgusted before it was back in place.

He stood taller, his body tensing with his anger.

"I kill cannibalistic little fuckers beyond the point of being human ever again.

"I don't kill cherub faced babies because your dad's a fuckin pussy who had you and everyone behind that wall brainwashed, believing in fucking fairies and bullshit utopias."

I crossed my arms, glad they were hidden beneath his hoodie. I had fairy tattoos; didn't take a genius to know that was leveled at me. I opened my mouth to respond but he wasn't done yet.

"Your dad sent them to the same place he had you and your uncle taken."

"Me and—what? Why would he do that?"

"How would I know that, Arlen? He's your dad. The same man throwing a tantrum because Romero doesn't need him anymore, same man who paid Noah to keep you locked away and supplied birth control so he could stick his dick in you. And then your ma sent Beth out here to—"

"Now you're just full of shit, Ma would never—"

"Use her own daughters to help further your dad's agenda and then play the victim?"

Ouchie. She damn sure would do somethin like that. They all would. But the truth felt like a barely closed wound bein torn wide open again. I didn't want to sit and think about all the implications right then. I needed a different pain to focus on.

"You interrupt me again and I'm gonna kick your balls into your stomach!" I glared at Grimm.

He threw his head back and laughed.

Not a little chuckle or a three second I'm-too-cool-to-show-emotion laugh, but a real gut bustin laugh.

I marched towards him, knowing exactly what to do for the reaction I wanted.

My hand was connectin with his face before I had one second to reconsider. The sting on my palm had just registered when he grabbed hold of me by the throat, slightly liftin me off the ground.

"Get…off," I croaked, clawing at his arm.

I heard someone yell in the background. It was Spanish, so I assumed it came from Katya.

Grimm let me go, sweepin my feet out from underneath me in the process. I landed on my ass; he swooped down and flipped me onto my stomach, makin me land face first in a pile of leaves, pushing his weight on my back to keep me down.

I lifted my head and yelled up at him "What the entire hell do you think you're doin?"

"You're a pain in the fucking ass, Brat. If you want to hit like a little kid and throw a tantrum, you can get your ass smacked like a little kid." He tore my pants down, draggin my underwear with em.

"Don't you dare!" My shrill voice echoed across the tree tops.

"Shut the fuck up." He cupped my mouth.

Arousal was already floodin between my thighs. He brought his palm down right on my naked flesh. I yelped, immediately tryna get away. He did it again, and again. I counted twelve hits in rapid succession.

I was still on the ground, tryna catch my breath, my clit on fire, when I heard his zipper.

He yanked his hoodie off me, letting me drop back down only after he pulled my tits out of my tank top. Grippin my hips, he slammed into my drenched pussy with no pretenses, fuckin me so hard I dug my nails into the ground to try and keep still.

I was so wet I could feel it coatin my thighs, drippin down his dick and onto his balls. "You're a filthy whore," he grumbled, fisting my hair, pounding me into the dirt.

"Yes," I moaned in agreement, my ass still burnin from the heat of his hits.

"You're my pretty little pain-slut."

"All yours," I breathed. He let my hair go and grabbed somethin behind him.

"You could have just asked for it, Brat. You want me to hurt you? That's all it takes. Apparently you don't trust me enough to give you what you need or you wouldn't have pulled that bitch of a stunt. I know you're hurting, baby. I'll always make it better."

I blinked the thick burnin tears away. I needed him to stop talkin and make me feel nothin but us in this moment.

"Doin a shitty job of it. Maybe someone else can do better."

He laughed, but there was no warmth in it.

I was just thinkin I'd pushed too far, only to slightly relax when nothin happened, which was exactly what he was waitin on.

"Grimm," I whimpered as soon as I felt the coolness of the curved blade against my throat. It was still covered in the blood of its last victim.

My pussy clenched, loving the very idea, but my heart rate jumped to concerning levels.

"Remember that conversation about me being a possessive dick? If you ever say that stupid shit to me again, I'll slit your throat open and shove my cock inside as you choke on your own blood. No one will ever touch you again but me. I have no problems taking out any man who thinks it's an option." He pushed himself so deep inside me, it hurt.

His words made me feel fuckin wonderful, completely owned. I wanted more. The blade threatened to end me, make me bleed out all over the earthy terrain.

I trusted him to cut me just enough to satisfy the painful ache I craved and make it sting. He began thrustin in and out painstakingly slow, makin me take his cock inch by thick, hard inch.

"You want me to fuck you bloody? Remember you asked for this."

He added pressure to the blade. I moaned as it bit into my skin, the burn increasing the pressure in my lower stomach.

I felt the blood begin to trickle a split second before he pulled the knife away. Immediately, he had the blade pressing into the flesh of my shoulder, diggin in hard enough to make me flinch.

He was quick and efficient with whatever he was doin. In less than ten seconds, he had the blade tossed to the side and was shoving me further into the ground as he lifted my hips.

Cupping some of the blood running down my neck, he leaned back slightly to reposition himself and spread my left cheek open. Using his bloody fingers, he pressed into my ass.

I tensed, my breath catchin in my throat. No one had touched me there since that night.

I remembered the tearing and the pain, suddenly wanting to feel it from him. I knew he'd make it better. He repeated the same process as before, this time taking the sticky crimson from my shoulder.

"Next time, I'll carve the R," he flippantly said.

I didn't understand what he'd meant right away, realizing he'd carved the first letter of his name into my skin a second too late.

He had the head of his cock lined up at the rim, and was shoving the fingers he'd just used to lube me in my mouth.

"You're going to scream. Bite down," he commanded, fully burying himself inside my ass.

It wasn't an option not to do as he said.

My jaw slammed together as he viciously plunged in and out of the sensitive hole. I screamed, feelin my legs tremble. The pain and pleasure had unfettered tears streaming down my face.

He battered me completely. I couldn't take it.

My body was a live wire one minute and a ragin inferno of pure bliss the next. I cried out, the pleasure shredding me apart as I hit a peak I'd never climbed before and hurtled over the edge.

He rode my body for what felt like hours, leavin me a boneless pile of mush by time he climaxed. I was barely aware I was even breathin when he smeared his excess semen and my come into my bloody skin before bringing them back to my mouth. I sucked them clean like they were coated in an elixir.

Suddenly, he grinned and looked over his shoulder. "You enjoy the show you sick fuck?"

Oh, lawd. I pulled my mouth from his fingers and hid my face.

"Personally, Grimmy, I would have added a bit more rhythm, but I'll give you a solid eight out of nine!" Cobra yelled from the other side of the clearing, following it with a laugh.

I shook my head, fighting my own grin. I hadn't even realized the damn peepin Tom was watchin us.

Grimm maneuvered me so I was on my side and he could press himself into my back.

"You're fucking beautiful, Brat," he murmured, running

his hand over my hip. Both of us fell silent, spent, lying in the dirt.

I didn't care I had leaves all in my hair, my skin was stinging where he'd cut me open, or that I probably wouldn't be able to walk come sunrise.

I was addicted to the way he numbed the hurt in my brain by givin me a different kind of pain. He made my worn heart ache in the best way possible.

Grimm had never been the cure; he'd always been the disease. My fucked up remedy, a poison I would willingly ingest until my dying day.

"Knowing or not knowing what you do now, do you ever miss your old life?" he asked me, toying with a strand of my hair.

We were still lying on the ground, but clothed again, his hoodie a blanket. I was certain my body was nothin more than a stiff piece of cardboard at the moment.

We'd only been awake maybe thirty minutes, but I was ready to get this conversation over with now.

I looked up at his bearded face. Naturally, I could've just told him no, but it was somewhat of a lie.

I missed my uncle, and I missed Ma even now she'd completely broken my heart, but that was the extent of it.

Right then, I missed razors, and shampoo, showers, hot meals, Cali, and even Romero. I missed the paradise of burning bodies and the surprise of bumping into a man in a black hooded robe and white satanic mask at three in the morning.

I didn't miss the house, pool boy, or that ugly wall. Didn't miss Dad, or even Beth, my half-sister, who I assumed was dead at this point in the game. She'd never done anything but try and hurt me or the family I'd come to love. They may have been Savages, but even wolves had loyalty that coursed through their blood.

"What if I told you I didn't give a damn about my old life, cause that's exactly what it is?

Being here with you, killin our way back to our corner of dark paradise where the devil's awaitin…that's my life now, and I happen to like it much better."

"Oh yeah?" He settled his hands on my hips. "Death doesn't scare you anymore?"

"Oh, it does. But I love it, almost as much as I love you." I smiled and wrapped one arm round the back of his neck, bringing us closer together. I didn't expect him to say it back, didn't even care if he thought I was psycho for sayin those three little words so soon.

I'd been crazy about him far too long to give a damn. I could wait on him to love me back.

"That's irony at its finest, because I think you're the only thing I've ever been scared shitless of in my life," he said, his gravelly voice so soft it almost sounded like he'd whispered.

My lips parted, but only air came out. If I made a big deal of his brutally honest confession, he would shut down.

I knew what he was tellin me, and no words would replace the actions that needed to be taken.

I was scared of lovin him, and it was uncharted territory for both of us. We didn't trust the normalcy and feared the solid foundation. The thing with love was that you couldn't touch it, couldn't hold onto it and be sure it would never change.

I took a shaky breath, cupped his strong jaw, and opened my wound a little more, letting him in deeper. That was going to be my strategy until he found a home inside me.

"The mayor of Centriole isn't my real dad. My uncle and my mom had an affair. I didn't find out until I was nine and overheard an argument. I was raised away from him, but he knew the truth. We were…close. He let me be myself.

"I've always been a black sheep, an outcast in my own home.

"I think I know why the man who raised me set me up to die. I'm an original family disappoint. He never really wanted me in the first place; he just didn't want to be publicly humiliated by Ma." I laughed, but damn did the truth hurt to the ninth degree of hell. I'd never caused anyone harm back then.

I felt like I'd been pushed into becoming this version of myself. I'd been done a huge favor. Grimm cupped my face, makin me give him my eyes, peerin right down to my brittle core. He didn't care that I was bitter.

He didn't care I was full of hate. He looked at me as if I was golden, every single time.

"When you break from the flock to be an individual instead of a mindless sheep, you're suddenly something foreign, a freak."

"The woman who raised me after I got out of The Order…she didn't like me very much either, she made that clear to me and my father. She left when I was nine. Haven't seen her since."

I took his hand and threaded my fingers with his. "Fuck those people."

"That's been my motto a lot longer than it's been yours, Brat."

I lightly nudged his shoulder, managing a small smile through my tears.

Chapter Nineteen

Arlen

We left at sunrise and arrived at sunset. Plymouth was much more of a town than a city, but it was full of vitality. Just like Rivermouth, the welcome sign was a tribute to Romero, but this sigil had *memento mori* scrawled across the ram's head.

People were walkin outside looking completely unbothered. There was a rundown diner with raw pink, freshly butchered pigs hangin in the window. Kids tossed a ball back and forth in an empty field.

The houses I was able to see were like lil cabins, cute and tidy. The majority of them had some type of sugar skull, leviathan cross, or ram head décor in their yards or windows.

A church with a giant inverted cross in the middle of a fire pit looked like the most cared for building around.

Clearly, this town took their worshippin to an extremely disturbing level. Anyone who saw Grimm or Cobra stopped what they were doin and waved or yelled out *ave Satanás*, like they were rootin for a damn sports team. Sometimes it was truly disconcerting how deep this all went.

Lucy's sat at the very edge, and I wasn't sure what to expect, but this…wasn't it.

The sign was a giant piece of white wood with the name written in bold blue font, stamped with a small leviathan cross in the corner. The actual building looked like a mini apartment building in major need of some siding.

A large dictation of the Sigil of Baphomet was painted on the side in red with the same *memento mori* scrawled across it. Dark curtains prohibited anyone from seeing a peep inside.

There was no sign of the acolytes, so I was assumin they hadn't arrived yet. Grimm cut the bike's engine in a parking spot beside a decent lookin sedan. A second later, Cobra's Charger pulled up beside us.

Katya smiled and waved at me from the passenger seat and I returned the gesture, lookin away when I heard a door open.

A man with salt n pepper hair stepped out adjustin his belt buckle, and pecked a familiar lookin redhead on the cheek. A huge smile spread across her face when she saw us, gesturing for us to come in.

When she turned back around, I saw the inverted cross on her left shoulder where her silken robe had slipped down.

"Grimm, where exactly are we?" I asked, hissin slightly as he lifted me off his bike and my body reminded me it was in dire need of some real rehabilitatin. Thankfully, he had the hindsight to keep a tight grip on me, because I felt like I was standin in quick sand.

"It's a place fine upstanding men like myself sometimes come to receive pleasure, and then we go on our way," Cobra answered, climbin out of his car. "You're lookin sore, sis," he smirked, laughing when I flipped him off.

"You brought us to a whore house?" Katya asked, joining the conversation.

"Kat, they're called brothels now," Blue laughed, sidling up to Cobra.

I quirked a brow at him, knowin full well he'd just been cozy with Katya the day prior.

She seemed unbothered by it, goin as far as smiling at the two of em together. Parker curiously studied Lucy's, keepin whatever he was thinkin to himself.

Cobra instantly lost his playful appeal.

Was it only obvious to me he was trying to make Kat jealous? With a soft sigh, I turned back to Grimm, who was undoing the bag from his bike.

"Why are we at a brothel?"

"Because it's where Rome told us to be, where our lead is, so we can go end this, get home, and start working on the next generation." He looped the bag of his shoulder and then headed for the building, leavin me to follow.

What the did he mean? I hoped to high hell it wasn't a damn baby.

"Damn *cabrona*, I would love to find a man who bossed me like that. I've yet to meet one with balls bigger than mine." Kat looped her arm in mine and urged me forward, payin no mind to the look on Cobra's face.

I had to swallow a retort, refusin to get in between whatever they had goin on. I heard an old Creed song blastin through a stereo system as we drew closer.

Grimm stepped right inside, leaving the music to pour out as we followed him in.

The room smelled of cigarette smoke and potpourri. It had been converted. If/when illicit activities happened, it was clearly very private. There was a large bar in the back left corner where two men sat nursing drinks.

A few more were playin a game of cards.

Women sat around seemingly content, dressed in comfortable lookin lingerie. A Baphomet banner like the one Cali had in her bedroom hung on a wall.

"Grimm, Cobra, bout time ya'll showed your faces around here. How long has it been? Six months, almost?" the redhead asked as she approached with a genial smile on her pretty face.

I side eyed Grimm but his expression gave nothin away. "Rome told you we were coming?" he asked, getting right to the point.

"Yeah." Her smiled slipped a bit.

"Your regular rooms are ready, and room four's been prepped for your friends. No one will bother you. Romero's message is with Tucker." She gestured to the bartender.

"Come on, Brat," he said over his shoulder, pushing past her and headin towards the wooden stairs. We went up, going to the door with a golden number two on it. He pushed it open and gestured for me to enter before him.

"Meet me down at the bar in five," he said to Cobra, who had stopped at a door across the hall.

My assumption about this being an apartment building was correct. There was a cornflower blue sofa pulled out into a neatly made queen sized bed with a wicker basket atop it. There was a simple kitchenette, a full sized bathroom through another door, and simple light gray painted on the walls. It was clean and cozy-ish.

Approachin the bed, I looked at the contents loaded in the basket and could have wept. Body wash, shampoo, a two pack of women's razors. There was a toothbrush, the holy grail of hygiene products. No one wanted their breath smellin like pork loin.

"I'm going to give you and the basket a few minutes alone," Grimm half-joked.

"The shower works; just give it a minute. There's a platter in the fridge to eat for now, and the bed is fresh. We won't be here long, but I want you to sleep a little because you know what happens next."

"Do *you* ever miss your old life?" I found myself repeating his own question back to him before he could go anywhere. I was genuinely curious.

I waved my hand around the room. "We're standin in a town that worships you, in an old fuck pad you were at months ago, so... don't go gettin the big headed notion I'm jealous, I am, but not cause you were with other people.

"That's to be expected...we weren't together, and you got to get your kicks from somewhere," I quickly explained.

He palmed his hair back, shaking his head with a slight twitch of his mouth. "The only thing different about my life is that I have you in it. What's there to miss?

"I don't miss fucking the mannequins who lie there and moan like I've stuck a Jesus piece inside them. I know my dick's pretty fucking amazing, but that doesn't do anything for me, just like they never did. They were irrelevant, Brat. Sure as fuck don't have shit on you."

"That was real sweet, but you could've stopped at the whole, *I am your entire life and you need me* portion,*" I softly joked. "You can go do whatever you gotta do. I'mma get acquainted with your shower. But...I'm sorry for what I said. Well, mostly all of it, actually. I wouldn't really go mess with another man, that wasn't very nice." I was rather proud of myself for that spiel.

Holding my hands clasped together, I waited for him to say somethin.

"Come a little closer. Let me tell you a secret."

Squinting my eyes, I slowly inched towards him, stopping when we were nearly chest to chest.

"I already knew that, Brat." He gripped my jaw, adding a bit of pressure, leaning down so his mouth was skimming mine. "No one's gonna touch you the way I touch you, see you the way I see you, break you down, use you, and then build you up like I do. You're not going anywhere. You're mine."

He kissed me, sealin his proclamation roughly, giving it back twice as hard when I reciprocated, nippin my lower lip and soothing the split skin with his skilled tongue before he finally let go.

He was out the door without another word, leavin me alone to clean every crevice on my body and some time to think.

I grabbed the basket and went into the bathroom, seeing a stack of plush towels on a rack.

Pulling the plastic shower liner to the side, I spun the brass nozzle nearly as far it would go, and then waited. Pipes groaned and it sounded like footsteps running inside the wall, but eventually the spicket shook and water began spraying out.

I wasn't goin to bother lookin in the mirror till I was finished; no need to see what the hell Grimm had been looking at the last few days. I may have been an emotional, unstable, occasionally badass lil bitch, but I was still a lady.

I slowly peeled off my clothes, definitely feelin everything Grimm had done to me. There were dark bruises between my thighs, and the scabby skin where he'd cut me flexed with my every movement.

My ass would never be the same again, of that I was certain, and he'd buried himself inside it for what seemed like a good hour.

Going to the bathroom was not on my top five things to do list, but I did need to pee.

That hurt, too.

Yeah, this was gonna be a pain.

But so worth it. Thirty minutes, maybe hours later—who knows?—my scalp was clean, my fur was gone, and my muscles had some much needed relief. I hadn't been in a real shower in so long, I could've stayed there for months.

Sinking down in the porcelain tub, I let the spray come down on me and shut my eyes for a minute. Everythin I'd learned should have dramatically impacted me, but I didn't really feel any more hurt than I already had—with the exception of Ma.

Not even *her* actions surprised me as much as they voided the last bit of love I had for her.

People would do anything to hold onto a semblance of power. The mayor was no different; he was just the shittiest kind of person, because he hid behind smoke and mirrors.

It didn't seem right to think of him as my dad at this point, when he had never really been such a thing. I'd had tutors and nannies, never real parents. My ma gave that up to join him in his quest to rule a city.

My real father was good to me, but we weren't permitted to spend countless hours together. He'd died in the worst way possible, but I refused to dredge up that initial feelin of loss. I'd numbed myself to it from the moment his life left his body.

This all seemed to have happened so long ago that when I thought of it, it was like seeing it from stranger's perspective. It only made me wonder: why now? Why was the mayor going through such lengths to find me?

Why was he having Noah keep me locked away? What purpose did it hold? Knowin Ma and Beth were in on it only added fuel to my fire and a deeper sense of urgency to figure out what the hell was goin on.

When the water began runnin cold, I made myself climb out of the shower, wrappin a towel around my body after wringing out my hair.

Brushing my teeth, I let myself see my reflection.

Nothing had changed. I still looked the same. Switchin off my moral compass hadn't made me look any different on the outside. But *everything* was different.

I had a past and a present. Like I'd told Grimm, it was a past I wanted to leave behind. I was ready to end this and go home. I was ready to move on and live again.

I stared in the mirror and found a genial smile liftin the corners of my mouth.

The faint red line on my throat was a reminder he'd had the curve of his blade against it less than twenty-four hours ago. Turning, I laughed, shakin my head when I saw the perfect inverted cross beside a G embellished in my flesh.

Chapter Twenty

Grimm

Our lead came written on a napkin.

Tucker, the bartender, had it wrapped around the V tattoo of the neck of whomever he'd got the information from.

"Forkfurt Penitentiary?" Cobra read from beside me, chugging down a shot. "How the fuck is anyone living in that place? It's falling apart."

I waved for Tucker to come over when he was finished with his conversation. I felt a heavy pair of tits pressing into my left arm as I lowered the right.

I knew who it was; I'd seen her watching me from the second we arrived. I wasn't going to give her any of the attention she was seeking.

Being so brazenly touched didn't sit right with me, never had, unless it was Brat.

I couldn't keep my hands off her, couldn't *not* touch her.

Without glancing over, I shoved the bitch attached to the

tits away from me. I heard her teeter on her heels, and then fall, landing on her ass with an outraged gasp, making Cobra laugh. I still didn't look over—that would mean I gave a fuck.

"With you and Rome being locked down, I feel a little left out. Don't suppose you wanna do the whole ménage thing?" Cobra asked.

Had he been anyone else I would have reached over and broken his spine vertebra by vertebra, and then I'd probably piss on him just for the hell of it.

"She's…"

"Don't hurt your precious brain trying to explain. She's the reason we're here right now, why were about to go invade a prison. I get it, bro. Rome was, is, the same way. I was joking, fucking psycho," he laughed, holding his hands up in a defensive gesture.

"Isn't that what you've got with Katya? That is why you chose to initiate her, right? Because we both know the mute with the dreads won't be around much longer, and Blue is fifty-fifty."

"No. Katya is a cool-ass chick. And I like Blue, she's my friend. I *am* capable of being just friends with a chick, Grimmy."

I scoffed in the back of my throat.

"Since when? You only stayed clear of Cali because you knew what would happen otherwise. You won't touch Brat, because, well, you know what would happen otherwise." I let it go at that, holding back the rest of what I wanted to say until a better time.

"You'll find someone," I felt the need to add. And I meant it.

He was the nicest out of all of us. He openly laughed, had a non-stop sense of humor, and at the end of the day, when push came to shove, you wanted him on your side.

We'd all been through shit. We were all tediously fringing on a blurred line of insanity. Cobra was more fucked in the head than I was, and Romero was so fucked up he had no semblance of empathy until Cali.

This world wasn't what went to utter shit; the people had. I admittedly had it the easiest—if you could discount the fact I was raised by my now estranged father, a reformed cult member, the current leader of a redneck tribe of cannibals, I could almost be considered normal.

The death shit didn't count. Death was nothing but an appointment that couldn't be cancelled. It was a natural part of life that too many saw as unnatural.

In death, life still meant what it always had. The definition didn't suddenly change. Death was nothing but an inescapable fate. We were all going to be ash and bone in the end; I just happened to hand out the ultimatums.

One day, I'd be like everyone else, nothing but a rotting corpse. I was a demon, a nightmare that would eventually meet a tragic end. It was inevitable.

But that wasn't fucking today.

Until now, I hadn't gave much thought about the years beyond. Now, I had someone to offer the world to.

She was willing to reign over the dead right beside me. By the time we sank into the ground, they'd whisper fables about us.

Having what I needed from Tucker, I headed for the stairs, telling Cobra we were leaving as soon as the acolytes arrived and to meet me upstairs in ten minutes.

I didn't want Brat in this fucking place, but it made the most sense for a rendezvous point. This was our town, specifically for me.

Cobra had one a few miles east. Romero had done it so we always had places to regroup if need be. Usually, it was the three of us. Shit had certainly changed.

Using my key, I unlocked the room door and stepped inside.

She was lying on the bed wrapped in a towel. Her hair was fanned out around her head, long lashes closed over her eyes.

How the fuck could anyone want to change her? How could I ever doubt what she'd become? Any version of her was beautiful. She was a goddess, a masterpiece. Fuck anyone who'd never seen it.

I walked to the bed, reached down, and ran my finger over the line on her neck. Her eyes flew open, and the second she saw me, she smiled, showing a mouthful of pearls.

"When do we leave?" she asked, bouncing up like a cork screw.

"Calm down, killer." I chuckled at her enthusiasm.

She launched herself at me, unashamedly letting her towel fall away as she wrapped her arms around my neck.

"Brat, I was gone less than an hour."

"Shut up and let me cling."

I kissed the side of her face and she leaned into it like she always did, starving for affection. As her man, it was my job to make her never want for a damn thing—starting with that, which reminded me of something I shouldn't have said.

"Why fairies?" I asked her, tracing the one on her arm.

"I like the idea of things that have the freedom to fly away."

"Because you couldn't."

She nodded, touching the one a little lower. "This is my winged succubus; I only got it because she looked badass."

She lifted her shoulder where a dragon was wrapped around the symmetrical black and white circle that represented yin and yang.

"Guessin you know all about this one."

Then, she held up her wrist. "My henna owl, cause she's majestic, wise, and rare."

"Like you," I said, leaning in and trailing kisses down her neck. She smelled like fucking peaches.

"I'm not fuckin wise, Grimm," she laughed.

"But you're majestic and rare?" I moved to her chest.

"Well, kinda." She shrugged. "Now tell me somethin about you. And make it good." I heard the slight change in her breath, felt her pulse jump. Her hands settled on my shoulders as I moved lower, kissing and suckling on her golden skin.

"I belong to you."

"I already knew that."

"Did you know I belonged to you from the very beginning, before I even knew I did?"

"Aw, Grimm."

"And this." I sat her on the edge of the bed, lifting her soft thighs over my shoulders, before placing a hand on her navel to make sure she couldn't go anywhere.

Right over the largest fucking fairy tat she had. "This is my favorite tattoo, because the wings lead straight to your pussy."

I had my mouth on her clit and my tongue working up and down her slit before she could reply.

It didn't take her long to thread her dainty fingers through my hair. I looked up, eyes traveling over the sinewy curves of her tiny body, and grinned. "Roll your hips, fuck my tongue, and don't stop until you're coming in my mouth."

That was all the directive she needed. She pulled herself closer, using my hair as leverage, and shoved me nose deep inside her.

I happily, greedily sucked and ate her like I was at my last meal, and she was the entrée.

Her pussy tasted like pomegranates, and her melodic moans were the key to Pandora's Box. Fuck, this girl was all my favorite sins in one imperfect vessel.

When the door clicked shut, I knew she heard it, but she didn't stop me, In fact, she pulled me even deeper.

I was acutely aware of Cobra's presence, never pausing in my ministrations. I heard him take a seat in the old wooden table chair after he dragged it a little closer.

I'd seen the way he watched her the night before. I remembered the flair of excitement in her eyes in the parking deck at the thought of an audience.

This was a onetime thing.

I'd usually pass who I was with right over to him if we weren't smashing her between us.

But he couldn't touch her; I'd take his hand off before that happened, and I knew she wouldn't let him.

When I heard him undoing his pants, I knew it was good enough, regardless.

Brat's legs began to tighten around my head, her movements not as sporadic.

She moaned my name and I almost came my damn self. I could hear Cobra roughly fisting his dick where he sat, knew he was hard from the full visual in front of him.

I nipped at her clit, digging my fingers into her thighs where I knew she was the sorest.

I growled when she roughly tugged on my strands in response. Her arousal was dripping down onto my beard. I was swimming between her thighs.

My hair felt like it was about to detach right with my scalp. Brat didn't give a fuck. She only cared about coming all over my taste buds.

I bit down on her swollen nub and made it happen. Her hips would have lifted clean off the bed if I wasn't holding her down.

I undid my pants, flicking her clit back and forth with the tip of my tongue, triggering another spasm from her body. I had her pinned by the throat, legs still over my shoulders, dick hard and pushing inside her with no warning.

As soon as she was lucid enough, she grabbed for me, urging me to tear her ass up like she knew I would. I fucked her like a whore every single time. She loved this shit as much as I did. Fucking each other up in bed had become our thing.

I looked at her pussy and swore I saw my reflection staring back at me. She was so wet I felt like I needed to dick her down a little harder to ensure she felt every inch of me branding inside her. Her face contorted, frozen in an over-whelming state of pleasure.

"Damn, this is intense," I heard Cobra groan. Brat's pussy clenched in response. I'd almost forgotten he was even in the room.

I switched positions, spreading Brat as wide as I could, sitting back on my haunches so Cobra had a better visual of my dick moving in and out of her tight, saturated pussy.

"Make her scream," he soughed, cupping his balls in one hand and stroking himself with the other.

Brat angled her hips, allowing me to bottom out. She shut her eyes and bit down on her bottom lip, trying to muffle her moans.

"Open your eyes, Brat. Don't fight it. Let me hear how good my dick feels." I grabbed her tits, firmly, and squeezed, kneading the shit out of them.

Hey eyes flew open the same time as her mouth, giving me and Cobra what we both wanted.

He groaned again, the sound had my own balls lifting and Brat digging her nails into my wrists, pleading with her sexy ass eyes that she wanted to come. I pulled one hand away and slapped her clit, rubbing the sting away with my fingers.

"Don't stop," she moaned, locking her legs behind my ass.

I slapped her clit again, forcefully pounding into her as her pussy locked down like a vise, come covering my length.

"Goddamn," I heard Cobra huff as he busted his nut, barely audible beneath Brat's screams of pleasure.

It wasn't until I was on my back, so sweaty I was sticking to the sheets, savoring the taste of Brat's pussy that I realized he was gone.

She lay on top of me, her trembling frame fitting perfectly with mine.

"My real name is Gerald," I randomly told her, my voice a little gravellier than usual.

"Gerald is a stupid fuckin name," she laughed, still out of breath.

I lightly slapped her ass and smirked. It was a stupid fucking name.

Chapter Twenty-One

Arlen

Cobra came bargin into the room just as I finished scrambling to button my shorts.

I could smell the smoke outside the windows from the fires being started around the town. The call of carrion birds and people shoutin is what had awakened me, though.

"How the hell did they find us again?" I asked, hearin another scream from down below.

"Well, Dreads, is missing, so I think that's our answer.

"Where the fuck's Grimm?" I finished lacing my boot, tossed my hair up in a ponytail, and followed Cobra out into the hall.

He'd been snuggled up right behind me, freshly showered, when I dozed again.

I had lots of questions about Parker, who'd suddenly been demoted to 'Dreads', but I figured getting out of the building was a better option to start with.

Katya and Blue were at the top of the stairs. Kat looked ready to kick ass, whereas Blue looked like she was about to have a full blown heart attack.

I made sure she stayed behind us as we descended. The first thing I saw was an acolyte shoving a damn sword through the lower groin of a Venom fucker.

"They arrived right before the last group did," Cobra explained, helpin me off the last stair. I smiled when his silver eyes searched my face, assuring him all was peachy between us after the earlier event.

I liked having another man watch Grimm have his way with me. I didn't know the logistics, but it made me feel good.

The redhead who had greeted us was cowering behind the bar, the bartender lying dead beside her, his throat making a perfect, gaping O.

Another one of the girls was flat on her back beside the card table, the whole back portion of her head missing. The exposed brain matter looked like raw hamburger meat.

Aside from those minor casualties, the other three bodies belonged to men with the V tattoo. Six acolytes stood around the room like lethal sentries, all in their signature long black robes and white masks with the inverted cross. These satanic fuckers were really startin to grow on me.

"Let's go. They got him at the church," Grimm's voice boomed as he came in the front door.

"I'm driving," he directed at Cobra, coming to grab my hand.

I obediently followed him outside. The smoke smell was ten times worse and the fluttering of wings was hidden behind dark clouds.

There was lots of shoutin and the devil's church lit up like a beacon in the distance.

"Why aren't we goin on the bike?" I asked Grimm, climbin into passenger seat of Cobra's Charger after he pulled the door open for me.

I slid all the way over so Cobra could get in beside me, takin position in the middle. Blue and Katya got in back.

"The only thing they could do that wouldn't attract too much attention: mutilated my tires," he responded as soon as he was in the driver's seat.

"We didn't know," Kat said.

"No shit, you were just the dumbasses he used as a cover," Grimm replied, flying down the road.

I nudged him with a scowl. It wasn't her fault Parker was a shit person.

"If I find out you *were* trying to take my girl away, I'll find everyone you love and slaughter them right in front of you."

He braced a forearm across my chest, and hit the brakes.

If it wasn't for that and Cobra grippin my shoulder, I would have flown through the windshield.

"Grimm—"

"And what's happening to them will be child's play compared to what I'll do to you." He cut me off and pointed at the church, indicating the cause of the smoke.

The iron Leviathan cross was glowing a bold orange. Tied to the front of it was Parker. The back held a man who was already too melted to be identifiable. Embers carried pieces of them on the air.

Parker's flesh was already splittin open, and somethin that looked like chunky blocks of thick cheddar was leaking out of him.

That was more disturbin and vile to me than him not being dead and the townies cheering the fire on. His voice was vastly fadin but his screams were audible nonetheless.

The substance leaked onto his clothes, and like a wick, his shirt fed the clumps to the hungry flames, fueling the fire.

It had just begun to consume him entirely as Grimm gunned the engine. I don't think any of us really had anything to say at the moment.

The acolytes followed us in a large SUV.

"We go through the valley and wrap around, surprise em from the back."

"That's smart," Cobra replied.

I looked from side to side, waitin on an explanation. "Are you gonna tell me where we're goin?"

"To cut the head off the snake."

We hit the Valley one bathroom break later, just as the sun came back again.

Grimm pulled the Charger to the side and cut the engine. Once he was out, he held out his hand and slid me towards him.

"It's best to travel light. The sun can be more of a pain in the ass than you are once we go in." He gestured to the tall rocks making up the walls.

"What sun? There's barely anything but darkness in

there," Katya said, coming to stand beside me. She'd changed into an outfit much like mine, shorts and a tank top, but still had a large glitter bow attached to her ponytail.

She was right. It looked like the valley of death, irony at its finest.

"You want to go through there? It's the valley of shadows."

"There's not shit to be afraid of. The valley is mine, and the shadows are my bitches."

I closed my eyes, shakin my head as Cobra laughed and held out his hand for a fist bump.

"I bet that made ya feel real badass, didn't it?" I asked.

"Brat, we both already know I'm badass." He took my hand and began leading me forward.

Three acolytes from Lucy's followed closely behind us. The other three were circling around in their SUV.

Cobra fell into conversation with Kat and Blue. By their responses and lack of remorse over Parker, I knew Grimm's first assumption was correct: he'd been using them.

I truly hoped the two of them made it all the way through this.

They were outcasts—just like I was not that long ago. We were all lookin for somewhere we belonged.

This hell was easier to survive with family who willingly went through the worst of days right along with you.

Or in my case, you had a man by your side who opened your eyes a bit to how beautiful it could be. Even the valley with its dark shadows, pinkish walls of rock, and odd lil critters occasionally peeking out at us held a quality of natural beauty.

I glanced over at Grimm and saw he had what looked like a smirk on his face.

"Why are you in such a good mood?" I asked. I couldn't help but smile at him. He was so damn gorgeous.

"Why wouldn't I be? I'm going to do what I do best, and after that's done, I get to take you home."

"Yeah, about that next generation thing…were you talkin about kids?"

He was quiet so long, I began wondering if I'd shoved him back in his bubble.

"I know you're only nineteen, but I'm damn near thirty-years old, Brat. If not now, when?"

"I don't care about your age, Grimm."

"I wouldn't give a shit if you did."

"I love it when you get possessive," I smirked. "Is this coming from you getting to play daddy in the woods the other day?"

"No, but I look forward to daddying the fuck out of you whenever you get out of line."

For real? He was going to owe me a wet floor sign he kept this up.

The thought of havin my reaper's babies one day was enough to make my ovaries implode. Hell, any woman would sign up for that job just to experience the epic ride his cock was. And his wicked tongue.

Still, this was pretty damn huge.

"Shouldn't we figure out our future first?"

"Already know what I'll be doing six years from today, and so do you, because your ass will be right beside me with a big stone on your finger."

"I…will? *You* believe in…?" I asked with a quirked brow.

"Our vows will be made before our friends, the forces of darkness, and all the gods of the pit, at the church of Satan."

Ooookay. I waited for a punch line. I should have known

that as Grimm had told a joke a total of maybe five times, that was the truth drenched in dark humor.

I almost tripped over my own two feet when I realized he was as serious as he could be. Holy hell, I could see the virginal sacrifices now. He took his Satanism way too seriously for me to say that joke aloud.

As if he'd heard it, Cobra laughed under his breath. "You'll see it all go down when Cali marries Rome." He nudged me with a canteen of water, and I gladly accepted.

I wondered how much longer we'd be walkin.

"Do you need me to say those three little words, Brat?"

"Nope," I answered honestly. At least, not right then I didn't. I would be patient, but I would want them eventually.

"You'd really marry me?" I asked.

He shrugged like that was an answer.

"You'll be mercy. I'll be death."

"You be my Jack, and I'll be your Sally," I quipped in response.

I wasn't sure if he knew what I was referring to but his soft laughter told me he did.

Our conversation ended as he pointed to an opening in the Valley wall a few feet ahead of us.

Apparently, we'd reached our destination.

Chapter Twenty-Two

Arlen

It looked like a haunted fortress of crumbling cellblocks and empty guard-towers.

"Well, you definitely picked the right time of day," I mused.

Grass nearly as tall as me surrounded the decaying brick building. The acolytes fanned out so fast I couldn't even see them anymore. They were like mice: mute, sneaky, and fast.

Carrion birds gathered on the roof of the prison. They seemed to be everywhere we went.

Grimm pulled the hood up on his newly acquired black ensemble, his eyes getting that calculated, deadly look in them he wore so well.

Katya surprised me by adjusting a stiletto knife in her boot.

"Will they have guns?" Blue asked.

"Yes, but they won't pull the trigger unless it's a last

resort. They don't know the structure of this building, and they'll realize soon enough we didn't come alone," Cobra answered her.

"There's ten of us—"

"Much more than that. Romero wouldn't send us anywhere without ensuring we were ten times stronger than whatever the fuck we're up against. In this case, there are twelve people— that's including Noah, and we all know he can't fight his way out of shit."

I could only assume he'd gotten all this information during one of his many vanishing acts for him to be so specific.

We approached the building and my nerves zinged. They all looked ready to fuck shit up, except Blue. She actually looked Blue.

Katya was definitely the backbone of their duo. She seemed shy, reserved, and sweet.

I had a gut feelin she would be the first and only one of us to go. For the first time in a while, I felt guilty.

"Blue, you stay with us. Cobra, take Kat. I'll meet you in the west wing."

"Go kill some shit, sis," Cobra grinned, droppin a kiss on my cheek before all but dragging Kat away.

"Be safe," I mouthed to her, catchin a small thumb up before I couldn't see her anymore.

"Take this," Grimm said, nudging me with a familiar black gun.

"You actually got it back?" I tucked the solid piece of metal in the waistband of my shorts.

"Cobra did."

Ugh, no further information needed.

"Wait, what about you? What are you gonna use?" I stopped walking and turned towards him.

"I have everything I need. I was going to make you stay behind me…knew your ass wouldn't listen. Also what you need, because I need it too. I promised to make sure you got what you wanted.

"Regardless, no one is going to fucking touch you. We need Noah and Vance alive, but kill whoever else moves. Just try not to get trigger happy, because foundation, and don't shoot our own people." He smirked at the last part, knowin my aim was pure shit. "And you stay close to her," he ordered Blue, suddenly serious.

"Stay close, got it. I don't need to hear that twice." She nodded.

How was I ever gonna thank him for any of this?

He'd turned his whole world upside down for me. He was getting ready to massacre in my name. What notion could be sweeter than that?

"Thank you is a real dismal way of—"

"Brat we've been through this, you—"

"Shut up and listen, Grimm. Damn. If my dad wasn't hell-bent on getting me back, your friends from the brothel would still be alive, your towns wouldn't be being invaded, and—" He gripped the back of my neck and brought me flush against him, forcing his tongue in my mouth to shut me up.

Blue shifted uncomfortably in my peripheral.

Grimm pulled away and looked down at me. "You wouldn't have been taken by Noah for some bullshit reason that never existed; I wouldn't have come to find you. We'd still be eyeing each other from across the room, neither of us making a move. You know I'd take you any way I could get you."

He let me go and stepped away, his face shrouded by his hood. "You ready ?" he asked, holdin out a gloved hand.

I looked at the old prison as the first scream of pain tore

through the air. My heart was pounding like I'd just approached a twelve foot drop, ready as hell for me to go over the edge.

I couldn't say me and this new Arlen were well acquainted yet, but we understood one another just fine. My petals had wilted and thorns took their place. The demon in my head was wide awake, and the venom in my veins churned a thirst for carnage I couldn't wait to satisfy.

I was a plague none were prepared for. I'd never felt stronger, and with Grimm forever lurking in the shadows, watching over me, I felt damn near invincible. To touch me was to touch death, and death always won.

"I'm ready," I said, lookin back at Grimm with a bright smile, and taking his hand.

Just like the hospital, sound echoed.

People's yells of surprise, footsteps, and one single gunshot so far.

Grimm had seemingly vanished, but I knew he was close, I could feel him, and was proven correct when a body seemed to come from nowhere. Blue and I had been on our way up an old staircase when the man came tumbling down.

His head hit the solid metal railing, leaving a ringing crack and blood behind as he free fell to the level below, landing at an obtuse angle with a nasty soundin splat.

I wondered what it said about my relationship when I knew it was my man who killed someone simply by the way they were executed. Clearly, we were very compatible.

"That's eleven," Blue whispered.

We wound up in a long hall lined with cells. I heard a muffled sound comin from the end like a woman was in pain.

Blue and I slowly edged towards it.

There was a ton of dark spots inside the building, but the vaulted skylights that had been installed when the prison was built made it easy enough to see.

The sound was comin from a cell halfway to the end. I had the pretty lil dagger Grimm had given me in hand and was ready to cut shit. The weight of the gun reminded me it was there too, but that was my last resort.

As we closed in, I realized it wasn't pain I was hearin.

Blue made a sound of disbelief, shaking her head. Two people were fuckin in the midst of all this. I reckoned they didn't know what was goin on for that same reason.

I debated for a millisecond if I should let the chick live, but nah. Fuck all of that; I was takin no prisoners.

They didn't see me until it was too late.

By the time the man realized I'd entered the small cell and gotten the full view of his freckled ass, there was nothin he could do.

I went in full force.

I was on his back with my blade slicin into his throat, making him bottom bitch. He tried to fight back for half a second; the blade sliced deeper, right through arteries, tissue, and muscle. His cock was still nestled between the woman's legs he'd been screwin, and as his body jerked I wondered if this would be considered necrophilia on her end.

Seein as they were on a dingy old cot, we didn't all fit nice and comfortably together.

The man was making weird noises as he bled out. I shoved his head full of brown hair out of my way, and covered the woman's mouth, mufflin her scream as blood sprayed us but, mostly all over her pretty blonde hair—shame.

"Someone's coming," Blue whispered, surprising the hell out of me by doing a similar move Katya had done.

She took over mufflin the blonde's screams by yanking the dirty pillow out from beneath her head and slamming it over her face.

Jumping up, I rolled the man onto the floor as fast and quietly as I could, then straddled the blonde. She fought like hell to free her face, Blue was stronger than she was though, and my bloody knife goin through the bottom of her jaw solved our problem real quick.

The air she expelled was forced right into the crimson pillow. Blue jumped right over her, grabbed me, and pulled me behind the old rusty door just as another Venom entered.

Hawke.

I reacted instinctively.

He spun around to yell and saw me. There was only brief look of surprise that reflected on his face as my boot landed squarely in the center of his stomach.

He went backward, trippin over the body, and goin down. When he attempted to bounce back up, he slipped in the blood of his friend.

It covered his shirt, arms, and jeans. I clenched my white-turned-red dagger between my teeth, knowing I would need both hands, and charged.

"Wait," was all he got out.

I managed to hit him hard enough that his head smacked against the stone floor when he fell back again. I straddled him, but because I was just as slippery as he was, I couldn't get the grip or angle I needed on the dagger due to his struggling.

I wrapped both my hands around his damn throat and squeezed. I squeezed with everything in me, digging my nails into his skin and feeling my muscles burn.

I blocked the veins responsible for the oxygen flowing to his brain, knowing it would start to swell as he suffocated.

I watched the color drain from his face and the capillaries burst beneath the skin, making it look like he was bleeding from the inside out.

I waited as his blood pressure plummeted, his heart struggled to beat, and his lungs seared with the burnin sensation I knew all too well when they were deprived of air.

I watched the life leave his body, and mine felt elated. He dropped down with a quiet thump. I simply stared at him. After a second, I spat in his face and stood up with Blue's assistance.

"He got off easy," she mumbled, clearly picking up on my body language. I briefly wondered if that was from personal experience, but we didn't have time for conversation.

"Come on," I said, removing the bloody knife from between my teeth. I rolled my lips together to rid them of the taste.

We left the room behind, heading down the remainder of the hall. The prison seemed oddly quiet all of a sudden.

I knew he was behind me without havin to turn around.

"Damn, Brat, you did good." His hands settled on my hips, and he spun me to face him, a full smile waitin to grace me. I swooned inside.

"You saw em?"

"My favorite part was when you choked him out. I might let you try that next time you ride my dick." His smile shifted to a smirk.

"How did *you* see that?"

"Just assume I never really left you alone." He took my bloody hand, pullin me down the hall.

"Is that why there's like, two drops of blood on you?" Blue interjected.

"No, there's only two drops of blood on me because I don't always make a mess."

"Is it done already?" I asked.

"No, but there's somethin you need to see."

Chapter Twenty-Three

Arlen

I was thoroughly confused.

In what would have been the food hall, there seemed to be a standoff. At the center of it was Noah, Vance, and Vitus' uncle, Rex, all with guns held to their heads by their own people.

Vitus stood behind them like he was a crowned prince. A man with darker features was right beside him.

Acolytes, too many to count, stood by every exit. Coming through a cellular's speaker was Romero's voice, soundin rather smug.

Cobra and Katya stood off to one side, both lookin like they'd dove in tomato soup, Kat still looked prim and proper despite that. Her face was serious for once, as was Cobra's.

I refused to cower into Grimm when Vitus looked right at me, a smile lightin up his face. Bile rose in my throat at the sight of these men, but that's all it was. They made me sick, made me hate, and they'd hurt me, but they didn't fuckin scare me.

Blue stepped closer to me as an act of silent support. Vitus's eyes shifted to her. The immediate curiosity I saw there had me pushin her behind me.

Grimm squeezed my hand, bringin me closer to his side and helpin me block her.

"You have two minutes to tell me something I want to hear before everyone in that room tears you a new asshole." Romero's voice filled the silence.

It was odd not to see him front and center; it only solidified how he felt about Cali that he wouldn't leave her side while she was carryin his lil spawn.

"I want to meet you face to face. I'll come to where you are, and, as an act of faith, you can have my father, my uncle, and Noah. I was gonna toss my cousin in too, but I'm told he's dead." He winked at me, the ballsy fuck.

This wasn't what I'd been expecting him to say at all. I couldn't even play the *but they're his family* card. Family wasn't defined by blood. I was walkin proof of that. Mine stood around me, half wearin satanic masks.

"He has leverage," Grimm said quietly.

"Continue," Romero commanded with no change in his vocal inflection.

"I just need a week. I'll meet you face to face and then we go from there."

"You haven't told me why the fuck I wouldn't just kill you now and still get what I want."

"Well, you could've killed me the second I became a problem. But you didn't. You've been waiting for me to show my cards. *That's* why you take these fuck-ups off my hands and meet me in a week. We can iron out the details of why later."

The room went so silent you could hear a pin drop.

"He's gonna take the deal," I mumbled, a split second before he did exactly that.

"One week. I'll get a hold of you, not the other way around." The line went dead.

"What just happened?" Blue asked from behind me.

I didn't fuckin know, and at that moment, I didn't care. Four of the men I'd came for would be dead. Three were right in front of me, comin back to my home turf. Four out of five was pretty damn good odds. I didn't care how they got there. I wanted them so badly I was nearly salivating at the mouth.

Vance's eyes locked with mine and I think he got the message clearly.

His ass was mine.

Chapter Twenty-Four

Arlen

We rode in the backseat this time.

For the first few hours we exchanged theories on what the hell kinda information Vitus could possibly have that made him feel so invincible.

"Vitus is naturally going to take his father's place. If you want to live out here, there's one man you don't make an enemy of. Sure as shit what his dad did," Cobra vented.

I'd worked that out already. I was on to more pressin matters.

Like the fact that my muscles were feelin my warrior moves from a bit ago, that I'd just faced the men who'd put me in this position in the first place, and how *badly* I wanted Grimm right then.

Our prisoners were bein transported in the back of a large, windowless van between two SUVs. I stared out the window at the black sky for a minute before adjusting my head in Grimm's lap.

He was replying to Cobra when I reached for his zipper. I worked it down, and adjusted again so I could slide my hand down his pants. His cock was already hard—clearly, he felt how I did. We just wanted to kill and fuck. Nothin was wrong with that.

He was solid and warm in my hand. He lifted slightly, allowin me to free him. His erection stood tall and proud in the darkness of the backseat. I encircled it, rubbing a throbbing vein with my thumb.

It was so smooth.

He grabbed a fistful of my hair, forcibly guiding my mouth down onto his cock, making me take him all.

I fought not to gag as the head hit the back of my throat. Grippin him with my hands, I lay on my side and started sucking him hard.

This I'd done quite a few times before. I knew how to cup his balls, swirl the tip of my tongue around his silky tip, and deep throat him back to back.

During a small lapse in silence, I was certain the suction noise echoed around the car. Knowin they heard me had my blood crusted thighs clenchin together.

I worked him harder, moanin in delight at the first taste of his pre-come. He scooped up some of the saliva running down my face, and then slid his hands down the back of my shorts, using it to lube between my cheeks before easin two fingers inside my puckered hole. The burn was delicious.

As he finger-fucked my ass, I eagerly sucked his dick.

I was a whore, greedy for his come to spray across my tongue as our friends sat in the front seat. My breathin became impossible to control. I wondered if I could get off with his thumb working my rim.

Poppin his cock out of my mouth, I turned my cheek into his lap, licking his plushy sack before gently easin his right nut between my lips, then the left, paying them equal attention.

I felt his abdominal muscles tightening, and heard him tell Cobra to watch the road, a breathy laugh following.

"Put my dick in your mouth," he gruffly commanded, turning me onto my stomach.

I did as he said, easily slipping his saliva drenched member back where it belonged. He took hold of my hair again, and proceeded to savagely fuck my face, driving his fingers in and out of my ass at the same tempo.

"That's it, good girl," he praised.

When he twitched, I was ready. He didn't warn me, didn't even have to force me lower.

"Goddamn, Brat. Fuck," he cursed softly, grippin my hair so hard my eyes stung.

I happily deep throated as he came, milkin his balls so I got every drop, feelin the tangy liquid slide down my throat.

After a complimentary twirl around his tip, I tucked his cock away before lying on my back again. I knew my face was a wet mess, just like my eyes were watering from his grip on my hair and makin myself not gag; I smiled up at him anyway.

"We'll be home in less than ten," he said. Due to the fact he wasn't touchin me, I knew what that meant. The word 'home' made my heart swell. *Home* was with him. *Home* was with our family.

Home was where Vance would soon find out how great it felt to be fucked in the ass without givin permission.

"Why did Romero cut the mayor off?" I asked to distract myself from the inferno goin on inside me, licking the roof of my mouth for any trace of his semen.

"*Cabrona.*" Katya tsked, making me grin.

"Sorry about that," I volunteered, not really sorry at all. I wondered if I should be worried that I didn't care *that* much, but then I'd *have* to care for it to be an option.

"No the fuck you're not," Cobra laughed.

"Girl, I could watch that spank bank material every day. You two are hot together. There's nothing wrong with being sexual. It's human nature. We're animals after all, savages who figured out how to walk and talk."

"We agreed to just be friends, Kat. You can't say those things. Now I'm in love," Cobra sighed dramatically, making Blue giggle. Bless her, she was so sweet.

Grimm took hold of my face, makin me give him my eyes before he answered, gently rubbin my cheek with the thumb that was just inside me. "We're filthy," I laughed.

"We're the best kind of filth, Brat," he smirked, pressin that same thumb to my lips for me to suck.

"You know Rome, so you know he isn't one to be controlled. That's what the mayor was doing. Romero found new suppliers outside Centriole. Now he won't take any form of contact from him. There goes the mayor's real power," he finally answered, pulling his finger away.

"Makes....sense," I cocked my head, furrowin my brows.

"What—"

I reached up, pressin my hand over his mouth to hush him, and he bit me.

"Ouch, you fucker." I jerked away.

"Don't fucking hush me."

"Ya'll are damn idiots, you know that? If the mayor wants to hold his power, he needs the same thing Vitus needs to make nice with Romero. And what better leverage is there than his 'daughter'? I'm best friends with the devil's fiancée, in love with Grimm, and adore Cobra.

"Romero's bitch of an ex could have easily told this to Noah, and, well, boom! I'm your leverage. Lock me away as a pawn. I reckon he didn't count on being ignored, so he brought in the Venom." The more I figured it out, the faster I talked, and the more pissed I became.

All the people he'd sent outside the wall, the babies lost, the death of my real father. Using me, brainwashing Beth into what she had become. His offenses went on and on. He deserved to pay penance for his sins just like every other dick on my shit list would.

I began wonderin what it was the Venom would get out of this, especially now that Vitus had given up Vance.

What the fuck were all these people hiding?

Chapter Twenty-Five

Arlen

At three in the morning we arrived home.

The main gates, manned by armed acolytes, swung open. Cobra drove the long distance to the main house, and parked in front of what I considered a mansion.

It was all so familiar, but like I was seein it for the first time. The main ceiling fixture was a black ram head in the center of an inverted pentacle that held four light fixtures.

The wall fixtures were deep golden colored ram heads serving as placeholders for candelabras in the shape of inverted crosses.

It was all comforting, somehow.

"Get ready," Grimm laughed softly.

I was starin at the smooth hardwood floor when he said that; I didn't see Cali until she rushed me. She grabbed my arm and hugged the hell out of it, and partially me.

I was so thrown off by her huggin me at all, I just stood

there. "I missed you so much! I can't hug you because my fucking stomach gets in the way." Someone had clearly swapped my Cali with another. When did she like hugs?

I looked down and saw a perfect bump beneath a silk nightie. She wasn't that big at all, though since she was normally the size of a toothpick, she probably did feel like a hippo.

"I missed you," I said quietly, trying to hold back tears and failing. Huggin her back, I felt a light sheen on her skin.

"Are you okay? You're sweaty."

She laughed and stepped back, right into a shirtless Romero.

His dark eyes flickered over me, and the fucker actually half-smiled. "Blood looks good on you. Welcome to the fam."

I blinked. Was this real life?

Cali moved onto Grimm, inspecting him closely, then full on embracing Cobra, who lightly rocked her back and forth.

"This place wasn't the same without you guys." She smiled sheepishly, her blue eyes curiously stopping on Katya and Blue for a brief second.

She looked between me and Grimm and her smile grew. I had so much to tell her, knowin I could tell her anything because she would understand it all better than anyone else. Seein the huge ruby on her ring finger, the bump, and overall aura she had, I knew she had her fair amount to tell me too.

But it was three in the morning.

I was dirty, she had obviously been busy, and Blue and Katya looked like they were about to fall asleep on their feet.

And then the acolytes came in.

We all moved out of the way as the Venom men, plus Noah, were dragged through the front door and towards the hall that led to the 'playroom', as the boys called it.

None of them were lucid. Their heads lolled, feet limply following behind their hoisted bodies as they went past.

"Get them settled, and then meet me down here," Romero said, walkin Cali back towards the stairs.

Grimm wordlessly took my hand and did the same, keeping a few paces behind them.

"I wasn't done talking." Cali yawned.

"You guys need sleep," Romero replied as we branched off at the top of the stairs.

"Aw," I softly sighed when I realized he'd meant her and the baby.

Grimm shook his head at me, stopping at a black door and pushin it open.

The smell of him hit me first, and I knew right then that this would be my favorite place to be. His huge blacked out tufted bed sat against a wall, neatly made up in silk linen and a plush lookin comforter.

The metallic dresser and armoire matched it perfectly. There was a closed door on each far wall. He sat me down on the cushioned ottoman bench at the foot of his bed, not bothering to turn on a light.

Kneelin, he pulled my socks and boots off my feet, and carried them off where they made a lil thunk on the hardwood floor. I dug my toes into the silky soft, faux fur rug under me. I leaned over, resting on my elbow with my chin in my hand, closing my eyes when a soft light spilled from what I assumed was his bathroom.

"Come on, Brat." He lifted me off the ottoman and practically carried me to the shower.

It took me way too long to realize he was ass naked. I felt the alluring steam and attempted to help him undress me.

"Why so tired all of a sudden?" I yawned.

"You're crashing from your sugar high."

"I haven't eaten any sugar."

He chuckled softly, placing me inside a glass shower with slate walls.

"It doesn't matter. You're home now, where you belong."

I nodded, leaning back against his chest, my front facing the opposite direction. The hot water felt *so* good.

"Was gonna run you a bath, but I can do that another day."

"That's sweet, Grimm," I smiled, pressin my cheeks back on his erection, making him laugh again.

"Must not be crashing too hard," he mused, gently parting my legs.

"Is that sausage?"

"You sound like me; haven't even opened your eyes yet and searching for food," Cali laughed.

That did the trick.

I squinted against sunlight, burrowing deeper into the amazing silk pillow. My body felt so languid. I smiled, still feelin the sensation of Grimm between my legs.

He'd been so sweet, so unlike his norm, washin me up after and tuckin me in. Ugh, I loved that man.

"I know that smile," Cali sighed wistfully.

Opening my eyes fully, I looked down the length of the bed to where she sat Indian style on the ottoman, bump facing me.

Her white-blonde hair was longer, pulled to the side in a fish-tail braid. She had on a halter dress that matched her eyes, lookin all soft and innocent—a damn lie.

"Hurry and get moving, we have breakfast to eat and people to torture."

"*We?*"

"I crashed last night after I got crashed." She laughed at her own joke, making me do the same. "Anyway, Rome, Cobe, and G spent a long time in the playroom. Now, if you're a good girl and eat your cheerios, we get to play too."

I sat up, belatedly forgetting I was naked. I grabbed the sheet as Cali scoffed.

"Like I haven't seen those bean bags before."

"If mine are bean bags, yours are beach rings," I retorted, climbing out of bed.

"You got clothes in the closet," she told me, pointing to the other closed door.

I went to the door she'd pointed at and pulled it open, seeing Grimm had ensured I would have more than what I could possibly need. Everythin was nice and organized, his stuff on one side, mine on the other.

"Do you know what's goin on?" I asked her.

"Vitus now has six days. Rome got whatever he wanted from Noah and Vance, and Grimm may or may not have killed the other guy, not that I blame him. And *you* need to eat, so we can play. I haven't gotten to play in months, and now Noah is just in that room helpless and scared out of his mind."

I put on a pair of gray cargo pants, skippin underwear,

pulled a comfy bra over my head, and grabbed a skin-tight black T and some socks. I put deodorant on, but that was it.

I could smell the scent of Grimm on my skin. I wasn't takin that away.

After a quick brush of my teeth and hair, I was ready for the day.

Cali said 'play'. I didn't want breakfast; I wanted blood.

"I want to rush in there and fuck them up on sight as badly as you do, but Rome taught me to go in slow, prolong the pain and make them feel it. They deserve every moment of their suffering. Plus, I am growing the future heir of the Badlands. I got to feed this kid a granola bar and some almond milk."

Heir? It hadn't really occurred to me the life she and Rome's kids were going to have. The life me and Grimm's kid would have.

"You ain't worried?"

"Um, no." She side eyed me, understandin exactly what I was tryna say.

"My kid will be surrounded by a family of deviants. The devil's their father, death will be their cousin, and their uncle's a Savage."

"Grimm would be their uncle too."

"But your baby will be their cousin. You should get started soon so my son has someone to play with."

"It's a boy?!" I exclaimed, a lil too loudly as we entered the kitchen, secretly overjoyed at how acceptin she was of me bein with her brother. This was Cali though, one of the most open minded people I'd ever met, so it wasn't all that surprising.

"We don't know that for sure." Romero jumped in from where he stood, cutting up an apple, while Cora and Grimm leaned against the counter. "I don't give a fuck what they are, they're mine."

"See, how sweet he can be? He's going to be a good daddy," Cali quipped as Cobra pulled out a barstool for her, and then me.

My attention was pulled to the hot plate of food Grimm slid in front of me and the glass beside it. Rome sat down a saucer of apples, granola, and sausage patties in front of Cali, who wasted no time digging in.

"You met the other two officially yet?" I asked her, spotting them out on the patio, lookin content.

"Blue is shy and real sweet. Katya is cool; I almost killed her for lookin at Romero like he didn't have any clothes on, but Cobra mediated. Plus, who can blame her? He's incredible."

Romero looked directly at her. "I told you I wouldn't fuck you till after lunch. Keep stroking my ego and soon your tongue will be stroking my—"

"Here, look at this," Grimm interrupted, sliding a small laminated book between our dishes.

I twisted my lips, taking a sip of what I found was the most amazing fuckin homemade lemonade on the planet, with *fresh* lemon, so I wouldn't laugh at the look on Grimm's face.

I focused on the lil book he'd just sat beside me.

"Leviathan cross of crucifixion, vise, garrote, hand-saw, tongue-puller, blow-torch, *seven* pairs of red tipped pliers, a fuckin *Cradle of Judah*?" I ticked off randomly. The book was at least ten pages long.

"Fucking great, isn't it?" Cobra asked, peering over our shoulders.

"They don't call it the devil's playground for no reason," Grimm added, liftin a strand of my hair to twirl around his finger.

"Where did you get a Cradle of Judah and a…he-ter-ricks fork?" Cali asked Romero.

"Babe, you know I can get whatever I want."

"Why are you showin us this?" I asked.

"Because you two will be putting on the show, so if you see something that's missing…." He let us fill in the blanks.

"What show?"

"My people want to watch, they get to watch. Plus, it sends a message not to fuck with me again. Speaking of," he turned his dark ass gaze on me, "what do you want to do about Centriole?"

I sat there, suddenly tongue tied, partially shaken that he was focusin on me directly. I didn't care how tough you thought you were; these three men were terrifying. I wasn't afraid of Grimm, cause I knew he'd never hurt me outside of our debauched fuckin.

Romero didn't have to say a single word. He had an aura about him. He was the owner of a medieval level torture room, enough said.

And Cobra, for all his jokes and sense of humor, it was clear he was fucked up too.

"What can I do? It's behind a stone wall," I finally responded.

"But if it wasn't?"

"I'd probably give everyone inside it a large dosage of reality." I shrugged.

"That's very…ominous."

"The elaborated version was draggin every civil leader into the middle of the street and slittin their throats cause I know damn well they're aware of how they got their positions.

"I'd shove most of those rich pretentious fucks inside the

revolting prison cells the mayor has outcasts locked away in for simply seekin refuge. And beyond that, put someone more competent in charge of them, and tear that hideous wall down."

"That's an excellent fucking answer." Romero grinned at me.

"If the wall comes down, it's ours," Cobra cut in, his gaze shiftin to Katya and Blue as they joined us.

"That's the beauty of it all. Walls fall down." Rome smiled, one of those evil genius smiles when a grand scheme has come together.

"You're going to tear it down?" Cali asked, dunking her granola in milk.

"*We'll* be tearing it down," Grimm corrected. "No one's doing anything till Baby S is here. Can't just run at a wall and expect it to crumble. In the meantime…" he trailed off, lookin at me expectantly.

"What else do you need, Brat?"

"A cattle prod." I was only semi-joking.

"We have three," Romero confirmed.

It was pretty damn luxurious for a torture chamber.

The tools were organized behind a chain- link fence that sectioned off the massive room.

The bigger ones were placed systematically about. There were plush couches and a damn bar in the far corner. I think what may have been a stripper pole at one time had been turned into a shackle bar, currently where Vance sat in nothin but his drawers.

Noah was stomach down on a long wooden table with some sort of device holdin his head in place.

Rex was most certainly dead. Half his bloodied body was submerged in a metal tub of what looked like leeches. The wet sounds emanating from it made me shudder.

Cali had swapped her blue dress for a shorter black one and some knee high boots. She looked like she was ready for a shoppin trip, not to kill someone.

I, on the other hand, was wearin my same outfit from earlier, and Katya, who had opted to join us, was dressed down.

Blue was positioned comfortably on the other side of the room, beside Cobra. She looked at him the way he looked at Katya.

"She has us," Cali said as if she'd just read my damn mind, struggling to pull a long metal contraption out of a chest.

"I think a good girl is what he needs," I shrugged, conscious of the fact I'd just said that in front of Kat. She didn't seem to care, which was really my point.

I wasn't tryna be a bitch, but I genuinely felt that way. Good girls could be bad, too. Regardless, Cobra deserved someone who would love all of him; lawd knows the man had issues that ran deep.

I turned and met Grimm's eyes from across the room, blowin him a kiss. He tried to fight a smile and lost. I completely melted. I felt him watchin me twenty-four-seven and I loved it. He moved away from the bar and began makin his way over to us, Romero followin.

"Whoever she is will be getting her ass kicked by both of us if she dares ruin that smile always on his face," Cali said, and looked right at Kat, provin she knew knew where my mind had been.

I scooted her out the way to get whatever she was struggling with, trying not to laugh. Her loyalty was iron-clad.

"I got it," Grimm said, coming up behind me and, embarrassingly easily, pulling out what looked like an extended pair of forceps with rusted metal teeth. He raised his brows at me.

"Now, you know full well your sister is the one who wants to play with whatever that is."

"It's a tongue puller. Had you curious did it, Pixie?" Romero grinned, helping Cali from her crouched position.

"Are you ready?" he turned and asked me.

I looked through the chain links at Vance and Noah. I was beyond ready.

Chapter Twenty-Six

Arlen

Vance died first.

With a room full of acolytes and death by my side, it went flawlessly.

"Swap him with Noah," I said, returning the wicked grin Cali had given me.

This was half her idea, half mine. She deserved this as much as I did.

Without questioning our reasoning, Grimm unshackled Vance, leading him by the metal ring around his neck to the table Noah was shackled on.

Romero turned a lever in a circular motion, and the large metal panels resting against the top of Noah's head and jaw loosened.

"It's a vise," Grimm explained.

Romero dragged Noah off the table, and the man began to pray as soon as his knees hit the ground.

"Not this shit again," he sighed.

Grimm shoved Vance down on the table in his place. He didn't make a sound, didn't even try to fight back as his arms were stretched above his head and secured in the ropes. Where was the fun in that?

Grimm spun the vise back shut, securing Vance's head in place.

I circled around to stand in front of him as Cali had Romero lift Noah off the floor.

"You're an ass man, right Vance?" I asked, stroking the hair on top of his head.

"Well, we know Noah is," Cali said, coming to stand by me.

We'd decided it would be best not to take unnecessary risks, and placed her where she couldn't possibly be hurt.

She held the position by Vance's head, and just like we wanted, Romero and Grimm easily lifted Noah up onto the table behind him.

Each held an arm as he struggled, and I dragged his boxers down, exposing his ugly blob of a dick. I ignored his cries, doing the same to Vance so his ass was exposed.

"You know what to do," Grimm said, dragging Noah's cock closer to Vance's ass.

"Please, show mercy," Noah mumbled, choking on a cry.

I started to laugh. Was he for real?

"This fucking pussy is not related to me," Romero snapped.

"Spread his ass," Grimm demanded, unabashedly grabbing Noah's cock, pulling on it like a rope.

Romero let his arm go and gripped Vance's cheeks, pulling them apart.

I moved out of the way, adjustin my grip on the prod Grimm had handed to me before we began.

"You hear that, Brat? He asked for mercy." He smiled at me, force feeding Noah's cock into Vance's hole.

I smiled and lifted the prod, tappin the zapper once, twice.

The acolytes were shiftin about by this point in excited anticipation. As soon as Noah's tip touched center, Vance reacted, yellin out all kinds of obscenities. "Here honey, you're going to want to bite down."

I looked at Noah's face, how the tears leaked off it, the slobber as he begged like a fuckin coward. I was disgusted. I saw myself in his place, pleading for it all to stop, and he did nothin but watch.

He hurt me, and he'd hurt my family countless times in the past.

I wanted him to *beg* for mercy, and then I'd give him death.

I jammed the prod up his ass and hit the button. He was forced to go balls in as his whole body convulsed forward.

Vance yelled, givin Cali the perfect opportunity to use her tongue puller. She clamped the device down and didn't let go, holding it in place even as he began to bleed.

"Move," I demanded, pullin the prod out and jamming it back in.

He screeched, gaggin as he jerked again. It took a good few minutes, and some leakage of crimson from his own hole, but he started to move. Noah thrust in and out so slowly I began to get bored.

Without warning I shoved him, removing his blood tinged cock from Vance's bright cherry asshole. He fell onto the stone floor with a loud thud; before he could even think about recovering, I placed the prod on the tip of his dick and hit the button.

"You could have done better than that shameful performance, Noah. I remember," Cali callously stated.

Romero blinked, slowly, as if he'd just been switched on.

"Maybe he knows he can't compete with Vance," I shrugged.

"Fuck this," Romero mumbled at the same time Grimm physically moved me out of his way, pickin me up and placin me by Cali.

"Pull out Lilith!" Romero demanded.

"Good fucking choice," Grimm affirmed.

Me and Cali shared a look, neither knowin what they were talkin about.

Romero grabbed Noah by the leg and began dragging him across the room.

Cali let her forceps loosen when Grimm stepped up to the vise. "Watch," was all he said before he began turning the balled lever.

I moved closer, watchin the two iron planes inch together, compressing what was in their way—which happened to be Vance's head.

Grimm's muscles slightly tensed as he continued turnin the lever.

None of us paid any mind to Vance's screams. He kicked his legs, shiftin his bloody ass back and forth, struggling in his restraints. I knew it hurt, knew he felt the non-stop pressure on his bones as they prepared for a farewell crunch. The more he hurt, the better.

The bottom jaw cracked first. Teeth cracked and crumbled. His life ended when the top of his skull fractured, and out came pouring pieces of his brain in a mass of cerebrospinal fluid and golden red liquid.

"This thing is sick." Cali grinned, runnin her fingers along the top of the vise.

Lookin at the way his face had permanently contorted, I felt like I'd done some vigilante justice.

Grimm stepped back, no emotion on his face whatsoever. He took my hand, and led me across the room to where Romero was.

Cali quickly followed, leaving her forceps on Vance's back.

Romero's steel toed boot was restin squarely on Noah's back so he couldn't go anywhere. Cobra looked like he was about to burst with glee so I knew whatever was bein dragged from behind the fence was some fucked up piece of equipment.

I was certainly correct.

"What the hell is that thing?" I asked Grimm.

"It's our version of a Nuremberg virgin, obviously with Lilith on top."

Was I expected to know what that was?

He positioned me in front of him, wrappin his arms around my middle. I snuggled myself into his embrace, kissin his cheek. We watched the acolytes get to work.

Whatever they had dragged out looked like a giant wooden mummy tomb dotted with round holes. Some were open, some were covered.

When Cobra did the honors of opening the two wooden doors like one would a cabinet, I saw it was affixed with long iron spikes on both the doors and the back wall.

"Rome, you've been holdin out on me," Cali pouted.

"No, you just never asked what was in here. Bet your ass memorizes that book now." He glanced back at her with a smirk.

"Get him inside," he said to two acolytes, steppin back to wrap his arm around Cali's waist. I tracked his thumb gently massaging her bump and smiled.

"You know, you may be an asshole of epic proportions, per Cali's usual words, only bein bested by Grimm when's he's a broody dick, but you ain't that bad. *And* you care about the elderly."

"I don't brood," Grimm said, squeezin my side.

"Well, you may be annoying as fuck, and a chick I only kept around for Cali's sake— and Grimm's, because he went soft on me—but I'm glad you're home. But don't tell anyone about the old folk. I got a rep to obtain," he joked.

"That was so adorable I have tears," Cali laughed, wiping wetness from her eyes.

"You have tears because you're an emotional bitch, babe."

He really just undid all progress with that sentence, but Cali just laughed it off and elbowed him.

We watched Noah loaded into the 'Lilith', and he fought for once, as best he could under the circumstances.

Grimm kissed my neck, and then rested his chin on my shoulder, speakin lowly into my ear.

"It was built to replicate the real thing. Those spikes won't hit any vital organs.

He'll feel ten stabs through his flesh all at the same time." As he explained, Cobra slammed the doors shut.

The thick padlocked hinges interlocked, and the room erupted in cheers a second after a piercing cry that sounded more animal than man pierced the air.

Grimm placed another light kiss just beneath my ear, nippin the lower lobe before he spoke again. "Two spikes in the shoulder, two in the lower back, and one in each ass cheek."

He shifted, pullin me further back into him; I could his hardened cock through the fabric of our pants. "Three spikes in the chest, and one in the stomach. Do you hear the way he's screaming? The spikes are binding with each bloody wound. Listen to him struggle, making them go deeper.

"That closed in space, nowhere to go and only darkness to see. It only exacerbates the pain and misery."

I gripped his hands firmly in mine. This was a whole new form of dirty talk.

Cobra opened the doors, revealin a flash of Noah's bloody body, tearin the spikes free, just to slam them shut again, bringin forth another loud yell, this time seeming to echo through the entire house.

Blood poured from the bottom of the Lilith and leaked from the open holes. But he wasn't dead yet; beneath all the chanting you could hear him moanin in pain.

His death wasn't meant to come fast. He was meant to suffer in agony, just like the Mayor of Centriole would.

"Take it to the Leviathan. We'll burn him sometime tomorrow," Romero ordered, nearly draggin Cali out the room.

"Come on," Grimm said, leading me after them.

We weaved in and out of the gathered in the house. *Ava satanas* and *memento mori* reached my ears more than once.

"What does *memento mori* mean?" I asked as soon as we made it to his room without incident.

"Remember death," he answered, watching me kick my shoes off and shimmy my pants down. "They celebrate death as much as they do the devil."

I lifted my shirt off, droppin it to the floor. I stepped back to get a good look at him as he removed his own clothes.

"They celebrate me finding you." He closed the gap I created and clasped my hips, easily lifting me up onto his dresser. The metallic metal cooled my ass cheeks.

"I ain't nothin to celebrate," I laughed.

He cupped my face a lil harder than was necessary, ensuring he had my full attention. "You're the only woman I would get down on my knees and bow to."

"Grimm—"

He shut me up with his mouth on mine, tearin the fabric of my underwear as he removed them.

"You said you didn't need those words Brat, but you deserve them, and you only deserved to hear them if I meant that shit." He pulled back, makin sure he had my eyes. "And I do. Whatever version of yourself you want to be. I'm going to love the fuck out of you, always."

"You're gonna make me cry," I mumbled.

"Think I already did," he smiled, slowly lickin the tears from my cheeks. "Do I need to make it better?" he teased, unclasping my bra.

I cupped his face, pressin a light kiss on the tip of his nose. "I love you, Grimm, needed to remind you of that, and yes, I think I'm owed some sex. *After* you tell me how Noah's goin to die in that box."

He pulled his cock out and brought me closer, wrapping my legs around his waist.

I knew he could feel how wet I was for him. I felt it on my thighs. He positioned one hand a little above my head on the mirror attached to the dresser, and grasped my thigh with the other.

"He's either dead already, or, the more likely option," he slowly pushed inside me, capturing my low groan in his mouth, "he's going to drown in his own blood as it fills up his lungs."

He began to fuck me, biting down hard on my shoulder. I grasped that perfect, toned ass of his, beggin him to go deeper.

Liftin his hand, he grabbed my neck and slammed me backward, never losing his momentum. Somethin fell off the dresser, breaking as it hit the floor.

I heard the mirror crack and slowly splinter due to the

force of our bodies movin together. The first shard fell soon after.

"Ow," I hissed, feelin an exposed edge dig into my skin.

I instinctively moved forward, but Grimm shoved me back, holding me in place.

"Grimm—" I began, feelin the blood trickle down my flesh.

He grabbed my wrists tightly, stretching them above my head, pinning them to the broken mirror before saying, "Shut the fuck up and take it."

The deviant, savage look in his eyes had me doin just that.

He drove in and out of me relentlessly, stretching me, destroying me. The louder I cried out, the harder he fucked me. He didn't slowly take me to the edge; he shoved me over it again and again.

I came so much my eyes leaked tears. There was no relief, just steady constant tension and my pussy contracting around him. The pleasure shredded me.

I began struggling to catch my breath.

He lifted me up and carried me to bed, droppin me down bloody back and all, ridin my body the rest of the night.

Chapter Twenty-Seven

Arlen

The remaining days leading up to the meeting were perfect; the day of the meetin, things kinda went to shit.

The damn thing only lasted maybe twenty minutes. Five of those were spent in silence, ten roughly in shock; the other ten were brief negations and high emotions.

Vitus arrived punctually—eleven in the morning, to be exact.

He wasn't the problem, though. Well, he was, but not in the way I would've thought.

He came with information and confidence.

I sat beside Grimm in the dining room, our delegated meetin spot. Cali was beside me, and Romero was at the head of the table.

Acolytes stood on the offense and defense, watching for the slightest hint of a threat from him or any of the four men he'd brought along.

By the smile on his face, I should've known this wasn't going to be a great conversation.

"I gave you three men and didn't ask for anything in return. All I'm asking for now is an alliance."

The silence after that stretched for a full five minutes.

"Why the fuck would I form an alliance with you?"

"Because I'm going to go out on a limb and say you want to destroy Centriole as badly as I do. And I don't want any part of your empire. I just want an alliance with it."

"Keep going," Cali said, waving her hand in the air.

"There's not much to it. They have someone inside the prison I want back."

Romero laughed, scrubbing a hand over his face. "Are you shitting me? Did you think I'd help you out of the kindness of my heart?"

"No, but if you really do consider these lovely people at this table your family, you'll do it for your niece or nephew."

I shifted; Grimm reached over and took my hand. Sittin here staring at Vitus' smiling fuckin face made me feel as if daddy long legs were all over my skin.

"You're not making much sense, Vitus. Spit it, out or get the fuck out of my house." Romero stood up, clearly ready to be done with this.

"See, that's why I like you, Romero. You're a take no shit kinda guy. I have a few planters inside that can help us when you accept my alliance.

"We had Beth with us, and came to find out," he leaned back dramatically, "she was pregnant, by Cobra. And if one of you wants to dispute that, it's understandable. But she said he was the last man to touch her before we got her. My dad was going to use the kid as leverage himself when the mayor didn't come through with his end of their deal.

"She ran away, got herself caught up with some people

who knew some people and, you can guess why her being back inside Centriole would be relevant to any of you."

What. The. Fuck?

No one said a word. I thought the bitch was dead, and now here she may be, pregnant with my niece or nephew? By fuckin Cobra, of all people? *Our* Cobra.?

"If any of that is remotely true—that's a real huge *if* by the way—then why was he hunting down Arlen?" Cali asked, not missing a beat.

"Well, probably because he doesn't believe Cobra would care enough about his kid to claim it. And then, he'd still need leverage.

"We all know he isn't going to let a little savage from the Badlands knowingly grow up in his precious city, especially if his daddy is a heathen.

"Don't believe me, tell me go fuck myself. All you need is a simple DNA test. Actually," Vitus hummed thoughtfully, "*that* right there is our leverage against him. Keep him happy and out of our hair for a little while. If you think that's *all* I know, it isn't. But I have to have some leverage of my own. *Just* in case." He stared dead straight at Romero, and I got the inkling that wasn't all for show.

What the fuck else could there be outside of that? Goddamn Romero in all his secrecy. I glanced around when no one said anything.

Cobra had a completely unreadable expression on his face, and Grimm looked slightly irritated.

None of them were surprised my sister could be carryin his kid. To be frank, neither was I. I just didn't want to imagine the conception.

"What do you want?" Romero finally asked.

"I don't—"

"What the fuck do you want; only a dumbass would walk out of here without securing a guarantee."

Vitus waited a beat, then another.

"Give me the girl with the blue hair."

What?

"Fuck that," Cali said at the same time Romero said, "Done."

"You can't fucking do that, Rome!" Cali yelled, pushing back from the table.

"I have to."

"What does that even mean?" I snapped.

"We can't just send her with him, Rome." Cobra interjected, runnin a hand through his hair.

Romero ignored that at first, walking into the kitchen. "You don't pick pussy over your fucking kid. We both know how high the chances are of the little shit being yours."

"Why the hell do you care, anyway? You specifically told me you didn't want Blue."

Course, it was at that moment Blue herself was dragged down the stairs, Katya right behind her.

She was like an open book. She looked hurt, a little pissed, and then she saw Vitus and seemed to fit the pieces of what was going on together.

"What is happening?" Katya asked, placing a protective arm around Blue, just to be pulled away by an acolyte.

"Blue is going to spend some time with Vitus," Romero replied.

At his words, Blue immediately took a step back, but the acolytes prevented her from going anywhere.

"Please don't make me do this," she pleaded softly. Her struggle played out on her face when tears broke free.

I think my heart broke more because she didn't try to

fight. She accepted her circumstance with a swallow and a tense nod.

Katya, on the other hand, was down on the floor like a damn wildcat, bein restrained by the acolytes and cryin and yellin curse words in her native tongue. But she was the only one.

It was calmly veiled chaos.

"I like you already," Vitus grinned victoriously when Blue took his hand.

Cali stood beside me, as helpless as I was. I think the saddest part of all this was that Romero was right. He *always* was.

"It's okay, I've been through this before," Blue told me on a near whisper, forcing a sad smile.

That didn't make it okay. That made it worse. I stepped forward to say somethin, but Grimm pulled me back.

"Wait," Romero said, walking towards them. He walked right up to Blue with something in his hand. By time any of us knew what it was, he was pressing it into the side of her neck. She cried out and instantly tried to jerk away. He was movin away again as fast as he'd gotten to her. A large red welt was now visible on her flesh.

"What the hell, man?" Vitus asked, actually lookin concerned.

"I just marked her. She's one of ours. I want her back *alive*."

"I'll be in touch," Vitus said, not looking pleased by that at all. He took her anyway, gently still. His men followed him out, and that was it.

Romero held a hand up for silence. "Before any of you say anything else fucking stupid and insult my intelligence, Grimm seemed to be the only one who trusted me enough to know what I was doing. If you think

I was suddenly caught off guard, you're as stupid as Vitus is." That was his fuck off speech, I assumed.

He left too, taking Cali with him.

Cobra helped Katya up where the acolytes had left her and helped her back upstairs. If it weren't for the heaviness in the air, it'd almost be like all of it never happened.

Chapter Twenty-Eight

Arlen

He hadn't left his room in hours.

Katya was on the patio staring at the remains of Noah, which meant he was alone.

We walked down the hall, and paused outside his door. Cali found her balls before I could. She knocked twice, and then walked right in, leavin me to follow.

"Wow," I murmured the second I entered. "I forgot how different his room was from the rest."

"He likes color," Cali shrugged, making her way to his bed.

Cobra's room was done up in blues, yellows, and a dark green. It looked like somewhere someone royal would reside.

Hearin the shower water runnin, and unsure how long he would be, I followed Cali's lead.

Grimm and Romero had gone on some secretive as hell run an hour after Vitus left and had yet to return. The fact

Cobra stayed behind let me know he was feelin some kind of way, which was to be expected, but he didn't have to do it alone.

I settled beside Cali on his bed, fluffing one of the gigantic pillows.

"Do you know how many come stains we're lying in right now?" Cali asked, staring at the ceiling.

"For real? Ew, shut up," I laughed, playfully pushin her shoulder.

"Damn, I'm thinking I should stay home more often," Cobra said, walking into the room with nothing but a towel around his waist, and his red hair a shade darker from his shower.

Cali and I shared a quick glance with one another after focusing on his body longer than necessary.

Cobra wasn't as bulked up as Romero or Grimm, but he made up for it with toned definition and colored tattoos.

"Stop givin me those incestuous looks." He pretended to shield himself from us.

I rolled my eyes. "Put some damn drawers on, and then come sit with us," I sighed.

"We came for moral support. However you need it," Cali added.

Without responding to us, he went to his dresser and retrieved some briefs. He respectfully added a layer of black sweats before crawling between us, smellin strongly of male body-wash.

The three of us sat with our backs against his headboard in absolute silence for a few minutes.

"Do you wanna talk about?" I asked, knowin Cali wouldn't.

He took my hand and then Cali's, just holdin them for

comfort. It dawned on me the longer we sat without sayin a word that he was lonely too.

"I fucked up," he finally said.

"We all fuck up, Cobra, that's life," Cali replied, placing his hand on her bump.

"But I really fucked up. I might have a kid, and now Blue is…Romero knew," he finished, confusing me and Cali both.

He puffed his cheeks up, and then let out a noisy stream of air. His silver eyes stared off blankly into space as he got lost in whatever was goin on inside his head.

I had an inklin he liked Blue much more than he'd let on, because Cobra killed chicks left and right, and now she was with Vitus.

My stomach still coiled just thinkin of his name. Throw a potential baby by my scandalous bitch of a sister into the mix, and I couldn't imagine how the man felt.

Beth deserved everythin she had comin to her, in my opinion. We didn't have a full disclosure about everythin yet, but we would. And if this turned out to be true, I'd be damned if I let the only untainted member of my family be used as a pawn in war.

"We've all been through the ringer, Cobra. And if you do have a kid, so what? You know we won't let anything happen. Fuck Beth. We'll bring him or her home, and that kid's going to have the best fucking life ever. You have to remember you aren't alone. Blue's going to be okay. You're going to be okay, too," Cali said.

I nodded my head, agreeing with her every word.

Romero and Cali had gone through hell.

Grimm and I had gone through hell.

Now, it was Cobra's turn.

Grimm

Did it seem like we would have trouble in paradise?

Sure as fuck did.

The Savages, though…

We're a family, blood or not, and every family goes through shit from time to time.

We were back on track a week later, trying to figure out the best course of action. Vitus had been right.

The DNA test was the best option to get Frank, the mayor, to back the fuck off.

And so life went on.

My life, specifically.

I grinned up at Brat, and she smiled back.

She loosened her fatal grip on my hair, urging me to come higher.

Not bothering to wipe my face, I rose up and rested

between her spread legs. I lightly trailed my fingers over the bruises on her neck.

She'd got her little ass shitfaced off hooch. If I thought Brat was a pain-slut sober, her drunk was a whole new fucking animal.

Last night was a special occasion. Brat took her initiation like a champ, rode me like a pro, goat blood and all, until I took over. My aching balls and happy dick agreed I'd made the right decision. I craved to make her pussy bleed.

"Tell me how happy I make you," I demanded.

She leaned up, licking her arousal clean off my face, beard and all. "You're gonna milk this forever, aren't ya?" she asked with a laugh.

"I can't put into any more words how happy you've made me. Tell me how happy I make you."

"You just fed me some delicious pussy for breakfast, and let me put a ball and chain on your finger; I'm very fucking happy, Brat."

She grinned at her diamond, and looked up at me with full adoration. Every time she gave me her eyes, I loved her hellion ass a little more.

The most damaged parts of her soul still shone strong enough to give me a peace I'd never known. That fucking brimstone flaring inside her would forever be my altar to worship.

She was mercy. I was death.

She'd always be Sally. I'd be her Jack.

A goddess like Persephone, to a dark lord like Hades.

Queen of death.

Queen of me.

For always.

Arlen

Death came to me in the form of a man.

He replaced the halo that had fallen from my head with a crown forged of bone, blood, and desert roses.

He gave me life, but didn't know it yet.

Looking back at the path I'd walked, I couldn't believe the woman I'd become, but she was someone I could be proud of. This whole journey was like watching a movie on the big screen.

I sat on the couch with Cali and Katya, relaxing for the final weeks before our lives turned chaotic again.

Across the room stood a man straight out of the darkest of nightmares, and in his arms was a small bundle wrapped in pink. She was our key source of happiness, it seemed, a temporary stress reliever to hold onto for a few moments.

He looked up at me with joy in his eyes as he gently handed her to Cobra. Romero, the bulldog of a dad he was, stood hovering over their shoulders.

I wasn't sure of the precise moment this gorgeous man had come to mean *so* much to me. I think he had had me at the first choke-hold. It just took some time to get the wind in our sails.

He was an angry gray cloud, hovering over my head, just out of a reach. And then the drizzle started, but I didn't think much of it, because a little rain wasn't that big a deal.

Before I knew it, he was a thunderstorm that was rapidly becoming something more.

He was as lethal to me as he was alluring—he was my Tartarus hurricane.

I don't know what gave him the right to sweep in and wreak havoc on my fuckin soul, but I was so glad he had, because he'd destroyed me in the most beautiful way possible.

He showed me how beautiful hell could be and all the wicked delight to be found in the dark. What seemed like a tragedy at first wound up being a blessing in disguise.

In this world, I was forced to change, to enter uncharted territory to find my true strength and authentic self.

What survived may not be kind, but it was me. As my eyes came to rest on Cobra, I knew that for the best.

It was going to take a helluva lot of bloodshed to make this right.

I had a feelin in the pit of my stomach that his journey would be the one that pushed all of us to the breaking point, and exposed everything.

We would win the war, but there was no guarantee we would all be amongst the living when it was over.

Bonus Epilogue

Romero

I had an empire.

I had my own personal hell right outside my door.

I had an army at my beck and call ready to annihilate anyone who fucked with me.

I had two brothers, a family that would do *anything* for me.

None of that shit mattered.

It couldn't touch what was right in front of me.

My beautiful, dark fucking queen was the best thing that ever happened to me. In her arms was my best motherfucking achievement.

Adelaide Deville came into this world six days early, on the sixth day of May, at six sixteen in the morning. Her hair was dark blonde, her eyes still newborn blue. She was quiet and calculating, already as beautiful as her mother and as lethal as her father.

There may have been an accident where the doctor ended up dead, but Uncle Cobra and a nurse got her out just fine while Arlen stood by as doula.

It was almost as if she was aware we were a week away from going to war, and needed to be present right fucking now.

Cali knew I was standing in the doorway, just watching the two of them, probably thinking I was there to collect my extra limb. She'd just finished feeding, now fast asleep on her chest.

Her hypnotic blue eyes met mine, and she smiled.

She still looked at me like I was the only man in the fucking universe, and she was still everything to me.

"You know you got this," she said as I finally approached our bed.

"No, Pixie, *we* got this."

Bloodshed is what we did, but she *was* right.

No one came to the devil's playground and beat him at his own game.

Heathens

COBRA X BLUE

Playlist

1. Lana Del Rey—Gods & Monsters
2. Meg Myers—Motel
3. Meg Myers—Numb
4. Billie Eilish—Bitches Broken Hearts
5. Selena Gomez—Back to You
6. Breaking Benjamin—Without You
7. Breaking Benjamin—Tourniquet
8. Breaking Benjamin—Psycho
9. Bring Me The Horizon—Mantra
10. NF, Fleurie—Mansion
11. NF, Britt—Can you Hold Me
12. Aquilo—Silent Movies
13. Flora Cash—Sadness is Taking Over
14. Marshmello—Silence
15. Pvris—You and I
16. Tender—Sickness
17. Halsey—Eastside
18. Red—Let It Burn
19. Juice Wrld—Lucid Dreams

20. Daughtry—It's not Over
21. Drake—Take Care
22. The Weeknd—Try Me
23. Shaman—The Devil in our Wake
24. The Fountain—Bad Omens
25. The Fray—Never Say Never
26. The Fray—Look After You
27. The Script—For the First Time
28. Eminem—Legacy
29. Eminem—Not Alike
30. 5FDP—I Refuse
31. 5FDP—Seasons Change
32. 5FDP—Will the Sun Ever Rise
33. 5FDP—Stuck in my Ways
34. Three Days Grace—Nothing to Lose
35. Gin Wigamore—Holding on to Hell
36. Julia Michaels, Trippie Red—Jump
37. Ariana Grande—Breathin
38. 30 Seconds To Mars—Rescue Me
39. Kanye West—Yikes
40. Troye Sivan—BLUE
41. Twenty-One Pilots—Heathens

Prelude

"*Fléctere si néqueo súperos Acheronta movebo*"

My world is cruel, merciless, and full of despair.

There are no superheroes, knights in shining armor, or handsome princes to save damsels in distress.

It's kill or be killed.

Man eats man.

Survival of the sickest.

Cannibals, gangs, and hedonistic warfare are what thrive in the Badlands.

I once fought every day to be an exception.

I had crippled wings and a splintered halo. My soul had turned a little blacker than I'd like to admit, but my heart was still solid gold.

I did my best to stay on a moral high-ground.

And then I met Cobra.

He was sin personified, deadly and venomous—just like his namesake.

We were total opposites, yet the only thing that could make the other complete. Our bond ran deeper than either of us could have expected.

In the midst of anarchy, as the walls came crashing down, we used one another as our reason to continue breathing.

However, hearts, flowers, and pretty poetic words our story is not.

Sometimes it's ugly, and sometimes it may hurt, but I would never take back a single moment.

We found our own version of paradise, only after going through hell together.

In the end, I was simply a blue-haired girl who fell deeply in love with a redheaded heathen.

Having been on the receiving end of that sound a dozen times, I knew it meant one of two things. Either he was disappointed, or his cock was content. Obviously the first option was preferable.

When we entered the room we shared, I took a fortifying mental breath, knowing what was coming next.

Sure enough, as soon as the door was shut Vitus' hands were on my hips and I was being turned into his chest.

"Look at me," he commanded softly.

I breathed in the smell of him, smoke from the fire and the liquor he'd used to fuel it, gathering my bearings before I forced my eyes to meet his.

Vitus was a far cry from ugly.

He was ruggedly handsome, well built, and had captivating greenish-blue hues. His personality, on the other hand, left much to be desired.

He brought his hands up and cupped my face. "You know you could be happy if you gave us a chance."

I covered his hands with mine and fought the urge to rip the damn things off, unable to form an acceptable response.

I'd never understand how he could go from the man who ordered a whole family be executed to a doting lover in five minutes flat.

It was more than a little unsettling.

"One day, you'll agree with me."

Not likely. What kind of woman fell for a man who acquired her through a trade? A man who was essentially keeping her against her will?

We always ended up right back at square one.

From the time I'd arrived, he'd made it abundantly clear he wanted me to be his in every sense of the word.

Sometimes, I wished it could be that easy, that I could wipe everything else away. I'd be protected from everyone but him. I'd have a roof over my head and food in my stomach.

I would have someone in my corner who gave a damn, even if the feeling was misplaced and he was a terrible human being.

If I had to pick a monster to love, I'd already done that, and it wasn't Vitus.

I was willing to risk the fear of being alone for the simple fact that I refused to settle, regardless of how fucked up this world was.

At my prolonged silence, he released a deep breath and slid his jacket from my shoulders whilst simultaneously lowering his mouth.

I shoved all thoughts of right and wrong to a dark corner of my mind, giving him the access he was seeking.

His tongue tangled with mine and I got another sigh. This one was content. As soon as I began to reciprocate, he used his body to walk me backward. His hands were everywhere.

I grabbed the back of his neck and kept his mouth pressed to mine. My shoes came off, followed by my cotton dress, leaving me completely naked with my nipples beading from the cool air.

He pulled back slightly, his eyes hungrily feasting on every bare inch of my skin. I didn't hide or shy away.

By this point, he'd already seen me nude on multiple occasions. I wasn't ashamed of my body.

Not anymore.

My stomach was not as flat as a board, but it wasn't a pudge either, and my ass jiggled when I ran. I had an ample chest, pinched lips, and big pale brown eyes.

So while I wasn't going to win any beauty pageants, this body coupled with the sweet and innocent aura I naturally emanated had saved my ass plenty of times.

I stepped forward and closed the small gap between us, but that's all I did. Vitus always led. He had a control problem I'd quickly learned to placate.

His clothes joined mine and we found our way to the mattress.

In a matter of seconds, I was on my back with him perched above me, eyes holding mine.

He ran his large hands from my ankles to my thighs, kneading the flesh with his fingers.

"No matter how many times I fuck your sweet cunt, it's never enough. I think I may keep you forever," he mused, spreading me wide.

His hand slid down my torso to my pussy, where he skillfully stroked me. Calloused fingertips ran up and down my slit, lightly circling my clit.

I sunk my teeth into the side of my cheek to stop a small whimper from escaping.

"Tell me how you want it," he rasped.

"H-hard," I stuttered around the sour taste that flooded my mouth.

"Good girl," he crooned as I gradually grew wetter, his eyes trained between my legs. My body was a traitor to my mind.

I kept my mental torment under lock, forcing a small smile.

He returned it with a genuine one, leaning low to brush his lips over mine.

When he replaced his fingers with his cock, I reached up and wrapped my arms around his neck.

With one solid flex of his hips, he was inside me.

At my soft gasp, a cocky grin came to his face. He pulled out and thrust back in, moving at a steady tempo. I didn't cry, didn't beg for him to stop or lie to myself about what was happening.

Within my first few days here, I saw firsthand what happened to the captive women when he and his gang were through with them.

Deal or no deal, I knew he wouldn't hesitate to be rid of me the moment I lost his interest.

So I spread my legs wider and accepted every thrust, moaning in his ear to encourage him.

His hands grabbed hold of my ass, spreading the cheeks so far apart it burned.

He rammed himself into me over and over again as if he wanted to break me apart. His groans of pleasure and the slapping of our skin filled the air.

I could do nothing more than hold onto his broad shoulders and allow my body to be brought to release as he found comfort between my legs.

Surrender had never been so painfully bittersweet, but I didn't have any other choice. I would do whatever I had to do to survive.

This wasn't just sex.

It was my lifeline.

Chapter Two

BLUE

He shut his eyes and drew me into his side.

A hand came to the back of my head, forcing my cheek to his sweaty chest.

"Sleep, Blue," he commanded.

I remained silent, my body language completely mute with the exception of my racing pulse.

I waited for his breathing to deepen, counting the seconds between my slow burning shame.

I wished he would leave.

My head was pounding and my eyes burned. I swallowed a few times and willed all the self-loathing away.

I'd been going through this since I was seventeen. I knew the drill, but it never lessened the degradation I felt in the end.

It's over now. You're okay. I soothed myself with lies, applying temporary balm to wounds that would be torn wide open again tomorrow.

His come was already drying on my thigh. The fact that he pulled out brought me little comfort—not when it wasn't one hundred percent failproof. It would be just my screwed up luck to wind up pregnant on top of everything else.

Not allowing myself to dwell on what we'd just done for what felt like the hundredth time, I preoccupied my thoughts with the bodies that had been cruelly burned in the yard before I was all but dragged in here.

There was so much blood, so much screaming. And death.

Acts of brutality didn't shock me anymore. I'd grown desensitized to it in a way that I myself couldn't understand.

There was emptiness in my chest where empathy was supposed to be. I wasn't angry or bitter, just comfortably numb. But that was only towards the acts themselves.

The aftermath was always too much for me to handle.

I knew I wasn't anything like the people I'd been living with the past few weeks.

The Venom were merciless killers. It was a gang made up of men and a few rough-around-the-edges women that had banded together. I swore their sole agenda was to wreak havoc on the weak for entertainment.

I was no saint; I'd taken my fair share of lives and didn't regret a single last breath I'd witnessed being eradicated from dying lungs. However, all similarities ended there.

I didn't kill for sport, and I didn't kill for pleasure. I killed to ensure I would see another sunrise. On rare occasion, I killed to protect someone else.

Propping my chin in my hand, I studied the man beside me, his dark curls, fresh scruff, and the soft rise and fall of his bare chest. There was a jagged scar on his right side that had healed with the skin slightly raised.

I wanted to hate him. Part of me did for what he'd done to Arlen. But there was a part of me that just..didn't.

I felt nothing for him, emotionally or even physically. I

just couldn't condemn him for being a vile person when I craved a man who was just as bad.

However, I certainly wouldn't miss the bastard when he was put six feet under. When it was time for him to pay for all his wrong-doings, I would be one of them who preached he deserved it.

Looking him over, I wondered how he could sleep so soundly when his daily life was anything but peaceful.

With a little huff, I slowly moved away from him, wincing from the soreness between my thighs.

The emblem on his neck—a snake wrapped around the letter V, a representation of the horde he belonged to—seemed to watch my every move.

It reminded me of a certain someone else, too, but I didn't want to think about him.

I'd done enough of that lately.

Lying flat on my back beneath the comfort of a sheet, I stared up at the paint chipped ceiling.

As I listened to the pitter patter of raindrops on the prison's rooftop, I reflected on how I wound up here.

I'd been pawned for someone else's barter with no liberty to object.

My fate was sealed the second the only man I'd ever been interested in chose my frenemy over me.

It wasn't all that surprising in the end, and I think that cut even deeper.

I guess I never thought I'd be in this position again, lying beside a stranger and feeling utterly alone.

It called forth memories that were better off exactly where I'd left them: buried in the graveyard of my past.

After another minute or so, my restless energy had me quietly slipping from the makeshift bed. I kept one eye trained on Vitus as I shoved my feet into a pair of Jersey-lined flats and scooped my navy dress up off the floor.

I cast one last glance his way before creeping out of the room.

Once in the hall, I drew a small breath, inhaling the pungent stench that always seemed to be clinging to the stale air, exhaling as I moved towards the restroom.

Vitus had taken residence in what was once the administrative office, placing the bathroom just a few quick strides away.

Voices in the near distance, approaching from the east wing of the prison, had me hurrying through the heavy wooden door.

I used my hip to push it shut and immediately turned the flimsy lock.

It smelled little better here, but that couldn't be helped. Walls that had once been white were now a faded, depressing yellow. Heavily dusted lights projected the same miserable color.

I quickly relieved my bladder, squatting above a toilet in one of the only stalls that didn't have old piss on the floor and menstrual blood smeared on the wall.

When finished, I made my way to the sink and studied my dulled reflection in the grime layered mirror.

My blue waves were longer now, falling beneath my breasts, and less vibrant, blonde roots were gradually beginning to make an appearance.

Eyes slightly puffy from another night of unrest stood out harshly against my alabaster skin.

Aside from all that, I looked as I always had—minus the exhaustion and permanent brand on the side of my neck, of course.

But I'd take being tired over being dead any day of the

week, and the symbol burned into my flesh had become my safety net in this damned forsaken prison.

"I'm okay," I told my reflection, speaking some positivity into existence.

I had a never-ending list of reasons why I should break down and throw myself a big ol' pity party. Half the time I walked around on auto-pilot, but I refused to become so hopeless that I accepted this as my end game.

Turning the sink on, I patiently waited for the water to travel through the rusted pipes.

A decent bit spurted from the spicket for all of three seconds before slowing to a dismal drip.

Cupping my palms to catch any amount of the lukewarm liquid, I did my best to wash up.

I started with my face, then my neck, and finally between my legs. It wasn't going to do the same job as the showers, but I never went in there unless Vitus was with me.

The first confrontation I'd gotten in was with a woman who came in after I did...and I can assure you there's nothing dignified about fighting ass naked.

A sound from outside the door, much like a woman's plea being cut short, had me pausing.

I shut the faucet off and strained my ears, concluding I was hearing things when it didn't come again.

I dried my hands on the hem of my dress and exited the bathroom, stepping out into the hall at the same time that a now fully clothed Vitus did.

Our gazes met for merely a second before they were intercepted by two of his men.

My attention went straight to the woman sandwiched between them. She looked half-dead.

I tilted my head to the side and furrowed my brows, wondering who she was.

She had a head full of messy brown hair hiding her face from view.

The clothes she wore, if they could even be called that, had a distinct moldy smell and were practically hanging off her emaciated frame.

She moved painfully slow, her blackened feet barely lifting off the floor. The men on either side of her were holding onto her arms. I doubted she could stand without their assistance.

They stopped directly in front of Vitus, ignoring my presence as they usually did.

When they began to converse, it was in low whispers, well aware I'd be listening.

He made a few hand gestures and then reached out to lift a strand of the woman's hair. He rubbed it between his thumb and forefinger before letting it fall back into a nest of tangles and frizz.

I didn't miss the slight intimacy in his gesture, or the way his eyes lingered on her face. This gentleness was unlike him.

I'd seen how he behaved towards plenty of other women since I'd been here, and with the exception of me plus one or two others, he was always unnecessarily cruel.

It was this train of thought that had me stupidly stepping forward without thinking. I'd barely gone an inch closer than I already was, making no sound whatsoever, yet the miniscule motion was still enough to garner Vitus' full, heavy-weighted attention.

I backtracked, blinking a few times to clear any warring curiosity from my face, slipping back into my usual persona of nothing more than a sweet, unassuming and naive young woman.

That's what most people thought me to be, anyway. In a

sense, they were right—I was pretty damn sweet. I was also the same girl who'd gutted a man while he was in the shower.

My inner savage was complicated.

I was a lamb, but even lambs have teeth.

Vitus scrutinized me for a second longer before telling his lackeys, "Get her some food and then take her to the showers."

They heeded his directive without protest, continuing down the hall with the woman still secured between them.

For him to feed, clean, and house her meant she was definitely important in some way or another. I wondered if she had anything to do with him and the Savages' plans to infiltrate Centriole, The Kingdom.

Judging by her appearance, that was a stretch.

I watched the three of them disappear down the hall and then looked back to Vitus.

He offered no explanation, simply staring right back at me with shuttered eyes before finally saying, "Come back to bed."

"Who was that?" I asked, staying exactly where I was.

"Come back to bed," he repeated. The tic in his jaw was the only indication that I'd just pissed him off.

Swallowing down the rebuttal that would raise unnecessary conflict between us, I set my pride aside and went to him with a mind full of intrigue and thoughts of a certain Savage once again bubbling back to the surface.

Chapter Three

COBRA

Popping noises filled the air as cartilage and ligaments snapped away from bone.

Gnawing on the inside of my lip, I let the rope go and watched his body slump awkwardly against the tilted platform.

Isaac, as his nametag deemed him, had passed out.

Again.

I mean, he'd also pissed himself and thrown up, but at least he was awake when those things happened.

I surveyed his separated hips and shoulders, dislocated elbows and knees, confirming what I'd figured out about a half hour ago.

This whiny fuck had been telling the truth. He didn't know any of the inner workings of Centriole or have a single clue about what Vitus' agenda could be. He was nothing more than a lowly employee sent out to monitor the power grid.

He'd been going about his business when an acolyte snatched him up and dragged his ass straight to the devil's playground.

I glanced at the clock hanging above the mini bar, timing

myself at a little over two hours. I'd tortured him for an hour longer than necessary—that wasn't too bad, if you ask me.

I gave a sharp tug on the knife I'd stabbed into the wood beside his face. The blade came right out, leaving a small indent behind.

Looking at Isaac, I debated what I wanted to do to him next. I could leave him exactly as he was, or end it all now.

His death was inevitable; whether it came in the next two seconds or in a few hours, making him wait wasn't going to change the outcome, and I couldn't care less about his pain.

Fuck, I *relished* his pain.

I'd always had a strong affinity when it came to making motherfuckers beg, bleed, and scream.

I needed the release that came with their anguish and despair.

It was my self-imposed buffer that kept me from analyzing the bullshit inside my head.

Coming to a decision, I flipped my buck-bone blade around and dug it into Isaac's chest.

Starting right beneath his throat, I made a jagged line down the center of his torso. He only jerked once, but that was more than likely his body going into immediate shock.

My blade was slightly dull and could use a good sharpening, which made me have to work a bit harder to finish my task, but I didn't mind.

I wasn't in a rush.

Me and Rockwell sang about someone watching him.

The longer I worked, the more my muscles relaxed. A sense of tranquility washed over me.

I couldn't tell ya when Isaac's eyes had flown open, because by the time I noticed, they were rolling around, nearly bulging from their sockets.

He made a low keening sound for a minute or two, and

then his head lolled. Isaac was gone, dead, and soon to be in a shallow pit.

Agonal breathing had his insides looking like the head of a boil ready to burst at any given second.

It was fucking fascinating.

Adipose tissue rubbed against my knuckles. The texture reminded me of the scrambled eggs I'd eaten hours ago.

When I reached where all six inches of his limp dick hung, I stopped and wiped my blade clean on his fuzzy balls.

I took a step back and admired my handiwork. Blood and fluid meshed together, dripping from the wooden platform to the concrete floor.

Satisfied, I shoved my knife in my boot and made my way to the industrial sized sink that sat behind the mini bar, passing different tools and contraptions on my way.

Everything inside this room was meant to cause pain and suffering.

Had I been anyone else, I would've shit myself the second I walked in.

Since I was admittedly a sick fucking individual, I thought it was all glorious.

I scrubbed my hands clean, shut off the stereo system, and made for the exit, leaving Isaac's mutilated body strung up in starfish position.

Stepping out into the empty hall, I saw the faint glow of a lamp coming from the living room and made my way towards it, shoes thudding against the immaculately polished hardwood floor.

"That guy didn't know anything," I announced, hitching a thumb over my shoulder.

"They never do," Grimm replied, offering me his jar of hooch once I claimed a spot on the sectional.

I gratefully accepted and took a healthy swig, sucking my teeth as the bittersweet ferment traveled down my throat.

Romero had yet to say a word, but I knew whatever deviant scheme was floating around inside his head would be shared aloud eventually—or at least the parts of it he felt like sharing. The man was notorious for springing shit on us at the last minute.

His dark eyes were fixed on the round screen of a baby monitor.

I didn't need to see it to know it gave him a clear view of Cali and Adelaide, his baby girl. Sometimes he would sit and watch them for hours. It was safe to say he was thoroughly obsessed with his family.

"So much shit has changed," he started after an elongated silence, tossing the monitor down on the cushion beside him.

Me and Grimm shared a look, readying ourselves for whatever else was about to come out of his mouth.

"It used to only be the three of us. Now our family is growing, and it's only going to get bigger. I need us to focus on securing our future. I've gotten a lot of offers for partnerships, more people want to be initiated, and I think it's time to expand the compound.

"Grimm's ready to have his house constructed, which means you should be too, but before we can do any of those things, we have to finish this. It's been long enough."

There wasn't a need to question what the '*this*' was, or how he intended for it to be finished.

He was talking about Centriole, The Kingdom, the city where all our problems currently laid root. He was talking about wiping Vitus from the face of the earth.

In short, he was talking about war, cuz that's exactly what the fuck was coming. And we'd be the ones on the offense.

"When?" I asked what me and Grimm were both wondering.

"We hit the city in two weeks."

"And Vitus?" Grimm asked.

"Let me handle Vitus. I'll make sure his end is satisfying for all of us."

His voice sounded as coolly detached as it always did, no evident tension in his posture.

Unlike him, the peace of mind I'd achieved minutes ago quickly fled, leaving behind emptiness that settled in my chest. My fingers flexed around the jar of hooch and I took another swig.

Romero and Grimm being the intuitive fuckers they were both noticed the slight motion.

"Whatever you're thinking, remember this isn't on you. Taking Frank out was inevitable. For Arlen, our new suppliers, and us," Grimm said.

I gave him a wide grin. "Aww, are you worried about me, Grimmy?"

Romero interjected with a smooth, "I am," leveling me with a look that conveyed how serious he was.

"I second that," Grimm added.

My brows slammed together, my gaze bouncing between them.

"The fuck?" I laughed. "Is this a feelings intervention?"

"If it is?" Romero tested.

Ah, hell. It was usually my job to lighten the mood and keep things from getting too serious. Can't say I liked where this conversation was heading.

"Yo, relax you two. I knew this shit was coming." I attempted to diffuse the tension in the room.

"You knowing it was coming and being ready for the

potential aftermath are two very different things," Grimm retorted.

Since when the fuck did he talk so much? Arlen was a bad influence.

I took another sip of hooch and then passed it back to him.

Swallowing, I searched for the words to say that would appease them.

"You two don't need to worry about me. I'm good, and if I ever get not good, I'll be okay, eventually."

Romero studied me for a beat and I knew he was seconds away from calling me out when I stood from the couch.

"Now if you two kiddies will excuse me, I'm going to hit the sheets." I rounded the sectional and headed for the stairs before either of them could get out another word.

I could feel Romero's soulless eyes burrowing into my back, right along with Grimm's.

He waited right till I was at the bottom step to ask, "And what about that pretty girl with the blue hair?"

I faltered, *barely*, calling him every kind of asshole there was.

"I know lots of girls. Gonna need you to be more specific. Maybe you should start in alphabetical order," I shot back just loud enough for them to hear me before heading up the stairs.

I knew she would be brought up sooner than later. I wish I could say I didn't give a fuck about what happened to her, but I'd be lying to myself, and they already knew the truth I had yet to admit out loud.

There were few chicks I cared about. Blue just so happened to be one of them. I couldn't pinpoint why, and honestly didn't want to try and dissect the details. I had enough to deal with without adding that kind of complication.

All I knew was from the moment I saw her in that shitty ass hospital, I'd known she was different.

It wasn't love at first sight, it was something deeper.

Making my way down the darkened hall, I pushed open my bedroom door and paused briefly.

"Do you need something?" I asked Katya, stepping into my room.

She was sitting on her knees in the center of my king-sized bed, wearing a barely oversized t-shirt. I knew there wasn't shit underneath it. I could damn near see the lips of her pussy.

They'd sat on my face on multiple occasions, I could pick them out of a line-up.

"That's certainly some greeting," she scoffed. "That's not how you react to Arlen and Cali."

"No shit. Arlen and Cali are by default my sisters. They've also never showed up in my bed with no underwear on. Somehow I don't think Rome or Grimm would appreciate that."

"Well, I've been waiting for you," she replied, running a hand over my comforter.

"Any particular reason why?"

I shut the door with my foot but moved no further than that. I crossed my arms and waited for her to continue.

Her eyes roamed over me from head to toe and a look came across her face that told me everything I needed to know.

Had this been a couple weeks ago, I wouldn't have hesitated. She would have been on all fours with my dick in her ass and her face in a pillow within seconds.

But as sexy as she was, I wasn't going to touch her again. If I continued to fuck her it would come back to bite me in the ass in the long run.

Her eyes finally met mine again and I could see she'd been expecting this reaction, or lack thereof.

"It's because of Blue, isn't it?" she groaned.

I cocked my head to the side and studied her.

"For her to be such a good friend of yours you don't really act like you give a fuck about what she's going through."

"What she's *going* through?"

Her tone of voice grated on my nerves. It wasn't right. I was big on loyalty and she just proved hers was shit.

"I think we're done here,"

"I think we should talk."

"Sorry, Kat, Grimmy and Rome just talked me all out," I chirped, kicking my boots off.

She puckered her lips and tracked my movements as I headed towards my bathroom.

"Cobra," she huffed.

I stopped and whipped my shirt off, then my belt. Course, now she was no longer looking at my face.

Her eyes were trained on my body, greedily drinking in every part of me covered in ink.

"Kat," I called to get her attention.

"What?" She blinked twice and her gaze snapped to mine.

"I'm going to be straight up with you. Don't take this personally, but my dick has caused me enough issues. You got a nice sized sample already. It won't happen again. I'm not going to fuck you tonight. I'm not going to fuck you tomorrow, and I'm not going to fuck you a week from today."

I didn't wait to see her expression or hear anything else she had to say. This was the nicest way for me to let her down, and a courtesy I didn't usually extend.

Any other chick would have been dead the second I was

finished with her—after some good natured fun in the play-room, of course.

I walked into the bathroom, not bothering to turn the light on.

I shut the door and locked it behind me just in case Kat didn't take me seriously and attempted to sneak in while I was in the shower. I wasn't sure what I would do to her, but it wouldn't be anything good.

She was beginning to show signs of possessiveness, and that's one thing I didn't fucking deal. More importantly, I didn't want that from Katya.

I'd been serious about hitting the sheets, so I sincerely fucking hoped she'd be gone by the time I was done.

I was jonesing for some peace and fucking quiet, but it wouldn't be for me to sleep.

I knew I was going to lie on my bed and stare at the ceiling until morning came.

If I did somehow catch an hour or two, I could only hope they'd be full of nothing but empty dreams.

I turned the water on to scalding and lost the rest of my clothes while I waited for the temperature to heat up.

When I finally stepped beneath the double shower-heads, I welcomed the stinging burn on my flesh.

It had been a long ass day. No, a long ass fucking week; time seemed to be endless.

I shut my eyes and rested my forehead against the cool wall, thinking over everything that had happened the last few months.

Course I knew this shit was coming, but Grimm was right when he pointed out I wasn't prepared for it.

I had no problem terrorizing people or painting the whole damn city of Centriole red.

In fact, I was looking forward to it.

I had no problem taking down Frank, the mayor.

He may have been Arlen's uncle, but he was a major pain in the Savages' ass and couldn't be trusted.

What I had a problem with was the fact that I may be a father when all was said and done.

That wasn't an easy pill for me to swallow. I always thought if I had kids, it would be with a woman I worshipped.

Me as a dad in the state I was in now? Shit was damn near hysterical. And with Arlen's whore of a sister, Beth? That was manically depressing. I had no issue with women getting theirs, but she had community pool pussy; anyone could take a dip.

I was ashamed to have even touched her. If my dick rotted off, it would be my own fault.

Then, there was Blue.

In the midst of everything going on around me and all the things I should be focused on, there was one unusual girl steadily at the forefront of my mind.

It didn't make sense to me on any rational level. She was the one thing in my life that was completely unexpected.

Fucking Blue.

Why did Rome have to bring her up?

Just thinking of her had my dick rising to attention. She was the prettiest damn thing I'd ever seen. She looked like she'd stepped right out of a classic black and white film.

But it wasn't just her looks that snagged my attention. It was everything else too. Her sad eyes haunted me day in and day out.

She may have played the naïve and innocent card with everyone else, but I saw what was beneath it.

Grabbing my body wash, I lathered it on and took hold of my dick.

With the pad of my thumb, I massaged the tip, bracing one hand on the wall.

Skimming down to the base, I gripped it tightly and began to stroke to the mental image of a blue-haired vixen with heart-shaped lips.

Her ample tits, the curves that accentuated her juicy ass, that milky skin, and those big, round fuck-me eyes.

I wondered if she tasted as sweet as she looked. How she looked when she came. What she'd sound like as she tried to scream my name with my hand around her throat.

It didn't take long for my balls to swell and tighten.

A low grunt slipped through my lips as my dick jerked, shooting a stream of come onto the wall where the water slowly washed it away.

The satisfaction was fleeting, just like everything else in my life. It was a shitty substitute for what I really wanted.

I couldn't get this girl out of my head. It'd been weeks!

I could fuck a million different faces and nothing would change. None of those people would be her.

I knew a man like me was toxic for a woman like her, but that didn't stop me from wanting to drag her ass over to the dark side.

I thought sending her away was for the best. For once in my life, I'd tried to do the right thing.

It was a little too late for me to realize that had been a huge fucking mistake.

If I ever got a second chance, I would do everything in my power to make her mine.

Chapter Four

COBRA

I could sense the tension in the air before I reached the kitchen.

Not the bad kind; more the type that came with excitement.

Everyone was there, with the exception of Romero and Katya.

"Mornin," Arlen greeted from Grimm's lap, giving me a smile that took over her whole face.

It was infectious; I couldn't help but return it as I made my way to the fridge.

I pulled out some freshly squeezed orange juice and poured a glass, glancing out the window above the stove as I sipped it.

Outside, acolytes moved around the compound, starting their daily tasks. With the black hooded robes cloaking their bodies, they looked like a bunch of black dots.

I had no idea how they wore those with the sun blazing high in the sky all day, but they never complained, and no one had dropped dead from heatstroke yet.

There was a first time for everything.

As I turned back around, I caught sight of Isaac's body being dropped into the pit in front of our iron inverted cross.

"Katya's usually here to ogle you by now. Did you finally tell her to stop throwing her pu—vagina at you?" Cali asked in amusement, drawing my attention to her.

"Yes, I did. She now knows I'm not interested in her, but can you really blame her for the ogling? I have a lot to admire."

"I've never ogled you."

"Ah, come on sis, there's no need to lie. I saw the way you looked at me the first time we met."

She rolled her eyes and took a bite of the bagel in front of her.

"That ain't how I remember it," Arlen said.

"How would you know? You were knocked out." Grimm smirked, kissing her lips when she glared back at him.

Changing the course of this conversation before it could go where it didn't need to, I sat my glass in the sink harder than necessary and angled my body towards Cali.

"How'd she sleep?"

"Almost made it through the night," she replied, beaming down at Adelaide.

She was crazy as hell, but oddly, motherhood suited her.

"Where's your other half?"

"He's right here," Romero answered, strolling through the open floor plan.

He went straight to Cali, placing a kiss on her cheek and then Adelaide's as he gently lifted her from her mother's arms.

Romero, like me and Grimm, was a good six feet, muscular, and covered in tats.

Here he was, cradling a swaddled up blob that had started sucking on its tiny fist.

I grinned openly at the visual.

"The fuck you smiling at?"

"Stop talking like that in front of her, Rome," Cali snapped.

"It slipped," he said unapologetically.

She shook her head at him, and Arlen laughed under her breath.

"You won't think it's funny when you're dealing with it, too."

"Brat's mouth is a lot filthier than mine," Grimm replied.

Watching them all together brought Rome's words from the night before to the forefront of my mind.

Our dynamic had been so simple with just the three of us and the acolytes.

Since the day they'd saved my scrawny redheaded ass from being a man's nightly fuck-buddy, we'd been inseparable.

Romero was the devil in the flesh, a damn king in his own right.

Grimm, well that one's a given. The man collected souls as a hobby.

And then there was me.

The black cobra tat coiled down my arm represented everything I was, a lethal monster of my own making.

The inverted cross tatted beneath my eye represented what I stood for.

Together, we'd built the foundation for the Savages, a satanic cult no one with half a brain fucked with.

But things had most definitely changed.

Romero had Cali, and she'd made him semi-human again. Grimm had Arlen, someone who accepted every immoral part of him. Our acolytes had families of their own.

I was still wrapping my head around the fact this pair of

assholes had found themselves two kickass women to hold onto. I'd be lying if I said I wasn't a tiny bit envious.

And right now, it was all at risk.

I felt I played a role in how we got here. Nah, scratch that, I knew I'd greatly contributed to this clusterfuck we were dealing with.

It was another black mark on my character card.

Personally, I couldn't give two fucks about myself, but this was my family, and I gave all the shits about them.

If I thought it would end things peacefully with no repercussions, I'd give my life for theirs with no hesitation.

I was the most expandable and the least likely to be missed. I was gonna die a painful death eventually—it came with the territory. At least that way, it'd be worth it.

This was the Badlands, though, and every undeserving asshole seemed to want a piece of our home.

Peace was a foreign word they'd never understand. They'd kill me just for the fuck of it and still come for them.

Inside the house we were as safe as could be. The compound was damn near a fortress of security.

It would take a damn big militia to get past the acolytes, but they weren't just people in robes. They were family, too. We couldn't risk their lives just cuz they'd happily die protecting our more than capable asses.

The Badlands was more than just the compound, though, and we couldn't stay locked up forever.

With Romero's kid here, Grimm's baking in the oven, and me possibly having one of my own, we couldn't afford to sit by and wait to strike out even the smallest threat.

Plus, the fun for me was in the carnage.

"I got an errand I need you to run," Romero said, drawing me out of my mental tangent.

He passed Adelaide back to Cali, dropped a kiss on her lips, and motioned for me to follow him.

The second we stepped outside, my brows shot up and I whistled. "Exactly what kind of errand is this?" I asked.

Sensing Grimm behind me, I moved to the side but didn't look away from my latest pride and joy.

The plum colored seventy-three Plymouth had been my project for the last couple months.

With the metal guard rail, floodlights, and beastly Maxxis tires that could handle anything, I'd created the perfect machine for Badlands terrain.

"Where'd you get the right engine?" I asked Romero.

"I need you to pick a package up from Luther's." He easily dodged my question.

"That can't be it. You didn't have to finish this for me to do that. You didn't have to finish this at all. So what's up?"

"Think of it as a bonus incentive," Grimm answered.

Bonus incentive?

There was something I wasn't being told.

I looked between them, getting nothing but well-mastered stares of impassivity.

"You two realize I know I'm being left in the dark about something, right?"

"Do you trust us?" Grimm asked.

"Is that a trick question, or just a really stupid one?"

"Right now, it's the only one that matters."

Hearing his somber undertone, I bit back my smartass response.

"I trust you two with my life."

"Good. Car's already loaded with everything you'll need," Romero cut in.

I didn't know what the fuck was going on, but I *did* know

that evasiveness would be all I got, the more questions I asked.

I also knew Rome never did anything without a reason.

I'd been by his side for years, and had only questioned a plan of his once.

Resigned and knowing I'd gotten all the details I was going to, I ran a hand through my hair and asked, "When do I leave?"

Romero's face broke into a smug grin and he held up a car key.

"Now."

Chapter Five

BLUE

A flurry of movement out in the yard caught my attention.

Three dogs were feasting on a carcass. They were too far away for me to tell what it was they'd managed to catch, but they were certainly making a messy meal of it.

Their muzzles were stained red. I could practically hear their jaws gnashing on bones as the animal was torn apart.

Shaking my head, I continued on my way. As I was passing by the old cafeteria, I paused again, this time because the woman I'd seen two nights prior was sitting at one of the tables.

No one else was in the large room but her; people never actually ate in there. The kitchen barely functioned outside of two faulty microwaves, and due to a rat problem, food was stored elsewhere.

I'd seen her the day before through an upper window, wandering around outside. The men had looked at her with disgust and the women had given her a wide berth.

The hostility on their faces gave away how they really felt. It was the exact same way they felt about me.

We weren't welcome here.

From what I'd seen so far, though, it was apparent that this woman had history with these people.

Whatever her connection to Vitus was kept her safe, just like with me.

The one thing I had that she didn't was the symbol on my neck. The inverted cross Romero had burned into my flesh was now a permanent scar. It made me stand out even more, but it also was my claim to his hierarchy.

I was technically a Savage, and that had turned out to be a welcome buffer. I never thought the mark of the devil would wind up being a blessing instead of a curse.

Unsure of how long I had until Vitus came to find, or sent for me, I decided to make my way over to her.

She looked much better than she had in the hallway. Her bundle of tangles had been chopped off, leaving a pixie cut behind. Her rags had been swapped for clothes that fit, and all the skin that had been marred with dirt and whatever else was clean.

She seemed lost in her own little world, twirling a spoon in a half-eaten bowl of broth. Her head turned towards me as I drew closer, and it took effort not to visibly react to what she looked like.

This was my first time being able to see her up close. The gaunt lines on her sunken face and dark circles beneath her eyes were nothing in comparison to the painful looking burn scars covering her entire left cheek.

I stared at her, and she at me.

Her brown eyes were dead, empty of light and aged far beyond her years.

In spite of her haggard appearance, I knew she couldn't have been much older than my fresh twenty-four.

"I'm, Mavi, but everyone calls me Blue," I casually introduced myself, sliding onto the bench across from her.

Noticing she was trembling, I folded my hands on the table in front of me to appear as non-threatening as possible.

Less than a minute rolled by when I realized my second assumption was just as wrong as my first.

This woman wasn't shaking because she was scared; she was shaking from the withdrawal of whatever drug she'd been doped up on.

There were multiple syringe marks up and down her wrists.

A light sheen of sweat was beading on her forehead, and her posture was stiffer up close than it had seemed from afar.

Dropping my gaze to her fingers, I saw the nails were chewed down to the bloody stubs.

This had Vitus written all over it. Drugs weren't something people had lying around. Those who sold them were able to live comfortably due to their high bartering demands.

The question that needed answered was *why?*

"Blue, huh? So you're Vitus' new dolly." The woman finally spoke.

There wasn't any bitterness in her tone; it was just a statement, one I didn't agree with.

"I'm nobody's doll," I replied evenly, more taken back by the harsh quality of her voice than the ridiculous label.

"Is there something I can do to help you?" I asked as her trembling increased to the point her spoon was repeatedly tapping the side of her bowl.

She ignored me, her eyes roaming over my person, stopping on the brand on my neck.

And there it was.

The flicker of recognition and a slight smile before it all faded into a look of utter sadness.

"You're one of the lucky ones."

"You think this makes me lucky?" I touched the bumpy tissue on my neck.

"They're going to take care of you. He's going to keep you safe. Safe. You'll be safe."

I gathered I couldn't converse with her on a normal level. Her responses were robotically monotone and curt, or didn't make much sense.

Still, I felt compelled to figure out who she was and what had happened to her.

I leaned back and decided to go with a different approach.

"The lucky people sent me here as…collateral."

"Me too. Tillie. Too."

Tillie? At that obscure statement, I found myself looking her over once more. She didn't have any tattoos and lacked the mark of the Savages.

I tried not to be vain, but she didn't look like the type of woman any of the men I'd gotten to know would touch.

She zoned out again, staring into her bowl of green liquid. Silence settled between us.

I waited to see if she would speak without my prompting. I never expected her to say what she did next.

"My name's Beth."

Beth….Beth…Beth…

My spine stiffened as realization set in.

"You…*You're* Beth?" I repeated, louder than intended, positive I'd misheard her. "You're Arlen's sister?"

"Half-sister," she corrected harshly.

I found myself scrutinizing her once again. She couldn't have resembled Arlen any less. Her sister was gorgeous and had an exotic look about her.

I'm sure before life dragged her through the dirt, Beth was pretty in her own way, but there were no similarities between them. Their hair wasn't even the same shade of brown.

My mouth opened and closed but no sound came out. I was at a loss of words.

Why was she here?

She was supposed to be tucked away inside Centriole, under strict guard.

Furthermore, she was supposed to be pregnant. It was my understanding that was why I was even here.

Vitus was supposed to be helping infiltrate an entire city to find the woman sitting right in front of me.

I honed in on her stomach. She clearly wasn't. But that didn't necessarily mean she hadn't been.

I'd been around women who'd lost all signs of pregnancy as soon as their baby was born. With Beth being in such an emaciated state, that could easily be the case.

"Did you have a baby?" I asked, keeping my tone soft.

She nodded her head slightly.

My gut rolled as I thought back to her condition the first night I saw her, piecing two and two together.

I asked my next question, knowing I wasn't going to like her answer.

"What," I started and stopped, "where is your baby, Beth?"

She lifted her shoulders in a subtle shrug and stared down at the bowl sitting between us. I wanted to reach across the table and throttle her.

"Beth. Where. Is. The. Baby?" I slowly enunciated each word.

"He's gone," she barely whispered.

"The baby's gone?" I breathed out, feeling a tightening in my chest.

Did gone mean he was dead? Or had Vitus simply taken him away from her?

I told myself I didn't want to know any details, had no desire to figure out what happened, but I knew I needed the truth.

Vitus had purposely built a whole agenda based on a lie, and I'd been swept up into his conspiracy. That in itself gave me the right to know what the hell was going on.

"Beth, can you make this make sense for me?" I twirled a finger in the air between the two of us.

Hearing voices, I glanced over my shoulder and spotted two Venom members coming down one of the halls. They were talking to one another, paying us little attention.

"Promise to help me, then I'll tell you everything," Beth rushed out, speaking normally for the first time since I'd sat down.

"What do you need my help with?"

I wasn't sure how I could help her accomplish anything when we were both wards of the same prison.

Her eyes were wild, darting from the two men, then back to me. "Tonight. Cell block D." And with that, she was gone, scooting away from the table, knocking her bowl to the floor, and all but running out of the cafeteria.

"Great," I muttered to myself, staring into the empty hall she'd retreated down.

I debated going after her, but thought of better it. I didn't want to draw attention to myself or overwhelm her.

The two men laughed at her expense. I remained exactly where I was as they passed behind me. From my peripheral, I saw them staring at me.

Their expressions were indifferent. I looked away before they could tell I was watching them.

The words "*Savage cunt*" drifted back to me as they entered the hall Beth had just gone down.

I bristled for a second before simply brushing the insult off. They could call me anything they wanted, as long as they left me alone.

I sat for a bit longer, trying to figure out what Vitus could really be up to and why he involved the Savages, continually coming up blank.

A prickling sensation on the back of my neck had me looking over my shoulder again.

I immediately spotted another of the Venom watching me from the opposite side of the room.

Even with distance between us, I knew the color of his eyes was bright green. His hair was sandy brown.

I had never heard him utter a word but I'd caught him watching me multiple times when no one else was around, just like he was now.

His gaze held no malice or lust, but something else. Concern maybe?

"Or maybe I'm losing my mind," I laughed humorlessly.

Rising from the table, I boldly walked to where he was standing, holding eye contact the entire way.

He was unnaturally attractive and not that much taller than myself.

From what I'd been able to tell since I'd been at the prison, he wasn't longstanding Venom, nor a newbie. He was somewhere in the middle.

I'd made it a habit not to talk to any of Vitus' men, holding down my role of naïve little Blue, but I was tired of playing the role of a helpless damsel. I was tired of not knowing what was going on around me.

All I'd concluded so far was what I'd already known.

Nothing was ever as it seemed. That could be the Badlands' catchphrase.

"Does Vitus have you watching me?" I asked the man.

When he remained silent, I looked up at him and quirked a brow as if to say, *well?*

He came forward, and for a brief moment I thought he was going to walk right into me. At the last second, he side stepped, brushing my shoulder with his.

He whispered something that sounded like, "*Ave Satanas,*" and continued on his way.

His steps never faltered.

Hope bloomed in my chest knowing those words were linked to Cobra.

When I whirled around, though, there was no sign of the green-eyed man anywhere.

For a second, I thought I may very well be losing my mind, but if I was certain of one thing, it was that I wasn't crazy.

If he'd really said those two words, there was only one person who would have sent him here.

It seemed Vitus wasn't the only one with ulterior motives.

Chapter Six

BLUE

There's the calm before the storm, and then the storm hits.

And it hit hard.

The sense of foreboding started in my gut the second I returned to my room.

It worsened as the evening progressed.

It was to the point where I considered not going to meet Beth, but really, what other choice did I have? She was my only hope of getting answers.

So there I was, entering a part of the prison that was unused and in worse shape than the rest of the entire building.

Weeds were sprouting through tiny cracks in the floor and mold was growing along one wall.

After flipping a few random switches, I realized the power didn't work here either.

Even with the moon shining down through a large skylight, it seemed ten times darker than it should have.

I stopped and searched for some sign of her.

If Vitus woke and saw I wasn't beside him, he'd assume I'd gone to the bathroom. It wouldn't take him long to realize that wasn't where I was, which meant my time was limited.

Hearing movement above me, I looked straight up and spotted Beth watching me from the third level of cells.

"I did it all for him," she sighed, her voice carrying down to me. "I left home, betrayed my sister, slept with strangers. I did everything he wanted."

"Did it all for who?" I questioned.

"Vitus, who else?"

I wasn't sure what to say to that, so I kept quiet. It seemed even the cruelest of men could be loved.

"We both want Zane," she added after a minute of silence. "Promise me you'll find him before he does." She stepped closer to the rusted banister.

I couldn't see her clearly due to the lack of light but I could feel her heavy stare.

"And where is Zane, Beth?" I asked.

"Do you promise?" Her voice shook this time.

She stepped forward again.

"Beth," I warned, understanding her intent.

"I'll find him," I lied, "but you have to tell me where he is first."

I didn't fucking know who Zane was. Maybe the baby? But how would Vitus not know where he was?

"Where is Zane, Beth?" I asked again in a firmer tone.

She abruptly turned her head and stared off into the shadows as if someone was there.

"Vitus threw him away."

It was the last thing she said before she jumped.

Chapter Seven

BLUE

A traumatizing smack echoed all around me.

I heard her bones shatter on impact. Her head hit at an angle, shooting blood in every direction as it busted open.

She lay twisted at an unnatural angle, a bone in her leg sticking all the way out.

What the fuck had just happened?

I blinked and sucked in a breath. I took a step back, and then another. Before I knew it, I was simply walking away. I wasn't sure where I was going, but it damn sure wasn't to Vitus.

So many questions assaulted my brain. I needed to get away; I needed a minute to breathe. The sound of her body hitting the ground would be stuck in my head forever.

A sudden bang echoed throughout the prison. The entire building seemed to vibrate. Yelling filled the air immediately after.

I rounded a corner and stopped, squeezing my eyes shut, trying to get my thoughts in order.

I'd been standing there for less than a minute when I was

grabbed from behind. A hand covered my mouth and an arm came across my chest, forcing me to hold still.

I struggled as best as I could anyway, blindly throwing an elbow back into a hard stomach and earning a soft grunt from whomever had a hold of me.

"Don't fight me," a deep voice said directly in my ear. My name's Bryce. I'm here to help you."

Immediately, I stopped and let myself go slack.

"I'm going to let you go now, but I need you to stay calm." His arms fell away and he stepped back to give me space.

I turned around and found myself face to face with the man with green eyes.

"You," I murmured, not at all that surprised. "You didn't have to grab me like that. What are you even doing all the way over here?"

"I can explain everything as soon as we get out. We need to go now. Stay close and keep quiet," he commanded.

Without further preamble, he set off at a brisk walk.

Unsure of what else to do, I followed after him. He led me into another portion of the prison that wasn't used.

We had to maneuver around old cots, a rusted toilet, and fallen debris. Every few minutes, Bryce would look over his shoulder and make sure I was keeping up.

I felt the breeze minutes before he led me through an old rusted door.

Outside, the shouting had grown louder.

"Come," he urged, picking up his pace.

I followed his lead, not really believing any of this was happening.

He veered into the overgrown weeds that nearly reached my navel.

I did the same, keeping up as best I could. I relied on the

back of his head and the moon to guide me in the right direction. After a minute or two, he stopped and bent down.

There was a rattle, and then he was standing up, peeling back a piece of the chain link fence.

"Blue!" Vitus' voice carried on the wind.

"Go, hurry," Bryce ordered.

I shivered, gave one last glance at the prison, and climbed through the hole.

Bryce came through right behind me. Wordlessly, he placed the fence piece back how it belonged.

"Blue!" I heard again, this time much closer.

"Now what?" I whispered.

"Now, we run."

He grabbed my hand and dragged me into the woods.

Chapter Eight

COBRA

I adjusted my facemask and looked around the dimly lit barn.

I could deal with a lot of foul smelling shit, but human flesh being cured wasn't one of them.

Luther stood beside me, marking items off a checklist.

Like everyone else, he was getting ready to transition his business to a new supplier, thanks to Romero.

I shifted my attention to where his niece was making quick work of a man hanging upside down from a meat hook.

She was about nine or ten now, and handled herself like a pro. I watched her carefully make the relief cuts on the man's wrists, chest, and neck to help remove his skin in large sheets instead of individual chunks.

When she was finished with that, she used her little blade and began to flay.

The man writhed in his restraints, no doubt feeling his skin being pulled off his muscles, and the nerve endings dying. His agonized screams were muffled by the dirty cloth shoved in his mouth.

"Where is this package I'm supposed to pick up?" I asked Luther, breaking my gaze away from the live display.

"It's not ready yet," he answered dismissively.

I looked to the ceiling and counted to three, searching for patience I didn't have.

He glanced over and shook his head, chuckling at my inability to hold still. "What's the rush? Didn't you miss me?"

"Need a smoke," I told him, ignoring his question.

As soon as I was outside, I lifted the facemask to the top of my head and sucked in a breath of cool air.

The temperature was beginning to drop at night, a sign fall had arrived at the Badlands.

Reaching into my back pocket, I took out my joint and a lighter. I placed it between my lips and sparked up.

I chiefed it three times and rolled my neck to loosen my shoulders.

The sooner I got whatever fuckin package this was, the better. If Rome sent me all this way to pick up a belt, I was going to kick his ass when I got home.

I was just about to go back inside the barn when I heard the low whir of an engine gradually getting louder.

Instantly on alert, I looked across Luther's property but didn't see anything. Not even headlights.

Someone was definitely coming, though, and they were moving pretty damn fast from the sound of it.

Shoving my facemask back down, I snubbed out my joint and went back inside.

Something heavy hit the rear door and the whirring cut off.

Luther all but shoved his fuckin clipboard into my hands, and rushed towards it.

"Fuck's going on?" I asked, watching him hurriedly undo the heavy padlock, keeping the rear exit sealed off.

"Your package has arrived." He looked back at me with a shit eating grin and pulled open the doors.

I saw the acolyte administered Jeep. Saw a sweaty and muddied Bryce.

Then, I saw her.

The unusual girl with the blue hair.

I was fucked.

Chapter Nine

BLUE

For once, I was thoroughly exhausted.

My feet ached.

My head hurt.

Hell, my ass hurt.

All I wanted to do was sit down and figure out what was happening.

Bryce was chugging right along like this was an everyday occurrence for him. Knowing who he worked for, I wouldn't be surprised if it was.

Only one of us was dressed for trekking through the woods in the middle of the night.

It obviously wasn't me.

"We're almost there," he said, looking back to make sure I was still behind him.

"I swear you've said that at least four times now," I grumbled.

"I actually mean it this time," he replied. I could hear the smile in his voice.

"What's going to happen now I'm gone?"

"Depends."

"On?" I questioned.

"It depends on how Vitus plays his hand. You don't need to worry about any of that. My liege has everything taken care of."

That was nothing short of diplomatic. I nodded, even though he couldn't see me.

"There it is," he said after we'd walked a few more minutes.

I peered around him and almost melted with relief. A blacked out Wrangler was parked on the side of a rural road. The sigil of Baphomet was embellished on its hood and the driver side door.

Two people in long, black hooded robes and white masks stood outside of it.

"Um…who are they?"

"Acolytes," he replied, holding out his hand to help me down the hill we had come upon.

I accepted and let him lead me down, not letting go until I was by the passenger side door of the Jeep.

One of the acolytes turned to look at me, but didn't speak. I couldn't tell if they were male or female. Whichever, it was unsettling to have their sole attention.

I offered them a smile and made a point to stare at the window until I heard the lock click.

I scrambled into the Jeep and swore I heard one of them laugh under their breath as they got in the back with their companion.

Bryce climbed in the driver's seat and quickly got us on the road. It didn't take long for him to say his piece.

"Romero sent me to Vitus a few months ago. No one knew where I was but him. Everyone assumed I'd been working at a skin farm."

"I wasn't around a few months ago," I pointed out.

"I was not sent there specifically for you. Once you became more of a… priority, the plan was readjusted. My duty was to gather intel, to keep you safe, and to get you out when the time was right."

I took a few minutes to process all that. I wasn't real ecstatic about the whole me being a sudden priority thing.

Romero wasn't someone I wanted to owe any favors to, but he was the reason I'd just gotten out.

Speaking of…

"What was that loud noise?"

"The foundation of that prison is weak. I simply gave one of the weakest columns a little push," he said casually.

I knew there was more to it than a *'little push',* but his answer was satisfying enough.

"You did all of this alone?"

"I wasn't the only Savage on the inside, no, if that's what you're really asking."

I nodded, wondering what else he knew. I assumed he had a way to communicate with Romero while on the inside to relay information.

"So Romero knows about…" I trailed off. Maybe I should have been asking what he *didn't* know.

Everything I'd come to learn about that man amplified how cunning he was, always ten steps ahead of everyone else.

"What he doesn't know already, he will know very soon. As it stands, my task is not finished quite yet."

At that, I looked down at my lap.

If he knew Vitus was full of crap, why make an alliance with him in the first place? If he knew so much, why didn't he do anything to stop what had happened?

As if he read my mind, Bryce dropped another Easter egg for me to ponder over.

"Vitus and my liege have a long, sordid history. That's all I'm allowed to say on the matter. He'll question you himself."

"He'll question me?" I gave a quick glance his way, crossing my arms over my chest. I hoped my voice didn't convey how uneasy that made me.

"Yes, once you're home."

"Home," I repeated to myself.

He had to be referring to the compound. Did I want that to be my home? I wasn't sure.

I think I was ready to get far, far away from all of this. The Savages, the Venom, people in general.

I wasn't sure if I was ready to deal with Katya.

I didn't how I was supposed to face Cobra, knowing what I knew now.

How could I look him in the eye and tell him his child was missing? That he may be dead?

I turned my face to the window and focused on the passing scenery.

My eyes stung. I blinked to clear the wetness coating my lashes.

My heart ached.

Yet, the emptiness I felt didn't abate. If anything, it grew deeper.

The first thing I saw was a pretty farmhouse with a wrap-around porch.

The second was the cheery red barn surrounded by rolling green hills.

"Where are we?" I asked, my voice laden with drowsiness.

"It's a surprise." Bryce parked the Jeep in the back of the red building and cut the engine, hopping out before I'd fully roused myself.

"I don't like surprises," I mumbled.

He pounded on the barn door with his fist and signaled for me to get out.

Releasing a weary sigh, I climbed out of the car and went to join him, stretching as I walked.

The rear doors of the Jeep opened at the same time, and I almost jumped out of my skin. I'd forgotten there were acolytes in the backseat. They hadn't uttered a single word the entire drive.

They walked off together, taking a path that ran along the side of the barn.

When I reached Bryce's side, he turned slightly towards me.

"It would be for the best if you didn't mention how the child demised," he said quietly.

His words confirmed what I'd originally suspected. The baby was gone.

"I don't know how he..."I swallowed around the sudden lump in my throat and looked down to hide my pensive expression.

"Then you are very fortunate," he stated somberly. "Tell him it was stillborn."

"And what's the truth?"

"That it was stillborn."

No more words were said between us. He straightened just as the large barn door swung inward.

I lifted my head and had to blink twice. I didn't notice the smell, the bodies, or the man who was practically standing in front of me.

All I saw was him.

The crazy redhead who kept trespassing in my thoughts.

His eyes met mine and whispered they were going to drag me to the darkest pits of hell.

My stupid irrational heart immediately responded, "*Yes, please,*" and I instantly knew I was screwed.

Part Two

Oh, heaven knows
We belong way down below.

Chapter Ten

BLUE

How can one look make someone feel so damn much?

It was enough to paralyze me.

It was enough to take away all the bad for a few blissful heartbeats.

However, reality refused to be ignored. Everything came rushing back, including the overwhelming smell trying to suffocate me.

"What is that?" I cupped a hand over my nose and finally wrenched my gaze away from the gorgeous man in front of me.

I honed in on a little girl standing by a bloodied man hanging from a meat hook, a friendly smile on her face.

If I was seeing things correctly, he was missing large pieces of flesh.

In fact, there was flesh everywhere.

Shelves were lined with jars of things that would give me months of nightmares. Metal tubs full of lye were dissolving who knows what.

I turned my gag into a cough and backed out of the barn, the stench making my eyes burn.

Cobra was quick to follow, his silver eyes completely focused on me, which only added to my complete humiliation when I turned to the side and nearly doubled over from a coughing fit, as if my lungs could spit out the foul odor they'd just ingested.

I was aware of the rear door slamming shut, and then Cobra's hand was rubbing my back.

When I was done, I awkwardly regained my posture.

"You good?" he asked, yet to remove his hand.

I sniffed a few times, relieved that the smell seemed to be well contained in the confines of the barn.

I gave him a small smile and nodded. "As long as I don't go in there, I will be."

"Yeah, it's an acquired taste kind of thing." He laughed softly, pulling his facemask off.

He removed his hand, too, and I immediately wanted to put it back. Then, I remembered everything that had happened and all the things he didn't know, and it felt like a vise tightened around my heart.

I took a small step back, swallowing when his brows furrowed in displeasure.

He reached out and grabbed my lower wrist to stop me from going any further.

"Cobra, we need—"

"Not yet," he cut me off. "I can see it all over your face. Whatever you're going to tell me isn't good."

"But I—"

He shook his head again.

"The first thing we're going to do is get you cleaned up. Can we do that?"

I looked up at him, really looked at him, and there went another piece of my heart.

He looked exhausted. His eyes were tired, but it was the

kind of tired sleep wasn't going to fix, full of a deep rooted pain; I hated myself for knowing what I did. I hated that I would have to add to whatever burden already crushing him.

It was disarming to go from uncaring to feeling so much of his sadness that it physically hurt.

"We can do that," I breathed softly.

"Thank you," he said, seeming genuinely relieved, me with an authentic smile. "Come on." He nodded to the walkway the acolytes had taken, and slid his fingers from my wrist to my hand.

A trail of electricity followed their path.

We walked side by side towards the farmhouse I'd seen from the Jeep.

The warmth of his body helped ward off some of the evening's chill.

I kept quiet, unsure of what to say or what subject to broach first. I didn't want to blurt out the news about his baby in a cold, tactless manner. That was too delicate a subject, and I could tell he was already in a decaying mental state.

I couldn't even summon anger to rant at him over his decision simply for the fact that I wasn't angry with him at all. He didn't owe me anything, had never promised anything, and if it hadn't been me, it would have been Katya. She wouldn't have lasted a week.

Think positive thoughts, I told myself.

I needed to take a chapter from his book and not focus on all the heavy right then.

"So you're my surprise?" I teased, desperate to shatter the silence.

"Guess so. Best fuckin surprise ever though, right?"

"Considering I don't like surprises, I have to say this one tops all the others."

"Hmm," he hummed in response.

We reached the farmhouse and he led me up the stairs, going straight through the front door.

I was surprised by how homey it was. The inside theme matched the outside. It was clean, cozy, and smelled of cinnamon.

"Luther wanted to make it as comfortable as possible for Annie, his niece," Cobra explained, taking me up to the second level.

"I take it Annie's the little girl in the barn?"

"Yeah. Don't call her that to her face though, she might try and kick your ass," he laughed.

"Duly noted," I grinned. "But what *was* she doing?"

"They're skin farmers."

"Oh." That was really the only response to something like that. I'd heard of skin farmers before but this was my first time seeing them in real life. Definitely wouldn't be one of my top career choices, but if they liked it, I loved it.

Cobra walked to a door at the end of the hall and pushed it open, nudging me inside first. It was a simple room, medium sized. It had a full iron bed made up with dark grey bedding, a matching dresser, stark white walls, and a large rug covered the floor.

The door clicking shut had my breath catching in my throat.

Cobra chuckled at my oh-so-obvious reaction. I could feel him right behind me. His presence took over the whole room. If I moved back the slightest bit, I'd be pressed against him.

"Relax, Blue. I don't bite. Hard."

The amusement in his voice had heat rushing to my cheeks.

"So damn sweet," he mused, now standing beside me.

"Not always," I confessed quietly, forcing myself to look him in the eye.

"Yeah, I already knew that, babe," he winked, not missing a beat. "Come on, bathroom's through here." He snagged my hand in his and tugged me forward.

The room flowed perfectly from one to the other. There was a toilet, raised sink, and a simple bathtub/shower taking up one wall.

"Go ahead and get cleaned up, there's shit under the sink. I'll go scrounge up some gear for you."

"Thanks."

"I'll be right out here."

I nodded and watched him leave.

As soon as I heard his footsteps retreating down the hall, I shut the door and let myself breathe again.

Chapter Eleven

BLUE

I stood in the doorway wrapped in a towel, brazenly staring.

He was shirtless, stretched out on the bed, ankles crossed with one booted foot over the other, a heavily tattooed arm slung over his eyes.

This man was beautiful.

His red hair was cut just as I remembered it, faded on the sides and long on top, swept back away from his face. He had a bit of stubble now that made him even more appealing.

His body was a wet dream.

Perfectly sculpted, sun-kissed, and covered in panty dropping ink. I wanted to trace each image with my tongue just so I could learn where one began and another ended.

"Enjoying the view?" he asked abruptly, turning his head to look at me.

"I um, thought you were asleep."

"That doesn't answer my question."

I twisted the top of my towel so it was tied tighter, and cocked my hip. "If you're asking if I'm attracted to you, the answer is obvious."

"And are those for me?" I asked, spotting a small pile of feminine clothes on a round stool.

He nodded, but said, "Come here," before I could take a single step towards them, sitting up so his back was supported by the headboard.

I went to him without hesitation, stopping right beside the bed.

He reached out and placed a feather light touch on my bare shoulder. "How was your shower?" he asked, dragging that same feathered touch down my arm.

"Amazing," I answered in a surprisingly steady voice. And it really was amazing. It felt superb to be under the strong spray of hot water again.

"You hungry?"

I shook my head from side to side.

"Tired?"

"I'm always tired, but I can never sleep," I shrugged.

He nodded, never stopping his trek across my skin. "Believe it or not, I know exactly what you mean."

He touched me again, this time starting at the hem of the towel, skimming his fingertips up the crevice between my thighs.

"So soft," he murmured.

My stomach clenched as his hand moved higher. I licked my lips and swallowed a shaky breath.

"Are we going to talk now?" I managed to spit out.

"We probably should, huh?" He dropped his hand and ran it through his hair in obvious frustration. "I expected you to be pissed at me."

"Well, I'm not."

"I can see that," he said, narrowing his eyes in suspicion.

I crossed my arms tightly over my chest and expelled a small breath. This was one conversation I was ready to get over with. If I couldn't have him, but he was happy, then that's really all that mattered.

In the end, he was going to need someone to lean on, and if Katya could pull him from whatever dark hole he was trapped in, I would stand in the corner and be a cheerleader.

"Just like ripping off a band aid."

"Huh?"

"Nothing, that wasn't supposed to be said out loud. Look, I can't be mad at you for what happened. It wasn't your idea, and you didn't owe me your loyalty or protection. Plus, what's done is done." I placed a hand on his shoulder and offered a small smile.

"Are you being serious?"

His face lost all traces of its usual playfulness and was replaced by a look I couldn't read.

"Yes…?" I dropped my hand down to my side and fought the urge to fidget. I hadn't meant for it to sound like a question.

I was more than a little mortified to be behaving like this. I was not a woman who got tongue-tied over attractive men or blushed from her roots to her toes just from them looking at her.

He made me feel like a love-struck teenager with a raging case of hormones.

He also wasn't mine. Something I needed to remember.

"So, how's Kat?" I cleared my throat and looked towards the stool, internally cringing at how peppy I sounded.

He opened his mouth to speak but I cut him off.

"I'm sorry. This is all kinds of awkward. I should prob-ably have clothes on before we discuss her. I already broke girl code by letting you touch me."

"Blue." He scooted over and patted the space he'd just

made. "I don't want you to put your clothes on. I want you to sit your pretty ass down right beside me."

"Cobra, I'm not going to have sex with you!"

His eyebrows rose in surprise, shock, or maybe it was amusement, based off the huge grin now on his face.

Oh, god. Why did I just say that? I could feel my face heating up.

"Well, that's good to know, babe. I'm not going to have sex with you either."

Oh.

"I'm going to fuck you so hard that you'll have a permanent imprint of my dick inside your pussy."

"Oh, wow. That's...creative," I replied stupidly.

He threw his head back and laughed. If the floor would have swallowed me, I'd have been forever grateful.

"You're bright fuckin red. Sit down, Blue; I'll keep my hands to myself. Scout's honor."

"Were you even a boy scout?"

"Nah, but I could've been."

"Right," I laughed, feeling a little less embarrassed as I sat down.

I was acutely aware of my nakedness beneath the towel as I settled on the bed, thankful it was thick enough to hide my hardened nipples.

"I think we need to clear up a misunderstanding. I've only fucked Katya once.

She's had my balls in her mouth twice. I'm not in a relationship with her. I don't want her."

"What? No...you two were together at the house."

"Nah, babe, not in that way. We messed around before you left and she...uh, gave me head twice in the two days after you left. but I never fuckin touched her after that. Now don't get me wrong, Katya is gorgeous, but she could never hold a candle to you, Blue."

I shook my head, unable to believe what he was telling me. "I…I don't even know what to say right now."

"Tell me I'm a fuckin idiot for letting you go. Then tell me why you look so damn sad so I can make you happy."

"I don't understand. If you had her, what do you want with me?"

"Blue, it was always going to be you. I just had my head to far up my own ass to know it.

"I knew the second I saw you in that hospital that you were different. I was tryna set you free.

"If you'd stayed, I'd have trapped you in hell with me. Thought you deserved more than I could ever give you."

His words cut deep. It wasn't just the honesty in them. It was him sitting there telling me he thought he wasn't good enough for me. I wanted to scream at him that yes, he was a fucking idiot for that logic alone, but I knew I'd never reach him that way.

"So you and her aren't….?" I asked instead.

"I may do a lot of stupid shit, but I know better than to fuck the friend of the woman I want."

He wanted me? My stomach somersaulted.

I pulled my lower lip between my teeth and focused on the area rug. Why was all of this just now coming to light?

"I'm glad we cleared that up. But where does that place us now? You understand I've been sleeping with another man almost every night the last few weeks?

"And we have to talk. I can't just jump from one man to another. I don't know where to start with all this."

His throat clearing had me glancing back over at him.

"Are you always this trusting?" he asked, looking at me.

"What?"

"I asked you if you're always this trusting."

"What does that have to do with anything I just said?"

"Just answer the question."

Confused, I searched his face for a minute to see if he was joking before I replied.

"I'm *never* this trusting. You're just special."

Something between a cough and a laugh slipped from his throat. "Been called a lot of things, babe. Special has never made the list. I think you might be alone on that one."

"That's cool with me." I shrugged and gave him a small smile, slowly starting to relax again.

His eyes dropped to my lips and he shook his head. "Too fuckin sweet," he muttered.

"If you can think I'm sweet, I can think you're special."

"I suppose that's fair, but I know you're not *that* naïve, Blue. I'm a fucked up person. I'm not ashamed to admit that, and have never tried to hide it."

"We're all a little fucked up, Cobra. It's not a competition."

"And here I was going for a gold medal."

"I know you're trying to be an ass. It's not working. You're adorable." I laughed. "But really, I have no issue with who you are."

"Huh, is that so?"

A small squeak flew from my mouth and suddenly I was on my back, staring straight up into a pair of silver eyes.

They were endless. Bottomless pools of pain, anger, and sorrow. I knew then that I'd happily drown in them if it meant I could make him better.

Offering help wouldn't be good enough. Even full of pain, his eyes reflected something fierce, primal, and utterly savage.

My mouth dried up as I realized he was letting me see him, completely, with no walls up.

It excited me, sending an adrenalized jolt racing down my spine and wetness between my thighs.

"Scared yet?" he asked, using a knee to part my legs.

"Nope," I breathed.

"Silly little monster." He leaned down and brushed his lips over the inverted cross burned into my neck. "I can feel your heart racing inside your chest."

And it was. It was beating so hard I was surprised he couldn't see it.

He moved his lips to my ear and nipped the lower lobe.

I swallowed a groan. "Did you hear anything I said?"

"Heard everything you said."

"So what happened to talking?"

"Isn't that what we're doing?"

"I need to—"

He silenced me by tearing the towel away and positioning himself between my legs.

"Nothing you tell me is going to change my mind about you, Blue. I know shit is going to be far from easy. I have a lot of fuckin issues and I'm guessin you do too, but we can figure it out. Just let me have this."

His solid cock separated by nothing but the fabric of his jeans rubbed against my throbbing clit, eliciting a needy moan.

He looked down and blew out a breath. "You have the prettiest pussy I've ever seen."

"Cobra." I reached up and cupped his face, smoothing my thumbs over his stubble.

Every solid, inked muscle all the way down to the V was pressed against my naked body.

I shut my eyes and tried to remember my agenda.

He hadn't even done anything and my body was on fire, needing him, craving him like nothing I'd ever craved before.

All the problems, all the painful truths, everything went up in smoke and it was just me and him.

"Look at me," he demanded.

I sucked in a breath and opened my eyes, seeing a hardened expression now on his face.

"I told myself letting you go was a big fuckin mistake. If I ever got the chance to fix it, your ass would be mine. This is the only chance I'm gonna give you to tell me to stop.

"This is the only warning I'm givin you that this isn't a onetime thing. I've waited weeks for you."

I knew something about that last part was significant, but I couldn't grasp it right then.

"Why would I need a warning?" I asked, genuinely confused.

"Because you should want more than a sick motherfucker like me to pin you down and shove his dick in you.

"I'm not a gentle teddy bear, and if you're going to be with me, you'll have to accept that. I'm a Savage. And that means you would be, too."

I threaded my fingers through his hair and made a spur of the moment decision I knew I couldn't take back.

This was insanity, I know. But I also knew in my heart of hearts that it was the right decision for me.

He was *exactly* what I wanted.

"So what happens after I tell you that I'm kinda obsessed with your strand of sickness?"

Something akin to a growl erupted from his throat. He balled a fist in my hair, slamming his lips against mine.

He stole all the air from my lungs, devouring me with a raw need. It was the most intense thing I'd ever felt.

I used him to breathe.

When he finally pulled away, he kept me in place with a hand around my throat. His eyes slowly traveled down my body, taking a second to admire my breasts.

"You're so damn beautiful."

He let go long enough to shove his pants down, completely commando underneath his dark jeans.

The second I saw his cock, I had to bite my lips and squeeze my thighs together, nearly moaning aloud.

My body was keyed up and desperate for this dark, brutal man.

"Do you want me?" he asked, stroking himself.

"I *need* you," I damn near cried.

I needed him to fuck away every trace of the man I'd just spent the last few weeks with, and if after tonight he changed his mind, then all I knew was that I never wanted to forget him. I wanted to touch and learn every part of him.

With another growl, he flipped me onto my stomach and shoved my face into the mattress.

He was behind me then, biting down on my right globe so hard I had to smother my loud yelp with a pillow. Next thing I knew, he was positioning me on my knees.

One hand came around and tightly gripped my throat, forcing my back to arch against his chest. I felt his throbbing cock against my thigh.

"Gonna fuck you now," was the only warning he gave me.

He slammed himself into me so damn hard I bit my lip and drew blood.

"Damn, you feel so fucking good," he ground out in a guttural voice. "Better than I imagined."

He rolled his hips, grabbing a fistful of my wet hair with his other hand, fucking me so brutally we started to move across the bed.

I got lost in the feeling and sensations of everything him. He fed me his dick inch by thick glorious inch, keeping his tight grip on my throat.

"Oh...fuck..." I panted, feeling my pussy begin to clamp down.

He was going to make me come from penetration alone, something I'd thought was a myth. His movements picked up. He fucked me faster, gripped my throat tighter, and pulled my hair harder.

"Shit! Cobra!" I screamed his name; every muscle in my body went taut as a ball of heat exploded in my core, flooding his dick with juices.

Another growl flew from his mouth. He pulled out, flipped me around like a ragdoll, and slammed back inside me.

He pounded into me harder than before, his hand still wrapped around my throat so tight I could barely breathe, and my eyes were beginning to water. I didn't dare tell him to stop.

I loved every bit of his roughness. I'd never get enough.

I could tell he was still holding back, and it pissed me off. I wanted it all. I wasn't afraid of the darkness lurking in his eyes; I wanted to drown in it.

I dragged my nails down his forearms and across his back, wrapping my legs around his waist.

"Fuck!" he shouted, lurching down to capture my mouth with his, pumping his come inside me and triggering a second orgasm.

I whimpered beneath him, my limbs turning to Jell-O.

We stayed together after he pulled out, his gorgeous eyes staring into mine.

That promise I'd seen before was back, knowing I wasn't going anywhere.

He moved off me and lay on his side, pulling me flush against him so we were in a spooning position.

He placed a hand on my stomach and gently massaged it.

"I don't know what to say right now," I admitted, my voice hoarse.

"Don't say anything. Just stay with me.

Chapter Twelve

COBRA

Fuck.

I'd repeated that word a dozen times since she'd succumbed to exhaustion.

What the hell had I just done?

I ran my hands over my face. My goddamn heart was still racing. Her moans were on replay in the back of my mind. They were going to be my new workout soundtrack.

She'd looked me in the eye and told me she could accept more, yet I'd still held back.

I wanted her again.

I wanted her in every fucking way I could have her.

She looked even more beautiful than I remembered, but that fuckin sadness in her eyes…Did I do that to her, or was I just now noticing it existed?

Could I fix it?

Fuck.

I needed a drink.

What was she going to do when she saw all my flaws?

The shit wrong with me wasn't fixable.

The pain would never leave. It wasn't physical; it was

constant mental fucking anguish, worse than depression, because there was no cure or treatment; it was just something I had to live with.

I wasn't sure what it was she had to tell me, but I knew from the look in her eyes it wasn't going to alleviate any of my current issues.

"You look like shit," Luther's voice carried from the kitchen doorway.

"Good evening to you too, fuckhead."

"I thought the girl would help," he said, coming to sit across from me at the table.

"She did—she will," I corrected. "I just got her back."

"That you did. Now you can quit being so damned depressed and moping around."

"Ouch, that hurt me right in here." I patted a hand over my heart.

"Do you want to talk about it?" he asked, turning serious as he broached a touchy subject.

"I don't know how to talk about it." My voice went dry. "All I want to do is make people bleed and cause a fuck load of pain. You know her birthday is coming up?"

"Yeah, kiddo, I know. It's your birthday too." Luther sighed.

I swallowed thickly, thinking of my sister and how full of life she'd been before everything fell apart.

Everyone knew loss. We'd all been through some shit.

I wouldn't argue that Romero hadn't had it worse than me due to the fact he'd been locked up like a fucking animal since the day he was born.

The difference between us was that he thrived in darkness, while I was forced to endure and adapt to it.

He'd never had to perform for a group of pedophile pieces of shit and fuck his twin sister until she came.

I remember cutting her body down from the cherry tree, and then being forced to put her in a trash bag.

They tossed her body in a creek and never looked back.

I was on the receiving end of their perverse games for a solid two years, until two dark-haired boys painted our trailer with their entrails and let me out of my cage.

"Is it sick that Blue reminds me of her?"

"No. I think that's a good thing. I think she's a good thing, for you. You didn't need someone like Calista, that's for damn sure," he laughed. "Why don't we reload the car? The sooner you get your woman home, the better."

"Yeah," I puffed up my cheeks and nodded. "That sounds like a good fuckin idea."

"You can go in. I got the rest," I told Luther.

"All right. I'll see you when the sun's up. You can introduce me to Blue."

I nodded and bent down to grab my duffel bag. I shoved it in the trunk on the side of a gas can, and slammed the lid shut.

I stood where I was and looked around the property. My

instincts had never once let me down, and right then, they were telling me something wasn't right.

Keeping my guard up, I moved towards the house.

I had just placed my boot on the back porch step when I heard the sound of shattering glass.

I spun around to see the barn catch fire. With all the chemicals and flesh stored inside, the entire rear end was covered in seconds.

The screen door hit the wall and Luther charged out in nothing but a pair of jeans.

"No!" I shouted, trying to catch him as he charged past me, but he was too fast. "It's a—"

Trap.

The word died on my tongue.

He made it less than halfway there when a fucking arrow zipped through the air.

"Fuck!" I yelled, watching it find its mark.

"Sonofabitch," he groaned, and stumbled off the path. He wisely turned to come back, grabbing for the arrow sticking out of his shoulder.

I jumped off the step and ran towards him, hearing the yells of his employees that lived on the property coming over the hill as they made a run for the barn.

They were a bunch of dumb fucks that weren't thinking clearly.

The barn wouldn't spontaneously burst into flame.

I reached Luther and grabbed hold of his good arm, propelling him to the house.

"You're not the brightest crayon in the box, are ya?" I asked.

"Fuck you. This shit hurts," he laughed, unable to pull the arrow out.

"Motherfuckers," I muttered when I barely missed taking a hit myself. "Who the fuck shoots arrows?"

Over the yelling and pandemonium behind me, I could hear the sound of approaching vehicles.

"You need to go get Blue and—"

There was a wet *splat*, and a spray of blood hit the side of my face as a second arrow found a home in his left eye.

Chapter Thirteen

BLUE

I jack-knifed into a sitting position, goose-bumps erupting across my flesh.

A quick survey of the room told me I was alone.

Hearing yelling from outside, I climbed out of bed and went to the sole window in the bedroom.

I pulled back a corner of the curtain and peeked out. Seeing the barn going up in flames, an unmoving body a few feet in front of it, and all the people rushing around had me jerking backward.

I needed to get out of the house.

Rushing to the stool, I hurriedly dressed in the clothes that had been placed on it, a dress and a pair of combat boots a size too small.

There was no underwear or bra, but I could worry about that later. All I could think about was Cobra. I had no idea where he was or if he was okay.

Leaving the room, I froze in the hall when a gun went off.

My palms clammed up as I forced myself to keep walking.

Before I could reach the end of the hallway where the stairs began, I heard heavy footsteps slowly ascending them.

Walking backward, I ducked into the first room on my right and quietly shut the door.

It had one of those knobs with a simple lock, but that was better than nothing. I pushed it in and took a second to figure out my best option.

This was a man's room.

The masculinity of it made that apparent.

Knowing I had mere seconds before the person on the stairs realized someone was in here, I began to pull open all the drawers for something I could use to defend myself.

In the bottom of a dresser beneath some t-shirts, I found a heavy black handgun.

I pulled the clip and saw three bullets. There weren't any other casings nearby, but this was better than nothing.

I flicked the safety off and tested the weight of it in my sweaty hand.

When the doorknob jiggled, my stomach dropped. Swallowing the excess saliva in my mouth, I turned around and expelled a deep breath.

Adrenaline coursed through my veins and caused my hands to shake. I did my best to hold steady and aimed the gun right at the door.

"Up here!" a man yelled a split second before kicking the door in.

I jumped slightly as wood splintered, causing me to pull the trigger.

"What the fuck?" the man yelled, grabbing the side of the neck where the bullet grazed him.

I gritted my teeth as my ears rang and fired again, this time hitting him in his stomach.

He placed his hand over the wound and hunched over

slightly. His black shirt prevented me from seeing the blood, but his hand was quickly becoming red.

Hearing footsteps running up behind him, I ran forward and shoved him out of my way.

He fell into the doorframe, still clutching his middle as blood ran freely from the wound in his neck, right over his Venom tattoo.

I didn't feel even a little bad about it.

Facing the woman who had just reached the top of the stairs, I aimed and fired my last bullet.

She dodged it, barely, and came rushing at me.

"Ah!" I cried out as she tackled me to the floor.

We landed in a heap. The air was knocked out of my lungs, and my head bounced off the hardwood. The gun fell from my hand as we struggled.

Getting a good look at the woman beside me, I recognized her from the prison.

She recovered before I did, bouncing to her feet with the agility of a cat, and moving to stand over me.

"You've been a real pain in the ass," she sneered.

I didn't acknowledge that ridiculousness with a response; instead, I did the only think I could think of and swung the toe of my boot into her pussy.

She hissed in pain and took one step backward. That's all she was able to do. Her head jerked and the tip of a knife popped out of her throat.

I gasped as Cobra made an animalistic growl and twisted the blade to the side, widening the wound before pulling the knife from the back of her neck.

She released a whoosh of air and blood sprayed out, coating the walls. I scrambled out of the way as fast I could, but it was impossible to dodge the mass of fluid.

I felt it on my face and running between my breasts.

"You good?" Cobra asked nonchalantly, grabbing my hand and pulling me towards him. His hand was sticky and there were bloodstains on his face.

"Yes," I breathed, relief coursing through me seeing he was okay.

"Fuckin A, babe. We gotta go now," he kept hold of my hand and pulled me with him down the stairs.

Two bodies lay haphazardly on the floor below, one in the living room and one in the doorway of the kitchen.

I didn't question them.

He led me right through the front door. Thick smoke and the smell of burning flesh filled the air, making it hard to breathe.

The barn seemed to shudder before a portion of it caved in with a loud *boom*.

I held onto Cobra's hand as tight as I could, feeling like my heart was about to beat right out of my chest.

We ran to the opposite side of the house where an old-school muscle car was parked and already running.

"Get in!" he called to me, letting my hand go. He made it to the driver's side in record time.

I flung open the passenger door and damn near dove inside.

I barely registered that Annie was in the backseat with a shotgun across her lap.

The instant my ass hit the leather seat, he gunned the engine and floored it.

Chapter Fourteen

BLUE

He'd been driving for hours and had yet to say a word.

He hadn't even looked at me when he'd stopped to refuel.

As the adrenaline wore off and realization of what happened kicked in, I wanted to blurt out an apology.

But that wouldn't bring Annie's house back or resurrect any of the people she'd lost.

I didn't dare ask about the man who was with her in the barn—seeing as she was with us and not him, I had a pretty good idea he was dead.

This was my entire fault.

I rubbed my cheek on my shoulder to try and get the dried blood off.

Every few minutes, I'd look in the mirror to check on Annie. She didn't look upset per se, but I figured she wasn't an emotional kid.

I was staring out the window when he placed his blood crusted hand on my knee and gently squeezed.

I covered it with mine and laced our fingers together.

It may have seemed like an insignificant thing to do, but for me, for us, it spoke volumes.

Neither of us knew what was going to happen today, tomorrow, or even two hours from now, but that was okay.

We would figure it out together.

Chapter Fifteen

COBRA

This was all so fucked.

I knew they'd be coming for her.

The second Vitus realized one of us had taken her, our alliance went to shit.

We shouldn't have been there.

Why the *fuck* did Rome send her there?

Luther was gone.

The skin farm was burning to the ground.

Annie was a fuckin orphan for the second time—though it's not like she fuckin cared. Kid was a bonafide psychopath.

I needed to relieve the pressure in my head. The pounding in my skull had me seeing black dots. I couldn't remember the last time I'd slept. I was an idiot for letting myself get this bad.

I looked over at Blue to see if she was still awake, and saw her staring out the window. She had yet to say a word the entire drive.

Without even thinking about it, I reached over and placed my hand on her knee, giving it a tight squeeze.

My heart flipped like I was fuckin girl when she put her hand over mine and laced our fingers.

I didn't deserve someone like her, but I sure as fuck wasn't about to let her go now.

Pulling past a sign that read *Polk County,* I coasted past a decrepit old gas station, an abandoned bank covered in graffiti, and a strip of stores well past looted.

Turning a sharp corner and narrowly dodging an old shopping cart in the center of my lane, I spotted a body on the sidewalk.

Their stomach was torn open and crows were beak deep in organs.

In a parking lot further ahead, a circle of men were beating the shit out of someone. They all turned, hearing the sound of my car approaching.

I'd have to tread carefully here. This wasn't one of our marked territories yet, which made us fair game.

Blue took in everything with a blank, almost disinterested expression on her face. It was a lot different than how I remembered her reacting to violence at the brothel.

"My name's Mavi." Her soft voice broke the hours' long silence.

That was random as shit, but I'd take it.

"But everyone calls me Blue," she added.

"Is that because of your hair?" Annie asked.

Understanding what she thought she was doing had me swallowing an amused laugh. It was sweet, though. I immediately committed her name to memory.

"Nope, it's because when I was a little girl, I wanted everything to be blue."

"That makes sense," Annie shrugged.

"What about you?" she asked, finally looking over at me.

"What about me?"

"How'd you get your nickname?"

"They said I'm like a cobra—deadly, dangerous, and kill all my victims viciously."

"Fits you just fine," Annie nodded, stroking the gun on her lap like it was a fuckin cat.

Blue's brows furrowed as she finally picked up on the fact that our tiny human passenger wasn't an innocent little girl.

Spotting the sign for the old motel I was looking for, I headed towards it, checking my mirrors periodically to make sure none of town squatters were following us.

"Aren't you going to tell me your name now?"

I swallowed and rolled my neck. I couldn't remember the last time a chick had wanted to know what my real name was. They were mostly just interested in being fucked by a Savage.

"Cody," I replied after a minute.

"Cody," she repeated under her breath. "I like that."

"And my twin's name was Carrie," I found myself saying.

I waited for the surprise and the million questions but they never came.

"I like that too," she simply said, tightening her grip on my hand.

Chapter Sixteen

BLUE

"Home Suites," I read aloud.

It was the first words I'd spoken since Cobra had told me the name of his sister.

Twin sister, I corrected myself. And he'd said it past tense.

I wasn't going to attack him with questions; I would wait for him to tell me in his own time when he was ready.

"This place looks like shit," Annie said from the backseat.

"It really lives up to its name, doesn't it?" Cobra joked.

I puckered my lips at her choice of words but didn't comment. The kid had a shotgun on her lap and seemed to be handling her new circumstance just fine.

"I need to contact Rome. We need to eat, and I have to take a piss. The man who runs this will let us use a room as long as we don't cause trouble," Cobra explained.

"Us cause trouble? Blasphemy," I deadpanned.

They both laughed.

"Sit tight. I'll be right back," he said, climbing out of the car.

"Do you feel safe?" I asked after ten minutes passed,

glancing in the backseat at the dark-haired girl.

"Do you not feel safe?"

"Right," I turned back around and crossed my arms over my chest.

The room was nothing spectacular.

It had two full sized beds, running water, and a toilet.

That was all the good things.

The television didn't work, the carpet was filthy, and only one light worked in the whole room.

But we made do.

I swallowed my last piece of jerky and stood from the bed, stretching my arms above my head.

Cobra watched me from where he was leaning against the wall.

We hadn't said a word to one another since we'd came into the room and he'd handed me some food.

If I couldn't still feel him between my legs, I'd have thought I'd imagined us having sex. There was an awkwardness I didn't know how to breach.

I silently went into the bathroom and shut the door. It didn't seem much cleaner than the prison's bathroom. The shower was a no-go zone. A nice sized spider web was stretched across the corner and the drain was completely black.

Sighing, I went to the sink and looked at myself in the pieces of glass that were left of a full mirror.

The dress I had on was black with little pink flowers, much lower cut than anything I'd normally wear, and hit just above the knee.

I turned on the sink and quickly realized there wasn't any hot water.

Hearing the door open and shut behind me, I glanced over my shoulder to see Cobra walking towards me.

For someone who hadn't slept in who knew how long, he looked as delicious as he always did in dark denim, black boots, and a fitted dark gray T.

"I'm sorry about your…" I trailed off as he came right up to me and dropped down to his knees.

"What are you doing?"

"Finding out if you taste as sweet as you look." He ran his hands up my legs beneath my dress and pulled my thighs apart.

"No, we need to talk."

"So talk," he shrugged, bunching my dress around my hips.

"Cobra." I pushed against his shoulders, my knees nearly buckling when he flattened his tongue against my clit, dragging it down my slit.

"Cobra," I groaned, threading my hands in his hair.

He took two fingers and pulled my lips apart, shoving his tongue inside my pussy as deep as it would go, slowly fucking me with it.

I bit down on my lip as hard as I could to stifle my moans, cognizant that Annie was in the other room.

"Damn, Blue. Your pussy might just be my new favorite meal," he groaned and pulled away, teasingly sliding his tongue up my slit to toy with my clit before plunging it back in.

It was enough to make me come.

"Fuck," I whimpered, grabbing hold of his head as my back arched.

"That's next." He rose to his feet, lifting me up in the process and walking forward until my back hit the wall. "Talk to me, Blue," he murmured, kissing from my jaw to my neck. His warm breath made my stomach clench. "What do you need to tell me?"

"Not like this," I objected.

He clucked his tongue at me and began to unbuckle his jeans. The look in his eyes damn near made my heart stop. He was not okay. And my body was about to be used to relieve some of his pain.

"Cobra," I breathed, grabbing the side of his face. I was desperate to get through to him.

I felt his tip at my entrance and prepared for him to thrust into me.

"Tell me," he demanded, grabbing hold of my throat.

"Please," I whispered, crying out when he bit down on my neck and slammed into me.

He set a brutal, rapid pace, digging his fingers into my ass to keep upright as he mercilessly pounded into my pussy. His cock stretched me, filling me to capacity.

I buried my face in his neck, forcing pressure on my throat to muffle my moans, burrowing my nails into his shoulders.

"Tell me," he growled, nipping my lower lip.

"Fuck…you," I choked out.

He jerked me back, knocking my head into the wall, forcefully rolling his hips so I had to take every inch of him.

I moaned wantonly, my pussy quivered, drenching his dick and balls.

"Fuck me back," he rasped.

With no more objections, I obliged and began to meet him thrust for thrust, tightening my legs to pull him deeper.

He dropped his mouth between my breasts and licked away the dried blood I hadn't gotten to yet.

Knowing I had to tell him sooner or later, my eyes began to burn, tears gathering on my lashes.

"The baby…stillborn."

I expected to him stop, not go harder. He made a sound in his throat and a dark look came into his eyes. If he thrust into me any harder, we were liable to break through the wall and into the next room.

"I'm gonna come," I gasped, opening my mouth on a silent scream not a second later.

He kept going until he was groaning, flexing his hips and squeezing my ass as he emptied into my pussy.

Both breathing heavy and covered in sweat, he gently pulled out and lowered my shaking limbs back to the floor.

"How do you know what happened to the baby?"

The rawness of his voice tears at my heart but I have to give him this truth.

"Beth was at the prison, she was never in Centriole. Vitus lied he…" I stopped seeing him walking backward, a look I couldn't read on his face.

"Fuck," he breathed, running his hands through his hair.

"Cobra," I swallowed.

He ignored my plea, dropping a kiss on my forehead.

Then he was gone, leaving me alone in the bathroom.

Chapter Seventeen

COBRA

I never claimed to be good at this relationship shit.

Actually, I'd never been in a single relationship in my fuckin life, until now.

Wasn't one for sitting around and discussing feelings either.

I'd always dealt with my baser emotions like rage and grief by purging lives.

I would have to go back to her and kiss major ass for how I left her. Right now, though, I was ready to play.

I fuckin needed it.

Luther.

The reminder of Carrie, which made me think of our parents, and now the baby…my head was a mess.

I hadn't even wanted the damn baby, but it wouldn't have mattered if I did because there was no fuckin baby anymore. I would have done what I needed to do to be a father. I'd worried about this shit day and night for what?

My fucking kid was dead.

Fuck!

I flexed my fists and rolled my neck, pulling out my buck bone blade.

I had questions. Lots of questions.

But first…

I rounded the corner, coming up behind one of the men who had been beating the shit out of the girl now lying dead in a parking lot.

He turned at the last second but it was too late. I was too fast.

Before he could even fuckin blink, my knife was slamming into the center of his forehead, splitting its way into his brain. I pulled it out and grabbed his companion by the hair, slitting the fucker's throat when he tried to call for help.

I let his body drop, adrenaline coursing through my veins like lava.

I tracked them down, one by fuckin one. Some tried to run; others were completely oblivious.

My mind wasn't on the blood, the screams, or the pleas for mercy.

It was on Luther, a childhood friend who had just become a needless casualty of war.

It was on my mom, who was beaten like the girl in the parking lot the day me and my sister were taken.

My dad, who'd tried to save us and had his fuckin head blown off.

My sweet sister who couldn't handle being in love with her twin brother, and hung herself from a cherry tree.

And that sweet, blue-haired girl I knew I could never let go, even if I didn't deserve her.

Chapter Eighteen

BLUE

The sun was high in the sky by the time he returned.

I'd yet to fall asleep, far too worried about where he could have gone or if he was okay.

My body hated me for it.

My muscles were screaming at me in protest with every step I took, sore beyond belief. There was bruising between my thighs and teeth marks on my neck.

He had a valid point.

I didn't look like I'd simply had sex.

No, I looked as if I'd been thoroughly fucked.

I gave up contemplating how a virtual stranger could mean so much to me, because the fact was he did.

We both had pasts full of pain but I was certain we could get through it, if he would let me in.

When the door flew open, I jumped out of my skin while Annie simply blinked.

Squinting against the sunlight now flooding into the room, it took me a second to take him in.

"Are you okay?" I jumped to my feet. He was covered in blood.

"Fuckin fantastic." He gave me a bright grin, flashing all of his perfect white teeth.

"You could have taken me with you," Annie commented, looping the strap of her gun over her head.

I shook my head at her. She was going to be a lethal woman. I could see it now. She'd let me braid her hair earlier and answered all of my questions in a tone that said I was boring her. That was the extent of our interactions; she didn't really say much.

She'd yet to shed a single tear over the loss of her home, or Luther, who I'd learned was her brother. When asked, her response was, *"We'll all be dead some day. His just came sooner. Yours could come today."*

That was the end of our conversation.

"Let me wash my face and then we'll hit the road, yeah?"

He looked right at me when he asked the question.

Aside from the fact that he was covered in fresh blood and old, his eyes were brighter than they'd been when he left, and his mood seemed all around better.

Is this what he needed to be happy? Blood and carnage?

What did that mean for me?

I turned away from him and nodded.

His stare lingered on me for a minute, and then he made his way to the bathroom.

When the sink kicked on, I walked out of the room, needing fresh air.

I sat on the hood of the car, leaning my head back to bask in the sun.

I felt as if I was stuck in a perpetual orbit, moving from place to place but not really going anywhere.

Cobra and I needed to have a nice long chat, because we would never get anywhere if we avoided all the hard conversations by twisting our bodies together.

If he could give me the rough sex and the man I knew he could be, I would never complain about anything again… unless he was one of those people who habitually left the toilet seat up. Then we'd have a slight problem.

Hearing the sound of a loud engine, I looked over my shoulder to see a large dark pickup racing towards me.

From my vantage point, I was able to count five men in the bed of the truck, plus however many were squeezed in the cab.

I didn't need to see their facial expressions to know why they were coming here.

Sliding off the hood of the Plymouth, I calmly walked back into our motel room, not bothering to shut the door.

I walked right into the bathroom, momentarily losing my train of thought at seeing Cobra's shirtless back.

The sigil of Baphomet. I mean, the whole pentacle, ram, and symbols. The word *sinner*, with a second cobra tatted around it was right above it. At the very bottom it read, *By The Blessing Of Satan.*

By the shading alone, I knew it had taken someone a long time, and the detail was amazing.

For him, this wouldn't just be a tattoo.

Like the inverted cross inked beneath his eye, they represented the life, the world he belonged to.

If we were really doing this whole *I'm his and he's mine* thing, then I would have to learn to accept that I'd be a Savage, too. And it was all or nothing with them.

"Blue?" he called my name, staring at me in the partial reflection of the mirror.

I blinked and tried to play off that I was just mesmerized by his back. "Um, did you maybe make some people angry? Because we're about to have company," I finally spat out.

"Yeah, we should probably go now." He turned off the sink, not bothering to reclaim his bloody shirt from the floor.

On his way out, he grabbed my hand. "We'll talk at home," he said softly, dropping a kiss on the back of it.

Home.

There was that word again. I hadn't a home in seven years; until it was true, I wasn't going to hold my breath that I was going to have one now.

I gave him a slight smile anyway, and followed his lead.

Right outside the door, Annie stood with her shotgun in her hands, aimed at the truck now pulling into the parking lot.

With her feet planted apart and shoulders set, she pulled the trigger, blasting one of the men right in the chest.

"Whoa! What are you doing?" I flinched, grabbing my right ear.

The man flipped backward out of the truck bed, his blood spraying onto his comrades.

I just watched a child shoot a man out the bed of the truck. All I wanted to do was wrap her in my arms and carry her to safety, but she was liable to shoot me too.

Had I met her before I saw her sweet angelic self skinning a man alive, I wouldn't have been as shocked.

"They aren't here to chit-chat, and you two were taking to long."

"Get in the car," Cobra said, urging me forward with a hand on my back.

I jogged to the passenger side and waited for Annie to slide in back before climbing in.

Cobra rounded to his side just as the men began hopping out the bed of the truck. None of them had guns, but they had everything else, from an ax to a metal slugger.

"Buckle up!" he yelled at us, shifting into gear.

The Plymouth lurched, jumped the small curb of the sidewalk, and then shot forward. At the same time, the man in the pickup tried to cut us off, clipping the rear end.

"Motherfucker," Cobra growled, looking in his side mirror.

"Have you learned anything about picking fights?" I asked, grabbing hold of the door handle.

"Yeah, that I should have brought you with me. Think we could have had a lot of fun." I saw his mouth kick up in the corner and bit back a smile of my own.

He swerved away from the truck, pushing the muscle car faster and faster to the point when he took the next corner, the tires burned rubber and we slightly lifted off the road, taking my heart with it.

"Cobra, I refuse to die in this death trap!"

"Babe, relax. I got this."

I stared at him ready to say something snappy, but seeing the exhilarated look on his face and his wide smile had me biting back one of my own. He was like a little boy with a shiny new toy.

"You truly are crazy," I said, shaking my head.

"And you fuckin love it," he smirked, reaching over to grab my hand.

"They're coming," Annie cut in, sounding all the way over our bullshit.

He whipped the wheel right, left, and then right again, taking us out of the city that looked ready to crumble at any minute.

I saw the sign that said *Now leaving Polk County.*

Blocking our exit was a man sitting on what looked like a moped.

I glanced at Cobra when I felt the Plymouth gaining speed instead of slowing down.

"You're not going to hit him, are you?"

I pretty much knew the answer and was already double checking my seatbelt, but figured it didn't hurt to ask.

"Of course not," he scoffed. "I'm just gonna move him out of the way."

"You're going to mess the car up," Annie said, sounding worried for the first time.

"Nah, why do you think I put the guard rail on it?"

Neither of us had time to respond. The man actually tried to move, but it was too late. His tiny bike began to roll forward, but the front of the car was already smashing into him.

His bike went down and he came up, rolling right over the guard wheel and on to the hood.

Cobra hit the brakes and he flew off, hitting the ground like a pile of bricks. He never stood a chance.

Cobra hit the gas again and rolled right over him, a sickening crunch and inhuman scream following in our wake.

I glanced in the side mirror and saw he'd become one with the asphalt, hardly recognizable as a person.

"You fuckin see that?" Cobra whooped, glancing in his rearview.

"I will never ride in a car with you again," I breathed, thanking the powers above we were all still in one piece.

"I'd never let anything happen to you, Blue. Ever. You're safe with me." He looked over at me and smiled.

Losing another piece of my heart, this time for something worth it, I smiled back.

Chapter Nineteen

COBRA

I was nervous.

Like a kid bringing a date home to meet Mommy and Daddy kinda nervous.

Blue woke up just as I was approaching the twelve foot barbed wire fence that surrounded the compound.

The acolytes manning the guard shack saw me coming and let the gate slide open, pulling the hyenas, Max and Toby, out of harm's way.

"I forgot how big this place was," Blue mumbled, staring out at the expansive desert-like field. The sun was setting, giving it all a pretty pink glow.

"By this time in two years, that will all be different shit," I explained as we drove along.

"You guys are still growing?" She looked back at me with wide eyes.

"Hell yeah we are. It's only going to get worse after we take Centriole."

She nodded and looked up at the flagpole we were passing, Romero's symbol flying on it.

It was something she'd have to get used to.

She went silent for a minute before asking, "What happened to the man who rescued me?"

I started to laugh, quickly turning that shit into a cough when she frowned.

"He'll be around," I replied casually.

If she wanted to paint Bryce as her rescuer, I was cool with that, though he and I both knew he was doing exactly what Rome had told him to do.

Before long I was pulling around the circular drive and cutting the engine.

"You good?" I asked her, asking myself the same question.

"Are you sure you want to do this?" she asked.

I swear she braced herself as if preparing for my rejection. I felt like a dick for how I'd been going about things.

She needed to know I planned on worshipping the fuckin ground she walked on.

"I fucked up by letting you go once, Blue. Don't ask me to do it again, I won't. And if you ever try to leave me, I have no issue chaining your ass to my bed. After I tattoo my name on it."

She shut her eyes for a minute and nodded. When she looked over at me, there was a soft smile on her face. "Then I'll be fine, as long you're with me."

Damn.

Too fuckin sweet.

Did I hand this girl my balls now or later?

Annie sighed in the backseat, reminding us her crazy lil ass was still present.

"Come on then," I said, opening my door.

I went around to Blue's side and helped her out, pushing the seat forward for Annie.

I could feel her palm sweating and wrapped my arm around her shoulder.

"There's not shit to be nervous about, pretty girl," I reassured her as we approached the front door.

I didn't tell her I was just as nervous as she was. I'd never cared before but Blue was mine; she needed to be comfortable here.

I stood there, hoping my family of psychos didn't send her ass right back out the door.

Chapter Twenty

BLUE

I hadn't been expecting everyone to be in the living room.

We walked in and all conversation ceased.

There wasn't a pair of eyes that didn't land on us. I could only imagine what the three of us looked like standing there together.

A redheaded heathen, a girl with blue hair, and a kid with a shotgun.

"They're back!" Calista broke the ice, smiling at us from beside Romero.

I smiled back at her, feeling oddly relieved. The last time I'd seen her, she was pregnant. Now she was right back to the size she was before, looking more ridiculously youthful than she had already.

"Annie," she greeted with a smirk that freakishly matched the one Romero was now sporting.

"Aunt C. Uncle Rome," Annie smirked back. When her eyes landed on the baby in Arlen's arms, an actual smile blossomed on her face and she walked right into the fray.

Arlen gave me an enthusiastic wave.

There was one person missing.

"Where is the fuck is Kat?" Cobra asked before I could.

The silence that transcended answered the question for me.

"She left, didn't she?"

"You say that like she's done it before," Arlen replied.

"Twice before, actually," I said more to myself than them, feeling an old hurt resurface and a little more than embarrassed.

"I'm gonna let her get settled," Cobra cut in as my saving grace.

I squeezed his hand appreciatively.

He and Romero shared a look I couldn't decipher, but no one objected to our quick departure. The girls told me they'd see me in the morning right before we disappeared upstairs.

Walking into Cobra's room was like a breath of fresh air. It wasn't overtly masculine and the bright colors worked well for him and his personality. Completely unexpected.

"Where did she leave you?" he asked as soon as the door was shut.

I sucked in the breath I'd just released, knowing I needed to tell him exactly who I was.

I walked further in the room and sat down on the edge of his bed, twirling a strand of my hair.

"Me and Katya were more frenemies than friends. Of course, we didn't announce that to people. We were from the same city. We had good lives. Then, she convinced me to take off with her at seventeen.

"She convinced my parents it would be a good idea for me to get out and see the world, which is laughable now that I think about it. The first time she left me was with a man she was sleeping with for a roof over our heads. That guy was such an asshole."

I paused and looked up to see him watching me intently before continuing.

"He...turned his attentions on me once she was gone. I had nowhere to go; she'd taken all my things. It was either him or the street. But he got mean when he drank."

"Think I know where this is goin," Cobra stated.

"I killed him when he was in the shower, stole his truck and everything I could gather up and left," I rushed out.

"And the second time?" he asked.

I shrugged and curled my shoulders, looking down at the floor. "The second time was after we reunited. I couldn't go home because I didn't have one anymore. Our city was raided a year after we left. I don't know how she knew where I was, but she has a habit of popping up wherever I am.

"We got in an argument over something so stupid I can't even remember. She took off and I was on my own for a long time until she found me again with that guy, Parker. And then we met you."

The room was silent for a few beats.

"Okay," he cleared his throat. "Do you want me to hold you while you cry or would you like to take a shower?"

I choked on a laugh and looked up at him. "How can you be so at ease about this? Do you know how I lived for all those years?"

"Babe, I'd rather not picture that."

"You don't think you're good enough for me, but I thought from the moment I saw you that I was the one not good enough for you. I'm a whore, Cobra."

"Shower it is," he said, ignoring my mini rant completely.

"Bathroom's through there." He gestured to an open door as he walked backward.

"Where are you going?" I asked, standing up. "Cobra?"

He ignored me, walking out the door and pulling it shut behind him.

As I stepped out of the shower, I wondered if I'd gone too far.

Cobra had emotional turmoil of his own to deal with; I had no right to dump off mine.

Grabbing a plush yellow towel, I wrap it around my body and used another to dry my hair.

When I was done, I carried it with me into the bedroom, pausing the second I stepped through the bathroom door.

I blinked. The lights had been dimmed and a cracker and cheese tray was on the bed.

"What is this?" I asked, looking to where Cobra was standing.

"This is for us."

"I see that but what brought all this on?"

"Blue. From day one, we've been surrounded by pure fuckin chaos and it ain't over yet, babe. We're about to go to war. So, tonight, I just wanna talk and I wanna fuck."

I laughed and my heart completely melted all over again. I had to blink multiple times to hold back tears.

"Sit down." He gestured to his bed.

Having a bit of déjà vu, I walked over and climbed up onto the massive king sized mattress, and settled against the headboard.

Shutting my eyes, I let out a deep contented sigh.

"You look good in my bed," Cobra said, sitting down on the other side of me.

"Good. I don't plan on ever leaving it." I looked over at him and smiled.

He reached out and traced his knuckles down my cheek. "Don't ever call yourself a whore again."

I opened my mouth to object, but he cut me off.

"You did what you fuckin had to survive.

" I wouldn't care if you fucked the whole Badlands if it meant your pretty ass would wind up here in my bed.

"You wanna know what a real whore is? It's me. I would fuck any willing pussy or ass as long as he or she looked good in the face."

"He?" I furrowed my brows.

He laughed under his breath, rubbing his thumb across my lower lip.

"Yeah, I love pussy but sometimes I like to bat for the other team. Hell, I fuck men to torture them."

"Okay, maybe you do have me beat," I joked. "And that last part sounds like a whole other level of conversation we need to have, but first tell me what made you...stop."

He moved the cracker tray to a nightstand and picked up a mason jar of hooch, taking a healthy swig before passing it to me.

"Well this sounds real fuckin cliché, but honestly, you. I didn't even understand it at first. I had this longing for something I didn't even understand. Then I saw my brothers and how happy they are. Then this shit with Beth happened, and I knew I had to change."

I took my second sip of hooch and passed it back to him.

"How do you feel about the baby?" I asked timidly. It wasn't my intention to pry but I couldn't let him bottle something like this up.

He took another large sip of hooch and then released a deep sigh, staring up at the ceiling. "At first I was pissed, ya know? I'd just started to accept that I might have a kid, even if their ma was a devious bitch. To find out my baby was still-born... I don't know. Indifferent? I'll be good, though. Eventually."

I held back telling him I knew he'd be an amazing father. Cobra was wild and unpredictable. Deadly and venomous just like his namesake. But this man was so freaking loyal and loved his family fiercely.

I knew we would be revisiting this subject in the near future, and I'd pushed him enough. The mood was quickly deteriorating and that's not what I wanted.

I tugged my towel loose and dropped it on the floor.

His eyes went from my face to between my legs; I smiled to myself and moved to straddle him.

He immediately sat down the hooch and gripped my hips.

Sitting right over his hard cock, I let my eyes drift from his silver eyes, over his muscled chest and down his torso. "You are so gorgeous," I sighed.

"I was thinking the same fuckin thing about you."

I leaned down and pressed my lips to his, tasting the tangy, sour hooch we'd just consumed. "I want you," I murmured against his mouth as I worked to get him out of his jeans.

He immediately moved to assist me, freeing his cock and kicking off his pants.

I didn't need any foreplay; I'd been ready since I'd stepped into the bedroom.

I gripped him in my hand and slowly lowered myself down, letting out a moan as my pussy stretched to accommodate him.

Placing my palms on his chest, I began to rock my hips, getting used to the fullness of him inside me.

"You feel good," I breathed, beginning to move faster.

He ran his hands from my breasts to my ass, grabbing handfuls of the flesh and squeezing, beginning to thrust into me from underneath.

My legs started to burn the harder I rode him, my breaths coming in little gasps.

"Damn, you are a fuckin goddess," he groaned, grabbing hold of my hips and flipping us over.

He placed my legs on his shoulders and fucked me faster; I reached down and grabbed hold of his ass, forcing him to bottom out.

The sound of his headboard bouncing into the wall mixed with my wanton moans, skin hitting skin, and the squelching sounds from my pussy every time he thrust in and out filled the air.

Sex had never felt this amazing. It'd never been this fulfilling.

I stared up into his eyes, letting him see everything I had to offer him. He dropped my legs, wrapped them around his waist and lurched down, slamming his mouth over mine. Our teeth clashed, tongues tangling as his dick continued to pound into me.

I pulled away, gasping, feeling the most intense orgasm of my life building in my core.

"Don't stop," I demanded on a moan, as his cock began stroking the sweet spot inside me.

"I plan on fuckin you all night," he laughed. He moved one of his hands between us, bypassing my clit and moving to my ass. He began toying with my rim, dipping a finger in and then pulling it out, causing my pussy to clamp down. "Plan on fuckin this ass too."

Yes! I screamed in my head.

"Cobra…I-"

"I can feel it. Let go, babe. Come all over my dick."

He covered my mouth with his as I exploded around him, catching his name as it spelled like a chant from my lungs. I arched into him, holding on as tight as I could.

"Fuck. Blue," he moaned, finding his own release.

We lay together, trying to catch our breath before he slowly pulled out and said, "That's one."

"What's one?" I rasped.

"I made you come once. I'm going for seven. We're just getting started. I don't want you able to walk tomorrow."

He laughed at my expression, taking hold of my ankles and flipping me onto my stomach.

Chapter Twenty-One

BLUE

Things were absolutely amazing for a full four days.

Beyond the sex, which there were just no words for—Cobra was dedicated to all the different ways he could make come.

On the one occasion my self-loathing set in, he held me.

The man who got off on torture *held* me and told me everything he loved about me. And then he fucked me again.

Our bubble together was my sole happy place.

The day Romero said it was time to talk, I wasn't fully aware of the history in the house. I sat at the dining room table with Cobra right behind me, his hands on my shoulders. Cali and Arlen were there too, as were Grimm and Romero, obviously.

From the second I sat down, I felt like I was facing judge, juror, and executioner. The man was intense without even saying anything. I mean, he was gorgeous just like Grimm; they had the whole dark and alluring thing down pat.

However, I preferred the man I was falling madly in love with.

I adored his red hair, sense of humor, and that darkness

that lurked just out of sight, coming out at the most unpredictable of times.

I was pretty elated that he didn't walk around with a thundercloud of hellfire over his head like they did.

"We need to discuss your initiation," Romero began.

"I'm sorry, my what?"

He didn't say anything for a minute, simply staring me down. I'm certain he knew he scared the crap out of me.

"Rome," Cali hissed, clearly on the same page as I was.

"Your initiation is you basically doing something that proves your loyalty to the Savages and lifelong commitment, and some other details," Cali explained.

"Oh, well what did you do?"

"Got knocked up," she laughed, then held her hands in a defensive gesture when Romero glared at her. "I was kidding. That's a long story for some other time."

"What do you want me to do?"

"Tell me everything you learned from Vitus and then tell me if you truly want Cobra and everything that comes with him, because he is a Savage, and you will be too. So you can kiss your precious morals goodbye."

Wow, he certainly didn't sugarcoat anything.

Cobra squeezed my shoulders to reassure me and let me know he was there, which only solidified my decision.

I knew without a doubt I would walk through hell if it meant being with this man. I was going to be his future and help him heal from his past.

The bits and pieces he'd shared with me already were heartbreaking.

He'd given me pieces of his heart and I was damned sure going to collect the rest of them. I would show him he was worthy of all the love everyone in this room had for him.

For him, I would hand my soul to the devil. I would give up my morality for savagery.

"Okay…I'm not sure what you consider new information. This is all over someone named *Tillie*, right?"

As soon as I said that name, I felt a spark of tension. Cali had looked from Romero to me; he didn't look away for even a second.

"All I know is that Vitus is looking for someone named Zane, and that he has something to do with Tillie.

" You may know where this Zane is because you and Tillie were closer than she and Vitus?"

"Also, Beth told me this, and she's dea—gone," I hurriedly added, choosing my words carefully out of respect for Arlen.

The room was too silent once I was finished.

Cobra moved his hands from my shoulders to around the front of me and gently squeezed.

"Who's Zane?" Cali asked Romero at the same time Arlen asked why her sister was at the prison and not in Centriole.

"Rome," Cali began.

"Zane is Tillie's son. She had him when we fucked around off and on."

"Did you know where Beth was?" Arlen was asking Grimm.

I made a point of studying the table, feeling all sorts of awkward witnessing other couples argue.

"What the fuck does that mean?" Cali asked, clenching her fist around the baby monitor.

She sounded equal parts hurt and pissed off. Had I known this would have upset her, I'd have worded it differently.

"You're okay, babe," Cobra leaned down and whispered in my ear, sensing my growing discomfort.

"Cali, don't start this shit," Romero snapped.

"You did all this because of her? Why are you still keeping things from me? Fuck you," she snapped right back, launching the monitor at his head before walking out of the room and straight out the back door.

"You two are fuckin assholes," Arlen laughed humorlessly, pushing away from the table and going after Cali.

Silence reigned.

I looked up, hearing a heavy sigh, seeing Romero sink down in a chair. Grimm hadn't said a word.

"He's not my kid," Romero said after a minute. "He's Vitus'. But I helped her hide him. He hasn't pulled his 'alliance' yet, even knowing we took Blue. He doesn't know we're aware Beth is dead and so is…" He looked at Cobra and trailed off.

"We leave in a few days. We'll take the city and Vitus. I have scouts inside looking for Zane, but so far he hasn't been located."

"So all Vitus wants is his son?" I spoke up. Now things made sense. I'd known he had have of been after something highly valuable to concoct this scheme.

Not much would beat out his son.

"He wants his son, and he wants my kingdom. He isn't going to get either." His words dripped contempt.

In that moment, I understood that for this beef, Vitus wanted the girl and the kid, while all Romero wanted was to win, as painfully as possible.

I didn't see where Cali came in.

"She loved her too. The bitch was good at playing people but I knew her too well for it to work against us. Beth wasn't half as smart. Thank fuck she's dead."

I didn't even want to begin analyzing that mess of a statement.

"This is the only secret she'll know," Romero said with a pointed stare at me.

How many secrets did he have?

Realizing he was speaking to me, I swallowed my fear of him to respond. "I don't know your secrets to tell. It seems to me you don't need assistance pissing off your wives, anyway."

"Our wives?" Grimm asked.

"I...saw their rings."

"I'm going to find my queen," Romero said, standing up. "Maybe she's got some backbone after all. Have her ready to roll out the morning of," he directed at Cobra on his way out of the room.

"Guess I should go too." Grimm stood and followed behind him.

"Did I mess up?" I asked Cobra as he helped from my chair.

"Nah, babe, you were fuckin perfect," he took my hand and kissed the back of it.

"What did he mean by have me ready to roll out?"

"You're coming with us," he stated slowly.

What? I knows he's not talking about their war.

"Ah, you're funny, but I don't think so."

"Oh, you'll be there," he laughed.

"No I will not," I objected with finality.

"Okay, Blue," he smirked.

I didn't care what he said, I was not going with them to take down a city.

Chapter Twenty-Two

COBRA

Adrenaline was running high.

Acolytes were fanned out moving towards the wall like a black, demonic tide, carrying the Sigil Of Baphomet with them.

We all sat in the Jeep waiting for our time to enter the city.

Romero and Cali were up front, I sat in-between Blue and Grimm. All with the exception of Blue ready to go tear shit up.

We were born for this shit.

Being ruthless killers was in our DNA. We'd been waiting on this fuckin day long enough. I had a fuck load of energy that needed an outlet.

My heart was racing so fuckin fast it felt like a bottle launcher getting ready to shoot out of my chest.

"Bryce in place?" I asked, wrapping my hands in finger-less gloves.

"Just dispatched our decoy," Rome replied, listening in on a headset.

"Why do we need a decoy?" Blue whispered to me.

"That." I pointed through the windshield to where the wall was, seeing the city guards rushing to find out what was going on.

"We had Bryce and a crew take out a weaker portion of the wall. The only good thing Vitus was able to help figure out." I explained.

"He's here?"

Damn.

Seeing her anxious expression I pulled her into my side. "You don't gotta worry about him ever again, Blue."

She looked at me with her big, beautiful fuckin eyes and nodded, trusting my words.

Fuck. She made my heart swell.

And she looked badass. Her hair in a braid similar to Cali's, cargo shorts full of bullets, a knife holstered and a gun in her hand, I'd have to fuck her like this later.

Cuz there sure as shit was going to be a later.

Blue was going to pass her initiation and be back in my bed by sundown with her pussy on my face.

She kissed my cheek just as Rome said, "We gotta move."

"Let's go," I said, taking hold of her hand.

Chapter Twenty-Three

BLUE

Oh, if my mother could see me now.

This was chaos.

The five of us moved towards the wall where all hell had broken loose. Acolytes had pushed well past the guards using their own comrades as shields against a hail of bullets.

We jogged past at least eight dead already and four wounded being dragged back the way we came.

It took me a minute to realize a fresh wave was surrounding us, moving in a formation that would protect their king and queen, Rome and Cali, at all costs.

"Is there a plan?" I yelled aloud to anyone that could answer me.

"Yeah, kill any motherfucker that looks like a problem," Romero called over his shoulder.

Because that really narrowed it down. We were attacking these people's city, I'm positive everyone was a problem.

I hopped over a dead body, barely managing to keep my footing as we continued onward.

We approached the archway of The Kingdom and ran

right through the wide open gates, dodging more bodies and people locked in struggle.

"Brace yourself, babe," Cobra warned, dragging me behind a car as gun fire came from every direction.

"What the fuck did you drag me into!?" I yelled at him as a body with half its head smashed in landed near our feet.

"Cobra," Romero called for him from the front of our tiny posse.

"Stay close to Cali, babe we're going for city hall."

Before I could object he dropped a fast kiss on my lips and then moved to Rome's side.

"Ya ready?" Cali asked, slipping back beside me.

Um no.

"I can do this," I spoke aloud.

"That's the spirit. Just stick with me, k?"

She flipped her long blonde braid over her shoulder as we set off again.

"Get ready," Cali sang, dodging around the acolyte beside her as he took a hit to the chest.

I did the same leaping over him.

When we hit the main city I understood why they were saying get ready.

People were being dragged from their homes and slaughtered right in the street.

Screams of women, men, and children filled the air. Like Romero had said, if they were a problem they were handled, age nothing but a number.

Blood coated the sidewalk and pavement as acolytes went from house to house in terrifying formation.

Hearing tires screech, I dove out of the way as mail truck barreled into our little group, smashing into three acolytes .

I heard their bones crack as I hit the asphalt, hands stinging along with my knees.

Trying to get right back up, I barely missed being clobbered by a golf club an older man had decided to swing at me.

I ducked at the last second and It whizzed by my ear. By time I was on my feet Cali had her knife in the man's gut, twisting it around in a circle before roughly pulled it back out.

Without even thinking of what I was doing, I had my gun aimed and fired at another man trying to rush her.

His head snapped back, his legs running for a second longer before getting the memo he was dead.

The adrenaline rush was incredible.

I fired again at a female guard who'd overpowered one of the acolytes, getting her in the back.

She was flung off, landing at the feet of another, her head promptly being stomped in.

Up ahead, Romero, Grimm, and Cobra had a mesmerizing system where they worked together.

Cali flashed me a grin, grabbing my wrist with her bloody hand and pulling me alongside her to do the same.

She was simply brilliant.

A bullet nicked her shoulder and aside from a sharp wince, the girl barely batted an eye.

When she swapped her blade for a bright pink gun I almost laughed.

I did my best to take out anyone that got to close to our group, slipping past an acolyte.

And that's how we worked our way to the City hall.

Killing anyone who got in our way and covering each other's backs.

There was Venom amongst us , fighting the good fight for once.

By the time we reached the large brick building it was clear this was going extremely well for the Savages.

The city had been hit from both sides at once. It wasn't until just then that I realized just how extensive Romero's reach was. This place never stood half a chance.

There wasn't one of us not covered in blood, sweat, and dirt. My own chest was heaving so hard I thought I was going to have an asthma attack, and I didn't have asthma.

Corpses littered the stairs, some no longer wholly intact. Acolytes surrounded the entrance and windows, not letting anyone out.

When they saw us they parted like the red sea so we could pass. I felt like royalty.

We marched up the steps and right into the building where cool air greeted us.

Blinking to adjust to the lighting change, I saw people on their knees lining the walls, cowering with their hands up in surrender.

I'd saw many in the streets doing the same but hadn't paid much attention to them with the whole kill or be killed stuff going on.

Acolytes stood with their heads bowed keeping them all in check.

"What the fuck, Pixie?" Romero's voice snapped me back to what was going on.

"Calm down, Rome. It's just a flesh wound," she sighed in exasperation.

"You're not allowed to get fucking flesh wounds," he mocked, dragging her into his arms to look over the rest of her.

Grimm shook his head and kept going. "I'll be going to get, Frank," he called over his shoulder.

"Come on, babe, we get to check for, Zane," Cobra said,

coming up beside me. I took the bloody hand and fell in step beside him, feeling the presence of two acolytes behind us.

"He's here?" I asked, looking around the building.

"The prison is under this building, got a tip that's where Tillie put him."

That didn't seem right to me.

"I thought Zane was a kid."

"He is. Around five or six."

Then why is he in a freaking prison?

"His mom has a lot of connections," he answered my unspoken question. "It's still a real fucked up thing to do," he added, voicing my exact opinion on the matter.

"Poor kid," I murmured. I felt even worse for him when we finally found our way to the lower level.

The smell had me wanting to go right back up the stairs.

"Jesus," I coughed, covering my nose with my filthy arm.

"Don't think Jesus had much to do with this, Blue."

It smelled of feces, vomit, and death.

Passing multiple cells jam packed of people who'd withered into nothing, I understood why.

The lighting was dim and the air was chilled. If I didn't already live in hell I'd swear we'd just found it.

Some of the remaining prisoners were naked, watching us with zombie-like expressions.

Turning down a narrow hall, we walked slowly to the end. When we got there we found three decapitated guards and a cell that had clearly housed a little boy.

"Looks like someone beat us to him," Cobra mused, looking around.

"Vitus?" I questioned, kicking one of the guard's limp hands.

"No, Bryce took Vitus before we breached the city."

I didn't feel anything from that omission but relief. More for Arlen than me, and all the other women Vitus had hurt.

"Why is this kid so important?"

"He's to the Venom what Adelaide is to the Savages."

"They worked with us to get rid of Vitus, probably planning to steal the kid away the entire time."

I looked from the cell to him in disbelief.

"If you knew that's what was going to happen why did you let it?"

"Because he's like Rome was."

Yeah, I had no idea what that meant. How could a five year old be anything like Romero?

I sighed, letting the subject rest for the time being. There wasn't much I could do about it anyway.

He was silent for a minute before maneuvering so that I was in front of him and he was behind me, signaling for the two acolytes to leave.

"I didn't tell you how proud I am of you. You're fuckin perfect, Blue," he softly said, sliding his hands around my waist.

"I certainly didn't see this day ever coming," I laughed, arching my ass back into him as he kissed my neck.

It was incredible the things he could make me feel with just a few words and feather light touch.

His hands moved downward, one cupping my pussy the other tugging on my shorts.

"We're doing that here?" I breathed.

"You mean am I going to press you against those cell bars and bury my dick inside you, yes." He dragged my bottoms and underwear off, kicking my legs apart.

"Cobra there's," my words ended on a gasp as he shoved two bloody fingers into my pussy.

"There are dead people all around us, your pussy is wet and my dick is hard," he growled.

His fingers pumped inside me and he worked his jeans down to rest low on his hips.

"Hurry," I whispered, grabbing hold of the iron bars for support.

I didn't have to tell him twice, he removed his fingers and replaced it with thick dick, diving himself into me with one thrust.

I cried out, my hand clenching the cell door in front of me.

"You feel so good, Blue. Love everything about you," he groaned, picking up his pace, hitting my G-spot in the process.

His words had my pussy growing wetter, my heart squeezing in my chest. "I love you, too," I breathed.

He immediately pulled out, spun me around and wrapped my legs around his waist, slamming back inside me with a toe curling brutality.

"Say it again," he demanded over my breathy moans.

"I love you," I repeated, threading my fingers through his hair. The look on his face was something between adoration and possessiveness.

I pulled his mouth to mine, letting him consume me completely me.

Our bodies came together but it was our damaged souls that sparked and came alive.

Epilogue One

COBRA

Centriole was ours.

Frank's body was strung up right outside the entryway to show who'd won.

Rotting bodies lay in the street.

The acolytes had done another sweep and spared those worth sparing and killed off everyone else.

As for Vitus, he was that evening's entertainment.

Zane, the kid, had really vanished without a trace.

Romero and Cali had made up, loud enough we all got to bear witness for a whole fuckin week.

Arlen forgave Grimmy the instant he brought her Frank's hand, the key to Centriole, and her mother's wedding ring. If that isn't romantic, what is?

As for me and Blue? We were fuckin perfect.

Every day, we worked on helping one another heal a little more.

I let her in my head and while she couldn't vanquish my demons, she knew how to soothe them.

I slept for longer than an hour when her arms were around me and her head was on my chest.

When shit got to be too much, I'd go to her and she'd sit in the playroom with me if need be; occasionally even joining in.

I was in love with the fuckin girl and hadn't been ashamed to tell her that morning when my dick was in her mouth. Then again in the shower.

We were Savaged and tamed.

Hellfire and holy water.

One broken, one lost.

Together, completely fucking whole.

If she hadn't shown back up when she did, I would have been a lost cause.

I had one motherfucker to thank.

He'd known from the very beginning that she was it for me. He made sure I was the one who brought her home.

As I stood beside him I couldn't help but feel grateful.

"What really happened to Katya?" I asked, watching the acolytes lead Vitus out back.

"The night she left your room after you turned her down, I had a nice chat with her.

"Grimm finished it off. Last I knew, she and Isaac both met the same end."

Watching Blue approach me, her fresh ink on her neck instantly made my dick hard. She got the inverted cross to show she was one of us, and for me to know she wasn't going anywhere.

"Thank you," I quietly told him and Grimm.

I was thanking them for more than just getting rid of Katya.

I was thanking them for saving my ass from years of abuse and making me second in command, giving me a family and two brothers who always had my back and never tried to change me.

Most importantly, I was thanking them for Blue.

The blue-haired girl had ended up saving me, and didn't even know it.

BLUE

Thunder rumbled overhead.

Any second now, the coal black sky would unleash its torrential wrath.

I sat with my hand intertwined with Cobra's, watching Vitus try to escape the semi-circle acolytes had formed around him.

They were softly chanting under their breath, the iron leviathan cross burning bright in the background.

Cali and Romero stood on one side of us, her head resting on his chest.

Arlen and Grimm were on the other, his hands cradling her tiny bump.

I heard their low keening a second before they were led into the clearing. Max and Toby, each guided by an acolyte.

Vitus saw them and tried to run again, but was shoved back.

A word was whispered and the beasts were unchained.

They launched themselves at him and shredded him into nothing.

With their jaws crunching bone, they ripped apart ligaments and limbs within seconds.

Vitus screamed until his throat was torn out.

Cheers went up around the yard as the hyenas devoured him.

I felt no pity for him.

I knew this held significance.

I met Bryce's gaze across the yard and gave him a thankful smile, then I looked up at the man beside me. He glanced down and winked.

He was my home now.

My redheaded heathen.

Epilogue Two

Romero

I said it once and I'll gladly say it again. All's fair in love and war.

You've got to use irrelevant people as pawns to set certain things in motion. I'd had this belief nearly my whole fucking life and had yet to be proven wrong.

"I got this," he said determinedly, peeling way too much of the shell off a boiled egg.

I shook my head, deciding to let him do it his way.

"We did well," Grimm said after a few minutes of silence, his gaze trained on the backyard.

"Fuck yeah, we did," Cobra grinned.

I slowly looked around me, taking everything in.

At the edge of the property, a few new acolyte recruits

were readying the pit for the evening's festivities with Bryce making sure they didn't fuck it up.

Adelaide, who was seven going on fucking twenty, sat at a round picnic table with Grimm and Arlen's daughter, Nyx, both fully immersed in their game of Go Fish. Annie watched over them, pretending to keep score.

I could hear her brother, Lucien, from up in his tree house with Camren and Braxton, Cobra's twins.

Turning my head back to the patio, my eyes found the pair of beautiful blue ones that had started it all.

"I couldn't agree more," I finally responded.

Life was fucking grand.

We still had hard days and colder nights, but being together made it all the more bearable.

This is where our story ended.

But the next generation was just getting started.

And they were a whole new breed of Savages.

Also by Natalie Bennett

Badlands Series

Savages

Deviants

Outcasts

Heathens

Degenerates

Hellions

Renegades

Miscreants

Old Money Trilogy

Queen Of Diamonds

King Of Hearts

Ace Of Spades

Pretty Lies, Ugly Truths

Sweet Poisons

Sick Remedies

Broken Crowns Trilogy

Beauty & Rage

Beauty & Wreckage

Beauty & Havoc

Standalones

Covetous

Dahlia Saga

Malice

Obscene

Depravity

Malevolence

Iniquity

Debauchery

Malicious

Stygian Isle

Del Diablo

Muerte

Deviant Games

Crucible

Malady

Calamity

Devil's Playground

Periculum

Maleficium

Daemonium

Coveting Delirium

Opaque Melodies

Melodic Madness

Keep In Touch

facebook.com/NatalieBennettWriter

instagram.com/authornataliebennett

Made in the USA
Monee, IL
03 March 2021

61887977R00448